I0586745

VENDEL RISING OMNIBUS

OMNIBUS EDITION: VOLUMES 1-4

LA WARREN

JEM PUBLISHING

Vendel Rising
Omnibus Edition
Volumes 1-4

Volume 1: It Begins With the End
Volume 2: Women of Rank
Volume 3: The Price of Power
Volume 4: It Ends With a Beginning

by: L.A. Warren

L.A.
WARREN
Science Fiction & Fantasy

Editor: Eanna Roberts (www.penmanshipediting.com)

Cover Artist: Ellie Augsburger (www.creativedigitialstudios.com)

Interior Design/Formatting: JEM Publishing

Published in the United States of America

JEM Publishing

———

ISBN: 978-0-9993888-4-6

❀ Created with Vellum

DEDICATION_

This book is dedicated to my one and only—my amazing and wonderful husband. Without your care and support, my writing would not have made it this far.

CONTENTS

IT BEGINS WITH THE END

WOMEN OF RANK

THE PRICE OF POWER

IT ENDS WITH A BEGINNING

IT BEGINS WITH THE END

VOLUME 1

THE BEGINNING_

New Terra Histories by Malita s'Lissa s'vlor

"To understand your enemies, you must first let go of your hatred. Only then may you forgive. Only then may you understand."

PROLOGUE_

May 31, 2136

THE DAY THE VENDEL INVADED MY WORLD IS A MEMORY THAT NEVER LEAVES me. It's the day I lived. The day I died. It's the day everything changed. I was defeated and broken. They destroyed me.

I hated them. I didn't want to forgive them. I didn't care to understand them. All I wanted was my revenge. What I got instead was something I never imagined possible...

Emperor Gregor Ulysses vlor'Malita claims to have our interests in mind, humanity's interests that is, and perhaps there is a kernel of truth in that statement. Earth, as it turns out, is but a small fraction of humanity.

But Saviors?

How do you justify that to the dead? How do we, the survivors, wrap our minds around that? We live with the impossible loss of everything and everyone we knew, but more than the collar, or the boot steps which announce the inevitable arrival of my vlor' master, one idea terrifies me.

What if the Vendel are right?

Are they, in fact, our saviors?

This is how my story begins...

CHAPTER ONE_

Sunday, January 30, 2035:

Bubbly chatter permeated the sunny day as the last few miles of the three-day, sixty-mile, Walk for the Cure passed beneath Elise Comwell's feet. Excited chatter bounced from one person to the next, amplifying as it rippled through the crowd. No one complained of sore feet, stiff legs, or aching backs; they were all happy to be near the end.

Two miles to go, Marybeth. For you. I did it!

Her new best friend, Alice, a tall, platinum blonde with a pixie haircut, walked beside her. For the past three days, they had traded stories about Alice's mother's and Elise's sister's battles with breast cancer. They cemented a deep bond of friendship through their shared tragedies.

"Where are your nieces?" Alice glanced over the heads of those walking in front of them. "I thought they were going to walk the last mile with us."

Elise pointed ahead. "Tom's bringing them. He didn't think little Crista would last a whole mile. They'll meet us in just a bit."

"How're they holding up?"

"Crista doesn't understand. She still thinks her mom will come home. Jenny and Sheila are trying to be strong."

"It's got to be hard on them, losing a mother at such a young age."

Elise gripped Alice's hand. "I think it has to be hard losing a mother at any age."

Alice returned the squeeze. "It is. I miss my mom every day. They say it's supposed to get better with time, but it doesn't. Or, at least, it hasn't yet."

A lump formed in her throat. It had been less than two weeks since her sister had lost her battle with cancer. She stopped walking long enough to give Alice a hug.

"I miss my sister. I still think she'll call me on the phone, or meet me for lunch, but then I realize she's gone."

Alice wiped at her cheeks. "Well, this is why we walk, right? To remember them?"

"To raise money to find a cure." Elise smiled. "And to make new friends."

"Yes, to finding the best, new friends." Alice glanced toward the finish line. "I think I see your little trio."

Elise stretched onto tiptoe. At five-foot-three, she didn't have the advantage of Alice's six-foot frame to see over the crowd, but less than a hundred yards away her nieces waited with their father at the finish line.

"Sheila! Jenny! Crista!" Alice called out, waving over the crowd. "We're over here."

Elise's nieces ran toward them. Tom stayed behind, taking a knee and setting up his camera for the finish line shot. As the girls drew near, Crista launched herself into Elise's open arms.

"Aunty El, Daddy's going to take our picture."

Crista squealed as Elise grabbed her under the arms and swung her in a circle. She propped Crista on her hip as she ruffled Jenny's hair. At nine, Jenny was too cool for the public display of affection and gave a huff.

Alice wrapped an arm around the shoulder of Elise's eldest niece. At ten, Shiela was going on twenty-one. Elise waved to Tom and gripped Crista's hand, ready to end the agonizing walk.

The cellphone of a walker behind them sounded. Another rang ahead. Two phones buzzed on either side, and then the warbling tones sprouted like weeds, drowning out conversations. A symphony of ringtones rolled through the crowd, bringing with it a rush of silence.

Elise exchanged a confused look with Alice.

Bubbly conversations popped and fizzled. Nervous whispers erupted and then died out to form an oppressive silence.

"Aunty El," Crista cried, "why have all the people stopped walking?"

Alice pulled her cellphone out and thumbed it on. She punched at the screen and then pointed a shaky finger to the sky.

"Spaceships." All color drained from Alice's face.

"What?"

An image of five ring-shaped objects filled the screen.

Tom raced toward them. His camera swung around his neck. He pumped his arms and devoured the distance with his long strides.

"Did you hear?" He held up his cell phone. "Girls, are you okay?"

Elise's gaze swept to her nieces. Crista clutched her sisters' hands, terrified of the silent adults. Jenny and Sheila stood to either side, their young faces scanning the crowd, confused and scared.

Elise kissed Crista's head and lowered her voice to a whisper so no one else could hear. "Don't worry, your great-grandpa should make an announcement soon."

Crista's eyes lit up. She whispered back, "Grampy Chuck?" Her little hand squeezed Elise's. "I wanna hear what he says."

Tom gathered Sheila to his side. Crista stared at him, not understanding what was going on. Jenny reached for her father's hand and he pulled her to him, sheltering and protecting his daughters.

Tears streamed down the faces of those around them. More than a few sobbed. Some looked skyward, eyes alight with anticipation. She was proud of her nieces, who didn't cry, and faced the sky with intelligent eyes.

Elise followed their gazes skyward, but there was nothing but blue sky and puffy clouds overhead.

"Elise!" Alice tapped her arm. "Director Comwell's going to speak."

Alice had no idea the famous family connection Elise could claim, and she hoped to keep it that way. True friends were hard to come by when the most powerful man on Earth was your grandfather.

Elise pulled Crista into a hug and lifted her into her arms. Tom gave her a thankful smile.

"Let's listen to the news."

Alice shifted the screen for Elise and Christa while Tom held his for Jenny and Sheila. The girls pressed close and hugged their dad.

The news anchor recapped. "Breaking news: The Global Corps Space Agency has confirmed a fleet of ships appeared in the space between Earth and the Moon."

"Aunty El," Crista whined, "I can't see."

Alice made a quick adjustment and turned up the volume.

The clipped voice of a woman continued. "So far, there has been no contact. We'll break for an announcement from United's CEO, Charles Comwell."

The face of the richest, most powerful man alive filled the display. Warm eyes radiated calm while his measured words entranced the world.

"Citizens of Earth, for that is what we are. We have been headed toward one unified global identity for decades. We are Citizens of Earth. And..." He leaned forward for effect. "We have visitors." Comwell's charismatic smile fixed in place while the full impact of his words sank in.

Elise looked up from the tiny screen. Those around them stared at their phones, fingers wrapped tight, heads bowed, spellbound by her grandfather's words. His calm and confident voice could soothe any crowd. Where she expected panic, his words brought peace.

We have visitors. Such a simple phrase. It made her feel safe, not scared. Only, his wink was too practiced and his voice too smooth. Something worried her grandfather.

Alice breathed out a sigh. "It's going to be okay." Her cheeks regained some of their color.

Elise shook her head, amazed as always by the effect her grandfather had on others. As a testament to his charisma, at the end of his announcement, those around them whispered reassurances to one another. They stood, hugged, tightened their shoelaces, and walked. Not to the finish line. Everyone had given up on the Walk for the Cure. There were bigger issues to deal with as people headed home to discuss the life changing news.

Perhaps upon realizing she wouldn't get her finish line picture, Crista cried. "What about our picture?"

Alice glanced toward the end of the race where the event organizers were packing up. "I'm game to finish this."

She gave Alice a sympathetic smile. A five-year-old didn't care about aliens from outer space. All Crista wanted was a picture of crossing the finish line for her mommy in heaven.

"Come on, let's do this." Elise winked at her youngest niece who grinned back with enthusiasm.

Tom released his older girls, giving a smile to Alice. "Hang on. Let me get in position." With a glance at Elise to watch over his girls, he jogged back to the finish line, took a knee, and set up for the shot.

She hoped her fears were misplaced, but an urgency to prepare for the worst tugged at her. Forcing one foot in front of the other, Elise tried to find some sense of normal. They crossed the finish line and Tom snapped their picture. Crista squealed and leapt into her father's arms.

"We did it, daddy!"

If only things were as easy as appeasing a five-year-old.

CHAPTER TWO_

Wednesday evening, February 2, 2035:

VERY MUCH OUT OF PLACE, ELISE FIDGETED IN THE FOYER OF THE SOCIAL Complex of Global Corps Headquarters, amidst hundreds of the wealthiest men, women, their spouses and leaders of the world's nations. Smiles filled their faces, portraying an eagerness she didn't share. Dread cut a deep pit in her stomach instead.

Her grandfather had shared the reports in the few days leading up to tonight. Aliens had been out there all along, exploring and colonizing space, while the rest of humanity hunkered down on Earth. And, if what her grandfather said was true, they were eager to strike up trade. An interesting twist to the greatest news story in history, and another reason to be excited: the aliens weren't alien at all, but human cousins who'd left Earth two thousand years ago. They had returned in peace.

Christopher Columbus said the same to the American Indians, the Spaniards to the Mayans; but look how that worked out. No more American Indians. No more Mayans.

A quick look had her thinking she was overreacting. Nobody appeared nervous, and these were the movers and shakers of the world. Even the scores of unobtrusive security men lining the walls stood at ease.

She bit her lower lip, pensive and uncomfortable. If what Gramps told her was true, the Vendel left Earth two thousand years ago. How they accomplished that feat had not yet been shared with Earth's leaders. She had grilled her grandfather after his initial talks with the Vendel. He seemed just as perplexed by their unwillingness to share and made it clear he intended to fill in the gaps when they opened negotiations. She hated not knowing and didn't have his patience for diplomacy. It felt all wrong.

The crowd circulated within the vast chamber, waiting. A string quartet played in a small alcove and the beautiful music drifted above the general hubbub to settle gently on the assembled crowd. Stiletto heels sounded a constant clickety-clack on the fine Egyptian marble, and the swish of silk added its counterpoint to the symphony in play. Round and round, the important people of the world smiled and waited for the arrival of aliens.

"Elise!"

She turned at the sound. Her grandfather strode towards her and deflected the constant stream of people determined to block him from his goal. He carried two champagne flutes, one already half empty.

He approached and gave a bow. "My lady, may I present you with your birthday drink?"

"Why, thank you."

Technically, she'd turned twenty-one the day of the charity walk, but he'd been busy with the Vendel and they hadn't had a chance to celebrate.

"Sorry to keep you waiting." Concern flashed in his aqua-green eyes, a Comwell signature trait passed down for generations.

She kissed his cheek. "You're an important man, Gramps. People need to talk to you."

His smile stretched and crinkled at the corners of his eyes. "And you're a very lovely young lady, whom I'm happy to have as my date for the evening."

With the deaths of her parents and her grandmother several years ago, she'd taken on the official duties of his social escort once she'd turned sixteen. It'd been a novelty at the beginning and quickly turned into an onerous chore. Tonight, with the prospect of meeting aliens from outer space, the novelty factor was back in full play. It'd been a long time since she'd looked forward to one of these events.

She took a sip and gestured to the crowd. "Are you sure this is a good idea? Putting everyone in one room makes little sense. We're painting a big target on our back."

Her grandfather placed a hand on her shoulder. "Relax, Elise. If they'd wanted to, they could've killed us a hundred times over already. That they haven't is promising."

"But shouldn't we be prepared? Just in case?"

His mouth twisted into a frown. "I know it's difficult for you to accept, but we have no choice but to play along. So far, they've negotiated in good faith. They understand the culture clash their return will cause, and they have a plan to mitigate it."

"Really?" She looked at her grandfather with a new sense of respect. "I keep thinking of what happened to the natives when America was discovered, or the indigenous Australians..."

He laughed. "Good analogy, but we're prepared."

"I hope so." Despite his assurances, she still worried.

Dale Armstrong, Global Corps Space Agency Director, and hopefully her new boss if she was selected for the deep space mission to Jupiter, joined them. He sported GC Space Agency's signature black dress uniform with Commodore pins on the shoulders.

"Elise, you look stunning," Dale said. He kissed her cheek. "That color brings out the green in your eyes."

Dale's wife, Elenor, joined them after disengaging from a nearby group of women. A flowing white silk gown draped her willowy figure, and she wore no jewelry except her wedding ring. She pecked Dale on the cheek.

"Elenor, your dress is to die for," Elise said with true admiration.

Elenor spun in a circle and the fabric floated around her in a dazzling swirl of pearl iridescence. "Well, I wanted to look my best for our guests." She glanced at Elise's grandfather. "Director Comwell, when will they be arriving?" Elenor searched the hall and waved to an acquaintance.

"Not until after we're all seated." He polished off the last drop of champagne.

Elise grabbed another champagne flute off a passing server's tray. Newly twenty-one meant enjoying the freedom of drinking at one of these functions. Much better than slipping in a flask. One more glass should calm her nerves.

A chime sounded and the great hall emptied as the assembled guests flowed into the large banquet room. Still no sign of the Vendel. People glanced around and nervous whispers filled the room. Men straightened ties as women fidgeted with their skirts. Anxious coughing bounced from one corner to the next, punctuated by an occasional sigh. An air of anticipation and excitement swirled through the crowd as people took their seats.

Elise felt their excitement; it almost overpowered her incredible nervousness, but then the large double doors closed, sealing everyone inside. The thumping in her chest sped up.

Her grandfather escorted her to the head table, followed by Dale and his wife. Gramps seated her to his right while the Armstrongs sat to his left. Four empty seats sat to her right and then four more next to Dale. A stab of shock made her sit upright.

Her hand shook as she took a slug of champagne, nearly spilling the straw-colored liquid on her dress. "Why did you seat me next to them?"

He leaned over and whispered. "They requested it. Something about traditions."

Her stomach flipped. "And when do they arrive?"

Her grandfather examined his watch. "Soon. They requested we all seat ourselves first and give them privacy to teleport into the lobby."

"Teleport? Why would they need privacy?"

Impatience flickered across his face. "I told you, we must handle them a certain way."

She thought he would say something more, but he drifted off into his thoughts, leaving her to twiddle her butter knife. At an irritated glare from him, she stopped. *Where were they?*

A single loud chime sounded, and the room stilled.

Light flashed through the cracks of the closed doors. The air crackled. Silence followed, broken by a loud knock on the outer door. Global Corps guards, disguised as butlers, swung the doors wide.

No smoke, no fog, no lightning, just ten large, muscular men walked in, marching in unison. The men in the back carried two crates.

Director Comwell stood, and the rest of the room rose amid the rustling of fabrics and the scuffing of chairs. She remained seated and stared at the tall, broad man in the middle who dominated the entire room.

Short, wavy, black hair topped his head, and over his left brow a tattoo swirled with what seemed to be a life of its own. His eyes were perhaps his most stunning feature. They simmered with an intensity she had never seen before and flashed with a silvery light.

Black shirts tucked into black pants, which tucked into black, calf-high boots. It implied a uniform of sorts.

What a way to make an entrance.

She glanced around the room. Women reacted with eyes wide and mouths parted as they breathed a little deeper and heavier in open admiration of the new arrivals. This contrasted with the men. They shifted their feet and looked small compared to the Vendel.

A few startled feminine gasps sounded. She suppressed one of her own.

Their leader scanned the room with a predator's intensity. His gaze settled on her for a brief moment, twin silver orbs pinning her in place. Even from such a distance, his eyes narrowed as he held her in his stare.

Then his brows shot up. His gaze flicked away to continue his survey of the room as if that moment of surprise hadn't happened. That's when she realized she was the only person not standing and popped to her feet.

The measured voice of her grandfather sounded down the length of the long banquet hall. "Emperor Gregor Ulysses vlor'Malita, welcome to Earth." He spread his arms out wide in greeting.

The Emperor inclined his head. A deep bass rumble vibrated outward from his muscular chest, melting feminine hearts in an expanding wave of masculine presence. "Your hospitality is most welcomed, Director Comwell. We are honored and eager to, once again, taste the fruit of Earth."

Elise eyed the Emperor. The hairs on the back of her arms lifted, and a chill wormed its way down her spine.

"We brought gifts," he said in that bass rumble.

Two of his men brought forward the large cases.

"These are our most treasured fragrances. May we offer them to your ladies?"

Her grandfather gave a shaky nod. This exchange had gone off script. He recovered with one of his enigmatic smiles. "Yes, of course. Ladies, please accept the gift of the Vendel." The crowd responded with soft applause.

The Emperor and one of his men stood watch as the rest distributed the fragrance. Gasps of appreciation sounded as women opened the bottles and inhaled. A few women sneezed. When they didn't distribute the fragrance to the head table, Elise felt slighted and tilted her nose trying to catch a whiff of the tantalizing perfume.

Only after the presentation was completed, and they had packed up their crates, did the Vendel proceed toward the head table.

As they walked down the aisle, the leader held her in his gaze. Over his left eyebrow that black tattoo of swirling lines danced beneath his skin. Thick black brows framed silver eyes that sparkled in the light of the crystal chandeliers overhead. Cold eyes, penetrating in their intensity, crinkled at the corners.

Despite the quickening of her breath, she couldn't seem to draw in enough oxygen. It was in that moment she understood what it meant when someone took your breath away.

———

THE VENDEL CONTINGENT MARCHED DOWN THE CENTER AISLE OF THE BANQUET hall as the world's leaders looked on. Tension twisted in Elise's gut and corkscrewed down her spine, deflating any earlier excitement and bringing back a landslide of anxiety. People shifted for a better glance, hungry, not for food, but for any hint of what would come.

What was proper protocol for greeting aliens even if they were human? She didn't know, and her grandfather hadn't briefed her on anything specific. Her entire focus centered on the men who advanced. Or rather, on the one man who strode with a singular purpose toward her.

The only sounds to break the oppressive silence were the tread of Vendel boots snapping against the tiles of the floor, some low whispers, and a few nervous coughs. There was something beyond simple nervousness at play here. Perhaps, she wasn't the only one with concerns over the tsunami of cultures clashing with this first meeting.

She held her breath, locked in a stare with the Vendel Emperor at the lead of this strange alien procession. The other Vendel around him took in the crowd, a calm superiority radiated off them with each step toward the head table. Powerful in their pressed, black uniforms, which strained across impeccable muscular physiques, their smiles eased as they gazed upon the women, while tightened when confronting the men. The Emperor, however, continued his stare, locking her in place.

Her heart beat a frantic tattoo under his scrutiny, and she fiddled with the fabric of her gown while struggling to maintain her composure. To her left, her grandfather gathered her hand in his grip.

He whispered, "And, I thought they were imposing on the vid-screen. In person... well..." He coughed and stood a little straighter. The tremor in his hand radiated to his voice. The muscles of her grandfather's jaw ticked as he ground his teeth together.

She squeezed his hand, uncertain which of them needed more reassurance. This crack in his stoic facade had her swallowing against a surge of panic. He was her anchor. She needed him to be strong, not the other way around.

The Vendel Emperor stopped a few feet short of the head table and gave a small bow. His gaze traced down her arm and caught her clutching her grandfather's hand. Above his brow, the unusual tattoo of dark swirling lines writhed beneath his skin. Her skin prickled as the tiny hairs on her arm lifted and stood up straight.

"Charles Comwell..." The smooth velvety tones of his voice wrapped around her in a blanket of seductive steel, warm yet unyielding. "It is my great honor to be here."

Her grandfather released her hand and extended his arms out wide in open greeting. "It's a pleasure to meet in person, Emperor vlor'Malita." He gestured beside him. "You have met Commodore Armstrong. May I please present Commodore Armstrong's wife, Elenor." He turned to Elenor with a smile.

Elenor reached across the head table to shake his hand. "Emperor vlor'Malita—"

The Emperor grasped her palm, turned it over, and kissed the back, silencing whatever else she had planned to say. "A great pleasure to meet the Commodore's wife. You are an exquisite vision, my dear. The Commodore is a most honored man to have you at his side."

His voice rolled across the distance in multi-toned layers causing Elise to shiver.

A flush pinked Elenor's cheeks. "Thank you. It's an honor to meet you."

The Emperor nodded to Dale Armstrong. "Commodore Armstrong, I look forward to working with you and the Global Corps Space Agency."

Dale extended his hand and gave the Emperor a firm handshake. His arm moved with a stiffness which was unusual. The Emperor radiated confidence in the easy way he carried himself. The contrast between the men was striking, even more so because she'd always considered Dale to be one of the most self-assured men she'd ever known.

Her grandfather coughed into his fist. "And this is my granddaughter, Elise Comwell."

She froze as the Emperor's entire focus shifted to her. Silver eyes sparkled as he regarded her with deliberation.

Her grandfather nudged her elbow. With a strange sense of detachment, she watched as her hand was engulfed by the Emperor's.

A shock pulsed between them, shooting through her arm and into his, then returning from him magnified tenfold, thrumming with a strange burst of energy. She blinked against a kaleidoscope of color edging the corners of her vision, but then the strange sensation vanished.

His eyes widened, then while still grasping her hand, he turned to the man standing beside him. The Emperor spoke something in a strange language which caused the man standing beside him to study her with an appraising intensity.

She pulled back, but the Emperor's grip held firm, encasing her hand in a sheath of warmth.

As with Elenor, he kissed the back of her hand. His thumb traced a circle on her inner wrist. Her pulse jumped a notch and that thrumming electricity returned, muted, but undeniably there.

"Your granddaughter is even more beautiful in person." He flashed a brilliant smile before releasing her hand.

Her gaze hardened as she turned to her grandfather.

He ignored her glare. "I'm hopeful she'll consider your cultural exchange opportunity. She's majoring in theoretical physics and artificial intelligence in the Global Corps Virtual University. I think she'll be an asset in paving the way to establishing a mutually beneficial trade between our peoples."

"Beautiful and smart. I believe you may be right." The Emperor's attention returned to her. "Miss Comwell, your grandfather has spoken highly of you during our preliminary talks. He also mentioned you have a unique skill—perfect recall? Is this true?"

She pressed the heel of her shoe into her grandfather's toe.

He hissed with pain when she shot him a look, promising a long conversation later.

With a smile her etiquette tutor would be proud of, she faced the Vendel Emperor and measured her words out in smooth even tones. "I'm blessed with an eidetic memory, but it's far from perfect."

He gave a slight bow. "Nevertheless, it is an unusual attribute. You are unique; intellect, grace, and beauty."

Heat spread through her cheeks, rising high to her ears and even down her throat. She turned her head, letting her long, brown hair mask her embarrassment. "I don't know about that; most men feel threatened by me. I tend to scare them off."

Mortifying didn't even touch on her feelings at this point. Another glare at her grandfather. Another look he ignored. She was alone in this and she didn't understand what her grandfather was up to, but now it made more sense why he seated her next to the Emperor. Cultural exchange? And why hadn't Gramps briefed her about this earlier?

The Emperor chuckled. "I'm sorry to have embarrassed you, Miss Comwell. Please forgive me, and I assure you, I do not scare so easily."

Perhaps not, but she wished he would. Between an overprotective grandfather, and her unique social status, dates were hard to come by. Add to that the quirkiness of her oddball intellect, her experiences with men had been... unique. Not that she was an untouched virgin princess, or a nerd with her nose stuck in a book. Quite the opposite occurred. She had a wild streak and plenty of willing men to take an heiress for a spin under the sheets—but she didn't have success in relationships.

The Emperor continued as if the intense exchange between them had never happened. "Director Comwell, may I please present my companions." He gestured to the men standing behind him. "High Tender Marcus vlor'Vardhal, Tender Zanthis lor'Malden, High Councilors Talen vlor'Adreti and Cardic vlor'Altus, Councilors Massen lor'Smethci and Riobal lor'Bracus, and Judicators Sessil Grader and Mireck Kender."

Each man gave a brief nod as he was introduced. By the time he finished his introductions, she had already forgotten half their names. High Tender, Tender, Councilor, Judicator, vlor' and lor'? The titles made her head spin.

The only one she remembered was High Tender Marcus vlor'Vardhal because he'd been the man the Emperor had spoken to right after that weird electricity zapped her hand. Also, he was a vlor' like the Emperor. It seemed to be a title.

For whatever reason, she took an instant dislike to the man. Maybe it was his beady brown eyes and matching short-cropped hair. He was short and stocky, too, at least compared to the other Vendel, although he still stood well over six-foot. All the Vendel were imposing in every measure: height, build—hell, their intimidation factor was off the charts. Standing in front of them, she felt diminutive and weak.

"Gentlemen, welcome," her grandfather said with a puff of his chest. From the way her grandfather rolled his shoulders back, trying to stand taller than his aging frame allowed, it was clear he felt their guests' natural dominance too. "Please be seated. We've prepared a meal which I hope you enjoy."

The Emperor stepped around the table and pulled out the chair next to her. A heady aroma filled the air around him, making her pulse leap in her throat.

He placed a hand on the back of her chair, holding it for her. "Miss Comwell, may I?"

With a gesture, he indicated she should sit. As he adjusted her chair, he reached over her shoulder, startling her, and flicked her napkin open laying it across her lap. His mouth hovered beside her ear.

"You are quite lovely, Elise."

He turned away and exchanged words with the man sitting beside him, the one introduced as High Tender Marcus vlor'Vardhal. They spoke in a different language, harsh and guttural. The men disagreed about something. Their argument ended as abruptly as it began when the Emperor put his back to the High Tender. The red-faced man crossed his arms, obviously the loser, but looked like whatever conversation they had was far from over.

The Emperor leaned forward, ignoring the High Tender. "Director Comwell, I'm sure this is one feast I'm certain to savor."

She fiddled with her napkin, smoothing it over her lap, looking anywhere but at the man seated beside her. Two of the Vendel, who hadn't been introduced, took up posts behind the Emperor. Slim black rods, tied at each of their hips, extended midway to their knees and looked a lot like police batons. She wondered if they didn't serve a more sinister purpose because the men oozed malice.

An awkward silence descended over the table. One she broke with a question. "Excuse me, but what is the proper form of address for you? Is it Emperor Malita or Emperor vlor'Malita?"

He leaned back, took a sip of water from the crystal glass from his place setting, and smiled. He flicked a glance at High Tender Marcus vlor'-Vardhal. "For you... it would please me if you would call me Gregor. In fact, I insist on it."

High Tender Marcus vlor'Vardhal coughed and shifted in his seat, but otherwise he remained silent. His dark brown eyes regarded her with intense scrutiny.

"That seems very informal." She placed more distance between herself and the Emperor.

"I insist," he pressed. "For the rest, Sire, or My Lord, would be appropriate."

"But you are not our ruler." Her words came out with more challenge than she had intended. "Or is that your intent?"

Why would he want her to call him Gregor? It seemed a very informal form of address. No way was she going to call him that.

The entire head table went silent punctuated only by the deep indrawn breath of her grandfather. He reached over and squeezed her knee under the tablecloth. "Elise," he hissed in a whisper. "Behave!"

Oh great. Open mouth. Insert foot. What would her etiquette tutor think now?

The Emperor tilted his head back and laughed. "A challenge at every turn. How refreshing. You are correct, of course. Presumptuous of me and very rude, but a matter of habit, I'm afraid." He leaned forward. "Director Comwell, you must forgive me. Your granddaughter is correct, and I meant no offense. My subjects would refer to me as 'My lord,' or 'Sire,' but I would not expect someone from Earth to use that address. I respect your autonomy. Emperor vlor'Malita is the proper form of address. The lor' or vlor' is added before a lord's name and their title before that."

He leaned back, using it as an excuse to speak low into her ear. "But for you, call me Gregor." There was no mistaking the hunger in his words. His throaty chuckle resonated deep within her, calling forth an answer she wasn't yet willing to acknowledge.

As the Emperor's laughter diffused the tenseness of her challenging question, her grandfather moved the topic towards something much more mundane. "What do the prefixes of your names mean?" He swirled the water in his glass as he shot her a warning look, as if to say, behave yourself. "Does it denote a specific title or rank?" He leaned forward, cutting her out of the conversation.

She pressed back, happy to stay silent.

High Tender Marcus vlor'Vardhal answered. "They denote social status. The lor' belong to the governing caste. The vlor' designate the ruling caste." He bowed toward the Emperor, placing fist to chest.

As he leaned forward to speak along the long head table, the Emperor pressed back to give him room. Which left the two of them leaning back while her grandfather and the High Tender discussed Vendel social structure. The Emperor tapped his fingers on the armrest of his chair, but did not engage her in conversation. She couldn't tear her eyes away from the rhythm of his fingers.

"And for those without the lor' or vlor'?" her grandfather asked. "And Tender, Councilor, and Judicators, are those titles as well?"

"Only lords are referred to as Councilor. Judicators are men taken from the working caste. They sit as a counterweight to the power of our lords." The smile he gave looked anything but friendly and did nothing to soften the hard lines of his face.

"What does a Tender do?" Elise tore her eyes away from the Emperor's hypnotic fingers. How was it possible for fingers to be so damned sexy?

High Tender Marcus vlor'Vardhal's hard-brown eyes narrowed. "We fulfill a vital role in training certain members of our society."

She wanted to press him, but stopped when her grandfather placed a cautioning hand on her knee.

"We are fascinated to learn about your culture," her grandfather said. "How does it work with governing and ruling castes?" He monopolized the conversation, frustrating her to silence.

"The lor' serve the working caste by governing them," the High Tender explained. "They meet in High Council and present their requests to the Ruling Council. The lor' govern, but the vlor' rule."

"And the Judicators?"

"They protect from tyranny." The Emperor gave a slight incline of his head toward the end of the table. "As a collective, they have the power to overturn any of my rulings, but they must then step down and select a new group to serve."

One man, introduced as a Judicator, returned the Emperor's gesture by raising his glass.

She could no longer keep silent. "So, does the working caste select representatives to meet with the 'lor? Do they have a voice?"

The High Tender snorted.

The Emperor answered in a soft tone. "Like many things, there are differences between how we govern. We are not a democracy." His eyes glinted, and he gave a soothing gesture to High Tender vlor'Vardhal she didn't think she was supposed to have seen. He folded his arms across his chest, ending further questions.

The servers delivered their meals. Cornish game hens decorated their plates and succulent vegetables sat to the side. Murmurs of approval sounded throughout the room.

"Director Comwell," the Emperor said, "if I may propose a toast?"

"Absolutely," her grandfather said.

He stood, and within moments all eyes were fixed on him. It was impossible to ignore the man.

Silence engulfed the hall.

He raised his glass. "A toast to the ladies. The food is delicious, but you are the true feast of this evening." His gaze settled on her for a moment before turning back to the crowd. "Your beauty brings tears to my eyes and joy to my heart. My earthly cousins are rich beyond belief, basking in your charms. To the true treasure of the Earth, I toast the radiance of the fairer sex."

Cheers rang out through the banquet hall. Everyone toasted, except Elise. Her fingers curled around her glass, gripping hard.

Why toast the women? Did the Vendel not have women? She glanced to her grandfather, debating whether to pose her question.

When she didn't join in on the toast, the Emperor's lips pressed into a thin line. It was over before she could blink, and they were soon embroiled in another conversation.

She allowed her grandfather to guide the conversation, curbing her insatiable questions about the Vendel. He steered talk toward matters of state and soon they were speaking about trade and plans for an integrated step-wise cultural exchange program.

The conversation shifted from topic to topic and came back, by degrees, to the main subject of the Vendel's visit and future trade. Each time her grandfather prodded and asked about Vendel history, and their path to the stars, the Emperor or the High Tender shifted the conversation to another topic.

As waiters removed the dinner plates, High Tender Marcus vlor'-Vardhal cleared his throat. "Director Comwell, if I may?"

"Yes?"

Bored to tears with the politicking, she folded her napkin and nearly succeeded in making a crane.

"We did not mean to leave out your granddaughter and Commodore Armstrong's wife with our gift. If I may present it to them now?"

Her head snapped up, and the napkin fell on the floor.

The Emperor picked it up and draped it over her lap. His husky whisper curled in her ear. "What a shame, I was wondering what you would make."

She fisted the napkin and placed the crumpled fabric on the table, embarrassed to find he'd been watching her fiddling.

His low chuckle had heat rising all the way to her ears.

High Tender vlor'Vardhal pulled out two bottles from an inside breast coat pocket. He passed a vial to Elenor, who took it with a polite murmur of acceptance.

Elenor opened the bottle and inhaled the fragrance. "Why, it's stunning. How did you bottle such a wonderful scent?" She sneezed. "Excuse me."

"Bless you," Elise said.

The Emperor exchanged a look with the High Tender.

"It is one of our unique skills," replied the High Tender. He handed the next bottle to the Emperor. "My lord, are you certain?"

The Emperor took the vial and twirled it in his hands. "This is a most elusive scent, and it would give me great pleasure if you would allow me to apply it to the inside of your wrist."

A danger signal flared, but she couldn't refuse. Not with her grandfather poking her in the ribs.

A tense smile fixed to her face.

The Emperor took the top off and applied a small dab of liquid to his fingertip. "It's best when slightly warm, like so." He set the bottle down and High Tender vlor'Vardhal stoppered it back up.

The Emperor turned in his chair so his knees brushed her thighs. He grasped her wrist in his muscular hand and turned it over. With the tip of his finger, he applied the liquid to her inner wrist. In no hurry, he allowed his touch to wander and caressed her wrist, tracing a line up her forearm and back down into her palm. She tried to pull her hand away, but his grip held firm.

He gazed into her eyes. "This is a special essence. It has a tendency to linger. There's a legend our people made this as an aphrodisiac."

Did he proposition her? She flinched at the intensity of his stare and found her answer in the heat of his gaze.

Electricity spiraled up her forearm where his finger touched her skin, sinking deeper as heat rushed into her shoulder. From there, the shock branched, heading up to flush her cheeks and burst into an uncontrolled explosion of multi-colored light. She gasped as her body awakened with a painful hunger. This was not the Vendel-Earth union her grandfather had in mind. Tiny tremors shook her body from the inside out, unsettling her stomach and making her voice quaver.

She ripped her hand out of the Emperor's grip and pushed back from the table. "Excuse me, please." She rose on shaky legs. Her stomach rioted, threatening to return her dinner to her plate.

"Are you all right?" He bolted to his feet, eyes glinting with concern. He cast a worried glance at the High Tender who shrugged.

"Yes," she said, if too sharply. She smoothed her tone of voice, trying to recapture her composure. "I need to powder my nose."

The Emperor stepped to the side to let her pass. She felt his eyes on her all the way to the exit doors of the banquet hall. As they closed behind her, she broke into a run and headed towards the bathroom and a sink where she could wash off the perfume.

Aphrodisiac her ass. That was a love potion amped up on steroids. She couldn't get the image of him ravishing her out of her head. Or worse, her ripping that black uniform off his body. And her wrist burned from where his finger traced that deadly line of fire.

And the rainbows? What was up with the rainbows flashing in her vision? A kaleidoscope of color still swirled in her periphery. Could the perfume have hallucinogenic properties?

She slammed the bathroom door and raced inside to the sink.

Get it off! Get it off! Oh God, get it off!

The floral perfume floated up to her nose, saturating her nasal passages with the potent aroma, even as water poured over her wrist. She staggered against the overwhelming desire for him to claim her. *What's in this perfume?*

CHAPTER THREE_

Wednesday night, February 2, 2035:

ELISE WALKED OUT OF THE RESTROOM AND INTO THE EMPTY FOYER. NO DOUBT she would hear about her behavior later tonight when she and her grandfather got home.

In front of her, the doors to the banquet hall opened and two elderly women stepped out, their steps echoing in the cavernous space. The women exchanged polite nods with her and disappeared into the women's restroom. She hesitated outside the doors, not wanting to go back to the gathering. Her entire body shook with the urge to run, because, inside, he waited.

Her wrist itched where the Emperor had rubbed in the perfume. Images of him kept swirling in her mind, intrusive and unwelcome. Despite her social obligations as hostess to their alien guests, she couldn't force her feet to move. Surely her grandfather would forgive her if she slipped away for a while? Who was she kidding? He would be furious, but she couldn't stomach another moment beside the Emperor. His overt interest went beyond casual flirtation, inappropriate for an official banquet, and the fact her grandfather did nothing concerned her even more.

A few stolen minutes wouldn't hurt, and she had pressing concerns of her own. She headed down a hallway leading to an array of private sitting rooms. It would only take a moment to check in at the university and get the edits on her thesis. The closest parlor was empty. She slipped inside and closed the door. She looked around. There, tucked into the corner, was a small workstation. With a press of her palm to the controls, the electronics came to life. Two slim metal rods rose out the top of the desk and the shimmering screen of mist and light formed.

A few flicks and she navigated to the Global Corps virtual campus where she looked for Professor MacCabe. He was usually online. As always, she sent her avatar, a nerdy pimply faced teenaged boy, in for a visit, rather than teleconference directly. To avoid favoritism, no one on campus knew her identity. Unlike her fake trust-fund friends, she liked to earn her grades rather than buy them.

"Alex!" Professor MacCabe's Einstein avatar greeted her arrival with an enthusiastic wave. "What are you doing on campus this late on a Wednesday night?"

Avoiding alien Emperors.

But she couldn't tell him that. Semester grades were due, and she was dying to know what he thought of her thesis. There was little time to make changes. An 'A' in his class sealed her seat on the Jupiter mission.

"Have you looked at my neural modeling paper?" Her avatar, Alex, pushed thick glasses up his nose and gave one of his programmed nervous shrugs.

"Yes." Einstein ran his hand though scraggly gray hair. "One moment, please." He leaned over a stack of research papers and thumbed through the mountain of folders. "Let's examine this theory of yours." He pulled the glasses off his face and chewed on the earpiece.

Over the next half hour, the two of them waded through her term paper. At one point, MacCabe's Einstein sat up with interest. They were in the neural phase processing section where she described her six-dimensional theory about neural interfaces extending into higher dimensions. It formed the basis of her theory for the anchoring of the subconscious in four dimensions, space and time, with subsequent extension into the fifth and sixth dimensions.

"This is promising work," McCabe said.

The door squeaked behind her. In the reflected view of the holo-mist, the imposing image of Emperor Gregor Ulysses vlor'Malita stared back, a look of concern etched deep in his face. Behind him, his Goliath bodyguards with the black batons took up positions outside the door.

Her stomach clenched, wondering how, or even why, he'd tracked her down.

Like a snapshot, her mind imprinted every detail of the enigmatic man into her mind. In one hand, he balanced a dessert plate that held a beautiful confection of chocolate lace swirls, a sprig of mint, and two forks. Under his arm, he clutched a bottle of wine. He gripped two wine glasses between the fingers of his other hand. His black uniform accentuated the sculpted muscles of a robust physique, and she would never forget his tattoo—dark lines swirling with a sinuous grace.

Pressure built in her chest, a sudden pounding that made breathing tenuous. A faint fragrance whispered past her nose, memory of the perfume she'd scrubbed off her wrist. Without thought, she lifted her wrist and sniffed, but all she smelled was the lilac scented soap she'd used to wash. Where was that tantalizing aroma coming from? This was not good.

"Professor, I have to go."

"But Alex?"

"I'm sorry."

She cut the connection because she couldn't risk MacCabe overhearing anything the Emperor might say. She turned off the console and faced the Emperor.

"What are you doing here?"

His eyes flashed silver in the soft light. "You missed a delicious dessert." He stepped away from the closing door and placed his treasure on a small coffee table in front of two wing-backed chairs.

"I'm not hungry, Emperor." And she wasn't sure how she felt about being trapped inside with him considering his men guarded the only exit.

His brows pressed together. "Please, call me Gregor."

"Honestly, I'm uncomfortable using your first name."

She crossed her arms, trying to put him off, but really, it was to silence the pounding of her heart. This man did things to her body. Never had she responded to a man like this. The way he tracked her down should have creeped her out. Instead, his interest excited her.

"Vendel do not have first names. Gregor is my given name."

"What about Ulysses? Is that a middle name then?"

A full smile warmed his face. "Ulysses is my public name, but you should not use it. And, before you ask, I can't bear for you call me by rank or title. We should not be formal when by ourselves."

He sat in one of the wing-back chairs, and regarded her with clear interest while she struggled to find her breath. Only when he uncorked the wine and poured did she suck in air. The intensity of his gaze made her feel like he was dissecting her under a microscope. She didn't have the strength to match that stare.

She should walk out, but her grandfather would be angry. There was no way to avoid insulting the Emperor if she left now. The obvious choice was to join him and make small talk until she could find some polite way to excuse herself.

All the questions rolling around in her mind, like what was a public name to a Vendel, and why was it something she should never use, faded beneath his intense scrutiny. She wanted to flee.

"I should get back. My grandfather is probably worried."

"Director Comwell knows I came to find you." He shifted in his seat. "In my culture, it's common for a vlor' to bestow a welcome gift to a woman of your station. I thought nothing of touching you the way I did. In retrospect, I may have crossed a line. Given the way you rushed out, it concerned me. I meant no offense." He gestured to the chair. "Please, allow me to make amends. Have a seat."

She flicked her gaze to the door and back to the chair. It was clear he would not let her leave, at least not unless she made a scene. With a defeated sigh, she slipped into the chair. Before she had settled herself, he handed over the drink.

He lifted his glass. "Shall we toast?"

No, but she lifted her glass and tried to keep sarcasm out of her tone. "To successful trade between our peoples."

A frown marred his elegant features. "An appropriate toast, but more suited to diplomats. It's just the two of us." He studied her. "Perhaps we could drop the formalities and enjoy a moment of each other's company? These can be difficult times, but I hope we navigate our way through them."

She refused to respond. If he didn't consider her a diplomat, then what role did he see her fulfilling?

"A toast to the true treasure of the Earth?" He lifted his glass in salute.

"You already used that one," she replied with a prim smile.

He searched her face and countered after a momentary pause. "A toast to you then? An unexpected treasure. I sense a connection between us. I'm hopeful that means we have a bright future ahead of us." He sipped and placed the glass of wine back on the table. "You're not going to toast?"

"No, Emperor."

"Hm, you still insist on formalities. I've made my wishes clear." He let his hands fall to the armrests. Silence descended between them. "Names are important in Vendel society, perhaps this is not the case on Earth?" As his brow quirked up, the tattoo over his brow quivered.

Names were names. "What's with your tattoo?"

"My what?"

She wiggled her fingers at the angular whorls over his brow. Only now, they were static and dark. "The tattoo over your left eye."

"Ah," he said, tilting his head back. "The imperial mark designates my birthright."

"Well, Emperor... I've never seen a tattoo that moves."

"Please, Elise, do not call me Emperor. I wish to be less formal." He leaned forward, surprising her with his speed. The warmth of his hand encased hers and his voice lowered. "I must insist you use my given name."

Her eyes widened at the touch. That odd electricity returned, muted from before, but undeniably present. She wasn't certain if he felt it, because he didn't react, but her skin hummed with the contact. However, what was clear was he didn't like being denied.

She swallowed. "Do you always get what you want?"

"Only if you toast with me." His intense focus fixed on her. He lifted his glass and waited.

Raising the glass to her lips, the wine tasted sweet and crisp. She licked her lips as she considered him. "Aren't you supposed to be giving a speech or meeting with the dignitaries? Won't you be missed?"

"The High Councilors will make sure they make the proper speeches. And I'll have plenty of time to circulate with the crowd later. As I said, I was afraid I offended you. High Tender vlor'Vardhal says I can be over-bearing, and he reminded me of the cultural gap separating our people. It would be horrible if I'd offended the granddaughter of our host during our first official state function. I had to apologize if I made you uncomfortable back there."

"That was considerate of you, but unnecessary." And as for making her uncomfortable, what did he think was happening now?

"Nevertheless, you feel fine? No sniffles or sneezes?"

That seemed off topic. Why did he care about sniffles and sneezes? "No, I just needed to work on my thesis assignment."

He waved toward the console in the corner. "Am I to assume visitors from space are less interesting than discussing neural chemistry with your professor? What was it now—defining the mind versus the brain? Neural modeling in sub-dimensions?" He made his voice soft, interested even.

How long had he been listening?

"Neural processing. Not chemistry. My thesis is about how the mind uses the physical framework of the brain to work. And it's not that I find you uninteresting, but rather, I was excluded from the general conversation. My grandfather does that at these events, and as you've pointed out,

I'm not much of a diplomat. I wanted to stretch my legs and check up on a few pressing concerns of my own." She gestured to the dark console. "Such as semester grades."

"I see. Even during what some might consider the most exciting moment of our lives, the mundane tends to pull us back to reality."

"Well, exciting would have been if you were green, three-eyed aliens with tentacles, but…"

His smile seemed genuine as he inclined his head. "Are you saying that since we're human, we're boring?"

"Not boring, just, not what I was expecting. I'm interested to see what your culture is like. After two thousand years, I'm curious to see how far it's diverged from ours."

"I think you'll be pleased to find we're quite similar, but also vastly different. Two thousand years is a long time." The tone of his voice turned serious, warning her of something.

"Different how? Do we have reason to fear you?" A spark of fear flared in her gut.

His eyes narrowed. "Elise, there is always a reason to fear, but you must trust me when I say I have nothing but humanity's best interest at heart." He pushed a dessert plate toward her. "You have not tasted the dessert."

"Neither have you. Do you include Earth as a part of humanity, then? If we're similar yet different, that leaves a lot of room for interpretation."

"You intrigue me. I'm not used to being challenged by a woman." His silver eyes bored into her. "But yes, we are all human."

"I noticed there are no women in your party. Where are they?"

He lifted his glass. "Not only intelligent, but wise. Perhaps that's why I find you so refreshing."

"You deflect my questions the same way you deflected my grandfather's at dinner. Why won't you answer my question about your women?"

"You're not put off by my position."

"Well, that's because I grew up around my grandfather. Power doesn't affect me like other people. He's always been Gramps first. I'm sure he'll have something to say about showing proper respect later though. Like your High Tender what's-his-name, my grandfather often tells me I speak before thinking."

That comment bought another genuine smile. It reached up to his eyes, making them sparkle in the subdued lighting. Neither of them spoke for a time.

He broke the silence first. "Honestly, I find it refreshing." He twirled the wine glass between two fingers examining the golden liquid inside. "And his name is High Tender Marcus vlor'Vardhal, although you will refer to him as High Tender Marcus."

At his words, her heart beat faster, her stomach knotted, and her breathing came just a little too fast. In trying to put the man off, she'd only drew his attention. "Emperor—"

He tilted his head and regarded her with that cocky grin. His eyes lit with amusement as he shook his head. "Ah, please Elise, call me Gregor."

Names meant more to the Vendel than she'd thought. It followed she shouldn't offend him by continuing to refuse his request. Ugh, her grandfather was so going to owe her after this state dinner.

"Gregor," she corrected and watched him settle back in the chair. "If I've offended you, I'd like to offer my sincerest apologies."

"No apologies required… Elise." The way he said her name sent shivers up her spine because of how he savored it, rolling the two syllables around in his mouth almost as if he was tasting them.

She rubbed her neck, feeling self-conscious. With every breath, she could see her chest rise and fall, acutely aware of her low-cut gown and exposed cleavage. What she wouldn't give for a shawl to cover up. Gregor's eyes spent way too much time focused there rather than on her face.

"I am hopeful you will consider our cultural exchange program. Your grandfather speaks highly of your skills."

She blushed. "Perhaps he's too vocal."

Gregor dismissed her comment with a wave of his hand. "He's proud of his granddaughter. What man wouldn't be?" He pointed to the console. "Take, for example, your thesis paper."

Her thesis paper? "What about it?"

"You'd be interested in our computer systems. Our technology is more biological than Earth's, but we use the sub-dimensions you mentioned with your professor in the framework of our computers. It will be easy for you to adapt to our technology." He arched a brow and waited for a response.

Again, she wondered how long he had been listening before making his presence known. More shocking was that he understood any of it. She tipped her glass to her lips and took a deep swallow.

He leaned forward to refill her wine.

"Do you think you would be interested?"

Despite her misgivings, she had to admit an interest. She'd been excited to be awarded a spot on the Jupiter mission, but knowing aliens existed, and other star systems were now within grasp... well that would be hard to pass up.

She nodded. "Exactly how much did my grandfather say about me?"

Gregor laughed. "He is very proud of you. The two of you seem close." His eyes pinched at that comment for some odd reason.

Another sip of wine. Her glass was empty and her head spun. She set the glass down, unwilling to drink anymore. And her inner wrist still itched. She rubbed at the faint trail of fire flickering up her forearm.

He leaned forward, his attention focused on her scratching. "What are you doing after dinner? We could discuss plans to bring you on board the *Gambit*." His eyebrows quirked up, but she refused to acknowledge the blatant proposition.

She stared down at the thick carpet. Heat blossomed in her cheeks with his proximity. A peek through her lashes revealed just how close he was. His crisp, clean scent rolled off him making her want to press forward for a kiss. There was something else there too, an underlying spice that had her head spinning. The heat flaring in her wrist shot up her arm, breaking her trance.

She bolted upright and shook her head. How did one say no to an Emperor? "Um... I don't think—"

The door eased open and one of the large gladiator guards poked his head inside. "Sire, High Tender vlor'Vardhal requires your presence."

Gregor turned toward the door with a resigned sigh. "It has been pleasant chatting with you, Elise. Perhaps another time. That is, if you're feeling well."

She cringed, heart thundering in her chest. He should have scared her half to death, instead, she'd been leaning toward him, nearly begging for a kiss. What was wrong with her?

CHAPTER FOUR_

Thursday, February 3, 2035:

ELISE WOKE THE FOLLOWING MORNING WITH A LAZY STRETCH AND ROLLED over to gaze out her bedroom windows to look upon her private garden. Memories of last night flitted through her thoughts and churned her stomach.

It was time to face her grandfather. After that conversation with the Emperor, she never returned to the banquet, but went home and straight to bed. She rolled out of bed and went in search of her grandfather, steeling herself to face his disappointment. He wasn't in his study, or anywhere else. She queried the house computer who informed her he was not at home. Confused, she sent a request to his virtual assistant to locate him.

Moments later, bleary eyes peered back through the holo-mist. "Good morning, Elise."

Good morning? Was that it? No yelling? No stern look of disapproval, or worse, disappointment? "Gramps, where are you?"

He rubbed puffy eyes and squinted into the screen. "I'm at Commodore Armstrong's house."

"You look tired."

"I've been up all night."

"Why?" Before he could respond, she added, "Gramps, I'm sorry I left the banquet, but..."

"I'm tied up at the Armstrong's right now. Can we do this later?"

"Yes, um… Why?"

"Something happened. Elenor's sick. The doctor is with her now."

"What's wrong?"

"She can hardly breathe. She's spitting up blood, and when she cries…" He averted his eyes. His voice cracked with emotion. "Her tears are red. The doc doesn't know what's wrong."

"I'll come right over."

"I don't know about that."

"Gramps, it's Elenor."

The woman had raised her, and Elise had taken part of her name from Elenor, or at least that's what her mother had said. There was no way he could keep her away.

"I'm coming. I'll be there in thirty minutes."

He vented a heavy sigh. "She might appreciate that."

She cut the connection and had their driver, Mark, take her to the Armstrong's house. Two hours later, thanks to a massive wreck closing the roads, they pulled up to Armstrong's residence. Parked outside was an official coroner's van. Her gut clenched at the sight. She raced inside, heart pounding, hoping what her eyes were telling her couldn't be true.

Her grandfather sat on the living room couch. A glass of Scotch hung in his hand, the amber liquid sloshing inside. He had his head cradled in his other hand and tears streaked down his face. Another cup of Scotch sat on the coffee table, untouched.

"Dale's upstairs." He downed the contents of his glass. He waved outside, sloshing alcohol on the carpet. "The medical coroner's team arrived just before you."

Boots shuffled behind her. She turned to see two men in white coveralls navigating the broad staircase with a black body bag. They placed it on a waiting stretcher. Dale descended the stairs behind the men. He walked them to the door, eyes staring vacantly ahead.

She watched, stunned, as they loaded the bag into the white van and drove off. The entire scene was too surreal. This couldn't be happening. It wasn't real.

Dale came into the room, brushing past her, unseeing, and grabbed the glass on the table. He collapsed into the overstuffed rocker. The two men sat in stony silence. The Commodore of the Global Corps Space Agency, her future boss, hunched back further into his chair and drank, looking as if his world had ended.

He sneezed and wiped his nose.

"Dale, I'm so sorry." She cringed at how pathetic the words sounded the moment they spilled from her mouth. What a fool. His wife just died. Elenor was dead? None of this made sense.

His gaze crossed hers momentarily before moving back down to the floor. She glanced at her grandfather, who shrugged and shook his head. He rubbed his nose with the back of his hand and sniffed.

Dale downed the last drop of the Scotch. She took the glass from his shaking hand. After she poured him another two fingers of liquor, she refilled her grandfather's tumbler. The movement kept her busy and her mind from thinking about Elenor.

She gazed out the window and tried to process what had happened while the two men dealt with their grief and she struggled to find hers. A numbness settled over her shoulders.

Dale spent much of the morning and early afternoon drinking himself into a deep stupor. He passed out just before dinner, and Gramps stumbled off to the internet console to work.

She went up to Elenor's room, her movements wooden and jerky. Sorting through Elenor's closet gave her something to do. She wanted to find the perfect dress for the burial. When her grandfather found her a few hours later she was curled up in a corner of the closet, sobbing into an expensive silk scarf. He sat beside her and hugged her tight.

"Come, we need to head home. Help me pack a bag for Dale. I don't think he should be alone tonight." He sneezed.

She jumped with concern. "Are you okay?"

"Oh dear, excuse me. I seem to be catching a cold." He pointed to his forehead. "Sinuses blocked." He stood and offered her a hand up. Together they found what they needed and descended to find Dale stirring on the couch. With the help of Mark, they loaded Dale into the car and headed back to the Comwell Estate.

Unease settled over her shoulders as a memory tickled. What had the Vendel Emperor said? *Perhaps another time. That is, if you are feeling well.*

A coldness settled over her chest. With a shudder, she wrapped her hands around herself. Were the Vendel responsible for what happened to Elenor?

She glanced at her grandfather, and then to Dale. Other than an occasional sneeze they both looked fine. And her grandfather suffered from allergies, but Elenor had sneezed at the banquet.

She leaned over to her grandfather and whispered into his ear. "Gramps, I think they did this."

"Who?"

"The Vendel. Is anyone else sick?"

Dale blinked bleary, red-lined eyes at her, overhearing her conversation. "What?"

"We don't know," her grandfather said.

CHAPTER FIVE_

Friday morning, February 4, 2035:

THE DAY BEGAN WITH A DULL DRIZZLE. GRAMPS'S HEAD COLD SETTLED INTO HIS lungs. Elise worried over him, playing nursemaid, bringing hot tea and sandwiches, while he set up for an important meeting of state. Unsettled thoughts of Elenor flashed in her mind as she listened to him cough.

Her hand shook as she placed the tea on the table beside him, and she tried to remember what he'd said about last night. Elenor had been fine at the banquet, then she didn't feel well. There was something about bloody tears.

Elise cast a sideways glance at her grandfather as he finished his preparations and held back the urge to feel his forehead. When she suggested they call a doctor, he shooed her out with a glare.

Moving to the guest wing, she checked on Dale. He refused to leave his rooms and come down for lunch. He too, coughed.

Fisting her hands, she made a decision, and returned to her grandfather's study. Holo-mist filled the air, framing the faces of the world's leaders. Her grandfather pressed his lips into a hard line at her interruption and almost had her turning on her heels, but this couldn't wait.

He muted the video feed with his finger. His red-lined eyes showed his intense fatigue, and the finger sandwiches she brought earlier remained untouched.

"Elise, I'm very busy."

"Listen, I think the Vendel made Elenor sick."

A few of the faces hanging in holo-mist turned their attention to her, but none showed any surprise. She recognized some of them from the various state dinners she'd attended over the years. Her grandfather pointed to the door. "We can't be sure of that."

"But..."

"We're investigating all the options." He flicked his fingers in dismissal. His deep sigh turned into a fit of coughing.

A step forward to comfort him was met with his raised hand. Palm out, he halted her advance. "Please. I need to pay attention to the meeting."

"Gramps?" *Why wouldn't he listen?*

"Why don't you call one of your friends? Or go to the flight line and practice your flight drills. Don't you have a competition coming up?"

He wanted her to go stunt flying? Or call one of her friends? The last thing she wanted was to waste the day with fake trust-fund friends. While fun, the Air Race World Championships weren't for another four months. Her instructor was out of town on his honeymoon, and it wasn't like she would practice her aerobatics without him. While she loved maneuvering her small Corvus Racer through the air gates, how could she think about that when her grandfather was sick?

Although, being stuck inside all day, knowing he'd be busy in his study with his meetings, made her want to leave. Dale wasn't helping matters either, not with shutting himself in with grief. Getting out was probably the best idea.

Another name came to mind. This might be the perfect opportunity to meet up with Alice. She would take Elise's mind off aliens and the heavy miasma of grief settling over Comwell Estate. It took digging to find Alice's contact info. Soon though, the holo-mist formed into an image of her friend's round face and shock-white hair.

"Elise! Hey! What's up?" Alice leaned toward the screen and lowered her voice to a whisper. "Have you been following the news? The bigwig Global Corps folk met the aliens at this uber-posh banquet. Now they're talking about sharing their technology. It's all biotech. Can you believe it?" Her bright blue eyes widened with excitement.

"Well, I suppose..."

Mention of the Vendel brought back an image of Gregor and an itching at her wrist. She rubbed the skin of her inner wrist remembering the odd electricity she felt every time he touched her.

"Oh, come on, you're not even a little interested? Have you seen the vids? Talk about drool-worthy man-meat."

"Where did you see pictures of the Vendel?"

Not that her identity was a big secret, but people treated her differently after they found out her grandfather headed Global Corps. For once, she wanted to just be an ordinary person. Fingers crossed, she prayed there weren't any vid-feeds of her circulating out in the Internet at that event.

"They posted them from the banquet," Alice answered. "It's all over the news."

Strange. She remembered no reporters inside the banquet hall.

Alice caught her confused expression, misinterpreting it. She rolled her eyes. "Here, I'm sending you some links."

The holo-mist flared green with the incoming message. Her finger hovered over the link. She squeezed her eyes and activated it.

Her breath hitched as she stared at the Vendel Emperor's face. Silver-gray eyes smiled warmly at the camera as the Emperor shook the hand of her grandfather.

With a sigh, she realized why she didn't remember. She fled after her brief meeting with Gregor, missing all the ensuing speeches and obligatory press. She remembered the champagne, his toast, and the perfume.

The itching in her wrist intensified.

"What do you think?" Alice asked. "Pretty hot, huh?"

"I suppose." Her dreams had been filled with sensual images of the man.

"You suppose? No supposing about it. That man is hot. And did you look at the others? I mean… yowza!"

Her apprehension surged. "Don't you think it's all too friendly? They left Earth like a couple thousand years ago. What do we have that they need?"

Alice laughed. "Oh dear, are you one of those?"

"One of those what?"

"A doomsayer!" Her friend laughed and sent her another link. "Here, check these out. Lots of people are talking doom and gloom and conspiracy theories. That they're here to destroy us, enslave us, take Earth's resources. You name it, the list goes on."

"I'm not a doomsayer. Just cautious." Lots of people were cautious, she wasn't the only one.

Alice waved her hand. "Oh, I'm just kidding with you, but Comwell has thought about all of that. I mean, he's handling it."

The absolute assurance Alice had in her grandfather astounded Elise. She wanted to scream.

"I'm sure if there was anything to worry about, they'd already be on top of it," Alice continued.

Elise didn't buy it. She tried to move the conversation forward, hoping to distract herself from anything to do with the Vendel, or her current issues at home.

"Listen, are you interested in going out tonight? Maybe we could hit some bars and find a couple of hot bodies for ourselves?"

"Actually, I have plans."

"Oh." Her shoulders sagged.

A wicked gleam lit up her friend's eyes. "You want to join me?" Her brows arched up.

"Are you kidding? I'd love to." Anything to get out of the house.

"Perfect!" Alice clapped her hands together. "I'm going to be a judge at The Spot in B-town. Come with me and be a judge as well."

"What kind of judge?" The Spot was well known for a hopping night life.

"It's a surprise. Here, give me your address and I'll pick you up."

"Better idea. Give me yours and I'll come get you." No way was Alice going to pick her up at the Comwell Estate.

CHAPTER SIX_

Friday night, February 4, 2035:

Elise picked Alice up just before seven. "So, what's the surprise?"

Her friend giggled. "We're going to be judges."

"I know, you told me that much. Judges at The Spot... but what are we judging?"

Alice rubbed her hands together and leaned forward. "Chest and Abs."

"What does that mean?"

A grin spread across Alice's face.

"Oh God," Elise said with a start.

Her night took a turn for the better. A night of judging hot bodies might result in an evening under the sheets with one. What might the Vendel Emperor's body might look like under the sheets? With an irritated shake of her head, she tried to erase that image. Thoughts of him popped up all the time. *So distracting.*

"Now step on it. It starts right at the end of Happy Hour, and if we're late, we lose our spot as judges."

"I'm not going to ask how you got picked for this." She poked Alice in the ribs, giggling. "But I like it."

"Good. Now drive."

Less than an hour later, Elise sat on a tall barstool in the middle of the dance floor at The Spot. The techno beat the DJ had blaring drowned out all conversation. Her voice was already hoarse from screaming.

Alice swayed to the beat of the music on the stool beside her and looked on with interest at the row of eager contestants who were busy shedding their shirts. Elise admired the rock-hard abs and sculpted chests, licking her lips as one hot guy gave her a wink.

She leaned over and yelled into Alice's ear. "How does this work?"

A man handed each of them a long ribbon of silk.

Another grin cracked Alice's face. "Did I forget to mention we judge by feel?"

Elise could barely hear over the music. "What?"

Alice pantomimed what was expected and Elise burst out laughing. This would be so much fun. She was so happy to have run into such a fun person like Alice during that charity walk. This was something she never would have done on her own.

The thumping of the music drove deep into her body as the contestants stepped onto the dance floor. The men grinned. She wasn't sure who would enjoy the judging more. When they handed the men the body oil, she found her answer. The glistening bodies swayed to the beat of the music.

At a signal from the MC, Alice tied on the blindfold. Elise took one more glance at the row of bare male chests before tying the black silk over her eyes.

Rough hands lifted her wrists, startling her. The male pressed her palms to an oiled chest. She jumped the first time, then let her hands roam until he stepped away. The next set of hands startled her with the following contestant, and the next, but she powered through, enjoying the slide of sculpted pecs and abs beneath her palms.

Her hands ran across more male flesh than she had ever dreamt possible. By the end, she'd lost the ability to blush, although her cheeks ached from the constant grin on her face.

She wasn't sure how, but they announced a winner. Unknown hands removed her blindfold. She blinked as she stared down the row of half-naked male flesh. Three of them winked at her. They awarded prizes to all the men.

Alice pulled her off the dance floor and to the bar.

Several of the men came over and bought them drinks. They chatted before the next competition of the night. As the men gathered on the dance floor, Elise leaned over to yell into Alice's ear.

"What now?"

Another wicked grin. Alice even licked her lips. "Buns and Thighs."

"What?" Her head whipped around to the dance floor and at the twenty-odd men standing in a ragged line. "How do they judge that?"

Her friend arched a brow and gave her an are-you-kidding-me look.

Her jaw dropped as the guys stripped out of their pants, revealing a remarkable array of boxers, briefs, and tighty-whities. When the girls who'd signed up to be the Buns and Thighs judges looked too drunk to continue, Alice popped up from her barstool like a Jack-in-the-box waving at the manager.

"Andy! Andy, we'll do it." She tugged Elise back to the dance floor.

They didn't leave empty handed. In her pocket, she had twenty numbers scrawled on napkins. Alice thought it strange she didn't hand out her personal number. When pressed, Elise refused to explain, instead, she made a game of it. For each guy who wanted her number, she demanded a kiss. Then she had them write their numbers on a napkin and hand it over. Definitely one of her top ten nights out ever, although, it was morning when they left.

CHAPTER SEVEN_

Saturday morning, February 5, 2035:

DAWN BROKE THE MORNING SKY WHEN SHE RETURNED HOME. ALL SHE WANTED was to sleep off her hangover, however, an all too familiar white van parked in front of the mansion gave her pause.

Men in white biohazard garb walked out the front door. She flew out of the car and staggered to the men carrying a body bag between them. Her heart lurched as the ground tilted beneath her feet. A shaking began in her chest, turning to tremors as it reached her fingertips.

Another man encased in a protective suit tried to hold her back.

Tears flowed down her cheeks. Memories of Elenor crashed in her mind.

"Gramps!"

The men sidestepped with the body bag. Respirators on their backs stressed their heavy breathing. The bag bowed between them, crinkling as it bent. Her stomach heaved as she fought down a wave of nausea.

The stranger held her when she lunged for the bag. "Miss, you can't be here."

"Just try to stop me." Her fingers clawed at the zipper of the bag. "Gramps!" *Please, don't be in there. Don't be in there.*

Familiar footsteps. A hand squeaking over a banister. A cough. A sneeze.

Those sounds drew her attention through the doorway and had her spinning out of the stranger's grip. Her gaze flew to where her grandfather leaned against the entry hall column for support. Pink tinged tears stained his cheeks.

She ran up the broad marble stairs, her legs strong and steady. "Gramps!" Well, mostly steady.

He held out his arms and folded her into a hug. "Hush."

"What happened?"

There was no doubt who lay inside that body bag. Five more men encased in white biohazard suits stood in the foyer. Canisters hung on their backs. Each had a small black case in their hands. The small red biohazard sign unmistakable.

"Sir, I'm sorry," the man said who had restrained her. "I tried to keep her away."

Her grandfather looked with bleary eyes. "Doesn't matter. This is my granddaughter. She's already exposed."

She took a shuddering breath. Exposed? She'd kissed all those men last night.

His body trembled and his shoulders slumped. "Come, let's go into the parlor." He started down the hall leaving her questions unanswered.

She followed, feeling deflated and very sober.

Three of the five men joined them while the others headed upstairs.

"Miss," one man said, his voice distorted by the respirator. "Please, I need to take a blood sample and a swab of your mouth." He gestured for them to sit.

She collapsed onto an ottoman, too numb to take the extra five steps to the overstuffed leather chair. "Tell me what's going on."

"Director Comwell, I need to ask a few questions." The man spoke with deference, shifting back and forth on his feet while adjusting the respirator over his face through the fabric of his hood.

"Go ahead." Her grandfather rolled up his sleeve as one man opened his case and rubbed alcohol on her grandfather's arm.

"Sir, I need a list of everyone you've come in contact with since Wednesday night."

He sighed. "Everyone at the banquet, Director Armstrong, and his wife, Elenor." He stopped while the assistant inserted a needle and withdrew his blood. Her grandfather jerked his chin toward her. "My granddaughter. We were all at the banquet. And the estate staff."

The man transferred the blood to a vial and then brought out a cotton swab. "Open your mouth." He scribbled on his tablet and then turned his attention to Elise.

Her answer was different. Last night had been exciting, but detailing her adventure with her grandfather sitting right beside her turned into one of the most mortifying experiences of her life.

The assistant taking her blood blushed as she recounted the crowded club. The man in charge pressed for details on how much physical contact she had with the men.

She stared at the floor and twisted her hands. "I ran my hands over their chests for the first contest..." She cast a sideways glance at her grandfather. Her breathing hitched as she continued. "... and then over their butts and the backs of their thighs."

The interviewer paused and cleared his throat. "Did you have intimate contact with anyone at the club?"

She groaned and buried her head into her hands. Across the room, her grandfather wouldn't meet her eye.

"Kissing."

"We will need his name," the man whispered.

Her head shot up. "There was more than just one." She did the math. Twenty abs and chests, twenty buns and thighs, and a few more. She'd kissed well over fifty guys the night before, spreading her contagion to those men. Those fifty would spread it to how many more by the time night fell? And those?

"I need all their names." A look of dread passed over the man's face.

Elise fished out the thick stack of napkins from her purse and thrust it at him. She shrank when her grandfather turned away.

"Was that all?" he pressed. "Nothing more... intimate?"

"No." She stood and walked over to her grandfather forcing him to look into her eyes. "Oh, get over yourself. I'm not innocent. Tell me what's going on."

"Dale's dead."

"I figured." The harshness of her words made him wince. Immediately regretting it, she knelt down, placing her hands on his knees.

Fatigue hung heavy in his eyes as he stared at her.

"I'm so sorry, Gramps. I know how close you were."

A sharp intake of breath and pain flashed in his eyes. "He and Elenor are not the only ones." He leaned forward and cupped her head in his hands. "More than a hundred from the banquet are dead. Twice that are sick with the sniffles, a head cold, sneezing. Nothing serious until they bleed." He sniffed and rubbed his nose leaving a pale pink tinge on the cuff of his shirtsleeve.

"Now do you believe me?"

Her attention lingered on the cloth and the stain. Her mind whirled. What had the Emperor said? An eidetic memory was great, but her auditory recall was crap.

"Have you spoken to the Vendel? Asked them?"

He looked down and his voice grew cold. "They cut off communications."

"Dear God." She gripped his hands hard. "They did this."

His stony gaze confirmed her fears. "I've been trying to reach you, but you forgot your phone... again." His voice broke. "It's spreading fast."

A spasm of coughing overcame him. When he quieted, he continued. "Thousands who weren't at the banquet are dead. That number is rising. Look." He activated a console in the armrest of his chair and a screen of numbers flashed in the mist. Red and black counts of those sick and those dead.

The two men returned from upstairs and one poked his head inside the parlor. "Sir, we're finished." He nodded to the interviewer.

"Director Comwell," the man with all the questions said. "You, your granddaughter, and the staff will be quarantined." He coughed and shifted from foot to foot as he explained.

"Gentlemen," Elise said to the gathered biohazard crew, "my grandfather needs rest. If there's nothing else?"

The leader shook his head. "We have the samples we need."

"Good. I'll see you to the door." She escorted the five men and their little black cases to their van and stopped the man who had interviewed them. "So, how bad is it?"

He shrugged.

"Do we know what's causing it?"

He shook his head. "I'm sorry, we don't. But with the samples, we hope to find out."

Her gaze wandered back up to the house. "And my grandfather?"

"I don't know."

"Has anyone recovered?" Hope burned to ash at the look returned in his eyes.

"I'm sorry. We're just trying to keep up with the cases and contain the epidemic." He handed his clipboard to one of the men in the van. "Miss, I have to go. I have a lot of work to do."

She thought of her night at The Spot. *What have I done?*

As the van drove down the long sloping drive, she cast her eyes skyward into the twilight. Her thoughts focused into a tight beam heavenward.

Whatever you did, I will make you pay.

She marched back inside. Her grandfather was slumped over in the chair. She helped him to his feet and got him upstairs. There was a desk in the corner of his room equipped with a holo-display. She activated the mist and found the program he'd shown her with the numbers with the current tally of deaths in real-time.

She called her brother-in-law.

"Hi, Tom."

Her insides felt like someone had carved them out, leaving her hollow and bleak.

A groggy Tom stared back at her through the holo-mist. "Hey, sis, we're going to be a little late getting over there today." He paused and then looked back with concern. "Why are you calling me so early?"

"We're under quarantine."

"What?"

"Gramps is sick." She stared through the holo-mist at his strong features. "People from the banquet are sick and many are dead. Dale and Elenor Armstrong died."

"What!" His eyes looked ready to pop.

She rested her forehead in her hands. "They're calling it an outbreak. Take the girls and get to the island."

The Comwell's had a private retreat, a secure facility for just this purpose. Alice had been right about one thing. Charles Comwell prepared for doomsday, and his family had everything they needed to survive decades, if need be, on a secured island retreat. They just needed to get to it. Or, rather, Tom needed to get the girls there before they were exposed.

It was too late for her.

Her gaze traveled over to the slumbering form of her grandfather. He appeared so fragile. On the pillow and sheets, pink tinged linens betrayed the truth of his condition.

She felt her forehead. It was cool to the touch. She inhaled through her nose. No stuffiness. No sneezing. Not a single cough.

A glance at the program her grandfather created made her gasp.

"What is it?" Tom recaptured her attention with a worried expression, but it was clear he still didn't get how serious it was.

"There are a hundred thousand suspected cases. Twenty-thousand confirmed dead. No survivors."

The numbers raced upward. Her stomach twisted. A sense of urgency pressed into her voice.

"Get out! Don't wait. Don't talk to anyone. Just run. Get to the island!"

"I'll come get you."

"And do what? I'm with Gramps and he's sick. Don't you understand?" They were all dead.

Tom's somber eyes stared back. He nodded after a long pause. "Elise, I love you." There was nothing further to say.

"I love you, too. Tell the girls I love them and give them a kiss from me." Hot angry tears threatened to burst forth, but she wouldn't let Tom see her cry. No need to let him see her terror.

"I will."

"Listen, if I..." She swallowed against the lump in her throat. "If I can, I'll fly down there... when it's safe to do so." Her small stunt flyer could make the journey to the island if she carried extra fuel. Risky, but she'd make it if she could. "This is spreading fast. Don't make contact with anyone. Do you understand?"

"I do."

She slammed the control button with a shaking hand, severing the connection before either of them broke down. It was time to be strong; Tom for the girls, and her for Gramps.

CHAPTER EIGHT_

Saturday morning, February 5, 2035:

ELISE WANDERED DOWN TO THE SOUTH WING TO CHECK ON THE FOUR OTHER individuals at the estate: Mark, their driver, Angel, their cook, and Mr. and Mrs. Jameson, who were the caretakers of the house and grounds. She found them in the staff break room, clustered around a holo-console watching the news. They glanced up as she entered.

"How is he?" Mark asked.

"Not good," she said.

"Elise," Mrs. Jameson said, patting the cushion next to her, "have a seat. They're talking about the sickness."

Mrs. Jameson's husband snorted. "It's a damn plague, not a sickness. Bet those bastards brought it to us."

Elise lowered down to sit beside Mrs. Jameson. She'd grown up with these people. Although employees, they'd become an extended family over the years.

The Jameson's were the over-protective parents who sheltered her, while Mark acted like an older brother, sneaking in driving lessons and showing the fine art of drifting, which she never mastered. For similar safety reasons, they never allowed her in the kitchen. They had rated stoves, boiling water, and hot ovens too dangerous for little girls. Angel, however, invited her in when her parents left on extended trips away from home, showing her how to bake and create edible masterpieces. She would forever associate Sunday mornings with Angel's special treats and the mouth-watering aroma of dough rising in the ovens.

Not all had been fun and games. They had viewed chores as a necessary character building exercise, and spared neither her, nor her sister from mundane labor. Mrs. Jameson imprinted a strict discipline, refusing to clean little girls' rooms. Elise learned hubris from her housekeeper. Perseverance came from Mr. Jameson who worked on the grounds. That man didn't know how to quit, and he didn't allow her to give up on her small garden plot either. She picked weeds for years, harvesting a frugal crop of stunted carrots and beans year after year, but they were all hers. With Angel's help, she turned them into tasty rewards for her hard work.

Her extended family huddled together, joined by the years and by their fears of this new threat. As a group, they leaned forward to see what they could learn.

The news agencies had precious little information to share. People were getting sick. They were dying. No one had answers. The newscasters advised everyone to remain calm.

"Don't worry, Elise," Mark said, "I've activated the security systems. We'll be fine if we stay on the grounds."

They were all thinking the same thing. The moment news agencies told people to remain calm was when panic set in. Her grandfather wasn't in any state to soothe the masses. Riots would ensue if Global Corps couldn't keep everyone calm.

"I'm going to go back and check on him," she said.

"I have soup brewing," Candice said. "It'll be ready soon."

"Thanks."

When she walked into her grandfather's room, his soft snoring calmed her. That, at least, was normal.

She turned toward the console and to the program displaying the numbers of those who were sick. It exceeded the hundreds of thousands mark and kept ticking upward. The dead seemed intent on catching the number of sick. Those who recovered remained steady at zero. Not a single survivor? Surely that was wrong.

After she called Candice to let her know not to bother with the soup, she went to her suite of rooms and gathered a pillow and blanket. She curled up on a chair beside her grandfather, holding his hand.

So hot.

All his clout in the world and they couldn't spare a single physician? Although, knowing her grandfather, he'd sent them all away. She held vigil alone.

After the death of her parents, he'd been her rock. He might be a leader to the world, but to her he was Gramps—the best man a girl could know.

Charles Comwell taught her everything she knew about strength, love, and forgiveness. *Don't waste energy on hatred*, he said, *your heart is too kind to hold on to such a damaging emotion.*

She'd be damned if he died alone.

CHAPTER NINE_

Sunday, February 6, 2035:

EROTIC TOUCHES FILLED HER DREAMS. A SENSUAL MAN WITH SILVER EYES traced fire along her skin. The Vendel Emperor's caress released pulses of multicolored light that spread over her body. Everywhere he touched, heat bloomed into a firestorm of need. She moaned with desire and an insatiable urge to be claimed.

With a start, Elise came to sudden alertness, breathing hard with the vividness of the dream. Lingering thoughts drifted in her mind, leaving her feeling flushed and aroused.

Bright light poured through the huge windows and showered the room with a warm glow.

A wrongness settled over her, spoiling the dream.

The room was quiet, too quiet.

She bolted upright, staring down at the still form of her grandfather wrapped in deep slumber.

He laid without moving. The rhythmic cadence of his breathing had vanished. She leaned over and stopped cold.

Blood stained his pillow and the sheets beneath his open mouth. His sightless eyes stared ahead. Her breath caught on a sudden constriction in her throat. Then, it was like a dam burst, and choking sobs clawed free of her throat. She howled with the loss of him. Her grief spilled into the too quiet room.

No one came running.

She brushed away her tears and stared at the back of her hand. No tinge of pink. In fact, even when she blew her nose, the drainage was clear. She felt well. No sign of being sick at all. No chills. No fever. No sign of the illness that killed her grandfather. First Elenor, then Dale... now her Gramps? All gone. An aching emptiness settled inside her chest. She closed his lids with trembling fingers.

They did this. The Emperor's face filled her mind. Even now her traitorous body flushed thinking about him, which made her feel sick to her stomach. That man had killed her grandfather.

There was no rewind button, no way to back up time. She couldn't escape the truth. She forced herself to stand, to move.

"Gramps, I'm sorry." The oppressive silence of his bedroom swallowed her words as she covered his face with the sheet.

Elise blinked back her tears and headed to the holo-console. She entered the biohazard emergency number and contacted his aides to have them make the necessary arrangements.

There was no answer... on either line. She tried several more times.

Nothing. Not even an answering service.

She shook her head. None of this made sense. A glance at the death-count sub-routine and her jaw dropped.

Fifty-million dead? And that was just in North America. In Europe, it was the same. In Asia, over twice that number had been reported. The African continent reported similar statistics. At least the numbers had stopped moving.

Wait. They stopped? Was the feed even working? She queried the reporting agencies only to find the sites were offline. The numbers were static. All had stopped during the night.

What the hell is happening?

She crossed the room and grabbed her phone. She called Tom. No answer. A quaking sensation radiated out from her core. She dialed again. Nothing. She punched in the numbers to Alice's phone and received a steady warbling tone.

Pulling up internet news reports returned the same results. Either she retrieved static pages from last night, or she got error reports. The servers and routers were functioning. There was no new content. The entire world had gone silent.

She needed to talk with someone, anyone.

A few minutes later she found Mark. His body lay in his bed along with a stain of his blood. She clutched her belly and rode the rising tide of nausea.

He hadn't been sick last night.

Her salivary glands went into overdrive. The thick acrid taste of vomit tickled the back of her throat, and she lost the battle, gagging as the contents of her stomach spewed forth. When there was nothing left to throw up, she ran to the kitchen to rinse out her mouth.

As she passed Angel's room, another blow fell. The grisly body count rose. The cook's body lay sprawled on the floor. Elise gagged against dry heaves. Blood and death filled her nostrils, cloying at the roof of her mouth.

She struggled at the door leading from the kitchen to outside. Her hands shook so hard that she fumbled with the latch. It took three tries to open the door. The Jameson's lived in the small cottage behind the garage. There was no response to her frantic knocking. She peered through the windows calling out. The door to their small house creaked as she entered.

"Mr. Jameson?" Her voice sounded loud, bouncing against the walls. She pressed forward, moving to the bedroom.

They lay together in bed. Bloody eyes. Bloody mouths. Hands clasped together.

She ran outside and collapsed in the garden. How did they die so fast? When did they get sick?

The sun stood high in the sky, proud and majestic, taunting her with its radiance. She sat frozen, unable to move for hours.

CHAPTER TEN_

Monday, February 7, 2035:

MIDNIGHT HAD COME AND GONE BEFORE SHE HAD THE GRAVES DUG. THANK goodness for Mr. Jameson's backhoe, because there was no way she would have been able to dig five graves by hand. It took hours to learn how to operate the thing, and the graves were the ugliest furrows she'd ever seen, but they would do. There'd been no one to call for help. She collapsed on the couch at two am, exhausted.

Somehow, she drifted off, because she didn't remember closing her lids. She groaned against protesting muscles as the morning sun shone through a crack in the curtains and forced her awake. Purpose propelled her into action, dragging her outside.

She surveyed the spot behind the garden she'd picked for her grandfa- ther's grave. It was near the rose bushes he loved so much. He would be at peace there. His had been the last grave dug. By then she'd figured out the backhoe. Of the five graves, it looked the most like a proper square hole in the ground.

She hoped the others would be okay with her putting them behind the Jameson's cottage. It had come down to a matter of practicality: where Mr. Jameson parked the backhoe where the soil was soft, and where her first tentative digs with the backhoe began, and finally, how far she could drag the bodies.

The rose bushes were some distance from the house. She hadn't figured out how to move her grandfather's body so far by herself.

By ten am, she had Mr. and Mrs. Jameson settled in the ground. It took much longer to bury Mark and Angel, but only because she had to figure out how to move the bodies. A wheelbarrow provided an inelegant, but practical solution.

At noon, she covered the last casket-less grave behind the cottage with dirt. Only one more to go.

She glanced up into the cloudless blue sky. Sweat soaked her back, streaked down her face, and trickled between her breasts. She had long since discarded her lightweight jacket as her labors heated her from the inside out. Dirt coated her hands and dusted her clothes. Her long brown hair, pulled into a pony tail, hung matted with sweat and dirt. The crisp winter air blew through her sweat-soaked clothes, chilling her within moments of stopping work. Her eyes lifted skyward, searching, and narrowed with the pain of her loss.

They had done this. Their visitors from space had brought this destruction to her world. Whatever safeguards her grandfather and the Global Corps Space Agency had put in place had failed to protect them.

She shivered as a gust of wind blew past. Before stepping inside, she said a prayer over the graves. There was one more to fill, but she needed a break before dealing with her grandfather.

Her thumb swiped at her phone, activating it. Tom's number flashed on the screen. She stabbed at the redial button and listened. No answer. Her fingers gripped the phone, trembled, and then she put it back in her pocket.

Back inside the mansion, she headed upstairs. Already her chest tightened with the thought of what needed to be done. After walking into his room, she stared at the shape of his body beneath the sheet. There would be nothing dignified in this funeral.

"Sorry Gramps."

She bit her lower lip as she set to her grisly task. A lot of thought had gone into how to move him and there was no easy solution. He'd been a large man, and she was a small woman.

With a tug, she freed the four corners of the bottom sheet. The coppery smell of blood made her wince. She wrapped his body tight and used several of his belts to secure the sheet. Then she grabbed the end of the bundle and dragged him downstairs. Each time his feet thudded against the stairs, she cringed.

Thud. Thud. Thud.

But, there was no other way.

The wheelbarrow waited at the bottom of the staircase. With great difficulty, she maneuvered his body inside. Her labor became much easier once she had loaded him in the wheelbarrow.

As she wheeled him out to the far garden, she said her goodbyes through choked sobs. The wood of the wheelbarrow roughened her palms. Her shoulders protested against the weight. But, she didn't readjust her grip or ease the strain on her shoulders. She needed to finish this, and was afraid if she stopped, even to adjust her grip, she would never find the strength to continue.

After she covered the graves, she walked to the end of the drive, to the barrier of the Comwell Estate gates. Locked, they kept her inside, quarantined and safe, but she didn't think it mattered anymore.

She buried those she loved. Outside, the city might be desolate. She was too tired to find out if it was as bad out there as it had been within her home. There was no movement. No people. No dogs barking. Not that she would hear them. Comwell Estate was too remote, but she would need to explore beyond the gates.

She would face the isolation of her world tomorrow.

CHAPTER ELEVEN_

Tuesday morning, February 8, 2035:

ELISE FORCED HERSELF OUT OF BED BY NOON. LYING AROUND ACCOMPLISHED nothing; there were things to do. The internet still broadcasted, but it delivered no new content. The entire world had gone silent. Fortunately, Comwell Estate had been built for self-sufficiency. She had wind, solar, and a deep geo-thermal well, not to mention a self-contained power plant. But it wouldn't last a lifetime. For that, she'd have to make it to the island, to the place she hoped Tom had escaped with the girls. If he'd made it there in time.

She had no idea how much fuel the power plant held, but when that ran out, she'd be reliant on wind and solar. In that, she felt comfort. Wind and solar would keep her comfortable until she was certain she wasn't contagious, then she would venture to the airfield and see about flying to the island.

There were other issues to deal with. Survivors provided more of a threat than anything else. Looting by people bigger, stronger, and better armed than her was her biggest fear. Down in the basement, she opened the vault. As an avid hunter, her grandfather had taught her the basics of how to handle a weapon. She wasn't good, but she had time to learn. She took stock of her assets.

Shelter: check.

Food: check. A quick inventory showed more than a year's worth of supplies. More than she cared about right now.

Water: check. There was a spring on the property. She counted this as limitless.

Power: check. Too tired to look at her fuel supplies. That could wait.

Protection: double check. Gramps kept an arsenal, and she had an active surveillance system.

Time to leave the safety of the estate and see how bad it was outside the gates. If there were other survivors, she would need their help... if they were friendly. Before that though, she double-checked the defenses for the grounds. The surveillance system functioned flawlessly. She locked all the house doors and set the intrusion alarms.

Thirty minutes later, she stowed an over and under shotgun on the dash of the car within easy reach. She strapped a pistol to her side, loaded, safety on. Her grandfather's side-by-side went in the passenger seat. And she had two back up pistols, one in her lap and the other nestled beside the side-by-side.

With a deep, trembling breath, Elise powered up the car. When it asked if she wanted to run the autopilot or drive in manual, she had a moment of indecision. While it would be easier to scout if she wasn't driving, her nerves hummed with restless energy to do something.

She thumbed off the autopilot and gripped the steering controls in her hands.

It was time to see what laid beyond the gates of the expansive Comwell Estate.

———

ELISE'S FINGERS ACHED FROM GRIPPING THE STEERING WHEEL. IT'D BEEN FIVE minutes since she exited and locked the wrought-iron gates of the estate. Still another ten minutes before leaving the long winding road that circled down the hills. Usually Mark drove, and despite teaching her how, she still felt uncomfortable behind the wheel, preferring to let the autopilot take control. Her grandfather commuted via helicopter. She never learned to fly a helicopter and regretted that now.

As it was, she was stuck with the car. Depending on what she discovered, she might drive out to the airfield. She could cover more ground in her stunt plane than she could by car. There was the problem of refueling. Shit. Considering how hard it had been figuring out the backhoe, what problems would she run into refueling an aircraft?

The winding road emptied into a narrow two-lane highway. She stopped. It was so quiet. Her chest vibrated with unease as her shoulders inched up to her ears. She checked her mirrors twice and her doors were locked.

Thankful for her grandfather's insistence on fortifying all their cars with bullet proof glass, she felt secure heading out. The car wasn't a tank, but nothing would get to her unless she opened the door. She navigated the tight turns heading down the ridge. When gaps in the trees occurred, she peered down at the city below.

The first abandoned car appeared when the narrow road dumped into a four-lane commuter highway headed to town. She slowed, curious about the vehicle sitting on the side of the road, wondering what had happened.

She pulled behind it. After making certain no one was around, she opened the door of her car. Her pistol shook in her hand.

"Hello," she called out. Her eyes narrowed as she spied a person in the car. "Hello?" Her voice croaked, sounding weak and unsure to her ears. She kept her pistol held in front, angled down, as she approached.

A little firmer, she raised her voice. "Hello?"

No response.

She moved up the side of the car, hopeful, but expecting the worst. A person sat in the driver's seat, but no one alive sat that still.

Blood sprayed across the front windshield. The seatbelt held the body upright. There were no other passengers. She slumped against the side of the car, her gaze flicking up into the brilliant blue sky.

A mile down the road, she came across the first wreck. Nearing town, the number of wrecks outnumbered the cars pulled off the side. Who'd been luckier? Those who died from the plague, or those who died in the crashes?

The lump in her gut grew heavy. Bodies filled the street in addition to the cars. Her mind created a grisly scene, her imagination filling in the gaps. A man in front of her opening the door of his car, coughing and sputtering blood, dying before he could climb out. To the left, a mother running with her children, dodging cars as they crashed around her, until she was struck down, her children flung from her arms. Over there, a trucker, one boot tangled in a rung of the ladder when he'd fallen out of his cab. The worst had to be the bus full of children. Those inside were dead. Outside, a string of small bodies led away into the grass at the side of the road.

Her stomach clenched as bile rose in her throat. Tears, so many tears, streamed down her face. Wrecks choked the streets, and the dead were everywhere. She had no choice but to turn around.

The metal gates swung closed behind her as she allowed the autopilot to carry her home. A watery veil of endless tears blinded her to the gathering storm clouds overhead. She forced herself out of the car and made it to the door of the mansion before the first drops fell.

She stood there for many long moments and lifted her fist as the first peals of thunder sounded all around.

"What have you done?" Her cries sounded pitiful and frail against the gathering storm.

Somewhere up there, the Vendel orbited in space. They had done this. They had destroyed her world.

But even worse than her tears, was the rising desire she felt when her thoughts turned to the Vendel Emperor. The skin at her wrist burned and her vision swirled with multicolored lights. Shame burned in her veins. How could she desire a monster? A glance at her wrist had another more concerning question blooming in her mind. What had they done to her?

CHAPTER TWELVE_

Wednesday, February 9, 2035:

ELISE SAT IN THE PARLOR READING ONE OF HER GRANDFATHER'S BOOKS. HER body was weak from not eating, but her appetite was nowhere to be found. A deep listlessness sunk deep into her bones as she wondered about her future.

Were there other survivors?

She had tried venturing out again, heading in the other direction. Once again, devastation forced her back to the estate. She was a prisoner, unless she attempted walking to the airfield, but then there was the issue of how to fuel up her plane. Was the runway even clear for takeoff?

The internet console flicked to life. *Blip!*

Her head swiveled.

Blip-blip.

She bolted from her seat, hands shaking to adjust the controls.

"Hello? Is anyone out there?" Her voice cracked.

Silence. She leaned toward the console, panting with the need for human contact.

A female voice called out in a foreign language. "*Ist da jemand?*"

German? She fiddled with the controls and instituted a translation subroutine. *Is anyone there?*

Her heart leapt into her throat. "My name is Elise."

"*Ist da jemand*," repeated the voice in a different inflection. The voice was live.

Elise jumped with excitement. She responded, but the woman's voice faded. Whoever it was didn't understand or couldn't hear her reply. She recorded her greeting and had it translated into German.

Nothing.

She screamed her frustration as she struggled to be heard. For two painful hours, the voice kept reaching out, rising in desperation. Nothing Elise did elicited a response.

But, there was another survivor.

She wasn't alone.

CHAPTER THIRTEEN_

Sunday morning, February 13, 2035:

ELISE GAZED OUT THE FRONT BAY WINDOW. THE SUN RAINED DOWN CHEERY brilliance, bathing the garden in bright light, but like her hope, that too would fade. Storm clouds were rolling in. Four days ago, she had heard the woman's voice through the console, but nothing since.

In her lap, one of Gramps's romance novels laid open and forgotten. She pulled her knees to her chest and sat back on the couch. Her eyes were dry, devoid of tears. With a deep sigh, she extricated herself from her melancholy. Her stomach rumbled, but she wasn't interested in eating. Ten in the morning, it was past time for breakfast. She had to force herself to eat, telling herself good nutrition was the key to survival. Instead, she walked out the front door and into the sunlight. The comfort of its warmth helped a little. Inside, she was so bitterly cold.

A gentle breeze blew across her skin, relaxing her mind. It felt like any of the countless days before it, bright, blue, and beautiful with a hint of chill. Her gaze turned skyward, seeing nothing but the clouds rolling in, coming to block the sun.

The world might be dead, but she was alive. The estate could sustain her, but eventually she'd have to move on. Not today. Not tomorrow. Not even for months to come. Before next winter, she decided. Staying put forever wasn't an option. Before the food ran out, she needed a plan. The rumbling protestation of her stomach forced her back inside.

Food.

Gramps always enjoyed eggs and bacon, but she didn't have the energy to mess with that. Instead, she pulled out a packet of instant oatmeal. She combined water and oat flakes, mushed it around, then shoved a spoonful of the paste into her mouth. It would do.

A red light flashed on the corner security monitor. The sensors showed an intruder in the entry foyer. Her breath caught. She'd locked the doors. How'd they get in? How'd they get through the gates without the outer perimeter alarms going off?

She placed the bowl on the counter and crossed the kitchen to grab the pistol she kept close at all times. Then she opened the drawer to retrieve a Taser.

Flee or fight?

One deep breath, one step forward. She crept out of the kitchen to investigate.

Male voices sounded from down the hall.

"Are you positive of your readings?" a deep baritone accompanied the tread of heavy boots.

"Absolutely," a second voice answered.

Elise sidled up against the wall, trying to make herself small. Two males weren't good odds against a single female.

Frustration filled the first voice. "I've never seen readings like these. I think the whole device is acting up."

"Talk any louder and you'll run her off," came a third male voice. It seemed familiar, but she couldn't place it. Silence.

Her breath thundered in her ears.

"The outside is secured, my lord," a fourth called out.

And now there were four. Four Vendel males in her home. No way these were humans... earthlings. Whatever!

Her gut clenched.

She edged back toward the kitchen, deciding on flight, and thumbed off the safety of her pistol.

The second male sounded frustrated. "Snarking detector is acting like there are hundreds of them here."

"Not hundreds... just the one." That voice, a rich timbre, had been in her dreams from the night she'd met him and he rubbed that perfume into her wrist. An aphrodisiac he'd called it, and something much more. "Now maybe you can get about the business of collecting her?"

Silver eyes. Black hair. Strong hands. Fingertips which had left a trail of fire on her wrist massaging that perfume into her skin.

A surreal calm swept through her body as her vision narrowed into a singular focus. The hammering of her heart, the quickness of her breath, her shaking hands, all of it stilled. Reason fled and rage took its place. She tightened her grip on her weapon and stepped around the corner.

The High Tender stood at the end of the long hall, to the side, halfway in another room. Two men flanked the front door. Between them loomed the man responsible for murdering her grandfather, Elenor, Dale, Mark, Angel, the Jameson's, and God help her if Tom and the girls hadn't survived.

Gregor Ulysses vlor'Malita's dreadfully handsome presence filled the space at the end of the hall, standing dead center and lined up for a kill shot. He destroyed her entire world. Now, she would kill him.

She lined up his chest with the sight of her pistol.

A slow inhale. A breath hold, just like her grandfather had taught. Her finger squeezed.

With a loud retort, the gun recoiled and pushed her back.

One of the men dove in front of the Emperor. Her bullet appeared in midair a couple feet in front of him, surrounded by a green light. It crept forward, slowly, inexorably pressing through a barrier of light.

The man protecting the Emperor grunted as the bullet slowed, hit his chest, and bounced—*bounced?*—to the floor.

The Emperor's head snapped up. His gaze locked onto her.

She kept firing. The large man grunted as the bullets bounced off his flesh. She aimed the last bullet high. It pressed its way through the green haze as if moving through molasses to land between the Emperor's eyes.

His head jerked back and then whipped forward. Fury lit his face as the spent bullet bounced—*what was with the bouncing bullets?*—off his brow to land at his feet. A tiny red dot marred his forehead. He should be dead.

He rushed her.

Beside him the High Tender screamed, "Sire, no!"

The pistol fell from her hand to clatter against the marble tiles. She seized the Taser, thumbed it on, and shot at Gregor's stomach. Electricity flashed between them.

His eyes widened in pain. It should have dropped him to his knees. Instead, he gritted his teeth and leaned into her.

Power thrummed through the insulated handle of the Taser. With deliberate care, he grasped her wrist and yanked the Taser away. The stubby weapon flew and rattled off the wall, falling beside the discarded pistol.

The High Tender rushed up behind the Emperor. He reached an arm around the Gregor's tall frame to press a slim sliver rod under her jaw. "Sire, you must let me deal with her. She is not yet—"

The Emperor ground his jaw muscles, holding her gaze. He flicked his eyes down to focus on her lips. "High Tender, know your place."

One of his hands secured her wrist over her head, his other cupped her jaw. He stroked her skin and pressed her body against the wall. "By the gods, but I am glad to see you."

She flinched against the intimate touch.

"Someday, you'll forgive me, but know this… you are, from this day forward, mine."

Electricity pulsed between his hand and where he gripped her skin. The shock waves thrummed along her nervous system, building with each beat of her heart until she felt like she would explode. Beneath it, an unreasonable desire for him sprang forth. It was unwelcome, yet undeniable. She fought the sensual craving and struggled against his grip.

"I belong to no one, least of all you." Even if he was all she wanted.

She closed her eyes and thought of her grandfather's lifeless body. It helped to push back the longing. Opening her eyes, the intensity of her desire reflected in his gaze, causing her to suck in her breath.

The corner of his mouth twisted up. "Elise Comwell, you very much belong to me. Do not fight what comes next. There's no way to avoid the inevitable and I don't want to see you harmed."

He gazed at her wrists and his eyes closed. "Do you feel it? Thrumming in our veins? Our connection is so strong. It's intoxicating."

"I feel nothing."

His eyes popped. "You lie."

Her heart slammed into her throat. Lying to him wasn't working. He saw right through her. "I don't know what that is."

"It's what ties us together… our bond." He closed the distance between them, his lips hovering over hers.

A single word filled her mind. No! But she had no time to voice it before the heat of his mouth was upon her.

The High Tender cried out. "No! You must resist the impulse. I must confirm her status before you stake your claim."

Sparks of color spiked through her brain. A frisson of heat exploded and raced outward, traveling along her nerve endings from the base of her neck down her spine. Energy gathered in her body, trapped without an outlet, and vibrated with pulsating potential.

He invaded her mouth, pushing his tongue inward to explore, to taste, to take. His body pressed her against the wall. She had nowhere to run, but she didn't want to flee. She wanted to kiss him back, to wrap her arms around his neck and hold on tight. Her self-loathing had never been so intense, but it didn't stop her from opening her mouth and letting him take what he wished.

Pressing her against the wall, he held her in place. All the while, when she should have been beating at his chest trying to free herself, she clutched desperately at his belt.

What the hell? This wasn't her. This was something alien at work.

The High Tender's screech continued, "Sire! On my authority, I command you to release the girl. Her rank is not established. You cannot claim her. Not until she's confirmed."

The Emperor ended the kiss just as abruptly as it had begun, leaving her breathless and pulsing with an odd electrical energy.

Red suffused the High Tender's cheeks and the muscles over his left jaw ticked.

The Emperor narrowed his gray eyes. He turned to the High Tender, his gaze hard and unyielding, and his breaths tugging hard and deep. "I concede. Do as you must, but I say she's mine. Our connection is unquestionable." Releasing her wrist, he kept a hand on her chin. "You have no idea how glad I am to see you well."

She held those eyes and poured all her hate and anguish into their brittle depths. It was that or give in to the hunger swirling in her veins. God only knew how hard her heart beat for more of that fiery kiss.

An errant thought crossed her mind. She should have aimed the Taser at his groin. "You fucking bastard."

"WOR do not swear to lords," the High Tender said. He pushed a slim silver rod against her jaw.

Gregor yelled. "High Tender, No!" He jerked her away, but it was too late.

Pain engulfed her world. The Emperor's shout was abruptly cut off and darkness followed.

CHAPTER FOURTEEN_

Sunday noon, February 13, 2035:

AN ELECTRIFYING JOLT OF PAIN THRUST ELISE FROM UNCONSCIOUSNESS INTO complete and brutal awareness. One moment she was lost in a world of blackness, the next she found herself strapped to a chair in the parlor of her home.

Sitting across from her, dominating her grandfather's chair, the Emperor regarded her with brows tugged tight and eyes pinched with concern. The black tattoo over his left eye moved as if the ink were a living thing. His gaze roved with avid interest over her body.

The intense scrutiny made her squirm. His blatant desire had her shivering with treacherous betrayal from her own body. Heat flicked up and down her skin with every sweep of his lustful eyes, chasing away the pain from moments before.

As she realized this, her neck and face flushed, burning with the knowledge of her body's rebellion. Where was this coming from? This wasn't a natural reaction.

His eyes flicked to a looming presence behind her. "At least we know the braklav works."

"Yes, Sire. She has Rank." The bass rumble of the High Tender appeared to agree. "I'll be ready for the testing in a moment."

The Emperor leaned forward, hands crossed. "I'm sorry for that, but there are some lessons you must learn. My protection extends only so far, and I can't protect you from the braklav. That is in the Tender's hands. Do not resist your training, Elise. Behave and the braklav will not touch you again."

What the hell is a braklav?

He settled back into the chair. The fingers of his left hand drummed out a rhythm as he waited. Two guards flanked him. The High Tender puttered about behind her while another guard stood to the side.

The Emperor watched her. She returned his scrutiny, unwilling to avert her gaze and show weakness, but her body trembled. Her heart hammered and her blood roared past her ears. She could barely hear. There was no way she would blink first.

She should have been scared, but she was too busy focusing on her anger and tamping down the odd response of her body. She hated herself for lusting after him. Now that he was here—in the flesh and no longer a figment of her dreams—it made it that much harder to concentrate on hating him.

His face broke into a smug expression that she wanted to slap off his face, or kiss. His lips looked delectable. His chest was broad and strong, perfect for leaning against. His arms bulged with cords of muscles she wanted to trace with her fingertips.

Stop. Just stop. He's the enemy, not your lover.

"I can't tell you how happy I am to see you." His left eyebrow lifted and the swirling tattoo writhed under his skin. "From the moment we met, I knew you were meant for me."

How was she to respond to that? What had he called her? Her eyes squeezed shut as she tried to remember. A treasure. Is that what she was to this man?

A metal rod touched the back of her neck and she flinched at the cold touch.

Colder words followed as the rod pressed to her skin. "First lesson," the High Tender said, "is the hardest, but most important."

Pain spiraled into her shoulder and dove down her right arm.

Elise gasped. "What the hell?"

The voice of the High Tender whispered in her ear. "When your master speaks, you answer."

The pain receded, leaving a dull ache behind and many questions flooding her mind.

He pressed the cold metal against her flesh once more, holding it steady. Fire scorched her skin.

"Oh, my God. Stop!" Her heart hammered in her chest and sweat broke out on her palms. "He hasn't asked a fucking question."

The High Tender touched the rod to the angle of her jaw. He spoke in a soft, paternalistic tone. There was no malice in his words, only the sound of eternal patience.

"The proper response is *High Tender Marcus, my lord, please stop.*"

The bonds on her legs pinched her skin. The ones around her arms cut her wrists. She gulped air as her mind whirled.

In front of her, the Emperor watched the exchange, doing nothing to intervene. He jerked his chin, and the rod pressed to her side. "Please stop with the profanities." He waved with the power of command. "This is an important lesson, opés. Pay attention." He nodded. "Continue, High Tender."

She tried to twist away from the silver rod, but the bonds held her in place. Pain flashed, ripping and tearing through her belly. The world went dark.

Warm fingertips traced the angle of her jaw, lingered on her chin, and then pressed against her lips. An answering heat within her echoed the touch. Her eyes fluttered open.

The Emperor smiled as he traced her lips. He knelt before her on one knee. "Ah, back among us, opés?"

She wanted to spit, or kick, or say any number of vile things, but she held her tongue. How long had she been out?

A corner of his mouth twisted up. "Lesson number one is always the hardest, but you are smart and will learn." He paused. "It's about obedience." His eyes twinkled, and he moved his finger off her lips only to draw it down to her jaw, her neck, to circle in the hollow of her throat. His words were soft, but his gray eyes hardened with steel. "Do you understand?"

She opened her mouth, but he pressed his fingertips to her lips.

"You must remember certain things. Be careful how you address me. From now on, you will only ever use my given name."

Her brows drew down at the removal of his fingers. He gestured to a small chair in the corner and one of the guards brought it over. The Emperor took a seat. His knees brushed her skin. The touch electrified and revolted her at the same time. A tear of desperation trickled out of her left eye.

The High Tender stepped around. In one hand, he held a black box. He placed it on the floor as he bent to one knee. In his other hand, he held the slim metal rod. It was the length of his forearm, no wider than the diameter of his thumb. He twirled it in the air as if it were an extension of his body. He made to place the rod to her leg.

Before the metal touched her, she looked at the Emperor. "Gregor, I understand." She flicked her eyes to the High Tender. "High Tender—" She'd almost said vlor'Vardhal but corrected herself before she made the mistake, "High Tender Marcus, my lord, please stop."

Gregor sat back and regarded her with a bemused expression. "She learns. I think she'll be easy to train."

Like I'm some animal? Never!

The High Tender dropped the rod to his side. It hung from a small chain wrapped around his wrist.

Relief flooded her body, and she shuddered, ashamed at how she had caved.

The High Tender snorted. "She has too much spirit, but that should be easy enough to break. The braklav will see to that." He ignored her and opened the black case. The High Tender hummed as he assembled a strange device.

Gregor's brows drew up as he considered her. "My given name is perfect on your lips, opés, just as you are perfect for me." The sound of possession matched the desire in his eyes. Such intensity in anyone would be strange. In him, it was overpowering.

Her eyes flicked to the floor to stare at the contraption the High Tender cobbled together. She had so many questions. So many profanities she wanted to launch at the pair of them. Tied to a chair as she was, words were her only weapons, but that tiny silver rod had taken even that small bit of defiance away.

Her heart sank at how she'd been tamed. A glance at her body revealed no outward sign of injury, but the pain... The agony from that rod had been unbearable. It shamed her that she hadn't fought back.

Gregor followed her gaze. "It takes a moment to assemble the Tenderstat."

The High Tender fit small black beads into a long crystal tube.

Gregor's eyes sparkled. She tasted bile, wanting nothing more than to slap that smug expression from his face. As tightly bound as her hands were, however, she could barely lift her wrists. She wriggled her fingers, working to keep the circulation going and prevent her hands from going numb.

A frown pinched at his brows when he noticed her movement. He reached for the straps. She flinched when he undid her restraints. His touch sent an involuntary shudder through her body.

He smiled. "You have no idea what you mean to me… to my empire."

Elise massaged the areas where the cords dug into her skin. "What do I have that you need?"

Gregor gave her one of his crooked smiles. "Everything."

Her anger flared. Like an avalanche there was no stopping it. "Bastard! What does that even mean? Did that give you the right to murder my family, or destroy Earth?" She slapped his face. The sting on her palm felt too damn good. "Are you a rapist, too? Is that what you mean when you say I belong to you?"

They must have done something to her. That had to explain her odd attraction to the man.

The High Tender sprang to his feet and pressed the rod to her chest. Her world exploded in fiery brilliance. Her body twitched, flopping like a fish in response to the pain pouring out of the rod. He twisted it on her skin. Icy cold tendrils entered her body, bringing an entirely different sensation of pain.

Gregor's voice remained clear and focused. "That's enough High Tender." He reached forward and pulled the High Tender's hand back from her chest. "Finish the Tenderstat so we can get her out of here."

"She is my charge, not yours. I will discipline her, as is my right."

Gregor gave him an icy stare. "Yes, of course, but first the Tenderstat. I'm eager to see how she ranks. You may discipline her later."

"And if her Rank is not as you predict?"

"We have a connection. The kiss confirmed it, and she survived the Activator."

His lips pressed into a thin line, a grimace of displeasure twisted at his face.

The other men in the room stood so still Elise had almost forgotten them. The uneasy expressions they exchanged between themselves, however, got her attention. Was it usual for a High Tender to fight with their Emperor?

Her chest heaved with residual pain, but she bit out a few meager words of defiance. "Whatever you think I can do, it didn't give you the right to destroy my world. And what the hell is an Activator?"

A heavy exhale accompanied a tight-lipped expression. "I don't have to explain myself to you," Gregor said.

Tears ran down her face. "Why did you do it?"

"I need Earth's treasure, little opés, as is my right. You are a part of that and will be trained to serve." He leaned back and crossed his arms. "I'm curious. All the others kick and scream. They babble on for hours and cry forever. Some can't tie together a coherent thought for days. You're different. You strike back, even knowing we'll only punish you for it."

Her heart fluttered. "What others?"

"You are not the only treasure of Earth, just the one meant for me."

There were others? Survivors? She was not alone. Which meant... she would have help in bringing down the Vendel and their Emperor.

CHAPTER FIFTEEN_

Sunday later, February 13, 2035:

STRAPPED TO A CHAIR, AT THE MERCY OF THE VENDEL, ELISE SHOULD HAVE been frightened. Instead, Gregor's words rang in her head, bringing hope and a fiery determination to fight.

She wasn't the only survivor.

"You didn't answer my question," she said. In fact, he flat out ignored it. Demanding an answer felt good. It gave her the smallest bit of control in a hellish situation.

Gregor turned to the High Tender who cradled a growing mass of black and clear crystal tubes in his lap. "See how she challenges me? She doesn't shrink in on herself with fear like the others. This is a great strength for one destined to be my s'vlor, don't you think?"

"Trouble." The High Tender glanced up and shook his head. "She's going to be a problem."

"Perhaps."

Gregor leaned toward her, and to her shame she shrank back under the intensity of his gaze. He reached out, but when the High Tender cleared his throat, Gregor paused, his fingers hovering inches from her cheek.

"You must wait, Sire." The High Tender focused on his task and didn't bother to look up. "She's my charge until then."

Gregor dropped his arm with an exasperated sigh. "So many rules."

"For your protection."

"Tell me, Elise, how many days did it take before you recovered?"

She paused, uncertain what he asked. The silver rod began its spin in her peripheral vision, an extension of that horrible man's arm. The way the High Tender handled it creeped her out. He brought the thing toward her. All she knew was the moment it touched her skin incredible pain would flow out of the thing.

She reared back. "Why the hell do you even care?"

The High Tender grumbled. With no emotion, he put the tip of the rod to her forehead. A tingling built to a steady throb, and it was clear that sensation would only worsen.

She pleaded with utmost sincerity. "High Tender Marcus, my lord, please stop."

Gregor tapped the High Tender's shoulder. "Easy, there's no need for that."

The High Tender's voice took on a lecturing tone, reminiscent of her professors in her online university. "This is why the Tenders train. You lords are too gentle with them." He turned his attention back to Elise and twisted the tip of the rod against her forehead. The tingling turned to a burn.

"She's no good broken," Gregor said in a warning tone.

She whimpered.

"I'm barely touching her with the braklav." High Tender Marcus's broad face and dark brown eyes looked down on her with parental concern, but this man was no kind parent. He was a monster. "Now answer him, or that burn you're feeling will turn into something that will make you talk."

Her gut clenched at the dispassion in his gaze. She croaked out a whisper. "But, I don't understand." She squirmed beneath the touch of the metal rod.

The High Tender closed his eyes as if bothered by her whining. He turned to Gregor. "Sire, we don't have time for this. I need to finish my task."

Gregor pulled at the High Tender's arm. The offensive rod lifted from her skin. "You're too quick to apply the rod when a simple question would suffice. Finish the Tenderstat and I will question her."

"You can't afford to be easy on them, not at this critical stage."

Gregor ignored the High Tender, turning his attention to Elise. After a long pause, he asked, "Is it possible you weren't sick at all?"

The High Tender slid a third clear rod through a flat black plate with five scalloped edges. He mumbled, "They all get sick." His hands worked at assembling the growing contraption.

"No," she said. "Everyone else did, and they died. What did you do to them? To me?"

"Curious," Gregor said.

Two identical egg shaped black discs, with five deep grooves on one side, were now separated by four of the foot-long glass tubes. Each tube was filled with black spheres the size of marbles. With a solid click, the fourth tube snapped into the device. The High Tender worked on the fifth, and what seemed to be the final tube.

Whatever he was putting together scared the crap out of her, so she focused on something else, something hopeful. "You said there were other survivors."

Thoughts of her brother-in-law and her nieces flashed through her mind. What were the chances? Without hope, her world was a dark place. She believed they made it, because she needed something to fight for.

"We need to be certain. Think before you give your final answer."

Final answer? Like this was some game show where she won a prize for surviving a great plague. Her mind reeled. Billions dead, and all he cared about was whether she had the sniffles.

She didn't hold back. "Everyone else was sick! Me? I was fine. Okay? Got it? Not a sniffle, a sneeze, or even a cough. You killed billions. My entire family is dead because of you. You're a monster. Why do you care if I sneezed or coughed? Everyone I care about is dead because of you."

"Lord vlor'Vardhal," he asked, twisting to face the High Tender, "what do you think? Possible?"

"Improbable," the High Tender said, "especially if she tests out as you hope. It's always hardest on those with greater rank."

She shifted in the seat, or at least as much as she could, considering she was still strapped in. Hatred for Gregor flowed through her veins. Her feet remained bound and were now numb. At least her hands were free. She brought them up slowly, watching them shake, and brushed the hair away from her face. The contraption the High Tender worked on was almost complete. Knowing what the braklav did, she could only imagine the pain that thing would cause.

The High Tender's beady brown gaze regarded her from where he knelt fiddling with the last rod. "After the banquet, did you feel sick? Think before speaking."

No need to think. Memories of the night after the banquet stirred in her head. She went to bed feeling well. The morning of Elenor's death, she was fine. Each day flashed through her mind. Nothing. She even recovered from her hangover in record time. The answer these men wanted wasn't there.

"You want me to say I was sick, but I wasn't."

The High Tender snorted in disbelief. "You had to have felt something—"

Gregor interjected. "Lying does not please me, opés."

Anger flared. White hot. Why demand answers to such an irrelevant question? They'd killed billions. People she liked, people she loved. They'd destroyed her world. And that name, opés, grated on her nerves.

"You bastard, I don't care if I please you or not, and my name is Elise, not opés."

The High Tender paused from his construction to rise with deliberate slowness. The braklav twirled around in a slow arc before he snapped it into his palm.

The resounding thud set her body quivering.

He shrugged. "I never give out warnings. That is lesson number two. Sire, excuse me."

Gregor pushed back his chair, scraping the wooden feet across the tiled floor. His brows pulled together.

The High Tender moved into the space vacated by the Emperor. He placed his hand on her forehead and pressed her head back against the chair.

"Tender Training is difficult to watch, Sire. You may leave if you wish."

Gregor gritted his teeth. "I know about Tender Training, I won't leave."

"You cannot protect her from the choices she makes."

"She doesn't understand that yet." Gregor ground the muscles of his jaw, while Elise looked on in horror. "By the gods, be gentle with her." He shook his head.

"That is not how it's done."

Adrenaline surged through her body, racing around her veins, seeking an outlet that wasn't to be found. It left her a quivering mess as she locked her eyes with the High Tender's cold brown ones. Her hand flew up to grip his forearm, to push him away, but he was too strong. He didn't budge.

Gregor looked on, his face a mask of concern. He gave her hand a reassuring squeeze, but he stepped to the side and made room for the High Tender.

High Tender Marcus touched the silver rod to her ear. Pain coursed down her neck and through her body. He dragged the silver rod down the side of her throat lighting a trail of agony in its wake.

Her determination not to cry out lasted a heartbeat.

With a twist of the rod, the pain intensified with an explosion of sensation. Screams erupted from her throat as he traced the outline of her body from fingertip to fingertip and toe to toe. He brought the thing up her left side and back down the right.

The mantra, "High Tender Marcus, my lord, please stop," spilled from her lips and fell on dispassionate ears. Hot liquid scalded her skin. Thousands of nettles flailed against her flesh and tiny knives flayed her skin. Her voice grew hoarse with her screams.

Pain beyond comprehension flooded her body, ripping at her soul. Her vision dimmed, then went dark. Desperately, she clung to consciousness unwilling to lose control in front of them, although her body went slack.

They spoke over her and she strained to hear them.

"High Tender," Gregor said, "that is enough."

"That is for me to decide."

"I dislike seeing her treated this way. She knows nothing of our ways, or what is expected of her. She doesn't know obedience is her only path."

"You know the risks. If we fail, I must destroy her. Neither of us wants that, not with what we face. I understand the difficulties in watching Tender Training, it's why we sequester them, but it's the only way. She's learning a valuable lesson right now. Trust the Tender Conclave to train these Earth WOR as we've trained all WOR. I know the proper path."

"I know, High Tender. It's just—"

"She awakens. Go to her and let me finish."

A residue of pain vibrated within her body with the fluttering of her lids. Cautiously, she opened them, only to see the High Tender standing before her with a calculating expression and that silver rod dangling from his wrist.

"Good, you're back," he said with dispassion.

She took inventory of her body, her skin, seeing no signs of the torture he'd inflicted.

"Now," the High Tender said, "you will always address Emperor Gregor Ulysses vlor'Malita by his given name. You will never use *profanities* against him again, or I will spend an hour with the braklav teaching you respect."

An hour? He'd touched her for mere seconds and she'd come undone.

The braklav dangled from his wrist. "Now apologize." The glower in his eyes left no doubt in her mind she would do as he commanded.

As he knelt to complete the fifth tube assembly, Gregor brought his chair back into position and sat with his knees brushing hers.

Her body responded to his touch, but she expected the surge of arousal, and tamped in down. She managed some control over the unnatural sensual response to this man. Maybe this was her first victory. She latched onto that. She needed something positive.

Gregor's expression told her he expected that apology, but there was also something else there as well. Concern. For her?

That metal rod had messed with her head, and her body shook from the after-effects.

"Forgive me, Gregor."

"Of course, you're forgiven." He shifted in his seat, looking uncomfortable. "The braklav stings, opés. You must learn to obey our rules. It's the only way to avoid its touch. I dislike having it used against you, but until you adjust to your new life, it is a necessity. What you need to understand is you are ultimately the one in control. Submit and all will be well."

Maybe killing billions went hand in hand with the torture of a defenseless woman? Submit? Like hell she'd submit to these men. She'd fight with every breath. She bit back a sob crawling out of her throat. Better to save her energy until she could find something to use it against.

"Back to what I was asking—before you called me a bastard—you're certain? This is important."

He was still stuck on the sniffles and sneezes? Incredibly persistent, she had to give him that.

"I wasn't sick. Why is that so important?" Her mind struggled to make sense of her predicament.

"Interesting." He didn't answer her question. "Lord vlor'Vardhal, do you think this will affect the testing?"

"The severity of the symptoms is telling, but not always predictive." The High Tender pressed the second disc to the end of the five rods. With a snap, the clear tubes slipped into the recesses of the second disc. Now he had a structure of two discs connected by five rods filled with black marbles. The thing glowed. He grunted his approval and stood.

Gregor took the device from the High Tender and cradled it in his lap. "What about the detector? It, too, had difficulty picking up her readings and locating her. Almost as if it were being blocked?"

The High Tender pulled a small pen-like device out of an inner coat pocket. "Time to find out."

"Whoa, wait," she said, terrified. "What are you doing?" Trying to jerk away while strapped to a chair was difficult, but she tried. Her heart went into overdrive.

Gregor stilled the High Tender's hand. His voice softened, trying to soothe her. "He's going to draw your blood. Be still, opés."

The High Tender grabbed her arm and pulled it straight. He felt for a pulse in her wrist and pressed the pen to the spot.

The jab of a needle pierced her skin. She flinched at the sting. Compared to the braklav, it was nothing, but the tension in her body was wound so tight a fly landing would have her jumping.

The device turned red as it took a sample of her blood. The High Tender pulled out a second device and repeated the process on her other wrist.

"Hold out your hands," Gregor instructed. He gripped the Tenderstat holding the center five tubes. "Put your hands out straight, palms facing each other, fingers spread."

"Is this going to hurt?" Her hands shook. She looked to the High Tender, but he jerked his chin toward the device and clutched the braklav in his palm.

She did as instructed, more afraid of angering the High Tender than Gregor.

"I promise, on my word as a lord, this won't hurt you." Gregor placed the device between her palms. "Now, see these grooves on the edge?"

Panic filled her with fear, but she would do this. She had to. It was either put her hands where Gregor said or deal with the High Tender and that damn silver braklav thing. Blood roared past her ears, making Gregor's voice sound very far away. Her body reacted on autopilot.

"Place your fingers in the grooves."

Her fingers trembled. She shook her head.

"No. I can't."

Gregor paused. His voice repeated the command, gently but firmly. There was no room to refuse. "Elise, you need to put your fingers in the grooves."

Out of the corner of her eye, a silver rod flashed. "What does it do?" She didn't move her hands.

"Please, listen to me, I don't wish to see you punished again. Put your fingers in the grooves." As he spoke, the metal rod touched her shoulder.

Tears pooled at the corners of her eyes. "Gregor, I'm so scared…"

The enormity of her situation weighed her down with hopelessness. Alone. There was no one who would come to her rescue. No family. No police. No military to save the day. These men had her at their mercy. She couldn't run and she couldn't even fight back. No way was she going to comply with their every request, but here she was, doing just that. Her entire body shook.

"Easy, opés." He reached out and stroked the back of her hand. "Unlike the braklav, this will not hurt. I've given you my word as a lord. It means on my life I will not break it. I promise, but I cannot help you in this. You must put your hands there yourself."

She blinked, not willing to trust him, but having no other choice. She bit her lower lip and did as commanded. The grooves were spaced a little wider than her fingers, and the material was warm to the touch. It didn't hurt.

"What does it do?"

Gregor pressed a switch and a thin bar trapped her fingers inside the grooves. "It's a simple test of your potential."

The High Tender leaned over and filled a small reservoir in the base of each rod with several drops of her blood. He nodded to Gregor.

The Emperor flicked a different switch.

The edges of the discs shimmered.

It kind of tickled. She glanced up, only to see Gregor's dark brows drawing together in consternation.

He tapped a finger to his upper lip. "Hm, not what I was expecting." He leaned forward and examined the tubes. "Even in one who is not WOR there is a glow."

The two men exchanged worried glances. What did that mean? Not what he expected? After everything, she was a dud? Wouldn't that be funny?

"Not possible," the High Tender said. "She survived the Activator, so she should light up at least the first bar." There was a strange emphasis placed on the word activator.

"I have an idea," Gregor said. "She claims not to have been sick. Is it possible her sample is flooding the registers? Let's try diluting it."

He pressed the first switch, and released her fingers from their prison. Gregor beckoned the High Tender over to the door. They spoke in low tones and it was obvious from the way the High Tender shook his head that he disagreed. Gregor glanced over and pointed her direction.

Fascinated, she watched their exchange. Which one was in charge? When the High Tender's shoulders hunched, she knew Gregor had made his point.

He wiped the blood well clean with a cloth from the High Tender's kit, then sat in front of her and lifted the device. He arched a brow. With a jerk of his chin toward her hands, he directed her to put them back in the device. His meaning was clear, and she complied.

He flicked the switch once again imprisoning her fingers.

The High Tender leaned forward. "We have never tested it like this before."

"Call it a hunch." Gregor pointed. "There, at the base of the thumb slot." He paused as the High Tender brought out the first pen with her blood sample in it and deposited a single drop in the receptacle. He moved to fill the other end. Gregor placed a restraining hand on his arm. "No, just the single drop."

The High Tender shrugged. "The minimum sample size is five millimeters. That will barely wet the sensors."

Gregor pressed the second switch. A white glow appeared at the edges of the disks. Then, it flashed. He leaned forward, an odd gleam in his eyes.

The rod at her pinky finger flared into life with a bright white light. That was kind of cool. Wait, maybe she shouldn't be excited about this.

Gregor leaned back. "Told you so."

The rod at her ring finger came to life and then the third tube blossomed into brilliance. The fourth light lit up and Gregor's smile went very wide.

"Congratulations, Sire, she is s'vlor," High Tender Marcus said. "She will be yours."

Not if she had any say.

By the time the fifth light lit up, Gregor beamed. The corners of his eyes crinkled, and he laughed. "I told you. I knew it!" He gave a great *whoop*, slapped his knees, and jumped to his feet. "I knew it!" He pointed to the five glowing tubes held between Elise's hands. "Fifth Rank WOR!"

She stared at the two men. This wasn't good.

"That was one hell of a hunch," the High Tender remarked.

"She lights up the Tenderstat with only a hundredth of the sample size. Do you understand what this means?"

"Do you?" The High Tender looked troubled.

Gregor waggled a finger. "Ah, but you are the best Conclave Tender Master in hundreds of years. You will train this one." He flicked his eyes to her while she stared, entranced by the Tenderstat and glowing lights.

The five rods flared with a brilliant hypnotizing light. As she stared, the glow intensified, responding to her will. The discs grew warm, and the sensation traveled up her arms to settle in her chest until she became one with the device. The light pulsed with the beat of her heart. She tapped her fingers in time with the rhythmic flashes. Either she controlled them or they controlled her. It was hard to tell, but the rhythm drew her in.

One. Two. Three. Four. Five.

Five. Four. Three. Two. One.

Her mind moved with the light as it framed out a melody. The first rod turned red.

The men stopped talking although she wouldn't have heard them if they'd yelled.

She and the Tenderstat were the only things in her universe, like it had some kind of pull on her. The rest of the world faded away. The second rod turned orange. Then a rainbow of colored light lit up the Tenderstat's five rods. Yellow, green, and blue sprang to life.

Elise stared into the light, watching it pulse, urging it to move faster and faster. She hoped to escape, and she poured these thoughts into the contraption she held in her hands. The color flickered and flashed. A rainbow marched forward as each color jumped to its neighbor's rod. A cascade of color leapt from tube to tube. It changed again, as the rainbow moved not just from rod to rod, but spiraled up from the ends towards the center and moved back out again.

A kaleidoscope of color swirled in the Tenderstat. It was the most beautiful sight she'd ever seen, and with it power washed over her. She could almost touch it and reached out to do just that, but like water, it slipped through her fingers. Frustrated, she cried out.

The Tenderstat exploded, shocking her out of her trance. The power dissipated. The tubes disgorged their contents of black marbles. In her periphery, the guards scrambled to capture the little black balls as they tumbled to the floor. She held two black discs in her hands, fingers trapped in the grooves.

She looked to Gregor, a brow lifted in question.

His expression was one of shock, or amazement. Satisfaction quickly replaced it.

"Satisfied?" His words were not meant for her, but rather the High Tender.

There was nothing friendly in that tone.

It didn't matter who was in charge. Both men scared her. Gregor claimed her—he said so—but the High Tender appeared to control her fate until he released her to Gregor.

She found the balance of power between them confusing.

"What happens now?"

Gregor finally answered one of her questions. "We take you home."

———

THIS IS NOT THE END!

VENDEL RISING: VOLUME 2
WOMEN OF RANK
is next!

Follow Elise's journey with the Vendel as she seeks her revenge.

Grab your copy now!

WOMEN OF RANK

VOLUME 2

PART ONE_

PROLOGUE_

New Terra Histories by Malita s'Lissa s'vlor

Life is but a collection of moments, some more memorable than others.

Every now and again a moment comes along, so intense that indelible memories are forever carved in our minds. We remember what we were doing, feeling, seeing, hearing, and tasting at the exact instant our lives changed.

I remembered two things: the warm, rich scent of a powerful man, and the agony of the braklav.

June 2, 2136:

ALIENS HAD LANDED. WE WERE NOT ALONE. THE VENDEL HAD SOMEHOW risen into the sky and traveled to the stars thousands of years before the rest of humanity launched our first rocket to the moon. In the deep reaches of space, an empire flourished and we knew nothing about them.

I never understood why no one thought to ask why the Vendel had returned. With so many planets, why come back to Earth? Why had they left to begin with? Perhaps we should've asked before inviting them to dinner.

Death began with a simple cough or sneeze. Like the Black Death of the Middle Ages, people who were hale and hearty in the morning, were dead by nightfall. Billions died at the hands of the Vendel.

For a few of us, we weren't touched at all. At least not on the outside, inside was a different matter. The Vendel collected us, tested us, ranked us, and remade us, although it would be a long time before we understood what that meant.

Gregor Ulysses vlor'Malita claims to have our interests in mind, humanity's interests, and perhaps there is a kernel of truth in that statement.

Saviors?

How do you justify that to the dead?

One idea terrifies me. What if the Vendel are in fact, our saviors?

This is the continuation of my story...

CHAPTER ONE_

Sunday, 13 February 2035:

CRADLED IN SOME MAN'S ARMS, ELISE SNUGGLED TIGHT AGAINST A WARM chest, and struggled to remember what was happening, because it made little sense someone should carry her. Her eyes refused to open, almost as if someone had drugged her. She wanted to free herself, but one arm was pinned between her body and the chest of the man carrying her, and the other hung with an unnatural lethargy, swinging with each beat of his step.

"Sire, she wakes." The deep voice shivered down her back and she furrowed her brows. Memories of pain echoed with his words.

There was more, something off about her entire being. An ache centered in her bones and burrowed deep inside her skull. It felt as they had ripped if something from her, something that was a part of her, but she was certain she had never felt *it* before.

The man carrying her shifted her weight and a heady scent of spice and musk filled her nostrils. She rested her head on the shoulder so conveniently placed for her use and luxuriated in the exotic aroma full of masculine promise. Another scent floated to her senses, carried by a passing breeze. Irritating to her nostrils, it smelled wrong; a mix of foreign aromas.

Wait. This isn't right.

She pushed against the hard chest and forced her eyes to open. Then she saw him.

Gregor held her against his chest and she tensed, realizing she'd been enjoying the embrace of a mass murderer on a planetary scale. How could she find his touch seductive? A deep self-loathing filled her and she wanted to die.

The palest blue eyes regarded her with an expression of concern.

Gregor gripped her tight, not the least put out by her struggles to get down. "You have come back to me, opés. I am pleased." He continued down a glowing corridor, filled with an unearthly opalescence, until he stopped in front of a circular door.

She wasn't pleased. Not at all. She wanted down, but he clearly had no intention of setting her on her feet anytime soon.

The door spiraled open and he carried her inside. Four men followed behind him, the three guards from before, and High Tender Marcus, the horrible man with the silver rod that dangled from his wrist.

"You feel good in my arms." To emphasize his point, he rocked her close, nestling the top of her head under his chin.

Her cheeks reddened as heat stirred in her core. She hated her body's response to this man. She'd dated her fair share of men and never reacted to any of them like this. It had to be that damned perfume making her body betray her like this. He said it had aphrodisiac properties, but it seemed to only work for Gregor. She felt nothing for the other men, and definitely not the High Tender. That man gave her chills. Knowing what she felt wasn't real didn't make it any less potent.

Pressing her palm against Gregor's chest, she found herself no longer pushing against him, but skimming the muscles underneath his shirt. With a jerk, she removed the treacherous hand and placed it on her throat where her pulse hammered beneath her fingertips.

The door to the small room spiraled closed behind them and one of the guards pushed a symbol with wavy lines and a series of dots on a recessed panel. Lights flashed on the walls and the ceiling opened.

She tilted her head and gasped. Open space extended hundreds of meters into the distance. She looked down, trying to regain her senses, and yelped as the floor disappeared, leaving them stranded over a gaping pit that was hundreds more meters deep. Vertigo overwhelmed her and she flung her arms around Gregor's neck, tucking her head beneath his chin.

He chuckled and held her tighter. He bent his head to whisper into her ear, "There is nothing to fear. We are in a lift tube, a transport device. A force field supports our weight while moving us up."

She pulled away, but he held her close.

He gave a low hush meant to soothe. "It's perfectly safe."

"Where am I?" her voice cracked.

She swallowed against rising nausea, because she already knew the answer to her question, but she needed the distraction to hide her fear of the nothingness above and the void below. No way was she going to lose it in front of these men and show any sign of weakness. Well, at least, not lose it again.

The High Tender stood opposite them. He twirled the braklav, caught it, released it, and repeated the whole process, all the while he watched her with his cold brown eyes. When he realized her attention focused not on him, but the braklav in his hand, his face lit in a satisfied grin.

Gregor's lips brushed her earlobe. It wasn't a kiss, more of a promise. "Welcome to the *Gambit*. You are not on Earth anymore."

A shiver ran through her whole body, lighting her nerves from head to toe. She'd guessed as much, but having her fears confirmed made it real. When had she left? Must have had something to do with them drugging her. There really was no escape now.

A wind blew down on them as they sped up into the dizzying height of the lift tube. The breeze helped to tamp down her nausea, but she still clung to Gregor, praying for the maddening ride to be over. For the moment, it didn't matter if that made her appear weak in his eyes. She would allow this one moment of reassurance from the enemy and find her strength later.

Soon their speed lessened, and the wind eased until it disappeared. A white circle fanned out from the wall and formed a solid floor. A semi-circular doorway spiraled open to their left.

Gregor released her from his grip and settled her on the floor. "Take it slow," he said in soothing tones. "Your body is still adjusting after the Tenderstat testing. Perhaps a little help?" He offered his arm for support.

She glanced at his arm with mixed feelings, not wanting to take it, but knowing it was impossible to refuse. Unless she wanted to taste the braklav again, she had to obey, and unfortunately, she needed his help. Her legs trembled and she barely kept her balance standing still. If she took a step, she knew what would happen. This weakness terrified her nearly as much as the five large men and alien spaceship surrounding her.

She reached for his arm. "Thank you, Gregor." Her gaze flicked to the High Tender and watched the silver rod drop from his grip. A shudder went through her as she considered what would have happened had she refused. Her hand shook as she placed it in the crook of Gregor's arm.

A smile spread across his face. It softened his expression, smoothing out the corners of his eyes. She wanted to pull her hand away, mortified by how compliant she behaved, but his hand covered hers and held it in place. The braklav snapped in the High Tender's palm, then dropped and dangled.

Steadying her grip on Gregor's arm, her first step went without a hitch. Not too bad. Another. She was doing well. On her third step, her legs buckled.

"Why am I so weak?"

Gregor caught her and steadied her on her feet. "Aftereffects of the testing. Do not worry, it will fade."

Elise gritted her teeth and tried again.

He moved down the long hallway, letting her set the pace. She placed each foot with deliberate care, testing before transferring weight. She tried to look around, but the act of walking commanded her entire attention. Intel would have to wait for another opportunity, although the hall remained empty except for them. Each step brought one thought to mind.

She was trapped and there was no way out.

CHAPTER TWO_

The Gambit, Day 1

A LONG WALK THROUGH A MAZE OF PASSAGEWAYS ENDED AT A PAIR OF CLEAR doors. Inside, six men dressed in black stood at parade rest, guarding an inner round door reminiscent of a bank vault. A red light flashed over the outer doors. The High Tender approached and pressed his hand to a flat panel display.

Three more men, wearing brown tunics, sat behind a waist-high counter, with their attention focused on holographic displays. Only one glanced up as they walked inside. He fixed his attention on Elise. She shrunk under his scrutiny and took a step back, only to come to a stop against Gregor's solid body. Retreating into the safety of her enemy's arms made no sense, yet she acted on instinct, choosing Gregor for protection. What she should have done was stand her ground and level a hard-focused glare at the man behind the counter.

"Master Tender, is this the one?" The man's voice was deep and smooth, but his eyes glittered with the same hardness she had come to expect in the High Tender. The title did not go unnoticed, or the deference in the man's tone. Master Tender seemed to signify a position of leadership. There was more to him than she thought.

"Tender lor'Marthis, she is indeed," High Tender Marcus said. He grabbed her by the elbow, separating her from Gregor, and dragged her to the counter. She wobbled the short distance on her unsteady legs, struggling for balance, and barely managed not to fall. The corners of Gregor's mouth twitched down, but he didn't intervene, although she sensed he didn't like being separated from her. She didn't like it either.

While glad to be rid of Gregor, she hadn't exchanged him for anything better.

The Tender, a man of lower rank, an assumption made by the way he referred to High Tender Marcus, placed a pad filled with a gel-like substance on top of the counter.

High Tender Marcus barked, "Place your hand on the gel."

Elise knew better than to hesitate and hated her instant obedience. She needed to resist these people and not blindly follow orders.

The moment she touched the gel, her hand was encased in an odd warmth. Not gooey like she expected, but she jumped when an electric pulse flashed up her arm. It didn't hurt, it just came as a surprise. The gel folded over the back of her hand, moving with purpose until her hand was fully encased. Something sharp pricked her finger. Only then did the *goo* withdraw, leaving her hand as dry as it had been before touching the strange substance.

"What's the final count?" High Tender Marcus inquired.

"She makes ninety-two of the Fifth Rank. Much better than anticipated," Tender lor'Marthis said. He tapped the counter and read off the display. "After you transported off the planet, the residual readings dropped to zero. We have one-thousand and two. Tender lor'Elstat is bringing the last ten on board. We've exceeded our projections, Master Tender. Nearly all are Second Rank or higher. Only a handful of First Rank, and over three hundred to add to the s'vlor registry."

High Tender Marcus gave a satisfied snort. "Excellent."

Finally, an answer to her question. A thousand survivors. Or at least, that's how many they had brought onboard. They didn't mention if any remained on Earth. These people had Rank, which meant they made the Tenderstat glow like she had.

The Tender entered something into yet another display. "My lord, I have uploaded her information. She's ready for processing."

What the hell did that mean? Alien probing? Now that she would resist, tooth and nail if it came down to it.

Behind her, Gregor coughed.

High Tender Marcus clenched his jaw and placed a hand on the counter. "This one has been claimed by the Emperor. Please annotate it in your logs."

The man's eyebrows lifted, then he glanced at Gregor. "Sire, we collected over ninety women who are of Fifth Rank. Would you rather examine them before making a final decision?"

Gregor came to stand beside Elise. The exotic spice of his cologne wafted over her and the beat of her heart quickened. She held her breath and willed her body to ignore the heady sensations his presence brought. Mind over matter, or in this case, mind over body; she would beat this unnatural attraction. Instead, a flood of desire heated her from the inside out. With great force of will, she shoved this false sensation to the periphery where it merely smoldered.

"I claim this one, Tender. Enter it into the logs."

The Tender seemed ready to argue, but closed his mouth, then tapped the display. "Your preference is noted, Sire."

Gregor leaned forward. "Not a preference, Tender lor'Marthis. I *claim* this one. She is mine."

The possessive tone of his voice, laced with a suppressed eagerness, made her heart surge. It was becoming a reaction she expected. Not that she understood it, but she vowed to somehow learn to control it.

"Yes, Sire. Forgive me." Tender lor'Marthis flicked his gaze to High Tender Marcus, who gave a nod. "Done, Sire. She is registered and will show up on your inventory."

Inventory? Like she was property? The Vendel had some nerve to claim they were a superior race of humans if they still practiced a slave trade. She would be no man's slave.

"I will take her from here, Sire." High Tender Marcus grabbed her elbow and yanked her toward the inner double doors.

The six men standing at parade rest snapped to attention. The doors spiraled open and revealed a tunnel stretching in front of them.

When they reached the threshold, Gregor stopped them. "Lord vlor'-Vardhal, I would have a moment with her."

"Sire?"

"Just a moment."

The High Tender gave a short bow. "As you wish."

He stepped back, and the men surrounding them pulled away, leaving her and Gregor in relative privacy. He took her arm and pulled her even further from the penetrating gazes of the men. Bending down, he leaned in and spoke in a soft, but firm voice.

"Elise, you need to listen to what I have to say."

She jerked her arm, but he held it firm.

"This is important," he said.

"I don't want to hear anything you have to say."

A flicker of irritation crossed his face. "You will listen and obey. Down that hall lies the Confinement Deck. Once you cross that threshold, you are in the hands of the Tenders to train. You must obey them."

She jerked free.

He gripped her chin, and tilted her face up, forcing her to look at him. His height intimidated her, but she vowed to be strong. Remembering all those dead by his hand helped to tamp down the unbearable attraction, if only a little bit.

"Why do you care?"

"Because you do not understand what it means to be a WOR."

"I don't even know what a WOR is?"

"A WOR is what you are. A Woman of Rank. A woman who must be trained."

"Like a slave? Is that what I am to you? A line on your registry, was it? Property?"

"You are valuable, Elise, priceless, but now is not the time to argue. I'm trying to tell you I can't protect you in there."

"Protect me?" Like she would even want protection from a man like him.

"The discipline of the Tenders is strict, but obey their rules, follow their procedures, and you will do fine. Most of what you will encounter is simple indoctrination into our culture. You have much to learn. Our language, technology, society, everything you need to begin your new life will be taught to you. This does not have to be hard on you. You can choose to make your transition to your new home smooth."

She understood. Comply with their demands and her life would be easy, fight and they would torture her. She shrugged.

"That's it? You're sending me to some twisted Vendel cultural academy? Should be a piece of cake. What do I have to worry about?"

"You're being difficult."

"I want to go home."

"You are home."

"This will never be my home."

"I am your home, Elise. There is nothing you can do to change that, and once your powers manifest there will be even more to learn."

"What powers?"

"Powers that make you WOR. Do not test Lord vlor'Vardhal." Frustration edged his voice, and he ran a hand through his black hair, pulling it back through his fingers and exposing the tattoo over his brow. "I'm trying to help you, because I know you will fight this. You still think you have a

106

choice, but you need to understand what will happen if you resist the Tenders."

"Sire," High Tender Marcus said, "it is time. Others come after us and I must get her processed before they arrive." He ushered her back toward the threshold.

Gregor called out. "I will see you later, opés. Behave for High Tender vlor'Vardhal. I expect to hear good news regarding your progress." Hesitation framed his voice. "Remember my words."

Having no answer to give, she curled her shoulders inward and hid her face from Gregor as the doors hissed closed and removed him from her sight. Good riddance, but she would see him again. When she did, she would need to be prepared to deal with the ebb and flow of desire which made her weak in his presence. She turned to face her newest threat.

"You are entering the Confinement Deck," High Tender Marcus said. "We'll exit this tunnel and enter the processing area. You will obey every command. Do you understand?"

"Yes." With a look at the silver rod he gripped, she swallowed.

"Good, you might just be trainable. The emperor is much more lenient than I."

With each step, her trepidation grew. The muscle ticking in his jaw intensified her unease. This was a man who knew no leniency. For a moment, she glanced behind them hoping to see Gregor. The fact she sought shelter in Gregor's arms did not escape her notice. She sniffed at the conflicted nature of her thoughts.

The High Tender continued and she forced herself to listen. "You belong to the Vendel. Specifically, you belong to Emperor vlor'Malita. Your resistance is a waste of effort. Obey, perform as directed, and life will not be so hard. Do otherwise and we proceed with the consequences. You determine how easy, or difficult, your training will be. It matters not how often, or how long, I bring the braklav to bear upon you. That choice is up to you."

A chill wormed its way down her back.

They reached another set of doors which spiraled opened. A square, antiseptic room with perforated white walls greeted her. In the middle, a recessed red circle a meter across dominated the room.

"Stand in the circle," he commanded.

Ten people stood in the room. Four were of the large gladiator type. Pristine, black jumpsuits covered their frames. Short sleeves, rolled at the cuffs, displayed prominent biceps which left little to the imagination as to their qualifications to perform their duties. Their dark pant legs tucked into knee-high boots. And at each of their waists twin dark rods hung from the loops of their belts; like the ones she'd seen on the Vendel guards from the banquet.

Four other men cloaked in white tunics scurried as they moved around the room checking holographic displays, adjusting knobs, and carrying flat pads in their hands. At a far door, two women stood still, one dressed in green, the other in yellow. Elise's eyes widened when she saw them, feeling an odd kinship with them. They wore shimmering gowns of a flowing silk-like fabric which fell to the floor in cascading waves of color and light. A corset, laced in the front, shaped each of their waists and pressed the swell of their breasts upward and outward. Each wore a golden necklace with a large crystal dropped low to snuggle within their cleavage, and a single silver armband encircled each of their left arms.

She met their eyes and knew two things. While a kinship connected them to her, they were somehow less than her. They broke their statuesque poses to give deferential nods, almost a bow, as if acknowledging the feeling. Beneath Lord vlor'Vardhal's stare, she made her way to the red circle in the middle of the room. Her stomach heaved with the fear of what might be involved in getting processed by aliens.

CHAPTER THREE_

Gambit, Day 1

ALONE AND VULNERABLE, TERROR SWEPT THROUGH ELISE, RIPPING HER APART from the inside out. Alien humans surrounded her in a sterile white room. She'd been forced to stand in the center of a red meter-wide circle. Not exactly an alien lab table, but then the Vendel weren't quite alien. Hulking goliaths garbed in black guarded the doors. Four men in white tunics appraised her with clinical eyes. Two women, who somehow shared an inexplicable kinship, looked on with supportive and gentle, but ultimately unhelpful, eyes. And there was the High Tender, a dispassionate man who'd ushered her inside the red circle to await processing.

"Remove your clothing, shoes, and accessories," one of the men in white said. "Earrings, rings, necklaces. Everything must go."

His words made her spine stiffen. "No." The word spilled from her lips with indignation.

A worried look from the woman in green, and the sudden alertness of the High Tender, had Elise rethinking her response. Perhaps this wasn't the time to make her stand.

The braklav moved.

"All right. Damn it." She kicked off her shoes. Under her breath she muttered, "Fucking Vendel bastards."

The braklav spun.

Her fingers fumbled at the buttons of her shirt. Her head whipped up and her eyes latched onto the silver blur. "Just give me a fucking second."

The High Tender's lips set into a grim line as his head shook side-to-side. The braklav continued its spin, but at a slower, more menacing pace.

Elise stripped in front of her audience as her eyes focused on the blur. She yanked off her blouse and her pants quickly followed. She placed her mother's necklace and wedding ring on top of her clothes. She took off her earrings and patted her hair down to make sure all had been removed. Hugging herself, she tried to hide, but all she could see was a blur of silver.

He arched a single brow.

She shivered as she stood in the middle of the red circle in her underwear.

"Remove everything," he said in a cool detached tone that she was beginning to recognize meant business.

She glanced at the people, none of whom seemed interested in her half-naked body. Even the goliath men lining the walls looked on with bored expressions.

As she regarded the cold eyes of the High Tender, she hooked a finger under her bra strap, released it, and slid a strap off one shoulder. When that failed to raise an eyebrow from any of the men, she slid the other strap off the other shoulder and then dropped the bra with a defeated sigh onto the pile on the floor. Her panties joined the stack next.

The High Tender examined her from head to toe as if she were an object.

"Enjoy the show? Freaking pervert." Anger coiled in her belly and erupted as heat bloomed in her cheeks.

Her instinct was to cover her nakedness with her hands, but pride kept her fingers tightly fisted and locked to the side of her legs. She met his gaze and held it.

Dear God, but she trembled. Her toes curled against the cold floor. She bit her lower lip to keep her jaw from shaking. Didn't work. Any moment tears would spring forth, but for now, the nails digging into her palms, and her teeth biting into her lower lip, provided enough distraction to hold that treacherous sign of weakness at bay.

The High Tender gestured the woman in green to come over. The light rustle of her gown preceded her arrival. She and Elise locked eyes and the woman gave a look of commiseration. She retrieved a single bobby pin Elise had missed and tossed it onto the pile on the floor.

Two of the men in white came over and removed her possessions. Elise followed them with jerky eye. Her mother's wedding ring was in there. Would she ever see it again?

They opened a large clear door along the left wall and placed her things inside. The door shut and a light flashed. Nothing remained. All her earthly possessions destroyed in the blink of an eye.

She hated these people.

Standing naked and alone on an alien spacecraft, among enemies, completely vulnerable, she should crumble and admit defeat, but that was not the girl her grandfather had raised. Levelling her chin, she faced the four men in white who approached en masse.

It took every bit of strength not to flinch as they descended on her with odd devices in their hands. They worked as a team, poking and prodding, measuring and testing. After their exam, they brought shiny white bullet tubes forward and injected her with what she hoped were vaccinations and not something more noxious like that infernal love potion the emperor had inflicted upon her. Even now, a part of her wished he were here to help her through this—and that didn't make any sense.

Once the men finished their poking and prodding, the woman in yellow brought a gown similar to the one she wore. Rather than a corset, Elise was given a belt of golden links to cinch around her waist. The neckline scooped just below her collarbone, but where the front of the garment was reserved, the back most definitely was not. It fell low to her waist, leaving most of her back bare, and barely covered her hips.

The lady in green knelt before her and offered two yellow slippers that reminded her of something a ballerina might wear. Elise had no mirror but had a pretty good idea of what she now looked like. She was grateful the emperor wasn't here to admire the result, and that thought brought an uncomfortable heat to her cheeks. That she cared what he would think shamed her to no end.

One of the men went to the High Tender. "My lord, we are finished. She may be placed within the general population."

"Very well, but first I must dispense a lesson. Clear the room."

Elise didn't have to be a genius to know this was a bad thing. Her stomach clenched, but she curled her fingers into fists, trying desperately to be strong. Gregor wasn't here to stay the High Tender's hand like before.

The room cleared of personnel and her heartrate doubled.

"I instructed you to avoid profanities."

"Forgive me, High Tender Marcus, I forgot myself."

"Obedience," he said, "is it such a foreign concept?" The braklav snapped into the palm of his hand. "I would suggest you kneel."

Elise considered begging for forgiveness, but one look into his darkened eyes said her plea would be worthless.

"Emperor vlor'Malita asked me to go easy during your collection and so I held back with the braklav, but he is not here to interfere now. Our lords do not understand the importance of the initial steps in training. And since he already feels the bond growing between you, he is sensitive to your pain. It was a mistake I will not repeat."

Her gut clenched. She dropped to her knees within the center of the red circle, looking up at the High Tender as he walked around in a slow circle. His boots struck the cold floor, causing her to flinch with each of his steps. When he stopped, she trembled. The fabric of his uniform rustled as his arm lifted, and while she couldn't see the cool metal of the braklav, she imagined it well enough. Somewhere deep within her, beneath the shaking of her body, a burning core of anger flared.

It died though, as an explosion of pain and agony raced down her nerves with the first touch of the rod. Her throat opened up. A raw scream tore loose from her lungs, fanning the flames of her hatred for this man.

He touched her again with that merciless stick. A press to her breastbone and pain rippled outward, traveling to her shoulders and down her arms. White hot, a bolt of surprise, she could only respond with a gasp. He touched her thigh and stinging nettles dove deep into her flesh, diving into the muscles until bone breaking pain ripped a screeching protest from of her lungs.

She howled with the twist of the braklav on her belly. The cold tendrils spreading inside presented a sensation so foreign, at first it didn't register as pain until she collapsed, writhing on the floor, blubbering and begging for him to please, please, please stop.

"You're hurting me." Tears streamed down her cheeks with her pleas for mercy. She curled in on herself, hiding from the rod, but his booted heel pressed inward and his strong arm forced her back to her knees.

"Yes, it hurts, Ten-two, and it will hurt again and again and again, until you learn to obey and submit to our ways."

A bolt of pain to her back had her jerking away from his touch. Her teeth chattered as the pain pummeled at her again. "P-please!"

The rod traced down her neck, turning her skin on fire. She screamed out and bit her tongue. Seconds stretched to minutes as pain travelled along her nerves.

Her screams echoed against the cold white walls, bounced back, and reverberated in her mind. He touched her with the braklav, gave her time to recover, only to repeat the process over and over again. Her sobs and pleas fell upon his uncaring ears.

There was nothing tender about the High Tender's punishment. There was no anger in his touch, no emotion whatsoever, as he applied the braklav to her skin.

When she moved away, he hauled her back to the center of the circle, or worse, herded her there by prodding her with the stick.

Endorphins released in her body, turning her skin slick with sweat. They did nothing to numb the pain. Her shivers intensified and heightened her sensitivity to his touch. Scalding heat melded with freezing cold until she could no longer differentiate the two sensations. Even the embrace of numbness brought an agony she couldn't process.

"Stop, p-please." Her voice scratched her throat raw.

He zapped her with electricity and a screech tore through her lungs, followed by a defeated sob. That rod touched her again and again, tracing out every nerve on her body until she sobbed on the floor in an incoherent, blubbering mess.

Minutes stretched to eternity until time lost all meaning.

A small part of her died in that room. How she survived, she had no idea, but she vowed never to forget another one of the High Tender's commands.

Then suddenly, the pain stopped. One moment it filled her world. The next breath it vanished.

A voice boomed. "High Tender vlor'Vardhal, was I not clear?"

It took many long minutes until she regained control over her breathing to find the strength to look up. It was him, the other bastard in her life, only now he came as a blessed savior. She could kiss him, but she wouldn't.

Gregor's looming form stood near, grey eyes no longer pale but stormy, dark, and ominous. "I said be easy with her. The moment I leave her alone with you, I find her subjected to Tender Training?" He yanked the High Tender away by the scruff of the neck and pulled him to one of the far walls. Gregor's arm lifted and pointed to where she huddled on the floor. "You will break her before we even begin. Every one of them is precious!"

"Disrespect drips from her tongue, Sire. I'm teaching respect." High Tender Marcus shrugged out of Gregor's grip and straightened his shirt. "This is my domain, not yours."

"And she is mine, not yours."

"She has yet to survive Activation," the High Tender said.

"She will survive."

"You get ahead of yourself, Sire."

"And you step far out of line."

"I serve you, as I serve all of Vendel, as should you above your desire for this woman." High Tender Marcus pointed the silver rod at Gregor's chest. "You must control it!"

Gregor dropped his chin to his chest. "I am in control. Don't ever doubt that. Now leave us."

"I will escort her inside."

"No," Gregor said with the authority of command. "You will not. You've done enough damage. I must undo what you have wrought."

"Tsk," the High Tender spat. "There is no room for compassion here. We don't have time to coddle them."

"Leave!"

The High Tender jumped at Gregor's shout, but he said no more, only turned and exited the sterile white room.

Gregor approached Elise, his voice level and calm. "My poor opés, did I not warn you? You must obey the High Tender." He extended his hand.

Elise stared at the proffered appendage. She hesitated to accept his help, because she didn't understand it, but no way would she fail to obey again.

His well-muscled hand encased hers, the electric shock she'd come to expect on skin-to-skin contact with him pulsed between them, as did the tide of rising arousal. Since she'd been expecting it, she was prepared. For the first time, she managed to shuttle the erotic thoughts of him to a side-corner of her brain. The thoughts and feelings were still there, active, but not in control like before. Her mind was free to tend to the task of dealing with the Vendel emperor.

Gregor lifted her to her feet with minimal effort.

Oddly, after all the torture, her body moved without lingering effects, like none of it had ever happened. She clung to Gregor, if only because she desperately needed some form of human contact. He wasn't the person she would choose, no one would willingly seek shelter in the arms of a mass murderer, but he hugged her to a chest with a solid heart beating beneath it. His warmth radiated outward and that was what she needed more than anything else. The contact of another human, someone who sought to shelter and protect her, who didn't wish her harm. In an odd turn, he was the solace she needed.

"Come, opés," he said, and headed toward the far door. He pressed a pad protruding from the wall and spoke into it. "Lord vlor'Ates, you may return to your duties now."

The door through which she had entered spiraled open. The four men in white tunics returned and went right back to work at consoles around the room, as if nothing had happened. Several women cowered in the tube behind the men. They'd heard her screams. Their pale faces held wide, fearful eyes. The clothing they wore identified them as being from Earth.

Survivors.

Elise didn't want to know what they saw when they looked at her. She couldn't face the mirror of her defeat in their eyes. Turning away, she curled into the protection of Gregor's embrace.

She couldn't think about the braklav, the pain, Tender Training, or how easily she'd caved to High Tender Marcus's torture. And Gregor had stopped him. How would anyone endure such pain. She forced herself not to think about it. It was too fresh, too raw, and right now she needed to focus on something else, like Gregor. She would begin with him and work on the High Tender later.

CHAPTER FOUR_

GREGOR PRESSED A HAND TO THE SMALL OF HER BACK AND MOVED HER forward through the door leading out of that horrid room. He guided her out onto a large observation platform with a gentle touch. The contrast between how he handled her and the High Tender's torture jarred her senses. It didn't matter though, she still squirmed out of his grip.

"Don't you dare touch me." Running from Gregor was pointless. There was nowhere to go. Three feet in front of her, she halted against a waist-high railing.

The platform he'd moved her onto overlooked an immense space. The floor dropped twenty meters below and a domed ceiling soared an equal distance above. Overhead, fake white clouds billowed across a deep blue, and equally fake, sky. She hated it on sight and angled her gaze to look down and away from the mockery of Earth's sky.

Neat ordered rows of open-topped circular structures stretched out on the floor. Inside each of them was what looked like a round bed. A quick count confirmed twenty columns of fifty-one rows. Just over a thousand cells. But no bars.

The stillness of the space made her gut clench. Hyperventilating, she curled her fingers around the railing and blinked against black spots crowding her vision. Choking sobs made breathing impossible.

"Elise," Gregor said, coming up behind her. His hand brushed against her bare back. "Calm yourself."

The High Tender mentioned a thousand women had been collected and here was the proof. Beneath her high vantage point, beyond the round rooms, hundreds of women moved in a kaleidoscope of shimmering silk gowns like the one they'd put her in.

Gregor grabbed her waist and pulled her to him. "Be still."

She jerked out of his grip again and stammered. "Get y-your gr-grubby p-paws off m-me!" She couldn't catch her breath.

He refused to let her go and drew her into his warmth. "You're hysterical. You must calm down." He pointed with his free hand. "This is the Confinement Deck."

The soothing tones of his voice called to her rational mind to return from the chaos of panic.

"It's your home."

She gripped his forearm where he held her against his chest. "No." Her denial came out a choked sob, but he spoke the truth.

Across the distance, encircling the entire space, other observation platforms bulged out from the walls. Figures moved on them, large men in dark uniforms, their attention focused on the captives below.

Guards.

The aftershocks of Tender Training lingered in her mind, even if no signs showed on her flesh. For this reason alone, she didn't resist Gregor. Her need for comfort, after something so horrific, drove her into his embrace. It was wrong to seek solace in the arms of her enemy, but she needed comfort only another human could offer. Her reserves of self-sufficiency and strength had long since been depleted.

His hand skimmed her belly, sending ripples of traitorous and unwelcomed pleasure straight to her core. She bit her lower lip, focused on his words, and not on what his hand was doing to her body.

"When we descend, I'll show you to your assigned sleeping quarters." He gestured to the elevated observation platforms. "This entire area is observed by the WOR-guards."

The brusque efficiency with which he described her new accommodations, and ignored her distress, told her much about her new master. A line in his registry for certain, she was his newest pet.

"WOR-guards?" Did they not use video recording devices, or were the guards in addition to cameras? She needed to find out how much monitoring she would be subjected to. It would affect everything in her efforts toward escape.

"The WOR-guards monitor compliance with the Tenders' training regimen."

Monitoring compliance sounded like more torture. She made a mental note to steer clear of the WOR-guards.

"Obey their orders as if they come from the High Tender himself or risk the consequences."

"You mean more punishment. Torture like the High Tender put me through?"

He stiffened behind her. "Consequences are meant to remind you not to repeat the same mistake. Remember, ultimately you are in control. Comply and things will be easy for you."

"Everything is punishment with you Vendel." Denied curse words, she injected all the venom she could into the name for his people.

He stiffened again and she used the opportunity to try, unsuccessfully, to withdraw. His grip held firm. His lips brushed her neck. "I warned you, my dearest opés, that Lord vlor'Vardhal would not be lenient. You chose to test him and he applied the consequences for your actions. Although, I did not think he would touch you with the braklav again so soon, not when a whipstick would have sufficed."

A whipstick?

She didn't know how a WOR-guard punished, but no way could it be worse than the braklav. Her body held no residual pain from the experience, but the same couldn't be said of her mind.

It felt...splintered.

Gregor heaved a heavy sigh and placed a chaste kiss to her temple. "You must obey him in all things. WOR training is the realm of the Tenders. I have limited authority here. He will not subject you to Tender Training without my consent, but do not underestimate a whipstick."

"For a superior race, you're more barbaric than any of us. You disgust me."

"We're not superior to earthlings, opés. We're your cousins, born and bred, and built from the same DNA. We bleed the same, love the same, and fight for the same things."

"And murder on a much grander scale." She pinched his wrist and pulled at his arm. "Your touch disgusts me."

"I know exactly what my touch does to you. I feel it just as you do."

"You're wrong. I feel nothing for you. You did this. Are you so unsure of yourself that you need to use an aphrodisiac to force a woman to respond to you? You're a pitiful and weak excuse for a man, let alone an emperor. Even the High Tender bosses you around."

Gregor spun her around. His hands gripped her arms tightly and the tattoo over his brow swirled with an angry intensity. "You have no idea of the things you speak."

"Don't I?"

"I understand how hard this is on you, and I feel your anger and fear, but I am not the monster you think I am. With time, you will see your way through and past this. We will be together for a long time, opés. You can't sustain your hatred forever. Your feelings will turn toward affection. Our bond ensures it."

He didn't know her very well. "There's no fuc–," Not being able to use curse words put a cramp on her vocabulary. "There's no bond. There's no us. Get that through your head."

"You are wrong." His brow arched with conviction. "I felt it the first time I laid eyes on you, and I know you feel it, too. It is a rare gift for the spark between vlor' and s'vlor to ignite. Ours enflamed on first sight. For many, it barely lights. You and I have been blessed by the Gods. It has only happened twice in known history. Deny it all you want, but you cannot fight it. Run from it, but you will fail. Eventually, you will run straight to me."

"There is no spark," she lied. A brushfire burned in her veins. "You're delusional if you think I feel anything for a monster like you."

"Delusional?" He cocked his head. "I don't think so. We both touched the *callidor.*"

"What the hell is that?"

"I rubbed the *callidor* into your wrist the night we met, opés. It confirmed the truth of our bond."

"That voodoo love potion? Whatever was in that shit, and everything I feel for you, isn't real."

He silenced her outburst with his lips, using warmth and power to overcome her objections and her curse. Liquid heat devoured her as he drove his tongue past her lips. His passion destroyed her. She clutched at the fabric of his shirt, trembling in his grip, and opened to him, despising her weakness, yet unable to resist his rich, spicy taste.

Then suddenly, the kiss ended.

His breathing, ragged and deep, filled the air between them and mirrored her own panting. He cupped her chin, his fingers sweeping the line of her lips. Blown pupils revealed the depth of his desire and a wide-eyed concern lingered there, too.

"You must stop with the profanities. If your High Tender hears it..." Gregor tugged in a deep lungful of air and clutched her to him. His voice caught on an exhale. "I may be the emperor, but in this, in your training, I am unable to protect you. He holds authority over you until our blood mingles. You must understand, obey, and comply with the teaching of the Tenders. I would shield you if I could, but in this, I cannot."

He bent down and brushed his lips against hers, lighter this time, but more damaging than the fire of the previous kiss because now he showed compassion. He moved to her ear, whispering again.

"The *callidor* only strengthens what is already there. It cannot create something from nothing." He straightened and composed himself, checking to see who might have witnessed their passion.

"You're lying." Her words garnered a lift of his eyebrow and a swirl of the imperial tattoo over his brow, as if challenging her to deny the truth of his words. A truth she felt inside.

"That perfume did more than change me. It brought disease and death to everyone I held dear. I will never forgive you for that."

The shaking of his head confused her. "The *callidor* did not contain the Vector."

The memory of Elenor sneezing after inhaling the Vendel's gift flashed in her mind. "But, after the banquet Elenor died. She got sick after you gave her the perfume. That's when everyone started dying."

He pursed his lips. "This is not the best topic for us to discuss."

"Not the best topic? What exactly would be the best topic? You killed everyone I know. What other topic is relevant? If you want me to become your perfect pet answer the fuc—"

He pressed a finger over her lips. "Let me explain something, Tender Training is measured in hour-long increments. Lord vlor'Vardhal had you less than ten minutes before I knew what was happening. It took five minutes to get to you and pull him off. I will have to deal with the fallout from that, because as I said, you are his charge for now. You experienced less than a quarter of a true Tender Training session."

A cold sweat broke out on her back with the memory of what had happened in that cold white room with the red circle. It had only been fifteen minutes? Gregor had that wrong. High Tender Marcus tortured her for hours. The memory sang clearly in her mind. The eternity of pain and the cracks in her mind proved it.

"Swear again, or persist in calling me a bastard, and you will experience a full hour of what a braklav can do. I meant it when I said I do not want to see you harmed. You and I are meant to work in harmony, but to do that you must obey my commands, and you will have to obey Lord vlor'Vardhal as well as me."

"You would let him do that to me?"

121

He didn't say anything, but his look told her everything she needed to know.

Her lower lip trembled. "You said you cared for me."

"I do, but you must understand one thing. I am the leader of an empire. I have oaths to uphold to my people and obligations to the entirety of the human race. You will be trained. There is no other option. I hope you choose to comply, but one way or another it will happen."

Whatever warmth she'd sought in his arms had been misplaced and she vowed never to make that mistake again.

"Now," he said with a brusque efficiency. "I have the High Tender's job to finish."

"What is that?"

"Introduce you to your new home." He gestured out into the vast space, past the rows of beds and continued as if nothing had happened between them. "Beyond the sleeping area is a series of educational and training rooms. You will be given a schedule which you will follow."

He pointed beyond the small circular rooms to larger square structures, also with no ceilings. Women sat within the rooms. Few were empty. It bothered her how orderly it all appeared, how compliant the women behaved. Soon, she would be one of them.

"To the left are the privacy facilities, and to the right are the cleansing facilities. They are monitored."

Of course they were. It would make covert conversations difficult among the captives, but she would find a way.

"Beyond the educational rooms are the exercise facilities. You must spend two hours a day in appropriate exercise. You will need to devise a schedule for High Tender vlor'Vardhal's approval."

"I get a choice?"

"Of course, now that you are here we want you to be as comfortable as possible. You are incredibly precious to us, to me, and we want you to be as happy as possible. Any questions?"

Only ten thousand. "Yes."

"Now is a good time to ask."

She turned away from his smile, unable to process what it must mean. But if he was giving her a chance to ask questions she needed to take advantage. "Why must I address you as Gregor and not Emperor?"

"Women who are familiar with a man use that man's given name."

"We're not familiar." She didn't like the sound of that.

He gave her a look. "You're my s'vlor and I am your master. For now, that is enough."

For now, but what about later?

The lecture continued in an even cadence that made her skin crawl. "Names have significance in Vendel society, specifically as to who may use which names. You, for example, will never again use vlor'Vardhal when you speak to the High Tender, either as High Tender Marcus vlor'Vardhal or High Tender vlor'Vardhal."

"Why is that?"

"He has been assigned as your Tender. You will forever call him High Tender Marcus, a more familiar address. Just as you'll never refer to me as anything other than Gregor, whether speaking to me directly or speaking about me to others. Although for the High Tender, you may use High Tender vlor'Vardhal when speaking about him to others."

She didn't like the thought of being attached to High Tender Marcus any more than she liked being tied to Gregor. It was a bit confusing. "What about Marcus? Is that his given name? If he's my Tender why am I not familiar with him as well?"

Gregor stiffened, then relaxed. "Never. And that is one mistake I'll expect you to never make. Understood?"

Elise swallowed. "Not at all. Tell me why not, so I can understand."

He paused and seemed to take a moment to compose his answer. She surveyed the Confinement Deck and counted the numbers in swirling garb below. Just a few shy of a thousand. There were less than ten in the tunnel behind her waiting for processing with their wide-eyed stares after listening to her screams. The High Tender said they had collected them all. There must be other processing rooms.

Finally, he spoke. "A man has several names: a given name, a personal name, and a family name. A man's given name is an intimate form of address. A name he shares with his mother when he's a child and later his wife after the sacrament of marriage is consummated."

Her stomach dropped and she gripped the rail in front of her, feeling suddenly unsteady.

"But I am not to become your wife." She hoped that wasn't the case. Please let that not be true.

He gave her a long stare. "No, s'lor and s'vlor are property. But they do acknowledge the intimacy of the Bond by using their lord's given name."

"What intimacy?"

He gripped her hands and warm steel encased her fingers. "Don't worry about things you cannot change. I have claimed you, therefore, you will address me as Gregor. The rest will follow. Do not fight the truth, opés. I see it in your eyes. The denial is there, but I'm telling you, you are mine."

A surge of anger rose and she suppressed it just in time to avoid saying something she would regret. No more profanities, at least not where Gregor, or the High Tender, or any of the wor-guard could hear. "So, that's it. I'm a slave?" One he would eventually rape to establish this intimacy.

"Slave is a distasteful term."

"Just because you don't like the word doesn't mean that's not exactly what you've made me."

"You are not a slave, Elise."

She wasn't going to argue semantics with a monster. Changing topics, she asked another question that had been bothering her. "One of the men called High Tender Marcus, Master Tender. What does that mean?"

"Master Tender is a title designating his rank among the Tender Conclave. He is their leader."

"Is that why he bosses you around?"

Gregor laughed. "He does not boss me around."

"Sure seems like it."

"He disagrees with my interest in you and fears the intensity of our Bond. His concern is appropriate for the Conclave Master. Speaking of Tenders, you will have an opportunity to meet many Tenders during your training. Since you are s'vlor most will be vlor'lords who are High Tenders, like Lord vlor'Vardhal, but others will be lor'lords with the rank of Tender. You will refer to all other Tenders using their family name. For example, Tender lor'Marthis, the lord who you met at the entry port, may participate in your training, but he is not assigned to you."

"Your naming system is complicated. I hope I'm not expected to get it all right at once?"

"You have plenty of time to work on it." He placed his hands back around her waist and stepped back, pulling her with him. He held out a hand to her. "Fifth dinner will be served shortly, and that leaves precious time to get you settled. Now come."

He led her down into her prison, all the while speaking of daily routines, schedules, classrooms, and subject assignments as if this was any other normal day. Only there was nothing normal about this day.

That morning she'd been picking grapes in her garden, on a planet whose population had been obliterated by these people, by him, and now he talked about mundane mealtime routines and exercise facilities. A fifth dinner?

How was a person supposed to wrap their mind around something like this? She had no answer, except to take the next step, to take the next breath. And that kiss? It was the second time he'd kissed her, just as unexpected as the first. She wanted more and couldn't reconcile that thought with her desire for revenge.

At the base of the stairs, he stopped by a console. "Put your palm on the access plate."

She looked at the gel-like plate. "What does this do?"

"It logs you in and out of the Confinement Deck."

Her interest peaked at this. For an advanced society, so far, their technology had been relatively lacking, except for the lift tube and the teleportation. The lift tube scared her and she didn't understand teleportation, but this gel-like device was the first thing even closely resembling a computerized device.

One thing she'd excelled at back home were computers, specifically breaking into their operating systems. The phrase 'back home' looped in her mind. Thinking about home and the possibility she might never see it again had her throat closing up.

"One of your first priorities will be learning our language and culture. I suggest you focus on your studies." His voice lulled her with its gentleness.

"What about your technology?" She pointed to the gel-plate. "Your computers and such?"

He smiled. "Everything. It is imperative we educate you. An uneducated WOR is useless to the empire. Despite what you think, we have no intention of mistreating you. As long as you obey, your life will be rewarding."

As long as she obeyed... The warning was not lost to her ears. "What am I to you?"

"You are the most precious thing in the empire, a true treasure. It's why we came to collect you. Five Ranks in all."

"Lucky me," she grumbled, then she flinched wondering if this violated the terms of not spouting off.

"If you were not WOR, more than likely you would be dead right now. Few survive the Vector who are not WOR. You are fortunate to be alive."

Elise was unable to process the callousness of his words and stumbled to a stop.

Gregor took a step before realizing she was no longer with him. He turned and reached out a hand to lead her forward.

They killed billions to *harvest* a thousand women? Her mind couldn't even begin to wrap itself around the number of people who'd been sacrificed. Hatred rose in the back of her throat, but she controlled the visceral reaction. She would turn her hate into a strength, but now wasn't the time. Revenge would come, but when she was prepared. First, she needed to learn everything she could about her enemy, and fortunately they were willing to teach everything she would need to know.

She would learn their language, their culture, and everything about their technology. The gel-pads would be first. They granted access to the rest of the ship. From there, she'd find a way off this ship, for her, and for the thousand other women they'd taken.

They'd return to Earth. No. That's the first place the Vendel would look. They would need to hide someplace else. She would find a place. It was only a matter of time.

Her grandfather taught her nothing was impossible. As long as the task was broken down into bite-sized chunks, the impossible became possible.

She looked at her new home with a fresh set of eyes.

CHAPTER FIVE_

Gambit, Day 3

AFTER ELISE'S HARSH INTRODUCTION TO THE VENDEL, HER FIRST DAY continued with more reminders of the vileness of her new life. A WOR-guard, specifically assigned for the day, explained the rules of her new home. Dubbed Initiation Day, she shadowed the hulking form as he moved her from one activity to the next.

All around her, the wide, helpless eyes of other women, other captives, reflected the same terror swirling in Elise's gut. One glance around the impossibly huge space and all Elise could think about was *there was no escape*. Did any of these women realize they were no longer *on* Earth?

They had to know. Right?

When she opened her mouth to say hello to a frightened woman, her escort yanked her hard, spinning her against the wall.

"You are not permitted to speak."

"But…" She looked at him, mouth agape, wondering how she was to learn if she was not allowed to speak, but he clarified.

"Conversation with any of the other WOR is not permitted. You may, however, ask any questions of the WOR-guards, the Tenders, or your professors."

"Professors?"

"Yes." His grim expression slid into one of reassurance.

It made her gut churn to see kindness on the face of one of her captors.

"10-2, we want your acclimation to be as easy as possible. To that end, questions are encouraged. However, you're not permitted to speak to the others."

He used the designation she understood had replaced her name. More twisting in her gut followed. They'd stripped her identity. Names had become numbers. It was as if she didn't exist. Their tour continued as bile rose in her throat.

The introduction to her new home came with a long list of rules. Infractions would bring correction if she failed to obey. The purpose of the black rod hanging from the belts of the WOR-guards didn't take long to manifest as the shrieks of a woman broke through the somber silence of the Confinement Deck.

Her WOR-guard never gave his name, but he drew her toward the commotion with one hand gripping her arm. Another WOR-guard stood over the trembling woman who had been forced to her knees. Three long tentacles extended from the end of the black rod. With a dispassionate expression, he whipped the woman while her cries littered the air. Elise wanted to go to the poor thing, but the firm grip of her WOR-guard escort prevented her from helping.

"You're not to interfere with the correction of another." His free hand stroked the whipstick attached to his hip. "Obey the rules and there will never be a reason for the whipstick to be used on you. We only want to welcome you to your new home and help you acclimate as quickly as possible."

"By torturing us?"

"The whipstick ensures obedience. You chose whether its use is required. Obey the rules and…"

"Yes, I know, obey and life will be easy."

"Exactly, 10-2. You chose your fate." He echoed the words bandied about by Gregor.

"I didn't choose this." She gestured toward the crying woman. Ten welts decorated the pale flesh of her back. "This doesn't make sense."

"We're here to help and guide you." He droned on in a monotone voice, not understanding, or not caring about her feelings. "Our entire purpose is to look after your safety and assist in your transition to your new home."

Arguing with him came as a waste of effort. Elise chose to ignore whatever else he had to say, but that left her with Gregor's words echoing in her head. *Obey and life will be easy.*

After seeing what the WOR-guard had done to that woman, she under-

128

stood better what Gregor had meant. Refuse to conform and her life would be miserable.

Her tour continued.

The wor-guard ensured she understood her class schedule. In the morning, she would begin her indoctrination into Vendel culture. Tardiness to any activity was only one of many infractions she would be punished for, but the most damning had to be the ban on speaking with the other prisoners.

The Vendel had gathered over a thousand woman and housed them together in what they called the Confinement Deck. In the most elegant of all horrors, they forbid communication between the women. A standard punishment consisted of ten lashes. She'd been forced to watch three women *punished* during her tour, but to speak to another? That brought double lashes.

"Why can't we talk to one another?"

Her guide gave her a side-lined glance. "Your focus is to assimilate. There is no need to speak."

"But..."

"Speaking to another WOR is a serious infraction. Continue to disobey, and the Tenders will deal with you. I suggest you do not break that rule."

She'd wondered at the oppressive silence. One thousand women occupied the expansive Confinement Deck, but not a single one of them spoke. At least not to one another.

With her head spinning, her day finally wound to a close. Her WOR-guard escorted her to her sleeping cubicle and waited for her to climb into bed. With her emotions a tangled knot, her body was an exhausted shell after the events following her capture. Sleep did not come easily, however. The cries of those subjected to the whipstick rang through the Confinement Deck. Elise found little respite in sleep.

Exhaustion finally pulled her into a restless slumber, but her first full day with the Vendel began in agony when she failed to wake to the morning bell. The stinging burn of the whipstick pulled her from deep sleep and left her gasping for breath. Ten strikes. Ten lines of fire marked her back and still burned as she stood in line for her first meal with the Vendel.

Tardiness to her first class brought another session of the whipstick with another unnamed WOR-guard. She made it through the rest of the day in a fog, and barely paid attention in class until she realized what they planned.

Gregor hadn't been kidding. The Vendel intended on fully assimilating their Earthly treasures into their world. She'd thought they restrict the subjects taught, but that didn't seem to be the case. From lessons in the Vendel language, to social class structure, they also taught the basics of Vendel technology.

The rules were simple. Obey, listen, and learn.

Elise made it through her first day, and then settled into an odd routine of avoidance. Whatever she needed to avoid the burn of the whipstick drove her every decision.

And as the days passed, she reflected on Gregor's disappearance. She thought he would have checked in to see how she was adjusting, but he didn't. His absence unsettled her, because in some messed up way, she missed him. That upset her even more.

The High Tender, however, was a man she saw several times a day. Tenders trained, they explained, but what they would train the women for wasn't clear. Scores of Vendel *professors* taught the women everything they needed to know about their new home and assisted with the process of assimilation. The Tenders weren't involved in their new education, which had Elise wondering. What exactly did a Tender do?

That question found no answer in the following days and weeks. A rigid routine ruled her life. She avoided the whipstick as best she could. Days and nights blended together into one endless hell as the insidiousness of the Vendel's plan worked against her resolve.

The normalcy of her day and the strict routine slowly worked to numb her mind. She, along with the others, moved through the motions of living until those motions became commonplace. Memories of Earth and the death of loved ones disappeared beneath the monotony of daily life.

The Vendel were slowly winning, and Elise fought a losing battle. Alone. Because, despite being surround by a thousand victims, she suffered in silence. They all suffered in silence.

CHAPTER SIX_

Gambit, Day 21

THREE DAMN WEEKS! TWENTY DAYS WITHOUT ANY SIGN OF GREGOR AND EVERY single one of those days had been spent under the watchful tutelage of High Tender Marcus.

The Confinement Deck messed with Elise's mind. The Vendel executed an extraordinary strategy of pacification which wore her resistance down. Each day she woke and struggled against the urge to give in. Pathetic as her effort was, however, she did find the energy to fight.

Sitting in her round sleeping quarters, she dressed in the scarlet gown provided sometime during the night. She slipped the layers of silk and gauze over the towel wrapped over her hair and secured the belt around her waist. Each day a new gown was provided, some variant of red or green. She preferred yellows and blues, but her favorite colors never appeared.

The Vendel's skill in subjugation was admirable, but her will surpassed theirs. She had to give them credit, though. They began by drowning her and her fellow captives in elegance and smothering them in kindness. From the beautiful gowns, to the silken sheets of their bedchambers, and even to the delectable food they ate, they luxuriated in Vendel grandeur. As long as the rules were followed, life was easy, pleasurable even.

When the captives failed to comply, the whipsticks came out. She hadn't asked Gregor about the whipsticks when he'd mentioned them. She inferred their use and hadn't wanted to know more, but she soon knew more about those long black rods than she ever wanted to know.

Wielded by the WOR-guards, rule infractions were ruthlessly dealt with through a swift application against bared flesh.

Consequences Gregor had said. It explained all the backless gowns.

A chime rang overhead. The ten-minute alarm pulsed in the air, warning the women to begin making their way toward their next scheduled activity.

It was one of the few sounds present on the Confinement Deck. Despite the presence of a thousand women, the most oppressive tactic of the Vendel was the silence. Insidious in its application, the speaking ban was their most ingenious. The women could answer the Tenders, converse with their professors, and respond to the commands of the WOR-guards, but speak to another woman? That brought a WOR-guard and his whipstick running.

They'd been effectively gagged. Not being able to commiserate was the worst torture inflicted upon the women. Touch was forbidden as well. There were no hugs to soothe the sobs that sounded day and night. They had nothing but the briefest of looks to ease the overwhelming grief of the loss of their loved ones, survivor's guilt, and the shock of captivity.

Even their names had been taken. Numerical designations based upon the order in which they'd been collected had been assigned. Hers was 1002, shortened to 10-2. She hadn't caught the significance in the white room, but High Tender Marcus had used the-number-that-was-not-her-name. In the twenty-one days since, not once had her name spilled from his lips. They'd been dehumanized.

Which was why it was the first thing she took back, their humanity. Modifying a code based off a cypher used by soldiers interred in prisoner camps decades ago, she devised a secret code. It was clunky and frustrating to learn, but determination did things to people. It made them strong.

In the first week, she braved beating after beating to teach the code to those tenacious enough to bear the pain of the whipstick. They learned. They kept it secret, and the knowledge spread. Unified by resistance against their captors, and by the beginning of the third week, they'd taken back their names.

Rebellions didn't have to begin with a bang, they just needed to start.

Her grandfather's words spun in her mind. *To make the impossible possible*, he would say, *you don't need to move the mountain. Chip away at it.*

132

Begin by moving grains of sand and, before you know it, boulders will fall. Soon, the mountain will come crashing down.

He'd been a brilliant man, but she was stuck moving her mountain without any tools. The task was insurmountable...impossible even, but she was resolute. Perhaps this secret code was that first grain of sand. And the cost had been low. A whipping was child's play compared to what she'd endured with the braklav.

The five-minute chime sounded. A stronger warning, louder and more insistent.

Unwrapping the towel, she shook out her long, brown hair. If she didn't get a move on, she would be late for breakfast, but she had to tie her hair into the mandatory braid. Even it didn't escape captivity. The WOR-guards refused to have anything covering the blank canvas of a bare back.

A tapping sound jerked her head up. One of the goliath WOR-guards in his imposing black uniform stood at the entrance of her enclosure. Not only did their sleeping quarters lack ceilings, they also didn't have doors.

"10-2," he said, calling her by the-number-that-had-become-her-name.

"Yes, sir?" She didn't know his name. Didn't care what it was. It didn't matter. One WOR-guard was like any other.

"I suggest you hurry. You don't want to be late." The WOR-guards were generally helpful and supportive, urging their charges towards assimilation. That they administered corrective punishment didn't register as something abhorrent in their minds, at least not that she could tell.

Reaching for the five arm bracelets designating her Rank, she slid them on her arms and completed her daily outfit. They were a constant reminder of why she was here.

"Yes, sir, I was just finishing getting dressed." She dodged around his large frame, exiting her room, and ran to the dining facility to join the others queuing up for the morning meal.

Arriving at the dining facilities, she said nothing to greet the other girls in line.

Words were forbidden with the whole no-speaking ban.

It didn't mean she didn't say hi. Her fingers fluttered using the code, telegraphing a generalized *Hi* to those in line. Her greeting was repeated back with smiles, nods, and the briefest blinks of acknowledgement.

A brunette with a short-cropped hairstyle tapped out encouragement to a woman in front of her with fresh whipstick marks on her back. *Strength, Mira.* She turned to Elise and gave a nod of hello.

Paula, Elise tapped. *Hi.*

Ex-military, Paula, had been one of the first to learn the code. She was

Fifth Rank, and like Elise, had an inherent strength of personality. She wasn't afraid of the whipstick, not if it meant spreading word of the code. They shared something else as well, or rather, someone else. High Tender Marcus belonged to both of them as their designated training Tender.

The woman standing in front of Paula tapped out, *Mira, be brave.*

Elise smiled. The code was rudimentary, but the message came through like a beacon of hope. Solidarity brought them closer. Such a small thing, but it mattered.

The sound of a whipstick striking flesh sounded behind them. They all flinched when the cry of the woman split through the air. Muffled sobs followed the beating as a WOR-guard hauled a woman in blue silks past the food line.

Strength, Laquita! The message fluttered down the line in a series of taps, encouraging support. Even now they adapted the code, shortening it and making it more efficient.

A WOR-guard drew up beside Elise. He darkened the space around her in his black uniform. "10-2," he said in a harsh clipped voice.

She shrank away from him. "Yes, sir?"

"High Tender vlor'Vardhal is unable to meet for your training session. He has instructed you to attend the yoga session scheduled at that time instead."

Her head snapped up. High Tender Marcus was the only Tender who met one-on-one with any of the girls. There were four others he made special time to take aside, all Fifth Rank, but he spent twice as long with her.

With his message delivered, the WOR-guard continued on.

Breakfast passed quickly and she moved to her first, and favorite, class of the day. In Tech, she navigated through the Vendel artificial neural network, or am-net, feeling more and more at ease with the new technology. Gregor had been right. She took to their technology easily. Her eidetic memory helped in that task, because she only had to see something once to know it forever.

The am-net was the equivalent of an Internet, only it's computing power and capabilities far surpassed anything Earth had yet imagined. She'd already hit several security walls she was certain she hadn't been meant to find. Clearly, the Vendel were limiting access.

She pulled up histories on the design of the am-net and devoured the content, looking for weak spots to launch an attack, while simultaneously teaching herself the equivalent of Vendel coding language. Two hours passed in what seemed like minutes.

After Tech, she moved to her language classroom.

While waiting for the professor to arrive, she plugged into the am-net system and pulled up a piece of code she'd been working on. She'd grown up hacking computer systems almost from the moment she learned to read. Right now, she worked recreating a rudimentary game, Pong. It amused her professor to see her work on something simple, but the project served to teach the fundamentals of their systems while appearing innocuous.

Logic was logic, and electrons worked the same whether they sat in an earth microchip or the biologic gel of the Vendel systems. Phase two, cracking the bio-gel scanners, was underway, buried in a simple game of Pong.

She didn't think about getting caught. Gregor and his consequences rattled in her mind. Whipsticks she could handle. It was the braklav she feared, but he said he wouldn't let High Tender Marcus use that silver rod on her. So, she pushed, learned, and chipped away at the mountain.

Professor Ziddak entered the room, and behind him 312 and 234 walked in.

She paused to tap the edge of the console in greeting. *Hi Chandra, Aomi.*

Chandra jerked her chin in acknowledgment. Aomi smiled a greeting.

Their professor took his position at the front of the room and raised his hand to give the gesture for the ritual greeting.

Her voice melded with those of the twenty other women in the room, speaking in unison. "Good day, Professor Ziddak." She stumbled over the Vendel syntax. Eidetic memory was her strength, not auditory recall. Learning the Vendel language proved her greatest challenge.

Professor Ziddak clasped his hands in front of his chest. He was a small man with beady little eyes, but his smile lit up the room. "Good day, ladies."

Aomi and Chandra took their seats to either side of Elise.

Chandra, Fourth Rank, scowled and sat down, as her blonde curls bounced.

Five bands of Rank encircled Aomi's arms. Her fingers fluttered, tapping out the code on the folds of her dress. She pointed to Chandra. *Wog's.*

Aomi was one of the few Asian women taken. The virus had been particularly devastating in the Asian countries. Asia died within days. She was young, nineteen, thin as a rail, and had long, flowing black hair. Quiet, meek, perfect little Aomi, with her dark walnut eyes and porcelain complexion, kept a secret from the Vendel. She didn't have perfect recall, but her IQ was off the charts. The Asian beauty entered college at twelve, and already had two doctoral degrees under her belt, both in obscure branches of biotech. Her shared passion for learning ensured a close friendship with Elise. They bonded instantly once they could communicate.

Elise squinted at Chandra. It meant *Sorry*. There was a lot more squinting going on now that the code was taking off. Their shared pain became a fountain of solidarity and a silent core of strength.

Chandra shifted in her seat, her discomfort obvious, as was the fresh whip marks covering her back. *Sneeze. Wogs whip. No fair.* Deep blue eyes narrowed in pain. Her blonde curls bounced over her shoulders as she tried to find a comfortable position. Her hair was too short to tie into the mandatory braid.

Elise envied Chandra's freedom of not having to confine her hair. Funny how the littlest things mattered.

Strength. She needed to refine the code. It took forever to communicate anything. They were limited to the clipped conversations of five-year-olds. That frustrated her.

She brought her attention back to the classroom and her assignment. Professor Ziddak came to stand behind her and peered with interest at her screen. "Where are you in your study manual, 10-2?" She cringed at the false display she'd chosen to hide her real work behind.

Professor Ziddak was not a lor' or vlor'lord, but rather a common man. She wasn't sure if it was because of his slight stature, or because he wasn't one of the lords, but she liked him. He seemed genuinely interested in his students and eager to teach his language. He reminded her of Professor MacCabe back on Earth, and it was impossible to hate him.

"Sir, I was doing a drill on time and dates."

"Ah," he tilted his head and clucked his tongue on the roof of his mouth. "Excellent. How about we review for the whole group?" He turned to the classroom. "Ladies, let's begin with minutes and progress up the timescales all the way through to the Sun cycle."

Class began with another drill. She activated a visual of the timescales and dutifully followed along with the sounds of the class, reciting along with them. Language class ended two hours later and her throat was sore from attempting to make the sounds unique to the Vendel tongue. At noon she was released, not to attend her usual two-hour session with the High Tender, but for something much more enjoyable.

Yoga.

As she walked to the exercise fields, her mind muddled over the problem of the clunky code. She changed into the grey and white exercise clothes and headed to the large yoga room. At a glance around the room, she stumbled to a stop. There were easily over two hundred women present. She hadn't seen a single one of them before.

A quick look confirmed why. These were s'lor, lower Ranks with only two or three bands encircling their arms. A few had only one. Yet another form of control? She'd only been around those of Fourth and Fifth Rank these past three weeks.

A thin woman greeted her with warm eyes and a delighted smile. The girl's gaze latched onto the five bands of Rank Elise carried on her arms and her eyebrows lifted in surprise.

412, Sharon Hightower.

10-2, she tapped out, *Elise Comwell.*

The girl smiled, gestured to the empty space next to her, and rolled out her yoga mat. Elise did the same and put her towel neatly in the upper corner.

In front of her, a series of scrapes sounded. It took a minute or two before her mind placed it into code. It had been a relay. Passed on through several individuals.

Elise? 3-Day?

The class filled as more women took their places. The mandatory exercise would begin soon. Her breath caught. *Yes? You?*

The tapping spread out along with a hushed excitement building like a wave. With barely over a thousand women collected, the likelihood of any two knowing one another was nearly impossible.

The return response was *Alice.*

When had Alice learned of her last name? Not that it mattered. What the hell? Her heart double-timed with the realization of what this meant. Alice was alive!

The instructor walked to the front of the class and started the breathing exercises. No one said a word. Everyone sat perfectly still, in yoga pose, as the covert message was passed. But excitement buzzed in the air.

Elise risked the wrath of the WOR-guards and faked a coughing spasm. She rose and staggered to the WOR-guard gesturing to her throat as she approached.

The glower in the man's eyes faded when he saw her distress. He released the whipstick from his hand and nodded.

She walked to the water dispenser. Her eyes flicked furiously over the rows of women. Not a single one of them moved, but she made out a tall, seated woman with a shock of white, blonde hair. It couldn't be, but her friend was there.

She wasn't alone. She had a friend. Someone who knew her, someone she could lean on for support. Moving back to her mat, she joined the others in Warrior pose.

Sauna. Meet?

Yes!

CHAPTER SEVEN_

Gambit, Day 21

AFTER YOGA, THE WOMEN WERE EXCUSED TO THE BATH FACILITIES TO WASH AND change for their afternoon studies. Long rows of benches easily accommodated two hundred women at one time with plenty of elbow room. Neatly stacked towel bins lined the edges of the large square room. On the floor, lines marked off individual areas at each bench space. Every woman had a five-foot buffer zone around her in which to undress and not talk.

All very regimented and controlled.

Finding Alice in the large space might have seemed daunting, but towering at six-feet tall, Alice stood out in any crowd. They locked tearful eyes when they saw each other. Elise stood across from Alice, not more than a few feet separated them, yet it felt like a vast chasm. The women surrounding them stared, then quietly turned to give them a moment of privacy. A mere ten feet of space. It was a boundary neither would cross. The WOR-guard did not patrol in the bath facilities, but that did not mean it wasn't monitored. Oddly, the bath facilities were the only structures on the Confinement Deck to have ceilings. She was certain it was to provide an illusion of modesty for the women.

Neither of them drew attention to themselves as they undressed.

Alice tapped, *Sauna*, and Elise nodded. The steam would hide them.

They grabbed their gray and white exercise clothes and dropped them down the designated laundry chutes. Elise wrapped a thick towel around her body and padded off to the steam sauna. Thick billowy clouds engulfed her in dry heat.

The door opened and several women entered. *Alice?*

Here!

She went toward the sound until she found her friend. They hugged and for a moment just held each other. Alice cried and Elise joined in, letting all her grief pour out. However, she pulled away, breaking contact. This was too risky. They sat down on the wooden benches.

"I can't believe it's really you," Alice said. "I'm so happy."

"Shh, be careful," she said in a whisper. "They can't find out we know each other."

Alice lowered her voice. "Why not?"

"I'm sure they'd never let us near each other again. They control everything."

"Yes, but now that we have this code, we can organize and fight them."

"Thanks, I took it from a history lesson."

"You started the code?" Alice's voice rose and she gripped Elise's hand. "I heard it came from the Master Tender's s'vlor." Alice gulped. "Oh, no. That's you? I've heard such bad things."

"About me?"

Alice's whisper grew cold. "There's this girl, Sarah, Second Rank, one of the last brought on board, 10-4. She told me about the woman who was in processing before her. She said...well, she said you screamed for a really long time."

Memories of the braklav and what High Tender Marcus had done flashed in her mind.

"Is he really your Tender?"

"Yes."

Alice continued in a low whisper. "She didn't say much more, except the doctors mentioned how he was good with difficult s'vlor."

"I doubt the physicians would've spoken so freely."

Alice shrugged. "She said they were talking amongst themselves. That one of them said when High Tender vlor'Vardhal wielded the braklav he could bring s'vlor to the brink of death and back again without leaving a scratch. That's almost an exact quote of what she told me, but she likes to exaggerate. No one likes her. She's a horrible person. I've learned the hard way to steer clear of her."

"Dear God." Elise sat up straight. "Does she know the code?"

Alice snorted and said, "Someone would have to brave a whipstick to teach it to her. She likes to kiss ass and has ratted out everyone at least once. I don't think anyone will bother."

"Good." That's the last thing any of them needed. To be stopped so soon would be devastating. "Look, we've been in here too long. Some WOR-guard is going to get suspicious."

"Right," Alice stood. "How are we going to get together?"

"When are your meals?"

"I have third breakfast, first lunch, and second dinner."

"I'm first, third, and fifth."

"Ouch, that's a horrible schedule. Why did you pick that?"

"It wasn't my choice. High Tender Marcus made the decision."

"Oh," she paused. "Sorry."

Elise shrugged. "I'm sure it was intentional. What about your exercise time?"

"Noon yoga, obviously, and then I work out during first breakfast."

"Any way you could move that? Say, after fifth dinner or before first breakfast?"

The hour chime warning bell rang. They were running out of time.

"Look," Alice said, "I'll go every third morning just before first breakfast. We can run, if that's okay. Talk with the code. Anything more and it might get suspicious."

"Deal."

Elise exited the sauna first and walked to her bench. She stared at the floor, her emotions spinning with the thrill of finding one person among Earth's survivors she knew.

She wasn't alone.

Such a small thing, but it meant the world. Like a seed, it took root in her heart, filling in the holes left behind by the unspeakable loss of everyone she ever cared about, and the faceless billions who perished at the hands of the Vendel.

It shouldn't mean so much, and it didn't change anything about the hopelessness of her situation, but it mattered. They hadn't taken everything.

Her mind shifted as a tantalizing aroma of spice filled her nostrils, sending heat racing through her blood. Between one step and the next, her heart hammered in her chest as she gulped deep lungfuls of the intoxicating scent. She couldn't help but breathe deeply. A prickling sensation danced across her skin and goose bumps spread up her arms. Her head snapped up as her nose sought the source of the exotic cologne.

Gregor waited at her bench, a self-satisfied smirk plastered on his face.

His silver eyes flashed in the bright lights, and over his left brow his imperial tattoo danced as if alive.

She shook her head to clear her senses. It had been three weeks since she'd seen him and she wasn't prepared to fight her body's response. Her legs trembled. She wanted to devour him, trace her hands over every chiseled muscle, kiss those lips until passion replaced that heady smirk. God, she wanted to wrap her legs around his waist, strip him out of his dark uniform, and have him right there on the floor.

Her hand flew to her mouth, suppressing a gasp.

She flooded her mind with other emotions, remembering anger, hatred, and resentment for the man. Desire faded, remaining muted perhaps, but with every breath his unique scent threatened to unravel her self-control. She struggled to ground herself and pushed the unnatural desire for the man aside.

His absence these past three weeks had been a blessing. A part of her had dismissed him, focusing instead on the Vendel history and culture classes she'd been required to attend. In many ways, it had been a relief to attend to intellectual pursuits while ignoring the reality behind her true situation. It dulled the pain of unspeakable loss.

With him standing in front of her, black uniform wrapped tight across a broad chest, dark, wavy, bed-head hair, so sexy—she groaned as lust surged anew and the need to be claimed by him drowned her—she couldn't pull her eyes from the firmness of his square jaw or the strength of his gaze.

Alice padded softly behind on bare feet and walked over to her bench. She glanced at the silent man making the room feel small just by his presence. Her eyes widened and her mouth parted. She toweled off and tapped out silently. *High Tender?*

No! Emperor! Go!

CHAPTER EIGHT_

Gambit, Day 21

Stunned by Gregor's sudden appearance after a three-week absence, Elise could only stare. Around her, the other girls dressed quickly. Modesty had long since been taken from them, first from the processing they'd all had to endure, and then by the lack of privacy over the ensuing weeks.

Alice dropped her towel and slipped into her gown. Grabbing her things, the blonde made a quick retreat. Other girls hurried to dress as well, and soon Elise and Gregor were very much alone.

She stood, clutching nothing more than a towel. Heat burned her cheeks.

He vented a soft laugh while running his gaze down her body with a deliberate pace. "Opés, you're trembling."

He wore the same dark jumpsuit as the WOR-guards, but on him it was so much more. The WOR-guards blended into their surroundings, silent with their whipsticks, invisible, watching and waiting for the women to make a mistake. By contrast, Gregor filled the room just by breathing.

She managed to croak out the appropriate greeting, his first name, an intimate form of address. A weak, "G-Gregor," stuttered from her lips.

He rocked back on his heels, taking his sweet time bringing his gaze back to her face. It bothered her and, by the suppressed mirth in his eyes, he knew it.

"You look well."

"It's rude to stare."

"I see you haven't lost any of your fire." He shook his head. "Get dressed. I'm taking you out." He gestured to a neatly folded gown on the bench.

The one she had put on this morning had been green and there was no sign of it. This one was deep scarlet. Matching slippers had been placed on the floor.

He watched the play of expressions on her face as if reading her every thought.

She hated being so transparent.

"While the green highlights the color of your eyes, this shade compliments your skin. I haven't yet decided which color I prefer."

"You've been picking out my clothes?"

He reached out, gesturing to the towel. "I'll take your towel."

"Turn around."

Memories of the braklav came crashing into her mind. High Tender Marcus's words sounded loudly in her head. Obedience was required. Shivers of remembered pain rioted through her body, but she'd be damned if she would drop the towel.

His brow arched, making the imperial tattoo dance. "That wasn't a request."

She took a step back and firmed her chin. "You've taken everything else away. Do you have to take my dignity as well?"

There went his brow again. Seemed it was his response to everything.

There had to be some humanity in him. "Please, turn around."

He picked up the scarlet gown.

Her skin burned beneath his stare. Such blatant scrutiny made her feel very much like property. She forced her hands to stop trembling as he advanced.

He held the fabric up.

With the constant vigilance of the WOR-guards, obedience had become second nature, and modesty had long since fled. It was different with him, though.

He positioned the opening of the dress over her head, the demand certain in his eyes. While the silk and gauze fabric fell down around her shoulders, he yanked the towel out of her hands, baring her body to the chill air of the room. He stared hard into her terrified eyes, not once looking down at her naked flesh. He made his point, while she shrugged her arms into the sleeves of the gown and settled the cloth to cover her nakedness. It might have been a concession on his part, it was hard to tell. The message was clear. He chose, not her.

He drew his finger along her jaw and cupped her chin. "Choose to resist and you will lose. Accept your place by my side and things will be easy for you."

Neither of those options appealed to her. She would pick a third option and fight to win. Their eyes locked and waged a battle of wills, one he broke with a shake of his head.

"I do admire your spirit, opés. Be glad we are alone."

"Why?" She didn't feel safe alone with him.

"Because, if High Tender vlor'Vardhal had been here, you would be on your knees with the braklav stroking your flesh. He is not nearly as forgiving as me."

"You're no better than him. You're both monsters."

He took in a breath and blew it out on a heavy exhale. "I intend to spend the rest of my life convincing you otherwise." With a spin, he had her turned around and his fingers began the deft task of lacing the corseted ties to the dress.

She'd been so distracted she hadn't noticed how very different the cut of this gown was from those she'd worn previously. The dress snugged her body, cinching in her waistline and accentuating her breasts. The plunging neckline dipped very low indeed, and it had a back.

"Come, opés." He pressed a hand to the hollow of her back. His other slid down her arm. The heat of his palm warmed her flesh, grazed over the bands of Rank on her arm, and traced a trail of fire to the curve of her elbow. Eventually, his fingers found and clasped hers, resulting in a surge of electricity pulsating between them. An involuntary breath yanked her gaze upward where she met an answering intensity in his eyes.

"That is the bond thrumming in our veins," he said. "It's what ties us together."

"I don't know what that means."

He escorted her out of the bath house, around the long rows of circular sleeping areas, and brought her to the base of the large stairs leading up to the observation platforms. He stopped in front of a gel-pad. "Press your palm here."

"Why?"

"Must you always challenge me?"

"I have a curious mind. Why do my questions challenge you?"

He gave her a look.

She shrugged. "You say you want me to learn, to 'assimilate', but then you don't like me asking questions. You make no sense at all."

He huffed a laugh. "I suppose I'm not used to s'vlor being so inquisitive. I will endeavor to be more accommodating to your questions, if you—"

She held up a hand. "I know, I know...if I obey, but it's just not that easy."

"Nevertheless, your life will be more difficult if you don't." He pointed to the gel-pad. "As for these, they are to log you in and out."

"Is there more to it than that?"

He cocked his head. "What do you mean?"

"In some of our prisons, a device like this would act like a lock. The door wouldn't open if the right person didn't activate it." She took in a deep breath, hoping her questions didn't raise suspicion. The answer would be vital to any escape.

"No one has the authority to log you out except for your High Tender."

"But you're taking me out, not High Tender Marcus."

He hesitated. "I'm the one exception to the rule."

Paying a keen eye to how the device worked, she pressed her palm to the gel. Knowing more about the technology behind the devices than when she'd arrived, she had a better idea of what to look for. Sure enough, it was connected to the am-net.

With a hand pressed to the small of her back, he guided her up the steps.

She tripped on the billowy fabric of her dress and he caught her in his strong grip.

"Careful, opés."

The nearness of him intoxicated her senses, sending another jolt of lust surging through her body. She curled her lower lip and pressed her teeth into it. The sharp pain focused her enough to think straight. Gathering the fabric of her dress, she stepped up.

He cupped her elbow and assisted her up the long flight of stairs to the top of the observation platform. When they reached their goal, she spared a glance down into the vast space below. It made no sense, but over the past weeks, she'd grown used to her new home and had started to feel comfortable in the elegant prison the Vendel constructed. She couldn't say the same about wandering outside these walls and lurched to a stop, afraid of what waited beyond the door.

"Opés?" The concern edging his voice centered her. "Is everything okay?"

She hated drawing any strength from him. "Just nervous." Admitting her fear at leaving the Confinement Deck surprised her, perhaps as much as it surprised him, considering the look on his face.

He took her hand in his, that electric tingle spread outward, and worked its way up her arm to settle at the base of her skull. Warmth followed, fanning outward to the rest of her body. He had to feel the racing of her heart. The drumbeat wouldn't stop. It sounded so loud in her ears it deafened her. Could he hear it as well? Being around him...feeling his touch...having his presence all around her made it hard to breathe.

He gripped her upper arm. "There is nothing to fear."

She took a steadying breath and placed a hand on his arm, felt the strength of the muscle beneath the black fabric, and shivered. "You have no idea what I feel."

He swept a strand of hair off her face, tucking it behind her ear. "You have it all wrong. I care very much about how you feel." He pressed his palm to the flat of her back. "I understand how hard this is for you." He leaned close and whispered in her ear. "Take a breath. Try to relax." His lips brushed her skin, causing yet another shiver to travel through her body.

She cleared her throat, taking the moment to steady her nerves. He was a liar, everything he did hurt her in some way.

He pulled back and there was a shift in his demeanor. "Lord vlor'-Vardhal tells me you're excelling in your studies." Gregor switched from English to Vendel. "He says your progress with our language is coming along well."

The attempt to distract her was appreciated, but he would never be able to ease her mind.

She slipped into his native tongue. "High Tender Marcus's extra instruction, especially with your language, has been most helpful."

"Well, I hope you appreciate your surprise. Normally, you wouldn't be allowed off the Confinement Deck until the Blood Rite, but I didn't want you to miss this."

She didn't like the sound of 'Blood Rite,' but the fact he was bending the rules seemed important.

"What?"

"Consider this a gift. I felt you needed a gesture of goodwill from me to you."

A round door opened before them and they entered the long tunnel that had delivered her into the processing room. He brought her forward to the pair of heavy-set Fort Knox-inspired doors she remembered all too well. He placed his palm on a gel-pad.

When she lifted her palm, he gave a shake of his head. "No need for that. This one can only be activated by a man. It notifies the Tender on the other side to open the final door."

On cue, the large doors eased apart and Gregor ushered her through. Again, his hand guided her with steady pressure. He led her to the counter.

This time there was only one man sitting behind the waist-high countertop. He glanced up with a look of surprise. "Sire? I was not notif—"

"Tender lor'Sanderford. Process my s'vlor out."

The Tender gave Gregor one look before he placed a palm pad on the counter. Elise dutifully placed her palm into the warm gel and decided any break for freedom would not be coming through this path.

Gregor guided her out the clear double doors and headed down a broad passageway.

She stopped and asked, "How big is this ship?"

He sucked on his lower lip. All she could think about was licking that lip. Shaking her head, she tried to clear her mind. She hated herself for wanting to kiss him.

He, too, stared at her lips. "Well..."

Her cheeks burned and that was nothing compared to the heat she felt elsewhere.

"The *Gambit's* design is based on a torus—like a big doughnut. It's nearly ten kilometers in diameter."

She rolled her eyes. "I know what a torus is." Blast it, but if a single smirk could throw her into such a state, she was lost.

"Come, my quarters are still a long way from here."

"Your quarters?" Hell, no. "I'm not going to your quarters."

She refused to take another step and crossed her arms over her chest. Stupid move, but all she could think about were his words about the implied intimacy between a vlor'lord and his s'vlor. She wasn't yet ready to consummate that intimate bond. Not that she thought she would have a choice in the matter, but no way was she calmly walking to his quarters to let it happen.

He grabbed her wrist and tugged her forward. "Relax. I just want to share something with you." Then he mumbled, "Lord vlor'Vardhal would spear me if I did anything else."

"He would?"

Gregor's head snapped up. Perhaps she wasn't supposed to hear that last part, but he grinned. "Yes, opés, he would. Don't worry." He glanced down at their clasped hands and sighed. "This is about as close as you and I will get for a very long time."

She should have felt good about that. "Promise?"

"Clasping hands, and a kiss or two is all you have to fear. Although, I'm rather certain your resistance to my kisses is but an act."

Cocky bastard, she didn't dignify him with a response about the kisses. Problem was, he was right and he knew it. "And you swear? Nothing more?"

He shook his head. "I tire of this. We have a long walk ahead. It's time to go."

With a tug, he pulled her forward and her trip through the *Gambit* began, and with it so did her mental inventory of every twist and turn, and every person they passed, along with every nuance of their dress and mannerisms. An invaluable tool, she thanked the odd quirk in her genes which allowed her to catalogue every detail she saw.

Soon they passed through an archway with its opalescent walls and moved onto a long sloping ramp spanning an immense park-like area beneath. The designers of the *Gambit* didn't seem to worry about economizing on interior space. Beneath them, rolling manicured lawns, large sweeping trees, delicate shrubs, and artistically tended gardens spread out on either side, arching upward toward the horizon until they were lost overhead to the curvature of the ship. Her mind hadn't been equipped to grasp the size of her new home.

He stopped. "This is one of our circumferential parks and runs the perimeter of the ship. It makes for a great place to relax."

A group of joggers came down one of the winding paths. The runners' hair, drawn up in ponytails, swung to-and-fro with each bounding stride.

She gasped. "Those are women!"

He scoffed. "Well, of course they are."

"But, I thought..." She fell silent with the realization of what the women were wearing. The grey and white exercise outfits were very familiar. "Are those WOR?"

"No, WOR would have bands of Rank on their arms. Why do they surprise you?"

"I didn't think there were any women on board."

"Why would you think that?"

Because so far, she'd only seen Vendel men. "Considering you captured a thousand females, I figured you didn't have any women of your own."

His eyes danced with amusement. "Ah, you've made an unfortunate assumption." He chuckled. "We didn't collect you for that reason."

Whatever, those women wore the same workout clothes she was forced to wear. In fact, from what she'd seen, the fashion sense of the Vendel was rather uninspired. Tunics and jumpsuits of varying colors predominated the local fashion scene, and workout clothes. That was the best news she could have hoped for. Her gown marked her as WOR just as surely as did the bands of Rank on her arms, but the exercise gear freed her. When she did eventually find a way off the Confinement Deck, and she would, she wouldn't have to worry about a disguise.

"Don't tease me because I assumed only men were on board your ship. All I've seen are men." She pointed to the women disappearing behind a copse of trees. "Those are the first women I've seen. And they aren't mentioned anywhere in your classes on governmental structure."

He scoffed at her comment.

"Do you treat all women as chattel? Are your women so far beneath you that they aren't even included in our assimilation classes?"

"Another unfortunate assumption on your part." His eyes darkened. "Men fulfill civic duties that women don't share, but women are an important part of our society. Your studies are meant to teach you about our governmental structure."

"You should be teaching us about your society, even the pitiful subjugation of your women."

His eyes darkened. "Do not jump to conclusions too quickly. Our women enjoy quite a range of freedoms." He leaned on the railing and watched her lips. "Unlike men, they can move freely between the social classes. Through the bonds of matrimony, they harness immense power."

"What does that mean?"

"Only that you should not judge my people until you have had a chance to learn more about them."

"How can I? I'm not stupid. The access you've given us in the Confinement Deck is restricted. We learn only what you want us to learn."

His eyes narrowed. "It's called assimilation."

"I call it brainwashing." She jutted her chin forward and dug in for an argument. "Open up our access and let me decide." The more barriers she could get released the easier it would be to crack the Vendel computing system.

"No."

"Why not?"

"Because you refuse to learn the most basic lesson."

"And what is that?"

"Obey."

She turned away from him, fists clenched, and stared off into the distance. "Like a good little slave?"

He had no reason to give in to her demands. Arguing with him would only lead her to a dead end. She needed a different tact.

"Yes, that's exactly what I mean. Trust will open more doors. The more you resist, the tighter the controls will be. The more you comply, the more freedoms you will enjoy. Surely, you see this?"

Right, obey and her life will be so much easier. For someone who held all the power, it was such an easy demand to make, not so easy to comply with, but she acknowledged the truth in his words.

She bowed her head in acquiescence. "Forgive me, Gregor, but look at it from my viewpoint. I struggle with making sense of your world. Your customs are hard to understand. I'm trying to learn, but I question everything. It would help me to assimilate better if I had access to more information." There she threw his word back at him.

Gregor didn't respond. He rubbed his chin and pushed off the rail. His eyes dropped to the low neckline of her dress. "Come, on the other side of this ramp is the lift tube that will take us up to my quarters."

He wasn't going to give in to her demands. She needed to accept what she couldn't change and focus on what she had power over. What she needed was a mental focus when dealing with him, something to latch onto when things got difficult.

A willow tree came to mind. Its long fragile branches swayed in the breeze, giving way beneath the terrible force of the wind. Because the willow bent, the storms didn't break the heartwood at its core. She needed to become like the willow and bend. Only then would she remain strong enough to beat Gregor.

He herded her toward the other side of the bridge with a gentle, but firm, guiding hand. "Do you remember the lift tube from before?"

She allowed herself to be led and composed herself to meekness. Demure, acquiescing, and submitting to his control, she approached familiar doors set into the wall. He seemed to like their verbal sparring, but it was clear he preferred when she submitted to his will. Whatever it took, she'd be the damn willow. He pressed a palm plate and they waited. The door spiraled open and she stared with trepidation at the wide circular space.

Gregor noticed her hesitation. "I can hold you. You could rest your head on my shoulder like last time."

She returned a false smile to his banter. "Face your fears or they'll consume you, right?" She stepped forward, but her bravado failed the moment she stepped inside.

The first signs of panic threatened: hammering heart, fast-paced breathing, knees knocking, and that flutter in her gut about sent her to her knees. It didn't help knowing the floor was going to drop out from beneath her feet and there would be nothing to hold on to. She looked to the only person she had for support.

"Gregor?" Her plea came out a faint croak.

Gregor gave a half bow. His eyes were open and sincere—warm even. "Come, I want you to become comfortable using these on your own, but your first lift tube ride on your own can be a little disorientating." He beckoned with his arm. "Stand in front of me. I will hold you."

Switching from English to Vendel he gave a command.

He wrapped his arms around her waist. The entire length of his body pressed against her. That heady scent, full of raw masculinity and exotic spice, filled her nostrils. She took in a deep breath and closed her eyes. Goose bumps sprung up on her arms despite her attempts to remain unaffected by his touch.

"Just focus on the far wall and you'll be okay. Your nervousness will fade as you get used to riding the tube."

As long as he thought the goose bumps were from the lift tube and not him, she didn't care.

Just like the first time, a wind tickled her skin. This time, she didn't make the mistake of looking down. The floor would be falling away and she didn't need to see that. When the breeze began to fade, she knew their destination—his private rooms—were approaching. A different set of nerves settled in her stomach.

She tried to prepare for whatever he had planned and was very much aware the High Tender was not present. Actually, now that she thought about it, it wasn't entirely clear if High Tender Marcus was, or wasn't, supposed to be chaperoning this visit.

The wind disappeared. She opened her eyes in time to see the wall opposite form a door and open.

"This is it." Gregor nuzzled the side of her neck and pressed his lips to the soft spot behind her ear.

A pulse of arousal flared, one she quickly stamped out. "Your quarters are off the lift tube?"

Gregor pulled her forward, grasping her wrist. Always, he had a hand on her. He took her through a series of rooms, describing each as they delved deeper into his retreat, but she wasn't paying attention. The further she moved into his private realm the faster her heart beat. What were his plans? What did she want them to be?

Where the hell was High Tender Marcus and why wasn't he watching over her?

CHAPTER NINE_

Gambit, Day 21

GREGOR'S LIVING SUITE GREETED ELISE WITH THE PICTURE OF CONTROL. IT spoke much about the man who inhabited it. White chairs and sofas, full of clean lines, dominated the room. The space was devoid of color, with the exception of the walls. Here the vibrancy of the man who ruled an empire shone.

Artwork and sculptures of surprising beauty filled niches along the walls. Lighted accents displayed each masterful piece to perfection. There was one wall, however, which remained a startling void of color. A solid gray. Her eyes latched onto it, ignoring all the rest for the starkness it represented. Soft music filled the room, floating around with tranquil melodies, trying and failing to calm its unwilling guest.

Butterflies danced in her belly, rebellious in their flight. She welcomed them. They reminded her to be strong.

A clean, fresh scent, crisp like an ocean breeze, swirled in the currents of the room. She inhaled deeply, noting the contrast between this room, light and fresh, and Gregor, a man both dark and compelling.

Warm light suffused the entire area in a muted glow, again, a calming influence which attempted to drain tension out of her body and failed.

During their walk, Gregor's hand had been constantly on her, but inside his domain he released her to wander. Perhaps he allowed her a moment to admire the various pieces of art, or maybe he knew she had nowhere to run. She suspected it was so he could better observe her from afar, although she had a feeling he'd been watching her every move on the Confinement Deck these past few weeks.

In her slow circuit around the room, her heart slammed in her chest, beating out a deafening tattoo in her ears. Since he seemed comfortable to let her be, she took the time to examine the niches in the wall and admire the artwork. Gorgeous glasswork constructions of alien sea creatures and underwater seascapes amazed her with their intricate craftsmanship. Despite their incredible beauty, however, her gaze kept turning to the gray wall.

Memories of his touch lingered in her palm, at the small of her back, and behind her ear where his lips had caressed her skin. Whatever this bond was he kept speaking of, she couldn't ignore its growing strength. She would need to come to terms with what it meant, and if she couldn't control it, she'd need to temper its influence.

He messed with something behind a long bar. A glance toward him had their gazes locking. Holding. The ghost of a smile curved his lips, then he glanced down and lifted two champagne flutes filled with bubbling liquid.

She cocked her head. "You brought me here for a toast?" What else did he have planned for this intimate rendezvous?

"Come." He crossed over the expanse of the room to stand before the gray wall. With a gesture, he indicated she should stand beside him. Handing her a glass, he pressed a patch on the wall. He rattled off a series of commands, which with her limited understanding of the Vendel language, she didn't follow.

"I wanted to give you something. It's not much. Consider it a gesture of good will from me to you...a path toward building a bridge toward our future together."

She looked at him in puzzlement. "What are you talking about?" The butterflies vanished. She didn't understand what he could possibly give her that she could want.

"None of the others will have this opportunity. Today we are exiting Earth's local space and engaging the WOR-drive. I thought you would like to say goodbye." He closed the distance. "This is my gift."

Her heart raced and her breathing quickened. She couldn't help it, but her body responded to his touch. A sharp breath in and his rich scent filled her nostrils. No one smelled that good. Her head tilted back. Her mouth parted.

This wasn't right. It wasn't normal. It reminded her of the banquet, of

156

that perfume, the *callidor* he'd called it. He was just so overwhelming and he felt so good up close, and his scent, full of spice and musk, made her want to yield. She shook her head, but it did nothing to clear her mind, or dampen the reactions of her body.

He continued on, as if unaware of the trembling in her knees, but if that was the case then why did his grip around her waist tighten? He pulled her close, supporting more of her weight.

"This is a great day for the Vendel." He sounded so damn proud.

There was an energy surging in the room, some pulsating current flowing between the press of their bodies. If their bare skin touched now, would she feel the electric jolt that surged through her the first time his fingers had swept across her skin?

He took in a deep breath and spoke into the air, "Viewscreen."

The slate gray wall dissolved. Thousands of twinkling points of light filled the screen. In the center, a star brighter than any other shone with a hot yellow light. Drifting down from the upper corner, sinking into sight like a lazy blue globe, was Earth. Cotton-white clouds draped over deep blue oceans. A typhoon coiled over Taiwan, ready to make landfall.

He held her tight and lowered his mouth to her ear. "Earth is your past. It's time to say goodbye and embrace your future."

Her entire body shook with suppressed fury. The champagne flute fell to the floor with the crash of breaking glass.

She fisted the fabric of his shirt and sagged against him. Her voice broke with the pain of the deaths of billions. "You thought this would please me?" She beat against his chest. "Damn you, damn you to hell!" Tears spilled and she broke down in sobs.

He set his glass down and held her. "Elise?"

She pushed against him, but he only held her tighter.

"Why? Why would you bring me here?" Twisting did nothing to free herself of his grip. He was so much stronger than she. He was like granite. The harder she pushed, the more his grip tightened. Each inhale brought his heady scent streaming to her senses, an aphrodisiac of potent proportions. Her fist beat against his chest. "Please, let me go."

"No."

Her head tilted back. Her eyes traced the path from his strong jawline to lips she wanted to kiss. Her gaze lifted to latch onto eyes of silver fire. "For once, just leave me alone."

"I will not. You need to accept this. Fighting the inevitable will only bring you pain." His brows drew together at his last statement, as if he were the one in agony.

"You don't get it." She shook her head. "I'll never accept you."

His lips pressed together as he gave a quick shake of his head. "You don't understand what's at stake."

"You murdered my world. Billions dead! My grandfather. My nieces—" Her voice broke. "Don't tell me I don't know what's at stake. You have no right. I judge you, Gregor. I judge everything you've done. You're nothing but a monster." Wetness pooled at the corners of her eyes. She blinked rapidly as she tried to keep her tears contained.

She wanted to hate him, but with each intoxicating breath his essence filled her with a sensual desire. A burning heat curled between her thighs, pulsed with an intensity she couldn't ignore. A groan escaped her lips, as she could no longer deny her rising excitement at being held in his arms. She was a freak to be aroused by him, an abomination. For this reason, she hated him even more.

"Do you not feel it? Even now it surges in your blood."

"No! Whatever this is, it's fake, something you did to me. Something only a freak and a monster does to another human being. Are you so weak that the only way you can get a woman to desire you is to drug them? Drug me?"

He released her and she stumbled from his grasp, gagging and choking on her sobs. Worst of all, she wanted back in his arms, and that feeling terrified her more than anything else.

"You may have drugged me, but I'll always hate you." She gestured at her body. "Whatever you did, I'll fight it. Don't ever think I'm not fighting it."

She glanced at the screen, and noticed Earth had moved a third of the way down. She wished she could see her home, but the blue of the Pacific and the typhoon raging on the island nation of Taiwan filled the view screen.

Wait. No longer a nation. The world held no people.

She walked to the wall. Earth was out of reach of her hand, but she tried to touch it anyway. "You not only killed us, but the planet, too. You're heartless." She wrapped her arms around herself. It was the only comforting hug she would get.

He stepped behind her, and by some grace of God, he did not touch her, but the heat of his body leapt the distance between them and warmed her back. She'd scream if she felt that electric pulse right now, but he didn't advance further.

"You're wrong."

"No, I'm not." Was he a fool? "When you killed the people, you left no one behind to tend the world. Nuclear facilities are just one of the things that will cause ecological disaster without humans around to tend to them. All life on Earth will perish because of what you unleashed."

Her skin pricked with electricity. His touch did this. He wrapped an arm around her waist and pulled her against his chest. The bastard couldn't keep his hands off her body. He rested his chin on top her head and breathed out a sigh.

"You have it all wrong, my opés. What do you think we've been doing these past sun cycles?"

Torturing and assimilating her and a thousand other women. Her breath caught. "What do you mean?"

"Earth is very important to all of humanity. It's impossible to explain everything, but in this you must take me at my word. No disaster will result from the culling that occurred. Earth, and those few who remain, are essential to the survival of the human race."

A hollowness in her chest occurred because her heart skipped several beats. "What?"

He brushed back her hair and kissed the top of her head. "My duty is to humanity. Earth is but a small slice of my empire. To keep an oath, I sacrificed what was necessary to save what I can."

"Sacrifice?" What the hell was he talking about? "You speak like you're a surgeon cutting out a tumor, like you made a clinical decision, but you ended billions of lives. You're not God. What gave you the right to decide?"

"For the greater good, that's exactly what I did."

"You said culling. What exactly do you mean by that?"

He spun her around to face him, the intensity of his gaze had her heartbeat accelerating. His eyes, a shade that changed from silver to the differing shades of blue depending on his mood, stared down on her with a dark intensity. A sadness pulled at the corners of his eyes, and for once the tattoo over his left brow remained dormant. "You are a very curious woman, Elise. We would be here for cycles if I answered all your questions."

"I have a curious mind. Now answer my question."

"Your mind will get you in trouble. I have warned you about this. You must put your rebellious nature behind you. WOR training is not easy. You need to understand you will be trained and High Tender vlor'Vardhal will use all measures at his disposal."

"Like torture? The whipsticks and the braklav?" A shudder rippled down her spine with the remembrance of that pain. "Tender Training? Is that what you mean? Have you ever considered just asking for our help? You know sometimes you get more with a simple please and thank you than a damn stick. You're all a bunch of damn assholes."

His eyes flared wide for a moment, then a chuckle escaped him. "See, that is what I am saying. Language such as that is grounds for punishment. A WOR-guard or a Tender would be taking care of such disrespect right now."

"But they aren't here. You are. What are you going to do? Punish me because I called you a name? That's ridiculous." Challenging him was foolish, but she couldn't stand there and do nothing. "You still haven't answered my question. Are there survivors left on Earth?" It could mean so many different things, like maybe Tom and her nieces still lived.

His gaze went to her lips. "I'm not going to punish you, nor am I going to answer all your questions."

To taste him would be delicious. She pressed her palm against his chest in anticipation of such a kiss, when her mind screamed for it all to stop. "But imagine if you did."

His brow shot up.

"You want to forge a future between us?" She grabbed at his shirt. "Then answer my damned question."

He lowered his head and brushed his lips over hers. "Yes, yes, my opés, there are very few who survived. Now, stop fighting me." His lips pressed against hers and she struggled to breathe as he claimed his kiss.

She pressed away, but an iron grip held her firm. Heat flooded her body as electricity pulsed between them and the bond ignited.

Her hands no longer pushed, but clutched at his shirt, pulling him close as the heat of his mouth overwhelmed her defenses. So much for resisting.

He tasted divine. She wanted more.

His kiss intensified, and she met his passion with a rising heat of her own. His fingers wrapped in her hair, clutching, and pulling her close to mold her body against his until she could no longer deny the strength beneath his black uniform. Their breaths mingled. His exhales filled her lungs. The dark flavors of his mouth drove her higher, building up her need.

She was being devoured, claimed by the strength of his kisses, and she didn't care. Elise Comwell yielded to a monster.

The initial urgency of his kisses lessened as he explored her mouth with greater deliberation. Her body responded with its shocking betrayal, wanting more than she was willing to give as she opened for him, allowing his tongue to tangle with hers. All the while, her mind struggled to find an advantage, to regain control, and failed.

The bond thrumming in her veins wasn't something she could fight. She kissed him back, hating him, but despised her body's reaction even more.

Somehow, she had to control this passion and turn it into a tool to free herself from this nightmare. Her tongue traced the fullness of his lips, grazed against the hardness of his teeth, and explored the landscape of his mouth, eager and insistent as she met his need with her desire.

A low groan escaped him and he clutched her tighter still, pressing her up the full length of his body. She felt every ridge of muscle in his hardened physique. He pulled back and their eyes locked. Her breathing was as ragged and uncontrolled as his.

She turned her head and stared at the viewscreen. The star field and Earth disappeared, and in its place a kaleidoscope of color took over. The view outside stretched into oblivion and snapped back in a multi-colored swirl of light. It reminded her of the Tenderstat, hauntingly familiar, resonating with something deep inside her chest.

Tears streamed down her face.

His voice cracked. "You surprise me, opés. The bond is stronger than I anticipated. Go ahead. Hate me, but your body betrays your true feelings." He stroked her long brown hair, twining his fingers in her curls.

Her voice remained steady, but she found the strength to match the chill of his words. "Don't ever forget that I am fighting you."

A loud crash interrupted them.

"Sire, release her." The booming voice of High Tender Marcus vlor'-Vardhal thundered through their intimate moment.

She stiffened in dread.

Gregor didn't release her. "Since when does the High Tender enter my quarters without permission?" His voice held a low, brittle tone.

"Since when does a vlor'lord run off with an s'vlor in training and engage in activities reserved for Binding?" The High Tender's voice went arctic cold. "You know you cannot take her without permission, and you most certainly cannot engage in such behavior."

Elise shivered, certain the temperature in the room plummeted twenty degrees as the two men locked icy stares.

"I don't need your permission, Lord vlor'Vardhal," Gregor's voice rose in annoyance. "She is mine."

"You do not have rights to her...not yet. And certainly not for...this." The High Tender moved to take Elise.

Gregor blocked him, placing his body between her and the High Tender.

She turned away and squeezed her eyes shut, wishing to disappear. The dark, rich taste of Gregor lingered on her lips. Breathing was nearly impossible, and she struggled to regain control of her body.

"Sire," the High Tender said with a throaty growl. "This behavior isn't appropriate until after the Binding. Blasted! You know this better than anyone." The High Tender's voice rose to fill the room.

It occurred to her being caught in a tug-o-war between these powerful men was a bad place to be.

"It was only a kiss," Gregor's voice rose in challenge.

High Tender Marcus took a long time to answer, but when he did, his words were measured. "Sire, my duty is clear, as is yours. I hold authority over her training. I insist you abstain from this behavior. I do not wish to involve the High Judicators, but I will." His lips twisted with distaste as he spoke those words

Gregor took a step toward the High Tender. "You challenge me? Am I not your emperor?"

The High Tender's voice cracked. "Sire, release the girl."

"You would, wouldn't you? You'd take this up with the High Judicators?"

The High Tender stared down the Emperor. The tone of his voice was solid, but he took a step back in capitulation. His voice lowered as he pleaded. "You saw what happened with the Tenderstat. I've never seen colors during a testing before, and never has one shattered. We do not yet know what it means. Do not force me to act against you."

Silence fell with a sudden stillness between the men.

What did he mean about the Tenderstat? And how could a High Tender act against the Emperor? What was a High Judicator? Her ignorance about this society frustrated the hell out of her.

Gregor spoke to the High Tender with great care. "I never had any intention of taking her before Binding. On my word as vlor' and as Emperor, I swear that as truth." He raised his palm out cautioning the man to silence. "There is no need to wait for the Binding. Do you understand?"

The swirling colors on the far wall captivated her attention. That was something called WOR-space and it called out to her, tugging on a part of her mind she had never felt before. It terrified her because it felt so familiar. It was a part of her, and she a part of it, even if she didn't understand what it was.

The High Tender made as if to speak and was silenced with a gesture from Gregor. "This is my will. Don't force me to make it a command. I have sworn oath, that should be sufficient." He paused watching the High Tender.

"This is madness," the High Tender whispered. "If you take her before the bond is mature, before you control it, you will sacrifice everything. I cannot allow it."

"I will not sacrifice the Binding."

"These Earth women are not like Vendel. They are much freer with their..." The High Tender waved vaguely at her with a look of disgust flashing over his features. "She would tempt you. It would be best to leave her alone."

"Trust in your emperor."

"Passion clouds your judgment."

"Will you interfere?" Gregor demanded.

The High Tender fell silent for a time, but when he spoke his words came out thick and strangled. "You may spend time with the girl, but I want to know where you take her and when you bring her back. Her training must come first." The High Tender extended his hand to Elise.

She stared at it, unwilling to let go of the safety of Gregor's protection. To her surprise, Gregor handed her off to the High Tender, practically pushing her toward the man.

High Tender Marcus yanked her out of Gregor's grip and dragged her out of Gregor's apartment before she could blink. She glanced over her shoulder to see Gregor's deep scowl as they departed.

The High Tender didn't say a word during the long walk back to the Confinement Deck. He held her hand in an iron grip and released it only after depositing her back on her bed.

After he left, she curled into a ball and shook.

Images of passionate kisses and silver-gray eyes invaded her dreams. She didn't know what bothered her more, Gregor's stupid toast, or the heated response he elicited in her body with that kiss.

With a glance at her luxurious prison, she still had no clue how to begin her plans for revenge.

CHAPTER TEN_

Gambit, Day 31

Elise began her morning like every other, at the track. It had been one full Vendel cycle, ten Earth days, since her encounter with Gregor.

She was thankful in a way; engaging with Gregor assured defeat. Her body was simply too rebellious in his presence. Although the trip to his quarters resulted in some gains. He revealed truths, even if he'd withheld other answers she demanded.

Not everyone had died. A culling he'd called it. It gave her hope. If survival depended on having the right set of genes, her nieces could still be alive. But Tom? The thought of her nieces struggling on without his guidance twisted her gut. She needed to believe they'd made it.

Why fight for freedom if there was nothing to go home to? And Gregor said his people were safeguarding Earth. That had to mean something.

Another thing had changed on the Confinement Deck. He said he wanted to build a bridge between them, and she'd complained about the lack of education about women in Vendel society. So, she was pleasantly surprised when a course in women's study had been added to the curriculum.

Gregor's bridge, rather than helping though, only enraged her more. Women had little control over their lives. They owned no property, and everything they earned went under the umbrella of their male sponsor—father, husband, brother, son-in-law, whoever their closest male relative

was ruled their lives—Vendel women were beholden to patriarchal benev-
olence from birth to death. There was some mention about matrimonial
unions being tied to the matriarchal line that confused her, but the Vendel
knew little about women's rights.

Which brought up the question of what happened when a woman had
no male sponsorship to fall back on? That answer would play an important part in her plans. If she couldn't act independent of a man outside the
Confinement Deck, her break for freedom would face a significant hurdle.
And she certainly didn't need another impossible task heaped upon all the
others she already faced.

Elise completed her warmup routine. Where the hell was Alice? She
wouldn't be able to stall much longer and would have to move onto the
track to begin her run.

They met every third day, coordinating it so their meetings didn't
appear arranged, a difficult task under the watchful eyes of the WOR-
guards. She stretched out her hamstrings, one more time, but when Alice
failed to show she had no choice but to head out.

After her first lap, however, Alice jogged up behind her, catching her
with an easy stride. "Got stopped by a WOR-guard."

On the tracks, the chances of the WOR-guards hearing them speaking
was low. They huffed out broken syllables on the exhales of labored breath
and painstakingly formed words.

"Sorry." Elise sympathized with her friend but didn't ask what Alice
had done to earn the whipstick. "I hate this place. I hate them."

"Yeah, but it's weird though...how you get used to it?"

"I know." Complacency was their biggest enemy.

"I wake up, put on a beautiful gown, go to class, and learn amazing
things. Each day it gets harder to remember."

"Yeah, until they whip you."

"Right. Until a WOR-guard reminds me I'm a prisoner."

It was true. The Vendel had built a perfect prison. If they behaved, they
lived an idyllic life. "I see it in the other girls as well."

"It bothers me, how easily they've won," Alice said with a frown.

"They haven't won."

"Yeah, I guess with the code we kind of have something over them,"
Alice said. "More and more of the girls are learning. At least those who
speak English. I feel bad for those who don't. They're so isolated."

"The Tenders will figure it out." She slowed the pace to make speaking
easier. "They'll punish us."

"The one time they used that silver stick thingy on me, I thought I was going to die."

"What about 10-4? What's her name?" She vented a frustrated sigh. "God, I hate these numbers the Vendel gave us. I hate even more that I'm using them. It's so dehumanizing."

"Her name is Sarah. Bitch turned me in to the WOR-guards yesterday. I was late for language class. She marched up to the first WOR-guard she saw and told him." Alice's fists clenched and she stumbled.

Many had fallen victim to Sarah's brown-nosing with the WOR-guards.

"No one has bothered to teach her," Alice said, "and she's too stupid to figure it out."

"I made a more fluid code...faster."

"If you're worried about the Tenders, you might want to keep it to yourself."

They finished another lap.

"I don't need a code to talk to myself."

Alice laughed. "True. Teach me. When they bust us, at least you and I will still have something."

They ran for thirty minutes and Elise introduced Alice to her new revised code. At the end of their run they separated until the next time they'd see each other. They each headed to their respective classes.

Her first class was linguistics with Professor Ziddak. His weasel face lit up when he saw his students. They'd been here for just over a sun cycle, made up of three cycles, or thirty days. He told them in three more sun cycles, ninety days, only the Vendel language would be allowed. Any Earth languages would be forbidden afterwards. He tried to reassure them they weren't expected to be proficient but made sure they understood the use of their native tongue would be added to the list of infractions correctable by the WOR-guards.

Elise was suddenly appreciative of the extra tutoring sessions High Tender Marcus gave her two hours every day. While she could barely stand to be in his presence, he spent their time together drilling her in the Vendel language. Fortunately, his tutoring had advanced her proficiency above that of the other women.

She followed Professor Ziddak's lesson plan, pretending to be involved. Instead, she put her hacking skills to use, working on viral subroutines and releasing them into the am-net as avatars. Little minions she sent out with very specific tasks. Some fetched schematics of the ship. Others brought back power grid network interfaces. She'd even sent a few to probe into societal structure, trying to piece together Conclave relationships and important things like what power a High Judicator may or may not hold over the Vendel Emperor and what happened to a woman who lost all her male sponsors.

Her viral subroutines were something the am-net had never encountered before. She had no idea what she was looking for, but anything she could learn about this new culture, computer systems, economic system, or personal tracking systems was something she might be able to use against Gregor.

The lesson droned on and Elise let loose a new squad of her little army into the am-net.

CHAPTER ELEVEN_

Gambit, Day 121

THE DAYS BLENDED INTO ONE ANOTHER WITH A DULL MONOTONY. FOR NINETY days, three Vendel sun-cycles, she'd seen no sign of Gregor.

Whether he chose to stay away, or whether High Tender Marcus kept them apart, she had no idea. For the first few cycles, their passionate kiss had filled her dreams, but as days turned to weeks and then to months (or cycles turned to sun cycles), that fire died and was replaced by something much more insidious—the routine of daily living.

She, along with the other women, grew comfortable with their new life. She fought the urge to give in, but it was too easy to let it happen. It had been over a sun cycle, three cycles, since the sound of a whipstick struck. They were all incredibly well behaved.

The language ban went into place early in the morning of Day 121 of their captivity. Not a few minutes later, the strikes of whipsticks ringing out reminded them exactly what they were.

Sobs sounded constantly throughout the Confinement Deck, followed quickly by flurried tapping of the secret code offering support and solidarity.

For those who'd forgotten, they now remembered their place.

Elise managed the language ban easier than the others. Due to the private sessions with High Tender Marcus, she was near fluent.

On her way to meet him, the familiar sound of a whipstick and the

169

cries of its victim sounded behind her. In this one thing, she was grateful, and she intended to express her gratitude to High Tender Marcus when she saw him.

She stepped into the small room for her private lesson and pulled up short. The High Tender wasn't there. Instead, the man who had filled her dreams for cycles waited.

For someone who'd made such a fuss about claiming her, where the hell had he been all this time? Not that she was going to let him think she'd missed their verbal sparring, his touch, or those full lips of his, but why show up now?

The gleam in his eyes sharpened and he gave her one of his quirky half-smiles. "Good afternoon," he said in clear, crisp English.

Was he trying to trick her? Why would he do that? He lounged at the single desk in the large room, leaning back in a chair, with his feet propped on the table in front of him.

"It's nice to see you."

Elise answered in fluent Vendel. No way was she going to break the language ban. "Hello, Gregor." Butterflies danced in her belly and her heart pulsed beneath her breastbone. "Where is High Tender Marcus?"

"He and the other Tenders are busy. They have much to prepare. I have missed you." Gregor gestured for her to take the seat opposite him. His brows drew down.

Perhaps he expected her to throw herself at him, but she wasn't going to pretend she was happy to see him. Despite an immediate heated response, she suppressed the power of the bond firing passionate signals within her body.

"Is that so?"

He kicked his feet off the table and sat up straight.

She crossed the few steps and sank into the seat. Her fingers twitched in the silken folds of her dress. "Tell me what High Tender Marcus is preparing." She'd found anger and a direct approach worked best to suppress the bond.

"Our time apart has threaded steel into your blood and tempered our bond. Unfortunate, but not unexpected."

She laced her voice full of sarcasm. "Forgive me if I'm not falling all over myself here, but I'm distracted by the cries of my friends being whipped by your men."

"By the gods, but I love the challenge in your voice."

She recoiled, remembering too late how unwise it was to bait him. She'd enflamed his desire. Not smart when the control she held over the bond was so tenuous. Even now heat coiled within her and she couldn't keep her eyes off his rich, full lips.

Gregor tapped his fingers on the table. "The High Tender left me a lesson plan." He flicked the embedded tabletop display to activate a glowing blue screen. "I'm supposed to discuss verb conjugation with you." He looked at her. "But it seems your grasp of our language is quite advanced, so I see no reason to waste what limited time we have on that."

His gaze focused a beat too long on her lips. It seemed they were both thinking the same thing.

Squirming in her chair, she attempted to direct him back to the task at hand. "High Tender Marcus's extra tutoring has been most helpful." Had the temperature in the room spiked?

"I'm glad you've found his attentions helpful. Since he will be your Tender, it is good you've been able to learn from him. He will be your primary guide as you learn the WOR-skill." He tapped the bio-gel and the screen went dark. His gaze lingered on her lips.

She coughed and pointed at the interface. "Aren't we going to go over the lesson?"

He blinked. "I have no intention of doing that."

"But...High Tender Marcus's instructions?"

"He is busy, and we are alone. I can think of a much better way to spend our time." His voice held dark and sultry promises.

She wanted to surrender to the heat simmering in his words but reined in the passion burning in her gut. "I don't want to go against High Tender Marcus's wishes." And this was the heart of her problem. Along the way, she'd become an obedient slave to these men.

"You're right to obey him, but you should not fear him." His voice was a harsh whisper. "His only goal is to train you."

"I don't fear him." That was a lie. The High Tender with his braklav terrified her.

"You do, but you should not. Obey him and he will be your most obedient servant." Gregor stated that as fact. It made no sense and fit into nothing she knew of the man. "You fear me, too, don't you?"

She found herself nodding. She did fear Gregor, especially how he made her feel, because none of it made sense. To look at him was to fan the flames of desire. And truth be told she wanted his hands on her, his lips pressing against hers. She needed to be stronger than whatever hold he held over her, but she didn't want that either. The desire to yield grew by the moment.

His silver gaze locked with hers and held her with strength. "I'm the least of what you need to fear. You're picking the wrong enemies."

"Why would you say that to me?"

"Only that there are worse things than a few stolen kisses or the fact you enjoyed them so much. You spend too much energy fighting when you should be embracing me. You're missing the real threat."

"What the hell are you talking about?" She crossed her arms. "You're my enemy. If your kisses aren't enough to make me cringe, then I can't imagine who else could?"

His tone turned deathly serious. "It's not who, but what. Annihilation is the true threat."

"You've annihilated everything I ever cared about."

And she wanted his arms wrapped around her right now and his lips pressed against hers, but that wasn't the issue right now. Which made her a freak.

Wait. "What the hell are you talking about?" She smoothed the fabric of her dress and tried to think. "If you're going to babble about nonsense," she said, "then maybe we should begin the lesson. I don't want to give the High Tender reason to use the braklav on me. If you want to tell me something, then by all means, please get on with it. You have my undivided, captive, attention."

By the narrowing of his eyes, he didn't like the emphasis she put on 'captive', but tough, she didn't care about his feelings.

He leaned forward, more tapping on top of the desk. His long fingers captivated her. "The braklav is only used as a last resort. You decide how you will be trained. How we get from here to there is completely up to you. Easy or hard. The choice is entirely in your hands."

"But I don't want to be trained to be your obedient lapdog." She twisted in the seat, trying to find a more comfortable position. "This is how you approach everything. You say I have a choice, but there is no choice. Either I obey or you torture. That's not choice."

"We've been training WOR for centuries. Our methods are effective."

"Your methods are barbaric."

A loud chime sounded.

He blew out a frustrated breath. "Your arguing has wasted what little time we had together." He stood and gestured for her to do the same.

Alarm bells went off in her head. "You didn't answer my question. What's the real threat if not you?"

He pursed his lips. "The Tenders are ready."

The Tenders were ready? For what?

She refused to move, at least not until he explained what was going on. "Ready for what? And answer my question!"

"Come."

"Have you ever heard the phrase 'you'll get more offering the carrot than the stick,' or 'you'll catch more flies with honey than with vinegar'. For someone who wants to steal kisses when the High Tender isn't looking, it's something you might want to pay attention to."

His brows twitched. "And what exactly do those phrases mean?"

"Only that if you answered a damn question, I might not fight you so much."

"I don't have to be nice," he said coolly.

"But imagine if you were?" She stood and walked past him in a rustle of silken skirts.

He grabbed her and pulled her close. "And if I answer your questions, you'll fall into my arms? Is this what you're promising, Elise?" He leaned close and the heat of his breath whispered over her skin. "Don't make promises you're unwilling to keep. You call me monster, even though I told you I had no choice in what had to be done. The bond ties us. You cannot fight it. I don't have to be nice to take what is already mine."

She opened her mouth to say something, but he silenced her with his cold words.

"But, let us try this and see how it sits with you." He yanked her up against the steel of his chest. "Today, the Tenders will be administering the Activator. It's the second step in your transformation to becoming WOR."

"The second?"

"Yes. The first was the Vector, which you already know, selected you based upon your genes."

She nodded. "Right. The perfume from the banquet that killed everyone."

"I already told you it wasn't in the *callidor*. The *callidor* merely accelerated our bond. The Vector selected you, and those who carry enough WOR-genes still survive on Earth. I did not destroy your home, merely pruned it back to its roots, and silenced it against an advancing threat. Despite what you believe, I'm doing everything in my power to protect humanity."

A loud bell tolled outside the room, growing even louder and more insistent. His grip on her arms tightened, as did his voice.

"The Activator will turn those very rare genes on, and transcription will begin. We'll consider ourselves lucky if only one-in-ten of you die. You are our most precious resource and we don't want to lose any of you. I don't want you to die."

"More deaths?" Her breath hitched in her chest.

"An unavoidable loss."

"You expect to lose a hundred of us?" She beat at his chest. "A hundred!"

He shook her. "Listen! You wanted to know. Well, I'm telling you. A few will lose Rank. A smaller number might gain Rank, if they aren't driven insane first—those will be put down."

"Like dogs?" There was no remorse in his features. These were just numbers to him.

"As the Activator triggers your very rare genomes, changes will occur. They're painful."

The grip on her arms loosened and he pulled her to his chest, holding her to him now in an embrace. "I would not wish this on anyone. I do not wish it on you. But it is necessary to transform you into a WOR." He smoothed her hair and pulled her braid over her shoulder. "I have no idea what will happen to you."

"Then don't do it." Her entire body shook in his embrace, and despite her revulsion she found herself clinging to him.

A deep remorse filled his voice. "I need WOR. Humanity faces a grave threat and you are my weapons."

"I'm not a weapon, Gregor. I'm just me."

"You are so much more than that." His grip tightened around her and he kissed her temple. "You mean so much more than that to me."

The feather-light touch sent a ripple of heat fluttering to her belly.

"So, tell me, would you have preferred ignorance?" he asked.

"How am I supposed to answer that?"

He brushed her lips in a chaste kiss, the touch so fleeting she barely felt it.

"I would love nothing more than to bring you pleasure, but that is not possible. Not for you and not for me. You were destined by the gods to become WOR, a powerful weapon for the empire. You are a tool that I, as Emperor, will use to save my people. You must trust me when I say it is better for you not to know what is to come. So, forgive me if I prefer to spend what little time we have enjoying each other's company rather than arguing over petty issues of morality, not when the survival of our species is at stake." Again, he held her with those eyes of his, silver, magnetic, and piercing her very soul.

She pushed away, stunned by his words and unable to process the enormity of his revelation. Through the bond, his touch had her head spinning. "You're confusing me and trying to manipulate me with the bond."

He released his grip. "Is this not what you wanted? Answers?"

She staggered. "I wanted the truth."

"Did I not explain it well enough for you to understand? Is that not the 'carrot' you spoke of?" The shade of his eyes deepened in hue, and his imperial tattoo simmered beneath the surface of the skin above his brow.

Her arms throbbed. There would be bruising from his grip.

"It doesn't give you the right to destroy our lives, our homes, our families, and our world! You should have asked. You should have told us the truth and let us make our own choices."

"To do what you ask would have taken time I do not have, and I need all the tools available for the task at hand, not just those offered up out of the goodness of people's hearts. Knowing what I just told you, would you have volunteered?"

Few would have offered themselves up to an alien empire.

His glare caused her heart to skip a beat. "I do not need your permission to do what is right."

She sucked in a breath and struggled to hold it while her heartbeat settled. "What you did wasn't right. It was inhumane. Whatever gave you the right to play God with other people's lives?" Her voice cracked.

"My birthright gives me the responsibility. And I have taken an oath to see it done." A heaviness hung over him. He reached for her arm. "Come, you are late." His lips pressed into a thin line as he pulled her to the door.

She followed mutely, stunned by his words.

They arrived at the exercise fields where rows of women stood in precise lines. Her fellow captives had no idea what the Vendel planned next.

High Tender Marcus stomped up to meet them. "She is late."

Ten groups of women stretched out. Elise made her way to the far left—tenth group, eleventh row, second one in...1002, her slave number.

Gregor and the High Tender exchanged words.

An assembly of men approached the formation dressed in tan suits. In their hands, they carried black cases. At their wrists, silver rods dangled. These were the Tenders and the High Tenders, men to be respected and equally feared. The Tenders fanned out until one stood at the head of each row with two WOR-guards at the ready.

High Tender Marcus spoke from the center of the field. His deep voice carried easily so all could hear. "Ladies," he paused until he had their

175

attention. "The Tender's will be coming down the rows. You will hold still and do as you're told."

The Tenders advanced. High Tender Marcus approached the head of her row. Paula, the woman designated as 1001 or 10-1, and one of High Tender Marcus's special trainees, shook. High Tender Marcus opened a vial of blue liquid. The first WOR-guard placed a thin golden necklace around Paula's neck, while the second stood behind her.

High Tender Marcus placed the vial beneath Paula's nose. "Breathe deeply, 10-1."

Paula inhaled through her nose and a smile of bliss spread across her face.

The High Tender brought the braklav to the base of her skull.

Wide-eyed terror filled her face as he pressed, then her scream joined those of others echoing across the Confinement Deck. The second WOR-guard lowered Paula's unconscious body to the ground and moved to stand behind Elise.

Other WOR-guards flashed their whipsticks as they patrolled. Not a single woman broke rank. They had nowhere to run.

Elise eyed the High Tender as he stepped in front of her. "Emperor vlor'Malita said he explained this to you?"

She stiffened. "Yes, High Tender Marcus."

He shook his head. "That is a shame." A WOR-guard snapped the necklace around her neck and stepped aside. High Tender Marcus brought the bottle and held it under her nose. "Inhale."

No way in hell she was going to resist her High Tender's instruction, even though every instinct in her body told her to. Some lessons went bone deep and her mind still remembered the touch of his braklav. She took a deep breath and the perfume flooded her senses. Indescribable pleasure raced through her body with the inward breath.

The braklav pressed against the base of her skull. Anxiety leapt in her chest moments before brutalizing pain exploded outward and splintered her mind with agony. A deafening shriek escaped her throat. One-in-ten chance of death.

Blackness engulfed her.

CHAPTER TWELVE_

Gambit, Day 122

Soul sundering agony pounded against Elise's skull. Every breath struggled to find an easy way inside...and failed.

But Elise did breathe, and with each tug and pull, lancing pain filled her with life. Consciousness followed in fits and starts, and slowly she clawed her way back from the brink of nothingness. She survived activation...whatever the hell that had been.

A groan prompted an aborted attempt to roll to her side. Bad idea. An overpowering wave of nausea stirred up her gut and the sensation battled with the knife splitting her skull in two for worst feeling ever. The churning of her stomach promised an epic event forthcoming.

Just breathe, dammit, and get through this.

Chapped lips provided a distraction. She latched onto that and moistened them, then tried to do something about her cotton-mouth. That took another moment of distraction, and the urge to empty her stomach eased up a bit.

"She's coming around," a dispassionate voice spoke somewhere from the right. It was fifty decibels too loud.

"Thank the gods, she survived." Couldn't forget that voice. It belonged to Gregor and his normally possessive tones were filled with relief...and concern.

The voices melted away with a roaring sound. She wanted to scream and cover her ears, but pain locked her body in agony. The void of nothingness reached out, trying to claim her, but she refused its embrace. Instead, Gregor gave her the lifeline she needed through the power of their bond. His touch grounded her with a zap of electricity.

"She shouldn't be awakening so soon." Warmth caressed her cheek. Pain fled beneath the gentle glide of his fingertips against her flesh. "Does this tell us anything?"

"The strongest always wake first, but even this is unprecedented."

Her mind began to clear. That voice belonged to her tormentor, the High Tender. Every instinct told her to lay still. Not that she could move. Her body remained locked, imprisoned in a cage of pain. She listened to the men, hoping to learn something important, praying Gregor would touch her again.

"This promises much, don't you agree?" Gregor's voice, full of sin and sex, was something she would never forget. He touched her temple. An electrical impulse pushed back the pain, banished it into the void. His fingers massaged her skin, stroked her hair, and brought a whimper to her lips.

A tear trickled from her eye. More please. She needed more.

"If this is any indication of her potential, we may yet hope."

"Have you heard any more word?" The High Tender's question had her flinching, the harsh syllables slammed against the fragility of her mind.

Gregor sighed and stopped his slow massage. "The S'Lorek continue their attack. The s'lor are useless. I've pulled them back. The s'vlor barely hold off long enough to allow the populace to flee. I need your linking project to show progress...soon. We're running out of time."

Gregor's frustrated voice reverberated in her ears. Too damn loud.

"Sire, The Neural Mine Conclave is working on it. Their best man is assigned. He would have been a Tender if not for his low birth. They assure me he is making progress."

The long, slow strokes in her hair calmed her mind. Even the rebellion in her stomach faded to a distant memory. For the first time she embraced Gregor's touch, not for sensual pleasure, but to take away suffering.

"So, what of Elise?" Gregor said. "Her reaction to the Vector, the Tender-stat, and the Activator is promising, right?"

"Ack! You're too familiar with this one. It makes you soft when you need to be firm."

"I disagree." His grip tightened in her hair, but she didn't care. The tug splintered a shard of pain and the fragments spun away.

"You persist in using her Earth name. We take those away for a reason. She must learn what she is to become."

"She knows."

Gregor mentioned turning all of them into weapons. Although how that would happen remained beyond her comprehension.

"You've told her then?"

"I mentioned a little."

"This is what I mean. You coddle her with explanations when you should lead. S'vlor are meant to follow. They need to know when given a command they must act, not question. Hesitation means death."

"True, but I sense something different in her."

He lifted his hands and pain slammed back with a vengeance. She would have cried out if speech had been possible. Instead, she wallowed in a flood of anguish.

"With respect, Sire, I've been training s'vlor for a very long time. She is your first and only. You must defer to my expertise in this."

"But she is mine. I know how best to handle her."

"You must treat her as the tool she's to become."

And there was the difference between the two men. This was how she would drive them apart. Elise kept pace with their conversation, enduring the resurgence of cutting pain, sharp needles dug into her brain, slicing her essence away, but she would maintain consciousness.

"While I respect your expertise and your position among the Tender Conclave," Gregor said, "I will forge my own path. Even you say our bond is unprecedented. Has it not occurred to you the stronger our bond grows now, before the Blood Rite, the easier it will be to control her? I intend to foster it, with intimacy if need be, despite your protests. When it comes time for the Binding she will be taken well in hand."

There were those words again. More ceremonies. More hurdles she would have to overcome, or rather, shackles they would put on her. Either way, the pressure of time weighed heavily on her.

"What I see is reckless behavior. Your fondness—"

"Do not think for a second I do anything without purpose, Lord vlor'-Vardhal. The Imperial Oath is ever present in my mind."

The High Tender blew out a heavy breath. "Forgive me, Sire, I did not mean to imply otherwise."

"Enough about what I do with her in private. Tell me about her recovery. Is it predictive? Given her reaction to the Vector and what we saw with the Tenderstat, does her recovery from Activation mean anything at all?"

"Her potential is promising, but it means nothing with her continued resistance. Your refusal to use Tender Training only impedes her progress."

Gregor made a growling noise. "It has unintended effects."

"So you say."

"I tell you, I sensed a dissonance."

"Merely a side effect. Tender Training is a powerful tool and it universally compels WOR into obedience."

"I'll do whatever is required to have her trained, Lord vlor'Vardhal, except break her."

"At least in that, we are agreed."

Strong hands took hers and held them in a cage of warmth.

"How is she?" High Tender Marcus paced around the room. "Can you sense her mind?"

"She fades in and out, but I sense her through the bond."

"Good."

Gregor lifted her and cradled her against his chest. "Opés, are you with us?"

As much as she hated it, the cure for her pain was him. Everywhere he touched, her suffering fled.

Her lids fluttered open. She lifted a shaky hand to the back of her neck, to where the worst of the pain radiated down her spine.

"Everything hurts."

Gregor wrapped his fingers around her hand and moved it out of the way. He cupped the back of her head and massaged her neck. Pain dissolved in a rush.

She moaned with relief.

"The pain was necessary. It will fade," the High Tender said.

Gregor's words flooded her thoughts. Her pulse quickened thinking of her friends. "How many died?"

"None, so far." Gregor hesitated. "It's too soon to know."

She pressed her hands to her eyes. It didn't help, but she tried to squeeze the tears and keep them inside. "It hurts so much."

"I'm not leaving you, opés," Gregor said.

"Sire," High Tender Marcus said, "I must see to the others."

Gregor shifted until his hip rested against her legs. Pain lessened there as well.

"It's best to let her get some rest," the High Tender continued. "She is out of danger."

"I will stay."

"We should go."

"My touch soothes her. I will stay." He brushed a finger over her brow and along her jawline.

She sighed with relief washing through her, wanting nothing more than to push him away, yet needing him to stay.

High Tender Marcus's voice sounded from the edge of her enclosure. "We will speak later, Sire."

"Until then," Gregor said. "Shh, opés, I am here for you."

Her hands wrapped around him and she buried her head under his neck.

"Hold me..."

Shudders wracked her body, spasms which he controlled, locking her within the strength of his embrace.

"I feel your pain," he said, rocking her gently. "Give it to me, and I will make it disappear."

And she did just that, until he absorbed every last drop of it. Sometime later, minutes or hours, she couldn't tell, exhaustion pulled at her. Her arms grew heavy and her head bobbed with the need for sleep.

Gregor laid her out on her bed. "You must sleep, opés. If you need anything, an access pad has been placed next to your bed." He kissed her forehead and whispered. "I'm sorry for everything you have had to endure, but know that all of it is necessary."

She gripped his shirt. "Don't let him touch me, please?"

Grey eyes stared down at her with tenderness. "Opés?"

"Tender Training...p-please, don't let High Tender Marcus do that to me."

He brushed his lips against hers, a chaste kiss. "I have no intention of ever using that on you. Promise me you will do everything in your power to learn and it will never be necessary."

Residual pain from Activation, or her incredible exhaustion, had her giving him a nod and promising exactly that.

A smile beamed on his face, bright and genuine. After giving her another kiss, he departed.

She rolled over, intent on sleep, but found the embrace of dreams elusive, instead she stared blankly at the access pad he'd left behind.

Had she really just agreed to train...for him? It was true. She'd done so willingly.

She crawled off the bed to huddle in the small space on the floor between the bed and the counter. The access pad cradled easily in her lap. She turned it on and found it linked to the am-net and all the learning libraries she had access to in the classrooms.

As she had done as a child, when she couldn't sleep, she immersed herself in study. She put in place her privacy routines, ensuring her activity would not be tracked. Once her system was secure, she queried her viral subroutines, virtual soldiers as she liked to think of them.

One of her bio-constructs, Bobo, had been sent to explore the interface connections of the universal gel-pads restricting access throughout the ship. She studied the retrieved designs and sure enough right there was a hacker's wet-dream, a flaw in the neural interfaces she could exploit to disable the bio-interfaces. Saturated throughout the am-net, and resident in every interface, she now had a back door into their system.

A victory!

Right when she'd given in and come so close to letting Gregor win.

She tapped out a series of instructions and sent Bobo on its way. It had a new mission.

Now, all she had to do was to walk past the WOR-guard perimeter, press her palm to the pad, and activate Bobo. Then she could go anywhere within the ship, even to the command decks. No one could follow her movements. Easy-peasy-simple-as-pie, except she had no way past the WOR-guards.

A light from inside the cabinet to her right caught her attention. She cracked open the lower door and peeked inside. Every night she'd been instructed to place her clothes inside and each morning new ones had been put in their place. She had assumed the Vendel accomplished the swap via their beaming technology. Inside, the lower shelf of the cabinet retracted down, and beneath that, a pair of hands took her discarded dress and replaced it with a fresh crimson silk gown.

She remembered a phrase from home: *'Don't jump to conclusions because it's a long swim back.'* Such an idiot. Evidently, manual labor still existed in this world.

Oftentimes, the simplest of explanations was the most obvious. It made sense that a prison of a thousand women would need some sort of support staff. It never occurred to her they'd be beneath their feet, literally. Her image of the technologically advanced Vendel beaming clothes in and out of cabinets had clouded her judgment. If she could find a way down there, there'd be no reason to bypass the WOR-guard perimeter.

She had finally found her way off the Confinement Deck. The first boulder fell.

CHAPTER THIRTEEN_

Gambit, Day 123

"GOOD MORNING. HOW DO YOU FEEL?" THE HIGH TENDER'S BOOMING VOICE made Elise wince.

She opened her eyes to find the High Tender staring at her from the foot of her bed. "My head hurts, but it isn't as bad as before."

He nodded. "Good." He sat at the foot of her bed.

Elise pulled her feet back. She didn't want to touch him. Grasping her pillow, she used it as a shield. She waited while the High Tender made himself comfortable.

"You've surprised me."

That wasn't what she expected. "How?"

He gave her a level look. "You recovered from the Activator in record time. Which means you're currently the only conscious WOR. I'm at a loss with what to do with you." He furrowed his brows in thought. "Emperor vlor'Malita has suggested using this time to begin acclimatizing you to the rest of the ship. I have some concerns about this." He levelled a knowing glance at her, which made her blush.

Elise's heart lifted at the thought of being given access to the ship. It was exactly what she needed.

"So, I have the problem of what to do with you until the others complete the process of activation."

"High Tender, please, what is this process? What are you doing to us?" She grabbed at the pillow for support, fearing the unknown.

He regarded her for too long, but finally he seemed to come to a decision because he stood and began pacing. "The emperor showed you the WOR-space?"

She nodded.

"He mentioned the WOR-drive, then?"

She shook her head. "No."

His lips twisted, and he settled into what she'd come to learn was his lecturing tone. "The WOR-skill is integral to our drive systems. And Women of the First Rank run the WOR-drive. There are many more First Rank WOR than any of the other ranks. Women of the Fifth Rank are exceedingly rare. To have found ninety-two on one planet is unheard of."

He watched her closely, as if waiting for her to process this information. She struggled to fit the pieces together.

"What do these women have to do with running interstellar drives?"

"You tell me."

He was leading her down a definite path. Only she had no idea how the two fit together. "Does it have something to do with the neural interfaces in the am-net. Something unique to a WOR?" She arched her brow. "I honestly have no idea."

He gave her a look, as if she had missed something obvious.

Her head hurt too much to piece it together and she put the pillow in her lap, exasperated with his game.

"I'm sorry, but I just don't see how an interstellar drive is something I, or any other woman from Earth, can help with. We barely know how to work the most basic of your devices."

"Let's try this differently. Do you believe in psychic abilities?" He crossed his arms and watched her closely.

"No."

She hesitated when he continued his stare, lifting a brow. He couldn't be serious? But the look on his face said otherwise.

She took a breath. A fluttering began in her belly. Surely, they were mad. "You're telling me, the WOR-skill is a psychic ability?"

"Yes and no." He pointed at her head, making a swirling motion. "Inside your genetic code is a very rare set of genes. When activated, certain changes occur within your body. Mostly within your brain."

She gave a nod. "Gregor mentioned turning me into a weapon. But can we back up?"

"Back up?"

"Yes, I want to know about the Vector. It started it all. Why the deaths? Why did it have to kill everyone?"

"It killed those without the minimum number of WOR-genes to survive. An unfortunate side effect."

She gathered her legs in her arms. "What percentage survived?"

"That's not relevant."

Her eyes moistened with tears. Her grandfather, nieces, brother-in-law, and everyone else were unfortunate side effects?

"It's relevant to me. My nieces might still be alive."

"If they are, they are no longer your concern."

"If I had enough genes to become WOR, and they share some of mine, doesn't that mean they might have survived?"

His head shook. "I understand your nieces were young. They likely did not." He stood silently while she processed this, watching her final round of grief.

She wiped her tear-streaked face on the pillow and whispered, "So, the Vendel came to Earth to find women with these genes, to turn us into Women of Rank, and practice psychic abilities for the empire?"

He snorted. "In the simplest of terms, that's correct."

She lifted her head as the pieces fit together. "If the First Rank operates your drive engines, what does a Fifth Rank do?"

"You will do much, much more."

"Gregor mentioned weapons. What kind of weapon am I supposed to be?"

"A very powerful one, we hope. So, now I must decide what to do with you while the others recuperate. Do I give you to the Emperor? Or, do I keep you busy here on your studies?"

"Shouldn't I feel different?"

"You will, but the collar around your neck inhibits your ability to touch the WOR-skill. Once we're done matching compatible lords to the other s'lor and s'vlor, we'll begin training in WOR-skill."

Her necklace was a collar. She swallowed against a sudden constriction in her throat. It had seemed like such a pretty piece of jewelry, a long, delicate chain.

"And Gregor is compatible?"

"I have no doubt your compatibility will exceed the required threshold. With this new phase of training, you'll be spending much more time with him as he trains you through each skill level."

She glanced up. "Do I have a say in what I do while the others recover?"

"Do you have a preference?"

"I don't want to be here while they...well, I'd rather not have to see or hear..." She didn't want to be around to watch any of them die. "If there's nothing to do here other than study, I'd rather spend my time learning about my new home." She wanted off the damn Confinement Deck so she could start working on her escape plan.

"I don't have the time to chaperone you. You'll be alone with him." He eyed her dubiously.

She made a point of swallowing before answering. "If I'm to be living in his shadow, I might as well start by learning to tolerate his presence."

His eyes glittered with caution. "You seem to tolerate him just fine. That's not what I'm worried about."

She flushed with embarrassment. "That was...well, it was confu—"

He held up a hand and stopped her from saying more. "I want to be clear. Sexual promiscuity is not acceptable in our society. I expect you to remember this and behave accordingly when you are out and about. A few kisses might mean nothing to you, but for our people to see the Emperor engaged in such behavior, especially with his s'vlor, is...well, make sure it does not happen."

Elise blinked. "You can't possibly put that on my shoulders." She stared him down, but now that he mentioned it, a little sexual promiscuity sounded like a perfect wedge to put between these two men. "So, what are you going to do with me?"

"As much as I dislike the idea, I need him to watch over you, and I do not think it is a good idea for you to remain here."

Perfect!

"Come, let's get you ready."

"Now?"

"Yes."

This was a surprise. High Tender Marcus helped her into a new gown. Layers of gauzy white fabric drifted down to settle just above her ankles.

"Did Gregor pick out this gown?" It wasn't the typical green or red.

"No. He's been busy." He handed her the five gold bands designating her Rank. "Put these on."

She fingered the collar around her neck. "Does this thing control me like the braklav? Will Gregor use it to give me pain?"

"No, it cannot hurt you. It allows him to guide your use of the WOR-skill, to teach you until you can be properly bound to him. Do not worry about the collar. It is not permanent, and it is not like the braklav."

Elise smoothed the fabric of the gown. High Tender Marcus stepped behind her and tied the back laces of the corset. The white fabric floated around her in a cloud.

She placed her hand to the palm plate at the base of the stairs and paused to check on her little ghost. Bobo was there, quiescent, waiting for a command. A fleeting sense of accomplishment and a new optimism flooded her heart. At the counter before the double glass doors leading out of the Confinement Deck she checked again. Her palm rested on the gel and Bobo waited.

The High Tender coughed. "Are you feeling up to this?" Concern lined the features of his face at her hesitation.

Elise removed her hand from the gel. "Sorry, yes. I'm fine. The bio-gel feels funny that's all. I still can't get used to *goo* that slides over your hands. I apologize for being distracted."

"Professor Marzak mentioned you had a lot of questions about the devices."

"I've been trying hard to learn." It was the truth.

Professor Marzak was the technology instructor whose job was to teach about Vendel technology. Educating grown women how to operate the simplest of devices was not as thrilling as it may have seemed to the genius professor. The bragging rights of his position were his only reward, and—as she had learned over a lifetime of study—a star pupil on whom to dote. She worked hard to become that student.

The suspicious look in the High Tender's eyes made her pause.

"I've always been good with computers. Or at least, I used to be." With effort, she raised her gaze to meet his. "Your systems are not that different from what I'm used to. I've found quite a few parallels."

"Professor Marzak said you're a fast learner. Keep to your studies, and I'm sure you will begin to feel quite at home."

That was exactly her intention.

For the second time, she found herself free of the Confinement Deck. With the High Tender, unlike Gregor, it was easy to focus on the world outside her prison. She inventoried everything and filed it all away for future use.

Despite her earlier capitulation to Gregor, she focused on the positives. She had an alternate way off the Confinement Deck and secured a back-door through the access panels which would allow her freedom of movement. Next step was to find a way off the *Gambit*.

Her mountain was finally beginning to crumble. One boulder at a time. Persistence and perseverance were the tools she needed. And faith in herself. She'd nearly lost that last crucial piece.

She renewed her vow to free herself and her fellow WOR captives. And while she was at it, why not help those Earth survivors who struggled in the wreckage of her world?

She would learn. She would train. And she would be victorious. But first, she would become the perfect student and deceive them all. The Vendel had no idea what they'd unleashed.

PART TWO_

CHAPTER FOURTEEN_

New Terra Histories by Malita s'Lissa s'vlor

June 22, 2136

IT IS THROUGH THE WOR-SKILL THAT THE VENDEL SHAPED THE WORLD around them. I never understood why men, and not women, taught those new to its power.

Such stringent rules and protocols? Oddball training sessions and these arbitrary levels of skill? It all just got in the way. They crippled hundreds of women and delayed my mastery by months; many painful months, tortuous times which I will not dwell on here. I should call them sun cycles, but even now I cling to my Earth ways.

When it came to learning the WOR-skill, I was slow to learn, something which bothered Gregor and High Tender Marcus to no end, considering I was a genius in every other thing.

I would have enjoyed learning about my abilities so much more if they hadn't resorted to alternate techniques to train me. But if they hadn't, my sisters would never have been born, and I would have truly gone mad rather than simply insane.

My fellow captives were brought forward in stages with gentle guiding hands. One tender step at a time, their vlor'lords led them through Bar, Rod, and Wheel skills, nudging them along the way.

Not me.

High Tender Marcus yanked me along, screaming from the inside out, until I was abraded and raw. But what can you say to a blind man trying to teach the sighted to see? The Tenders understood the taste and texture of the WOR-skill, but the colors...oh the colors...

These men were fools.

They didn't know the power and depth of the beauty I saw.

They wanted a weapon, but I would become so much more.

CHAPTER FIFTEEN_

Gambit, Day 123

ONE HUNDRED AND TWENTY-THREE DAYS. IT HAD BEEN FOUR MONTHS SINCE Elise's capture by the Vendel. In that time, everyone she knew had died. In some strange twist of fate, the new friend she'd made at a charity walk had survived the Vector which had killed Earth's population. Like Elise, Alice had been tested and brought on board *The Gambit*, but it had been months before they'd been reunited.

They talked every day, supporting each other through the brutality of the Vendel. Not with words, but through the secret tapping code Elise had modified from an old Earth prisoner camp code devised by the inmates. Like those tortured men, Elise and the other survivors clung to the secret code and lent emotional support to one another. Forbidden speech, they had nonetheless found a way to communicate. Everything had settled into a monotonous routine. They'd begun to forget the Vendel were the enemy, but then came Activation.

Like the Vector which killed those who didn't have the required genes to survive, the Activator turned those genes on, but it too came with a price. One in ten, Gregor had said, wouldn't survive.

That final cost had yet to be paid. As with the Vector, Elise suffered few aftereffects. She had been the first to awaken after Activation, and it would be many days before the others woke, if they woke at all. This left High Tender Marcus with a dilemma, as he couldn't supervise her while also tending to the rest. In another twist of fate, Elise found herself released from the Confinement Deck and delivered into Gregor's hands. Her exploration of the world outside that horrid place helped her heal, but it also spurred her determination to find a way to escape.

Where her previous trip off the Confinement Deck with Gregor had been an easy stroll, High Tender Marcus dragged her through the *Gambit's* torus at a fast trot.

Her body ached from the after effects of Activation. A throbbing pulse in her temples felt as if the High Tender's braklav still wedged itself at the base of her skull. She hurried beside him, afraid of the dark scowls he tossed in her direction, and the threat of more pain from the braklav if she failed to keep up.

She hustled beside the High Tender, struggling to keep pace, until they reached a lift-tube. There, he had them stop, waiting for the door to open. He drew her inside where she shamelessly huddled beside him. Any moment and the floor would drop away to nothingness. Unlike Gregor, High Tender Marcus provided no reassurance and forced her to endure the fear of floating on an invisible pancake of air alone.

He rattled off commands and they rode the solid currents upward. Another ten-minute half-walk half-jog and he shoved her inside a pod-like vehicle with windows staring out into a featureless gray void. A second terrifying lift-tube ride left her shaking. Instead of stopping inside the long tube, they rose to the very top where the ceiling spiraled open. The invisible force field of air carried them up another few feet until the ceiling closed beneath them, forming a floor. They had arrived in the center of a massive domed space filled with dozens of men who spoke in muted whispers; although with the pounding in her head, they might as well have been screaming.

She was well on her way to having the mother of all migraines. The overhead lights had her blinking in pain and she squinted against the glare. A raucous scraping noise grated against her ears and covering them only made things worse. Blinking against the too bright light, she glanced around at her new surroundings.

She and the High Tender stood at the center of the concentric rings of consoles. Men in gray and white uniforms stared at them. Their conversations stopped, but they picked up again with a fast-paced urgency. Glowing holographs hung over the men's workstations, drawing her eyes as much as theirs. She wanted to crawl into a dark hole and cover her head to hide from the light and noise, but High Tender Marcus cupped her elbow and drew her off the lift-tube platform and directly into the busy space.

Angular stripes decorated the sleeves of most of the men's uniforms. A few had silver stars adorning their collars—those wearing them turned penetrating stares her direction and paused the longest from their work to stare upon her.

The High Tender pulled her through and past the concentric rings to the far side of the room. The air vibrated with an unexplained tension. She'd felt something similar on trips to Global Corps Headquarters, the one time she'd interviewed for the Jupiter Launch Mission. This was a place where *things* happened. It had to be the *Gambit's* bridge.

Something bad was at play. It carried itself in the way the men moved, even those who sat still. A sense of desperation lurked in the tight creases at the corners of their eyes and hovered in their pinched expressions. Even the depths of their frowns generated despair.

Not one smile graced their features. No one joked or laughed. Gregor had said their very survival was at risk. The very air reeked of the understated terror of it. Whatever *it* was.

High Tender Marcus moved her past a large hologram. A multicolored spaghetti array of glittering lights crisscrossed the display. A vast network of intersecting lines connected twenty-one glowing spheres of light. Hundreds of smaller lights littered the field. Several of those, and one of the spheres, had gone dim.

Twenty-one planets in the Vendel empire had to match the twenty-one spheres of light.

One light dim?

From her studies, she'd learned about colony ships, or C-ships. Ten of those had gone silent. Gregor said she should fear annihilation. He didn't say the Vendel risked losing a war. Exactly what kind of weapon did he think she would become to fight against an enemy capable of taking out a planet?

Two men stood in front of the holographic display and spoke quietly to each other.

One pointed to the dim sphere. "Saphirah is silent. There's no response to our hails." Three small stars decorated his collar. When he saw her staring, his eyes narrowed and the muscles of his jaw bunched. "The Emperor is just ahead."

High Tender Marcus kept her moving past the men.

She turned from the hologram to look where he indicated. Gregor faced away from her and wore his signature black trousers tucked into knee-high boots. A simple black shirt strained against the expanse of his muscular frame. A man with five stars on his collar took a gel-flimsy from Gregor and left with a bow. As if he sensed her from across the crowded room, Gregor's head snapped up. Dark shadows obscured his eyes and a scowl framed his lips.

"Sire." The High Tender closed the distance, towing her behind him.

"Lord vlor'Vardhal, this is a surprise." The dark foreboding visage vanished and Gregor's expression softened. A smile replaced the scowl.

"Saphirah? When did this happen?" The quaver in the High Tender's voice surprised Elise.

"We just received the news." The scowl returned and Gregor's eyes darkened.

"I understand." High Tender Marcus glanced at Elise. "The Confinement Deck is too busy to watch over your s'vlor, and I am needed to care for the others." He took a deep breath and gave her a little push. "I thought you might take her, but if you are too busy with command…" He glanced at the large holograph behind him with the spaghetti lines and frowned.

"There is nothing I can do about Saphirah," Gregor said heavily. His voice shifted to a lighter tone. "I would, however, love to take care of my s'vlor." He stretched out his hand.

She needed to convince Gregor she was willing to work with him, but found herself too numb to do much other than force a fake smile. Upon taking his hand, the familiar tingle jolted between them.

The High Tender glanced at their entwined fingers and ground his molars. He walked away without another word.

She took a deep breath, closed her eyes, and brought up the mental imagery she'd decided to use when dealing with Gregor—she would be a willow bending in the wind.

Bend. Do not break. Survive at all costs.

This was how she would win, earn his trust and work to destroy him.

He pulled her close. "How do you feel?" An unusual tenderness threaded through his words.

"My head hurts." It was the truth. The Activator, along with the braklav, had done a number to her head.

He kissed her temple and her suffering eased. "Do you want to rest, or are you up for a tour of the ship?"

A sudden relenting of her pain had her staring at him dumfounded. She blinked, then withdrew her hand and rubbed it where his lips had pressed against her skin. "Um...High Tender Marcus mentioned you might show me around the *Gambit*."

The overly bright lights had dimmed. The harsh sounds had quieted. The throbbing in her temples had vanished with the press of his lips. The spike at the base of her skull, however, remained, no longer sharp and stabbing, but blunted.

"Are you okay?" The concern in his features reflected in the dance of the tattoo above his brow.

She rubbed at her temple. "How did you do that?"

He touched her forehead. "The bond does many things. It connects us. Taking your pain is but one small thing."

"You *took* my pain?" How?

A tightness pinched the corners of his eyes and he furrowed his brow. She traced his jaw, just as surprised by her gesture as he was, if his sharp intake of his breath was any indication.

"I did."

"You didn't have to do that."

"My opés, it's the least I can do after everything you've suffered."

She didn't know what to say. He was her enemy and she shouldn't be thanking him for anything, but she could use his uncharacteristic tenderness to her advantage. It was time to learn about her new world. Anything that could help in an escape was something she would use.

He glanced around. "This is the Command Deck. Come, let me show you the rest of the ship." He led her to a wall, which opened with a whisper to form a doorway, and led her to the center of a small circular room.

She didn't realize it was a lift-tube until the floor swiveled out from beneath her. In her surprise, she grabbed for the nearest solid support.

Gregor wrapped an arm around her waist and chuckled. "Sorry, opés, I forget this is all new to you." He kissed the top of her head. "I have you. Do not fear. I will never let you fall."

Her immediate instinct was to recoil, but a sickening burn of desire had her nuzzling into his embrace. The bond flared before she could temper her reaction. It took all her focus to not tilt her lips for a kiss.

Gregor seemed to interpret the way she clung to him as a fear of heights, because he tightened his hold. If he had leaned down to take that kiss, she would have been swept away.

He pulled her closer still. "I promise you will get used to all of this. I want you to feel comfortable in your new home."

With their gentle descent, a soft wind blew against her cheeks. She leaned against his chest and inhaled his heady aroma the entire way down. He smelled too good to deny herself the small pleasure.

A platform swiveled out from the wall to form a floor, and a doorway appeared in the wall to let them out. Again, he led her out holding her hand. "You will enjoy this."

She placed a hand on his arm. "I'll try. At least my head doesn't hurt so much anymore." She gazed into his eyes and held them for a fleeting instant before turning her attention to where she gripped his arm.

He lifted her hand, kissed it softly, and then let go. "Things have been difficult for you, but they won't always be this way. I promise this. I hope we can put aside our differences and enjoy each other's company for the span of a day?"

Easy for him to say when he held all the power, but she didn't dare tell him that.

Maybe he took her silence for assent, because he continued with his tour. "As you know, the *Gambit* is a torus. We started in Command and Control, located on the inside of the ring. We traveled along a major lift-tube, those move from the inside of the ship to the outside, and now we're on the outermost edge of the ship. Minor lift tubes span the ship from top to bottom."

She breathed in his scent and placed her hand on his arm, letting him lead. Touch, smell, and taste, he was irresistible, or rather the bond tying them together made him so.

"The ship is ten kilometers in diameter and one kilometer thick. The center of the torus is about two kilometers wide and is the foundation for the WOR-drive. Are you with me?"

She already knew most of this due to the virtual subroutines she'd let loose into the am-net to gather data, but she wasn't supposed to know anything about the structure of the *Gambit*. That wasn't on any of her approved lesson plans. "Major lift-tubes connect inside-to-outside."

He continued with a firm grip of her hand. "Minor lift-tubes span top-to-bottom levels. The pod circuit is a series of concentric transports running around the various levels encircling the entire ship."

"Where are we going?"

"For a pod ride." He grinned with enthusiasm.

"Stars?" She couldn't help herself, but she wanted to see stars.

"Not stars. I'm going to show you WOR-space, or rather the WOR-bubble the fleet travels within."

"Excuse me?"

"WOR-space is a construction of the fifth and sixth dimensions. The

First Rank WOR create a bubble of three-dimensional space which encases the fleet while we travel. We call it a WOR-bubble."

"Not very creative."

The corner of his mouth tilted upward with her teasing. "No, but it works."

"Is it gray?"

The grin slipped a little from his face.

"High Tender Marcus took me on a pod ride on the way to see you. Does flat and featureless kind of describe it?"

"He spoiled my surprise."

The pout on Gregor's lips was almost endearing. Almost, but then she remembered all he'd put her through.

She shrugged. "Sorry. Honestly, he rushed me over so fast I didn't get a chance to appreciate anything. I'd love to have another look. And you said the whole fleet travels in this bubble of space?"

"Of course."

"So...can you fly between the different ships?"

This could be groundbreaking information. Not that she would be able to hide a thousand women inside the other ships of his fleet. They'd be found instantly, but it meant there was a way off *Gambit*. Actually, this meant a few things. There was nowhere to go while the *Gambit* travelled within this WOR-space bubble. However, the upside was there had to be transport ships within the holds of *Gambit*. This implied possibilities for getting off the ship when they exited WOR-space and entered normal space.

She couldn't hide within the fleet, but among twenty worlds and thousands of colony ships, there had to be a safe haven somewhere.

All she had to do was find this flight deck, a large enough transport ship, and a pilot willing to commit treason against an empire, or one she could threaten with whatever psychic abilities Gregor intended to train her in. While sounding preposterous, attempting the impossible no longer phased her. She was up to the task.

"Oh, yes," Gregor said. "There are several flight decks on all the ships."

"And can you fly between the ships in this WOR-bubble?"

"There's actually quite a bit of traffic back and forth, not to mention the jump-jet circuit."

"I'd love to see one of your hangars."

He shook his head. "Not today. They're too far for the time we have. I don't want to stress you. Maybe another time."

Another time then, but she could see the pieces falling together. One huge problem loomed before her. No matter what she did, her success depended on learning the WOR-skill. To do that, she would have to work with Gregor.

Her tour continued and she soaked up everything.

Life support was nothing like she envisioned. Biologically minded, the Vendel designed the bulk of life support into the structure of their walls and ceilings. Tiny bacteria constantly processed carbon dioxide into oxygen within the spongy matrix. An army of bio-pods swarmed the ceilings, absorbing airborne contaminants, and returning the waste to vats for further recycling.

Gregor showed her how the biological machines traveled along pre-programmed routes and then returned through specialized corridors following a scent trail back to the vats. There were also larger bio-carts that managed most of the general janitorial duties. He stopped one and showed her the artificial eyes on the little dog-like box, but she didn't care about that. It was the access corridors the bio-carts used which she found fascinating. They were the perfect size for a woman to crawl through.

He also explained how Confinement Deck clocks were off-set from Vendel ship-time by twelve hours. Day on the Confinement Deck was night for Vendel crew and vice versa.

"Why is that?"

"It makes it easier for the support staff."

It was the only explanation he gave, although she figured it was easier on the support staff to serve sleeping WOR than awake captives.

After some time, he guided her to one of the Circumferential Parks for dinner. She remembered this park from their first time out. Although he said this was a different one, explaining how there were five parks spread out among the different top-to-bottom levels of the ship.

A picnic spread had been laid out for them. They nibbled on finger foods while he talked about his ship and the people on it. His pride in his people was evident from the way he spoke and in the respectful bows given to him everywhere they went. He walked his ship without an escort. No security team kept him safe. Crewman they passed greeted him with genuine smiles but didn't pause in their duties. They were respectful without being reverent, which had her looking at Gregor in a different light. Instead of a monster, was it possible Gregor was a benevolent ruler?

She nodded, murmuring *mmm*, and *hmm*, at appropriate intervals and found herself smiling with an ease that surprised her. She even managed to laugh at his jokes. It felt odd, like they were on a date, except he was the last person on Earth she'd want to spend time with.

Her stomach clenched at that thought. They were no longer on Earth.

After they ate, he took her on a stroll and pulled her off the main path to a row of bushes bursting with a riot of flowers. He plucked a vine from a plant teeming with hundreds of tiny white flowers and coiled it into a wreath.

"Come here." A sweet, light fragrance filled the air as he settled the circlet over her head.

"It smells wonderful."

"A beautiful flower for a beautiful woman." He held her gaze and swept down to plant a lingering kiss on her lips. His mouth melded with hers, perfectly molded to match her lips.

The bond burst between them, powerful and unrelenting, but she had managed to master some semblance of control. As long as she didn't deny the attraction their bond aroused, she could mute the potency of the connection. Gregor slid his hands into her hair, tilting the wreath. With his heady aroma of spice and musk, combined with the light floral scent of the flowers, her senses enflamed.

A deep rumble vibrated up from his chest. "Kiss me, Elise."

Play it, play him, a strange voice whispered in her head. *It won't be so hard to give in.*

She struggled to restrain her passion, knowing it would consume her if she allowed it, but that was hard with Gregor's moans eliciting an answering need within her. With great hesitancy, she pulled him close and lifted herself up on tiptoe. Wrapping her hands around his neck, she wound her fingers in his hair.

There was a momentary look of surprise in his eyes, quickly replaced by a sense of triumph. He planted a trail of kisses from her brow to her eyelids, down her cheek, to the angle of her jaw, and finally back to her lips.

With a sigh, she parted her lips. His touch shocked her system and the bond spiked electricity down her nerves, lighting a path of desire to her core, rippling and tingling all the way to her fingers and toes.

Such a pleasant defeat.

He hauled her tight against his chest and ran his hands along her back, leaving a trail of blistering heat. She leaned into him while little shudders racked her body. Tilting her head back, she needed more and he deepened their kiss. He lifted her up against the hardened planes of his chest and the kiss became her universe.

Here was the true battle, but it was okay. For now, she needed him to believe she had surrendered. He had to think she was his. Only then could she learn what she needed from him. Later, when the time was right, when she was stronger and ready, she would fight. Until then, she would eagerly give in to his kisses and let him think she wanted him as much as he wanted her.

They kissed for many long moments. The fervent heat of his kisses turned his breathing ragged and deep. Only then did his grip on her waist loosen and he settled her back on her feet.

Why he didn't take this moment further than a simple kiss?

Not once did he reach for her breasts, or cup her bottom, or move his hands anywhere below her waist.

The High Tender's warning returned, as did Gregor's odd oath that night in his quarters. Intimacy was forbidden until the Binding Ritual. Did that mean sex? Kissing seemed to be allowed, but what about petting? A hand job? What about a blowjob?

Perhaps it was something she could use to place a wedge between Gregor and the High Tender and rip them apart? If she could make Gregor break his oath, what would be the consequences?

She traced the outlines of his chest and built up the courage to proceed. The pleasurable sounds Gregor made, combined with the bond, ignited a firestorm of passion in her blood. A very small part of her mind screamed in revulsion, but oh, how her body wanted more.

A disembodied voice in her head shouted, *Go, go, go!*

She lifted on tiptoe to kiss him and slipped a hand to his belt, letting it linger there, then she very carefully brushed her fingers below his waist-line feeling for the telltale sign of his arousal.

He grabbed her wrist with a strangled cry. "No opés, that must wait."

A nibble of tiny kisses followed, and his low throaty chuckle gave her an answer. This boundary wasn't one he wouldn't cross. The kisses he laid down her neck had her moaning and clutching at the collar of his shirt. He twined a hand in her hair and pulled her head back, opening the curve of her neck to his assault. Her body betrayed her with every kiss, dragging her mind kicking and screaming up that steep cliff of arousal. How she wanted this man, but he remained the enemy, as difficult as that was to remember.

She swept her gaze up his body and remembered him saying something to High Tender Marcus about controlling her through the bond. Maybe he was using his kisses to manipulate her?

"Please, stop." Terrified by how far she had fallen, she pushed against him.

It felt so right to be with him, as if she truly belonged in his arms, but if he gained any more control, she would be lost.

"You have no idea what this does to me," she said. *Or how much it costs...*

His eyes smoldered, heavy with passion. "Let it happen, feel the bond swell between us."

"No!" She let out a strangled cry, horrified.

His brows drew together. "Do not pull away from me."

He pressed his lips to hers and a sharp current spiked between them. His taste was electric and overpowering, an addictive drug she desired more than life itself.

Her fingers went to her throat and gripped the cool chain around her neck. How easy it was to forget. But she didn't. She didn't forget. She didn't forgive. She didn't allow the needs of her body to overrule her soul.

"I'm sorry. I can't...a few kisses doesn't make it all go away."

He tried to soothe her. "Of course not, but you should not deny the bond."

She pushed against him and freed herself from his embrace. Spinning on her heels, she stomped a few feet off. There was nowhere to go, but she felt a need to put distance between them. When he stood so close, it was impossible to think.

"Do not walk away from me."

His words passed over her with an icy chill and stopped her cold. Implications of power threaded in his voice, who held it and who did not. It was a threat she could not ignore.

She closed her eyes. *Stop fighting and be the damn willow. Bend and dear God, do not break!*

One of his hands clasped her arm as the other brushed back the hair from her neck. He kissed her on the nape and she shuddered with desire. The hairs on her arms stood on end.

His warm breath whispered in her ear. "S'vlor never walk away from their masters." He traced a long line of kisses along the soft flesh of her neck. "I do not ask you to forget, Elise. You have a lifetime to work through what happened. Eventually, you will understand and accept your place in my worlds."

She spun around and found herself encased in his arms. "It's not as easy as you think. I need time to figure things out." Time she would never give him, because she would be gone, and out from beneath his rule.

"What do you find so hard?" He looked down with a smoldering hunger burning in his eyes.

She gestured between them. "This! Being held in the arms of my enemy." She lowered her voice to a whisper. "Being kissed...by you...and feeling..."

Gregor stared at her for a long hard moment. "It's not the being held or the kissing that bothers you." He planted a final kiss on her forehead and released her. "I wish I could give you the luxury of time to accustom yourself to your new home and your place within it, but unfortunately time is something I am short on. Speaking of which, it is time to deliver you back to High Tender Marcus. Never forget, my dear Elise, as much as you wish to believe it, I am not your enemy."

His dear Elise. Not his opés, but his Elise. What did it mean when he used her name?

A battle had been waged, but for the life of her she had no idea who had won. Her body? Her mind? Gregor?

What she knew for certain was that she knew more about her prison than she had before. That had to count for something.

CHAPTER SIXTEEN_

Gambit, Day 126

SCREAMS, GROANS, SHRIEKS, AND WORSE CLAWED THEIR WAY THROUGH THE AIR of the Confinement Deck. Elise worried over the lives of her friends, but the WOR-guards forbade any contact. A better name for the hulking guards would be *woe*-guards, because they brought nothing but pain and misery.

Three days, and none of the women had yet to regain consciousness. Their cries echoed through the vast chamber of her prison, keeping her awake late into the night. Her only reprieve from the heartbreak of their ongoing agony were the excursions off the Confinement Deck grudgingly allowed by High Tender Marcus. She was grateful for the trips outside, yet equally riddled with guilt for wanting to escape the agony of her friends.

High Tender Marcus moved her sleeping area far from the others, but distance didn't help. With each passing day, the WOR-guards removed a few more sleeping pods—casualties of the Activator's work.

Otherwise, things continued as they had. Gregor selected her dresses, scarlet or emerald hues of diaphanous fabric or shimmering silk. The back laces declared his victory. By covering her back, the message was clear. She had progressed beyond the need of a WOR-guard's whipstick. That he had that much confidence in her compliance made her want to wretch.

She kept up the façade, laughing and smiling. They snuggled and held hands. She didn't draw away. Every word he said she devoured, but ever present on her mind were thoughts of escape. Today he promised a treat, although he wouldn't say what his surprise might be.

She had come to anticipate his gifts with a reserved skepticism. He'd asked about her hobbies and when she mentioned her love of stunt flying. His eyes lit up with excitement. Next she knew, he had her immersed in the Vendel equivalent of a virtual simulation of a small one-man craft he called a jump jet. He said it was a big deal with the Vendel, a racing circuit popular throughout the empire.

It was more than a big deal. It was the most intense and freeing experience of her life. The controls confused her at first, no joysticks or rudder controls for her feet like her stunt plane back home. Instead, the jump jet was controlled using her palms and a gel-interface. She *died* too many times to count in the simulation, but the experience had still been exhilarating.

His next surprise had been the farms. *Gambit* had five Circumferential Parks. Sculpted and manicured, they ran the perimeter of the ship built exclusively for the rest and relaxation of the crew. The farms were different and built for sustenance. In a ship ten kilometers in diameter, the farms took up the entire underbelly. Never had she imagined large tracts of land, orchards, or even forests, rivers, and lakes would exist on a spaceship. He even took her fishing on one of the lakes.

The last of his surprises had been a tour of the inner workings of *Gambit's* protein processing plants. That hadn't been nearly as fun as the others. Disgusting didn't even begin to describe that horrifying trip and she hadn't eaten *meat* in the days since.

Every day a WOR-guard escorted her out of the Confinement Deck and she met Gregor at the entrance. His handsome face lit up at her arrival, his brows quirking in that dashing way of his, and the imperial tattoo danced as only it could.

"Hello, Gregor." She stretched up on tiptoe and kissed him.

He wrapped a hand around her waist and pulled her close. Then he returned her kiss with a chaste one of his own. Releasing her, he took a step back and reached into his breast pocket where he pulled out a gel-flimsy.

"A gift for you, opés." He handed the device over.

She took it with some confusion. "What am I supposed to do with this?"

"Well, you can start by activating it."

The display lit up in a glittering blue, and rows of numbers and letters appeared. She glanced at him. "Gregor, why do I have a list of the ship's coordinates?"

Excitement sparked in his eyes. "This is your surprise."

She shook her head, feeling like she'd missed the joke. "I don't understand."

He leaned in and kissed her cheek. "Lord vlor'Vardhal is busy in the Confinement Deck and I have a High Council meeting I cannot miss. Since neither one of us can chaperone you, I am sending you on a tour of the ship...alone."

"You're doing what?" This simply wasn't happening. She turned back to the WOR-guard who had escorted her out, but he'd already disappeared back down the long tunnel returning to the Confinement Deck. There was no guard waiting to accompany her on this excursion.

"Alone? High Tender Marcus will have a fit."

"No. In fact, we came upon the idea together."

"Aren't you afraid I'll try to escape?"

Gregor tilted his head back and laughed. "Gods no! Where would you go that we wouldn't find you?"

"I didn't mean—" She tried to frame an appropriate amount of shakiness to her voice. "I just figured I'd have an escort." An upwelling of hope speared through her heart at the thought of an unescorted foray through the ship. There was so much she wanted to explore.

"At some point, I must trust you. I think now is a good time to start." His brow arched in question. "Unless there's a reason I shouldn't?"

"Well, no. I'm just a little shocked."

He gripped her hands. Penetrating gray eyes pierced her and held her in place. "You are my s'vlor, my opés. You and I are meant to work in harmony...not against each other. This is an important lesson for you to learn."

"But the WOR-guards and the braklav?"

"Serve me, and they will not trouble you. Trust must start someplace. I chose today."

"What if I get lost?" Not that she would. A perfect schematic of the entire ship, lift tube and pod system was permanently etched in her brain.

"I will find you."

She wanted to explore the parts of the ship he'd avoided or hadn't gotten around to showing her, like that flight deck and those access hatchways the bio-carts used. Those empty holes in *Gambit's* schematics were begging to be filled.

"How?"

Freedom to explore *Gambit* was great, but the kind of exploration she had in mind couldn't be done under the watchful eyes of her captors. Unlike the Confinement Deck, the corridors of the *Gambit* didn't have continuous monitoring devices, but she wasn't foolish enough to believe they were giving her free rein. They had to have some way of tracking her movements; she needed to find a way around their system, and she already had an idea about that.

"Just press any palm-pad and I will know where to find you."

"Won't you be watching?" She pointed to one of the recording devices planted at the Confinement Deck check-in desk. "You should know where I am."

He pressed the tip of her nose with his finger. "If I need to monitor your movements I could, but that is not what today is about. I said today was about trust, but it is also about extending freedom, me giving you my trust and you showing me you are worthy of accepting it." Concerned filled his voice. "I thought you would be more excited."

She smiled and looked into his eyes with a meekness she didn't feel. "Sorry, I guess I wasn't prepared for something like this, not after everything—"

He pressed his finger to her lips, silencing her. "It is time to move toward our future, opés, and leave the past where it belongs."

"I will try." She stepped toward him and wrapped her arms around his waist. "Thank you, Gregor. This means a lot to me."

He kissed the top of her head. "I know."

Since he was in a giving mood. "Can I ask for something else?"

"It depends."

"I was just thinking about the other girls."

Tension stiffened his body's stance in her arms. "My power is limited there."

"I know, but it's hard on us, not being able to speak to one another. Is there any way you could get the Tenders to lift the prohibition on speaking? After everything we've been through and now with Activation, it would be helpful if we could support one another. It's been months since we've had that freedom. I could tell them about all of this."

"All of what?"

"What lies beyond the Confinement Deck for one thing. About how working with you is easier than resisting. I can't do that if I can't speak to them, and there will be questions. It would really mean a lot, and I think it would go a long way to helping them see what I've come to see."

His chest rumbled with a soft laughter.

"What?" She leaned back far enough to gaze up into his eyes.

He stared back at her, warmth flooding his eyes. The corners of his lips turned up. "Your language slipped, you must be more careful."

"What do you mean?"

"You said months when you should have said sun cycles. The Tenders will not be so tolerant of mistakes as I am."

She punched him playfully in the chest. "See, that just supports my point. If we could talk to each other, we could practice your language with each other and we'd be more proficient. It's really to your benefit to have the ban lifted. And, it's not like we're going anywhere." She tossed his words back at him. "Like you said, there's nowhere we can go you won't find us. A thousand women aren't going to run away."

At least not yet. Still working on that plan.

"I will talk to Lord vlor'Vardhal, though I make no promises."

Grabbing the fabric of his shirt, she kissed him with more passion than she intended. "I was just thinking about the lift-tubes. Who will I grab for support without you there beside me?"

"Somehow, I think you will manage. Not that I mind you clinging to me."

"Or the kisses?"

He laughed. "Or your kisses." He pulled her close. "Your ardor is appreciated, but for certain things we must wait."

Of course, he'd made that very clear.

"Now, I must get to my meeting with the High Council." He leaned to whisper in her ear. "But we will not have to wait forever. An insatiable hunger grows within me."

She gave the expected answer. "And I." The sweet smile she plastered on her face made her cheeks hurt.

"You have your task. Lord vlor'Vardhal has required you to report in at each destination on the list. If you get lost, activate the nearest palm pad and I'll come for you."

That wasn't nearly enough time for what she had planned. "I'll learn better if I have to figure it out on my own, even if I get turned around, or even lost. That's always the best way to learn a new place." She shrugged. "I mean, if that's okay with you."

"I don't think Lord vlor'Vardhal intended for you to wander..."

She tried for an innocent expression. "If you're not sending guards as escort, does it really matter if I get lost? There's nowhere you won't find me."

"I love your stubborn streak. To building another bridge between us, my opés." His voice was full of conviction and it was difficult not to believe him.

"You have half the day, Elise. Go and explore. See if you can follow my directions."

"Thank you." She threw her arms around his neck and kissed him. "Thank you for trusting me with this." He was such a fool.

"Call for help if you need it. I will see you at third lunch."

The oddball meals on the Confinement Deck mirrored those of the ship. She thought the schedule was a sadistic means of control for the women, but it was a necessity of shipboard life. Another assumption which had turned out to be wrong. When feeding twenty-thousand crewmen, eating in shifts made sense. Especially since the personnel quarters lacked cooking facilities. She gave the gel-flimsy a hard look and assessed her situation, trying to work out how best to prioritize.

The first destination on Gregor's list was one pod ride and a short lift-tube away, the Culinary Conclave, better known as a chow hall. For the first time in four sun cycles, four long Earth months, she found herself alone, but she was far from free.

Immediately she found a public access corridor with low foot traffic. There she pulled up her viral subroutine, Bobo, with its backdoor into the am-net security protocols. Pausing to glance at her gel-flimsy, she waited for a lull in the passing traffic.

She prayed this worked. "Please don't get caught. Please don't get caught." A sudden and violent swirling of colors in the periphery of her vision had her swaying and holding onto the wall for support. She shook her head to clear her vision and steady herself.

Putting her hand to the palm-pad, she activated Bobo. The viral subroutine enacted its programming and opened a doorway in an otherwise seamless wall, granting her access into a restricted space.

The easy coordinate system of the *Gambit* left huge gaps in the volume of the doughnut-shaped ship. A maze of service corridors, filled with nothing but the biologic robots of the Vendel, existed alongside the human passageways. These would become her pathways and in them she would travel throughout *Gambit,* unseen and untracked. Bobo not only allowed her access into this private space, but the viral code logged a trail of her travels along the human passageways for Gregor and the High Tender to follow.

Mission success.

Third lunch with Gregor wound up much more passionate than she had planned, but one look at the pleasantly surprised expression on his face, she knew she'd be able to take advantage of that as well. His stoic restraint against her sensual advances couldn't hold up for much longer.

CHAPTER SEVENTEEN_

Gambit, Day 127

THE NEXT MORNING ELISE WOKE TO A SOMBER CONFINEMENT DECK. THE WOR-guards assembled a few women—a handful who had awakened from the Activator—and escorted them to a subdued first breakfast.

Alice's white hair stood out among the others. Elise sprinted to her best friend, tears streaming down her face. She risked a beating from the WOR-guards with her hug and her words, but it was worth it. Alice had survived.

"Alice!"

Sallow and gaunt, the Activator had taken much out of Alice. Even her shock of blonde hair had dulled in the light. Alice's beautiful blue eyes, normally vibrant and light, sunk inward, giving her a defeated look.

"You look...so tired," Elise said.

A WOR-guard stood ten feet away, his hard gaze giving a warning she ignored.

She didn't care. Alice needed her. She brushed her hand over Alice's temple, feeling a slight flush of heat beneath her friend's skin where a low-grade fever simmered. "How do you feel?" Her gaze cast toward the WOR-guard, but he didn't move toward her, although it was clear he'd heard her speak.

Alice's red eyes stared back from a face lined with pain. "Someone put my head in a blender and set it on puree. Why do you look so damned happy?"

"I've been up longer than you."

"What did they do to us?"

"Practiced their bio-tech."

The anger in Alice's voice relieved Elise, just a little. Perhaps they hadn't taken the fight out of her friend.

"They call it the Activator and it switched on these special genes we all have," she explained. "The pain is from those genes rewiring our brains."

"Why?"

"I've been told it's to bring out latent mental abilities and turn us into tools for the empire."

"That's lame." Alice placed a hand up to shield her eyes. "My head hurts like hell. It's so damn bright. Don't they believe in pain killers? And what's up with these necklaces?" She twirled the necklace dangling around her neck.

"They have something to do with suppressing our abilities. I think it's supposed to control us." She didn't have the heart to tell Alice the High Tender had been dosing all the girls with potent pain killers. Alice likely still had some of the drugs onboard. "Are you hungry?"

Another glance at the WOR-guard revealed him standing idly by listening to them talk, making her wonder if Gregor had intervened about the talking ban. If so, she needed to find a way to thank him, and do so honestly.

"No," Alice groaned. "Yes. Hell, I don't know. My stomach is wearing a hole in my belly, but the thought of food makes me want to puke."

Alice didn't seem to realize she was speaking freely in front of a WOR-guard.

Elise pulled her toward the food line. "Let's put something on your plate. You can take your time eating."

"Ugh."

Elise led her friend through the line and ignored her protests as she piled food on Alice's plate. Alice took a tentative bite and then another.

"You'll feel better with a little food in your stomach."

Alice chewed and swallowed, the entire act of eating taking even more energy from her friend. She let out a deep sigh and slumped. "Is it ever going to get better?"

She reached across the table to give Alice's hand a brief squeeze. "As long as we're alive, we have hope."

Bleak eyes rebuffed her words. "As long as we're alive, these bastards torture us."

Elise leaned in close and whispered. "I'm working on that. I'm going to get us out of here."

"Remember, the best kept secret is a secret known by one." Alice searched for the WOR-guards. "If you figure something out, I'll be there, but until then…"

"Oh, Alice. We've got to stick together. I can't do it all on my own."

Alice's look of terror was answer enough. She whispered, "I'm scared."

CHAPTER EIGHTEEN_

Gambit, Day 132

THE WOR-GUARDS KEPT CLOSE WATCH ON THE WOMEN. NOT TO CORRECT them, but to make sure their recovery continued to progress. Ten women fell from physical exhaustion that first day, and twice that number the next. More were waking and as they did, they spoke to one another, providing much needed support and encouragement.

On the fifth day, Elise found the courage to count those they'd lost. It wasn't the one hundred Gregor predicted. They lost nearly twice that. One hundred and eighty succumbed to Activation. The WOR-guards and Tenders didn't allow the survivors to grieve, for that Elise held a silent vigil. They used the secret tapping code to say their goodbyes to the friends they'd lost.

Alice, along with far too many others, retreated into a fog of despair. Elise could barely get Alice to eat and the few words Alice strung together were more often unintelligible than not. The entire atmosphere on the Confinement Deck turned bleak and desperate. If the Vendel filled the ceiling with dark clouds, and poured down rain and lightning on the women, the mood would be better for it.

Repetition became their routine. Eat, exercise, eat, exercise, and eat again. Lights out and repeat the process. Classes had been cancelled until...well, until the final tally was complete. For the Vendel it was the number who survived that mattered, while she counted the dead.

The Activator pushed most over the edge and demoralization became rampant. They had allowed the Vendel to seduce them with fancy clothes and stimulating education. Activation reminded them they were nothing more than a commodity to the Vendel, something to be cared for, kept safe, but ultimately controlled.

Elise had to find a way to end this brooding silence, a difficult thing to accomplish since her forays off the Confinement Deck had come to a halt the moment the women started to wake. She'd accomplished nothing in five days. The Confinement Deck had never felt more like a prison than it did now.

On the fifth night, with sleep eluding her, she rose out of bed. The quiet tread of patrolling WOR-guards was the only sound breaking the silence of the night. When the patrol came and left, she counted the seconds until they reappeared.

A silent prayer for not getting caught and a childish wish for a cloak of invisibility gave her strength to get out of bed. Upon rising, a wave of dizziness had her gripping the side of the bed. Spots of color flashed then vanished as the lightheadedness receded. She moved as silently as she could to the showers after the patrolling WOR-guard turned the corner and headed down the row of sleeping pods.

In the bath facilities, the benches stood in long silent rows. Around the periphery, stacks of clean towels waited for the morning press of women. At even intervals, distributed between the white stacks, smaller piles of gray and white exercise clothes had been placed with obsessive precision. On the far wall, huge laundry bins dotted the long locker room. She tip-toed over and gave them a thorough inspection. All the bins were full of discarded towels. She leaned over and pushed the towels aside, but the bin was just too deep for her to reach the bottom.

She'd have to get inside. As she got ready to climb inside, a whirring sound filled the air. The bottom of the bin released. The dirty towels tumbled into a large vat of steaming water, full of soapy bubbles and bleach. She jerked back before the steam could scald her face. She'd be bleached, drowned, and boiled if she tried to leave that way.

There had to be a way down to the lower service levels. She stared at the ceiling trying to think. One of the recycling bio-devices crawled overhead. They were ubiquitous devices all over the *Gambit*, although she'd never seen them on the Confinement Deck before. The devices must only come out at night while they were sleeping. She tracked its progress while another of the devices appeared at the far end of the room, and then another.

The first reached the edge of the ceiling, readjusted, and continued down the wall. The second and third devices plodded along and followed the first. They accomplished the same precise pivot and crawled down the wall. At the base of the floor, the wall slid aside and the first bio-pod disappeared down a narrow tunnel.

She scrambled and raced over. The second device slipped into the tiny corridor. Something warm bumped her arm and she recoiled in alarm. It was the third device trying to line up to the service corridor. She peered into the dark tunnel. It was just barely big enough. Maybe if she squirmed on her belly? But the fit was tight.

Time was running out. It was time to get back to bed before the WOR-guards discovered her absence. As brave as she felt, she feared the pain of the whipstick more.

A second larger access door slid open beside the first. A larger bio-cart trundled out. Behind this opening, a square, lighted tunnel stretched into the distance.

Gregor explained how the smaller air scrubbing bio-pods didn't need to see to make it back to the recycling vats. They followed a scent-marked trail, but this was a larger cleaning robot. It had optical sensors, which meant it needed light to see. That tunnel was her way out of the Confinement Deck. The door to the access tunnel slid shut.

Elise slipped back into her bed, undiscovered, and excitement hummed in her veins. Tomorrow night she would escape.

CHAPTER NINETEEN_

Gambit, Day 137

THERE ARE SO MANY OF THEM. AOMI'S EYES FLICKED TO THE VLOR'LORDS standing in precise lines in front of them.

Speed dating at its worst, she tapped out. The code remained useful for private conversations.

Elise stood beside Aomi at the end of a long row of tables and benches, her breathing not nearly as fast, nor as deep, as her Asian friend. Elise worried, knowing what the men standing across the room meant for the women. Paula was there as well, hanging back as she usually did. The tightness in the former Marine's eyes betrayed a rising anxiety she failed to contain. The rapid shifting of her feet made her look like she desperately needed to pee.

If Paula would allow it, Elise would go and comfort her, but the stoic woman held herself apart from the others. She wished Paula was more receptive to attempts at friendship. Both of them had been taken under High Tender Marcus's wing, something none of the other women truly understood. It would have been nice to have someone to talk to who understood how difficult he could be.

Aomi stretched out her hand to grasp Elise's for comfort. Her almond gaze flicked along the precise line of vlor'lords standing across the room. Eighty-nine to be precise. One for each of the Fifth Rank WOR present.

All the women looked at the newcomers with trepidation. Since their capture, the only men they'd been exposed to had been the Tenders and the WOR-guards. To see vlor'lords had to be more than a little disturbing. Add to this all the recent changes occurring within the Confinement Deck and everyone was on edge.

Over the past few days, the WOR-guards had reconfigured the left half of the Confinement Deck where they stood. The classrooms on this side were now divided into five separate rooms, one for each Rank.

After Activation, along with its horrific aftereffects, they had lost faith in their captors. A sad testament to say they'd ever developed trust in the men who'd taken them, but the truth couldn't be denied. They'd come to understand their place and accepted it. Obey and they would not be hurt. This alteration to their strict routine put everyone on edge. The men standing before them were not there to harm, but rather to claim.

The right side of the Confinement Deck remained the same. Their lessons about Vendel society and technology resumed in the small class-rooms. They spent this morning back in class for the first time since Activation, but even there they'd found yet another change. Their entire day of instruction had been compressed into half a day. Afterward, the Tenders took all of them to the exercise field, divided them by Rank, then led each group to the newly configured rooms.

Which is where Elise and the other women of the Fifth Rank gathered now. Theirs was the smallest of the five newly constructed rooms. She stood with Aomi, Paula, and a few others in a small group near one end of long rows of tables and eyed the vlor'lords with concern. Of the original ninety-two Fifth Rank women, they'd lost five of their original number. Gregor had told her this would happen.

He'd been right, knowing beforehand that some would die hadn't helped her to deal with the loss. If anything, the foreknowledge had made things harder. In fact, the past cycle had been the worst ten days since her capture, but she appreciated his honesty. His willingness to answer her questions had built a bridge between them and that brought a measure of trust.

While she still considered him an adversary, the time he spent showing her the *Gambit* had been almost pleasant. She honestly looked forward to seeing him, spending time with him, holding his hands, and being held by him. As she opened up to him, he rewarded her with more freedom, and the best gift of all: the ability to once again talk to her friends without fear of a whipstick.

None of it changed her plans. A hundred and eighty women had lost their lives to Activation. Her stomach still twisted at the callous disregard the Vendel held for human life. For that reason alone, she needed to free her friends. As long as Gregor and the Tenders controlled their fate, their lives would always be at risk.

She turned her thoughts toward the positives. Chandra had risen from Fourth to Fifth Rank after Activation. She had shared nearly identical schedules with Aomi and Elise previously, and the three of them had developed a close bond. Aomi and Chandra had helped Elise on the original code, refined the syntax, and morphed it into an effective language.

To her delight, Alice had risen from the Second Rank to join the Fifth as well. Unfortunately, the brown-noser, Sarah, had too. That bitch paraded around the past few days as if she were some damn queen, like the other women she had joined hadn't been Fifth Rank from the very beginning.

High Tender Alec vlor'Martun, a surprisingly gentle man for a Tender, escorted the three newly risen WOR into the room. Upon seeing Elise and Aomi, Chandra hurried over. Alice followed a bit more slowly. Chandra gave Aomi and Elise a hug. Making friends had been difficult through the isolation imposed by their captors, but they had managed to bond, becoming as inseparable as they could, given the constraints of their captivity.

Now that they could speak again—*thank you, Gregor*—Elise quickly introduced Alice. She tried to include Paula in the introductions, but Paula turned away, again holding herself apart.

Sarah stood away from the group as well, but for a different reason. She received a chilly reception from those gathered. Word had spread about her tendency to backstab and seek favor with the WOR-guards, leaving her with few friends.

High Tender vlor'Martun went to speak to the vlor'lords and left the women without a word.

Aomi nudged her shoulder. "Have you been listening to a word I've said?"

"Huh?"

Aomi pulled her long black braid over her shoulder. "I asked if you had any idea what was happening?" Her friend looked to her with an expectant expression.

Those are the vlor'lords, tapped Elise, to her friends. The other girls became silent as they listened to the conversation. *They are going to be training us and the Tenders have to figure out some sort of compatibility rating.*

How do you know this? Aomi flicked her gaze toward the row of men.

The emperor has explained a little of it, too little, but some.

With the code, anyone could listen in on a conversation. Someone, she wasn't sure who, tapped, *What the hell does that mean?*

Expletives were one of the first new words added to the codes. They came frequently in conversation and had been whittled down to just a few taps.

I don't know exactly. But somehow, they plan to run everyone against each of the lords. Speed dating is probably the best analogy, at least in the rotating part. I have no idea about the speed part. They come up with some sort of compatibility score and, based on that, the field of eligible lords is narrowed down. I believe we'll all just have one.

Unexpectedly, Paula joined them. She flicked her gaze toward the row of men, her eyes narrowing. *Match us to train for what?*

I'm not sure. If you meet a minimum threshold, you'll be matched to that vlor'lord. He'll claim you and you'll belong to him.

A look of disgust passed over Paula's features.

Elise shrugged. She didn't like it either.

Chandra whispered. *You've already been claimed, right? By the emperor?*

Yes.

Alice jumped into the conversation. *What are you going to do while all the rest of this is happening to us?* Alice glanced around the room, probably looking for WOR-guards.

I'm not sure, but I think it's time to learn about this WOR-skill.

A bubble of excitement ran through the group. As much as she hated the Vendel, the thought of bending time and space with her mind brought a certain thrill. How something like that was possible, she had no idea.

High Tender Alec vlor'Martun returned and gripped a gel-flimsy. His gaze flicked up to the women and back down to the gel-flimsy.

High Tender Alec vlor'Martun pointed to Aomi. "234."

"Yes, High Tender vlor'Martun," Aomi said with a dip of her head.

He pointed to a seat at the long table. "Sit here." He scanned his list. "12?" He glanced up.

"Yes, High Tender vlor'Martun?" a timid voice called out from the back of the collected women. The girl lifted her hand and identified herself.

"You are to sit here." He indicated her seat. He called out another number. "29?"

As he announced each woman's numerical designation, he indicated their assigned seat along one side of a long table until he filled that row, then he moved to the next table and began again.

With the exception of a slight shifting of feet, none of the men across the room moved as High Tender vlor'Martun seated the women.

Five long rows slowly filled. Alice and Sarah were the last to be called. "5 and 10-4 take your seats here." Alice and Sarah bobbed their heads and took the last remaining seats.

Elise looked around the room feeling lost. "High Tender vlor'Martun, what about me?"

"Silence, 10-2. The Master Tender will be here shortly to collect you. Stand to the side and be quiet."

She took up a spot next to the wall and waited.

High Tender vlor'Martun read off a second list of names. Each name brought forward a swaggering vlor'lord from the regimented line of men. One by one, High Tender vlor'Martun lined the men opposite the women.

The vlor' were the royal caste in Vendel society. As they strutted, marched, and paraded past, Elise noticed two things. First, they were young, under thirty or forty years, but more importantly, they were nervous.

It wasn't the kind of uneasiness from a person who was scared. They shifted their feet, clenched their hands, pursed their lips, and coughed with anxiety. All the things nervous people did. It was more...as if they were being tested and feared failure.

Sometime during this process, nine other High Tenders entered. At a nod from High Tender vlor'Martun, the Tenders took up position at each end of the five long tables, leaving a spot free for High Tender vlor'Martun at the front table. Finally, it was done. Eighty-nine seated women stared nervously at eighty-nine Vendel lords standing before them.

"My lords, welcome. S'vlor these are the vlor'. They are your guides and will take you through an introduction of the WOR-skill and teach the first skill of the Bar." He scanned the room. "Lords, please take a seat and introduce yourselves."

A shiver went down her spine. This was the beginning of her training, but where was her trainer? Where was Gregor?

Scraping sounds filled the room as chairs dragged across the floor. Deep male voices made introductions as the men reached across the table, the act looking rehearsed, and took the hand of the s'vlor opposite them: a slight bend at the waist, followed by an almost reverent bow of the head followed. Then the men lifted the women's hand, turned it over, and pressed a kiss to the back of the knuckles. Startled gasps echoed around the classroom as this ritual repeated itself eighty-nine times.

The memory of a hot breath and a trail of fire flashed through her mind. Gregor had introduced himself exactly as these men did. This ritual had to be important. Was this unique to vlor' and s'vlor, or was it just the way a Vendel man greeted any woman?

"S'vlor, listen up." High Tender vlor'Martun continued his instructions once introductions were complete. "Your vlor'lord will place three items on the table in front of you."

The room filled with rustling noises as the men removed these items from their jacket pockets. A small tray, not much larger than a hand, was put on the table. They filled the tray with a vial of water. A red, fist-sized ball went to the left of the tray, and a rosebud was placed to the right.

What these items had to do with the WOR-skill remained a mystery. Silence filled the room, as Elise was certain all the women had to be thinking exactly the same thing.

"Now," began High Tender vlor'Martun, "we begin with a meditation. The WOR-skill is a set of abilities accessed only after you have firm control of your innermost thoughts. You must learn to calm yourself and seek the peace within. Your vlor'lord will guide you in this. Place your right hand in the tray of water, palm down, and put your left hand on the tabletop beside the rose, palm up."

The women did as they were instructed, while Elise watched from the edge of the room.

"Feel your vlor'lord's touch as he places his hand in yours." Some of the girls jumped when this happened. The Tenders made notes on the gel-flimsies they carried. Others didn't move at all. Sarah, who sat at the end of the table right in front of Elise, lifted her fingers to lightly stroke the wrist of her vlor'lord.

"Listen to his words as he directs you through the exercise."

The vlor'lords leaned forward and spoke to their assigned s'vlor. The girls closed their eyes and the low hum of deep voices filled the room. Elise strained to hear what the vlor'lords whispered, but couldn't make out individual words.

High Tender Marcus entered the room. She knew, not because she saw him, but because all of the High Tenders stiffened and bowed as one. He held the braklav and twirled it absently. With a jerk of his chin, he motioned for her to join him. She eyed the braklav with concern and stepped quickly to his side.

Once outside, she greeted him as was expected. "Good afternoon, High Tender Marcus." She said it with a smile, although her teeth clenched.

"Good afternoon, 10-2." He guided her past the other four, much larger classrooms and toward the far end of the Confinement Deck. Passing by the open doorways, similar scenes occurred inside. Long rows of women and men sat across tables with red roses, balls, and trays of water.

High Tender Marcus took her down the exercise fields and headed toward a long row of much smaller rooms at the far end of the Confinement Deck. She'd never been allowed back here before. He ushered her inside one of the tiny rooms where Gregor paced beside a square table with three empty chairs. On top of the table were three items: a red ball, a rosebud and a tray half full of water. His lips twisted in that smirk she'd come to know so well.

"Opés, it is good to see you. Come, we have an exciting day." His eyes danced with excitement in the bright light of the room.

Her gaze shifted between Gregor and the High Tender. She didn't like being caught between these two men. Nothing good ever came out of it.

"Good afternoon, Gregor." She kissed him on the cheek, avoiding a more amorous lip-locked entanglement in front of the High Tender who wouldn't have approved.

Gregor settled her in a seat and sat beside her.

The High Tender took the third chair across from her, his mouth twisting at the slight display of affection.

Gregor's imperial tattoo danced beneath the skin of his brow, restless and eager. "Do you have any questions?" Glittering steel flashed in the reflection of his gaze.

Was this another of his concessions? One of his bridge building exercises? It was hard to tell. They'd been getting along when alone, but she remembered the High Tender didn't like Gregor coddling her by answering questions. Her gaze shifted to High Tender Marcus as uncertainty built within her.

"Opés," Gregor said gently pulling her attention back with the gentleness of his voice. "What would you like to ask?"

She glanced again at the High Tender, her head moving on a swivel, back and forth, between the two men.

Gregor noticed the direction of her gaze and frowned.

She didn't know how to act around the High Tender. If it had been just Gregor she would have been more at ease.

She directed her next words to the High Tender. "I don't want to play games today. Maybe we can just do whatever the exercise is?"

Gregor crossed his arms. His gaze flicked between High Tender Marcus and the odd assortment of items. Silence stretched between them, filling the room with an oppressive weight. No one said a word.

She certainly wasn't going to fill the suffocating gap. The thudding in her chest pounded loud enough with a restless rhythm, a loud drum beat filling the awkward pause with dissonance.

"I am surprised you are so eager to begin." Gregor placed his elbows on the table.

"Can we just get on with it? Whatever we're supposed to be doing? If you want to explain what's happening to the other s'vlor, I'd love to hear it, but since most of my questions go unanswered, I'd rather avoid the frustration. I have a feeling I need to concentrate and I'm finding that difficult."

"Are you trying to anger me?"

"No, Gregor. I'm simply being honest." Her attention flicked back to the High Tender.

The few times she'd been in the presence of the two men together, things never went well, but she reminded herself this was a battlefield. She needed to bend to survive, give so she could take. With a long breath out, she buried her anger and portray the meek woman they wanted to see.

"I'm sorry." She glanced sideways at the High Tender certain Gregor caught every nuance. "I'm a little scared. I didn't mean to be rude. High Tender Marcus marched me back here and explained nothing. I'm a little keyed up. Then I see you here and that always stirs up such strong emotions. I never know what to feel, or which way is up."

She'd learned a few things about Gregor. Blue colored his passion. Silver his displeasure. Right now, his eyes glittered with a pale and brittle light. When he was pleased he used her name, and when he was not the possessive label, opés, came out.

"What you see before you, opés, are three items which the Tenders have used for generations to train the WOR-skill. They are focusing devices aimed not so much to bring out your abilities, but rather to pair compatible vlor' and s'vlor, Yin and Yang, to borrow from our combined Earth history. You and I will perform the exercises because it is required to validate compatibility before training can begin and will serve as an aid in focusing your mind during future exercises. Your state of mind needs to be calm and focused."

The High Tender's chair creaked as he shifted his weight.

"What if we're not a match?" She glanced at the High Tender.

"We are most definitely matched." Gregor drew her attention back to him with his sharp tone. "Did I not say you belonged to me?" He pushed the three things aside and the tenor of his voice hardened, steel bridging the gap between his words. "Stop looking at him. I am your focus."

A shiver went down her spine and her gaze snapped back to meet the silvered glare of Gregor's direct gaze.

"Sorry."

He let out a breath and stretched his neck side to side. "This will not work if you are anxious. I know how your mind works. You have questions rolling around in that head of yours. None of this will work if you're not focused on the task at hand. It is a waste of both of our time, so let us deal with your questions."

Without thinking, she looked to the High Tender. He kept the braklav spinning. The constant sliver blur flashed in her peripheral vision reminding her of pain.

Gregor slammed his fist on the table making her jump. "Stop looking at him!" His glare was, cold, unrelenting, and full of disapproval.

"I'm sorry!" she said with a yelp. "He makes me nervous. Him and that thing in his hand."

Gregor reached out. "Give me your hand."

The jolt of their bond surged up her arm and dove directly into her heart. She gasped with the adrenaline spiking in her blood.

"Take a deep breath," he said, stroking the back of her hand. "This will be hard enough. Tell me, what is wrong?"

"I'm not trying to be difficult." She glanced down at her lap and dropped her voice to a whisper. "I'm scared." Terrified really of the silver rod spinning in her peripheral vision. Her gaze shifted left. "What happens if I fail?" Because deep down she didn't believe what they claimed was possible.

"I see."

"If I can't do this…" She couldn't help but swallow against the thickness growing in her throat. "If I'm not successful, what are you going to do to me?"

"Elise, I understand what you fear, but you must trust me. This exercise works only if you relinquish control. I have already told you Lord vlor'-Vardhal will not touch you with the braklav, but you must work with me. This is my promise to you."

He'd given her his promise, even if it was backed up with a threat.

She'd be a fool not to take advantage of it, so she took a deep breath and asked. "Tell me why one of your planet's lights went dim. How did you know I'd be yours? Did you know the moment you saw me or only after we touched? It was that first touch, right? That was this bond?"

High Tender Marcus slammed his fist on the table. "Sire, why do you bother explaining anything? She is s'vlor!" The skin over his knuckles turned white from where he gripped the braklav.

Her lungs struggled, but she took each breath in and out. Why did he care so much if Gregor answered such simple questions?

Gregor turned to the High Tender. "Elise and I have had an interesting conversation about answering questions in the past. She promised to work with me if I worked with her. Is that not so?"

That wasn't exactly how it had gone. She promised to be nice and he'd inferred the rest. "I only meant to say, it matters how you treat me."

The High Tender slapped the braklav in his palm, but Gregor placed a restraining hand on his arm. He nodded for her to continue.

Sometimes there was great power in confessing the truth. Gregor wouldn't be able to say she lied to him. The High Tender wouldn't be able to punish her for lying. "If you and I are building bridges, then I'll give you the truth, but you already know you don't want it."

"Even in surrender, you challenge me." He drummed his fingers on the table and they sat in silence once again. "Tell me, what is the truth? Will this be worth my time? You've asked me to be nice and treat you with respect and compassion. Will I regret it?" He sat back, crossing his arms, and eyed her with interest.

She hesitated to answer. Clearly, he demanded her surrender, but she didn't know if that was something she could fake. The words she chose had to give him what he wanted without giving too much.

"I only meant to say that if you were nice, compassionate even, if only from time to time, it would make the rest of it easier for me. Does it matter how you treat me? I believe so, but even then, I have every reason to hate you and none to feel otherwise. My emotions are conflicted—no, sorry, not my emotions—I know exactly how I feel. I hate you. I hate the Vendel. With every fiber of my being, I hate all of you."

The High Tender grabbed the braklav, but Gregor placed a restraining hand on his arm. "Continue."

She went on, knowing the danger in her words, but it felt good to speak her mind. "If I knew of any possible way to hurt you, I would in a heartbeat. When you touch me, my skin burns. When you kiss me, I want more. It confuses the hell out of me and I hate myself for it. I'm trapped and I see no way out except to work with you, and that makes me very angry." It was the truth, only by learning the WOR-skill would she get enough power to fight them.

"If you're hoping for my enthusiasm," she continued, "I don't know if I can promise it. I'm going to try and work with you, but I'll probably fail. I can't help but fight you. I know it doesn't make any sense to keep fighting when I've already lost, but I can't admit you've won. You want my honesty, Gregor. I can't be more transparent than that. But when you treat me with kindness and dignity, like answering my questions and giving in to any reasonable requests I may have, then yes, it helps me to work with you instead of fight against you. Is that honest enough for you?"

"It's a start. How can I get you to put that aside and learn what I must teach?"

"I honestly don't know." She glanced at High Tender Marcus. "I'll learn whatever I'm supposed to learn, because I know what he'll do if I don't."

High Tender Marcus pointed the braklav at her. "See how she defies you?"

She pulled back, cringing.

Gregor shook his head. "No, I do not think that is what my opés is saying, Lord vlor'Vardhal." He leaned toward her. "Go on, Elise, continue."

She sucked in a deep breath and blew it out, slow and measured. "Is it worth your time to answer my questions? Probably. Will you regret it? Maybe. Trust will always be a challenge between us. I don't understand what's happening with the bond and that scares the hell out of me."

"Lord vlor'Vardhal is correct. Even in surrender, you challenge me, but it's enough." Gregor drummed his fingers on the table and they sat in silence once again. "Your honesty makes you strong. That is what will save my empire, and I don't mind taking time to explain things to you."

"This is a mistake," the High Tender grumbled. He paced the room, moving behind her. The deep tread of his boots sent shivers of fear up her spine. In his hand, the blur of the braklav threatened. "She will cost you everything."

"I disagree," Gregor said. "And the decision is mine to make. Trust in your Emperor, Lord vlor'Vardhal. I have vowed to save us all."

CHAPTER TWENTY_

Elise didn't like not being able to see the High Tender. Not that she could do anything about where he chose to stand or walk.

"Are any of her questions so damaging?" Gregor turned to address the High Tender. "If she is so intent on *hurting* me, then I need her to understand why that is not a good idea. I have come to learn my opés needs incentive to work toward my goals rather than against them."

High Tender Marcus moved back into her line of sight, twirling the braklav in the air. His lips pressed into a thin line. With a flick of his wrist, the braklav snapped into his palm, landing with a thud.

"As you wish, Sire." He paced, making a wide circuit around the table. "10-2," his voice dropped into a lecturing tone, "the compatibility scale measures the strength of the future biologic and mental link between vlor' and s'vlor. The sole purpose is to see how the man and woman react to one another. How well can he make her perform? How compliant is she to his direction? How willing is she to please him? Over two cycles, we have a general idea who a woman will bond with best. A degree of attraction— emotional and physical—ensures strong bonding potential. In some cases, we find no compatible match and resort to a stronger set of emotions."

"Torture?" She twisted around to get a view of the emperor.

High Tender Marcus's beady eyes drilled into hers. Dark and severe, his gaze made her shudder.

"If she's not compliant, we bring the s'vlor back here and leave her with a potential vlor', a whipstick, and the imagination of the lord. If, after that, we are unable to achieve a compatibility score of at least eight of ten, we eliminate the woman."

"You kill her?" They were barbarians.

"After Activation, a non-bonded WOR is a liability."

"The bond?" She turned to Gregor, confused. "We already have a bond."

"Once compatibility is confirmed," the High Tender continued, "and after some basic proficiency in the WOR-skill is achieved, the Blood Rite is performed."

"Blood Rite?" She'd heard them say those words before. Bonds and Blood Rites? She would never understand.

He gave a nod. "Your blood will activate Emperor vlor'Malita's WOR-genes, allowing him to train you."

She didn't like the sound of that. "You mean control me."

High Tender Marcus exchanged a look with Gregor.

Gregor answered. "The WOR-skill is...difficult to contain. The power accessed by a newly activated WOR can be volatile. I will guide you while you learn and temper your emerging abilities. It's for your protection and the safety of everyone."

"Safety?"

"You must understand the dangers."

"I'm no threat." She tapped her chest. "I mean look at me."

"It's the power you'll touch which is dangerous. WOR need to be contained until they are trained."

"You mean enslaved." Her stare bore into Gregor, but he refused to flinch against the animosity she threw at him.

"Our WOR see it as a privilege to serve the common good."

"Do they have a choice?"

Gregor shook his head. "It is a sacred birthright. A woman cannot refuse. Why would she?"

"I would." She slammed her hand on the table. "I do, but then you know this...as do all the woman out there right now being paired up with future masters. You simply don't care about what is right or just."

"You need to understand our history." Gregor leaned back, splaying his fingers wide on the table. The muscles of his jaw tightened, clearly, he was trying to remain calm in the face of her questions. He's the one who encouraged her to ask. It wasn't her fault he wasn't comfortable with her questions. She'd push until he shut her down.

"Please, enlighten me. Tell me how being *your* slave is *my* privilege."

The two men exchanged another look, but it was Gregor who spoke.

"The first woman who expressed the WOR-skill wound up enslaving our people." His tone softened. "WOR have abilities the rest of us don't. The first Vendel woman to express this talent abused it horribly. It took a long time to figure out how to control her. Then we discovered what made her WOR. Those abilities are meant for the common good."

"The emperor is correct," the High Tender said. "Once we harnessed the power, and used it to the benefit of all Vendel, we made surprising advances. It didn't take long before we outgrew our neighbors. You think what we did to Earth was wrong? The best thing the Vendel ever did was leave Earth when we did. We had become gods compared to our neighbors. Given more time, we would've done to them what the first Women of Rank had done to us."

The High Tender continued. His voice took on a lecturing tone. "The WOR-skill is a potent power, 10-2. We travel the stars using psychic energy. Twenty women of the First Rank operate the WOR-drive in alternating shifts. Through their use of the WOR-skill, we travel at speeds impossible in normal space. There are no engines, no warp-drives, no hyperspace. We have WOR-space. And that is just using the abilities of First Rank WOR. There are tens of thousands of the First Rank among the Vendel. Power between Ranks is exponential, not additive."

If twenty First Rank women could fold space-time and transport a fleet of five ships through space, what exactly could she do as a Fifth Rank WOR? She shook as the meaning of his words became clear.

She looked across at Gregor. "What kind of weapon do you think I'll be?" What the hell did they intend for her to become?

"You don't fit any of our standard patterns, Elise," Gregor answered. He took her hand in his and threaded his fingers with hers. "As to what sort of weapon we think you'll be?" He shrugged. "Don't really know. But to answer your other question, one of our planets has gone silent. We've lost billions of people to an intelligence we don't understand. The s'lor who keep the lines of communication open hear the screams of our people before they go silent."

"So, enslaving a sub-segment of your population is justified for the common good? How many WOR are there?"

"Not nearly enough," High Tender Marcus said.

"Which is why Earth is so important," Gregor added.

"If Earth had so many WOR on it, why didn't the WOR-skill manifest in other women in the two thousand years since you left?"

Another look was exchanged between the men.

"Sire, we don't have all day. At some point, we must begin with the exercise."

Gregor blew out a breath and tapped the tabletop. "I agree." The stony slant of his eyes bore into her. "For the common good, Earth has been managed."

What did that even mean?

"That's the same argument you've been using since my capture. You decimated Earth for the common good. You captured me for the common good. Now, you're going to contain my power, again for the common good? Yet, I have done nothing wrong. It's easy for you to justify your actions because you hold all the power."

Her hand strayed to the necklace wrapped around her neck, the one meant to control her through training. High Tender Marcus said the necklace wasn't permanent, but when it was removed how would they control her then?

"Who controls you?" She looked between the two men. "Who governs your power?"

The High Tender gave a derisive snort.

"I'm serious."

"You have no idea of the destructive force of the WOR-skill," the High Tender said. "Do not sit in judgement on what you do not understand. For the greater good, all WOR are contained."

"You enslave WOR because you can, not because it's right." She couldn't keep the defiance out of her voice.

The High Tender's braklav twirled in his fingers, blurring with its speed. "We're wasting time, Sire."

"The WOR-skill is a terrible gift," Gregor said. "You will gain access to portions of your mind you have never touched before. You'll be able to manipulate the very fabric of space. This ability is dangerous if not guided appropriately. I have told you to trust me." He stroked her hand. "We are under attack. One of our planets has been destroyed. You know this, because you were there the day it happened. We lost twenty-billion lives when Saphirah went dark. All life was destroyed."

"Destroyed?"

"Everything." He gave a nod. "We call the enemy the S'lorek. Our s'lor are defenseless against them. Our s'vlor barely protect the populace while they flee, but even they can't protect a planet during an evacuation on that scale. Despite what you think of me, the Vendel are not a violent people. We do not have weapons to fight this war beyond our WOR—beyond what you may become."

She didn't want to believe him.

Aliens destroying planets? Her head swam with images of death and destruction on a planetary scale.

Gregor said he was trying to save everyone. He sounded sincere.

He leaned forward, grabbed the rosebud, and set it down in front of her. Then he placed the tray of water and the red ball back in position. The deep timbre of his voice reached out, drawing her back to him. "So, opés, if you want to know why *I* killed all those people on Earth, here's you answer. I'm losing a war I don't understand, against an enemy I cannot fight. I need weapons. I need you."

"That still doesn't give you the right—"

"It doesn't? I'm running out of WOR. Our enemy loves them best. I need weapons, and a concentrated source of high-ranking WOR. Earth has been a genetic melting pot for eons after the Vendel left and ripe with untapped WOR. You know what, opés?" Gregor placed his hands on the table and stood, looming over her.

She cringed at the sudden movement. The fury in his face, and the absolute certainty in his eyes told her he regretted none of what he'd done. The dark tattoo danced over his eye and hardened steel flashed.

"The Vendel are at war. If Earth had kept broadcasting into space, it would have attracted the attention of the S'Lorek sooner or later." He wiped his upper lip and lowered his head within inches of her face.

She felt the heat of his breath and his heady aroma of musk and spice made her head spin.

"The S'Lorek are knocking at our borders. By harvesting Earth, I may… I will stop them. By sending Earth back to the dark ages, I may get them to ignore the home of humanity. So, if you're done with your self-righteous, downtrodden victim routine, it's time to get to work. The good of the many outweigh the good of one. You're not more important than the whole of the human race. Your freedom is insignificant. I'm willing to do this the easy way and work with you, answering your questions, but you will cooperate. If not, I have no problem resorting to the braklav. One way or the other, you will be trained."

He sat back with a thud and glowered, looking down at her over the bridge of his nose. The High Tender sat silent. Elise tried to breathe.

The loss of billions of Vendel didn't justify the destruction of Earth's population. Only madmen thought such things.

"It never occurred to you to ask for our help. For volunteers?"

Was he insane? Colors spiraled at the edges of her vision. Multicolored hues flickered in a kaleidoscope of chaotic jewels. The tips of her fingertips tingled and a prickling sensation in her lips had her biting down on the plump flesh. A deep breath staggered into her lungs, struggling to find its way inside. Another breath shuttled inward, filling her lungs with oxygen.

"Even if what you say is true, if you're trying to save your empire, why would you take one unnecessary life?"

"Not every decision is easy."

The absolute certainty in his voice terrified her, because he believed every word of what he said. The dark tattoo danced on his brow and hardened steel flashed in his eyes.

The High Tender's pacing intensified. Every time he came into her field of vision, he spun and caught the braklav in his palm. The silver rod twirled in the soft light of the room, an ominous threat if she failed to comply.

No moral argument warranted Gregor's conclusion.

"With all your knowledge of biotech, you couldn't have found another way?" Her gaze shifted between the men.

"The Vector's lethality was designed," the High Tender said.

"Why?"

"Only someone carrying at least five of the twenty WOR-genes survived the Vector. With each passing generation, more WOR will be born than not." High Tender Marcus snapped the braklav in his palm and gripped it tightly.

He couldn't be serious. "You turned Earth into a WOR breeding ground?"

Gregor spoke. "I serve humanity, by blood and oath. The death of a few is acceptable when considering the survival of the species."

"When did we stop being human in your eyes?" She wanted to yell—to scream—instead her words came out a whisper.

"Not all of my choices are easy. I serve the Vendel. You asked what I fear? I fear the extinction of the human race and I've vowed to do what I can to save us. The price Earth paid was small."

"Are you mad?"

"Mad? No, Elise. I'm resolute in my goal."

He glanced at the High Tender who twirled the braklav, then he placed his hands palm down on the table.

"It is time to train, opés." He glanced at High Tender Marcus who gave a nod.

Elise swallowed, hard. The slow nod she gave was only because she needed to learn the WOR-skill before she could use it against them. The red ball and rose received a dubious look.

"What do you want me to do?"

CHAPTER TWENTY-ONE_

GREGOR AND THE HIGH TENDER WERE WRONG. THERE HAD TO BE ANOTHER way.

"Put your hand in the water..." Gregor's tone had softened now they'd begun the focusing exercises.

Cool water closed over the back of her hand. The sensation calmed her at first, but the moment she acclimated, an electrical jolt shot up her arm.

Gregor gave an encouraging nod. "Form in your mind an image of the rose."

Whatever this exercise was it was stupid. He was stupid. This whole place was stupid.

The WOR-skill was stupid!

Her hand was wet and the rose was sitting right there. She stared at it, no reason to form an image in her mind when the rose sat right in front of her.

For four months—four sun cycles—these men had controlled every facet of her day, from what she wore, to what she ate, to when she slept, and when she woke. They tortured her and beat her and killed her with kindness.

If this is what they'd been building up to, then why did her first step to becoming an all-powerful superwoman begin with a tray full of warm water and a stupid red rose? Ridiculous didn't even begin to describe it.

She would have laughed if she weren't sitting in a fancy prison, inside a small white room, with a High Tender who had an overly fond fascination with his torture device. Twice he'd used that thing on her. The last time had messed with her head. Gregor said he had sensed a *dissonance*, whatever that meant, and thankfully he forbade the High Tender from using it on her again.

"Focus, Elise." Strain edged into Gregor's calming voice.

"I'm trying," she lied. Everything about this moment stirred up memories of exactly what these two men had taken from her.

Gregor had sat in her grandfather's chair, gloating over the capture of his treasure, while her hands and feet had been bound. The High Tender had knelt on the ground, constructing the device which confirmed and consigned her to this fate. Spiraling colors on the Tenderstat proclaimed her Fifth Rank and allowed Gregor to stake his claim.

Her grandfather died in her childhood home. As had Dale, and Mark, and Angel, and Mr. and Mrs. Jameson. She'd been left to dig their graves and bury them all by herself.

The damn braklav never stopped moving. "Sire, her mind is drifting, guide her back."

Of course, her mind was drifting.

Tension creeped into Gregor's voice. "Feel the water on the back of your hand. Imagine the water as an endless ocean. Empty your thoughts into it and let them float away."

She curled her fingers into her palm, frustrated. "It's not that easy. Why do I have to do this?"

"Your place is not to question," the High Tender snapped. "Follow the exercise."

"Easy, Lord vlor'Vardhal," Gregor said. He tried to soothe her. "Relax your hand and close your eyes. This exercise is not difficult. Let's try some deep breathing to calm you." He took a deep breath and blew it out.

Clearly, she was supposed to copy him. She tried, but it did nothing to ease her mind. Instead, her head swam with more images of those final weeks.

Dragging her grandfather's body down the staircase while his feet thudded on the steps, loading his body into a wheelbarrow, blisters on her palms as she wheeled him outside and the heat beating down as she fought with the tractor to dig his grave. In death, he'd been denied the dignity he'd earned in life. They had taken that from him.

Her last conversation with her brother-in-law, Tom, replayed in her head, pleading with him to flee. Never knowing what had happened to him and her nieces would bother her for the rest of her life. She was supposed to have joined them on the island retreat. If she'd been brave enough to face those empty, tortured streets and had driven to the airfield, could she have flown to the island? Refueling an aircraft took a lot more planning. Planning kept her holed up in Comwell Estates, right where Gregor and the High Tender found her, waiting like an idiot to be taken. She'd made it so easy for them.

"You're hyperventilating," he said. "Slow down. Take deep, easy breaths."

"She makes a mockery of your control."

"Silence, Lord vlor'Vardhal, or I will ask you to leave."

High Tender Marcus thrust the tip of the braklav at her face. "It's a simple exercise, 10-2. Resistance will not be tolerated."

"Lord vlor'Vardhal, stand down!"

They'd taken everything. She'd never really resisted. Even her escape plan was a joke, a mess of magical thinking. To think she even had a chance at escape.

The stupid water bowl and rose. Her fingers curled.

They'd killed everyone she'd ever loved. Captured, imprisoned, and enslaved her and she'd let it all happen never putting up a fight. She'd even let her guard down, only to have them do it all over again. Another round of deaths followed with Activation.

The bowl shook beneath her hand.

Whatever this power was, once she learned how to use it, she would turn it upon them. Crush them. She'd fight until there was nothing left and take as much as they'd stolen from her.

Just don't touch her with that silver rod. Her insides clenched every time it came near. Like now, a twirling blur, she cringed against the silver flash as he pressed it to her shoulder. Fear bubbled up inside.

"Stop, High Tender Marcus, please. I'm trying." Panic raced through her, she wanted to run, but there was nowhere to go.

"That is not helping with this exercise." Gregor brushed the braklav off her shoulder.

The High Tender retreated to the far wall.

Gregor reached out. Their palms touched and scalding water slipped between their skin. The bond thrummed between them, spiraling up her arm and tunneling into her nerves. The electrical vibrations traveled a path it had never taken before and headed directly into her mind where an expansion of her consciousness stole her breath and left her with sudden clarity.

Just breathe he had said. Impossible when you had left your body behind.

Colors of every hue imaginable swirled around her and ignited in an explosion of burning radiance. Her mind stretched impossibly far, then pulled taut and balanced on a knife's edge. Then, currents of power slammed into the core of her being. Her consciousness spiraled outward—unanchored, she flew into another realm of existence.

The world shifted, folding in on itself, then exploded. Impossibly, space twisted, deforming and rejoining in right angles atop right angles. She spanned the dimensions of space and time and traversed newly formed places, which branched and subdivided into new realms.

Back in the room, walls buckled and warped. Lights flickered. A deafening alarm sounded. The false sky of the Confinement Deck darkened and swirled with newly formed clouds, where jagged bolts of lightning flashed. Ozone burnt the air and lightning struck the room.

The High Tender gasped. He held his chest where a dime-sized hole appeared. Perfectly circular, the edges cauterized with the surge of current she pulled from the air. He staggered and gripped his chest. Wide, terrified eyes turned toward where her body slumped at the table.

Gregor leapt to her limp body and cradled her in his arms. "Elise! Elise!" The floor canted and buckled beneath his feet.

High Tender Marcus clutched at the hole in his chest, his breathing labored. He held out the braklav. "Sire, I must stop her!"

A contingent of WOR-guards arrived, their booted feet clomping against the shaking ground, black whipsticks swinging at their hips. She pulled on her new abilities and cast them back. She was the tempest, centered within a maelstrom of fury. Klaxons sounded and more men arrived.

Gregor stumbled to his knees, nearly dropping her body.

"By the Gods," High Tender Marcus said, "what has she done?" The braklav trembled in his grip. "I must stop her."

She reached for the power to kill the High Tender, excited to inflict terrible pain. The braklav was nothing compared to what she would inflict upon him.

"No. I will do it." Gregor kissed her forehead and whispered a command. "Opés, you must stop."

The bond slammed into her and severed her access to the divine force, causing her to howl with unimagined pain.

Gregor staggered too, pain furrowed deep within his brow.

"You cannot escape the ties that bind us. The WOR-skill will destroy you without me to temper it." He lowered her fragile body to the ground and kissed her brow. "I offer you a concession, a promise from me to you, a bridge of trust I am extending." He paused to let his words sink in. "Work with me and all will be forgiven, but know this: force me to act against you and I will not stay the Tenders' hand. Choose wisely, my opés."

She'd never been so alone. Elise regarded the warped floors and walls. They stretched out and twisted beyond comprehension. The strong steady beat of Gregor's heart, and the very palpable pull of his anger, caused her to shake with uncontrollable fear.

Threads of power swirled all around her, an intense latticework of dimensions, but she could no longer touch them. Gregor had her blocked. Her connection to the WOR-skill weakened. Power coursed all around her, but instead of that intuitive contact she managed moments ago, the fragile threads slipped past her frantic grasps.

CHAPTER TWENTY-TWO_

Gambit, Day 140

THREE DAYS LATER SOMEONE RIPPED THE COVERS OFF ELISE'S SLEEPING BODY. She grabbed for the sheets and their vanishing warmth as cool air brushed against her skin. Groaning, she curled into a fetal ball.

"Elise, get up!" a familiar voice yelled in her ear.

Why are people bothering me?

Someone kicked her.

"Stop that!" she cried out.

"Dammit! Get up! The WOR-guards will be here any minute."

The WOR-guards? She blinked and rubbed at the sleep in her eyes.

"First breakfast starts in five minutes." Aomi's long, black hair glinted in the too bright light.

Chandra opened Elise's cubby and pulled out a red silk dress. "Get up," she said. "You have a minute to get dressed, two minutes to make it to breakfast, any longer and we're all going to be seeing the end of a whip-stick." Chandra's blonde curls bounced on her shoulders.

Elise had never overslept before, but then she'd never stayed awake for three days running.

Alice stood outside her sleeping pod. It was hard to miss the tall blonde. "Hurry up, one of them just rounded the bend!"

Aomi and Chandra lifted the dress over Elise's head, guiding her awkward hands into the appropriate holes. Aomi fastened the linked chain around her waist while Chandra helped her get the shoes on. The three of them hurried out of the pod and around the corner before the WOR-guard could see their rapid flight.

They slowed to a fast walk and headed toward the breakfast line.

Alice knocked her on the back of her head. "What's up with you?"

"Hey, that hurts," Elise said.

"That was nothing compared to the whipstick," Alice said. "This is the second day you haven't gotten up with the bell. You're lucky Chandra's bed is next to yours."

"No shit," Chandra said. "But today I couldn't get you to wake up. I ran to get Aomi and Alice to help. Elise, you have to get it together. If someone like 10-4 found out, you'd be toast for sure."

"Her name is Sarah."

Elise despised the Vendel's numeric naming convention, Sarah's name might sound like a CB sign off, but then that was the point. The numbers dehumanized them, took away that which was so personal. What was more intimate than a name?

"Screw the bitch's name, 10-4 is apt for her. She keeps all those vlor'lords smiling for days," Aomi said, grumbling. "Do you see what she does during training? Ugh, she strokes their hands and licks her lips. You don't even want to know what she's doing with her feet under the tables! I bet she was a whore back on Earth."

"Nah, whores get paid. I bet 10-4 gave it away for free, and to a lot of people. Tramp is the better word," Chandra said.

"Nevertheless, her name is Sarah. The Vendel call her 10-4, but we shouldn't. Our names are the only things we have left of Earth."

"Elise," Alice said, "10-4 has embraced her new Vendel home with enthusiasm. Now that she's Fifth Rank, she's horrible."

Elise stumbled.

Alice grabbed her arm and kept her from falling. "Seriously, what's up?"

Elise tapped her fingers, using the ultra-private code known only to her and Alice. *You don't want to know.*

She had based this code off the original one she'd devised for the women, but it was only a matter of time before the Vendel discovered the women's secret communication. Another form of control. Take away their names. Take away their communication. Well, Elise had taken both of those back. It was a small form of resistance, but it mattered. It all mattered.

They made it just in time. The WOR-guards closed the doors after they

246

stepped into line. Elise filled her plate with a salad and went to sit down. Her head hurt and all she wanted to do was sleep.

The other women ate in silence.

After Activation, the Tenders had rearranged the daily routine. Fifth Rank ate the first rotation of each meal. After that, they continued their studies on Vendel society and technology. First lunch followed and then five grueling hours of training in WOR-skill filled the rest of the day until dinnertime.

It wasn't that the training was physically hard, but after hours of staring at the rose and red ball, Elise's head hurt.

For the past cycle, she sat with Gregor and practiced the focusing exercises. Master Tender Marcus took a few days off to heal from whatever had happened in that room. Gregor never spoke about it and treated her with kid gloves every day that followed. It wasn't that he was fearful of what she had done. Rather, he appeared terrified of what might have happened to her. Evidently, it was possible for a WOR to burn out. Yet another potential way for her to die. Despite the ravage of her first brush with the WOR-skill, life returned to the monotony of its routine.

For the others, the field of eligible vlor'lords whittled down each day until there were less than ten candidates for each woman. The High Tender felt it would only be another cycle before they could begin confirming lords and s'vlor.

Elise's and Gregor's compatibility score came in at a solid ten. It had taken just two days to confirm. When High Tender Marcus returned, he let it slip how unusual it was to establish a perfect score; just another oddity that was Elise's new life.

Gregor, of course, beamed. He went on and on about how she had been made for him. It made her stomach twist.

Today, when they arrived for WOR class, High Tender vlor'Martun had rearranged the classroom yet again. He replaced the long rows with massive circular tables. The insides had been cut out to make room for an inner ring of seats. Five seats on the inside sat opposite an equal number arranged on the outside. A small cutaway gave entrance to the center of the table.

As they arrived, High Tender vlor'Martun directed the women to their seats. A single desk stood to the side of the group with two chairs. Elise didn't need High Tender vlor'Martun to tell her where to sit.

Gregor sat with his feet propped on the desk. He reclined with his hands crossed behind his head looking perfectly relaxed.

As High Tender vlor'Martun made his assignments, Elise approached the Emperor. "Good day, Gregor."

He nodded. "Yes, it is, opés. Please have a seat." Gregor kicked his feet off the table and rose. He pulled out the other chair and helped to seat her at the table. She turned to watch the room fill with waiting s'vlor and the lords. Alice was seated at a table at the far end of the room. Aomi, Chandra, and Paula sat inside the nearest of the large round tables.

"What is all this?" she said.

"Next phase of training."

"But, I thought they were still working through compatibility scales?"

"True. There will still be some shuffling of vlor and s'vlor, but they are ready to start training the first skill. The rest will sort itself out over next cycle."

"Oh."

The room filled. Sarah took a seat between Aomi and Chandra, who both stiffened. Sarah ignored them.

The afternoon wore on.

High Tender vlor'Martun lectured, explaining the first skill of the Bar. He droned on for twenty minutes about force diagrams, centering yourself, and imagining your mind pushing a set of balls along folding vectors.

With her tenth failure, she heaved a frustrated sigh and rested her head on her hands. "This is impossible."

"You're not focusing, opés," Gregor soothed. "Let's try the focusing exercises again and regroup."

She lifted her head and stared at him. *Again? How many times were they going to start from the beginning?*

"It's idiotic. Why turn something so simple into such a convoluted series of incomprehensible tasks?"

Gregor kept his frustration in check, mostly. It was his turn to sigh, and it was much more controlled than hers. He was actually being quite patient, considering her complete failure to accomplish anything. She hadn't been able to touch the WOR-skill since that very first focusing exercise.

Sarah, on the other hand, set the four balls spinning on the tabletop and beamed with her success at the vlor'lord opposite her.

A touch of edginess crept into Gregor's voice as he talked her through the focusing drill.

Those four little balls sat unmoving on her desk the entire session.

Gregor's gaze shifted to the tables, taking note of the squeals of delight as eighty-nine other women moved their little balls without much difficulty. Psychic abilities all around, except for Elise, the retard of the group. She'd never been on that side of the bell curve before and didn't like it much.

Why is it so simple for them and impossible for me?

Gregor took her through the focusing drills, again, the odd little rosebud and red ball routine. That was the easy part. She imagined the little rosebud unfolding and folding. In her mind, she picked the petals, one by one. *I'll destroy him. I'll destroy him not. They'll destroy me. They'll destroy me not.* After she stripped the poor rose bare, she carefully put her imaginary rose back together.

Easy.

The stupid balls, however, defied any effort to obey her will.

Not a wiggle nor a wobble.

The four tiny balls sat on the table perfectly content to remain that way forever.

She tried to explain how their methods were wrong. She could *see* how to make it work, but Gregor stopped her every time she tried to do it her way. Perhaps worried about her accessing the WOR-skill outside their rigid protocols.

Even High Tender Marcus refused to hear what she had to say. He'd chastised her when she'd asked to try it her way.

"We've been training s'vlor for millennium, 10-2, what could you possibly know about the WOR-skill? You're simply not applying yourself."

That earned her a scowl from Gregor. After class dismissal, Gregor left without a goodbye. He signaled to the High Tender with a jerk of his chin and the two men exited the room with their heads buried in deep conversation.

She remained in her chair. The other women and the vlor'lords milled about, in no rush to leave.

Damn Tenders and their rules.

She looked at the four little balls and tried it her way, because she could, and because no one was paying attention. Rather than constructing complex lines of force and folding vectors, she imagined the balls simply moving into position. She wanted that ball to move up and the other to move down.

The little balls rolled obediently into place.

Ha! It works.

Once she removed the stupid scaffolding of force, lines, vectors, and that weird folding ritual, the little balls did exactly as she wanted. She stole a glance around the room.

The vlor'lords said their goodbyes to the women.

It looks like a damn cocktail party mixer. She'd taken to speaking to herself in her head. It was the safest place to vent. *A well-dressed cocktail party.*

The daily dresses the s'vlor wore seemed commonplace now, but back on Earth they would've rivaled the richest celebrity event. The lords, decked out in their house uniforms, looked just as dashing. An air of flirtation and cautious investigation drifted through the room. Now that the field of vlor'lords had been narrowed down, the interactions between s'vlor and their potential candidates became more inquisitive than fearful.

The women eyed the men speculatively. They fell into the only roles they knew; a tentative touch, a shy giggle, demure eyes, a glance held just a little too long, a casual swish of silk and a timid smile, all social cues with one purpose in mind. These women didn't understand they were giving the vlor'lords exactly what they wanted.

Sometimes, it seemed she was the only one who remembered these men were the enemy. If it wouldn't land her in trouble, she'd grab those stupid little balls and whip them across the room. Maybe even hit one of those lordlings with the little projectiles. With an irritated flick of her eyes, she imagined the four little balls doing just that—sailing off the table to smack into the far wall.

Sailing wasn't exactly what happened. Flying was too weak of a word. The four balls rocketed off the table. Little missiles flew through the air and burrowed themselves deep into the far wall like buckshot out of a gun. Elise ducked and the room went silent.

"Holy shit," a female voice exclaimed.

"What in the worlds was that?" a male voice bellowed.

"Don't be frightened, little one." That one also come from a male.

Contempt rose within her. *Don't comfort her, you bastard.*

Cries of alarm reverberated through the room as the vlor'lords tried to figure out where the sudden noise had come from. Elise knew. And she sure as hell wasn't going to tell anyone. But how could she hide this from the Tenders? That wasn't part of the first skill of the Bar. Elise imagined her little projectiles sitting on the table just the way Gregor had left them.

One by one the tiny balls materialized in front of her with a tiny *pop*, reforming from thin air right where they belonged. She stood in alarm.

Did I do that?

High Tender vlor'Martun examined the room. He passed her table, eyed the four balls resting peacefully, and moved on. The other High Tenders collected into a huddle at the very front of the room. She filed out of the room with the rest of the bewildered s'vlor. Whatever the noise had been, they had only minutes to get to dinner before the wor-guards began flashing those sticks. No one was ever intentionally late to dinner.

She hurried to catch up to Alice. "Hey, how're you doing?"

"Pretty good," Alice said, excited. "I got two of the balls to wiggle. Did you ever think you'd ever be able to do that?" Alice swung her arms wide.

Elise had to lengthen her stride to keep pace with her tall friend.

Her friend flashed a grin. "As a child, I always wanted to use my mind to make things happen. All those stories about magic and sorcerers...the Internet vid shows with those people with superpowers. This is a dream come true." Alice did a little skip. "Lord vlor'Calcask says today was nothing. He says it's the tiniest bit of what we'll be able to do. All we have to do is work hard and focus our minds."

"Hm," Elise murmured. That hadn't been what she was going to say.

"Edgard told me I did really well today, and High Tender vlor'Martun let him teach me for three of the rotations. Isn't that a quirky name?"

Elise stopped short. "He told you his name?"

"Yeah," Alice said. "Why are you looking at me like that. Don't roll your eyes. He's actually kind of cute, in a geeky roman gladiator kind of way. Are all the Vendel born with such huge muscles?"

"He didn't ask you to use it, did he? Call him by his given name?"

It was Alice's turn to be evasive. "Well, he said it wasn't proper just yet, but I was welcome to call him Edgard where no one else could hear. He said it'd be okay."

Elise smacked her forehead with the palm of her hand. "Do you even know what that means?"

"Why do you care what I call him, or what he calls me? Relax a little."

"Alice, what does he call you?"

"Just a pet name really." Alice shrugged. "Opés. It's kind of cute."

Elise shook her head.

"Why are you giving me that look?"

"Names are significant in Vendel society. It's something they haven't taught, because I think they want to keep everyone from getting upset."

"If you know something tell me," Alice said.

"You're not supposed to use a man's first name."

"You call the emperor by name," she countered.

"Not by choice. In fact, it was one of the first things they taught—hell, trained—me using the braklav. In Vendel society when a woman uses a man's given name she's broadcasting an intimate relationship. Only wives and consorts use the given name, and, as I've come to find out, that's generally only in private. In public, even they use formal names and titles, except during matrimonial rites."

"How'd you find all this out?"

"Please, Gregor was dying to tell me what it all meant. Just another way to put me under his thumb." Elise ground her teeth and stepped a little faster.

"But we're not wives or consorts." The tone of Alice's voice dropped. "Are we?"

"No, we're not. And, I'm guessing opés is a term they use for their WOR, for us. I thought it was an annoying pet name of Gregor's, but I guess it's more than that. If this Lord vlor'Calcask has asked you to use his first name, well—in his mind—you already belong to him."

"Shit," Alice said.

They hurried to the beginning of the food line. Alice remained silent. Elise took a plate and handed it to her friend. Alice piled food on it and went down the line.

"But, then he's really kind. I mean, he's trying to help me figure out the first skill. He's funny, too."

Elise found Aomi and Chandra and joined them at their table. Alice came along and sat down quietly. The four of them sat in silence, eating, while the wor-guard patrolled.

Aomi scraped her fork on the plate tapping out the secret code as she did. *What's up with Alice?*

I told her something she didn't want to hear.

Alice looked up from her plate and stared across the table. She tapped, *But it doesn't mean we're supposed to be intimate with them? It's that we become property, right?*

What the hell are you talking about? Chandra scratched out a hasty question.

Elise was telling me something on the way over here. How much do you know that we don't know? The suspicion, and worse, the pain of Alice's words hurt.

Sorry, I didn't want to make you upset. Elise scraped up a pile of lettuce and shoved it in her mouth. One of the WOR-guards passed their table, paused, and eyed the full plates. They jumped and began eating. Four women staring at full plates of food would draw unwanted attention.

Spill it. Aomi glanced at Alice and then leveled the look at Elise. It was time to explain, and, with the code, everyone within earshot would hear as well. Perhaps it was time to share the news.

First off, we're property. In their minds we're not people, just little pets to train. Don't ever forget that. They don't see you the way you see them. The only difference between you and me right now is that the emperor laid claim to me from the very beginning. I belong to him. I have done from the start. Who you eventually belong to has yet to be decided. High Tender vlor'Martun is in charge of determining that. When he finally does, you'll be registered to your vlor' master on his inventory! The fact Alice has a vlor'lordling asking her to call him by given name means he's pretty certain she'll be his.

Elise scraped absently at the lettuce on her plate. The other girls stared sullenly at their food. No one was really hungry anymore. She continued trying to explain something she barely understood.

Just remember, everything the Vendel do is tied to biology and biotech. The Vector and the Activator were biological constructs. Like little machines sent into our bodies with one purpose in mind: to create WOR. They're picking out vlor'lords for each of you. Once they do, there's this Blood Rite. You exchange blood and your genes somehow get integrated into his DNA. I'm assuming by some sort of mechanism like the Activator, but I don't really know. I can't find anything in the am-net. WOR training is highly protected information, but I'm working on that.

Alice tapped out. *Why would...what would be the purpose of the Blood Rite? I don't see how you can swap DNA?*

Elise paused and considered. *There's a lot about the Vendel and their technology we don't understand. But they engineered the Vector, not only to pick us out of the herd, but to make sure only those people with some of the WOR-genes survived. Earth has become a WOR breeding ground.*

How do you know all this? Chandra flicked her curls in frustration. She stabbed a piece of meat with vengeance and shoved it in her mouth. Baby blue eyes flicked up and down the table. They weren't the only ones listening in to the covert conversation.

Gregor. He's thrilled that they harvested so many of us. In particular, so many of the Fifth Rank. So, the Blood Rite pairs you with a vlor'lord. But after we're trained there's another ritual. The Binding Ritual. I'm guessing—because it's the only thing the emperor hasn't forced on me—that it involves sex and the exchange of other bodily fluids. Whichever vlor'lord you get paired with remember you belong to him. All of you, body and mind. Each of those things are his to do with as he pleases.

The three women sat up in alarm. Elise had gotten their attention. Women on both sides of the table stiffened. One of the girls cried out.

Alice slammed her cup on the table. "No shit!"

Aomi's eyes widened and Chandra cringed. They weren't allowed to speak during meals. Alice remembered a moment too late. Two WOR-

253

guards descended on their table, she barely had time to tap out, *Damn WOR-gors.*

The two men glared at the women and yanked Alice up from her seat. She didn't resist and allowed them to take her to the far wall. Two other WOR-guards pulled the woman who'd cried out from the table and dragged her off whimpering to the far wall. The lash of the whipstick echoed in the room as each woman met the strike of the whipstick ten times.

Alice didn't make a sound. When they were done, she came back to the table and picked up her plate. Tears streamed down her face and she sniffled. A WOR-guard correction always ended a meal.

Whatever you're planning, hurry it up! Alice tapped in their secondary, and very private, code. Alice drew down her brows in a frown and headed out the door. Ten bright red welts marked her delicate white skin.

CHAPTER TWENTY-THREE_

Gambit Day 140

LATER THAT NIGHT, ELISE BUNCHED UP THE COVERS OF HER BED. THE LIGHTS had dimmed several hours ago. The sounds of those around her had faded into the gentle slumber of sleep. She desperately desired sleep, but would get none tonight. The desperation in Alice's coded words pulled at her and persuaded her to pursue another night of exploration, despite her fatigue. Elise had spent the last two nights exploring her escape route. She was exhausted and had planned to sleep tonight, but plans changed.

A WOR-guard passed her bed and continued down the rows of little round cells that posed as beds. She waited for the WOR-guard to pass again before making her move. With a wish for invisibility, she slipped into the showers. She carried a palm-pad. With a cautious glance around the locker room, he headed to the stack of gray and white workout clothes.

She moved to the access hatch and lined up her electronic construct, Bobo, to the door sensor. The panel slid silently aside and she crept into the hatch. A long tunnel extended into the wall for twenty feet before coming to a 'T' intersection. She crawled to the intersection, removed her clothes, and dressed in a gray and white workout uniform.

Last night she'd found an exit hatch along the outer edges of one of the ship's ports. The Confinement Deck straddled the 25th level of the *Gambit*, conveniently placed with easy access to the central pod-car track.

She wracked her brain trying to figure out how to escape. Unfortunately, Gregor's words haunted her every effort. Where was she going to go in a ship traveling through WOR-space that they couldn't find her?

It was a problem, but she challenged every assumption concerning the Vendel. Gregor also said over twenty First Rank WOR operated the WOR-drive, taking five ships, which made up the fleet through WOR-space. Was it an assumption or reality that there was no travel between the five ships while in WOR-space? The Vendel had beaming technology. Did they teleport between ships? Or was there a way to travel between...to travel within WOR-space? Where was the Vendel fleet going and how long would it take to get there?

All these questions needed to be answered before she could figure out a plan. Time was running out. The Blood Rite would be here in less than a cycle. That left less than ten days. Training through Bar, Rod, and Wheel took time. How much she hadn't a clue. The Bonding Ritual loomed in front of them all. If her suspicions were correct, any escape would be impossible afterwards.

The clock ticked and Elise had no idea how much time was left.

She tucked her clothes into a small crack in the ceiling. The exit hatch was easy to locate and she made it out without difficulty. She found her way to the central park and loped into a jog.

Several crewmen passed, all dressed in the casual gray and white exercise outfits. She gave them cursory nods and pressed on. The intended target for this excursion was a particular flight deck and a distinctly unusual woman. She ran until she came to a pod hub. A quick ride around the *Gambit's* torus brought her to Sector F.

An antiseptic space, Sector F was full of utilitarian lines, dry air, and a pervasive metallic taste. A swarm of bio-pods lined the ceilings, coming and going as they scrubbed the air and cleaned the ship. Through her research, she determined Sector F was the manufacturing and trade hub on the *Gambit*. The refineries, machine shops, and processing plants dumped vast quantities of pollutants into the air, which the bio-pods cleaned. The ceilings were nearly black with the moving carpet of the little devices.

Elise wandered to the personnel quarters. She read the signs and entered the single women's rooms. Nearly everyone should be at work. It was convenient that the sleep cycles of the Confinement Deck and the ship proper were opposite one another. If this had been their night, all of these rooms would be occupied with people bedding down to sleep. As it was, the hallways were desolate.

She tracked down the wash facilities and snuck inside. A quick look around and she found a pair of blue overalls that fit. They appeared to be relatively nondescript, but she was wary. The Vendel social structure was still very mysterious.

A quick examination in the mirror and she thought she looked similar to any of the other women. Gregor had been upfront about that as well. While there were definitely well-defined male and female roles in this society, women were well-represented in the workforce.

That discovery led her to scan personnel logs. Women were engaged in virtually every profession among the Vendel, but there were a few exceptions. There were no female WOR-guards. The Tender Conclave remained an exclusive realm of the privileged male half of the population. Otherwise, women appeared to fill nearly every niche onboard, working in concert with their male counterparts.

If she ignored the fact that women had no say in the political system, property ownership, or basic rights, it seemed almost civilized.

It was in the personnel logs where she found mention of the female pilot.

The flight deck she had chosen was small, but packed full of civilian trade vessels. Once she'd stumbled across the *Gambit's* ship inventory log, she was surprised at the number of privately owned citizen vessels berthed inside. The *Gambit* may be the imperial flagship, but it appeared to be a mini-world as well.

Berth 28F39.1 was her intended target. The pilot of *Copingham's Riot* was female.

Elise wandered the flight deck, trying to look as inconspicuous as possible. Her eyes and ears were open and took in everything, using her eidetic memory to file away every detail.

A squat bullet-shaped ship with asymmetric bulges protruding from its hull sat two rows down. *Copingham's Riot* had been scrawled across its bow in a feminine hand. All the ships looked similar and varied merely by differences in length, girth, or the number of odd projections coming off the hull.

"Hey, chickadee," a deep rumbling voice said, "care to hand up that k-site and the wrench next to it."

Elise stopped, and her breath caught in her throat. Looking left and right failed to identify the owner of the voice. She took another step.

"Ah, come on, sweetie. You're not gonna make me come down there and fetch it myself, are ya?"

Elise looked up and into one of the ugliest faces she'd ever seen. A cauliflower nose and puffy, beet-red cheeks highlighted a face too broad and too scarred to have ever been called handsome. The face topped a thick-set man with a barrel chest. His eyes twinkled and laugh lines crinkled as he looked down at her from the top of his ship.

She jerked her chin at the blue letters on the hull. "*Spider Devil*…what an unusual name."

"Not if you're from Colnag. Those little buggers infest everything with the coming of the tides. Have you ever been to Colnag before?"

"No, sir," she replied.

"Well, these red arachnids live in the oceans. But every five years, when the planet is under the greatest influence of its three moons, the high tides come and bring with them a flood of the red spiders. It's their mating season and they scurry up out of the tidemark and head into the hills. A living, crawling mass of the little critters swarm over everything. Disgusting," he said with a deep baritone voice.

"And you named your ship after them?"

"You bet. When the red tide comes, everyone gets out of the way of the red devils. Get it?"

"Yeah." She couldn't help but smile.

He wiped his hands on his overalls. The stains on the front of his blue coveralls were thick. He arched a brow and looked at her quizzically. "So, can you hand me my tools."

"Sorry."

A black case, filled with odd looking devices in neat and orderly trays, sat on the ground near the base of the front support rod. She had no idea what a k-site or arc wrench were.

"What do you need?"

"The k-site and the arc wrench."

She dragged the box of tools out from under the nose of the ship and looked up at him doubtfully. She shrugged. "I don't know what those are."

"You're kidding, right?" His eyes narrowed suspiciously.

Oh shit! Elise swallowed hard. This wasn't good. Her mind worked furiously.

The man walked to the nose of the ship and stood looking down with his hands crossed over his barrel chest. He kicked his boot and a metal ladder unrolled, clattering to dangle near the floor. "Look sweetie, grab that box, bring it up here, and let's have ourselves a little talk."

She glanced around, deciding on an escape route. How fast could she run versus how fast could he yell? The answer to that was plainly clear. Her hands balled into fists and she shook her head at her stupidity. Why hadn't she just stayed on the Confinement Deck?

"Listen, chickadee," he knelt down on one knee and extended his hand for the box. "I don't know what you're running from, but the Constables are due momentarily. If you continue to look so out of place then they're going to pick you up and take you back to your sponsor. Come up here and come inside. I won't bite, and at least we can let them finish their sweep, then you can go back the way you came." He extended his hand and beckoned with his fingers.

Elise stood still. "Why do you think that? I was just walking along minding my own business."

"Right," he said with a crooked smile. He jerked his chin at two men dressed in dark jumpsuits walking toward them. "Tell that to the Constables."

Elise considered. This man could turn her in just as easily as any other. The consequences wouldn't be any worse. More importantly, she had to figure out what gave her away. It was his smile that finally persuaded her to trust him. Anyone with a smile that wide, and a face that ugly, had to have a warm heart to go along with it.

He reached out and took the box as she stretched up on tip-toe handing it to him. Placing her foot on the first rung of the ladder, she climbed on board. He gestured to a small hatch in the fuselage and she ducked inside as the Constables came by the front of the ship.

"Good day, gentlemen," the man said.

"Good day, Dove. Are you gonna get that dust bucket running by the time we reach Malbra?" The older of the two constables spoke. He was a tall, thin man in the prime of his life. Salt and pepper hair, cropped in the common Vendel style, made him look distinguished.

"Shoot yes," Dove said.

"How much business are you losing right now with it grounded?" The second voice belonged to the younger of the two guards. She could barely make out his clean-shaven, good looks from the edge of the airlock door.

"Don't worry about me. I'll make due. That's what the Conclave is all about." Dove scratched his crotch and wiped his hands on dirty trousers.

"Hey, I hear Jeena's been taking up all your slack!" The younger man smirked.

"You bet! Damn smart lass, even better pilot. And I'm glad it's her and not one of these other fellows. Makes them think twice having a woman submit double earnings to the Conclave. Maybe they'll start pulling their fair share of the load."

"I hear she turned down Pendelton's matrimonial offer," the first Constable said. Wiry tendons stood out from his arms as he flexed them.

"Did she?" Dove said. "She should've tossed him out the airlock for asking. Hell, I bet Jeena would've cut off his balls and tossed them into orbit, if she could have gotten away with it."

The younger man slapped his hand to his thigh and laughed. "Shoot Dove, she may not have cut them off, but she sent him to the infirmary. Kicked him in the groin. She waited for him to stand up straight. When he got his breath, she apologized and kicked him again."

Dove planted his hands on his hips, elbows wide. "Well, I guess he deserved it. Ha! A man asking a woman to the matrimonial bed." He shook with disbelief. "Guess he got tired of snarking. Did she really send him to the doc?"

"You need to get out more Dove. It's the talk of the deck."

"Yeah, well," he gestured to his ship, "got to get the old boy flying again. Haven't really been out at the pubs for all the gossip."

The older man eyed Dove with interest. "Why haven't you made a play for Jeena? I've always thought you were kind of sweet on her. You'd make a great pair. It's not right for a woman to be alone. You'd be a right smart sponsor for her, too. Give her status."

Dove sighed. "No way in hell am I asking like that fool Pendelton." He shook his head, "A man asking a woman to wed is absurd." He waved at the men and they ambled off.

Elise ducked her head back from the doorway as Dove came in. He rubbed his shaved head and the stubble turned a darker shade of black. He smiled and gestured down the hall.

"Sorry, not a lot of space in here. Gotta save it for cargo." Dove directed her into a tiny cabin with a table, two benches, and a dirty countertop. "Thirsty?" He went over to the sink and a hiss of air and foam magically stripped the grease and grime from his hands.

"No, sir," she said.

"You're a really formal one, aren't ya'?" Dove stuck out a hand. "Gabe Doveland Maddus, call me Dove, everyone else does."

She looked at his hand and reached out tentatively to take it. "Elise." His grip was surprisingly gentle.

"Well, it's right nice to meet you Miss Elise." He leaned back, crossed his arms, and puffed out his cheeks. "So, what's a girl like you doing on the deck, dressed in mechanic's blues, with no snarking idea what a k-site is?"

"What is it?" she asked with a sheepish grin.

"Nothing." He pointed a fat finger at her. "But you didn't know that and that's when I knew."

Her shoulders slumped. "Did I stick out that badly?" If she was such an easy mark, she'd never make any headway with her scheme. The Vendel citizens would pluck her out of a crowd with ease. This whole thing was hopeless.

"Yeah. You were attracting stares from some of the pilots. I was relieved when you stopped at my ship." He ran his hands up and down his body. "Despite my looks, I'm a really nice guy."

She laughed. "Well, I give you my thanks." She glanced around the room and compressed her lips and sighed. "I guess I should be going." She paused. "What was it that gave me away?"

"Your hands are tiny, delicate, and clean. Your face is pristine without a smudge or a streak of dirt. And your very lovely hair, which cascades down your back in those beautiful waves of brown, should've been tied up very tight. Mechanics also don't often step so lightly or look around so carefully. I swear it seemed like you were taking mental snapshots to go over later."

That part was true. "Oh." She bit her lower lip in thought.

"So, what brings you down here? Where are ya' from?"

"Hm." Would he buy her story? "Can I have that drink now?"

He laughed. "Sure, tea, coffee, or something stronger?"

"Stronger, what do you have?"

"Good stuff." Dove puttered around in the small space. He brought out a flask and two small shot glasses. The liquid was a fluorescent blue and she eyed it dubiously as he poured.

She stretched out a tentative hand and examined the glowing liquid, arched a brow in question, and brought it to her mouth. He swallowed his drink in one smooth movement, then placed the shot glass on the table and poured himself another drink.

The pungent fumes burned her nostrils, but beneath that an interesting aroma begged to be free. With a toss of her head, the blue liquid poured into her mouth. It burned all the way down and a spasm of coughing kept her sputtering for several minutes. A slight taste of spice and fruit peppered the drink, but it was lost to the burning and the coughing. Her eyes watered and she blinked back moisture.

Dove laughed and refilled the tiny cup. He watched as she regained control of her breathing and then nodded to the glass. "One more, chick-adee, and then we'll talk."

"What the hell is that stuff?" Her heart raced, trying to compensate for the lack of oxygen. She gulped air and soothed the racking coughs. "I think I'll be fine, thank you."

The chair creaked as Dove readjusted his weight. He took a small sip and stared at her with an inquisitive grin and warm eyes.

"I was hoping I'd blend in a bit better. It was really that bad?" She raised the little cup to her mouth and touched her lips to the liquid. The spice aroma was pleasant. She took a tiny sip and let the alcohol percolate in her mouth and nasal passages. The faint fruity aroma was utterly foreign but pleasant.

"Yeah, next time you might want to smudge yourself up better." He sat back and folded his thick arms across an even thicker chest.

"I was looking for the captain of the *Champion's Riot*. I wanted to ask her a few questions, maybe even get some advice."

"Jeena? Now what in the devil's backyard do you need to talk to her about?" Dove eyed her suspiciously.

A knock sounded down the corridor, followed by a lilting female voice. "Dovey? You in here, honey?"

"Damn!" He eyed Elise with caution. "How the hell do you women do it? Is it some form of ESP?"

Elise shrugged and bobbed her head in a what-are-you-talking-about gesture.

He huffed and raised his voice. "Sitting in here, luv, and I got a present for you."

"A present," the feminine voice squealed. "Why Dovey, you shouldn't have…"

A tall, dark haired woman poked her head in the doorway. Her voice fell flat when she saw Elise sitting across from Dove. "Hm, not really what I was expecting." She smiled tentatively at Elise. "You got me a girl? Dovey, we've been snarking long enough for you to know where my tastes lie." She folded her arms across a full chest. The half-zipped red coveralls accentuated an ample cleavage.

"I didn't mean it like that. What's up with your snarks? I hear they're begging to climb into your matrimonial bed."

"Pendelton? He's no longer on my snark list. So, you heard what he did?" Her voice rose with indignation.

"Yes, luv and I heard about your answer." He grinned up at her. "As has everyone on the flight deck, by the way."

Jeena beamed. "You bet. That'll teach him to ask for a marriage oath. You'd think he'd know better."

Dove gave Jeena his seat in the cramped space.

"Jeena, meet Elise. She came looking for you and I scooped her up before any of our fellows did. You saved me the favor of tracking you down. Why are you here, anyway?"

"Aw, luv. I had some free time before my—your—next ferry run." She pulled out a tiny gel pad from her pocket with wires wrapped around it and two gel pads the size of silver dollars.

He glanced at the device with interest and flicked his eyes at Elise.

"What's that?" Elise asked.

Jeena snorted and Dove laughed. His eyes were teary when he answered. "You've got to be kidding, chickadee."

She didn't think it was that funny.

Jeena stopped laughing when she saw the expression of dismay on Elise's face. "You're serious, aren't you kid?"

Elise nodded. Obviously, she'd just made another social snafu.

"You don't have a snark pad?"

Elise shook her head.

"How old are you?" Jeena placed the device on the table.

Elise cursed her ignorance for the fiftieth time that day. "Twenty-one."

"Your ma' never gave you one?"

"My mother is dead," Elise said with a sigh. That part was true.

"So, what about your aunt?"

"Dead." If she counted Elenor as her aunt, that was true as well.

"Grandmother?"

"Dead."

Jeena glanced at her with concern and looked sideways at Dove standing in the doorway. "Do you have any living female relatives?"

"No."

"But you have a paternal sponsor right, or a matrimonial sponsor?" Jeena leaned forward and played with the wires on the snark pad absently.

With Vendel rigid societal roles, Jeena's comment reminded Elise about the patriarchal structure and a woman's place within it. Ties to a male sponsor formed the very foundation of a woman's place within society. As only men could own property and money, women depended on the beneficence of their sponsors. She would keep to the truth as much as she could, but she would have to lie to these strangers.

"No, my father is dead, as is my grandfather," she said.

Dove opened his mouth in an 'O' of understanding.

Jeena perked up as well. "You have no sponsor?"

Elise twisted in her seat. She had Jeena's interest, now to plant the hook. "I was hoping to find a way to—" She took in a deep breath and glanced at each of them in turn before continuing, "Well...I'm trying to find a way off the *Gambit* and I was trying to find a way to do it alone, without a sponsor, on a permanent basis...like you."

Dove whistled.

Jeena narrowed her eyes and tapped her fingers. "And so, you came here looking for advice?"

Elise nodded. "I heard about you and I was hoping..."

Jeena interrupted her words, "Listen, I don't help runaways. I turn in runaways. The Empire doesn't stand for unsponsored women. My situation is entirely unique, and it's only because I keep to the Pilot Conclave regulations that I'm allowed to live the way I do. It's why I can't stand pricks like Pendelton who think I'd let him crawl into my matrimonial bed because I need a snarking sponsor. I like my independence. I'm not going take a husband just to satisfy the male viewpoint. I'm not going to jeopardize my place either because you want to run away. My advice is to run home and pray your sponsor never finds out you were ever here."

Elise's heart sank. She hadn't expected such a negative response. Gregor's face, and his twisted little grin, flashed in her face.

She whispered, "He's an evil bastard and I can't stand to have him touch me."

"So, you do have a sponsor," Dove said. "If you didn't like his affections, why'd you take him to your marriage bed?"

"I'm not married," Elise said in an ominous whisper. She grabbed the forgotten shot and tossed it down her throat. It burned and gagged her, but she refused to give in to a fit of coughing. She stood. "I'm sorry for wasting your time." She shouldered past Dove.

He grabbed her arm. She yanked out of his meaty hands and glared. Dove let go and lifted his hands away, palm out.

"Chickadee, if you're not married and your father's dead, then who is your sponsor and why is he—dear gods—he hasn't taken your nuptial gift has he?"

It was time to pull the proverbial heartstrings and lie. "He's my uncle, and yes, every night, beginning the night my father passed away. I have no snark pad." She waved a hand at the device lying on the table. "He never gave me one."

What the hell is a snark pad?

It was a question she desperately needed answered. From the way they talked about it, it seemed was either a casual game or something more. But then, why would Jeena snark with Pendelton and Dove?

"He's ruined you," Jeena said in a low whisper. "By taking your nuptial gift, you'll never be able to lead a man to your matrimonial bed. The bastard! I bet that's exactly what he's thinking."

She leveled a finger at Dove and shook it. The tone of her voice went from a whisper to a shout. "See, luv, that's exactly what I'm always talking about. This one man has ruined her life. And what's the Empire going to do about it? Nothing. She's tied to this monster. By violating her, he's made sure she's unfit to wed. She's going to be dependent on him for everything. Every breath, every morsel, every drink, every scrap of clothing for the rest of her life. Everything!" Jeena stood and hugged Elise.

She stiffened.

Jeena pulled back and yelled at Dove, "See, she pulls away from a simple hug. I can't even imagine what he's done to you, kid." Jeena stroked her hair. "You poor little thing."

Dove's voice dropped in warning, "Jeena, what are you thinking?"

"I'm gonna help this girl."

"Jeena…" he cautioned.

"Oh, shut up, Dovey," she snapped. "You're gonna help."

Dove groaned, but Elise noted he didn't refuse. She hugged Jeena tightly. "Oh, thank you. Thank you. Thank you! You have no idea what this means to me." She noticed a clock buried in the wall and her face fell. "Listen, I have to get back…before I'm missed—before he finds out I'm gone. Can I come back?"

"Absolutely, kid," Jeena said. "Listen, come back tomorrow after fifth dinner. We'll talk then and start planning."

"I can't come back then," she said with regret. Fifth dinner was the beginning of her day. "I can only come about this time and stay for just a few hours. It's the only time I won't be missed. And even then, it'll only be hit or miss if I can even make it."

That was the truth, she reflected glumly. At some point, she'd have to sleep. She hadn't slept in days and there was no way she'd be able to keep going without sleep.

Jeena released her. "Dear kid, he really has you under his thumb, doesn't he?"

Elise nodded. "You have no idea how he runs my life." A smile twisted on her lips.

"Hm, no doubt the better to control you. Well, we'll just wait. If I'm not at my ship just come over here to Dovey's. He's not likely to get this spider-plagued, dump bucket running before we get to Malbra. We'll figure out something."

"What exactly are you promising, luv?" Dove's words grated.

Jeena pushed Elise to the side and squeezed around her to stand in front of Dove. She pinched his meaty cheeks with her fingers and planted a kiss on his lips. "I'm promising to never, ever, let another man think to lead me to my matrimonial bed." He wrapped his arms around her and kissed her back.

Dove leaned back. "And what if a man were to *suggest*? You could start using his given name, for a change."

Jeena kissed his nose. "Why Dovey, I'd kick such a man in the nuts and take him off my snarking list."

"Humph, would it really be so bad?"

"For me luv, it would be death." She ran a hand over his bald head and grimaced at the grease stain left on her hand. With an irritated sigh, she wiped her hand on his chest. "I like it the way it is, don't try to take that from me, Dovey. It is what it is, and I am what I am. I'm perfectly content to keep it that way. If you want a wife, you've had—still have—plenty of offers."

He rubbed his neck. "No, I'm good."

Dove jerked his chin at Elise, who'd been standing neglected and trapped inside the little room, watching what appeared to be a very odd lover's quarrel. He backed out of the door. "Go on little Chickadee, looks like your little foray to the flight deck has brought you luck." He rubbed his fingers on his pants and then rubbed the grease on her chin and cheek. "There, now you don't look so out of place. Tie your hair up, make it look messy, and get your pretty behind back to where you came."

She gave him a huge smile. "Thank you." On the way back to the Confinement Deck, her steps felt a little lighter.

266

CHAPTER TWENTY-FOUR_

Gambit, Day 141

THE NEXT MORNING ELISE WOKE TO AGONY. SEARING PAIN FLASHED ACROSS her back and then again on her legs. Attempts to twist away failed and she found herself yanked back to her stomach. Strong arms held her shoulders down. Two hands pinned her legs to the bed. She screamed as the all too familiar sting of the whipstick bit into her flesh.

Ragged sobs fell on disinterested ears. Tears soaked into her mattress, useless and impotent against the men who restrained her in bed.

Heavy booted steps, a particular sound she knew all too well, approached after the last lash had been dealt and announced the arrival of her Tender.

"What is going on?" High Tender Marcus asked with a hint of amusement edging his voice. How she hated his callous disregard.

"My lord, this one missed the morning bell." That voice belonged to wor-guard Lewsik. One of the supervisors known for a particularly strong arm. "10-4 brought it to our attention."

Sarah, that brown-nose bitch! Elise fisted the covers of her bed.

"Well, that's disappointing," High Tender Marcus said with a deep breath and slow exhale. "Give her an additional ten. The Emperor's s'vlor needs to set a better example. When you're done, bring her to me in the Fifth Rank classroom."

The WOR-guards held her down while Lewsik administered the additional lashes.

This hurts!

Screams spilled out of her lungs to merge with ineffectual tears. When it was done, they dragged her off the bed and escorted her to the showers. She could barely stand. That didn't deter the WOR-guards from their task. They stripped her naked and thrust her under the cold stream.

Stop it!

Did she say that or think it? She didn't know.

Water pelted over her head. "Stop! Oh my God." This time she knew she had said the words, but the plea fell on deaf ears as Lewsik attended to her the way a trainer would a dog. He lathered up a bristle brush and scraped her skin clean.

He tossed her a towel. "The gods won't help you, 10-2. You know the rules." There was no compassion in the set of his square jaw. His expression was as hard and unyielding as the bulging muscles of his body.

"Yes, sir." She choked out the words in-between sobs and managed to get the scarlet dress over her head on the second try. The small chain belt fastened on her third attempt. They marched her past the dining hall without stopping and deposited her in the classroom.

High Tender Marcus stood at the far end of the room examining the wall. He wore his usual brown jumpsuit, a darker shade than any other Tender she had seen, and glanced her way. A frown filled his face and his short haircut, which failed to cover a growing bald spot on his head, did an even poorer job of concealing the anger in his face. That combined with his coal dark eyes made her shake as Lewsik deposited her at the door.

"Thank you. That'll be all." The High Tender dismissed the men with a wave of his hand. He turned back to his inspection of the wall.

"High Tender, please forgive me." She found herself halfway to a curtsey before she realized he wasn't paying her any attention. She glanced around, unsure what was expected.

He turned and met her growing fear with narrowed eyes. They glittered like coal, devoured the light, and sucked the air out of her lungs. "You are not just s'vlor, not just s'vlor of the Fifth Rank. You are the Emperor's s'vlor. Your actions reflect on him."

"Yes, High Tender," she whispered.

He walked up to her with his hands clasped behind his back. She couldn't see his braklav, but imagined him fingering it in his palm. "I don't think you grasp what I'm trying to say. Your performance yesterday during WOR-skill training was much less than hoped for."

"I will try harder." She held her hands together, wringing her fingers, because she didn't know what he was getting at. From the glint in his eyes he had something definite to say.

"I'm curious, what did you think about yesterday's session?"

"I found it confusing."

"Interesting for someone of your intellect, and especially considering that you've touched the WOR-skill before. I would think training would come naturally. Which makes me believe you are intentionally holding back." The High Tender's eyes blinked with deliberate slowness. His voice lowered and turned menacing. "It wouldn't do for you to hold back. That's one thing I will not tolerate and let me remind you—you don't want to make me upset." The dark brown eyes of the High Tender narrowed to thin slits and she felt the temperature of the room drop to an arctic freeze.

She shuddered. "No, High Tender, I swear I tried very hard." She took two steps back without even realizing what she was doing.

He released his hands and the braklav came forward, twirling with menace. "I'm to believe you?" He took a step toward her.

"Yes," she said. Her heart beat wildly as adrenaline raced around her body, making her tremble. The instinct to flee overwhelmed her senses, but to run from this man was certain invitation to the administrations of the braklav.

"Explain then, opés," Gregor said from behind her, "why there are four little holes in the far wall."

Elise spun, heart racing. The looming shape of the emperor filled the doorway. He wore his black jumpsuit with the silver detailing and the knee-high boots. He held his arms crossed over his chest, looking impossibly handsome, and yet she cringed, hunching in on herself and even taking a step back toward the High Tender and the braklav. The thick muscles of Gregor's biceps twitched. His silvery eyes flashed with displeasure as the swirly black tattoo over his brow writhed with fury.

She froze. Her eyes flicked between the two imposing men. High Tender Marcus held the braklav. Gregor's stare held an even greater threat, made all the more imposing by the casual way he held his head cocked to the side.

She swallowed. "Gregor." It came out as a squeak.

The High Tender frowned and advanced.

She shifted her attention to High Tender Marcus.

"The emperor has asked a question," he said.

"I can't," she said.

"You can't? In that you are unable or unwilling to answer?" Gregor said.

I must have left holes in the wall.

"I'm...unable, Gregor," she said cautiously.

His brows drew down, displeased. "Answer me—yes or no—the fact there are four holes in the wall over there, far away from our table..." He jerked his chin toward the opposite wall. "Is this, or is it not, a surprise to you?"

"Yes, Gregor. I mean no." She scratched her head at the double negative. "I mean yes, it is a surprise."

"You think we're fools!" The High Tender's face turned red. The braklav became a blur in his hand and then she felt it against her throat. "S'vlor, I suggest you explain."

"I'm not lying! I didn't know the holes were still there." *Oh shit.* She hadn't meant to say it like that.

Gregor's lips twisted. "Now that is even more interesting. So, what did you think had happened to the holes?"

"Sire, this is ridiculous." High Tender Marcus pressed the braklav to her neck, but she did not yet feel its sting. He grabbed her wrist.

She flinched. Her eyes locked on to his.

The emperor held up a hand, as if telling the High Tender to hold still. He looked to the far wall and brought his hand to his chin, rubbing his lower lip with his finger. "No, I think she's telling the truth." Gregor shook his head. His eyes narrowed and his voice dropped the temperature in the room to just below dead cold. "It's what she is not saying that is the lie."

"Perhaps a touch of the braklav will loosen her tongue," the High Tender said.

"Please, High Tender Marcus, no," she whispered.

Gregor raised his hand, halting the High Tender. "Opés, sit down." He gestured to one of the chairs. "Tell me about the holes in the wall and maybe things will go easier for you."

Maybe? She collapsed into the nearest chair, grateful not to have fallen to the floor. High Tender Marcus released her wrist and the braklav no longer threatened her neck. She glanced at Gregor. He motioned with his hand for her to breathe in and out.

One breath shuddered into her body. Another followed.

Gregor and the High Tender pulled up chairs to face her. Gregor straddled his backward and rested his chin on the backrest. The High Tender sat with his legs crossed, knee and elbows spread wide. He twirled the braklav.

"I just wanted to see if I could do it my way."

High Tender Marcus snorted. "Your way? What can you possibly know about the WOR-skill?"

"This system you're teaching is wrong. You have all these steps—technical and perhaps correct—but as a whole, wrong. I can't follow it. It's like when my brother-in-law tried to teach me to juggle. I could toss one ball in the air and even two. But when he added three to the mix...his instructions just made me fumble all three balls. I couldn't even keep one in the air."

"What does any of this have to do with the emperor's question?" the High Tender asked. As he leaned toward her, she pulled back.

"He gave up on me. I got so mad at him. I picked up the balls and tossed them in the air. I don't even know when I started juggling. It just happened all by itself."

"Get to the point. Cute story but irrelevant." The set to Gregor's jaw told her she was in trouble.

She implored him with her eyes wide, hoping he would understand, praying he would forgive, but knowing he could not. "Yesterday, everyone got those little balls to move. Me? Nothing. Over and over, you took me through that complex pattern. And I tried. I really tried to please you. I followed up to a point and then I just lost it...all of it. I couldn't keep it together. I'd get to the same point and it'd unravel. It reminded me of juggling and I got mad. So, when you left, I wanted to try it my way. I didn't mean for it to happen and was really surprised when the balls flew across the room. Then I got scared and wished the balls back on the table, and there they were. I didn't know they had left holes in the wall."

Gregor stood and kicked the chair to the side. He swooped down to within inches of her face. She recoiled at the expression of fury in his face. His strong hand gripped her hair and held her head back.

"You should have told High Tender vlor'Martun immediately!" He released her and loomed over her. Darkness filled his face. "I thought you agreed to work with me, Elise. You promised and you lied. High Tender, she is yours." Disappointment hung heavy in his voice. "It's time you learned what obedience means."

"Please, Gregor, I'm sorry." Her gut clenched. "I'm so sorry." She jumped up and grabbed his shirt.

He pried her fingers off his shirt, practically throwing her at the High Tender, then he stalked out of the room without a backward glance.

The High Tender grabbed her. The braklav twirled and snapped into his palm. She tried to crawl back over the table but he connected the braklav to her throat and sent her into oblivion with a flare of agony.

CHAPTER TWENTY-FIVE_

Gambit, Day 141

SHE CAME BACK TO CONSCIOUSNESS IN A SMALL SQUARE ROOM. HER WRISTS were bound and suspended above her head. There was one other thing. She was naked.

"You're in one of the private lesson chambers in the Confinement Deck." The soft voice of High Tender Marcus spoke from across the room.

She searched for him.

He leaned against the far wall, arms and legs crossed, watching.

"High Tender, please forgive me." Her breaths came in erratic bursts.

"This is a formal training session." He watched carefully.

Her heart fluttered, but she understood and used the formal address. "My lord, High Tender Marcus, please forgive me."

"Oh, I forgive you. This training has been directed by the Emperor. I intend to carry out his command. Your behavior was unfortunate, and I've been instructed to make sure it never happens again."

"I promise." She begged. "Please, High Tender Marcus, I won't—"

"Silence!"

Her pleas died in her throat.

"I've been given an entire cycle to educate you. Welcome to Tender Training." He stepped away from the wall, twirling the braklav in his hand. "For the next ten days, from noon until two, you will report here. You'll remove your clothes and step to the center of the room where you'll

273

apply the restraints and wait for my arrival. You will not speak. If you say anything, beg for this to stop, I will add an additional day. Is this unclear in any way?"

She whispered, "High Tender Marcus, I understand."

"Good, then let's begin. Let me introduce you to the braklav. You've only tasted a fraction of what it can do."

The powerful man set to her body with deliberate purpose. The braklav traced each nerve in her body. Dull pain first. Low and intense, she rocked in agony. Sharp pain made her gasp for breath. Hot and cold, he scalded and froze her body.

Each time she heard his voice, he gave her time to digest the newest sensation lined up. Before the first ten minutes passed, his voice alone made her tremble in fear.

Sweat poured off her body. Her lips dried and cracked as she panted against the pain.

His attention turned to her muscles. The High Tender began at her neck and worked his way down, activating each muscle and forcing it to react. She cried out in anguish as her muscles convulsed.

He pressed the rod to her arm and traced it up to her shackled fingers. The cramps he caused left her whimpering but he did not allow her rest. He moved to her chest, ribs, belly, and lower still. Working like a talented musician he played her like a fine instrument, continuing down her body as his monologue continued. She knew exactly what he was going to do before the braklav graced her skin.

The braklav could shock, he explained. He turned his administrations back to her nerves. These he lit with wild flashes of pain and followed with a low buzzing just at the threshold of her sensory perception. He held the braklav as the intensity built, until she shook with anticipation of more agony to come, and then he let it all loose in one firestorm of lightning and anguish.

"Please, please, High Tender Marcus, please," she sobbed, "please stop. I'm so sorry. So sorry." She choked out the words and he stopped. Elise breathed with relief. She had made it through the first session.

"Your first day is finished, s'vlor," the High Tender said.

"Yes, High Tender Marcus," she said. Each breath came with heart stopping agony.

The High Tender undid the restraints and her arms fell lifeless to her sides. She wobbled and her legs gave way as she collapsed to the ground.

"You have ten more days," he said.

"Nine, only nine," she croaked.

"Right, nine... plus one. My instructions were clear. You were not permitted to speak or beg for this to stop."

She groaned and hugged her body, then rocked on the ground, choking out sobs.

"Your bed has been set apart from the others. During Tender Training your mind will be focused on Emperor Gregor vlor'Malita. His desire will become yours. His wish will be yours. His happiness will become your driving force. Until he is satisfied, I will continue. You may not speak to any WOR. You will eat alone, dress alone, work out alone. Your classes are suspended. Emperor vlor'Malita and I will meet with you in the mornings where you will train in WOR-skill. You know where you'll be for the middle hours of the day. In the afternoon, the Emperor will rejoin us for more WOR-skill training. I suggest you consider how to impress him."

It took two breaths before she could squeak out the appropriate address. "Yes, High Tender Marcus."

He threw her dress at her. "Get dressed. Don't be late." High Tender Marcus turned on his heels and left. His thick booted steps echoed through the door, leaving a memory etched forever in her mind.

How will I ever survive ten more days of this?

She made it two days before darkness filled her world.

CHAPTER TWENTY-SIX_

Gambit, Day 143

ELISE WOKE TO FIND HERSELF IN A STERILE WHITE ROOM, ALL HARD EDGES AND glaring lights. The light hurt her eyes. A sheet covered her body and a thin pillow rested beneath her head. Ghost pains rattled around her body and shot from limb to limb. She wanted to move, but her body protested and refused.

"Emperor vlor'Malita, she is waking up." A woman's voice, low and soft, radiated a tenderness Elise hadn't heard in a very long time. A shadow passed over her bed, followed by cold fingertips lifting her eyelid and a very bright light shining in her eye.

"How is she?" Gregor hovered at the foot of the bed.

Elise knew it was him, could feel his presence even with her eyes closed. The bright light moved to her other eye.

"Pupils reactive, her vital signs are stable," the soft voice said.

"What happened?" Gregor demanded. "Why did she collapse?"

"This wasn't from the braklav, my lord. She collapsed from exhaustion."

"Her training is no more or less rigorous than the others. In fact, she's in better condition than most." The bed shifted as he leaned against it.

"Perhaps."

"How much longer will we need to keep her in the infirmary? I need to get her back to the Confinement Deck and her training."

"You can take her back now."

Elise groaned. Her lids fluttered open and she sank into the warm caring eyes of a tall, thin woman with shoulder length brown hair. The woman's face disappeared to be replaced by Gregor's and the swirling dark tattoo. Elise shut her eyes and said silent prayer for strength.

"Come, opés."

"It may be a little while longer before she has the strength to stand or walk." The woman urged caution.

Elise tried to sit.

The woman helped. She lifted Elise's legs and swung them around to dangle over the edge of the bed. Her legs felt like leaden weights and her arms were no better. Little tremors made all of her limbs quiver.

Gregor lifted her off the table and deposited her on her feet.

She fell.

He caught her and lifted her into his arms.

"Perhaps, she should stay here a little longer, my lord," the doctor urged.

"You said this was not from the braklav?" Gregor shifted her weight.

"Correct," the doctor said.

"She is otherwise fine?"

"Yes, my lord," the doctor said. Her voice was laced with concern, but she didn't argue.

"Very well. I'll carry her back."

"As you wish, my lord. I would urge you to lighten up on her physical demands. It will take a day or two for her body to recover."

"I hear you. Her physical demands will be light. But I need her back in training."

The doctor walked to the door and it opened with a low swoosh. Gregor carried Elise down sterile white corridors and back to the Confinement Deck. He didn't take her to her bed, but continued down the center of the Confinement Deck, past the classrooms and the exercise field. She rocked in and out of awareness. Her mind drifted and her body hung in his solid grip. Gregor brought her to a small room. Her lids fluttered and she choked back a sob.

He deposited her in the middle of the floor and held her upright by her hands. Shackles snapped around her wrists.

She stared at his broad chest and blinked back the beginnings of tears. *You couldn't possibly have brought me back here. I thought you cared for me.*

Her gaze wandered up to his neck and, finally, meandered to his eyes. Hardened steel greeted her and he compressed his lips. Her eyes slipped past his into an unfocused oblivion. His thick scent of musk and spice filled her nostrils. He released her and she sagged against the restraints. Thick booted steps sounded from behind. No need to see. That sound was ingrained in her mind. High Tender Marcus had arrived.

His deep voice rumbled through the room. "Has she been released from the infirmary?"

"Yes. The doctor said her collapse wasn't from the braklav, but rather from exhaustion or stress. You may proceed."

Her head sagged forward and she choked back a sob. *You're monsters.*

Gregor put a hand around her throat and lifted her chin up. He leaned down and planted a brief kiss on her lips. "You cannot escape Tender Training. I told you, we would do this one way or the other. You chose the hard way. Collapse again and I will leave you hanging."

"Gregor—"

He gripped her chin. "You were warned not to beg."

A sniffle. "I only wanted to say…I'm sorry."

He released her chin and traced a line down her throat with the back of his fingers, an intense look spread across his features, then hardness fell once again. "High Tender, see that she makes it to the classroom. If she needs to be dragged, have the WOR-guards do it."

"As you wish."

Gregor walked away, leaving her and High Tender Marcus alone.

I felt nothing when you kissed me. Nothing.

The braklav held so much pain.

I can't survive the braklav's kiss. There's no reason to even try, but that doesn't mean you've won. I'm going to disappear and endure.

She wrapped everything important about herself into a tight little ball and compressed it. Her thoughts, feelings, desires, plans, and hopes for escape vanished as she banished that part of herself into darkness.

As the braklav touched her body, what was left of her mind splintered. *I can't fight your braklav, High Tender. So take everything. When you're done, I'll still be here, hiding in the cracks of what's left behind.*

He stepped behind her and said, "Day four, shall we begin?"

She shuddered and gave a nod, remembering not to speak.

In that moment, as Elise faded into oblivion, the braklav brought forth new voices. Shriek and Whimper stepped into the light, stretching into existence from the ravaged remnants of Elise's mind. Shriek took the pain. Whimper submitted. Elise no longer cared what happened to the body. It was merely a burden to her consciousness. She stepped back while Shriek gloried in agony and Whimper yielded to the High Tender's demands.

Days passed.

WOR-skill training called forth Elise from the blackness for morning and afternoon sessions. She studied and applied herself to learn, only to fade into the background during Tender Training. That time was for Shriek and Whimper to endure. They shielded and protected her from the High Tender. They took the pain and bent to High Tender Marcus's will.

Gregor took Elise through WOR-skill practice one painful step at a time. She feared failing him, and begged Shriek and Whimper to step in, but her new sisters refused. They feared Gregor. WOR-skill training belonged to Elise and Gregor. Tender Training belonged to the Master High Tender, Shriek, and Whimper.

Shriek howled and screamed at the many torments inflicted by the braklav. Whimper cried while the High Tender detailed the next round of instruction. Her sisters insulated Elise from the worst of Tender Training, but it soon became too much for even them to bear. By the seventh day a new voice cackled in the darkness. Malice joined the wreckage of Elise's mind and called for the High Tender's blood.

High Tender Marcus's true skill was in how he habituated their responses to the braklav. Whimper developed a reflexive desire to please. Shriek endured what they could not. Malice muttered, cursed, and planned.

Elise wanted it all to stop, desperate to plead with Gregor, but Malice bullied her into the background when the urge to beg became overwhelming. At night, Elise huddled in her bed, choking back sobs. The High Tender and the twirling rod dominated her dreams.

On day ten, the High Tender raised the braklav to within an inch of her belly and, with only a gesture, kept Shriek writhing for minutes.

Elise watched from the darkness and despaired.

The expression on his sadistic face was one she would never forget. He'd won.

It was a smugness Malice planned to destroy. She turned to Elise. *So, what do you plan to do, my sister? So far you have accomplished nothing!*

I don't know, she answered.

What about Jenna?

What about her? Elise asked.

Malice chuckled. *We need a way to be free of them.*

I was working on it, but now I don't know.

You cannot give up!

Malice forced Elise to take in everything she'd endured. Malice's rage fueled Elise's determination. She would not let the Vendel win.

Her fingers curled to make fists.

I have to get back to the flight deck.

Then I suggest you find a way to please these men.

Elise vowed to do exactly that.

Whatever it takes, I will please them.

She had a plan.

———

THIS IS NOT THE END!

VENDEL RISING: VOLUME 3
THE PRICE OF POWER
is next!

Follow Elise's journey with the Vendel as she seeks her revenge.

Grab your copy now!

THE PRICE OF POWER

VOLUME 3

PART ONE_

PROLOGUE_

New Terra Histories by Malita s'Lissa s'vlor

If someone thinks they are crazy, are they? I have no answer. But perhaps, it is only when someone stops asking that they truly are insane.

JULY 4, 2136

The braklav defeated me.

It transformed me.

The High Tender molded me to obey him and serve Gregor, my master, Emperor of the Vendel, and my enemy. I did whatever it took to please Gregor and endure my High Tender's wrath.

The birth of my strange sisters, *Whimper*, *Shriek*, and *Malice* gave me strength. When my trials became too much to bear, my sisters protected and sheltered me.

They suffered so I might survive.

They broke so that I did not.

They gave me strength when I was at my weakest.

They endured so that I might one day fight.

In breaking me, the High Tender gave me the means to defeat him, but that is another story.

I want to tell you how I met my new friends, because that is a story of legend...

CHAPTER ONE_

Gambit, Day 150

ELISE COMWELL AWOKE STIFF AND SORE, BUT WORSE WAS SOON TO HAPPEN. She had committed a great sin by sleeping through the awakening bell.

Again.

She had also missed her mandatory morning workout.

Damn! Alice would've been waiting. I need her.

Elise curled into a fetal ball, but it didn't help. Alice was the only reason she made it through each day.

What am I going to do now?

Today promised to be the last day of braklav torture. Over the past cycle, Alice had run a discrete distance ahead and encouraged Elise to press on despite the pain, not to mention what was happening to her mind.

While Shriek and Whimper took control during Tender Training, only Alice could coax Elise out of the darkness following it.

Not only had Elise missed her brief meeting with her friend, she had racked up an infraction with the WOR-guards. The braklav was an instrument of torture that left no marks, the whipstick wounded fragile flesh. There was no escaping the brutality of the Vendel.

A brief shower did nothing to ease the kinks in her muscles. Aware of the time, and the inevitable encounter with a WOR-guard, the hot water only made her muscles clench with anticipation of the lashes to come. She toweled herself dry, padded to her bench, and dressed.

Dead woman walking.

You're being overly melodramatic, Malice yawned. *We're not dead yet.*

Shut up, Malice! Shriek called out from the corners of her mind. *She's not as strong as you.*

Is that what you think? Malice cackled.

I'm falling apart, Malice. They're winning.

You're wrong, my sister, Malice muttered.

Tender Training drew interest from everyone. The WOR-guards scrutinized her every move. What they looked for she had no idea. The other women hovered at a distance and watched for signs of defeat to creep in, perhaps terrified that Elise would cave against the pressure of Tender Training.

You're their hero, Malice said.

I know, but I'm losing the war.

Your code keeps them together and reminds them they are human. Not slaves. The Vendel dehumanized you. They assigned you numbers, but you gave them back their names. If you give in, what hope do any of them have to resist? Malice's voice dripped with venom, the threat in her words clear. *You cannot give up!*

I know! I'm trying.

You're letting them win!

Leave me alone.

No. You can't afford to be weak.

I'm tired, Malice. I'm tired of fighting. It is hopeless.

You don't have a choice, Malice hissed. *You must win.*

I can't do that when everyone is watching me so closely. I can barely breathe!

Then become invisible again, sister. You must bend beneath their strength. Remember the willow? Bend against this storm. Give them what they want. Surrender, so that we can win.

Will the WOR understand my surrender?

They must. You are their leader. Tell Alice. She will explain.

Elise took a deep breath, held it, and slowly blew it out. It helped to steady her for what was needed.

Surrender stared at her with the weight of ponderous judgement, but it would only be a temporary capitulation. She only needed a short respite. Maybe.

Shriek? Whimper? she called out to her other sisters, the two who endured torment and pain. *Give me one more day, only two more hours and I promise to let you rest.*

Shriek shuddered and Whimper cried, but they agreed as she explained what she planned.

With her shoulders pushed back and her spine as straight as she could make it, she marched out of the bathhouse and approached the first WOR-guard she could find.

"Sir, I must report an infraction."

Elise wasn't allowed to speak to the other women, but she hadn't been forbidden from addressing the WOR-guard. Up until now, she chose to ignore them. Seeking one out would trip all kinds of speculation.

The alerted WOR-guard scrunched his face.

She took a deep breath and hung her head. "I slept through the awakening bell, missed my exercise routine, and didn't make first breakfast." She kept her voice contrite and stared at the large man's chest, refusing to meet his eyes.

"Excuse me?" His brow arched, confused by her report. "You did?"

It was difficult not to smile at his confusion. No one self-reported to a WOR-guard, not when it resulted in a session with a whipstick.

"High Tender Marcus has instilled in me that my actions reflect on Gregor. I wish to please him and failed. I deserve correction."

The man didn't answer, but his knitted brows and his pursed lips told her everything she needed to know.

She continued in a rush, struggling to get her words out before he could come to a decision. "I'll tell him myself later during Tender Training. I just thought it would please Gregor if I came forward on my own and accepted the consequences for failing to follow the rules."

"10-2, each infraction is punishable by ten lashes."

"Yes, sir." This was the price to be paid to be meek. Malice told her to bend. Well, she would bend beneath the whipstick. A harsh implement, but the whipstick couldn't break her like the braklav. She would endure.

"I can't administer that many at one time," he explained.

Her eyes lit up at his dilemma.

The man tapped his wrist device and spoke into it. Within a few minutes, a small group of WOR-guards surrounded them.

"What's going on here?" a second WOR-guard demanded.

"She's admitted to three separate infractions." The first WOR-guard snapped to attention.

"She reported herself?" The second WOR-guard lifted his brows. Disbelief edged his voice.

"Yes, sir. I can't administer thirty lashes at once." The first one ran a shaky hand over his head. He eyed her nervously. "I can't ignore it either."

The second WOR-guard glanced at Elise. "You didn't have to report this, 10-2. Explain."

The command in his voice made her jump. "Sir, I've spent the last ten days with High Tender Marcus in Tender Training." She paused as they exchanged knowing glances. All these men knew what she'd been subjected to. "I could've kept silent, but that would've made Gregor mad. I want to make him proud. I need to." Elise was surprised at how convincing the words actually sounded. By the looks on their faces, they bought it. "I hope to show him I've learned not to hide my mistakes."

The second WOR-guard paused to consider. He tapped a finger on his chin and then turned to the first. "Administer twenty lashes and suspend the rest."

The first WOR-guard looked relieved.

Elise swallowed her revulsion as she willingly knelt to accept the twenty lashes from a whipstick.

Step aside, sister, Shriek said. *I will bear this.*

Elise felt guilty allowing Shriek to bear this burden, but Whimper pulled Elise to the side.

This is Shriek's strength, Whimper whispered. *We shoulder the burden together sister. It's how we survive. Let Shriek do her part.*

The WOR-guard's arm drew back. Elise turned away and headed to the darkness of her mind where Whimper joined her. Shriek took control of their body and absorbed the pain. After the last lash, Shriek crawled into a corner, trembling.

Thank you, Shriek. Elise resumed her place while Whimper turned to comfort Shriek.

The WOR-guards put their heads together and whispered as they departed. "Can you believe what he's accomplished?"

"That's why he's the Master Tender. She was worried about displeasing him. Bless the empire, but the emperor is going to be relieved when he hears of this. Make sure the emperor is informed about what happened here."

"Yes, sir!"

That's the point boys. Spread the word. Little 10-2 has caved. I am the willow. I will bend. And when it's over, when ruin and devastation surround me, I will stand unbroken and whole.

Tinkling laughter filled her mind as Malice approved.

The touch of the whipstick left her back aflame. Shriek endured the

292

agony of the lashes but the residual pain would be hers to deal with until it eased.

It was time to meet Gregor and the High Tender for WOR-skill training. A new hurdle loomed.

The High Tender would need to be convinced with her capitulation. Whimper had already laid down the foundation from previous sessions, but he would test it again. Which meant Shriek was not yet done.

Gregor would be next. He'd be easier. Or at least, Elise hoped that would be the case. His cool detachment that had begun with the onset of Tender Training worried her, because he hadn't touched her since it started. The heat between them had vanished. That electric charge had fizzled and faded away.

It was time to bring back that spark.

Elise walked into the classroom that the High Tender and Gregor had appropriated for their morning drills. High Tender Marcus sat at one of the round tables while Gregor paced. He stopped short at her entrance.

"You're late." The aggravation in his voice was a bad sign.

She dipped her head in acknowledgment. "Forgive me, Gregor. Good morning." The High Tender greeted her with suspicious eyes. "Good morning, High Tender."

"Good morning, s'vlor."

Not once had the High Tender used her name, whether as Elise or as the annoying 10-2. To him, she was nothing more than an object. His patronizing, cool tone held the barest hint of question though. She wondered if he had heard about her encounter with the WOR-guards.

Elise fought the urge to respond. Whimper demanded she answer the High Tender's unasked question. She ignored Whimper with great difficulty. It was a dangerous step, but calculated. Her quarry was a different man.

She stepped to Gregor and bowed her head in acquiescence. "I overslept."

Gregor stiffened.

She glanced at the High Tender and continued before either could speak. "I reported myself to the WOR-guards and they administered correction. I told them I would let you know."

"You did?" High Tender Marcus stood and came toward her. The braklav twirled in his hand.

Gregor held up his hand to halt the High Tender. "You reported yourself?"

"Yes, Gregor." Elise kept her eyes focused on his boots and crossed her hands to the front in supplication. "I earned thirty lashes for everything. They delivered twenty."

Gregor said nothing, but made a gesture for her to spin around. She complied and jumped when his hand brushed her back and his fingers traced the lines of twenty lash marks. She dared not move and held her breath.

He moved the hair away from her neck and traced his finger along the curve of her jaw. It was the first intimate touch since Tender Training had begun.

"Today is your last session with Lord vlor'Vardhal. Tell me, opés, what have you learned?"

Whimper screamed.

Shriek crumbled.

Malice hissed.

Elise struggled to hold them together. The path to invisibility had never felt so uncertain. She had to make this work.

Turning, she clutched at his shirt. Tears streamed down her face and her body shook. "Gregor, I will please you."

How much of this is really an act? Malice giggled. *You're convincing even me.*

She managed to choke out the words. "Please forgive me, Gregor."

She collapsed against him. Ten days of torture, and the disgust at being beaten by the High Tender, broke upon Gregor's solid chest. Elise poured everything into that moment and clung to him for forgiveness, for strength, for absolution.

Please, believe this. God, I almost believe it!

His body went rigid. Had the cruel emperor become resistant to her surrender? The unmoving wall made her heart lurch.

It's not working! Shriek screamed.

Elise sniffed back her tears and wiped her face with her hand. Her hands clutched his shirt and she lifted her head.

She whispered, "I'm sorry. I will make you proud, I promise." She averted her eyes with the smallest bit of submission.

He held perfectly still, implacable, solid granite resisting her efforts to erode his stony exterior. Like the wind upon the rocks, this mountain did not move.

Elise let go in failure. This passionate man had withdrawn from her completely. It was imperative that she make him see her as human—desirable—and she was failing. The first rule of warfare was to dehumanize your enemy; because it was easier to destroy an object than a person. He'd destroyed his little opés. But could he destroy a lover?

If he trusted her, he might remove the extra WOR-guard patrol that kept her prisoner. Until they were gone she had no hope of returning back to Jeena and the flight deck where her hopes for escape rested.

Elise stepped away, defeated.

Gregor's strong hand encased her wrist in a grip of steel, and it trembled. "High Tender vlor'Vardhal…"

"My lord," the High Tender said.

Gregor's breath came in a throaty whisper. "Leave…now." The command in his voice was unmistakable and unarguable.

High Tender Marcus stood and, without a word, strode from the room. He shut the door with a thud on his way out, leaving his silent disapproval to hang heavily in the air.

Elise closed her eyes in victory.

With a yank on her arm, Gregor spun her around. She let him enfold her in his arms.

His hand lifted her chin. "I desire you more than you can know. Tender Training is difficult, but in your case vital. Are you ready, Elise? Are you ready to be mine?"

He used my name!

Malice cackled.

"Yes, Gregor. I'll be the best s'vlor you can imagine."

"You do not hold the Tender Training against me then, opés?"

She pulled him close. "I understand why it was necessary. It was wrong of me to hide anything from you."

Gregor leaned down and kissed her. It started slow but deepened quickly, stealing both their breaths.

Malice snickered.

Elise allowed her tongue to tangle with his, showing the depth of her enthusiasm. It wasn't hard. Gregor was an amazing kisser.

Gregor's throaty laugh was music in her ears. He pulled her tight. "Hm, this is nice, opés. I have missed our kisses."

She pressed her body against his. "I thought with Tender Training you no longer wanted me."

"No, that is not true." He stole kisses. "I was angry, but my interest has not changed, only intensified. Tender Training has a way of teaching certain things that are not easily forgotten. I have been impatient for this cycle to end and see what changes Tender Training have made."

"Let me show you what I've learned." She ran her hands down his chest and tugged at his shirt, pulling it free so she could touch his bare skin.

Emperor Gregor vlor'Malita reacted to her touch, gasping as she raked her nails against his flesh.

She reveled in her victory and sent the reluctant Malice back into the dark to wait with Shriek and Whimper. *Later girls, I'll let you come out to play later. But this—this—is all mine.*

She threw everything she could at him. His granite exterior softened to her touch until he became putty in her hands.

He kept her in the classroom the entire morning and cancelled the last Tender Training session.

Shriek and Whimper did not need to come back out and play. Elise tucked them away with a prayer of thanks. They were an integral part of her now, a permanent effect of Tender Training. Each had done her part and it was time to let them rest. When they were needed again, they would be ready.

Elise found enthusiasm to return Gregor's affections. She tested his oath with every trick she knew and left him gasping for breath more times than she could count. It was time for the hairs on his arms to stand on end. Her excitement left Gregor speechless as she planted kisses down his bare flesh. He barely kept his oath not to take her to bed.

CHAPTER TWO_

FIVE HOURS LATER, ELISE WAITED IN LINE FOR DINNER. SWEAT SOAKED INTO the welts on her back, making her skin sting. It seemed days ago that the WOR-guards had used the whipstick, when it had only been early that morning.

Her eyes closed of their own accord. She wobbled and would have fallen if not for a firm hand gripping her elbow. She blinked and regained her balance. Alice and Aomi gave supportive smiles, but concern pinched in their eyes.

Over? Aomi tapped.

Elise nodded.

Aomi sighed with relief. *Worried 4 U.*

Alice squeezed Elise's and tapped. *How R U? Tender Training?*

Bad.

I'm sorry.

Elise moved forward with the line. She tapped a private message to Alice in their super-secret personal code. *I need a favor.*

Anything.

Draw the WOR-guards off me tonight.

Alice filled her plate with salad and raised an inquisitive eyebrow.

Trust me. Elise pursed her lips.

Alice did not reply. They finished piling their plates with food and sat down at a table. Aomi and Chandra join them. It had been a concession of Gregor's to allow her to mingle with the other women again.

The women chatted using the code, otherwise keeping silent to avoid punishment by the WOR-guards. They avoided questions about Elise and the braklav. Talk revolved around WOR-skill training and their accomplishments. Over the course of the meal, they filled Elise in on the major happenings over the past ten days.

The most important news: their vlor' lords had been chosen. Alice had been matched with Lord Edgard vlor'Calcask as predicted. Aomi had been paired with High Councilor, Lord Talen vlor'Adreti. Elise recognized the name. He'd been one of the men who'd attended the welcome banquet at the GC Social Headquarter's building. Lord Valerius vlor'Damius would claim Chandra.

Are these okay? Elise asked the girls.

Edgard has been helpful. Hell, I've slept with worse. He's not the best looking man, but his body is hard enough.

Valerius is okay. Demanding though, Chandra said.

Aomi? Elise asked. The Asian beauty was silent.

She wiggled in her seat, and looked sheepishly at them. *Men scare me.*

Silence descended for a time. Alice glanced around. *Don't worry. I'll teach you some tricks. Keep him satisfied. Give him reason to please you.*

Aomi coughed away her nervousness and the meal passed while they traded WOR-skill training stories. Elise had nothing to add. She rolled the peas around on her plate with her fork and thought of the second skill. Her continued failure to learn the basics of *WOR-skill* frustrated not only Gregor and the High Tender, but her as well. How was it she struggled while everyone else seemed to make steady progress?

If I just nudge here and pull just so... The little peas did exactly as her thoughts commanded, surprising her. Intrigued, she tweaked the command and added rotation.

Chandra stomped on her foot. "You're not allowed to practice outside the classroom. When did you start working the fifth skill? I thought you were behind in your training?" Chandra shut her mouth, realizing she spoke out loud. She glanced up and down the rows, looking to see if she'd attracted the attention of any of the WOR-guards. None approached.

Elise looked at her rotating tower of peas. Six formed a perfect column and hovered a centimeter above her plate. She bent them into a loop and set them spinning.

The girls gasped.

How did you do that? Alice tapped out furiously.

It's easier this way, but they won't let me try it my way.

Show us.

They didn't get it at first, and kept brushing against the you-can't-do-it-that-way argument the Vendel had pounded into their heads. Elise showed them again, and again, until by the end of the meal, Alice got two peas to rotate.

She glanced Elise and tapped in their private code. *Favor granted.*

Later that night, when everyone was asleep, Elise counted out the steps of her WOR-guard. Her protective WOR-guard shadow had been decreased from three to just one of the broad muscled Vendel males. He made a circuit around the five empty beds to either side of Elise's semi-circular room and returned. She timed the circuit while waiting for Alice to provide some sort of distraction.

An ungodly commotion sprang up from down the long rows of beds. Elise paused to listen as Alice's screams called the WOR-guards to her bed.

Elise formed her blankets into the shape of a sleeping body and prayed.

Please let me get out of here without being seen.

Slipping out of her sleeping quarters, she sprinted until the showers came into view.

Almost there.

She slipped inside without being seen. At the service door for the cleaning robots, she activated her sub-routine, Bobo, and waited for the door to open, then she crawled inside, breathing heavily.

Made it.

As the access port closed, Alice's screams filled the air, growing louder. "They're crawling all over me. Get them off! Get them off!"

"Come on, get her in the shower before she wakes the entire deck." A WOR-guard's deep baritone rumbled from the other side of the hatch.

"What's wrong with her?"

"Who knows."

"She bit me!"

"I don't think she's awake."

"Well, I know how to fix that."

Alice continued a string of unintelligible words while one of the WOR-guards turned on the showers.

Elise left Alice to her WOR-guards and raced down the passageway. She made it to Sector F. A quick search through the linens produced a dirty blue jumpsuit. Dove's comments echoed in her mind.

Another quick search revealed an even dirtier jumpsuit. This she didn't put on, but smudged some of the dirt and grease onto her cheeks and chin. Her hair went into a messy bun and she secured it with a strip ripped off one of the towels. A quick look in the mirror, a few strategically teased strands of hair, and she appeared appropriately messy. The jumpsuit hung on her frame, and the saggy bottom added to her rumpled appearance.

Dove and Jeena had expected to see her a day or two after she'd left them. It had been over a cycle. Ten days!

Will they still be willing to help? Have they given up on me?

She raced to the hangar and pulled up short. A sharp metallic tang peppered her tongue and filled her nostrils with an acrid burn. She looked up, up, and up to the ceiling stretching far into the distance. It crawled with thousands of the black cleaning bio-pods. In the center of the vast space, a ship hung suspended in the grip of a crane, which itself was suspended, held by no force she could see. The ship moved along a silver guide wire and disappeared into a black opening.

Elise hurried to Berth 28F39.1.

Champion's Riot, longer and narrower than Dove's *Spider Devil,* sat in its berth. Elise's gut clenched, worried about her reception.

Jeena's bottom half dangled out of a hole in the underbelly of *Champion's Riot.* She wore red coveralls, clean, pressed and perfectly fit. One red boot perched precariously on a stepladder teetering on two of its three legs. The other kicked wildly. Elise hurried over to stabilize the stool, ducking to dodge the flailing leg.

"What...who?" Jeena's thrashing stopped and she popped out of the hole. "Well, I'll be. It's you! I thought you'd evaporated into thin air. How's it going kid?"

"I'm sorry I didn't come back." Elise felt her expression darken as memories of the braklav flooded her mind. "I couldn't get away."

Jeena's mouth opened in an "O" of understanding. "He caught you, didn't he? Bastard. How bad was it?"

Elise frowned. "Bad. But it's over now." She stood back from the stool while Jeena climbed down. "Does your offer still stand? Will you help me?"

With a stony look and a grimace, Jeena frowned. "We need to talk about that."

CHAPTER THREE_

A WAVE OF RELIEF WASHED OVER ELISE AT JEENA ANNOUNCED THAT SHE would help.

Jeena held Elise by the shoulders and gave a cautious appraisal. "How much did you find out about me before you tracked me down?"

"You're an unsponsored female with the full support of the Pilot Conclave. That's unheard of, and you have all the rights to earn and keep your money. You have no need for a sponsor, which is why I looked you up."

"Right, I have some of the privileges of caste and status given to males, without the obligations of citizenship or the restrictions of a sponsor. And I don't technically keep my money. It goes to the Conclave Master and he doles out an allowance. It's a formality. I report it to him and he lets me do with it what I want, but I don't technically own it." She scratched her neck and eyed Elise carefully. "But what have you heard about how I came to my unique situation?"

"A little." She'd researched the hell out of this very unique woman.

"It was a dark time for me, involving an accident, death, and rape. Is that why you came to me?" Jeena cocked her head and parted her lips.

"Yes," Elise ventured cautiously. "I'm sorry about what happened to you, and like you, I have no hopes for a sponsor."

"Let me explain a little, because I want you to know why I'm willing to help. Helping you puts me at risk, but I think things need to change. My story is long though."

Elise glanced around. "We have time."

"We don't have that much time. Let me tell you the short version. My family was en route to Sergra to meet me. My *entire* family: father, brothers, cousins, and uncles. My mother died a year prior, but had arranged for the matrimonial union. I was her only daughter and she matched me well. My family escorted my fiancé, his mother, and his female relatives to our wedding. Lord Saren lor'Sidlek was to be my husband and I would be the first in our family to move out of the commoner caste. My sons would be born lor' lords." Jeena's eyes grew wistful and she paused.

After a while she continued. "My mother asked his mother, and after intense negotiations, his mother consented to the union. He was quite surprised at the offer and delighted when his mother accepted. He arranged a lavish wedding in the highest lor' fashion, insisting on a full year to plan. After the marriage oath, I would've given him my nuptial gift." Jeena chuckled. "We had the worst fights that year. I hated that he insisted on the full ceremonial year of waiting. I was okay to get the permits and have my father sign over his sponsor papers. But Lord lor'Sidlek wanted everything proper for his new lady wife."

Jeena's expression clouded over. "I stood in the transfer station, just outside the docking bay doors. My presence there had been the gift of the Sergra Pilot Conclave Master. He allowed me past the security checkpoints."

"You weren't supposed to be there? Because you're female?"

"Yes and no. Only pilots were allowed there. I'd finished cadet pilot training, top of my class, star pupil. The Sergra Pilot Conclave was upset to be losing me to Lord lor'Sidlek and the Eroptan Pilot Conclave. I was giddy."

Jeena sat on the stool and motioned for Elise to sit on the floor. "I never noticed the men. Never dawned on me that they shouldn't have been there. They hovered at the edges, dressed in mechanic's blue. Lord lor'Sidlek was the first to step through the docking bay door. The rest of my family filed out behind him and Lord lor'Sidlek's women behind my family. The men opened blaster fire and mowed Saren down. My poor fiancé didn't even see my face before he died. I screamed and then the blast doors shut, sealing me in with the assassins."

Tears pooled in the corners of Jeena's eyes and trickled down her cheeks. "The shuttle pilot came out waving his blaster and joined the dead. The leader cursed and killed the one who shot the pilot, saying something about taking out their only escape route. That's when they noticed my pilot's red. They forced me into the shuttle. Fortunately, I'd completed my checkout runs on that model and could fly it. Otherwise, they would have probably have killed me as well."

"Oh, Jeena, I'm so sorry. I can't even imagine." Except she could. Elise's entire family, her friends, and nearly all of Earth's population had been exterminated by the Vendel.

"You asked if I would help. Kid, those three men had me alone in that shuttle for four weeks. They forced me to pilot for them, but their WOR-space ship never materialized at the rendezvous point. I tried everything to keep them off me. It worked the first week, but four weeks with three desperate men never goes well for the woman. Especially a woman without her snarking pad. By the time orbital patrol caught up to us, my life was ruined. I was damaged goods. Not fit for any man's matrimonial bed."

"I'm so sorry. I didn't know."

"I don't advertise. Most women in my situation have family to fall back on. Their fathers or brothers, even uncles take over sponsorship obliga-tions. My entire male lineage lay dead in that docking bay. No sponsor left and no hopes for a husband. Not after the rape. The Sergra Master spoke with the Eroptan Master and they presented me with an option. They took it all the way to the vlor' lord of our sector for approval."

She waved her hands over her body, "And so, here I am today. A woman without status, without sponsorship, and yet I own my own ship, manage my own business, and I made a killing in the jump-jet circuit."

She hopped up and motioned for Elise to follow. Jeena continued speaking as she walked away. "I have three things to give you. And one to show you."

Jeena took her inside *Champion's Riot*.

They wandered down the long central hallway of the ship. Tiny rooms protruded off the side of the passageway. Jeena brought her to a slightly larger crew's rest quarters than the one in *Spider Devil's*. On the table sat a gel-flimsy, a red jumpsuit, and a snarking pad.

Elise approached the table and the three items. "What's this?"

Jeena spoke over her shoulder. "The first is a gel-flimsy on basic piloting skills, training simulations, and everything you need to know about the jump-jet. The second are your new clothes, pilot red. You're ditching mechanic blue. I'm making you a pilot! It's what's going to get you off this ship, and hopefully, away from your sponsor. And the last, is self-explanatory."

Elise picked up the snarking pad and fingered the twin trailing wires. "Jeena," she said sheepishly, "I have no idea how to use this."

The low throaty laugh caught her attention. "Kid, that is the root of a woman's power. With it, you will garner favors, cement friendships, and make men lavish you with everything your sponsor should otherwise provide. They'll bend over backwards, hoping against hope you'll enter into negotiations with their mothers. You aren't obligated to tell them about your lost nuptial gift. That's for their mothers to know and you aren't going down that road."

"Marriage?"

"It's a social crutch, I know, but it levels the playing field. You'll need to find a sponsor eventually, and that is your ticket. Men might believe they hold all the power, but all citizenship does is burden them with obligations. Snarking is the currency of women and the road to a matrimonial union you choose. But it's not the only road. A smart woman only ever trades up in sponsorship. Her intended husband is very much aware of the need to keep her happy. For those of us who will never see the matrimonial bed, well, the snarking pad keeps us civilized."

A snarking pad? Elise still didn't understand what a snarking pad did.

Jeena placed a hand on Elise's shoulder. "Don't worry. I'm going to show you everything you need to know about the snarking pad. Dove is going to help. You need to learn because it's the only way you're going to entice a jump-jet entrance fee out of a man dying for a chance at matrimony."

"Jump-jet entrance fee?" Elise turned around. "What's that for?"

"You have been kept in a cave, haven't you? Jump-jets?"

Elise couldn't be more puzzled.

Jeena continued, "Only the most highly contested race in the empire?"

Elise shook her head.

"I see you have much to learn. For a novice like you," Jeena poked a finger at Elise's chest, "a win in the ship's finals, or even placement in the top ten, will give you enough money to live for a very long time. Long enough to disappear from your no-good sponsor."

"I don't even know what a jump-jet is, let alone how to fly one."

"But you have something none of the other pilots have."

"And what's that?"

"Aw, kid." Jeena put her hand over her chest in an expression of mock hurt. "You have the best, and craziest jump-jet pilot in the empire and Imperial Circuit Winner for ten straight seasons on your side." She lowered her voice to a conspiratorial whisper, "And, I'm a damn good instructor too! A bit unconventional, but good. Besides, I know your competition inside and out."

Elise's eyes lit up. She thought of the WOR-skill; her failure and her success. "I'm good with unconventional."

"Then it's set. That flimsy is everything you need to know about the jump-jet. Take it with you and study. It has basic simulations on it. Are you a good student?"

"I've been told I have an aptitude."

Malice came out of the darkness and purred in the background.

"Good, you'll need it."

"You said you had three things to give me and one to show?"

"I do." Jeena wiggled her finger. "Kid, you are going to pilot my jump-jet. Want to see it?"

"Hell yes!"

"Good, it's on the way."

"On the way to what?"

"Dove is celebrating his 6th. I promised I would be there when he took his *rejuv* shot." She jumped up. "And, we need to get going or risk being late!"

"His 6th?"

"Yeah, can you believe it? I feel old and I just celebrated my fourth century a few years back. He's up to his sixth. Not many citizens are selected for *rejuv* past their fifth. Except for the lor' and vlor' lords, of course. Dove is special though. He has talent! Best damn teacher I've ever met."

Whimper hissed. *How old is Gregor?*

I can't ask her that! Elise pulled up short. "Jeena, how old do the lords get?"

"A few are into their first millennium. The vlor' are guaranteed that much. The highest ranking officials are pushing way past that."

"How long ago did your fiancé die?"

"I stopped keeping track after my second *rejuv*. I wasn't much older than you. A pre-rejuv. Young and sentimental. Full of life and vigor. I remember those days well."

The flutter in her heart, thankfully, did not translate into her words. "I've always wondered how old the emperor is. He's interesting."

"I don't know a single woman who's not dying to snatch that man into her matrimonial bed. Now there's someone who can make a woman's heart sing. There're several contenders, and I hear he's received a serious offer, but he's delaying until he can get the Earth WOR trained. It's all rumor, of course, but who doesn't follow the vlor' social gossip?"

"Hm. But do you know how old he is?"

"Young! Just into his 1st *rejuv,* plenty of life ahead of that one. Many think he'll live long past his father's 22nd *rejuv.* Lord vlor'Malita has worked hard to fill his father's shoes. If anyone can bring us through the S'Lorek threat, Lord vlor'Malita is the man. I'd go to hell and back again for him. If he asked me to jump, I'd sail to the stars and never look back."

"Will he?"

"What? Ask me to jump?" Jeena asked absently.

"No, train the Earth WOR?"

Jeena placed a reassuring hand on Elise's shoulder. "We're all scared, kid, but he'll get them trained, and there are rumors there's a WOR prodigy in the batch. He'll take care of us. He's vlor' after all."

"How long is that going to take?"

"To train a WOR? It depends on Rank. Rumor on board is they culled nearly a thousand WOR from Earth, and hundreds are s'vlor. Those should take a bit longer, a year perhaps. WOR training is realm of the Tenders, and they're a closed mouth group. I think they're getting desperate now that the S'Lorek is close."

"Yes, the S'Lorek."

What the hell is a S'Lorek? Whimper crawled forward. *And why does that word frighten your friend?*

I don't know, Whimper, but I can't just ask. I'm expected to know what everyone else here knows. Her lack of knowledge about the Vendel would cripple her, or worse, expose her for what she was...an Earth WOR.

"Come," Jeena said, "enough of doom and gloom, Dove is probably getting anxious looking for me. You'll be a delight. He's missed you, been worried and all."

Jeena's comments made her want to retch as her head spun with new knowledge. She allowed Jeena to drag her out of *Champion's Riot* and down the long rows of ships.

Yet again, she'd underestimated the Vendel. Life extension? These weren't the hundredth-odd generational cousins of Earth. They were much more recent.

Elise struck gold with Jeena. All she had to do was not screw it up with her ignorance. But how would that work? The age-old question surfaced in her mind. How do you know what you do not know? How can you ask questions about the obvious? She skated on thin ice. Below her feet, the frozen water shifted, cracked and threatened to swallow her whole.

Damn. Why is nothing easy?

Because, Whimper said, *it wouldn't be fun if it weren't hard.*

There's nothing fun about this, my sister.

Not for you. Whimper fled into the darkness, her cackles reverberating in Elise's head.

What else lurked out there that she didn't know? That she didn't think to even ask?

"How long will it take to learn the jump-jet? To get good enough to race?"

"Depends how badly you want to get rid of your sponsor," Jeena replied with a wink.

"Now," Elise replied glumly.

Jeena tugged on Elise's messy bun. "I can get you ready for the qualifications in a few months. You may or may not make it past the *Gambit's* qualifiers and earn a spot in the circuit. It depends on how badly you want it. If you're any good, and are determined, you may just have a shot at the fleet circuit. Most of your training will be in the am-net training simulators. Since we can't guarantee when you'll make it back here regularly, I loaded everything you need on that flimsy. When you manage to get away, Dove or I will take you out in the jump-jet. You'll get palms on training!"

Palms on training?

"I'm determined to get you placed in the circuit. It'll get you a large enough purse that we can start looking at getting you off the *Gambit*. Is your sponsor a permanent resident on *Gambit* or was he hired for this expedition?"

"Can we not talk about him?"

"Sure thing, kid. Come, I see Dove." Jeena broke into a trot and waved a hand over her head. "Dovey," she yelled. "I've got a gift for you."

CHAPTER FOUR_

ELISE TRAILED BEHIND JEENA, LOST IN THOUGHT. AHEAD OF HER, THE ROWS OF bullet-shaped ships ended. A large space, filled with round tables in neat little rows, was crowded with people. Mechanic blue and pilot red predominated, but grey and white peppered the crowd.

She was going to have to learn the uniform color code. In her exploration of the ship with Gregor, she hadn't paid attention to the multicolored jumpsuits. Didn't realize it was important. It must have been so commonplace that Gregor hadn't thought to mention it.

A couple hundred people milled about. At the front, large yellow stripes decorated an elevated platform. Six to be exact. To the far left of the stage, Dove's stocky form bent low to listen to the shorter man beside him. When Jeena called out, he straightened and his face broke into a broad grin. The smile softened his features and he looked, if not handsome—Dove would never be called handsome—rather beautiful. Beautiful, because his inner light shone so brightly it overshadowed his physical ugliness.

Or maybe it had to do with how he looked with Jeena in his arms? The broad man had lifted the lithe pilot by her wrists and hoisted her up onto the platform. She hugged him and pecked him on the cheek.

Jeena searched for Elise in the crowd. When she spotted Elise, Jeena whispered in Dove's ear. He followed her outstretched arm and located Elise. He grinned anew and waved. Elise waved back, but remained where she was, waiting for the celebration to begin.

A man in a green jumpsuit bumped against her arm. "Exciting isn't it. Dove's earned this."

Elise glanced at the man. His green outfit was tailored, and like all the other Vendel men she'd met, he was tall, muscular, and fit. He had brown hair tied at his nape into a ponytail that dangled down his back. Green eyes flashed with excitement and matched the green of his clothes. A name-tag on his breast pocket identified him as Carek Tusel, Neural-Mind Conclave Member, Level 5.

"Yes," she replied without encouragement, and stepped to the side.

"You're new here," he continued, "and young?" He closed the distance between them.

"Yes." *Oh shit.*

Elise struggled for an exit. Unfortunately, just at that moment, a hush fell over the crowd as two men stepped up to the platform. A serious looking man in pilot's red followed the first fat man she'd seen since joining the Vendel. Mechanic's blue draped his frame and he waddled as he walked. The coarse stubble on his face was evident even at a distance. In his hands, he carried a black box with great reverence.

Carek Tusel put a hand on her elbow. "Come, follow me. We'll get a better view." He pulled her through the crowd and ignored the protests of those they passed.

Carek waved at Dove, trying to get his attention. Jeena, standing beside Dove, elbowed him when she saw Carek. Dove, who was desperately trying to look serious as the two men approached, gave her an annoyed look. She elbowed him again and pointed.

Dove jerked his chin in acknowledgement when he saw Carek, then did a double take when he noticed who Carek dragged through the crowd. His eyes widened.

The actual ceremony was relatively quick. The men stopped on the right side of the stage. Dove and Jeena stood on the left. The man in pilot's red opened the case and the one wearing mechanic's blue took out a slim white rod. One of the injectors Elise remembered from the processing room.

A shiver passed down her spine as she remembered the square white room, the little red circle in the middle, the braklav, and…all the rest.

Carek misinterpreted her shiver for a chill and wrapped an arm around her shoulder. She did not protest.

The fat man raised the injector up, presenting it to the crowd, and said a few words. Dove looked solemn, and ignored the little jabs in his side that Jeena inflicted with her finger. He stepped forward and the man pressed the injector against his arm.

Elise jumped when everyone around her hollered, whistling and yelling wishes of good cheer. Carek removed his arm from around her shoulder to whistle. The ear-splitting shriek had her covering her ears.

Despite her troubled thoughts, the mood of the crowd infected her with a profound joy. She found herself smiling. It had been a very long time since she'd felt anything but gloom, despair, anger, confusion, and pain. Every step she took balanced on what would cause the least pain. That easy emotion of joy no longer existed in her world.

It feels good to smile. When Shriek had come out to watch Elise didn't know, but she had to agree.

Yes. I almost think I forgot how.

And these are our enemy? Shriek looked upon the gathering. *They don't look like the Tenders, or the WOR-guards, or even Gregor.*

No. They don't.

But they were Vendel and each of them were responsible for what happened to Earth. She couldn't allow herself to forget that.

One by one, everyone filed on the stage to congratulate Dove.

Jeena stood by his side and Elise wondered exactly what sort of relationship the two shared. She watched the parade, uncertain of her anticipated role, and felt a little lost.

It was only when Carek nudged her elbow that she realized he was still there. He leaned down to whisper and she caught his clean, fresh scent. It surprised her, because, so far, everyone else managed to smell a little like the grease or metal of the ships and hangar bay.

"Come, the line's almost done. How do you know Dove?"

"We just met," she said, again without encouragement. *Who is this man?*

"Are you available?" Before she could respond, he guided her to the side and up the steps to where Dove and Jeena were saying farewell to the last person in line.

Dove glanced at Elise. His expression odd. A mixture of pleasure laced with wariness filled his deeply lined and pockmarked face.

She had been paying attention to the men and women congratulate him and felt comfortable leaning up to kiss his left, then right cheek and finally his forehead. The men had all just kissed the forehead, but the women did all three.

Carek kissed Dove's forehead, and then slugged Dove in the arm. "Congrats, cuz! To another century full of invention and..." His eyes raked up and down Jeena's outfit. "...passion. Hi, Jeena."

"Glad you could make it," Dove replied with a twinkle.

Jeena flashed a grin at Carek. "I see you've attached yourself well." She lifted her brow and cocked her head toward Elise.

"I have." Carek draped his arm around Elise.

She held very still, uncertain if it was rude to shrug it off.

"I'm assuming," he said, "this is the chickadee you've been going on about, cuz?"

"And you will do well to treat her kindly, Carek."

Jeena stepped between Carek and Dove and extricated Elise from Carek's arm. Carek snorted, but flashed his teeth and dipped his head in a bob. "Well, cuz, where's my drink? I came all the way over for this auspicious event and I'm thirsty."

"What did you bring?" Dove crossed his arms over his chest. "We'll drink that."

"Tsk, tsk, cuz, where's your hospitality?"

"With you, I've learned long ago to let you buy the drinks," Dove said.

Carek considered for a moment and glanced sideways to where Jeena had pulled Elise off to the side. "Tell you what. Not only will I pay for all our drinks, but I brought a case of Malbean spirits. It's yours for a proper introduction to your little chickadee."

Dove glanced at Elise. "Kid, how much time do you have today?"

Elise looked at the clock at the top of the stage and did a quick mental calculation, converting ship's time to Confinement Deck time. "Two hours, but no longer. I need to be back in plenty of time, before…"

"There you have it, cuz."

"Supernova!" Carek exclaimed.

Dove spoke with half a smile. "It is my pleasure to introduce Carek Tusel, Neural-Mind Conclave Member, Level 5, my cousin. He finds it difficult to *express* himself. Be careful, chickadee. Carek Tusel, may I please formally introduce you to…ah…Elise. She's a special interest of mine."

Carek's eyes widened. He said, "Just Elise?"

Elise straightened, unsure of the social dance.

Jeena rescued her. "Yes Carek, this is just 'Elise.' No fiancés waiting in the wings, no long-term entanglements. She's young, prejuv, available, but not looking for anything serious right now." Jeena glanced at Elise and said, "You have to be very specific with Carek, lest he get the wrong idea."

Carek's eyes flashed with amusement. He thrust out his hand. "Elise, it is my pleasure to make your acquaintance. Ignore my cousin and his girl. Anything bad they have to say about me is rubbish. Anything good is probably true."

"Nice to meet you, Mr. Tusel." Elise took his hand tentatively. It was warm and he shook her hand in a firm grip.

He rolled his eyes in dismay and clasped his hands over his heart, "Oh, no, no. That won't do. You wound me horribly. You must call me Carek. Mr. Tusel is way, way, too formal. Would you care to join me for a drink? Unfortunately, Dove and Jeena will have to join us. We'll pretend to celebrate Dove's 6th and then ignore them while we get better acquainted."

"I was going to show her my jump-jet." Jeena smoothed the front of her jumpsuit and lowered the zipper a fraction of an inch.

Both men paused to watch.

"Carek is buying, luv. Perhaps it might be worthwhile to introduce our little chickadee. She should start making connections among potential backers."

Carek put a finger in the middle of Dove's chest. "No, you don't. If I'm buying then it's a private party, for four. Not for the entire pilot conclave."

Dove conferred with Jeena in a flash of expressions, a personal code known only to them. Elise recognized the close familiarity the two shared which made words unnecessary. It developed sometimes between individuals who'd grown to know each other very well over many years—centuries perhaps? Finally, Dove shrugged and Jeena nodded.

"Hell, how do you two do that? ESP? You know, you should just make it all official."

Jeena opened her mouth to speak.

Carek silenced her. "Oh, shut up Jeena. We all know what you're going to say. Dove, you're a fool." He waggled his finger in Dove's face. "Come on, let's toast your 6th, so I can get to know your new friend better." He offered his arm to Elise.

After a moment of hesitation, and a worried glance to Jeena, who nodded encouragement, Elise allowed Carek to lead her off the platform. Dove put an arm around Jeena and Elise found herself surrounded by an enemy who looked a lot like very good friends.

CHAPTER FIVE_

New Terra Histories by Malita s'Lissa s'vlor

I HAD SUCH A VISCERAL REACTION TO THE TENDERS, THE WOR-GUARDS, and the Vendel lords. I hated them. The sight of those men caused my blood pressure to soar and the muscles in my jaw to clench.

I plotted their downfall every day.

But the Vendel people?

Fortune smiled on me the day I met my Vendel friends.

They gave me back my humanity.

They gave me hope.

CHAPTER SIX_

Gambit, Day 150

AFTER HER TEN DAYS OF TENDER TRAINING, ELISE SETTLED BACK INTO A routine. She began each morning with a run, followed by WOR-skill training with Gregor, a blessed two-hour break with lunch, and then more WOR-skill training with Gregor and the High Tender to finish the day. High Tender Marcus pulled off her personal WOR-guard patrol, making it easier to slip away to Sector F every other night where she trained with Jeena.

Each night she whispered her prayer for invisibility and a calmness came over her as she escaped the prison of the Confinement Deck.

When she couldn't make it to the flight deck, she practiced on the flimsy in the virtual world of the am-net. Her hand touched the gel coating and the bio-gel hooked into her senses and transported her into a world where flight became her universe.

Unlike WOR-skill training, Elise's aptitude with the jump-jet took off. Her eidetic memory allowed her to breeze through the technical manuals. Knowledge of thrust, momentum, and velocity was no different for the Vendel than it had been on Earth with her stunt plane.

The hardest part was in learning the controls. Her mind longed for a simple joystick. Flying using the palms of her hands—the seat of the pants analogy didn't translate into Vendel flight lingo—took longer to figure out. Once she did, Elise found success with every scenario Jeena devised.

Not that she was a perfect student. Dove kept a tally of her deaths in his particularly quirky way.

Carek had found his use as well.

Dove was more than willing to instruct her in the use of the snarking pad, but was a little hesitant as he got to know her better. As he wormed his way into a protective role, it started to get downright weird. Carek was more than willing to help Elise explore the full capabilities of the snarking pad.

Days passed, cycles turned and counted out Sun cycles. Back on Earth, she would call them months, and she was still no closer to a solution of how to escape. She sat beneath *Champion's Riot* going over jump-jet strategy with Jeena and thought how routine her life had become. How complacent she had become terrified her, but she didn't see a way past it.

"Kid? Did you hear me? I said Carek put up the fee." Jeena nudged her knee.

Elise startled. "What?"

"You're daydreaming again."

"Sorry. I'm worried." She shrugged. "It seems like I'm getting nowhere."

"But that's just it. I just told you."

"Told me what?"

"Kid, your jump-jet fee is set. You've been entered into the competition. We're on track."

"What do I owe him?"

"Nothing." Jeena chuckled. "If a man offers, a woman accepts."

"But it doesn't seem right. What does he expect from me?"

"Carek? Nothing, kid. He wants the pleasure of your company. You provide him with a necessary diversion and you don't have to worry about him. He won't push for anything more than a confirmed place on your snark list."

"I'm a diversion for what?"

"He's part of the neural mind conclave." Jeena gave Elise a look like that should mean something.

Elise shrugged.

"He spends his day hooked into the am-net—full immersion? Neural Conclave members lose a bit of themselves over time—hazard of the job. Carek's using you to keep in touch with reality and tap into his humanity. That's all he wants out of you."

Elise liked Carek, but was leery about developing too close of a relationship, which was challenging considering the intimacy of the snarking pad. He reminded her of those quietly brilliant men who hovered around the edges of society, except Carek was energetic, an animated storyteller, and a prankster.

Watching Carek tease Dove had become one of her favorite past-times. She loved the puzzle Carek posed. Despite an otherwise outgoing personality, he really did have his head in the clouds most of the time, or rather, in the am-net, although she didn't understand what full immersion meant.

"Now let's run that sim again," Jeena said. "I want you to work on hitting the bonus rings."

Elise suppressed a sigh. She didn't want Jeena to pick up on her fatigue.

The pace of training—physical, WOR-skill, jump-jet—confounded her ability to stay awake some days.

Train. Train. Train.

It was all she did anymore. Fortunately, Malice helped. Her sister snapped and growled when Elise's head dipped during WOR-skill training, or when her mind wandered during jump-jet flight lessons.

Despite her achievement with the jump-jet, however, Elise continued to lag behind in WOR-skill. It bothered not just her, but Gregor and the High Tender as well. Her continued failure was on all their minds.

Gregor was supposed to start her on the first skill of the Rod. Except, he'd promised her a surprise. His surprises tended to worry her, which made it difficult to focus on Jeena's jump-jet lesson.

Elise looked at Jeena. "I'm sorry, but I can't seem to focus. I need to get back to my sponsor…before he notices I'm gone."

Jeena patted her knee. "I understand. Maybe next time we'll take the jump-jet out for a spin?"

Elise smiled. "I would like that." When she flew the jump-jet, she felt free.

CHAPTER SEVEN_

Gambit, Day 181

ELISE HURRIED BACK TO THE CONFINEMENT DECK AND SLIPPED BENEATH THE covers an hour before the awakening bell rang. When she woke, it was to find instructions left by High Tender Marcus.

He moved her mealtime back and sent her to the track to run. The change in routine was a little strange, but she didn't question him. She—they—never questioned the High Tender. Her mind was a little crowded what with sharing it with Whimper, Malice, and the mostly silent Shriek.

Elise finished her run and headed to the showers. She washed quickly and rushed out, rubbing her hair with a towel. Staring at the floor, she padded on bare feet to her bench. Two pairs of black, shiny boots brought her to an abrupt halt.

Her breath caught and she raised her head to greet Gregor and High Tender Marcus. Her nudity meant nothing anymore. High Tender Marcus didn't care, and Gregor's restraint remained wire tight.

She stepped up to Gregor and gave him a kiss on the cheek. It had become a part of their greeting ritual. "Gregor, good morning." She held the towel in front of her damp skin. "High Tender Marcus, good morning."

The High Tender's expression was a mask of disapproval and made her flinch. Gregor, however, gave her one of his smirks and his smile broke into a crooked grin. The grueling pace of training left Gregor precious few opportunities to be alone with his property. Not that he didn't steal kisses when and where he could.

He raked his eyes up and down her body and said, "It's a pleasure to see you." His eyes twinkled with amusement when she didn't cover herself and allowed him an uninterrupted view of her body.

High Tender Marcus turned dark, judgmental eyes to the emperor. "I will accompany you."

Elise deferred to the High Tender, once again thinking how dangerous it would be to get caught in the middle of these two men.

Gregor stepped to the side to reveal a shimmering pile of deep green silk and lace. The High Tender rolled his eyes. What a funny expression on the stern man's face.

"Why Gregor, that's beautiful." She held the dress up.

"Yes, opés, it brings out the color of your eyes."

As always, Gregor tied the corset as the High Tender coughed into his fist. She looked at him and tilted her head. She was missing something.

Gregor tugged on the laces and the garment squeezed her waist. He ran a finger up her spine and across her shoulder. His finger came back to trace the edges of the collar she wore. A line of blistering heat marked the path of his touch. He pressed a hand to her back and gave her a gentle push toward the washroom.

"Go do you hair and put on your bands of rank. I'm anxious to leave."

Elise headed to the washroom and heard the High Tender's low rumble as she turned the corner. "Must you insist on corsets with the back ties?"

"She lives to please me. We've achieved that much."

"I achieved that with Tender Training."

Elise worked to straighten out the tangles in her hair. She finger-dried her hair at one of the drying vents. For a moment, she stood in front of the mirror, examining her reflection, surprised at the beauty uncovered by the dress.

The collar at her neck glinted in the soft light, reminding her of what she had become, a slave. She wasn't supposed to be able to remove it, but she'd figured out the clasp. She slipped on the five armbands which denoted her as a fifth rank WOR.

Taking one last glance at herself in the mirror. Elise spun on her heals and walked out.

I'm not your filthy slave, Gregor. I'm not your slave!

Malice cackled in the background. *Are you certain?*

Gregor smiled as she approached. She wanted to rip that smile off his face, but had to portray a meekness she did not feel. Her submission to him was the key to her freedom. She hated it, but fed it. There was no other choice.

He led her out and around the sleeping quarters. They paused at the palm pad at the base of the stairs. He logged her out, and then led her out of the Confinement Deck. The High Tender kept his distance and followed.

"You haven't taken me off the Confinement Deck in months. Are you taking me to your quarters?" She twisted around to glance at the High Tender.

"Sadly not, opés. But, I promise to find some time for us to be alone."

"Can't you just order him away like last time?"

"Not anymore." Gregor didn't elaborate.

He took her to one of *Gambit's* circumferential parks. A modest breakfast spread on a large quilt had been prepared for them. He seated her on the ground and took a seat opposite her. The High Tender retreated to a bench twenty-feet away, and sat where he could keep an eye on them. Gregor placed her back to the High Tender.

He jerked his chin toward the High Tender. "He thinks to act the chaperone. Despite my word, he's hesitant to leave us alone."

"Yes, Gregor." Elise looked down and eyed the food spread out. She was thankful for the High Tender's presence. A part of her hoped it would remain the routine as Gregor's advances only became bolder with the passage of time.

"Look at me," he commanded.

Elise brought her chin up and gazed into his eyes. "Yes, Gregor." She kept her expression blank, but inwardly she cringed.

"I expected more of a reaction out of you. This is a treat after all." He arched a brow in question. "How about some breakfast?" Gregor filled a plate with food. He held it out.

"Thank you." Elise leaned forward to take the plate. Gregor held it steady, but didn't release it. His eyes flicked to her lips and he leaned forward. Elise held herself perfectly still as he brushed his lips against hers in a soft kiss.

He leaned back and frowned. "What's wrong?"

"Is he staring at us? I feel his eyes boring a hole in my back. It's weird." She took the plate and set it down. Her hand reached out to rest on top of his.

"Are you not happy to be alone with me?"

She laughed. "Please, we are very much, *not* alone."

He frowned and narrowed his eyes. The tattoo over his brow danced ominously.

Elise placed a finger on his lips. "You know I won't lie to you. While I would like nothing else than to have you pull me into those bushes over there and take me with this passion you control so well, you don't seem to want to do that. Sitting not more than a few feet from High Tender Marcus while you kiss me, and he watches, is uncomfortable."

"I don't mind kissing you in front of Lord vlor'Vardhal."

"I do." She grabbed a pastry and took a bite. It gave her a minute to collect her thoughts.

"Hm." Gregor leaned back and stretched his legs out.

Good, no more kissing, Malice hissed.

Shriek and Whimper remained silent. They rarely revealed themselves. Elise took another bite.

Gregor's next words hit her with all the subtleness of a lightning bolt. "Opés, I want you to show me the fifth skill of the Bar again. Now."

Elise didn't hesitate and obeyed without thought. With her mouth still full, she looked at the food spread out on the blanket. She picked four grapes and they floated into position as she started them in their orbits. Once they were all rotating around a common center, she spun each along its axis.

Gregor reached into a tin and tossed a handful of crushed nuts on the blanket. "Add these."

Elise blinked and complied.

He tossed her an orange, an apple and two nectarines. "Add these."

The orange rotated outside the orbit of the nuts. The apple came next and she added the nectarines without batting an eye.

Gregor leaned over to a basket and pulled out a large grapefruit. "I want this one in the middle. You need to expand the rings to make room." He tossed the grapefruit into the air and Elise caught it with her mind before it landed.

The grapefruit hovered over her rotating construct while she considered how to fit it in. She had to push the innermost grapes outward before the grapefruit slipped into place. The outer orbits rippled and expanded to make room.

"Tilt the whole thing ninety degrees and elevate it so the High Tender can see."

She did *exactly* as Gregor instructed.

I'm his trained dog. I didn't even think. What just happened?

Her heart leapt in her throat as the implication of what she just did sank in. She'd struggled with this for the past cycle and never performed this flawlessly, but then she wasn't thinking, just reacting.

To Gregor.

A trained slave. This is what I've become.

The High Tender joined them. He grabbed a handful of fruit. "S'vlor," he said.

She regarded him, tears brimming in her eyes. "Yes, High Tender."

"I expect obedience." His tone slipped into the terror of Tender Training.

Whimper made mewing sounds.

Shriek shuddered.

Malice hissed.

Elise hushed them. *The High Tender is speaking!*

Don't disobey him. Shriek cowered. *I don't want to feel the braklav.*

The High Tender cupped ten grapes and held an orange in his other hand. "Make another construct." He flicked his eyes up and she followed his gaze as he threw the fruit into the air.

They couldn't disobey the High Tender. That brought the braklav.

Malice hissed.

Whimper moaned.

Shriek screamed. *Do it. Do it. Do. It!*

Elise reacted on instinct, determined to keep her sisters safe from the High Tender and his braklav.

All ten grapes sailed through the air. At their furthest point, she caught them and forced them into position. The orange fell and smacked into the ground. The rind cracked. She snatched it, sealed the crack, and shoved it into place.

Her original construct rotated in the air behind her, completely forgotten. She had been forced to tie it off when the High Tender tossed the grapes. If she hadn't, it would've fallen, and that would've made Gregor mad. They never made Gregor mad. He's the one who brought the High Tender to task.

One of the grapes in the second group wobbled. She nudged it back into a stable orbit.

Gregor walked over to her first rotating mass of fruit and pointed to the third grape. "What is this?"

She stared at him, not understanding the question. It was a grape. But he knew that. Why would he ask her such a stupid question? She looked at the first mass of fruit, rotating in silent precision.

It all fell into place as she saw the arrangement of the fruit mirroring her home solar system. With that sudden realization, both rotating masses came crashing to the ground.

"You tricked me." It was all she could manage to say.

"It was no trick."

High Tender Marcus stepped forward, kicking grapes out of his way. "S'vlor, your master asked you a question."

Fruit littered the ground. The grapefruit had split under the impact of its ten-foot fall. One of the oranges didn't look much better.

High Tender Marcus took a step. Gregor placed a restraining hand on the High Tender's chest and the advance stopped.

Sneaky bastards, Malice muttered.

Answer him, Whimper cried.

He asked a question. We must answer, or they'll use the braklav. Shriek rattled inside Elise's mind. *I'm not ready. I'm not prepared!*

We did that. That voice belonged to someone new.

There were too many people screaming, shrieking, and wailing in her head. Elise listened for the new voice. *Who are you?*

Her head shook trying to quiet everyone.

Gregor came over and knelt on the ground. He lifted her chin. "Opés?" He leaned in close.

She struggled to focus. *Who are you?*

Silence greeted her question.

Mumbles from Whimper filled her mind.

Shriek's cries echoed in her head.

Malice's hissing drove her to distraction.

Quiet! But her sisters could not be consoled. *Who are you?*

She cast the question into the dark crevices of her mind, certain she had heard someone new, but no one answered her call.

"Opés!" Gregor shook her shoulder. "Opés!" Concerned edged his words. "Take a breath! What's wrong with her?"

A breath? She wondered why she should bother. The edges of her vision dimmed and her heart thumped. She cast about in the dark. *Who are you!*

"Opés!" Gregor said. "Elise! Snap out of it!"

Now who was Elise? She didn't know that name. Hands from the darkness pulled her back into the shadows. She wanted to let them. It was warm and safe back there, but Gregor demanded an answer.

Malice kicked her into the light. *Go to him! Now!*

Elise opened her eyes. "Gregor?" It came out in a breathless whisper. Adrenaline flowed through her body and her arms felt shaky, almost like they belonged to someone else. "Why are you shaking me?"

"I asked you a question." Gregor searched her eyes, darting his gaze from one to the other. "Where did you go just now?"

Elise raised her hands and pushed his hands off her shoulders. "You're hurting me."

He released her, but his gaze held her with just as much force as his hands.

Her fingers went to massage her temples.

Whimper remembered the High Tender's words. *The question has not been answered. We have to answer the question. Bad things happen when the questions aren't answered.*

"Earth. You pointed to my home." She flicked her gaze to the High Tender. Elise stood and Gregor followed.

"It's not your home any longer, opés." He pulled her to his chest and she willingly went to him, even found some degree of comfort in his arms.

"I know. You're my home now."

He smoothed her hair and kissed the top of her head. "Yes, opés, I am. We learned something important just now."

"You meant to catch me off guard."

"I remembered what you said about juggling." He put a hand on her shoulder.

She shrugged him off and pushed out of his embrace.

"Call it my version of WOR-skill juggling," he said. "A test of sorts."

Elise stopped short. They had tricked her into using the WOR-skill, not the way she had been taught, but the other way. Her way. Intuitively. The urge to please these men had dominated her thoughts and desires until instinct took over. The realization made her stomach turn.

She hated her weakness. "Gregor, why do all the dresses you put me in have ties in the back?"

His expression filled with surprise.

She'd caught him off guard.

"Not exactly the question I expected, opés."

"Please, answer me."

Gregor rubbed the back of his neck. "WOR in training wear dresses bare in the back. It makes correction by the WOR-guards most effective."

The gang began to squirm in her head. *Hush, my sisters. We're learning here.*

327

He grabbed her hands and pulled her close. She allowed herself to be led and pressed against the hardened planes of his chest. He did not release her hands. "Once a WOR has progressed past WOR-skill training, she wears an outfit similar to the one you're wearing. The front is lowered to display the binding amulet. A back-tie corset is an expression of the intense mental and physical bond between s'vlor and master. The back tie is a choice a s'vlor makes to show her willingness to serve. Tell me, opés, is that not the truth for us? Are you not willing to serve me?"

What have you done to me?

Elise stared at the ruin of fruit littering the ground. "Tender Training, Gregor. I wear what you choose, but it is not my choice."

The High Tender shifted in his seat and twirled the braklav. She didn't think he meant to use it.

Cries from the darkness sounded in her head.

She soothed them and pushed them back. "You say jump and I jump. With Tender Training, you made me need to obey you, to please…both of you. You asked me to perform the fifth Bar skill. Something I've struggled with for months. You added a few simple requests, which by themselves were easy. Altogether, something I shouldn't have been able to do. I don't even know what skill level that is. I succeeded because I know the penalty for disobedience. I remember the braklav. That twirling rod is in my thoughts day and night. I don't dare disappoint you, or I risk the braklav. What you make me wear is your choice, not mine."

She glanced at the High Tender. "I can do so much more with the WOR-skill if you would allow me to learn it my way. Your silly rules and constructs are crippling my ability to learn and I can't please Gregor unless I learn." She gestured to the fruit littering the ground. "This should prove it."

Gregor stared at the High Tender, an odd expression of smugness plastered on his face.

The High Tender ignored Gregor, instead focusing all his attention on Elise.

She felt like a bug under a microscope. An awkward silence stretched between the men. Elise feared saying anything else. Her words bordered on insolence and Shriek would not allow her to say more and risk a session with the braklav.

When Gregor spoke, his voice exuded eternal patience and an unwavering calm that brought chills to her spine.

"That will be all, opés. You can find your way back to the Confinement

Deck and log yourself back in." He turned away and took a step toward the High Tender.

Elise didn't hesitate. She left the park and the scattered fruit littering the ground. Her feet didn't seem able to move fast enough for her mind. She wanted to run, but settled for a dignified retreat.

Before she got too far, she heard Gregor. "And what do you think of that, High Tender?"

CHAPTER EIGHT_

New Terra Histories by Malita s'Lissa s'vlor

MY SISTERS: SHRIEK, WHIMPER, MALICE, AND EVEN THE LAST SISTER WHO took longer to reveal herself, don't think I'm—we're—crazy. We get along just fine.

What Gregor and the High Tender accomplished with Tender Training terrified me. There was no escape from the braklav. No mercy from Gregor.

I divided my mind to survive. Shriek howled. Whimper cried. Malice pushed us forward. The final sister saved us all.

My breakthrough happened in the circumferential park with those silly pieces of fruit. I hadn't thought about vectors, lines of force or dimensional folding. All I did was give Gregor and the High Tender instant obedience without thought. The thrill over controlling the WOR-skill was tainted by the impulsive need to please those men. I reacted. I pleased them. I struggled to make them proud and, without thinking, the WOR-skill flowed out of my mind.

It was a beginning. My first success. But success wasn't good enough. I needed a victory.

CHAPTER NINE_

Gambit, Day 201

ELISE WALKED DOWN THE FLIGHT DECK DRESSED IN HER RED PILOT'S JUMPSUIT. The pocket over her left thigh bulged with a jump-jet training flimsy. The one over her right held her snarking pad. The collar was zipped up high, hiding her WOR training collar from prying eyes.

No one was entirely certain who she was or where she came from. What they did know was Jeena was training her for the jump-jet circuit and planned to enter Elise into the *Gambit* trials.

Larkin waved as she passed. A *prejuv* like herself, he was in his mid-thirties, not much more than a kid among the Vendel. Curly white hair topped his head, spilled over his ears, and fell down into his chocolate brown eyes. He winked at her as she passed.

"El! Come here," he called.

She angled over to him and his ship, the *Golden Pride*. She was early and had a few minutes to chat.

"What's up Lark?"

"So, I hear it's official and all?"

She crossed her arms and looked at him. "What?"

"Well, I heard you made the entrance fee for the novice competition. Who funded you?"

Elise didn't answer. She tapped her foot.

Larkin continued. "Hm. They told me you wouldn't say." He rubbed the back of his neck and brushed the curls out of his eyes. "Well, Jarvis, Anders, Prindle, and I..."

Elise arched a brow. Jeena thought it would be good practice, and good networking, to get to know some of the junior pilots. To that end, Jeena had introduced Elise and in the Vendel-way, snarking followed introductions. Elise had since become quite popular.

Larkin shifted from foot to foot. His gaze lingered on her chest. Elise stepped forward and put her finger under his chin. She lifted. "My eyes are up here. If you're going to speak to me, then stop staring at my breasts."

He glanced up sheepishly.

"Lark, why did you call me over here?"

A blush colored his cheeks. "Oh, well, like I was saying, none of us have much money, but we pooled it all together for your entrance fee. I brought it to Jeena and thought we'd surprise you. With all the work you're doing in training, and Jeena saying you're damned good, we wanted to pay, but I was surprised when she said you already had a benefactor."

Elise kissed him on the cheek. "Lark, that's so sweet."

"It's more than just the few of us. We didn't have enough, so we kind of got everyone to chip in."

"Who is everyone?"

"Every pilot on this flight deck, most of the mechanics, and some of the loadmasters too." Larkin's smooth face broke into a broad grin and his eyes crinkled at the corners.

Everyone?

Something he said caught her attention. "Did she really say I was good?"

Jeena hadn't given her a single word of encouragement in the months of training. Difficult to please didn't even come close to explaining Jeena's rigid standards. She was worse than the High Tender and Gregor when it came down to training.

"Don't tell her I told you. She told Dove. A few of us were standing nearby. She caught us listening, came over and threatened us. I'm not supposed to tell you."

"You just did. What's up Lark, not afraid of Jeena anymore?"

"Hey! You better not tell on me."

Elise laughed. "On you? Dear Lark, I won't."

He breathed a sigh of relief and then glanced down at her pocket. "Do you have to go right away?"

Elise pulled out the snarking pad, and gave him a sly smile. "Not right away. I have a few minutes to share with a friend." She walked under the canopy of his ship and sat on the floor, placing the snarking pad in front of her on the ground and unwrapping the wires.

Larkin sat down, his eyes alight with eagerness.

"So, what are you up for?"

"How about that massage you did last time. I *liked* that!"

"Back or front?"

"Do we have time for both, and maybe that bit at the end?"

"For you, Lark, always time." Elise attached the gel pad to his hand and watched Larkin's eyes glaze over as he entered her simulation.

Snarking was as natural as a hug between friends, or a peck on the cheek, except the Vendel turned all that on its head with snarking. The interface activated Larkin's pleasure receptors while she led him through an immersive experience. It wasn't exactly like having sex, but it was intimate, highly sensual, and elicited a sexual release: virtual not physical. As far as she was concerned, snarking was no different from sex, but since there was no physical contact, the Vendel viewed it as a platonic diversion.

Snarking replaced sexual intimacy between unmarried individuals in Vendel society and women ruled the snarking pads. They used them to cement friendships, establish alliances, and sometimes to determine matrimonial unions. Snarking

was the currency of the Vendel female, which meant Elise made it her priority to become proficient in the art of snarking.

Because she wasn't a virgin, and due to her personal experiences, her snarking sims incorporated all the senses. Through sight, touch, feel, taste and sound, the complexity of her simulations layered sensuality on top of eroticism. And in sim, she created an experience Vendel males couldn't get enough of.

Larkin's features relaxed as she increased the intensity of the stimulation. She set the timer and let the sensations flow over her mind as she guided him through the simulation. She forgot all about the WOR-skill, Gregor, and corseted dresses. Eight minutes later a buzzer sounded, pulling them out of their simulation.

She wrapped the cables back around the pad and placed it back in her pocket.

Larkin kissed her cheek and lay back on the ground, humming. "You have some pretty interesting tricks with that thing."

"I'll take that as a compliment," she said.

"Any way you could show some of the others how to do that?"

"What?"

"El, come on. You know what I mean. I'd just be nice if their sims were as rich as yours. You incorporate all the senses, it makes the rest feel flat by comparison. That bit with the water...*hot* water, nice."

"I need to go, Lark. Jeena's going to let me fly the real thing. Dove's all nervous."

Larkin laughed. "You haven't been by his ship yet, have you?"

"No. Why?"

"He's been decorating in preparation for today."

"Great." Elise stood and brushed off her pants. "Please tell everyone thanks, by the way, I really appreciate their support."

Larkin jumped to his feet, "Oh, I forgot!"

"What?"

"I'm supposed to ask if we can use it for a bet instead. We figured since all of us had pitched in, and Jeena thinks you may have a chance, that we could put it in the betting pool. Since you're a novice the odds are stacked against you. So, if—when—you win, we'll all make a killing. What do you say?"

"If I lose, you all lose your money. I can't do that."

"It was going to be a gift from all of us anyway. We're not losing anything."

"Listen, I gotta go."

"Think about it. Now that the entrance fees have been collected, the betting is going to start. The earlier we put it in, the bigger the payout."

"Fine, I'll think about it." She hurried off.

The whole deck? What had gotten into them? And now there's a betting pool, too?

She shuddered at the thought. And, Jeena, who rivaled the High Tender as a taskmaster, said she might actually be good?

Perhaps I do have a chance?

You're not supposed to be doing this for fun. Malice hissed. *Or, have you forgotten your purpose?*

Malice's words pulled Elise up short. *I have not forgotten.*

Good. Don't! These are not your friends. What would they do if they knew who you really were?

Malice's words of caution echoed in her mind as she trotted towards *Champion's Riot*. Hanging off the wings, the fuselage, the nose, and the tail of the *Spider Devil* hundreds of long black tassels dropped to the ground. Dove's entire ship looked like it had grown a hairy beard. She pulled up short.

"What the hell is this, Dove?"

Dove stood out in front with his arms crossed over his large barrel chest. His bald head shined in the light. Odd, since it was usually covered in a layer of grease and grime.

She smiled at the stern expression on Dove's face. "Larkin told me you'd redecorated, but honestly, I hadn't expected this." She gestured at the bearded ship and pulled on one of the tassels. It held firm.

Dove walked up and stuck a small black ribbon on her chest with a frown.

"Dove? What's going on?"

He gestured to the ship. "Each of these, my little chickadee, represents every one of your sim deaths. I've been keeping track."

Elise rolled her eyes. That number was well past one hundred now. "I didn't die every time in the sim."

He poked her chest. "No? But today, if you screw up, it'll be for real."

"Jeena's going to be with me. I don't think she'll let me screw up. Besides, it's her jump-jet. She's not going to let me trash the thing."

"I just wanted to make an impression on you. There's a hell of a lot of ribbons here."

"I promise to be careful." She kissed him on the cheek.

He rubbed his fat nose. "Do better than that. Everyone on deck is watching. They know it's your first time out. Did Larkin tell you about the collection?"

She nodded.

"Not everyone likes to take second place against a woman. Be careful and don't screw up."

"I've had better pep-talks."

"Tough. I just wanted to remind you why you're doing this. It's not for fun or for glory. It is fun and glorious to fly a jump-jet, but we're doing this to get you away from your sponsor. It won't work if he suddenly finds out about you. You don't need your sponsor's permission to enter, but he can pull you out of the competition. Keep a low profile, chickadee."

Her eyes widened. It's not that she'd forgotten, but he had a point. The thrill of this other life outside the Confinement Deck infected her with a sense of normalcy. When she was here, she could forget about being a prisoner, a slave.

"I do remember. And thank you. It's easy to get caught up in all of this." Elise fingered the black ribbon on her chest.

You see? It's not just me. Listen to him. Malice purred in agreement.

He snorted. "Humph. Look, Jeena's waiting for you at the jump-jet yard. I'm supposed to take you over."

"Let's go, then."

Dove led the way past the long lines of ships. About a third of the berths were empty. Loadmasters in burnt orange jumpsuits filled ships' holds with cargo, while blue mechanics swarmed the rest.

This deck held forty ships, forty men willing to put money down for the chance of a newbie to make it on the jump-jet circuit. The ground crews waved in greeting or jerked their chins in acknowledgment. She got thumbs up from the red clad pilots as they passed.

Jarvis Darmel scowled as she and Dove walked by. He was a member of the loadmaster conclave, a solid worker and a harsher boss. He'd loaded cargo for one of Jeena's trips and Elise managed to get in his way. One of the crates had tipped over and spilled its load of parts. Jarvis blamed her and hadn't forgiven her for distracting him. He insisted she address him as Mister Darmel, the only person on the deck to demand the more formal name.

"Don't mind old Jarvis, chickadee. Some men just think women should stay in their quarters all day long. Doesn't make sense to me. Shoot, if I had a wife who worked all day long, I'd stay in quarters myself. Would it come as a surprise to know he contributed a large share to that collection of yours?"

Elise jabbed him in the ribs. "Really?"

That would be a surprise. Jarvis didn't like her and made a point of letting her know it. Perhaps she'd been too harsh on the man?

They exited the commercial flight deck and navigated the corridors to the jump-jet hangar. Long rows of small crafts decorated the space. They reminded her of dragonflies standing at attention with their bi-wings spread and ready for flight. Three large thrusters sat at the rear of the craft and a delicate canopy perched at the very front.

They glittered in the harsh light as each jump-jet flashed its unique array of colors. It reminded her of walking through an iridescent swarm.

They approached a black and red jump-jet with four iridescent purple and blue wings. The tail thrusters were painted black with trails of red and purple fire racing down the fuselage.

The canopy slid back and Jeena stood up from the back seat. "Thanks, Dovey. Hey, Kid! Ready for your first real flight?"

"Are you kidding? Sim's great and all, but I've been itching for this."

Jeena eyed Elise's outfit. "Oh luv, please tell me you didn't put one of those awful ribbons on my student. That's no way to encourage the girl."

"You're right, it wasn't meant to. It's a reminder and Elise knows what I'm talking about. Bring her back safely, luv," Dove said.

Elise piped up. "Am I flying today or attending my funeral?"

"He's always like this, Kid. First flight jitters. Just ignore him. He's been a complete pain in the ass the past couple of days. Snapping at anyone who came close as he hung all those dreadful tassels all over his ship. Just horrible company."

"It's my first flight, not his, and I don't have any jitters. Perhaps it's good someone does." Elise stood on tiptoe and kissed his cheek. "I'll be fine."

The slapping of running feet and labored breathing came from behind them. She spun around. Carek ran up, tugging hard for air. He stopped short, smiled in pain, and held a hand out, palm facing them. He waved them to patience while he bent over and caught his breath.

"Why, Carek," Jeena crooned from the cockpit. "I didn't think you'd make it."

He sucked in air and straightened. Sweat streamed down his face and he mopped it up with a dark green cloth he pulled out of his pants pocket. Two silver discs glistened on either side of his temples.

"You!" He pointed an accusatory finger at Jeena and then gulped in more air. "You didn't tell me today was her first flight!"

"Oh, dear, did I forget?" Jeena chuckled. "Hm, must have slipped my mind."

"Did not." He waved his hand.

"Oh, please."

Carek glanced at Dove. "Hi, cuz." His eyes narrowed to thin slits. "Did it slip your mind as well?"

Dove smirked. "Nope."

Carek frowned but found nothing to say. "Well, at least Elise cared enough to let me know."

"Hi, Carek. You're late. You were supposed to meet me at Dove's ship." Elise gave him a peck on the cheek. "I even came early, in case you wanted to try out my new sim." She patted her pocket for emphasis.

"Maybe after?" His eyes lit with anticipation.

"No, sorry. I have to get back right after. I'm pushing my time as it is."

"My loss," he said again.

She reached up to his temples and touched the silver discs. "What are these?"

His fingers went to his temple, "Oh, shoot. I forgot to take them off."

"What are they?" Elise asked again.

"They're my neural interfaces. I'm supposed to leave them in the lab." He peeled the discs off his skin and tucked them gingerly into his left breast pocket.

"I didn't think you were working today. You said you were taking the day off to meet me here."

Dove interrupted, "You really told him about your flight today?"

"Of course," she smiled, "he's my benefactor. He has a right to be here. He gets to see if I blow myself up for real, or just flub my way through."

Carek flashed his white smile. "I don't think you're going to flub anything despite Dove's horrible sense of humor." Carek plucked the black ribbon off her jumpsuit. "Here, I'll just hold this morbid little reminder for you. Cuz, you really need a better sense of humor."

She gave him another peck on the cheek. "Well, I'm glad you made it. Sorry you had to work. I'd really have hated if you missed my first flight."

"Me too. Our Conclave Master has everyone working extra shifts. Almost didn't let me go."

"Problems?" Dove asked.

"We're not sure. There've been odd glitches in the am-net. Nothing that's affected critical systems, odd little subroutines that aren't acting normal. It's like the am-net is infected."

Elise's ears perked up. Her army of subroutines was out there, collecting information, sorting, sifting and other things.

"Don't really know what to make of it. Master Persins wants it all sorted out before we make it to Malbra. We're picking up extra shifts, staying over, trying to track down the little buggers."

Jeena called down from the jump-jet. "Kid, are you gonna fly today or stand around gabbing with a neural mind freak?"

Elise flashed Carek a smile. "Wish me luck!"

She vaulted into the cockpit.

Malice, I don't care what you think. I'm going to enjoy this. Don't spoil it for me.

I won't spoil it for you, sister. Just remember why you're here.

Like I can ever forget?

"You ready to fly, kid?"

"You bet your ass I am."

I still don't see how this helps us to escape. Whimper's plaintive voice called out from the darkness.

I win the jump-jet competition and that gets us enough money to buy a ship. One of the big ones. Big enough to take all of us home.

Oh, is that all?

Malice cackled. *Yes. Easy-peesy-simple-as-pie. And do you know how to get home?*

Shut up, Malice. Elise and Whimper shouted as one.

Malice grumbled, but she didn't leave. In fact, even Shriek came out to watch their first launch. All four of them grinned like fools as the jump-jet blasted out of the *Gambit* and launched into WOR-space.

The gray void of WOR space wrapped around Elise as she sped away from the *Gambit*. For the first time in far too long, she found herself free of her prison. Not that she could go anywhere. WOR space confined her as effectively as the walls of the *Gambit* and she was eager to be free of them, even if only for the span of a jump-jet training flight.

She exited the launch tube with a scream full of adrenaline and victory.

"Cool it, kid," Jeena warned from the backseat.

"Sorry, it's just so…incredible."

Not wanting to make a poor showing of her first real flight, Elise throttled back on the thrusters and entered a wide banking turn. *Gambit's* torus slipped back into view, along with a glittering trail of jump-jet course rings.

"You ready to try the rings?" Jenna asked. "Or do you want to practice a few turns?"

"I want to try for the rings."

Like snarking, the jump-jet simulations Jeena had her complete were virtually indistinguishable from the real thing. Elise was ready.

Ready to attack the rings.

Ready to fly.

Ready to take her first step toward freedom.

In her stunt plan back home, lift, drag, thrust, and weight dictated the laws of flight. To control her plane she used a throttle, rudder, ailerons, and elevators to navigate three-dimensions. A jump-jet didn't have rudders, ailerons, or elevators. It didn't use the physics of lift to control its flight. Instead, it had tail rockets, 360-thrusters beneath each wing, and a reverse thruster to stop forward momentum, but the concepts of flight remained the same.

She didn't have a stick to nose forward for a dive or pull back to climb higher. Instead, she had the pressure of her palms and the tapping of her fingers against the biogel of the control pads. Hours of simulation retrained her brain and re-established muscle memory.

She screamed away from the Gambit and fixed a smile to her face. Jeena coached from the backseat and guided her through the set of training rings. The silvery structures floated out in the sea of WOR space.

In competition, there would be fifty of them with five bonus rings. For her practice runs, Jeena set only ten, and Elise attacked them with all the bottled fury and desperation of months of captivity.

This was how she would prevail over the Vendel. Locked in the craziness of a jump-jet competition, she would find a way to free not only herself, but all her fellow survivors. And so she flew and rejoiced.

CHAPTER TEN_

Gambit, Day 202

Elise barely made it back to the Confinement Deck after her first jump-jet flight. She stowed her pilot's jumpsuit behind a little box at the cross corridor in the service crawlspace and slipped out of the service door when the alarm bell rang.

There was barely enough time to make it back to her bed. She straightened out the sheets and removed all evidence of her nightly ruse. The cupboard opened and she took out a scarlet red dress. The silky fabric floated around her slim frame as the front plunged down to reveal her modest cleavage, and finally, the dress had a back with three ties that cinched the waist.

Guess this means Gregor believes I'm truly trained.

She put on the five bands of Rank with a frown, and then slipped on her shoes.

On her way to training, she ran across Alice.

"Where were you this morning?" Her anxious friend glanced around, looking for WOR-guards and keeping her voice low. "I waited for you at the track."

"You don't want to know, my friend." She practically bounced on her toes, still dizzy with excitement over her first flight.

She had hit every ring on the circuit dead on. The grey sea of WOR-space made finding the silver rings challenging, but she'd located every single one. Even the bonus rings, which shifted wildly on approach, hadn't eluded her skill. Carek confided that she'd beat Jeena's first flight time, smashing a two-hundred-year-old record.

Alice pulled Elise out of her reverie. "Interesting dress. Is it something new?"

"Gregor's doing. He's trying to tell me he believes I'm officially his well-trained dog. Evidently, once we've been cowed by the WOR-guards, they let us wear dresses with backs. Before that, they don't want to ruin the dress with the strike of the whipstick. I guess he considers me tamed."

"Are you?"

"In an odd sort of way, yes and then again, equally no. It depends on who you're talking to."

"I thought I was talking to you. Is there more than one of you?"

Elise smiled. Was there? She didn't know.

"How are you doing with him? It's hard with Edgard. He's kind enough, but I couldn't imagine having the Emperor as my..." Alice's voice trailed off groping for the word.

"It's hard to say isn't it...master?"

"At least we don't have to call them that."

Elise took in a breath and blew it out slowly. "To answer your question, it's very hot and cold with Gregor...like I'm not really in control of how my body reacts to him. I don't understand it, except it has to do with the Activator."

Alice giggled. "I get that, but there's no hot for me. Edgard is totally hands off. I swear Vendel men are prudes."

"They're not. The Vendel view intimacy differently than us. Trust me, in their minds, Vendel men have a lot of imagination."

"What does that mean?"

There was no way to explain the snarking pad to Alice without revealing everything, and that would put Alice at risk.

"Only that when Edgard decides to touch you, it will mean a lot more to him than it does to you. There is nothing casual about sex in this society." *Nothing casual unless it was at the end of a snarking pad.*

They arrived at the Fifth Rank WOR classroom. A few women trickled in behind them. All the vlor' lords were present, including Gregor. The doughnut shaped tables had been removed and double rows of pillows stretched out down the length of the room. In between the pillows, identical flat gray stones stretched in a line. On top of each stone, a flash of steel glinted in the bright lights. Instead of greeting Elise, Gregor remained with the other vlor' lords.

Alice stopped short. *What's this?* She used their personal code, not the one known to everyone else.

I don't know.

Only two High Tenders were present: High Tender Marcus and High Tender vlor'Martund. They stood at the front of the room. High Tender vlor'Martund held his gel-flimsy in hand.

High Tender Marcus cleared his throat. "Over this past cycle, we have been testing your skill of the Bar. Most of you are progressing nicely through the first skills of the Rod. Congratulations. All of you have passed the Bar skills. We are delighted with your progress. Today we celebrate the Blood Rite."

High Tender vlor'Martund checked his gel flimsy and lined the women along the rows of double pillows. As each took her place, her lord came to sit on the opposing pillow. The women were instructed to kneel and to remain silent.

WOR-guards filed into the room once all the women were in position. At the front of the room, a pair of cushions sat apart from the others. Gregor's steel gaze captured hers and he gestured for her to join him there.

A long, sharp knife perched on the gray stone. The expressions on the faces of her fellow prisoners mirrored her emotions: fear, grief, dismay, and hopelessness warred within her. In stark contrast, interest, curiosity, and eagerness bloomed on Sarah's face.

Gregor's mood was unreadable and steel glinted off his eyes to match that of the long blade resting on the stone. More WOR-guards filed into the room and took up position all around.

"Good morning opés, the dress flatters you."

"Gregor, good morning." She wanted to ask more, but his eyes cautioned her to silence.

With the positioning of the cushions, her back was to the room. Gregor faced the assembly. She followed what happened by the booted steps of the High Tenders, tracing their progress around the room by sound. One pair of boots was known only all too well. A cold chill ran up her back.

Memories of hanging by her wrists, day after day, waiting for his approach, dreading his arrival and wishing she were dead, flooded her mind. Sometimes, he had let her hang to build the anticipation to an agonizing climax. Once, he'd let her hang for almost the entire two hours of Tender Training, coming only in the last ten minutes to drag the braklav along her body. That had been one of her worst days.

High Tender Marcus stopped behind her and she couldn't help but draw in a sharp breath. "You will place your hand, palm up, on the stone in front of you. Obey your master and do as instructed. My lords, you know your role."

Elise didn't move. Shriek refused to come out. Whimper cowered in the dark, pulling shadows around herself to disappear. Malice babbled incoherently, and someone else watched from the cracks of Elise's mind.

She begged for strength from her sisters, but they abandoned her to face whatever this was alone.

A strong grip encased her hand and shocked her out of her thoughts. Her eyes widened and she stared into the concerned face of the man who'd become her master.

"Where do you go, opés, when your eyes glaze over? I know you don't dare disobey, so your hesitation must be something else."

It took a moment. She blinked several times and swallowed the lump in her throat. A deep breath helped steady her nerves, but did nothing for the rising tide of terror swirling through her veins.

"Forgive me, Gregor. The sound of the High Tender's step brought me back to Tender Training. I lost myself to my fear."

"There's no reason to be afraid."

She cocked an eyebrow. A bold move to taunt him, but she'd learned he appreciated her honesty. "If you were sitting in my place, *Emperor vlor'-Malita*, my Gregor," she sighed, "would you believe those words? Or find comfort in them?"

His eyebrows shot up at her use of his official title, the one she wasn't allowed to use, but then drew together again when she used 'my' next to his given name.

"I suppose not." He gripped her hands and gave them a squeeze. "I will be honest with you, the Blood Rite will hurt, but it will be over quickly. If it makes you feel any better, I will experience much more pain than you. Place your hand on the stone as the High Tender instructed. Your compliance is required. Your obedience expected. It is not my intent to bring you more pain. I'm sorry for that, but this is necessary."

She sniffed and tears fell from her eyes, but she complied. Her fingers brushed the stone and her palm turned up. Gregor placed his left hand over hers and pressed down. His fingers encased her wrist and held her immobile.

High Tender Marcus came to examine them. Gregor nodded and gripped the knife in his free hand.

"My lords, if you are not ready speak now." High Tender Marcus vlor'-

Vardhal waited. After a length of time, while Gregor's hand encased hers in solid steel, he spoke again. "Now, my lords, claim your s'vlor."

Time seemed to slow as Gregor thrust the knife through the air and into the top of his hand. Her mind processed his action with cool detachment.

The knife pierced his skin and slowed. Gregor came onto his knees and drove the knife deeper. His face twisted in pain. A tiny prick caught her unaware as the tip of the knife pierced her palm. Blood poured out of his wound and pooled on the gray stone.

The heat of his blood burned and she pulled back, but his grip held her firm.

He continued to press down with the knife. The prick of pain turned to fire as he buried the knife to the hilt. Then the tip of the blade made contact with the stone beneath her hand.

Screams echoed around the room, but not from Elise. The pain shocked her, but she had endured far worse pain than this. It was nothing compared to the braklav. Gregor grimaced and took three deep breaths. Sweat beaded his brow and his dark tattoo danced.

Elise breathed easily. High Tender Marcus had taught her how to control her pain; how to be in command of the sensation, so that he might give her even more. This was gruesome, but tolerable.

The knife locked their hands in a grisly union of flesh and steel. Her blood joined his, pooling on the stone. Gregor lifted their hands a few inches above the stone and rolled them over. Her blood now flowed onto his skin. It would've dripped into his wound; except the knife was in the way, but then he grasped the hilt of the blade and yanked it out.

As the blade exited her skin, the vessels, freed from the pressure of the steel, bled with renewed force.

Gregor placed the knife to the side and then pulled her hand back down to the bloodied stone. This time their positions were reversed. His hand rested on the stone with her palm upon his. His free, uninjured hand pressed her bloodied hand down. Her hand slipped on the film of blood separating their hands, but he applied pressure and kept a firm grip.

"I claim my s'vlor," he said through gritted teeth. The tendons on his neck stood out, as if he were experiencing extreme pain.

She felt next to nothing.

"I accept all responsibility and obligation for this s'vlor's training, welfare and safety. In the name of the Vendel Empire, as a vlor' lord, as Emperor Gregor Ulysses vlor'Malita, I claim Lady Malita s'Lissa s'vlor to be mine in every way."

A burning began in her palm, different from sharp pain from the knife. An intense itching bloomed between muscle and bone where it turned into a deep throb. The pulsations intensified and deepened, building to a rising fury.

Pain!

She blinked back tears and bit her lip to keep from crying out.

The bright red blood on the stone flowed. Not out of their wounds, but rather into his. Their combined blood, mixed outside their bodies, flowed up and into Gregor.

His face stretched in a grimace and he huffed against the pain. His body shook and he dug his fingers into her wrist. A low groan escaped his lips.

The blood flowed into his wound until the stone gave up the last drop of blood. Gregor removed his top hand from hers and the puncture in her hand knit together and healed as she watched.

As it closed, the voices in her head mewed in terror. The lightning shocks continued until her hand healed completely, leaving a thin scar where the knife blade had entered. The pain didn't bother her and she endured it with a dissociated calm. Gregor, however, released her hand with a cry and fell forward.

She watched with detached interest. What would happen next? What else would the Vendel throw her way? As surely nothing else could surprise her?

Echoes of women's cries and men's screams bounced off the walls.

Malice giggled. *Ninety men and ninety women with ninety sharp knives. Ninety men and ninety women with ninety sharp knives.* She ran off babbling into the darkness.

Minutes passed and the cries became whimpers. Screams became groans. Gregor clasped his previously injured hand, and sat back, his face a mask of pain.

When it was all over, the s'vlor were rounded up by the WOR-guards and marched out of the room. One-by-one they were logged out of the palm pad at the base of the steps leading to the rest of the ship. The vlor' lords remained behind and she noted most of the men, perhaps Gregor included, were still racked with agonizing spasms.

The WOR-guard led the women down several corridors to a new suite of rooms. No enclosed football stadium-space, but rather a large, square, open lounge area greeted them. Clusters of chairs and tables peppered the space, all clean white lines, too much white in her opinion. The edges of the square room held low counters with stools and gel-pads, which gave access to the am-net. All ninety of them could easily fill this space and not be crowded.

Eight doorways lined the room, leading to long corridors. Elise, Alice, Aomi and Chandra huddled together for support.

Elise, what is this? Aomi asked.

No idea.

The WOR-guards shuffled the women around and led them away in small groups.

Stay together! She tapped out the words just as a WOR-guard came to their group.

"My ladies, please follow me to your rooms." He ushered them away in a tight group and led them down a spartan hall to the last door on the left. It swished open with a faint hiss and they stepped inside after the WOR-guard. A small living room greeted them and five doors.

"Names please," he intoned, and whipped out a flimsy pad.

Aomi began, "Well, I'm Aomi, that's Chandra–"

He interrupted her, "Those names don't exist. What are your given names?"

Elise understood and hurried to fill the silence. "Lady Malita s'Lissa s'vlor."

Chandra added, "Lady Damius s'Amia s'vlor."

"Lady Adreti s'Aury s'vlor," Aomi said in a whisper.

"I'm Lady Calcask s'Adreta s'vlor," Alice shrugged. "At least we're done with the stupid numbers."

Aomi shook her head. "Be thankful for the small things, right?"

The WOR-guard spoke, "This is the Fifth Rank training deck. This room will be your suite to share. There are four bedrooms. Please inform me of which room you will claim. The fifth door leads to a private wash-room. The main lobby has eight halls leading away from it. The six on either side lead to private rooms. You are not allowed in any of the halls except for this one, leading to your specific room. You may, however, socialize in the main lobby as your free time allows.

"The two halls at the end, lead to exercise facilities, dining facilities, and training rooms. The main door is guarded at all times. There is no other exit from this deck. Once you let me know which room you claim, I will have your lord's wardrobe selections sent to your closets. You have standard exercise attire in place right now."

Elise pointed to each door in turn and assigned rooms at random. After all, how different could they be?

He made notes and nodded. "You have the rest of the day off. I suggest you exercise and try to sleep. Rod training continues in the morning as well as etiquette and other classes."

This is not good. I have to find a way off this deck.

But how and when? She looked up. A single, unmoving bio-pod clung to the ceiling.

Well, I figured it out before. Just follow the bio-pods. They will lead the way.

CHAPTER ELEVEN_

Gambit, Day 205

ELISE SHIFTED IN THE SEAT OF THE JUMP-JET AND PREPARED FOR THE CATAPULT launch. The helmet encased her head with a snug fit, and the visor display scrolled the launch checklist. The webbed straps over her shoulders, and across her lap, held her firmly to the seat and her hands rested lightly on the gel-interface pads at her sides. She flicked her eyes up to the left, signaling a 'Go' for launch, and tapped her left index finger.

The command rocketed her jump-jet out of the *Gambit's* launch tube and pressed her back against the seat. Upon exiting the ship, the feature-less gray of WOR-space became her universe. She maneuvered the jump-jet to the beginning of the course and activated her ship's communications channel.

"Lark, you ready to get spanked?"

"What the hell does that mean?" His voice crackled over the communication channel.

"It means...I'm going to beat you. You know, spank your ass? Hands down, no question. You are going to lose."

"You come up with the weirdest expressions. I've been at this longer than you, El. Care to make a wager?"

"With what? I don't have anything to bet."

"Yes, you do," he said.

Elise glanced out the canopy window at Larkin's jump-jet hovering off her starboard wing. She could see the lights of Larkin's helmet through the canopy of his cockpit. "Women don't bet that," she said flatly.

"I wasn't talking about that, although I do have an idea for a new snarking sim I'm interested in." Larkin tipped his wings.

"Well, I don't bargain away that." She prepped for entrance to the jump-jet course.

"I want something else. Something nice."

A green light flashed on her visor signifying the course was set. "Lark, you ready? Fox or Rabbit?"

"Fox," he replied. "You haven't answered me?"

Elise tapped in her acceptance for Rabbit.

The jump-jet circuit had two separate races. The first was a speed trial. The job was to navigate through a series of fifty rings set up along a twisting course around the *Gambit's* torus. Five of the rings were randomly placed and shifted wildly as the pilot approached. They gave additional bonus points if the pilot could hit them. Few did.

Most jump-jet pilots avoided the bonus rings; it could be a terrible risk. Trying and failing jeopardized the entire race. A miss could put a pilot out of position for the next set of rings. Penalty points were deducted for missed rings. Top contenders could usually hit two to three of the rings. Jeena had been the only professional pilot to successfully hit all five rings during a competition in the past fifty years.

Larkin had her interest, however, with his bet, and she couldn't resist egging him on. There was no doubt in her mind who was going to win today. "All right. What do you want that I have?"

"I want to take you to dinner, on a date, with everything that entails."

"Lark, isn't that supposed to be my line?"

Counter to Earth culture, women drove romantic entanglements among the Vendel.

She and Larkin lined up their jump-jets at the entrance to the course. In the distance, the faint shimmer of the first ring could be seen.

"El, you'll never ask!"

And I never will.

"What's wrong with a little courtship and romance?" He seemed distressed.

Everything.

"Nothing."

How she wished for the unobtrusive company of Carek. His demands were simple and he wanted nothing from her beyond a casual friendship. This was not so from some of the others. To them she was an unattached female. It was considered rude for Vendel men to ask outright, which left quite a bit of room for subtle hints. Larkin, in particular, attempted to turn their friendship into something else at every opportunity. This request came dangerously close to crossing social boundaries.

For so many reasons it was out of the question. She could never explain to Larkin why that was, and it didn't help that he'd developed a serious crush over the past weeks. He was a great friend and wonderful training partner, but nothing more.

Training of every form dominated her life. Vendel culture class, and the new diplomatic and social sciences classes the High Tenders levied on the Fifth Rank WOR, filled her days with mind numbing study.

Gregor stuffed the Rod skills down her throat every afternoon. The High Tender insisted on teaching the WOR-skill in the traditional manner. Rarely, Gregor would allow her to try the skills in her own fashion. However, despite her successes, High Tender Marcus would not advance her skill levels until she'd demonstrated mastery using conventional means.

Each day, Gregor ended Rod training a few minutes before the other lords. He walked her to her suite and, in the brief minutes until her roommates arrived, he held her close, stroked her hair, and murmured in her ear his pride in her accomplishments. Sometimes, he stole kisses, sometimes he sat and they talked about the many worlds of the Vendel empire. He never asked about her childhood, her past, or anything tied to Earth, but opened up about his past. It seemed important to him that he share this piece of his life.

How could she explain to Larkin that his affections were wasted on the Emperor's slave? How did she reconcile her growing affection for Gregor? In those stolen moments, she could almost forget what he'd done.

"I don't have time for that right now. I really want to focus on the race. Are you ready?" Elise tried to put Larkin off.

"Yeah, but what about the bet?" Larkin wasn't so easily dissuaded.

"How about this, if you win, I'll let you take me out for a lunch, no dinners." She couldn't promise him a dinner. That ran up against her time limit on the training deck. "If I win, then you promise not to ask again until after the jump-jet circuit finals."

"Fleet finals?" he asked cautiously.

"No, Imperial finals?"

"Aw, shit, you're kidding, right?"

"Take it or leave it."

"Well, since I'm only going to get a lunch out of this, let's make it harder. Rabbit turns Fox at thirty-five."

"Thirty-five! What happened to twenty-five?"

Rabbit and Fox was the elimination race held between two pilots, and Elise's favorite of the two races. The Rabbit received a thirty-second lead and evaded the Fox down the twisting length of the course. All the rings had to be hit, but there was no time limit, and unlike the first race, a time trial, there were no bonus rings during Rabbit and Fox.

If Fox hit Rabbit with the laser weapons in the first half of the race, Fox scored two points. If, however, the Fox failed, the Rabbit's lasers became active at the halfway point, ring twenty-five.

Then it became an exciting duel.

The race could end several ways. If the Rabbit had a solid lead, the pilot could simply race to the finish line. Crossing first earned Rabbit a victory and two points. If Fox finished first, without scoring a hit on Rabbit, Fox gained a single point. It was in Fox's interest to score a hit on Rabbit, but sometimes earning one point was better than scoring none.

However, once Rabbit's weapons activated, another outcome became possible. It was Elise's favorite outcome. *Rabbit grew fangs.* If Rabbit 'killed' Fox, then Rabbit earned three points and gained a hefty lead in the point tally.

The competition played out over a series of three races. The two pilots took turns as Fox and Rabbit. The pilot trailing in points had choice for the last round and the pilot with the highest score progressed to the next elimination race.

"Tell you what Lark, I'll take thirty rings. But don't get too depressed when you get trounced."

"Famous last words, El. I'm already thinking about where I'm taking you for lunch."

Elise reprogrammed the course to switch on Rabbit's lasers at the thirtieth ring. She edged her craft in front of Larkin's and prepared for the race, thinking that it might be fun to let him win. Her display winked green and she hit the thrusters.

Thirty seconds later, he came after his prize. If Larkin really wanted to court her, he was going to have to earn it. She slid through the first ring, hitting it dead on. The second twinkled ahead and to the right. The jump-jet banked hard and she screamed toward the second ring. By the time Elise had swung past the third ring, Larkin started his pursuit.

He had to follow through the rings just as she did, but in between it was a game of chase. All he had to do was sight his laser on her ship and it would all be over. Elise passed over the fourth ring and began defensive maneuvers.

Larkin pressed the attack, but she evaded and wove a complex pattern, forcing him out of his intended path and thwarting his perfectly lined up sights. Her ship dipped through ring after ring and he followed, blasting her fleeing form without effect.

Ring twenty-five came and went and Elise remained untouched. He now lagged two rings behind and had some catching up to do. Elise pressed her advantage and dove through the next series of rings.

They wove their paths around the far side of the torus to the halfway point. Here, the rings came precariously close to *Gambit's* surface, only to later stretch out to the furthest boundaries of the WOR-space bubble.

Elise headed toward the torus, arrowed through the rings, and then twisted her ship violently around to scream toward the next ring at the boundary point. Larkin had gained a ring and laser fire streaked around her craft.

"Oh, no you don't," she screamed through the communications channel.

"Give it up, El. There's no way you can make it to the next ring. I've got you."

Never. The twenty-ninth ring loomed in front of her and the boundary lurked just beyond. Her only choice was to continue along her current trajectory, through the center, and then pull up and around to race all the way back to the *Gambit*. All the while, giving Larkin a clean, and steady, target to line up his lasers.

Inspiration struck. She didn't have to go forward to win, sometimes backward worked just as well.

She was nearly to the ring. The evasive maneuvers barely kept Larkin off her tail. Soon she'd have to straighten out if she were make it through the ring. Which was exactly what she hoped Larkin expected. He, of course as Fox, couldn't enter the ring until after Rabbit.

Elise steadied her approach and watched as Larkin lined up for the kill shot. When her display notified weapon's locked, she pressed down on the controls and looped in a tight corkscrew away from the ring, and directly toward Larkin. His weapon's lock failed.

Elise chuckled as he cursed over the communications channel. Her flight course leveled out and she headed directly toward Larkin. This was a game of chicken and she didn't think Larkin would react fast enough to reengage his lasers. If she could get inside his targeting solution, he wouldn't be able to lock on. Then, one of them would have to pull away. That person was not going to be her.

"Snark it! What the devil are you doing?" Larkin shouted.

Elise activated her thrusters and accelerated. "Winning."

"El," he cautioned. The space between the ships narrowed. She could hear him tapping out code over the communications channel. The weapons lock blipped twice and slid off her ship. She breached the boundary where his laser targeting systems could not lock on.

"Damn," he swore. "El, pull up."

"No," she said, enjoying his frustration.

"You can't chase me, you're still the Rabbit. You have no weapons!"

"You're right." Red collision alarms flashed. She could make out the lights on his helmet and visor now, but held her course steady. He swore a string of Vendel curses she couldn't follow and rolled his ship up and away. His retreat went wild and took him away from the twenty-ninth ring.

She banked hard and dove toward number twenty-nine.

While Larkin struggled to bring his jump-jet back into line, she orchestrated her maneuver flawlessly. She was halfway back to the *Gambit* before he managed to realign and navigate the twenty-ninth ring.

Perfect. The *Gambit* and the thirtieth ring hung before her eyes.

It was time for Rabbit to hunt the Fox.

Elise ducked through ring thirty and her weapons display bloomed into life. Larkin streamed toward the *Gambit*. Elise had no intention of racing toward the finish line. She lined up her sites on his ship and, without waiting for weapon's lock, fired when it *felt* right.

The visor display confirmed her 'kill' and she earned three points.

"Why you rotten little…" Larkin's words trailed off in another spray of Vendel curses.

Elise laughed. "Rabbit got Fox. Are you ready to be the Rabbit, Lark? You're gonna have to get two points in each of the next rounds to have any chance of winning your bet. I bet Fox takes Rabbit by ring twenty in the next race. Care to wager?"

He cursed and Elise accelerated back to the start of the course, laughing, and feeling more alive than she had in a very long time.

CHAPTER TWELVE_

Gambit, Day 221

High Tender Marcus led WOR-skill instruction with his droning voice and demands for perfection. Elise barely managed to achieve proficiency with the first two skills of the Rod, while the others seemed to breeze through the skills, working on the fifth skill. Not a single vlor' lord was present during this WOR-skill training session, which was unusual. The High Tenders paced around the room as the ninety Fifth Rank WOR went through the drills.

Her skin itched with the certainty the Vendel had some new surprise in store for the women.

Each High Tender had five to ten WOR under his personal supervision and instruction. High Tender Marcus had only four, including Elise. The women had been separated into the High Tender's personal groups to make it easier for the High Tenders to oversee the training.

With the vlor' lords present, the sound level in the room usually remained just below a quiet hush. The lords encouraged and soothed the women as they worked the forms, performed drills, or were introduced to the next skill. The High Tenders did not encourage conversation. They expected obedience and, in general, received it. As such, the room remained eerily silent without the encouraging voices of the vlor' lords.

Every time High Tender Marcus passed her seat, Whimper smiled and struggled to please, whilst Shriek cowered and Malice cackled in the background. Elise found the voices distracting and struggled to push her sisters to the back of her mind. A fourth presence stared out of the darkness, but had yet to reveal herself to the others.

Quiet permeated the room. That, in and of itself, wasn't unusual. At times, s'vlor trained in the absence of their vlor' lord, with their High Tender providing the required guidance. The uncommon aspect of today's training session was that not a single vlor' lord was present.

High Tender Marcus came to stand over her shoulder as she worked the first skill of the Rod. "Your vectoring solution is wrong s'Lissa. Solidify your base and clean up these lines."

"Yes, High Tender Marcus." Her reply came with instant obedience, something hammered in by Tender Training. Her lines were clean, damn him, but she and her sisters never disobeyed the Master Tender.

A pitcher of water sat on the table. It was supposed to be ice. The first skill involved phase transformation and began with shifting water through its various forms: gas, liquid and solid. It was one of the last steps in the first skill of the Rod.

She was doing a spectacular job of failing and couldn't get the simplest phase change, liquid to solid, to occur. High Tender Marcus's disapproval hung heavily in the air.

Elise complied, with the encouragement of Shriek, and reformed her vectors and folded the construct. High Tender Marcus grunted as the first ice crystals formed.

The lesson continued. Tension hung around them all, causing the women to shift and cough in their seats. The High Tenders continued instruction as normal until the bell sounded. Elise filed out of the room with her friends.

Chandra's luminous eyes beamed with excitement. *I got the sixth skill!*

Congratulations, Alice tapped, using the code. *I'm still stuck on the last step of the fifth. Can't seem to wrap my mind around that one.*

Maybe Elise can help. Aomi flipped her straight, black hair over her shoulder.

Me? I bombed the first skill, again. I have no consistency in any of this. Elise shrugged.

Aomi tapped, *Well, that's just because they're stupid. If they'd just let you do it your way...*

They exited the long hall and filed into the main lounge area where ninety vlor' lords stood around the space, their expressions grim.

The first thing Elise noticed was the dark tattoo dancing on Gregor's face. He stood at the head of the gathered vlor'. The second thing she noticed were all the chairs and tables pushed to the sides of the room. The center of the lounge had been cleared. The women came to a sudden, confused halt and the light chatter ceased.

High Tender Marcus spoke from behind the women. "Form yourself into rows according to High Tender group. You have less than thirty seconds to comply."

The women rushed to the center and arranged themselves as directed. Elise didn't move. The glower on Gregor's face, the flash of steel in his eyes, and the fists formed at his side, gave her pause. Her sisters squirmed in her head and a dull roar sounded in her ears.

"Elise!" Alice hissed, standing at the end of one of the rows.

Elise brought her head around to the sound. They weren't supposed to have those names. A fact immediately brought to Alice's attention as High Tender Anders vlor'Alturis pressed his braklav to Alice's neck.

Alice's shriek echoed off the walls, but the High Tender's words carried easily over her screams. "Those names are dead!"

The blonde croaked out a weak, "Forgive me, High Tender Anders." Alice's High Tender yanked her off the floor and deposited Alice back on her feet.

Malice hissed and propelled Elise toward the front row where three other women stood. She took position at the end of the line of her Tender Group. Her eyes locked onto Gregor's. The fury darkening his face sent Whimper and Malice cowering into darkness. Shriek took a breath and stood at Elise's elbow, waiting, anticipating.

Preparing.

In less than the allowed thirty seconds, the women lined up in ordered rows. Ninety vlor' lords and fifteen High Tenders looked on with dispassion.

One emperor fumed.

Gregor stepped forward. The High Tenders arrayed themselves loosely behind their charges. The vlor' lords came to attention.

"Ladies…" Gregor flicked his attention to Elise and narrowed his eyes. "Certain rules have been in place since the very first day you arrived. Specific rules that shaped our intent. As you have learned, failure to obey has consequences."

He stepped to the first row of s'vlor, at the end opposite Elise. Gregor passed each s'vlor, pausing to loom as only he could do. After an agonizing period of time, he came to stand in front of Elise.

She said nothing, but held his fierce gaze. Shriek stood up straight.

"Is there anything..." His gaze flicked to the row behind and back to Elise, "anything you wish to tell your masters?"

The women glanced around, exchanging bewildered looks. Fear laced their eyes, as did incomprehension.

Gregor scowled and leaned in to whisper in her ear. "Opés, is there anything you wish to tell me?"

Lots of things flashed through her mind. None were good. What had they discovered? What did Gregor know? Her mind raced, trying to determine how she had slipped up. What critical mistake had she made? Did he know about her nightly forays? About Jeena? About the jump-jet training? Had he found out about her silent little army in the am-net? There were simply too many secrets held in her head.

Elise stared back into eyes absent of compassion and said simply, "No, Gregor."

His lips twitched into one of his smirks. "Well, opés, that is unfortunate. And here, I thought we'd made such progress." He shook his head. "It was unwise to make fools out of the vlor' lords." He stepped back to stand at the head of the mass of Vendel lords. "Master Tender, the s'vlor are yours."

Those words rang with frightening familiarity in her head.

High Tender Marcus came to stand at the front of the s'vlor. "Ladies, is there not a single one of you willing to admit disobedience?"

The women whimpered.

A woman behind spoke out. "High Tender vlor'Vardhal, what have we done to displease you?" Her cries began a chorus of similar words.

High Tender Marcus allowed the women to speak.

Elise watched his eyes.

In training sessions, this man's eyes sparkled with warmth. He cared about all the s'vlor and worked to bring them along slowly, deliberately, without fear, in the discovery of the WOR-skill. In place of the liquid brown pools of warmth, Elise noticed the flat, dispassionate gaze she had come to know all too well in the little room at the end of the Confinement Deck.

High Tender Marcus had moved fully into Tender Training mode and not a single woman here knew what was to come. His gaze passed over Elise and he gave a slow nod, confirming what was coming. Yet, she still had no clue what had brought on this mass Tender Training session. The women's protestations died out and were replaced by ragged sobs and sniffles of fear.

It was something they had all done, she suddenly realized. It had nothing to do with her secrets. That at least was still safe. However, there was one thing, something small, something secret, something the vlor' lords had finally discovered.

Elise tore her gaze from High Tender Marcus and looked directly at Gregor.

She'd tapped out in the code, clear and strong. *You discovered the code.*

It was loud enough to be heard by everyone in the room. The women went eerily silent and the men stiffened as one, confirming the truth of her words. Then she did something stupid.

What took you so damned long?

Gregor launched forward, coming at her in a blur. He slapped her with the force of granite. Her head whipped wildly and Elise spun with the force of his blow. She crumpled. It was fortunate Gregor grabbed her, or the impact with the ground might have hurt. Before Elise passed out, startled gasps of comprehension and the thuds of several s'vlor falling to the ground filled the room. At least they had the privilege of fainting.

Gregor didn't allow her to remain unconscious. The braklav brought her back to full, painful awareness. When she did, there was not a single s'vlor standing. The women had all been forced to their knees.

"She's back with us, sire. We may proceed." The dispassionate voice of High Tender Marcus grated in her ears.

Gregor spoke and Elise heard his words as if from a great distance. There was no way the women could endure Tender Training. It would destroy them. Many of these women liked their new masters. It had only been her hate which had given her the strength to endure.

Shriek pulled at Elise's elbow and guided her toward the dark. *This is my job*, she whispered. *I will take the pain.*

Elise shrugged off her silent sister. *No, I can't let them destroy these women.*

What choice do you have, sister?

I must try.

Shriek let go and Elise remained.

High Tender Marcus spoke to the kneeling women. "Communication was forbidden, and yet you devised this code. You flaunted this in front of the High Tenders, the WOR-guards, and your masters for cycle upon cycle. This mistake will cost you dearly, s'vlor."

He paced up and down the rows. "I want to know who was responsible for the code."

Silence echoed his words. Elise realized with incredible pride what that implied. This group of women, Earth women, slaves, fodder, property, had achieved solidarity. They had been beaten and yet, in this one small thing, they held together.

And then it began. Voices rose from all around her.

"It was me, High Tender vlor'Vardhal."

"No, me. I devised the code."

"No. It was me."

"No, forgive me, but I made the code."

"I did, and I taught it to us all."

The words repeated again and again.

Elise's face stung from the impact of Gregor's hand. The women protected her, or tried to. All of them. These women knew the terror of Tender Training, had watched as Elise retreated day after day to the back of the Confinement Deck. They understood what had happened there.

High Tender Marcus stood quietly, as the cries of admission percolated up from the mass of s'vlor. His face clouded over with fury.

"Enough!" he roared. "You dare lie to me!"

Elise controlled her breathing. They couldn't take this for her.

But can we take it for them? That voice belonged to the silent sister.

Who are you? Elise searched the darkness of her mind, but the silent sister retreated to the shadows.

"Each of you will receive five days of Tender Training. I trust you understand what that entails."

There was no response from the women.

No. This can't happen.

Elise braved the reaction of the High Tender.

"Gregor," she said, in a cool detached voice full of strength. "They seek to protect me. I made the code. You know I did. We've had it since the very first day. With it, I kept our identities intact, our names, our heritage, and our anger simmering in the background. I've used it to fuel my hatred of you, the High Tender and all the rest. I've continued to use it, through and past, Tender Training. While pretending to be supplicant, I have flaunted this one victory in your face, without your knowledge. I have reveled in this small thing we had. I used it so that we might get to know one another and find strength. And I've used it as a weapon to try to beat you."

"No, Elise don't!" several voices cried out in unison.

"Silence!" The High Tenders spoke as one. The words died on the lips of the s'vlor.

Gregor spoke softly. "I have underestimated you, opés. Those are damning words. You claim responsibility?"

"Yes, Gregor."

High Tender Marcus interrupted, "My lord, what are you doing?"

"Lord vlor'Vardhal ten days of Tender Training, obviously, was not enough for this s'vlor."

"It was not without effect. You can attest to that personally." The High Tender's defense of her came as a surprise, but it was short lived.

"We have been fools," Gregor said. "It's time to teach this woman a real lesson. I'm not pleased, opés. We could have done this the easy way, but it seems you prefer to make things difficult. You have made a serious mistake."

Gregor put a finger under her chin and lifted her face to his. He looked down at her and his entire visage changed. "This is not your day. I sentence you to twenty days of double sessions with Lord vlor'Vardhal. Perhaps we will see how much fight is left in you after that."

"Yes, Gregor," she said in resigned acceptance. Her entire body shook with the implication of the pronouncement. Double sessions for two cycles. It was too much. She was defeated, but she had to save the others from the agony of Tender Training. "It was my code, my plan. They don't deserve Tender Training."

He rubbed a finger along the line of her jaw. She jerked away from his touch and watched as he pursed his lips.

Gregor cupped her jaw in his muscular hand and wrenched her face back around to look at him. "Opés. You don't understand Tenders at all. The punishment has been given. It will be dealt."

"Then, I will take it for them." Elise shuddered and silenced her mind as it calculated the math. High Tender Marcus hissed and the room went silent. Elise watched the cold steel of Gregor's eyes glitter as he considered.

"Lord vlor'Vardhal, would this satisfy the High Tenders. Can this s'vlor take the Tender Training of all the women?"

"The punishment has been spoken and must be dealt, but a single s'vlor can't endure that much Tender Training. It will kill her."

"Sorry, opés."

Alice stood, "High Tender vlor'Vardhal, I will share in the burden."

Alice tapped in their very private code, known only to the two of them, and therefore still secret. *We knew this day would come. I am here for you. We will endure. But we are not defeated. A secret kept by two is still a secret.*

Elise wavered on her feet. *You have no idea how bad it will be.*

One by one the s'vlor stood and repeated Alice's words. Each woman accepted her portion of the Tender Training with one exception.

Sarah screamed, "I knew nothing of any of this. My lord, I would have told you. You know I would." Sarah broke ranks and ran to her lord, High Councilor Lord vlor'Altus. Sarah wept at his feet and he reached down to pet the top of her head.

High Tender Marcus spoke. "My lords. Your charges will receive Tender Training to address this disobedience. Five days have been given by the High Tenders. If you agree, stand by your s'vlor now. If not, then remove your s'vlor to her rooms. She will receive a single Tender Training session but no more."

The lords moved toward the women. "Understand lords, the full five sessions will be dealt. If too many of you remove your s'vlor, the others will take up the slack."

Sobs echoed his pronouncement. Gregor, still holding Elise's chin in his grip, did not move. The vlor' lords came to their s'vlor. High Councilor Lord vlor'Altus pulled Sarah off to her rooms. She glanced at Elise in triumph and followed her master. None of the other lords pulled their charges away.

Tears streamed down Elise's face. "Give me their punishment. Please I beg of you. Gregor, please. They have no idea what's in store."

The High Tender came to stand beside Gregor. "Are you satisfied, Emperor?"

"No." He frowned. "I need more if I am to control this one."

High Tender Marcus raised his eyebrows in interest. "What more do you want?"

Gregor spoke so his voice carried across the room. "Five days is a lot to endure. As Emperor, I request a reduction to three sessions for the rest so they might return to WOR-skill training as quickly as possible. For this one, you will administer triple sessions. I need her crushed."

"Yes, Sire." His voice boomed, "High Tenders, you have heard your emperor."

Gregor turned to the High Tender and said, "One more thing, Lord vlor'Vardhal?"

"Yes, my lord."

"This one needs a greater degree of control. Do you understand?"

"Yes, Sire."

"Release me from my oath. She must be bound!"

Elise's throat hitched. Her heart hiccupped and then raced in a mad flutter. *Please, High Tender,* she begged and squeezed her eyes shut. *Do not allow this.* Her hands clenched and slickened with sweat. That would be worse than Tender Training.

"You take a great risk, my lord, especially with her not yet trained. But, you made that oath as emperor, not as a vlor' lord. I can't release you from your oath. Only the High Council can."

Elise had been holding her breath and let it out with these words of reprieve. She took a breath and then another.

Gregor's hand squeezed her jaw and he glared at her. "Then I will bring it to the High Council. Will I receive your support?"

High Tender Marcus pursed his lips. "It is dangerous to bind an untrained s'vlor, but I agree. It must be done. I support you."

"Thank you, Master Tender."

Elise faded to darkness as Shriek stepped into the light, stretching and preparing for the ordeal ahead. Whimper wrapped an arm around Elise's shoulder while Malice grumbled about Tenders and their braklavs. The silent sister was nowhere to be found.

CHAPTER THIRTEEN_

THE WOR-SKILL TRAINING ROOM HAD BEEN RECONFIGURED FOR TENDER Training during the confrontation with the lords in the common room. The tables had been removed and long silver rods had been secured to the ceiling. Elise knew immediately what they were for. The other girls figured it out when they saw the shackles dangling from the dull, gleaming metal.

High Tender Marcus began with Elise. The fourteen other High Tenders strung up their charges. Gregor pulled up a seat and made himself comfortable for the two-hour Tender Training session. The women's vlor' masters followed suit and pulled up chairs to observe the punishment alongside their emperor.

It was harder to endure with Gregor watching. She wondered what she must look like. Soon, however, she wasn't thinking about much other than the High Tender. Gregor faded from her thoughts while Shriek soaked up the pain.

At the end of the first session, the High Tender released her and placed her along the wall to huddle her sweat soaked body until the second session began. He moved on to his next charge. Paula was a strong woman in her mid-twenties. The lines of her body were sculpted and hard, but her expression betrayed fear.

The High Tender laid into her with his dispassionate calm and Paula cracked in under ten minutes, gasping for breath. She begged for a forgiveness that would never come. The High Tender calmly told her what would happen the next time she begged. Paula did not speak other than to scream.

Elise watched the other girls with cool detachment and wondered if she looked the same, or if her screams sounded so forlorn. Whimper kept her company while Shriek made ready for the next round. Malice growled and prowled in the darkness.

Gregor secured Elise back to the rod and observed the next session. Wave after wave of s'vlor entered the chamber. It filled with quietly apprehensive women as they wondered how bad it could really be. The chamber emptied as they left knowing all too well the answer to that question. High Tenders had no mercy and the braklavs allowed them to dispense great pain without inflicting permanent damage to a body.

The room filled and emptied several times. The other two s'vlor, who High Tender Marcus trained, took their turns while Elise recovered and waited for her next session.

Elise watched the women for four and a half hours before her next, and last, turn of the day. It gave Whimper time to contemplate the first two sessions while Shriek prepared for the last. High Tender Marcus took breaks for food. Elise was not fed.

Gregor attended all of Elise's sessions. When her turn came back around, the third and last for the first day, Gregor dragged her off her feet without a word. He placed her at the bar and shackled her wrists in place. It was very considerate of him to help. She didn't think she could have stood, let alone lift her arms to the shackles.

"Opés," he said with a smile, although his eyes danced with fury. The tattoo above his brow she ignored. It promised pain.

"Gregor," she answered, automatically.

"I have placed my request before the High Council. I'm anxious for them to meet." He placed a finger under her chin and traced a cool line down her throat and between her breasts. The smile fixed on his lips held pure malice. His eyes twinkled with unspoken promises. He traced a circle around her left breast and then moved his hand around her back. He cupped her bare bottom and yanked her forcibly against his body. Her shoulders wrenched with the strength of his pull, and he brought her painfully to her tiptoes and gave a chaste kiss.

"Yes, Gregor."

"Once you are bound to me, it will be impossible for you to resist, or lie to me, ever again. It's a quirk of the bond."

Day after day, the scene repeated.

The conversation was the same each time and ended with the same slow kiss on her lips. The fact that she was naked, and he brushed his fingers across her breasts, simply didn't matter anymore. The kiss was Shriek's signal to come out and play, while Elise faded into oblivion. Malice became more and more feral as the days progressed. Whimper struggled to please a Tender who simply did not care.

The High Tenders remained busy. Each man took care of his group of five to ten s'vlor. At two hours per session, it made for a long day for the High Tenders, so they split the women into groups and conducted Tender Training on alternating days.

Six days later, Tender Training ended, except for Elise, Shriek and Whimper. Malice was missing. Elise didn't know where that sister had gone.

The mood on the Fifth Deck was subdued, but not a single woman complained to Elise, or blamed her for Tender Training. The opposite occurred. Nearly everyone made an effort to comfort Elise and wish her strength for what she must still endure.

Gregor moved the remainder of her Tender Training sessions to her suite so that WOR-skill training might continue in the classroom. The bars were left in place as a reminder, so that the s'vlor would have every opportunity to contemplate the price of disobedience throughout their day.

Each night Elise fell into bed. When her body stopped twitching, sleep shrouded her mind. In the sweet release of her dreams, she dreamed of jump-jet training, silver rings, and escape.

CHAPTER FOURTEEN_

Gambit, Day 222

ELISE ATTACHED HER WRISTS TO THE BAR GREGOR PLACED IN HER SUITE FOR Tender Training. Her roommates, forbidden to speak to her, went about their morning routine in silence, except Alice, who became Elise's sole link to her friends. Their private code endured; a secret known only by two. With a flicker or a glance, Alice lent Elise the strength she needed to survive another day.

Shriek gazed up at the cuffs. *I can't do this.*

Whimper's tears emptied. *I too, am done. We are beaten.*

Malice hissed and retreated somewhere in the dark. It had been days since she'd said a word.

This left Elise alone in her body.

Nor can I.

And that was it. She was done. With a shrug, she left the body to endure by itself. Her consciousness separated from the flesh and floated away.

How did you do that? Shriek craned her neck.

Why didn't we do this sooner? Whimper wriggled free of their body and hovered beside Elise.

Shriek detached as well, and joined them.

I didn't know I could.

Whimper pointed. *The High Tender has arrived.*

Where's Malice? Elise peered at the body, but didn't see signs of Malice.

I should have been stronger. Shriek's disgruntled frown spoke of her frustration.

The High Tender walked up to Elise, and without a word pressed the braklav to her spine.

Oh, Shriek said, *Usually that makes me twitch. Do you think he'll do the fire thing next? It makes the skin feel like it's blistering and bubbling.*

Shriek, stop, Whimper said with a moan. *You don't have to tell me how it feels.*

The High Tender's lips pressed into a firm line. He touched the braklav to the base of her skull. Nothing happened. He moved it down, tracing each vertebrae as he went.

Nothing.

Without them inside to feel the agony, the body hung limp and unresponsive.

He stepped back, a deep crease furrowed on his brow.

"S'vlor?"

She didn't answer. She couldn't, because she wasn't inside the body. Elise watched, curious as to what would happen next.

Footsteps sounded in the hall and a new presence arrived. Elise turned, but there was only one person it could be.

Gregor has arrived. Do you think he'll kiss me today?

I don't like his kisses, Malice hissed. *What are all of you doing out there?* She poked her head out from the dark, but then disappeared again.

Elise shook her head. *Malice, come back. Join us.*

No! I don't like it when they're together. She scuttled into a darker corner, disappearing from the conversation.

Don't you think we should twitch a little? Shriek asked in a quiet voice.

Elise glanced at the unmoving body, watching it hang from the shackles. High Tender Marcus pressed the braklav to the skin over and over again but nothing happened.

I'm scared. It feels wrong being out here. Whimper hugged herself as Gregor approached the body.

"Opés?" His eyes narrowed and his hand reached out.

They didn't answer.

He brushed her hair aside. "My request goes before the High Council. We will become one, bonded together." His brows drew down in concern as her body failed to respond to his touch. He glanced toward the High Tender. "Lord vlor'Vardhal, something is wrong."

"A word, if you please, my lord." High Tender Marcus gestured with a jerk of his head for Gregor to join him at the far end of the room.

Now, this is interesting. The body hung from the shackles, forgotten, as Elise brought the girls over to hover above the men's heads.

Whimper babbled. *This feels wrong.*

Shriek moaned. *I'm scared.*

Malice hissed.

Shh...we need to listen. Everyone quiet!

"My lord, she's not responding."

"What do you mean?"

"I press the braklav to her skin and I get nothing."

"Not possible." Gregor glanced across the room at their body.

"And yet it is." The High Tender's lips puffed out with his breath.

"No s'vlor can resist the braklav. Explain." Gregor's dark brows drew down.

"There's no doubt she's feeling every bit of what I'm giving. The nerves are firing, but she's gone."

Gregor kept his face blank. "How is that possible?"

They watched the High Tender scratch his head. "I may have broken her beyond repair."

Gregor scowled. "Hell, she had us fooled. Is she faking this now, to avoid the punishment?"

"I wouldn't put it past her, but I don't believe so. I can't explain this withdrawal, but I do have an idea to pull her back out."

Whimper cried. *I don't like it when they get ideas!*

The High Tender walked back to her body. Gregor watched as the High Tender pressed the braklav to her skin. Again, there was no response.

"If she no longer responds to the braklav, perhaps watching her friends endure its touch will bring her around? We can start with her suite-mates."

No! No! No! All three of them wailed.

Gregor paused. He walked back over to their body. He tapped his index finger on his chin, and appeared to be deep in thought. "I won't ask their lords to consent to more just because I can't control my s'vlor." He traced a finger down her back, to her hips, and then back up her side.

She felt nothing.

"I've felt this before, a dissonance in her, but this detachment shouldn't be possible. Opés, where have you gone?" he whispered in her ear. "The High Tender wants to bring your friends into this. I don't think that will solve our problems."

He pulled her hair to the side, exposing her neck. Strong hands touched her skin. He rubbed the tight cords in her neck, lightly at first and then a little deeper.

"I never wished this on you, but my hands were tied. Your disobedience had to be dealt with. Tender Training is a singularly effective means of control and a useful reminder of your place…at least until we can be Bonded." His fingers moved to her shoulders.

"This is what I'd rather do for you. It feels good, does it not, opés?" Gregor moved his massage to her arms and up to her hands. He unshackled her wrists and massaged her fingers.

She looked at him, but did not respond.

What is he doing? Shriek screamed. *I don't like this.*

What would it cost us to just give this man what he wants? Whimper spoke softly and began to drift back into the body.

It costs us everything! Shriek screamed. *Have you forgotten about the jump-jet? Jeena? Dove? Earth?*

Earth is dead to us! Malice hissed out of the darkness. *No longer our home! Dead! Dead! Dead!*

There was some truth to what Malice said.

What do we do? Elise turned to her sisters, seeking guidance.

No one answered.

Gregor lifted the body and carried it in his arms. He headed to the bedroom. Whimper stomped into the darkness in a huff, not speaking to Shriek. Shriek followed, her shoulders hunched in defeat.

Where are you going? Elise asked.

I…I am too tired. You need to deal with this. I'm done. Shriek faded away.

Elise stretched out her hand to catch her sister, to bring her back. She came back with nothing.

Gregor laid her body on the bed and rolled her over to her stomach. The High Tender watched from the doorway, and the braklav dangled impotently from his wrist. Gregor continued his massage and worked down her back, taking his time, soothing her body.

Clenched muscles released and the tension in her body evaporated. She shouldn't feel anything, but Gregor's touch crossed the chasm from her body to her mind, pulling at her and drawing her back.

He moved to her buttocks and down the backs of her thighs. He spent an eternity on her calves. They bucked and went into spasm at his touch. Gregor worked out the cramps with a deliberate touch. He finished at her feet.

Elise shuddered as warmth flooded her body and a release from pain suffused her soul.

Gregor lifted her and carried her into the bathroom. He turned on the shower, until a warm mist filled the air.

The High Tender followed.

"Come, hold her while I strip out of my clothes."

"What are you doing?" Suspicion clouded the High Tender's words.

"I'm going to wash her hair, and I'd prefer not to get my clothes wet."

"And you think a massage and shower are the answers to our problem?" High Tender Marcus jerked his chin. He sounded dubious.

"Her body has shut down. It can't take anymore. Her mind...I don't know what's up with her mind. I sense her, but she is not in here." He pointed to her body. "I can't explain what I'm feeling, except I feel her presence. A massage and a warm shower might go a long way toward bringing her back. Maybe even a little forgiveness and leniency? Do you have any better ideas?"

Gregor pulled his boots off and stripped out of his clothes. He gestured for the High Tender to hand over the body.

"You still feel her? That's good, but is Binding the solution? She's nowhere near ready for a proper ritual and you're not fully prepared to accept the Bond. It's too risky."

"What else do we have? Tender Training has no effect. I must have control over her. I can think of nothing more absolute than Binding."

"It's too soon after the Blood Rite." The High Tender scuffed his boot on the floor and sat at the bench. "Is there even enough of her essence grafted inside of you to perform the Binding Ritual?"

"The changes are unfinished, but I am sensing her. Not to the degree of Lord vlor'Delatris. I certainly couldn't sense this secret code they kept from us. But I'm beginning to feel the swirling of her thoughts. I can almost feel her presence now. Reading her mind is beyond me at this point, but it's not unusual to proceed with Binding before that is established. Her strength of mind is intense. I can feel a little of her passion in my blood. It will only get stronger with time."

"Did she fool you with her desire for you as well? You may not be as *pleased* at the consummation as you had hoped."

"Our compatibility is a ten. Physically, she can't resist me. You've seen what happens when I touch her. Once she realizes this, she'll accept me." Gregor sighed. "For now, I need control of her mind, not her body. Even a weak bond will strengthen over time. After the final transformation, she'll be incapable of lying to me ever again."

"What about disobeying? We have nothing if her obedience isn't secured. You know what you must demand of her."

"I do, and I hate what is coming." Gregor sighed. "Please get some towels and clothes for Elise."

"You use her Earth name? We remove those for a reason." The High Tender opened one of the cabinets, and retrieved several towels. He watched as Gregor placed her body under the shower.

"Elise is the name she responds to best. She hasn't accepted her place in our world." He cooed in her ear and wiped soap off her forehead. "I'm going to give you a reason to care about the Vendel, Elise. I'm going to turn your rage into something I can use. I'm going to show you something worse than me to fear."

"What do you plan?"

Gregor's voice went icy cold.

Elise shivered despite the warm water pouring over her body.

"Ultimately, I defer to you, but I think you'll agree. She uses her powers differently. Beginning with the Vector, the Tenderstat, the Activator, and even the most severe Tender Training, she is wired differently from the rest. Her biology is something we've never seen. When she acts unconsciously, WOR-skill flows out of her effortlessly. When she thinks about it, she stutters and stumbles through the most basic of drills. I want to tap into her unconscious mind. That's where her power lies. To do that, I need her bonded to me."

Gregor scrubbed her hair now. He sat on the floor of the shower and cradled her head in his lap.

Steam filled the room and she breathed in the thick air. His touch was gentle. His voice smooth and it soothed her jangled nerves. The cadence of his words took her up and down in a gentle, lulling rhythm.

Where have you gone, my sisters?

"The control she demonstrated in the park...the ability to tie off the construct was impressive. Have you ever seen a s'vlor do that at this stage? I want her out of WOR-skill training all together. I want her to observe true WOR and let her abilities take form organically."

Elise closed her eyes and allowed the pain of Tender Training to leave her body and swirl down the drain. Gregor's touch awakened her and pulled her back to her body. Which was exactly where she wanted to be so she could feel more of his electric touch. But how could she want that from a man who had sentenced her to such brutal torture? Is that why the High Tenders wielded the braklav and not the v'lor lords?

She sighed as Gregor squeezed the water out of her hair and wrapped her in a towel. She felt pampered. Cared for. Cherished? Maybe even loved.

"Now, opés, if you can hear me, I'm going to wrap you up and put you to bed. Sleep. Tender Training is finished. You are forgiven. No more pain. Relax. Dream." He kissed the top of her head and carried her to her room. "You may speak with your friends again. They will comfort you." He laid her out on her bed, kissed her forehead, and pulled up the covers.

"And what about the S'Lorek?" The High Tender said with a snort.

"Later," Gregor whispered. "That will come later."

The men left her room, and their voices trailed down the hall getting fainter with distance.

"Get Lady Calcask s'Adreta to watch her through the night." Gregor issued commands to High Tender Marcus, tipping the balance of power between the men once again. "Check her yourself in the morning."

"I'll place a WOR-guard on duty."

"No guards. Have her friends tend to her. Make sure she gets up in the morning."

"And if she doesn't?"

"She will." Gregor spoke with conviction. "Do I have your consent to train her in this fashion?"

"Yes, but with reservations. I don't know if what you propose will be any different, but I'll allow a trial period."

"Thank you, Master Tender—"

"You have two days to bring her around, two cycles to show some improvement, and a Sun cycle to convince me to let you continue. If I'm not satisfied, she must return to WOR-skill training."

"Agreed, Master Tender."

CHAPTER FIFTEEN_

Gambit, Day 223

A SOFT SOPRANO SANG A LULLABY. IT CALLED ELISE OUT FROM THE DARKNESS. She rolled over and hugged herself tight, not wanting to wake.

"Elise?" Soft words percolated in her mind. Someone rubbed her head and straightened out her hair.

"Elise isn't here anymore," she murmured. Was that true? *No, no, I'm here, just not there. Don't want to be there anymore.*

A voice from the dark spoke, *You have to come back. We need you.*

Who are you? Elise twisted in the darkness searching for the unfamiliar voice.

We need you.

Don't let them win! Elise knew that voice. Malice's ire was unmistakable.

Malice, who is that?

Don't know...she's a lurker. Can't smell her either.

And the others? Elise asked. *Where are they?*

We're here, Whimper and Shriek whispered.

Elise struggled. It was so much nicer, warm and cozy, in the darkness. The plaintive voices of her sisters tugged and pushed her into the light, where the humming became louder.

"Elise? Are you ok?" The voice sounded like gentle Aomi.

"What's wrong with her? What happened?" Chandra's harsh tone demanded an answer.

"What would happen to you if those bastards put you through that much Tender Training? How she survived is a miracle. We only had three sessions. She had three a day for an entire cycle." That voice carried the unmistakable strength of Alice's tenacious will.

"I didn't know how bad it was going to be. I thought I was strong, like Elise, but I was so wrong. I would've done anything to get them to stop. Is Elise going to be okay?" Aomi's voice cracked.

"Elise, are you with us, baby doll?" Alice hummed and Aomi added her sweet soprano to the tune.

Elise floated on the words of the song. They wrapped themselves around her in a cocoon of love and support. She allowed the music to bring her back, but it came with a gut-wrenching lurch as she returned to her body.

"Alice, Aomi? Where's Chandra?"

A hand touched her foot. "I'm here. Oh, we've been so worried." Chandra bent over and sobbed.

Alice kissed Elise's forehead, her cheek, and hugged her tight and Aomi's delicate hands squeezed Elise's in a light grip. Elise reveled in the warmth of her friends. They sobbed and then they began to laugh. Soft sounds began at first and then turned lighter as relief swept through them.

"We're still here. Still together." Chandra sniffled. "They didn't take that away."

"Elise," Alice helped her to a sitting position.

Her body felt broken, the residual effects of Tender Training. "I'm…" she paused, "I'm a mess. Inside and out, a total mess. I have to get out of here."

Silence echoed her pronouncement.

Alice tapped in their private code, *There's no way out. They've won.*

Elise placed a hand on Alice's hand. *I can't let Gregor beat me.* She blinked away tears. "What time is it?"

"Just after lights out," Aomi said.

"Why are you out of bed?" That was a hard rule.

"High Tender Marcus dragged me out of WOR-skill training and deposited me at your bed," Alice answered. "I'm supposed to watch you all night. Make sure you're ok."

Elise stretched out the kinks and soreness left behind by High Tender Marcus's Tender Training. Her friends surrounded her and smiled as she settled fully back in her body.

"You're all here." She tried to sit, but Alice pressed down on her shoulder, a light touch which said not to try too hard.

"Why didn't they put a WOR-guard on me? This doesn't make sense."

"Our instructions were clear." Aomi shifted on the bed. *Talk to your friend. Let her hear your voice and bring her back from wherever she's hiding. Tell me immediately if she wakes.*

"You've been out of it for a while." Chandra glanced toward the door. "I don't know what he thought we could do, but we weren't allowed to leave. Not even for training."

Elise put her hand to her forehead. "The singing was sweet."

"Aomi has the most beautiful voice." Alice beamed at Aomi, who blushed at the compliment.

"I can't believe she's been hiding it all this time." Chandra stood. "Do you need a drink? What can we do to help you?"

"What happened to you?" Alice asked. "You didn't respond. You had me so scared."

"I can't explain it. Where are they?" Where was Gregor and High Tender Marcus? Odd for them to leave her alone.

Alice sighed. "I'm supposed to tell him when you wake."

"Have you?"

"I guess I have to, but you look so worn out."

"I am. Ten days of Tender Training the first time was bad enough. Triple sessions for another cycle of Tender Training? Alice, they broke me." She pinched her eyes tight. "I'm not the same."

"Broke you?" Aomi leaned over and placed her palm over Elise's forehead.

"Not how they think," she said. "I can't explain except they didn't stamp out my will to fight. I couldn't make Tender Training stop, so I had to learn how to endure. I changed inside. Triple sessions...well, I couldn't survive that. I can't explain it, don't want to, but in a way, I hid where there was no pain. High Tender Marcus did his damage and my body took it, but I no longer cared."

Aomi spoke softly, changing the subject. "I'm glad you liked my singing. You're our hope. Our light. There was never a reason to sing after being captured. I used to sing for joy, but there's been precious little of that since the Vendel destroyed our lives. I had hoped my singing would touch you."

Elise tried to sit up, but then fell back in bed with a groan. She reached over to touch Aomi's arm. "It was beautiful."

Aomi spread her lips in a sweet smile. "I had thought—I had fooled myself into thinking these people were kind. I let them win. Talen, High Councilor vlor'Adreti, has been patient during WOR-skill training. He's been gentle, guiding, supportive, encouraging. He *was* all those things. He held my hand through the hardest parts, but Tender Training? He sat and watched as my High Tender tortured me. I screamed and begged and he never even raised an eyebrow."

Chandra's voice grew quiet. "I believed even worse. Valerius, dark and handsome man that he is, I liked him. I mean…really liked him. He's been," she blushed, "well, he's been stealing kisses and I've let him. No holds barred, roving hands and all that. I would've taken more, but he always stopped things well short of a home run." She waved her hands in a dismissive gesture. "I thought, damn, but I thought there was something more between us. He not only watched the Tender Training, he placed the shackles on my wrists. Valerius told my High Tender it wasn't enough. That I needed to obey him without thought, without question, without… well, without free will. I've never felt so betrayed."

Alice gripped Elise's hand in encouragement. "I think we all forgot why we're here, or how we got here. These men engineered the destruction of our planet. They literally made us into WOR. We are tools, not people, which means we're not quite human in their eyes. They've brainwashed all of us into thinking, believing they are…well, shoot, I don't know?" Alice shook her head. Blonde curls bounced. "Good? Nice? Caring? We've all fallen for our vlor' masters in some way or another. Even more for some?" She looked at Chandra who blushed and shrugged with remorse.

"I didn't know," Chandra said. "I forgot and Valerius was really kind— and his kisses…" Her voice trailed off as she contemplated his betrayal.

Alice tried to soothe Chandra. "I felt the same toward Edgard. He watched me during Tender Training with his arms crossed. Never asked if I was ok. Just looked at me like I deserved all of it. As long as we do as they want, they are kind and gentle. I think we've learned our true value."

Aomi growled. "We're the dogs they kick when they're mad. What I wouldn't give to shove it all down their throats." She sighed. "Elise, I'm sorry it was so much worse for you. I can't imagine what it must be like to be the Emperor's s'vlor. He wanted to hurt you. I have never seen anyone so angry before."

"He was right to be mad," Elise said. "He thought I was obedient. You know how they are about those damned names. He made me pay for calling him *emperor* and not Gregor in front of all the other lords. I think it was that, and not the rest, that really set him off. I played him as a fool and that infuriated him. I have a plan though. I'm not done fighting." She sighed with the pain of it all.

How much do I tell them?

As little as possible, Malice growled. *You can't risk another mistake!*

"I needed Gregor to believe I was broken. I played the part of his perfect s'vlor in every way. That's why he was so mad. It wasn't the code. It was the rest of it. I embarrassed him in front of all the vlor' lords. I don't think he thought it possible for me to keep anything from him. The fact that I did, well…you saw what that did to him."

She settled fully into her body and took control. With the exception of Malice, her sisters remained silent and rested in the cracks.

"Don't tell the High Tender I'm awake."

"I have to," Alice said.

"What he doesn't know won't hurt him." Elise tapped in the code shared only with Alice. *A favor, please.*

What?

I have to leave.

Leave? What? How?

Explain later. Please?

Alice took in a deep breath and blew it out slowly. "Come on girls. We'll tell High Tender vlor'Vardhal in the morning that Elise is awake. Elise needs her sleep. He'll just come bother her if he finds out now." Alice shepherded the girls out of Elise's room. *Be safe.*

Thank you.

The door swished closed with a faint hiss. Elise stood. She stretched and was surprised she didn't feel worse. Gregor's massage and the shower had really helped.

Alice had said it was just after lights out, which meant it was morning for the crew on the *Gambit*.

Ten days lost.

The jump-jet circuit qualification rounds were due to begin, if they hadn't already started. She hoped she hadn't missed them. But what would a jump-jet prize do for her? Money for sure, but she had to get away. She had to get them all away and a jump-jet only held two people.

I'm going to need a much bigger ship. All for one and one for all. I need to find a way for us all to be free.

She went to the corner of her room and located the bio-cart access panel. As she had done every time before, Elise prayed for a cloak of invisibility to shroud her movements and hide her activities from the watchful eyes of her captors.

It was time to fly.

CHAPTER SIXTEEN_

Gambit, Day 223

THRILLED TO FINALLY BE RELEASED FROM THE TORMENT OF TENDER TRAINING, Elise rushed through the tunnels, stripped out of her dress, and donned her pilot's red jumpsuit. A lift tube ride and a pod circuit later, she ran across the flight deck until she found Jeena. A surge of adrenaline raced through her body, invigorating her from the inside out.

"Jeena!"

Jeena spun upon hearing her name. Her face broke into a big grin and then sank to a frown. "Kid, where the devil have you been? I've had to reschedule your qualifiers four times already." Jeena glared with disapproval. She scanned Elise and her anger faded instantly. "Damn, not again?"

"I'm sorry, but I couldn't get away and I had no way to leave a message."

"Well, there's no fixing it now. Are you good to fly? Because you're scheduled for the fifth run in just under two hours."

Elise pursed her lips. *Am I?* Her body protested even the smallest of movements. She felt like a living zombie, but one amped up on adrenaline.

Yes! Malice screamed. *We're ready!*

"Uh...yes."

"Listen, Carek is waiting, and Larkin, and the rest. Everyone's been worried, what with you not being around and not training." Concern edged Jeena's expression. She gathered Elise and walked her toward the jump-jet hangar. "Now the pilot you're racing in this qualifier is Wilma."

"Another female?" Elise was surprised. Most of the pilots were men.

"For the record, women make better pilots. The men haven't figured that out yet. Six out of ten of the last imperial jump-jet finalists were women and nearly half the top semi-finalists are women too. Not too bad a showing considering how few actually enter the races."

Jeena continued as she guided Elise to the jump-jet hangar. "Now Carek did a little creative work with the papers. Sometimes it helps to have a neural-mind conclave member in your back pocket. Helps even more if that particular person is a little sweet on you too. There should be no chance of your sponsor finding out you're involved. In the betting rings, you're *Chickadee*." Jeena held her free hand up in a what-have-you gesture. "Sorry, Dove insisted."

"Chickadee?" Elise said with a grimace. "So, what do I need to know about Wilma?"

"She's conservative. But first, you have two runs today. A speed trial and an elimination run. Your speed trial is later this afternoon, no worries there. With Wilma, pick Fox first. If you don't get her by the halfway point, scream towards the finish line. She's not going to go Rabbit with Fangs on you. She'll try to go for a clean win. On the second race, be careful. I'd suggest you play traditional as well and go for the finish line, but you tend to get crazy out there. It's up to you if you want to risk the points. If she doesn't score a hit on you by the halfway point, she's likely to make a dash for the finish line."

"Not very bold," Elise said. There were definite strategies for what seemed like a simple race.

"No, but consistent. Wilma's gone far with consistency. She's not the best pilot, but she's solid and has a lot more experience than you. If you beat her in this race then you'll be set for a second elimination after your speed trial. Now, let's talk about your speed trial. You need to play the speed trial carefully. You don't want to finish well."

"I thought the point was to get the best time."

"Yes and no." Jeena chewed on her lower lip. "Look, kid. You're a first-time novice contender. There are only a few of us who've seen you train. I didn't want you to get too cocky, but you've got a real chance."

"You're telling me I'm good? What's gotten over you? So far I've just been merely ok?"

Jeena gave a sheepish grin. "Hell, you're just a kid. Anyway, you need to do well enough to pass into the next round, but if you do too well, it'll draw unwelcome attention. We want the other pilots to think you're lucky, not good. You'll show them good once you get a spot on *Gambit's* circuit race. Then you'll show them spectacular. But before that, be just barely good enough."

"How good is good enough? How do I know how fast to time the speed trial?"

"That's what Carek is going to tell you. It's lucky you're in the last speed trials. I've been busy trading favors to get you rescheduled, again and again. It's going to work in your favor. He should be able to tell us exactly what time you need based upon the finishing times of everyone else."

"I'm not going to be in the lowest ranks, am I?"

"Yes, but there's strategy there, too. We want you ranked somewhere in the lower third. It'll give you a margin and generate some interest in the betting pools. Now, stay away from the bonus rings. I don't want flashy, just good."

They walked down the long hall and into the jump-jet hangar.

"You're taking away all the fun!"

Jeena gave her a dark stare. "And I've won the Imperial finals several times running. Have you? Take my advice, kid. It's worth it. Winning on the jump-jet circuit is six parts skill, three parts strategy, and one part luck. You need strategy to win."

"Elise!" Dove's deep baritone voice sounded over the noisy hangar. The ever-present noise dropped for a second and then rose again to its usual fevered pitch.

Carek stood by Dove's side and his eyes brightened. He was dressed in his green jumpsuit and his hair was drawn back in the ponytail he always wore. She saw a flash of green in his eyes and then nothing as Larkin ambushed her from the side.

Larkin swung Elise around in a circle. "El, you made it!" He spun her a few times and then steadied her on her feet. He pecked her cheek and released her as Dove and Carek came up. "We were all starting to get worried!"

"My little chickadee, you made it." Dove's eyes crinkled at the corners and his lips spread into a wide grin. "Jeena was getting frightful to be around. If you missed the qualifiers, she would've been unbearable for cycles. Thank goodness you're here!" Dove leaned over and kissed her cheek. "Good to see you. Are you ok?" he whispered the last into her ear where no one else could hear.

She nodded.

Dove and Jeena were the only ones who knew her *story* and why her visits to the flight deck sometimes stopped completely for days at a time. As far as she knew, they hadn't told anyone else about her sponsor uncle who'd taken her nuptial gift.

Carek hung back a little from the group. Twin silver pads lined his temples again. He looked tired and distracted. He must have slipped away from work again because he'd forgotten to remove the pads. She wondered what full immersion in the am-net must be like. With the Vendel and their biotech, it might be literal, but he'd always evaded her questions when she asked.

Larkin thumped her on her back, making her grunt. "So, *Chickadee*, good luck on your races today. I passed my qualifiers already. Maybe we'll fly against each other?"

Elise couldn't help but prod her friend. "You should hope not, Lark."

Larkin's face went red and his eyes narrowed into thin slits. "I *let* you win, novice and all. You won't find me so easy to beat next time."

"Famous last words." Elise arched a brow in challenge.

"Well, El..." his voice trailed off with promise, "I made dinner reservations for the last night of the *Gambit* finals at the Pinnacle Room."

"Sounds nice," Elise purred. "Who asked you out?"

Jeena giggled and Dove shifted his feet, suddenly finding a speck of metal on the floor incredibly interesting. Elise gave Larkin a wide-eyed smile and blinked demurely. Carek looked on in bewilderment.

Larkin scowled for a moment, but then brightened when he realized she was teasing. "Listen, El, good luck out there. I do hope you do well." He brushed the curls out of his eyes and waved his way off.

Dove collected Jeena and the two of them headed to Jeena's jump-jet. Carek stood in place, looking lost. He twirled a dainty silver chain from his fingers.

"Carek?"

He looked up and his eyes twinkled. Carek had a tendency to stare off into space and then step right back into conversations as if he'd been following every word. Today he seemed a bit off.

"Hi," he said, "We were starting to get worried. I tried to track you down, but Jeena told me to leave off. We kind of got into it a little. I'm sorry, but they told me about your sponsor and what he's done to you. I didn't realize."

Elise held perfectly still.

Carek raised a palm. "I'm the only one they've told. Your secret is safe." He shuffled his feet and looked down at the slim silver chain. "I wanted to give you something. I didn't want to be obvious like Larkin. I thought, maybe, you could wear it as a good luck charm, rather than as a promise bracelet?" He gazed deeply into her eyes and quickly looked away.

Elise wanted to laugh. Carek was over four hundred years old and here he was acting like a shy schoolboy.

"I think it's really sweet of you." Elise laid a hand on Carek's arm.

"Well, it's just for luck. I don't mean it as a promise bracelet, unless... well..." He stammered and didn't meet her eyes. At last, he said, "You don't have to keep it on. At least, not now, not yet. I mean, it's too early and all, and you have your problems." The words tumbled out of his mouth. He took a breath, blew it out slowly, and nodded to himself as if making a decision. "Just for luck, and then you can take it off. I wouldn't want him to see it, or get you in trouble."

"Carek, I would love to wear it. Even if only for my flights. Even if I have to take it off when I leave here. I'd be honored."

Carek relaxed and smiled. He took her hand and pushed back the sleeve of her jumpsuit. He brushed his thumb over the thin, silver scar on the back of her hand. It made her self-conscious having him touch where Gregor's Blood Rite knife had pierced her skin.

He frowned and his brows drew down in thought. "Um, let me put it on for you." Carek looped the silver chain over her wrist and turned her hand over, palm up. A miniature jump-jet figurine dangled from the chain. It had been painted in Jeena's colors. Carek attached the clasp and ran his thumb down her palm and over the scar on that side of her hand.

Lost in thought, he held her hand. Elise did not pull away. He felt good. He smelled good, too. Standing as close as they were, his clean fresh scent washed over her, so different from the pilots, mechanics and other flight deck crew.

Where do you go, when you leave here, Carek?

Who was this man who fronted the exorbitant jump-jet fee on a stranger, a novice? A young, prejuv, female pilot, at that? Had he done it for Jeena, for his cousin Dove, or for her? She had a suspicion he'd done it for her. Carek Tusel may not be searching for a wife, or romantic entanglements, but he was searching for something. Some form of companionship; *a connection to his humanity* was how Jeena had described it. Elise wished she could give him that bond.

His touch was so much different than Gregor's. A touch like that from the emperor would've felt like fire, sent her heart racing, quickened her breathing, and made the hairs on the backs of her arms stand on end.

Carek's touch was warm, soothing, and innocent. His touch asked for nothing, whereas Gregor's demanded everything.

Elise would give Gregor what he wanted because he would take it. He would draw out her body like he took everything else. Their inevitable union would likely consume them both. Just the thought of it made her heart race. But, what would it be like to share Carek's bed? A low roiling simmer could hold as much, or more, passion as an uncontrolled blaze.

She jumped at the unexpected thought and ripped her hand out of Carek's gentle touch. "Sorry," she said, to cover her unease. She hadn't really thought of him like that. Her cheeks felt noticeably hot. Why now?

Carek gazed into her eyes and flicked his attention to her cheeks. His brows drew down, deep in thought, and he seemed wary, as if he wrestled with some great decision. "We should go join the others," he said abruptly.

It wasn't what she'd expected. Elise had thought he might say something more personal and it made her uneasy.

He reached for her hand and placed it in the crook of his arm. "Elise," he said and paused for a moment in consideration, "have you ever seen the am-net?"

"You don't mean the interface pads, do you?"

"No, I'd like to show you the central core. I think you'd find it interesting. There are things in the am-net I need to show you. Things, which can only be truly understood by sensitive minds."

"I..."

His tone struck her as odd, as if he had just lost something dear to him. He was trying to tell her something.

"I would love to, but I thought it was ultra-secure. Only Neural-Mind Conclave members allowed." She paused and then heard his words. "You think I have a sensitive mind?"

"Level 5 conclave members have the ability to make exceptions to the rules. I can give official tours. Especially if there's a reason. You do have an exceptional mind. Just to pull this off shows me you're brilliant. That means something, by the way, coming from someone like me."

Now what does that mean?

"I wouldn't think your girlfriend would qualify as an official tour." *Oh, shit, why did I just say that?* "I..."

He put his hand over hers. "Don't you dare tell me you didn't just mean that." He gave a low throaty chuckle and patted her hand. "But, I think it's best to leave things as they are. You're not ready, I think. And I, well I..." He paused and rolled several phrases on his tongue before settling on, "I just can't right now. Just tell everyone it's a good luck charm, nothing more. We'll deal with more, later."

"I said too much. I'm sorry."

"Don't be, I liked the sound of it. But you have issues to deal with and there are some lines I can't cross." He squeezed her hand and kissed her cheek, lingering longer than customary before pulling away.

Elise closed her eyes, wishing he hadn't pulled away.

Carek led her on his arm to where Jeena and Dove stood by the jump-jet. Dove looked at their hands, frowned, but said nothing.

Jeena's eyes focused on the silver chain. Her brows went up and her eyes widened in surprise. "Carek, let's go over your numbers."

Dove moved away from the jump-jet revealing *Chickadee* etched in the nose of the craft. Jeena's eyes lit up and Dove crossed his arms over his chest. "Well?" he asked in his deep voice.

Elise let go of Carek's arm. He resisted and then released her hand. She walked up to the jump-jet, her little dragonfly, and ran her fingers over the name. It wasn't a name she would have picked. It was ridiculous, but Dove had given her that name. It was a good name. The perfect name. She loved it.

She looked at these people who were willing to help a stranger. Jeena taught her to fly and had donated her jump-jet. Dove had managed all the fine-tuning of the jump-jet engines, and had worked with her when Jeena was out on her transport runs. Carek had graciously donated an exorbitant sum to give her the opportunity to race. The pilots on the flight deck had given her live opponents to practice against as she honed her skills.

Tears welled up and threatened to fall. She'd had a lot of tears lately, but these were the first happy tears she'd shed in a long time. Whimper's tears were too painful to bear, and Shriek never cried.

"It's beautiful, Dove. Thanks."

"No problem, Kid. Hey! You've got about an hour before launch time, why don't you go relax." Dove rubbed his fat nose and left a grease stain on the tip.

"I'm not going to relax, Dove. I wish I could fly right now and get rid of these jitters."

Jeena's wrist call sounded and she tapped a finger to her ear, and spoke with the caller.

Carek pulled out a gel-flimsy from his pocket and walked over to Dove. He placed it on the nose of the craft. "Elise, if you pass through all fifty rings averaging fifteen seconds per ring, you'll make it in the bottom third of the rankings."

"I've blown through the rings a lot faster than that." *Fifteen seconds? I can do it in nine, maybe even less.*

"Yes, but we don't want you finishing high. You don't need the attention."

"Your numbers don't even take into account the bonus rings," she countered.

"Novice pilots *rarely* hit the bonus rings. When you get to the *Gambit* finals you can start pulling some of your tricks. But for now, we just need to get you on the circuit. You don't have to win during the qualifiers." Carek tugged on his ponytail.

Dove placed a fat finger on top of the gel-flimsy. "It's not the speed trials that'll be the problem. In order to secure your place in *Gambit's* circuit, you have to pass through four elimination rounds. Two races are set for today. The next two tomorrow. Are you going to be able to make it tomorrow, kid?"

"I can only hope. Things have kind of quieted down."

"I've got news." Jeena came around the side of the jump-jet. "Jenson just withdrew from the competition, which means you only have to make it through three eliminations, rather than four. They want to run them all today. Are you up for three duels and a time trial, or is that too much? Should I tell them no?"

"Yes," Dove exclaimed. "This is perfect. You can get your place on the circuit today."

"Yes, I'm up for it."

Jeena spoke into her device, then gave a flat stare to Elise. "Get your flightsuit on and hop on board. They've moved up your match with Wilma to right now. Be careful what you ask for kid, sometimes you get it!"

Elise scrambled into the tight fitting flightsuit. The helmet, with its opaque visor, fitted over her head with only a little rearranging of the messy bun at the back of her head. Carek and Dove missed their good luck kisses in the rush and had to settle for hugs. Well, Dove thumped her on her back. Carek gave her a hug. Jeena sealed the helmet and thumped the top.

Before she lowered the visor, Jeena said cautiously, "Beat Wilma but do it with respect. You don't want to make an enemy out of her. Don't take unnecessary risks. It'd be better to win on the third race than humiliate her like you did with Larkin."

"I get it. Don't worry, I'll be good." Elise grinned and the visor slid into place. Larkin ran up, as if the mention of his name had him materializing out of thin air. He had to settle for a vigorous wave as the jump-jet crane

392

lifted her craft off the hangar deck. Elise waved with enthusiasm and tapped through her pre-flight checklist as the crane moved her jet up to the catapult launch system, where it deposited her into a dark hole and the clamps engaged with a solid *thunk*. She waited until the catapult loading ramp maneuvered her into position. The jump-jet shifted sideways, out of the little dark hole, and into a much longer launch tube.

Twinkling in the darkness, the silvery gray of WOR-space waited for the arrival of its newest contestant.

CHAPTER SEVENTEEN_

Gambit, Day 223

A GREAT ROARING FILLED THE CANOPY AS THE CATAPULT LAUNCHED ELISE, pressing her back against the seat of the jump-jet. Her heart leapt as adrenaline surged through her body. Once free of the *Gambit*, she engaged the engines and headed to the staging area.

Three other jump-jets waited outside the jump-jet circuit. Elise tapped into their communications channels.

"Zander, Fox or Rabbit?" a male voice asked.

"Your pick, doesn't matter to me. I'm going to blast your ass before the end." Another male answered.

"Hardly, Zander." A low chuckle sounded over the com-channel.

"My, my, Zander, aren't you in a fighting mood?" The last, a low alto, belonged to a woman.

"Aw, hell, Wilma. Zip it. Once I blast this idiot's ass, I'm gonna come screaming up yours." Zander's voice crackled over the communications channel.

"I'll take Rabbit," the first voice growled.

"Looks like the little *Chickadee* has finally arrived." Zander's voice snarled. "You're late."

"Hello, Wilma," Elise said, by way of introduction, "sorry we didn't get to meet before our race. They just told me of the change in time. And I'm not late!"

"How nice," the first pilot purred. "I want the newbie, not this cocky bastard."

"Zander, pay attention," Wilma chided. "Malikai is showing you how to properly greet a newbie. He knows how it should be done. Chickadee, it's nice to meet you. The two *children* fighting here are Zander, he's grumpy, and Malikai, he's...well, he's not as nice as he seems. They're scheduled for the next race, we're up after them."

Malikai angled his jump-jet in front of Zander's and they positioned themselves for the start of their race. At the signal, Malikai raced ahead. Elise popped up a virtual of the *Gambit* and the jump-jet course. The string of fifty rings encircling it looped crazily out to the edge of the WOR-space bubble. Malikai, who took Rabbit, blew through four rings before Zander launched after him and almost made it to the fifth.

Wow, he's fast. Malice peeked out and took up position where she could watch.

Elise did the calculations. That was less than seven seconds a ring, six if he'd made the fifth ring.

Impressive.

Elise watched with a cool detachment as Zander narrowed the lead. One of these men would be up against her in a later circuit match. It was time to learn about her competition.

Malikai made it past the twenty-fifth ring and became Rabbit with Fangs. Rather than turn his lasers on Zander, he screamed toward the finish line. Zander hit him on the forty-ninth ring, earning a point and the lead.

In the second race, they switched places. Zander took Rabbit. Malikai hit him by the tenth ring, earning two points and the lead. Zander said a few choice words, add to Elise's growing repertoire of Vendel curse words.

Elise sat up and took notice. A hit by the tenth ring was very unusual. Malikai remained silent over the communications channel.

The only way for Zander to win the heat was to earn a minimum of two points in the next race. There were a few ways to do that. Malikai only had to earn one point to beat Zanders current score of two. Since Zander trailed in points he had choice between Rabbit or Fox for the final race.

Elise would have chosen Rabbit. Rabbit could win two points for a first-place finish or three points if it took out Fox after the halfway point when weapons became active and Rabbit grew Fangs. The only way Fox could get two points was to get the Rabbit in the first half of the race. Otherwise Fox earned one point for a hit after the twenty-fifth ring, or for finishing first. It was risky to choose Fox.

She wasn't the least surprised when Zander did exactly that. Nor was she surprised when Malikai breezed through the finish line first as Fox, winning the heat. Zander flew back to the *Gambit* in sullen silence.

Malikai came over to the two women. "Well, ladies, good luck. I wish you well. *Chickadee*, I'll be hanging out in the pilot's lounge later. Perhaps we'll see each other and can make a proper introduction." Malikai flew off leaving Elise with Wilma.

"Well, that's an invitation if I ever heard one," Wilma said. "Make sure you bring your snarking pad."

"What do you mean?"

"You've obviously never met Malikai. Fox or Rabbit?"

"Fox and no, I haven't." She lined up her ship behind Wilma's and waited for the start of the race.

"You should look him up."

"Why?"

She laughed. "Malikai flies veiled and you know what that means?"

"No, not really. I'm a novice remember, still learning all the tricks."

"Well, I give you some advice. We're not supposed to know who the veiled pilots are, but who would hide their identity? Not a commoner, unless he was a previous winner. Malikai has to be a judicator, a conclave master, a previous finalist, or perhaps even a lor' or vlor' lord. The jump-jet competition is open to all. We're all equal in the circuit. What makes it so much fun is that it's a level playing field. I'm pretty sure Malikai is a previous winner, or finalist, and I'm thinking he's at least a conclave master or Judicator, if not a lord. He's haughty enough. Anyhow, he's just given you an invitation. You should look him up. Could be a marriage opportunity in it for you."

"I have enough on my plate, thank you. Thirty seconds to go, you ready?" Elise checked her weapons display and remembered Jeena's words.

"Good luck, *Chickadee*. You'll need it." Wilma's jump-jet screamed out of the starting gate and headed toward the first ring. Elise watched the jump-jet disappear from her visuals, but followed the track of her ship on the course display. The seconds ticked by while Wilma extended her lead.

Finally, Elise was given the green light. She accelerated down the course and looped through the rings eating away at Wilma's lead. With Jeena's advice whispering in her head, she paced herself and slowed her advance. Wilma passed the halfway point where Rabbit grew Fangs, but kept going rather than turn and fight. Jeena had been right about Wilma. Elise pressed her palms down, adding acceleration, and closed the gap.

Wilma slipped through the rings, but Elise followed hard on her heels. A few shots of the lasers flew wild, on purpose, but by ring forty, it was time to end the hunt. Without waiting for weapons lock, Elise fired, scored a win, and her first point.

"Lucky shot, *Chickadee*. You won't get so lucky when I'm the Fox."

"I'm willing to try!" Elise laughed. "See you back at the start."

Elise was now Rabbit. To allow Wilma to lose with grace, Elise would have to give this race to Wilma, but that didn't mean Wilma wouldn't have to work for it. Past the twenty-fifth ring, Elise's Rabbit grew Fangs and weapons became active. When Wilma surged forward, Jeena's words were at the forefront of Elise's mind. She'd already decided to let Wilma cross the finish line first, and earn her points, but she wanted to have some fun.

Rabbit grew Fangs and Elise dodged wildly and looped around to get behind Wilma. She fired off several shots and laughed silently as Wilma dodged. Wilma almost flew into one of her shots. That would've been bad. Elise wasn't trying for the three-point win. After several rings worth of dodging and firing random shots, Elise went for a clean race. She stopped badgering Wilma and barreled down the course.

Ring forty-eight lay ahead and Elise pushed for the ring. Only one jump-jet could go through at a time. Wilma edged Elise to the side. By the time the ring loomed in front of them, Elise banked hard and broke off the approach. She used one of Zander's curses and tossed it over the communications channel.

"My, my," came Wilma's voice, "such words from a lady."

"I'm no lady. I should have had you, several times over." Elise feigned irritation.

"*Chickadee*, a word for a jump-jet neophyte. That little trick rarely works in competition. Best save it for fun and training. You could have won this heat if you'd just gone straight for the finish line. You'd have earned two points and left me with nothing. No need to even run the third race."

"Oh." Her voice sounded crestfallen, but her face was fixed in a grin. *Yes, Wilma that is true, but then Jeena would be mad at me.* "Lesson learned. You ready for the last race?"

"Sure, we're even in points, so I'll give you choice as the new girl on the circuit."

"Thanks, I'll take Rabbit."

Elise crossed the finish line three rings ahead of the lagging Wilma who never came close to scoring a hit on Elise's ship. The final score was three to one. It was a nice, clean and honorable race.

"Nice job. I hope to see you around later. Unfortunately, not on this year's circuit races."

"That would be fun. Thanks for the race, Wilma."

Elise set up for, and finished, the speed qualifier following Carek's advice. His math was perfect and she finished solidly in the upper portion of the lower third in the speed trials. It gnawed at her to do so poorly, but she understood their tactics.

Her second and third elimination rounds went without incident. As she did with Wilma, she won each heat in the third and final race. She did try to mix it up a bit, just to see how the numbers would fall out.

Larkin wanted to celebrate, but one look at the time and Elise knew she'd have to run all the way back to her quarters or risk discovery. She called out hurried farewells and raced back to her bed.

She barely made it. Despite the excitement of her first jump-jet competition, her sisters were relatively quiet. Malice hummed a simple children's melody. Whimper kept Shriek company in the shadows. The fourth sister, who watched from the dark, remained silent and refused to reveal herself.

Elise's dreams floated up and down, following the notes of Malice's song. Her thoughts spiraled in and out of silver loops, and she slipped into a blissful oblivion filled with a kaleidoscope of swirling light.

CHAPTER EIGHTEEN_

Gambit, Day 224

Sometime later, a presence loomed in Elise's room. The silent one urged caution and Elise scurried to the darkness rather than come awake. Her body lay beneath the sheets and they all watched, in silence and in fear, cowering in the cracks of her mind.

The High Tender placed a hand on her forehead and then on her cheeks. "She does not appear to be awake, my lord."

"Lady Calcask said she was," Gregor sat on the side opposite from the High Tender and cradled her hand in his.

She felt nothing and watched the slow rise and fall of her body's chest with detached interest. Not too long ago, Gregor's touch would have set her heart to fluttering with the zing of electrical energy flowing between them. To have that gone felt wrong.

The High Tender rubbed his upper lip. His brows drew down. "Perhaps, she was lucid for a few moments and then slipped back away?"

"What do you suggest?" Gregor lifted her hand and placed it on his thigh. He straightened out her fingers and traced the outline of her hand.

"I don't think any more showers or massages will help." Sarcasm dripped from the High Tender's tongue.

Gregor ignored him.

"I'd say let her rest. We'll return in the afternoon and see what happens."

Gregor growled. "You have only given me two days. I don't want to waste any more time."

"I understand, but if you force her now, it may be for the worst. Her body is still recovering from Tender Training. Her mind should not be far behind. Give her the morning to rest." The High Tender removed his cold hand from her face and stood.

Gregor paused and traced a finger up her arm to her shoulder. He continued the path to her neck, over her collarbone, and to the angle of her jaw. His hand was warm. His fingers soft.

She felt nothing.

He leaned down and whispered in her ear. "Come back to me, opés. Elise, come back." He brought warm lips to her mouth and pressed them down with a soft, but determined presence. Elise felt her body sigh and watched his eyes crinkle at the response. "Elise, I will be back."

His words spoke volumes and meant so many different things. Where concern edged his words, possession filled them too. Gregor was a powerful man, used to getting everything he wanted and all that he desired.

Her resistance frustrated him. He was incredibly passionate, and as quick to lavish her in kisses as he was to condemn her to torture. Warm and fervent. Cold and dispassionate. His moods shifted wildly in regards to his little opés.

Her denial must give this powerful man pause. Perhaps that's why she intrigued him so much. It was a victory of sorts, her putting him on edge. He was the leader of over a hundred billion, entrusted with an empire spanning twenty worlds and hundreds of colony ships, and yet, she bothered him.

Pay attention to this man. He will teach us much.

I will not speak with you until you tell me who you are. Elise shouted into the dark.

Silence! Listen! And learn! Take from him everything you can, for he will surely take more from you.

The voice retreated and Elise drifted off, dreaming of jump-jets, silver rings, and a rabbit chasing a fox. She was grateful for the chance to sleep. It had been a long time since she had rested, and it would soon be time to fight.

CHAPTER NINETEEN_

Gambit, Day 224

GREGOR RETURNED AS PROMISED LATER THAT DAY. HE SAT BY HER BED, ALONE, and his weight settled onto the thin mattress. His warm fragrance flooded her senses as he leaned over her body.

"Opés, it is time to rise. I have much to show you. I would like for us to come to some sort of resolution in this matter." He stroked her hair and drew it out straight. "I can forgive this secret code you hid. Your words were harsh, and spoken without thought, without respect, and it was for that, and not the code, that you were punished."

He leaned down and traced a line with his finger from her forehead, down her nose, to her lips, chin, neck and the all the way down to the hollow between the swell of her breasts. He lingered there.

"Ask me to forgive you and I will. We can forget this horrible nonsense and continue with a fresh start. Open your eyes and ask your master for forgiveness, and I will grant that and so much more. We were made for each other. It's time to wake up, Elise. It's time for you to join me and stop fighting your destiny."

His voice cracked and his breathing turned ragged. He moved his finger up and cupped her chin in his hand. Gregor pressed his lips to hers and kissed her with a gentle intensity.

Her mind screamed. Her skin burned. She wished to breathe all of him in.

The silent sister spoke. *Give so that you may take. We are powerless. I must learn!*

With regret for what it would cost, Elise agreed with the silent one. She had forgotten the willow tree and allowed her strength to turn her rigid and inflexible, like the oak. She had cracked and splintered under the storm. It was time to be the willow once more and bend.

She folded her arms around Gregor's neck. He paused and held perfectly still. Her fingers twined in his dark black hair and she pulled him back to her lips. He came willingly and she greedily took her fill of him. Gregor parted her lips and allowed his hunger to flow into her.

Elise kissed her master as tears trickled out of the corners of her eyes.

Gregor pulled himself over to lie on top of her, but then stiffened and withdrew as the intensity of their embrace increased and his arousal became evident. He lifted his lips from hers and pulled back to stare. The smoldering passion in his silver eyes frightened her, but his restraint, as always, remained rigid and unnerving.

He brushed away a tear with his finger. "It's good to see you, opés."

"Gregor," she breathed in a low whisper. "I...I am sorry, but I cannot ask for your forgiveness, for it is not deserved."

Gregor's eyes narrowed. He smoothed her hair and his expression softened. "I would grant it if you did. It would please me to do so."

Elise flicked her eyes to the side. "I wish to give in, to surrender to you, but I can't stop myself from fighting. Do I beg for a forgiveness I don't deserve? Or do I speak the truth and endure the consequences?" She twirled her fingers in the hair at the nape of his neck.

He laughed at her words. "And what is the truth, opés?" He touched her lips and arched a brow. "Are your kisses the truth? I feel the surrender in your body. I know it in my heart. Are your words true? Your words are your downfall. What am I to do with you?"

"My words are the truth. My kisses...are my undoing. Whether true or not, I cannot say. I have never known a man that I both hate and desire at the same time. Or do both with equal intensity and passion. That is truth."

"Hmm..." He brushed a strand of hair off her forehead. "You are not fit to endure any more Tender Training, although it would do you good. What happened to you? Where did you go?"

"I don't know. I disappeared. Has Tender Training ever made a woman crazy?"

He shook his head and kissed her lightly on the forehead, "No, opés, never. It makes women submissive and instills an obsessive desire to please. Most women that is, you seem to be an exception."

She dropped her hands from his neck and he sat up straight. His silver eyes regarded her with consideration. Elise grasped her head as pain flashed through her skull.

"Are you ok?" Gregor helped her to sit.

She opened one eye to look at him. "My head. It will be fine. My whole body hurts."

He smirked. "Did you enjoy your massage?"

She eyed him. "I can't say I remember...exactly."

"Well, I enjoyed giving it to you. And I must say, next time we'll have the shower to ourselves."

She ran her hand through her hair and blushed, making sure he noticed her unease. "I thought Alice...I mean Lady Calcask washed my hair."

"Your friend did not, but I think you know that." His eyes narrowed and she watched as he decided whether she was lying or not. He shook his head and stood. "Enough of this. Forgiven or not, your Tender Training has been suspended. I can't afford to have you incapacitated any longer. Do you feel up for a walk? I wish to show you something."

"I obey."

"Yes," he laughed. "You must at that. Come, wash and get dressed. I've brought a new dress for you."

"Back or front tie?"

He winked. "Back of course. I'll tie it when you're ready."

"So, where do I stand with you?"

"Warily forgiven, not forgotten, but I must press on. I need you trained and, so far, I have failed. Tender Training is suspended and I've taken control of you WOR-skill training. We'll try unconventional, as you wished, and see where that leads us. I have a surprise, and I trust we are through with this ugly business of lies and disrespect? Respect and cooperation is expected in all things."

"Yes, Gregor."

If he ever found out about her forays off the Confinement Deck, or the Fifth Rank quarters, or any of the rest, there would be no end to his fury.

We hate his surprises. Whimper cringed in the darkness. The others were silent.

Shut up!

Surprises or not, they had learned to endure. She was not defeated, and with the success of her jump-jet runs, they may just have a chance to find a way off the *Gambit*.

Only time would tell, and one thing was certain. Elise would bend, but she refused to give up. Unconventional sounded perfect. She agreed with the unknown sister. It was time to learn. It was time to make the Vendel pay.

PART TWO_

PROLOGUE_

New Terra Histories by Malita s'Lissa s'vlor

At some point, I think I was crazy. Perhaps there were several times where I danced back and forth across the line between sanity and insanity. It's difficult to know if there was a line at all.

Tender Training was an odd thing. While it had been bad the first time, the second time broke me. It transformed me.

I lost something the second time around—a piece of my humanity disappeared—but I believe I gained more than I lost.

Would I do it again?

Now that's a difficult question.

I learned several things as a result of my training with the Tenders. First, we could never make it back to Earth. Second, there was nowhere to run. And third, and this was the most important lesson, I had to find a different solution. For that, I needed to redefine the problem.

Not once did it occur to me I might fail. My grandfather didn't raise me to lose. He taught me to persevere until winning was the only option left.

I still didn't know what to do, but I kept moving forward. That was the secret to success. Keep moving forward.

One small step at a time. As long as I did something, no matter how small the step, the solution would reveal itself.

Sounds easy, right?

It was anything but easy!

I never formed a plan. It wasn't like one step led to the next. I had no idea how to defeat the Vendel. I just came to it in stages and by a great deal of luck.

To this day, I still don't understand how I was never caught sneaking off the Confinement Deck. Either I was truly lucky, or I had a better command of the WOR-skill than I thought.

CHAPTER TWENTY_

Gambit, Day 224

GREGOR TOOK ELISE TO COMMAND AND CONTROL. HE GUIDED HER THROUGH the rings of consoles and past the hanging holographs. He wrapped his hand around hers, maintaining a firm grip, while he pulled her along.

They paused at the railing where she had met him after waking from the devastating effects of the Activator. The Vector selected her from the billions on Earth and consigned her to become a Vendel slave. Activation turned on her genetic code and remade her into a weapon. What kind of weapon remained a mystery, and what she was to fight against remained even more unclear. She was nothing more than a tool, one that had failed its masters.

Tender Training broke her the first time, shattering her mind, and gave rise to the voices in her head. The second round? Something shifted inside of her, and she was still trying to sort out what that meant.

Not once did she waiver from her goal: free herself and her fellow captives and find a way home. She would never stop fighting Gregor or the Tender Conclave, but to escape and seek her freedom, she needed to learn everything they had to teach her about her new abilities.

It was time to stop fighting.

It was time to learn.

Gregor led her down a ramp and into the pit below. Five women reclined in body-hugging chairs. Technicians in yellow jumpsuits hovered over them. A strange feeling overcame her; an odd kinship filtered through her mind. She knew these women, even if she'd never met them before.

Strange.

They wore dresses similar to hers. A single armband encircled their left arms, not five like hers. None wore a collar. They were WOR of the First Rank. She felt the smooth metal of the collar around her neck and brushed against the bands of Rank wrapped around her upper arm. Someday, she would be free of them.

The six chairs faced toward the front of the pit. A display screen, similar to the one in Gregor's personal quarters, filled the wall and arched over her head. In the centermost position, a single seat remained vacant. Gregor ushered her there.

The five women opened their eyes and nodded, but none of them spoke. Intense concentration lined their faces and pinched at their eyes. Rigid fingers gripped the edges of their chairs.

"Opés," Gregor made a sweeping gesture encompassing the five women, "these are the First Rank WOR assigned to the oversight of the *Gambit's* WOR-drive. They help the technicians focus the drive and navigate us through WOR-space." He indicated the empty chair.

She sat, unwilling to show any hesitation. Her status following a second round of Tender Training remained uncertain. Until she understood where she and Gregor stood, she would obey and learn. She had so much to learn.

He helped her settle in the seat and then stood behind her, out of her line of sight. "The screen in front of you should look familiar."

A whirling mass of color and light twisted in a vortex of motion, overlying a gray shimmer.

"Is that WOR-space?"

"Not exactly. It's a portion of the three-dimensional bubble of space that the WOR wrap around the fleet. The colors and light you see is the activated WOR-drive. The WOR fold the fifth and sixth-dimensions through the center of the *Gambit's* torus."

Built like a torus, the *Gambit* resembled an impossibly large doughnut.

"What you see is the three-dimensional representation of those folded dimensions. Only WOR see it as it really is. With training, you will too. The display on the screen is for the technicians' benefit." He patted her head like she was an obedient pet. "What I want you to do is observe the WOR. See if you can follow what they do."

"What am I supposed to see?"

"The engines of the *Gambit* force us into these additional dimensions, but we can't survive in there. The WOR serve two purposes: two of them fold space around the fleet to maintain a three-dimensional space which we call WOR-space—it maintains our integrity as we travel the alternate dimensions; and the other two WOR guide the output of the drive down the center of the torus."

"But, there are six chairs?"

"One WOR pulls us through the dimensions to our destination. The final WOR is for emergencies."

"Emergencies? If that's the case, why is the sixth seat vacant?"

"Because you're here to train. Don't worry about emergencies."

"I'm sorry, but I don't understand any of this. How does this move us through space?"

"The WOR-drive doesn't move us anywhere. It connects us to our destination in two-dimensions, a line with infinite length and infinitesimal diameter. We exist everywhere along that line at once. The WOR *pull* us along the probability curve of that infinite length until we reach our target exit point."

"We've been traveling for months. If what you're saying is true we could travel anywhere instantaneously. Why is it taking so long?"

"WOR can't envision infinite probabilities. Instead, they look down the length of the line and pull us along bit by bit. In a sense, we crawl down its length."

"And this takes time?"

"Yes. Using the WOR-drive, we achieve supraluminal velocities, but we're still limited by time."

"This links your empire?" She was beginning to understand a complex problem, and realized her escape plans might truly be impossible.

"Exactly. Travel is finite, not limited by space, but rather by time. It will take another sun-cycle before we arrive at Malbra."

"What is it you expect me to do?"

She glanced at him, remembering a little of his conversation with High Tender Marcus. Gregor had wanted to try something unconventional to break through her block in learning the WOR-skill. This had to be a piece of that.

"You've used your WOR-skill enough to feel what they do. You and I will walk through the focusing exercises. Hopefully, you'll be able to view WOR-space and the WOR-drive as the First Rank WOR see it. Just like in the park, try not to think about it. Just relax and let the WOR-skill take over."

He has to be kidding.

"Are you ready to try? I wish you to please me."

The man was certifiably insane. He really thought she could do this. That she would do it out of a compulsive desire to please?

That is what he believes Tender Training did to you, Malice hissed. *Play the long game. We must win!*

"Yes, Gregor." She suppressed the shiver his words caused. Pleasing him, as much as she hated to admit it, had been ingrained in her through High Tender Marcus's triple bout of Tender Training. She wanted to succeed…for him.

It made her sick to her stomach.

Gregor talked her through the stupid focusing exercises. For a long time, she let his voice lull her into a deep meditation, but the space in front of her did not change. What was supposed to happen remained unclear.

Her sisters crawled out of the dark recesses of her mind. Malice, Shriek, and Whimper looked on with rapt attention, even the silent one, who refused to reveal herself, came out to watch. They were no help. Their running commentary only served to distract Elise from whatever hell it was Gregor expected.

By the end of the second hour, after she had accomplished nothing, she let her irritation get the better of her. "I can't do it." She tucked her head in her hands and rocked.

Gregor rubbed her shoulders. "It will come, opés."

Opés! She hated that word, but his touch was something else. *Intoxicating, it was a drug she craved.*

"I'm sorry," she said, on the verge of tears.

He breathed a sigh. "It's okay, opés. I had hoped you would sense something, but we shouldn't give up so easily. It's either this or WOR-skill training with the Master Tender, and that has not been going so well." He gave a throaty chuckle, but underneath she sensed a bit of strain in his tone. "I'm hoping some unconventional training might work for a truly unconventional WOR."

Her shoulders tensed.

He swept her hair to the side and leaned down. His warm breath caressed the side of her neck. "I have faith in you, opés. Please, relax. You and I are no longer fighting. Remember?" His thumb circled her earlobe and sent delicious shivers down her neck.

She closed her eyes and pushed back against the rising tide of desire surging in her veins. Why did her body respond so easily to the simplest of his touches?

Vendel biotech, the silent sister whispered. *You cannot resist his touch, because your response to him is engineered.*

I'm not speaking to you until you tell me who you are! Elise cast about in the dark, but the mystery sister fled.

Biotech? Does that explain it then?

Gregor startled her out of her inner conversation with a kiss pressed to the spot behind her ear. "Where do you go, opés, when you stare like that?"

The urge to cackle like Malice nearly overwhelmed her. *I'm speaking to my other selves, you bastard. I'm crazy, bonkers, certifiably insane! And you did this to me!*

"We will take a break."

"I'm sorry, Gregor." Liquid warmth spread from the site where his lips brushed against her skin. "I really am trying." Except, how could she try to do something she had no idea how to do?

"Opés, stay here," he said. "I must attend to some matters. Sit back and relax. I'll return and we'll try again."

"Yes, Gregor."

Saying his name was an obligatory response, and it grated on her. Each and every time she said his name, it made her hate him even more. She should be thankful for that requirement, because the more he touched her, the harder it was to hate him.

Two girls came in to replace two of the WOR. They settled into their reclined seats and wore masks of tension before their heads even hit the headrests. Their eyes pinched and their fingers curled around the armrests.

Elise got out of the chair and walked around the pit. She followed Gregor's movements as he exited the pit. She didn't need to see him to know where he went. His presence vibrated her blood, at least when he was close.

Her wandering brought her to stand before the huge viewscreen with the shimmering gray background.

So, this is WOR-space.

Doesn't look like much, Malice said. *Kind of dull.*

I don't like it. Shriek sniffed with disdain. *It feels funny.*

Only because we can't see it. Grumpy as always, Malice looked to pick a fight.

Shh! Elise stared at the dull shimmer.

She knew WOR-space intimately, at least from the cockpit of her jump-jet. Where were the silver rings of the jump-jet circuit? She traced out an imaginary course in her mind.

Her little dragonfly craft zipped and looped, accelerating through the course. Wild bonus rings danced in her mind's eye, elusive and challenging, taunting her to take a chance. In her imagination, she attacked each one, caught it, and dove through to the next.

Was it crazy to think a simple jump-jet circuit win would aid her escape? There was nothing else, and even if it did nothing, it was her only way to defy Gregor. She needed that tiny victory. Maybe someday, tiny would become something unstoppable.

A spinning vortex of colored light crept into her peripheral vision. Between one breath and the next, before she realized what was happing, the vortex exploded into painful awareness. Lines of color converged, folded, shifted and danced through the dimensions.

The latticework of lines reminded her of a long funnel, like a twisting tornado rotating with contained fury. The colored lines converged and wove themselves into tight cords, stretching and thinning until they were barely a thread. Her vision spun and exploded outward. Her consciousness separated and left her body behind, until she floated within a tunnel, supported by the lattice of woven light. From within, she saw infinity.

A familiar presence approached and she felt, rather than heard, Gregor as he stepped to within a few paces.

"How do you feel, opés? Are you ready to try again?"

Elise ripped her mind from the light and the infinite vision and settled back into her body. She swayed as her mind and body reunited. Dragging her gaze from the silver screen, she focused on silver eyes and a dancing tattoo.

She blinked. "Yes, Gregor."

They spent the rest of the day in the pit, and she managed to keep her discovery of the WOR-drive a secret, letting her sisters take it in, each in their own peculiar way.

Gregor bombarded her with questions. She answered them all.

Yes, she thought she might have seen something.

No, she couldn't describe it.

Yes, she was relaxed.

No, he couldn't help to get her more comfortable.

There was also *Gregor you're distracting me!* when he had rubbed her arms and brushed his fingers alongside her breasts.

She had seen the WOR-drive in action and peeked at infinity. At least she believed the infinite tunnel is what the WOR pulled them down.

At the end of the day, Gregor grudgingly walked Elise back to the Fifth deck.

"Don't feel bad, opés. We can't expect progress on the first day, but you think you felt something?" The eagerness in his tone made her want to give him some kind of hope.

"Maybe."

He wrapped his arm around her waist and pulled her to him.

"Well, that's better than nothing. We try again tomorrow."

Her roommates popped to their feet and bowed their heads when she and Gregor entered her quarters on the Fifth Rank Training Deck.

Elise managed to say goodnight without too many unwanted kisses.

Questioning glances from her friends led to a very brief recounting of her day. Elise directed a knowing glance to Alice. She had a full evening ahead of her in a jump-jet.

Without another word, she feigned exhaustion and excused herself for the night.

CHAPTER TWENTY-ONE_

Gambit, Day 234

THE REST OF THE CYCLE, TEN EARTH DAYS, PASSED IN A SIMILAR FASHION. ELISE followed Gregor around during her day as he took her to each Conclave and introduced her to the resident First Rank WOR. She spent her mornings and afternoons watching, learning, and hiding her growing knowledge from Gregor.

He had not yet shown concern over her lack of progress and she decided she would have to give him something soon before he became desperate for results.

Elise spent her days learning the WOR-skill and every other night with Jeena and Dove, preparing for the *Gambit* jump-jet circuit. The other nights she fell into an exhausted sleep and tried to find rest. When her exhaustion became too much, Shriek and Whimper took control of her body, allowing her to find respite in the darkness of her mind. She hid there, going over everything she had learned and trying to make sense of it.

Her only solace came from the cockpit of Jeena's jump-jet and the races she flew. Her dreams consisted of the silver rings and complex lines of force and folding of multiple dimensions. Her consciousness expanded as it grew into new potentials, avenues of thought and explorations previously unknown, but still terrifyingly foreign.

There was a sense she should be able to do more, perceive more, feel more, but a crucial piece of a complex puzzle continued to remain elusive.

Something blocked her efforts to understand, and the harder she tried to force her learning, the faster her limited control of the WOR-skill slipped out of her grasp.

Additionally, the more she learned, the more paranoid she became about being discovered during her nightly forays. She finally sat Jeena down to discuss her growing concern.

"Wilma mentioned that some pilots fly veiled." Elise rocked on the hard bench seat, wringing her fingers with unease.

Jenna gave a dismissive wave. "Sure, why?"

"I was wondering if I should as well."

"Why would you?"

Elise pursed her lips. "I'm worried I'll be recognized."

"Very few veil themselves. It's assumed they have status, but the veils give the illusion of equality."

"Then, why do it?"

Jeena shrugged. "I guess if you don't know the actual lord you're flying against then you're not technically competing against your Sector lord..."

"But others veil themselves. Wilma mentioned *others*."

Jeena thought about it for a moment. "True, I guess it depends. Previous Imperial finalists might do it so as not to intimidate their competition. Conclave Masters for obvious reasons. Low and High Judicators have been known to do so, but they rarely have the time for jump-jets. Lords for sure." She rolled her eyes. "I mean, who would willingly beat a lord..."

"What about me? I mean, why not me?"

"You're a novice. There's nothing special about you."

Elise bit at her lower lip. *Except for the obvious.* "What if my sponsor is watching?" *Like Gregor, or High Tender Marcus, or any of the High Tenders, or Tenders, or the WOR-guards.*

Jeena listened to Elise's argument about veiling and slowly nodded. "That is as good a reason as any."

"I don't have any way to purchase one."

Jeena laughed. "Kid, that's why you have Carek. I'll send him a message."

"I feel bad having him pay for everything."

"Why? He's your main snark partner. It's expected. Besides, you wear his bracelet, right?"

Elise blinked at that comment. What exactly had accepting Carek's bracelet meant? There was so much about the Vendel culture she did not understand.

CHAPTER TWENTY-TWO_

Gambit, Day 237

CAREK PROCURED THE REQUIRED BIO-DEVICE AND PRESENTED IT TO ELISE OVER lunch several days later. His caring eyes looked at her with a fondness that warmed her heart. It felt nice to be wanted by a man who demanded nothing in return.

"I think this is a good idea." He leaned toward her and fastened the veil around her head. "You should put this on the moment you leave the... um, your sponsor's quarters."

"I thought to only wear it here in the hangar. Do people normally wear it around the ship?"

He cocked his head and paused as if considering. "Well, I guess if you put it on once you get here that would be okay."

She smiled back at him. "Thank you."

His eyes dropped down to rest on the tiny dragonfly dangling off his promise bracelet. She made a conscious effort to always have it on when she was off the Fifth Deck.

"You don't have to wear it, El. I can't promise you anything more than just this."

She put a hand over his and frowned. "You look so sad when you say that. Is it wrong that I wear it? Do you want it back?" *Please don't take it from me. It means so much.*

He shook his head. "No. No. That's not what I meant." He turned her hand over and traced the creases of her palm with his finger, avoiding the faint silvery scar from the Blood Rite.

"I like being with you." His eyes bored into her, flaring with a smoldering heat before being banked behind a slow blink. He took in a deep breath and blew it out. "It's not usual for a man to be so forward with a woman, and you have issues, and I have…well, it's complicated. I didn't mean to overstep and sometimes I feel like…well, I'm not really sure."

"You haven't. And it means a lot to me." Her brows drew down, not understanding what he was trying to say. She smiled and tried to ease whatever issue he had.

The corners of his mouth curved into a grin. "I like it when you smile." He cocked his head to the side, as if listening to something. The silver pads were at his temples again. They seemed to always be in place these days.

He gave her a look and his smile twisted into a frown. "I'm sorry." He tapped his temple. "Conclave business calls."

"But you just got here. We haven't even had lunch."

Carek seemed more and more distracted during their snarking session, tired and withdrawn. She might have pushed him away with her talk about girlfriends. Something bothered him and she couldn't get over her paranoia that it had to do with her.

He glanced around the cafeteria and pointed to the far corner. "Zander's over there. You should go speak with him."

"Zander? Why would I do that? He's rude as hell."

"He also just got kicked out of the competition and is managing the betting pools. You should see if he's interested in snarking."

"Why would you want me to snark with him?"

Carek gave her a strange look. "It's not for me to say one way or the other." He stood and looked down at her. "I know you're new to snarking, but it's not really a man's place—"

"But the bracelet?"

He leaned down and kissed her forehead. "Means nothing. Not until a matrimonial union does a man have a right to any claim over a woman. Remember that, El. It's important."

As he walked away, she was more confused than ever. Vendel men were a strange lot.

Elise activated the circlet around her forehead and a thin mist obscured her features. She walked up to where Zander sat and leaned against the table. A large holograph captured his attention, full of numbers she didn't understand.

"Unless you're here to place a bet, go away," he snapped.

"I'm not interested in placing a bet."

He gave her an appraising look and his gaze swept across the obscuring mist, then lowered to check out the rest of her body, lingering a bit too long on her breasts. He leaned back, fingers laced behind his head. "And who might you be?"

"Chickadee."

He leaned forward, his palms pressing on the table, charcoal eyes widening with interest. "And what brings you to my table?"

She tapped her side thigh pocket and the bulge of her snark pad.

His eyes dipped with interest.

"So, what are the odds on me?"

His guttural laugh made her frown, but he couldn't see that with her concealing mist in place. "Not so good."

"What can I do to make them better?"

"Not much considering you're a novice without much of a showing."

"I've done well enough so far, better than others." She glanced at the screen, the numbers making sense now that she recognized them for betting odds.

"I've heard about your snarking sims." His pupils dilated.

"Really?"

"Oh yes, is it true?"

"Will it improve my odds in the betting pools?"

He laughed. "No." He flipped his wrist. "Maybe." One of his brows lifted. "I guess it depends."

She pulled out her snark pad and placed it on the table.

He leaned forward eagerly, stretching out his hand for the pads.

She slapped his hand. "Eager?"

He huffed a laugh. "As I said, I've heard your sims are unique. I believe that prejuv Larkin was bragging about one with a water massage?"

"Larkin needs to keep his mouth shut," she muttered. Hopefully he'd been discreet enough to use her competition name and not her real one. Dove and Jeena had been quite clear about that.

Zander tapped his finger on the table when she didn't move. "Did you come over here to tease me, or what? Because it's very cruel to make an offer and pull it away."

"Right now, Zander, my only question is what's in it for me?" The only true power women had in Vendel society was tied to their snarking lists, garnering favors as it were.

Zander leaned forward and cautiously picked up one of the pads, watching her the entire time to see if she would slap his hand again. When she didn't, he breathed out a sigh and gestured for her to have a seat. "Please, sit. I'm sure I can come up with something."

Elise sank into the seat and attached the pad to her hand.

By the time she was done with the simulation, Zander gasped for breath. He wasn't nearly so irritating afterward.

"Damn, that was amazing."

She leaned forward to collect the pad from him.

He placed a hand over hers. "Do you have time for more?"

"Depends? How do my odds look?"

His blush made her laugh. "Better and better. But I'm going to want to fly against you at some point, before I make any changes."

She shook her head and started to peel off the pad.

He groaned. "Please? One more sim?"

"You don't need to fly against me to know I'm good, Zander."

"I know." He sat back and glanced around the room. Several people had taken notice of them. "How full is your snark list?"

"Getting longer and longer by the day."

"I want a dedicated spot."

She pressed the pad back to his hand. "Done. I think you're going to like this one."

His eyes lit up. "Really."

She nodded. "Oh, yes."

Her betting odds improved dramatically afterwards.

Snarking fell short of virtual sex, but there was an undeniable degree of intimacy associated with the interaction. She managed to hack the snarking sim and drafted one of her virtual subroutines into service. While it managed the simulations, she practiced folding space and working on vectors and lines of force. It was the only time she could practice her growing understanding of WOR-skill without Gregor's oversight.

CHAPTER TWENTY-THREE_

Gambit, Day 239

GREGOR DID NOT SHOW UP THE NEXT MORNING TO TAKE ELISE OUT OF THE Fifth Rank training deck. She fretted in her quarters waiting. He failed to show up in the afternoon as well. When she escaped to the flight deck, late that night, she found what could demand the undivided attention of the ruler of worlds.

Carek sat on the ground under Dove's ship. The two silver medallions affixed to his temples flashed in the light. She couldn't remember a day recently when he hadn't left those discs in place.

The mood on the flight deck seemed subdued. Machine noise filled the deck, and the thick scent of fuel and oil assaulted her nostrils, but the people hunched as they walked, whispered as they talked, and scurried as if hunted. A few had haunted expressions and eyes stretched tight with strain.

Dove glanced up at the sound of her approach.

Her smile turned to a frown as he shook his head. His shoulders sagged. He patted the ground beside him in invitation and she came to sit next to him. Carek's eyes were drawn and his complexion pasty as if he hadn't seen sleep in too many days. She felt the way he looked and hoped she didn't look as worn out. It might give Gregor reason to ask uncomfortable questions. Carek's green eyes, normally brilliant and full of life, were wan and subdued.

"What's wrong? Has something happened?" she asked.

Carek took in a deep breath and his gaze flicked to her wrist, the one wearing his bracelet and Gregor's scar. Elise swore Carek looked more at the scar than anything else.

"We've lost Dunlaap," Carek said.

She glanced at Dove only because she had no idea what Dunlaap was and didn't want her ignorance to show in her expression.

Carek explained, "Dunlaap went silent last night, El." He gazed into her eyes and she swore he tried to tell her something not meant for Dove to hear. She had no idea what Carek hinted at.

"Larkin's family is from Dunlaap," Dove added.

Elise kept silent. If she didn't speak, one of them might fill in the blanks. What did it mean that Dunlaap went silent?

Dove swore. "Damn it. Here we have nearly a thousand of those women on board and not one of them is of any use."

Carek's eyes narrowed and he glanced to Elise. "The empire sent a large portion of our high ranking WOR to Dunlaap. Half of them went silent. There's reason to hope. We believe they may have escaped into WOR-space, but not before the S'Lorek annihilated Dunlaap. We can't raise anyone to know for sure."

The "we" Carek referred to was the Neural-Mind Conclave. Each time the First Rank WOR crept down the length of their WOR-drive construct, the Neural Mind on the *Gambit* was able to interface with the rest of the empire. Elise had learned that they took two such steps each day. Therefore, every twelve hours the Vendel of the fleet could keep their family, social, and business ties connected.

"Do you think Emperor vlor'Malita and the Tender Conclave will be able to train the Earth WOR in time?" Dove stared at Carek and wrung his hands.

Carek shrugged and turned the question to Elise. "What do you think?"

Elise's heart beat wildly at the directness of his question. The girls in her head squirmed. She shrugged and spread her hands out, palm up. "How can any of us know? But, he is vlor' and gave his word to save us." The last bit was a Vendel saying she had picked up around the flight deck.

Carek coughed and stared at his feet. "Of course. Trust in the vlor' and the emperor. He will see us through."

"Yes," she said, "I'm sure he will."

"Absolutely," Dove added. "They must be close to the Blood Rite, if not done already."

Elise fingered her scar. It itched like crazy.

"Shouldn't be long before they begin with the Binding Ritual. After they get control of those women's minds and their abilities, we should be set."

Elise frowned at this. *What does that mean?*

Carek dusted off the tops of his pants. "El, there's no one flying today."

"Right," she said, distracted.

He stared at his feet and made several false starts before finally asking his question. "It would be a good time to see the am-net. Do you feel up to it?"

Dove grunted. "Might as well." He jerked his head toward his cousin. "Take a field trip, Chickadee. Few have the opportunity to visit the tank."

"I'd love to, but I'd like to check in with Lark first."

Dove raised a hand and shook his head. "Don't bother. He might want to spend some time alone with you, but right now he's in the pilot's lounge and several bottles past oblivion. Jeena's with him. I don't think he would recognize you right now."

"Oh," she said, feeling his loss. She knew what it meant to have lost your family.

Carek leaned forward and touched her hand. His fingers brushed the silver chain and he smiled. Dove watched but pretended not to notice. Carek said she didn't have to wear it, unless she was flying, but it seemed to make him happy when she did.

It meant more to her than it should. She didn't know what her feelings were for Carek, except she cared deeply for him. They had no future, but there was always hope.

Or is there?

The corners of his mouth quirked up in a smile and then drew down as he caressed the back of her hand. "Come, it'll be interesting. I think you would find it a useful learning opportunity."

Elise tilted her head, but decided to go along. She really wanted to see the am-net. More importantly, if her little subroutines were infesting the Vendel mainframe, she wanted to check in with them directly and see how many had achieved their objectives.

"Well, I'm yours for the day. Lead and I will follow." Her words put a smile back on Carek's face.

Dove laughed. "Be careful, Chickadee. Most men would take that for promise of something more. Good thing it's Carek. Right cuz?" He grunted and unfolded his legs. Dove stood and offered her a hand up.

"And where would a man like me lead a woman like you?" Carek sighed.

She grasped Dove's meaty hand as he lifted her to her feet.

"Go have fun, little chickadee. They've suspended all non-essential flights for the Two Days Mourning. I'll see you later."

Carek stared at the ground.

Elise watched as he shook his head, shrugged and sighed.

He stood and held her in a penetrating stare.

"What's wrong?"

"Nothing, just thinking." He extended a hand, which she took. "See ya' later, cuz."

"Later, be good with my chickadee."

"Always." Carek turned to her. "I'll be a perfect gentleman. Let me show you my world, El."

"What's with all the comments?"

He sighed. "Just tired. We've been working extra shifts in the am-net. The Tender Conclave has commissioned a project and it's taking a toll. They're not the kind of people you disappoint, if you know what I mean?"

She knew that well enough, but all she said was, "Oh."

He led her out of the hangar and through the network of *Gambit's* lift tubes and pod circuits. He held her hand the entire way and walked like a man headed to his execution.

"What's wrong?" She tried to draw out the normally exuberant man. "Is it Dunlaap?"

He shook his head. "El, how do you intend for the jump-jet circuit to help with your sponsor difficulties?"

"If I win, or even finish in the top ten, Jeena's going to help me find a way to leave with the prize money."

"Sure, but how far do you think you'll be able to get? Won't he track you down?"

"Maybe, but it's a big empire. I'm sure I'll be able to hide."

"Hm." He fell silent for a time and they walked. He squeezed her hand. "You know, I could speak to him. Sort of let him know…well, I could stand up for you. I have some ability to put pressure on the average citizen. We could," he paused, hesitant, "we could marry?"

She stopped and stared at him, stunned by such a brazen remark. Vendel men never proposed. "I'm not looking to trade sponsors and I don't want a knight in shining armor to rescue me. I'll take care of it myself."

He stopped, bowed his head, then shook it. "By the gods, I'm a crazy man."

"God has nothing to do with it."

They walked in silence. Carek brooded and Elise fumed, confused over their odd conversation.

Is this our first fight?

He didn't release her as he guided her toward a large set of white doors. Above, printed in bold letters, she read *Am-net Neural Mind Conclave Headquarters. Conclave Members only beyond this point.*

She drew back.

He pulled her forward. "It's ok," he said. "I'm your escort."

The large doors swished open. The entry was an exact replica of the outer foyer of the Confinement Deck, and had her pulling up short. Four men sat behind a white, waist high counter. Carek walked up and pressed his palm to a gel pad.

"Hey, Telas. I'm bringing a guest in for a tour."

Telas eyed Elise in her red jumpsuit. He wore a green suit similar to Carek's and smiled at her briefly. "The Master's been looking for you. That High Tender just left and was looking for a status update. Master Varlen covered for you. I guess I now understand what kept you." He gave Elise another long look.

"Ah, hell. I don't want to talk to Master Varlen." Carek sighed. "Where is he?"

Telas answered, "He left the am-net for some rest. Said he'd be back before dinner and that you'd better be waiting for him in his office when he returned."

Carek swore. "Fine, just don't tell him I'm here now. I want to take El around for a tour."

"Don't worry. He left explicit instructions as to what would happen to the poor soul who tried to wake him." He winked at Elise. "You're safe. Enjoy your tour."

Elise nodded and Carek collected her and took her down an even more familiar tunnel. She suppressed flashbacks to her first experience onboard the *Gambit*. Thankfully, the long tunnel opened up directly into a huge space and not a tiny room with a center red circle. She didn't know if she would be able to deal with that.

"Come, let's get you dressed," Carek said.

"Dressed?"

"You need to get out of your jumpsuit and into an immersion suit," he explained. "Over here."

He escorted her to rows of white suits, gave her a head to toe look, then dragged his hand down the rack of suits and stopped near the smaller sizes.

"Try this one. Change in that dressing room and put your clothes in the locker. It'll palm lock to you so don't worry about valuables. And make sure you remove my bracelet as well as *all* your clothes. They're not compatible with the soup."

At the sound of *soup*, she raised her brows. She did not ask him to elaborate, although the twinkle in Carek's eyes suggested he waited for the question. She touched the collar around her neck. The jumpsuit hid it from view, but would the immersion suit do the same? She hoped the collar didn't interfere with the am-net, because there was no way to remove it, unlike the five bands she wore to denote her Rank. She turned and headed to the dressing room.

When she pulled the curtain closed, Carek called out, "I'm going to change into my suit. It's just down the way. I'll be right back. Don't go anywhere."

Elise stripped out of her clothes, all her clothes, and held the white suit up. It had the feel of gauze but felt strong, resilient, and stretchy. It had a nice high padded neck to it. At least she didn't have to worry about exposing the training collar. With a shrug, she donned the white suit. It clung to her skin without feeling tight. She wished there was a mirror present. A quick look down revealed more than she wanted to know. It was indeed skin-tight, something she would only have worn back on earth for a dare or after several shots of hard liquor and a few bottles of wine.

The collar at her neck, her constant companion since the Blood Rite, gave her pause. She could not remove it. None of them could. The neck of the immersion suit came up to just below her chin and fit loosely enough. Without a mirror, she couldn't tell if the collar was visible. She hoped Carek wouldn't notice the slight bulge.

His steps sounded outside. "Problems?" The lilt in his voice held a breath of humor and a little expectation.

"You might have prepared me." She pulled the curtain aside and stepped forward.

He cast his glance down her slender form and back up. He did not hurry and his lips spread into a wide grin.

"Enjoying the view?" She crossed her arms.

After standing naked in front of the WOR-guards, any modesty she might have felt in the past had long since vanished. She allowed Carek his slow appraisal and made one of her own. The muscles of Carek's arms and chest stood out beneath the fabric of the immersion suit, as did the dips and valleys of his cut abdomen and all the rest farther down.

"I'm enjoying it now." Carek finally brought his eyes up to her face. He smirked and his eyes twinkled. "And, I might say, so are you. The immersion suits leave little to the imagination, but are necessary if you plan on entering the soup."

She giggled. "I hope I made your day."

"In some ways," he replied cryptically.

She shrugged off his remark and asked, "So, what's this soup you keep talking about and how does it relate to the am-net?"

He took three steps toward her and reached up to her temples. Elise breathed in his fresh scent and lifted her chin. How she wished he would plant a kiss on her lips. Instead, he attached two silver discs to each temple.

"There. The immersion suit has its obvious purpose. The temple implants just make the experience more complete. Once we get to the tanks, I'll hook up the connectors. Ready for a swim?"

Elise hesitated. "So far this is nothing like I expected. Are you going to prepare me or not?"

Carek stood inches away. He looked down at her and she watched as his gaze passed over her lips. For a moment, it felt like he was going to kiss her, but he stiffened and his eyes narrowed. His expression faded to a blank mask as he stepped away.

"I have always found my guests find any explanations I give fall far short. I stopped preparing people decades ago."

"How many tours do you give?"

"You'll be my first tour for fun."

She arched a brow in surprise.

"Most are guided tours. People with business in the am-net. Special programs that they can't access through the gel-pads interfaces. Things for which only full immersion serves their needs."

"Well, I'm honored you want to share this with me."

"Yeah, well," he said and then his tone grew serious. "You are a remarkable woman, as I have said before. Brilliant, daring, courageous, and deadly determined to get what you desire. I find all of those things admirable." He tugged on his ponytail and continued, "I love my work and I love my people. I want to show you the Vendel in an entirely different way. I want you to see what I see. I hope you'll understand why it's worth saving. Why we must fight. All of us need to fight, each in our special way. We've lost two worlds to the S'Lorek. I don't want to lose another."

"You're very doom and gloom all of a sudden. I'd really like to see what you see, but I don't see what you, or I, can do against the S'Lorek."

"Hmm." He stretched out a hand. "I've learned to never underestimate." He led her to a wide railing and took her to the edge. With a flourish, he said, "This is the immersion tank."

Elise gasped. Below her was one of the largest tanks she'd ever seen. It reminded her of the water parks at home, except it wasn't a tank. It was easily the size of the Confinement Deck, and it glowed purple.

"You're taking me in there?" White humanoid shapes flitted in the depths, darting from place to place. Several others hovered at depth. "How deep is it?" Her heart raced realizing he was indeed intending on taking her for a swim in the purple liquid.

Carek wrapped an arm around her waist. "The deepest part is twenty meters. We won't go that deep. See why I didn't explain?"

"I wouldn't have believed you. So, what do we do?"

"Since this is your first time, instead of jumping in, I'll take you down the ramp so you get used to it slowly." He guided her down a set of stairs to a ramp. "Two things. First your hood." He pulled out two hoods and put one on. She watched as he tucked the ponytail into the back of his suit. He helped her with the white hood and got her hair tucked neatly inside. He then walked over to a cabinet and pulled out a white cylinder. He handed it to her and she took it with hesitation. It had a mouth-piece on it.

"Put it in your mouth to breathe. You can breathe the soup, but it can be an uncomfortable feeling unless you're used to it."

"What do you mean?" It had not escaped her notice that he'd only pulled one cylinder off the rack.

"The first few times it feels like drowning. You have to force yourself to breathe in the fluid." He laughed. "Don't worry, you'll be perfectly fine with that."

"This…" She held up the tube, "doesn't seem to hold much air."

"Trust me. Just keep it in your mouth and breathe normally. Oh, and don't breathe in through your nose."

"What about a mask?"

"No need. Just open your eyes, you'll see well enough. When we get to my node, I'll hook you in with the temple pads and you'll be busy seeing other things." He jumped onto a platform and reached down, gesturing for her to grab hold.

She grasped his warm hands and he lifted her without effort, leaving her to wonder again at the universal Vendel male physique.

He jerked his head toward a sloping ramp. She took a step toward it.

If other people can do this, so can I.

They walked down the ramp until the purple liquid came to her chest.

Carek stopped their descent. "Doing ok?"

She nodded.

"Good. We're going to continue walking down this ramp until we're swimming. This isn't like water. It has neutral buoyancy, so you're not going to float. That may seem weird, but keep a hold of my hand and I'll tow you along."

"Sure..."

"What I want you to do right now is dip down until your head is under the water and try a couple breaths. Let's make sure you're comfortable before getting in over our heads."

She did as instructed, surprised with how easy it was to breathe with the small canister.

Carek nudged her elbow and lifted her to the surface. "Good, how did that feel?" He watched her closely.

"Not bad. Pretty comfortable actually."

"Now try it again, but open your eyes and try to relax."

She hadn't realized she'd closed them. They did it again. Elise took a couple breaths and then cautiously opened her eyes. Carek's face filled her view. A purple haze covered everything, but otherwise, she was surprised how clear the water... *the soup* was. She looked over his shoulder and made out the shape of another person way off in the distance.

"How are you doing?"

She flinched. His lips hadn't moved. Elise stood and broke the surface of the soup.

Carek's head surfaced a moment later. He had traded his grin for concern. "What's wrong?"

"How did you say that underwater?"

"Not underwater, El, but in the soup. It's the immersion suits. I've linked ours together. All you have to do is think about what you want to say and the immersion suit will translate it for you. After a bit, you'll forget you're not actually speaking."

She cocked her head and narrowed her eyes. "Now that would have been useful information."

"Sorry, I guess I don't think about it much. For most people who come here it's obvious. Ready?"

"Yes," she said.

"Great," he grabbed her hand. "This is just like swimming. You can kick along beside me, or I can guide you."

"If you guide me, I get to hold your hand, right?"

His expression filled with regret. "I'm a fool, but I do enjoy holding your hand. Come on, little chickadee, worlds await."

Carek squeezed her hand and led her down the ramp and into the soup, then he kicked off and headed into the purple sea.

CHAPTER TWENTY-FOUR_

Gambit, Day 239

AFTER A FEW MINUTES OF BRISK SWIMMING, CAREK DOVE DOWN, TOWING ELISE with him. They stopped at a white sphere floating in the middle of the purple expanse. Several long threads hung from the device. He attached two to his temples and gestured for her to do the same.

"What do you think so far?" Carek crossed his arms and hovered in front of her in a lotus pose.

"What is this stuff? Is this the am-net? All this fluid?" *How does this form a computer?*

"Yes and no. This is one hub of the am-net, specifically *Gambit's* hub. Floating inside are biologics that act as nodes or nubs." He scratched his head. "It might do to think of it like your brain. The biologics are the nerve cells."

"Okay, but don't they have to connect through something. Is that the purple soup?"

"In a way."

"Then didn't we just destroy millions of connections by swimming through them?"

"Not really. The soup is their nourishment, but the connections are formed through sub-space. We stirred up billions of biologics, but all their connections are still intact in subspace."

"So, is it alive?"

Gambit was one hub, Carek had said. One? How many hubs formed the am-net? The computing power had to be astronomical.

"No, it's biotechnology. It's not alive." He unfolded his legs and kicked to her. "Here, hold my hands."

"Do we need to touch for you to show me whatever it is you brought me here for?"

He laughed. "No, I just want to hold your hands. Do you mind?"

"Not at all," she said with warmth. "Not at all."

He gave a sad smile she didn't understand. His emotional reactions had been off all day.

"For this part, you need to close your eyes. I'm going to take you on a tour. You'll hear me, just relax and follow along, and we'll talk at the end."

"Ok," she said with some degree of hesitation, but she closed her eyes, trusting Carek's guidance.

Her sisters poked their heads out of the darkness, interested in what Carek wanted to show her. She hushed them, but welcomed their company. Malice came to sit by her side, Whimper and Shriek were content to stay where they were, and the other lurked, as always, in the shadows.

A slowly rotating planet filled her mind's eye. Twin to Earth, it had blue oceans covering much of its surface and white clouds dotting its atmosphere. She counted eight large island continents, reminiscent of Australia in size. Ice capped the northern and southern poles. Three moons orbited the planet. One was smooth and round, somewhat larger than the Moon. The other two were much smaller and lacked the uniform smoothness of a sphere.

Carek brought her down through the atmosphere to a large city full of beautiful spires and sweeping ramps. People hurried to and fro along moving walkways and disappeared into towers soaring miles high. He swept her up and around the city until they flew above the land. They came to the edge of a coastline and he plunged her beneath the waves.

Beautiful reefs dotted the coasts and he gave her a moment to appreciate the wonder of the sea life. They went deeper until he brought her into a submerged city. Children played on the backs of porpoise-like creatures in a game of chase with little bubbles encasing their heads.

He took her inside the underwater domes and showed her the city parks. A group of two- and three-year-old children played on a lawn and giggled with delight. A couple pointed to the kids at play. The woman whispered into the man's ear. He beamed back and nodded.

Carek sped up time and Elise followed the couple as they checked into a clinic. The couple donated blood samples, then left. They returned the next week to donate sperm and an egg. Time flipped forward and an embryo grew inside a clear crystal globe. It matured into a little, perfect human. The man and woman returned several months later, accompanied by their friends on the day the pod was opened. The little baby screamed its distress at this rude awakening, while its father held it in his hands.

Elise clapped with joy at the birth of this precious child.

Carek took her out of the dome and they soared to the clouds and into space, leaving the beautiful world behind. He headed past six different planets, reminiscent of her solar system. They passed an asteroid belt, crossed the paths of five gas planets, and headed to the stars.

Ten enormous ships, each easily dwarfing the *Gambit*, traveled in the depths of space. They had just exited WOR-space and she sat on the command bridge as the expectant captain brought his colony ships to their new home. This stellar system lacked any habitable worlds, but was rich in all the materials necessary for life. They brought everything they needed to build their new home and maintain their fleet of c-ships. The bridge crew toasted their safe arrival.

Carek brought her light years away to a new planet. This planet was a mirror opposite of the first. It was covered in deserts and the empty basins of long dried up oceans. Only a few landlocked seas peppered its surface. Few clouds dotted the sky and a brown haze of dust covered the globe. Two suns and no moons decorated the heavens of this world.

He brought her down and showed her cities carved out of rock, which formed brilliant sculptures. As before, he picked a family and followed them for a brief period of time.

On this planet, a young boy stood with his mother, along with hundreds of other boys with him. The hot wind blew down on an open bowled amphitheater and provided little relief from the heat of twin suns. The dust cast a golden glow to the setting of the first sun. A mother caressed the top of the boy's head and then, at a prearranged signal, knelt at his feet.

She presented her son a carved dagger, which he took with solemn care. Along with the other boys, he gave the first of several oaths as a Vendel male. This First Oath he swore to Emperor, family, and to the Master of his accepting Conclave. The people in the open bowl burst into applause as thousands of happy onlookers cheered. The boy shed a single tear and walked away from his mother to his new master. Elise felt the joy and pride of the boy's mother and wept tears of sorrow and delight at this first important step in the young boy's life.

What beautiful people.

Carek spoke. "How are you doing?"

"It's beautiful."

"Would you like to see them again?"

"Can we?"

"Let me show you those worlds again."

Carek transported her back to the first world. They hung above the blue marble planet, which reminded her so strongly of Earth. She counted the island continents as they rotated into view.

"Do you want to go closer again?"

"Yes."

They soared through the atmosphere and across the rolling hills. Only the green pastures and dense forests were dry and parched.

"Is this the dry season?" she asked with concern.

"No," he said, flatly.

They came upon the city of spires. Where beautiful ramps had soared before, broken devastation littered the city. The spires had cracked and fallen, as if a giant had stomped on the town. An unnatural stillness hung in the air.

She gasped.

Carek remained silent.

He took her beneath the waves. The coastal reefs were quiet. No fish swam in the waters and the corals were coated in detritus, empty of life. They raced to the undersea domes, which were cracked and flooded.

"What happened?"

Carek did not answer.

He brought her up and out of the ocean and sped her toward the fleet of colony ships. Warped and twisted metal greeted them. Where ten ships had flown with grace, a field of debris littered space.

He took her to the dessert planet and the proud little boy. The sand had been scoured clean. Carved out of hard rock, the bones of the city withstood the devastation, but no signs of life were to be seen. It was dead, deserted, dried up. The few seas evaporated.

Elise sobbed. "Carek, what happened? What did this?"

"The first planet was Saphirah. The couple you saw were my parents, you saw my birth. The c-ship Bravo fleet was home to Dove. The twelve-year-old boy on Dunlaap was Larkin giving his First Oath to Emperor, family, and the Pilot Conclave. This is the devastation left by the S'Lorek. They sterilize planets. This is what the empire faces, Elise. This is what

Emperor Gregor Ulysses vlor'Malita must fight. This is an enemy for which we have no defense."

He paused and took in a deep breath, then blew it out slow. "It is why you must return to him. It's why you must stop this nonsense with the jump-jet finals. You cannot run from him, from us. We need you to fight for us."

She ripped her hands out of his grip and clutched at her heart. She gasped and the breathing tube slipped out of her mouth. Purple fluid filled her mouth, poured down her throat, and sought to drown her. She panicked and kicked for the surface, but strong hands held her in place and powerful legs encircled her waist. She clamped her throat shut against the water.

"El," Carek shouted, "you must breathe. You will not drown, but you must breathe before you pass out. Do. Not. Hold. Your. Breath."

Her eyes popped open. How had he found out? She choked in the purple soup as her sight dimmed. Elise spasmed and coughed. Air bubbles escaped her throat and floated above her head. It took two full minutes before she realized she was not, in fact, drowning.

Carek held her shoulders and wrapped his legs around her waist to keep her still.

"I'm so sorry, El, but you must understand."

"Don't touch me!"

Normally, she would wipe away her tears, however, the purple soup dissolved her misery and her tears floated away. She tried to extricate herself from Carek's embrace, but he held her firmly.

"Let me go."

He gave a shake of his head. "You would try to run and I can't let you out of my sight."

"Let me go!"

"El, we need to talk." He stroked her cheek and she jerked away.

She tried to pry out of his embrace. Powerful legs locked around her. Her struggles only succeeded in sending them into a spin. Carek was not budged by her efforts and allowed her to flail against him. He let her work out her anger and frustration until she finally caved in and relaxed, defeated.

Everything she'd worked so hard to achieve had come to this? How had he found out? How did he know? How could she survive this?

Shriek took in deep breaths. *I must prepare for the braklav.*

Whimper mumbled. *Lost! We are lost! No. No. No!*

439

Malice narrowed her eyes. *He has not yet turned us in. Why? Elise. If he has known, why did he not turn us in?*

Elise had to find the answer to Malice's question. Why hadn't Carek turned them in?

More Tender Training would destroy them. Gregor would not kill her. She was too valuable, but he would crush her until nothing remained.

She and her sisters had their limits. If not Gregor, then the High Tender would find them.

Carek lifted her chin.

Her eyes squeezed shut in anguish. When Carek pressed his warm mouth to her lips, her lids popped open.

In such startling contrast to Gregor, Carek's kiss was a tenderness without end.

His kiss? *Why is Carek kissing me?*

Her sisters screamed in her mind.

Shriek screamed. *What's happening here?*

Whimper moaned. *What is this?*

Malice growled. *I don't like this!*

Carek kissed her cheeks and her nose, and brought his kisses around to whisper into her ear. "I am damned, and doubly doomed, for I'm in love with an impossibility. Forgive me, but I love you."

Elise sobbed.

He returned to lightly kiss her mouth. And that was when she realized what was so different about his kisses. Carek didn't force himself on her like Gregor did.

"We need to talk." Carek did not release her from his grip. "El, please, look at me." He put a finger under her chin and lifted.

"How did you know?"

"I think I've known for a while, but I didn't want to believe the truth. I mean, who would believe such a thing? But then, I began to hope. You're a miracle. It's impossible what you've done. How you've escaped."

"How did you know?" she repeated.

"It was little things really."

"Tell me."

"I wasn't certain until today. You made two mistakes."

"What?"

"The Vendel left Earth long before knights in shining armor. It's not an expression any Vendel would use and we worship the gods, not God. We left long before your Jesus walked the earth. I said, *By the gods*, and you said…"

440

"God had nothing to do with it." She glanced far above, to the ripples in the surface of the purple soup. There was nowhere to run.

"Right, that's when I knew for sure who Dove's little chickadee was. Well, at least what you were."

"But you suspected before that?" What else had given her away? She needed to know for the next time. *Will there be a next time?*

"You have a scar on your hand. Vendel rarely keep scars, unless for a reason. And none would dare leave a scar where a Binding Knife would enter, especially a woman. That's what set me to thinking. I knew it couldn't be true. I tried to deny it. How could a s'vlor sneak out the way you do? Why haven't you been caught? I suspected, but by then it was too late."

"What do you mean, too late?"

"Didn't you hear me?"

She searched his face. "No."

He leaned in and kissed her lips again. "Against every custom in my world, I profess my love to you. I am damned and doubly doomed. Damned for loving you. Doubly doomed for breaking my oath, sworn three times, to the empire. I should have turned you in, and yet I kept finding something else I had to do. I am forsaken three times over."

"What happens now?"

"Don't abandon us to the S'Lorek, El. Tell me you will help. If you belong to Emperor vlor'Malita, as I suspect, then you must be the key that Master Tender, Lord vlor'Vardhal, keeps talking about."

She stiffened at his words. "I have risked much to rid myself of Gregor."

"I know. I have helped, even after my suspicions grew. I have seen your brilliance and your tenacity, which is why I believe the Master Tender is correct about your potential."

"You don't understand. I hate him. I hate Gregor. I need to be free of him. I can't live as a slave."

"My precious, El," he said, "the Emperor has requested the High Council meet. Do you know why?"

"To rape me. He says he needs to Bond with me." She couldn't suppress her revulsion. "The bastard is dying to complete his conquest, mind and body."

He pressed a finger to her lips. "Be careful with your words. We share a private communication in here, but those are treasonous words. What you've said is a part of it, but not the whole of it. He is seeking more than sex."

"Really?" What more was left?

"What do you understand of the Binding Rite?"

"An exchange of biologicals. I hate Vendel biotech, by the way. A Vector to kill billions, an Activator to torture us, and the Blood Rite to prepare us for this Binding Ritual. I know it's so he can have my body. I'm not naive."

"Let me explain, because you deserve the truth of what happened to you. What we've done to you."

"Fair enough."

"The Vector was designed here in the am-net. It had a very specific purpose."

"I know, Gregor told me all about it. Killing everyone without a certain number of WOR-genes and identifying women like me. A WOR breeding ground is what he left behind."

"Simplistic, but correct. The Activator?"

"Turned on the WOR-genes and altered our neural chemistry so we can use the WOR-skill."

"True, so tell me, you've practiced the WOR-skill, tell me—how do powerful women allow themselves to be subservient to men?"

"We have to learn how to use the WOR-skill and while we learn we wear collars which limit our ability to touch the WOR-skill. We're nothing more than chattel."

"I'm sorry for that, El. I truly am. But let me explain about the Binding Rite. It's not so they can take their WOR to bed. Most lords are married and perfectly content. It's considered by many to be a tremendous burden as it causes conflict with their wives."

She scoffed at that comment. "How unfortunate for them. What a terrible burden..."

Carek tried to find the right words. "Please, let me explain. Our culture is not like yours. No lord can—well, he's not permitted to have sex with his WOR until after the Blood Right and after she's demonstrated a certain degree of mastery over the WOR-skill. The exchange of biologics isn't effective until then."

"Exchange of biologics? You can't even say it. Gregor is going to rape me. He's going to ejaculate inside of me!"

"El!" Carek glanced around, but they were alone. "You must watch what you say."

"Tell me, Carek, why is Gregor pushing the Binding Rite? And why does he need to take it to council? What does that even mean?"

"It's the High Council. The highest ruling body we have. His peers will decide whether to release his oath. The Ruling Council has already decided the legal aspect. Recently, as a matter of fact."

"How, why?" And what oath?

"Lord vlor'Vardhal argued that the emperor's s'vlor has been resistant to conventional training. It is the judgment of the Ruling Council that an early Binding will help the emperor force his s'vlor through training by giving him absolute control over her. The Ruling Council has given the emperor the go ahead. However, he made a mistake and gave his sworn Oath not to touch you until proper Binding."

"What does that even mean?"

"Oaths are important rituals for the Vendel and they're legally binding. Emperor vlor'Malita gave oath as Emperor, not as a vlor'lord. Had he given oath as vlor' he could have been released by whoever he gave his oath to. In this case, High Tender Marcus vlor'Vardhal. But, he gave oath as Emperor. Only the High Council, the ruling vlor' and the High Judicators, can relieve him of that oath and allow a premature Binding."

"I don't understand. And, how do you know so much about this? You're not a lord."

"Several hundred years ago, I rose to my current position. Selected after the death of my uncle, who previously held it, for my forthrightness, my honesty and my loyalty to the empire."

"What position? You're not Ruling Caste. You're Working Caste."

"I'm a High Judicator. Do you know what that means?"

"No."

"Our lords wield tremendous power, especially the v'lor with WOR. The Judicators and High Judicators balance the power of our lords. We're drawn from the Working Caste and sit in Council. As a group, we have the power to overturn decisions, laws, and release lords from their oaths. Our decision must be unanimous, but it is binding. We're the few who serve the Empire above the Emperor. I mentioned I've sworn oath to my empire three times; first as a boy, then when selected as a Judicator, and again when placed in the position of High Judicator. El, I sit in judgment of my emperor. Can you not see the conflict consuming me?"

"I don't see any of it. I don't understand any of it."

Why hasn't he turned us in yet, Malice Whispered. *Why are you still free? Ask!*

"I'm well aware the trouble you've caused my emperor. I didn't know it was you, El, Dove's *Chickadee,* but I've heard the Emperor's arguments in council. The High Council meets soon and the vlor' rulers will release him from his oath. The High Judicators will follow and endorse that ruling."

Elise's hope flared. "But it has to be unanimous, right? You can vote no. I need more time."

He dropped his chin to his chest. "I love you. I have said it. It is true. I'm damned for loving you and doomed for not turning you in." He glanced up and shook his head. "I will not turn you in. When we are done here, I'll watch you walk away. I won't betray you. I'll never betray you. But when the High Judicator's cast their votes, I will vote with them. I'll release him from his oath, knowing full well what it will cost you."

"Why let me walk out of here, but then condemn me to him?" She shook her head trying to sort it out.

"Because the S'Lorek are out there. How many Vendel do you know? Not many. And yet the S'Lorek have touched each of us. I showed you my empire. My people. They are vibrant, brilliant and full of life. The trials of WOR indoctrination taint what little you know about the empire. It's a cruel process, but necessary. I know this and yet I condemn you to it. I need you to see the empire as I see it. We took your world from you, and there's no excuse for what we did, but you need to know why it was necessary. The S'Lorek would have eventually found Earth. Only in silencing the home world do we save it. Hate me. Hate the emperor. But don't hate the Vendel. We're worth saving."

His words hit her with the force of an avalanche. She tumbled down the mountainside, pummeled from every side by the force of his words. He smothered her with his passion for life, for humankind, and she broke under the onslaught.

The willow bent and cracked.

He reached out to her and she didn't have the strength to pull away. All her efforts at freedom stopped in this moment.

I have failed.

Defeat took the last of her energy and she crumbled beneath the weight of it.

Carek embraced her and she folded into his muscular arms.

"I'm not done hurting you, my love. The Binding Rite is more than a physical rape. It's much worse, and for this you will hate me. Binding will tie your mind to his. The Blood Rite has been preparing his body for the act. Your blood, your DNA, was taken into his body. It has been changing his genetic makeup as surely as the Activator worked on your brain. When his seed is planted within you, when the Binding is complete, you won't be the same."

"What do you mean?" The tone of his voice, the seriousness of his expression caused her to panic.

"Oh, El..." His voice cracked. "I'm giving the Emperor the keys to your very soul, because I'm the architect of your destruction. Binding destroys your free will. It will be bound to him. Lost forever. Do you understand?"

No! Shriek shivered.

No! Whimper wailed.

No! Malice mumbled.

It's not true, the silent one whispered, but even in her voice, Elise sensed fear.

"You will cease to exist," Carek continued. "Dove's *Chickadee*. Jeena's *kid*. You will vanish. In every outward manner, you'll be no different, but he'll rule you absolutely. Who you are will fade. Your independence, your passion, your vibrancy will die. Your thoughts will be his. Your will bound to his. This is how the vlor' control the WOR. It is how I will destroy the woman I love."

Everyone went silent in her mind. Malice said not a word, a cackle, a giggle or a whisper. Shriek bit her tongue. Whimper cocked her head. The other pondered.

Elise fisted her hands and spoke with a cold fury. "Release me."

"I cannot."

"I won't run."

Carek, so unlike Gregor, gave her the freedom she demanded. He unwrapped his legs and let her loose.

"El, Gods I'm so sorry." He wept. "I have forsaken my emperor, but my people...our people need you. Please don't dismiss us. The Master Tender has tasked me to devise a system to link the s'vlor and increase their power. We hope it will be enough to destroy the S'Lorek. Help me save my people."

"Take me back, Carek."

"El!" he begged. "Please!"

"This...is not love...Carek. Take me back."

Do not worry Elise, the silent sister said. *We are not yet defeated. Until we are Bound, we are still free. We fight.*

Free? Free to do what? We're a dead woman walking. Or at least a soon to be mindless automaton. Is there no limit to their cruelty?

We learn new things every day, Elise. We still have time.

At least one of us is still an optimist. Does this mean you're finally going to come out of the dark and join us?

The silent sister slithered into the dark, leaving Elise alone with her thoughts.

I didn't think so.

Shriek stood and stretched. *Looks like I'm not needed. Carek likes you. He's not going to tell on us. You should listen to the lurker.*

Are you taking her side now?

No, but I don't think we should give up. Shriek turned and walked away.

"Like giving up was ever an option," she said out loud.

"I didn't mean give up, I just meant you need to work for the emperor." Carek reached for her shoulder but she shrugged away from him.

"I wasn't talking to you." She turned away from him. "Take me out of here. Tell your emperor whatever you want. He'll destroy me when he finds out what I've been doing behind his back. I won't survive it."

Carek unhooked the wires from his temples and then did the same for her. His eyes cast down. "Didn't you hear me? I'm not going to do that."

"How can you not? Aren't you obligated to your emperor?"

He firmed his lips. "You didn't hear me, El. I'm not sworn to serve the emperor. I'm bound to serve the empire, one of very few men, the Emperor being one of them. Unlike him, I believe you must choose to help us rather than be forced to serve us. I very dearly hope you do."

Elise took in a deep lungful of the purple liquid and felt it glide down her throat and fill her lungs. Such an odd sensation.

Save the Vendel?

She gave a soft laugh.

They were mad.

And yet, you're considering it, the lurker whispered from the darkness.

CHAPTER TWENTY-FIVE_

Gambit, Day 239

ELISE SAT IN THE LIVING AREA OF HER SUITE ON THE FIFTH DECK AND TOLD her friends all about what Carek had said regarding the Binding Rite and what it would do to them all. This, of course, took time because she had to backtrack to the beginning and explain who Carek was, along with the rest of her excursions off the Confinement Deck. In short, clipped tones she described her late-night adventures to the stunned threesome.

Alice became very still. "You thought that would work?" Her brows lifted with a dubious expression.

Elise shrugged. "I did, at least until Carek explained what's in store for us."

"Your plan was to win the jump-jet final and buy a ship?"

"Yes! How else are we going to escape? Look, it may not be the best plan, but it's the only way to get everyone off the *Gambit*."

"And then what? It's not like we can go back to Earth. That's the first place they'd look."

"I know. It's not a perfect plan. There are tons of holes, but we don't have time for perfect. It's just the next step. Get off *Gambit* and find someplace to hide."

"Hide?" Alice didn't look convinced.

"Look, the Vendel aren't tied to a planet. They have colony ships. If they can survive in c-ships, then we can too. At least until we figure out the next step."

She wanted to explain her grandfather's process of breaking down the impossible into smaller steps, but they didn't have time for a lecture. Something changed in Alice's expression, as if she'd been having an inner conversation with herself, because she suddenly turned to Aomi and Chandra, who had been quiet during the entire exchange.

"It's time to teach them our code."

"What code?" Chandra looked between them, confused. "They already know about the damned code."

Alice shook her head. "Elise devised a second code. We didn't share it with anyone because we figured the Vendel would figure out the first one eventually. It was a pretty big secret for nearly a thousand to keep locked up. She and I have been using it."

Aomi and Chandra exchanged glances.

"I feel so left out," Aomi said with a frown.

"Me, too."

Elise gripped their hands and gave a light squeeze. "I know you do, but you understand now? Our vlor'lords can read our thoughts. We couldn't risk them knowing about it. And I never told Alice about what I was doing with the jump-jet. She knew something was up, but I kept it a secret to protect her if I got caught."

"I'm not mad," Chandra said. "I get it. I just can't believe you were able to escape the Confinement Deck. I can't believe you're still here."

"Where would I go?" While *Gambit* traveled in WOR-space, there was literally no place to go. They technically didn't exist in space, but rather along an infinite line of possibility.

Aomi smiled. "I can't believe you're looking for a way to get all of us free, Elise. It would be much easier to free just yourself."

"I would never leave any of you behind."

Aomi leaned forward and kissed Elise on the cheek. "And that is why I believe you will find a way. What can we do to help?"

"Alice will teach you our secret code. It belongs just to the four of us. Don't share it. Gregor has given me limited freedom to learn the WOR-skill by observing it. I'm hiding what I'm learning from him, but sometime soon, I'm going to have to show some progress. If not, High Tender Marcus will force me back into regular training. And despite what Carek said, I'm not giving up on the jump-jet. It's the only way I know to acquire a ship large enough for all of us to escape in. We're headed to Malbra. When we get there, we'll be back in normal space. That's when we can escape. What happens next...well, that's something I'm working on."

Elise had no idea what came next.

Alice stood and pressed out the wrinkles of her dress. "Then that's our plan...until something changes. Come on girls, I've got a code to teach you. Elise has..." She gave a vague wave of her hand. "Elise has whatever magic is up her sleeve. We continue as obedient and subservient slaves to our masters, at least until Elise tells us what comes next."

Aomi and Chandra rose. They didn't say much as they left for morning WOR-skill instruction. Beneath their somber faces, however, a hint of hope ran through them.

Elise prayed she wasn't leading them astray. There had to be a way.

She picked out one of Gregor's favorite dresses and slipped it on. He was late and she wondered if the evolving Dunlaap crisis would keep him away for another day.

Her body craved sleep. After Carek's revelation, a numb sense of calm overcame her. He wouldn't turn her in, but he would consign her to the Binding Rite. Time was ticking.

This must be what a prisoner feels on the eve of his execution. All the fight gone and only grim acceptance of the inevitable was left.

We cannot admit defeat, the lurker spoke, surprising Elise. *We're not done. As long as we're in control of our mind we have not lost.*

I'm not done fighting. She gave a deep sigh. *But I am tired.*

The fight's not over, Elise! Malice echoed the lurker's words, lending a measure of her strength to Elise.

Don't give up, Shriek urged. *I'm not done fighting.*

Nor, I, Malice said.

Elise pondered her next move while she waited for Gregor. He gently shook her awake some time later.

"Gregor!" She popped to instant alertness. "I'm sorry. I didn't mean to fall asleep."

He gave one of his smirks. "You're wearing one of my favorite dresses, opés."

The dress she wore was snow white, with layers of shimmering gauze. She liked the dress too, because the layers floated around her like a white cloud when she walked.

"I missed you yesterday and hoped it would please you."

He frowned. "Yes, well, I was forced to be an emperor yesterday and not your master."

"I hope it was nothing serious?" She gathered her hair and pulled it over her shoulder away from the back of the gown and the ties she'd left undone.

Gregor traced a finger up her arm and down her shoulder. He tightened the ties of the dress while they shared an intimate moment of silence.

When he was done, she turned around and placed her hand on his arm.

Gregor held still as she brought her hands to his tunic and unbuttoned his shirt.

"What are you doing, opés?"

Elise kept her eyes off his face. She opened his shirt and exposed the expanse of his chest. "Tell me about the Binding Rite."

"Why this interest in the Binding? I thought you weren't looking forward to it?"

Time to lie and dig for information. How much of the truth would he give her?

"We both know what happens when you touch me." She rose on tiptoe to kiss his lips. "How much longer are we going to have to wait before we can do more?"

How much time do I have left?

"Unfortunately, longer than I had hoped. Something has come up which occupies the High Council."

"Do I have anything to fear from this ritual?"

Gregor's expression became an impenetrable mask. He released her waist. "The consummation of our bodies is merely the final step in union of master and s'vlor. Nothing more."

Beast, bastard and devil. This man was all three if he was one.

"Will you swear on that?"

"Masters never take oath with their s'vlor. Come." He buttoned his shirt and led her toward the door. "Today will be interesting, opés. Let's see if you can put any of that genius intellect to use."

"I will try, Gregor. I am trying very hard to learn." Elise followed him out the door. She'd given him an opportunity to reveal the true purpose of the Binding Rite and he refused to share what it would do to her.

She hated him for that.

His plan for the day was another round of tours through the Conclaves. Each Master explained how their First Rank WOR integrated into their Conclaves. First Rank WOR, she learned, underwent the Blood Rite with the Conclave Masters, not a lord from the Ruling caste, and did not undergo the Binding Rite. When control of the Conclave passed hands, the WOR underwent another Blood Rite with the new Master. These women lived in relative freedom, compared to the s'lor or s'vlor. Relative freedom, but they were far from free.

The Conclave Masters introduced her to their WOR, who showed Elise how they used the WOR-skill to assist the Conclave.

Out of habit, Elise compartmentalized the training. She had to show improvement by the end of this cycle, or else High Tender Marcus would revoke his training plan. She followed each WOR as they practiced their WOR-skill and tucked all that knowledge away to chew on it later. Shriek and Whimper helped. Elise even felt the presence of the lurker absorbing knowledge of the WOR-skill.

When she realized why the Conclave First Rank WOR were so eager to help, Elise shouldn't have been surprised. Whether by Gregor's decree or High Tender Marcus, failure by these women carried with it a full hour of Tender Training for all *Gambit's* Conclave WOR.

With that knowledge, she focused on learning, rather than her plans for escape. No way would she be responsible for any woman's pain.

A mantra continued in her mind. The words never stopped.

A beast. A bastard. A devil. I hate him.

———

The Vendel Two Days Mourning passed while Elise made steady progress with the First Rank WOR.

Time passed.

Gregor's oath had yet to be released. The High Council remained engrossed in the Dunlaap disaster. Elise passed her time training, and enjoying what she viewed as her last days.

On the final day of her two-cycle trial, she found herself in High Tender Marcus's office for an assessment.

"Good morning, s'Lissa," the High Tender said.

"Good morning, High Tender Marcus."

Elise stood within his personal office full of odd holographic plaques displaying wire diagrams that shifted and moved as she watched.

He sat at his desk, busy working at the gel interface. "I will be with you momentarily."

No invitation to sit on either of the two leather chairs facing his desk, or the two couches facing one another. This left her to watch him in silence. Her attention wandered to the odd plaques hung around the room.

The wire diagrams represented each of the WOR skills progressing from Bar to Rod to Wheel in a progression around the room.

She looked at each, filing the images away with her eidetic memory. This was the first visual representation of the WOR-skill she had seen. It was wrong. They were missing key dimensional folds and some of the vectoring solutions were wrong.

Strange that they have it wrong, the lurker said.

Yes, she agreed. *How is that possible? They're supposed to be the experts.*

Displayed along the left wall, the five skills of the Bar sat in a neat line just above eye level. Beneath the Bar skills, three rows, with ten holographs each, displayed the first three sets of the Rod skill. The back wall had similar holographs, and she recognized the fourth and fifth Rod skill sets arrayed in ordered rows.

She walked over to the right wall, to what must be the skills of the Wheel. So far, none of the women had progressed past the second set of Rod skills. Wheel skills remained the domain of the high ranking WOR, the s'lor and s'vlor. Elise scanned the wall. It was arranged in the shape of a wheel, with five spokes radiating out from the center.

The High Tender remained occupied with his work and continued to ignore her. She glanced at him and then moved over for a closer inspection of the Wheel skills.

A central non-holographic plaque had the Roman numerals two through five inscribed in a deep ebony wood. The number two filled the center of the plaque while the other numbers, separated by concentric white rings, spread out toward the edge. The number five lay at the outermost top edge and seemed to float unsecured on the black wood.

Five spokes radiated out from the central plaque. One headed up, one each to the left and right, and the last two headed down to either side, sloping a little to the floor, slightly off-center.

Each spoke held ten holographs and three white rings encircled the entire display, encompassing two of the plaques from each spoke. The final four holographs of each spoke floated outside the last ring.

At the current rate the Vendel were training their WOR, it would be an incredibly long time before they got started on the Wheel skills, let alone begin work on the Fifth Rank rung.

Elise looked at each of the Wheel skills on the plaques. By the time she finished scanning the Wheel skills, and testing her recall, she felt the presence of the High Tender behind her.

"Impressive, isn't it?" His deep bass rumble filled the room.

"Daunting is more like it." She spun around and gave a polite smile she did not feel. "If these are what I think they are, and I'm sure I'm right, I'm stuck way over there."

He nodded.

"How am I supposed to get all the way over to here?"

"It takes time."

"How much time?" She scanned the wall again. "How long does it take to train a WOR?"

"Depends on Rank, of course."

She stepped close to the wall and touched the innermost double rung of plaques. "Are these the Wheel skills of the Second Rank?"

He nodded.

She moved her hand to the next double rung. "Third?" She lifted her brows in question. "So, this is Fourth and Fifth."

"Correct."

She dragged her hand out to the outermost ring of plaques. "Are you certain you and Gregor haven't made a horrible mistake? I'm far behind the other Earth Fifth Rank WOR in training, and I haven't even been practicing these past two cycles."

"Legitimate question." The corner of his mouth tilted down. "One, which I might say, is causing your master a lot of grief with the High Council right now. It's also his primary argument."

"What? Is it over his oath?"

He nodded, again. "They have expressed concerns."

"Aren't you supposed to be supporting him?"

"I have and am. That has been settled in the Ruling Council. His oath is another matter and not mine to release."

"I don't understand your government. High Council, Ruling Council?"

"You don't need to. You just need to serve your master."

Elise caught herself before she rolled her eyes. The braklav dangled from the High Tender's wrist and she would not give him any cause to use it. "Would it really hurt to explain a little to me?"

"Other than wasting my time, no," he said flatly. He gestured her to one of the couches and lifted a brow when she did not immediately comply.

She sighed and stepped past him to take a seat on the couch. He sat on the couch directly opposite her.

"The emperor believes your inability to learn by conventional means is due to a certain uniqueness in the way you access your abilities. I don't disagree with him, but not sure I agree either. But I did test you with the Tenderstat, and saw how it responded. Perhaps he's right and you have a mental block. He believes we're not showing you how in a way you can understand."

"I'm really not trying to be difficult." Elise fiddled with the silk of her dress.

"You've been exceptionally difficult and disobedient."

"I'm trying to obey." Elise forced her hands to stillness. "Since...well, I've worked hard to learn everything you've shown me." She shuddered in remembrance of the pain of Tender Training.

"Do you know why I have brought you here?"

She did, but he didn't know she had heard that conversation. She was supposed to have been out of her mind at the time.

"Are you checking up on me? Worried about my training?"

"Emperor vlor'Malita desired to try something unconventional. I'm sure you've wondered why he's been dragging you all around the ship. The First Rank WOR have been showing you what they do. Unfortunately, the *Gambit* doesn't have any higher-ranking WOR onboard. They're all occupied elsewhere. Which is unfortunate. I think it would be interesting to have you watch some of them."

"I have found it interesting," she said. "They appear to be involved in almost every ship's systems. What would the Vendel do without them?"

"I've brought you here to try a few things. I want to see what you've learned in these past two cycles." High Tender Marcus placed four steel balls on the surface of the table.

"Now, I'm sure you recognize these. What I want is to run through a series of exercises. Most will be new and I don't want you to use anything Gregor or I have taught you. I want you to think about what the *Gambit's* WOR have shown you and let it flow from there."

"What am I supposed to do?"

"I want you to start the balls spinning."

"Rotating on an axis or spinning around a common point?"

"Either."

Elise thought about it and arranged lines of force.

He frowned. "What are you doing?"

"What you asked?"

"I can see what you do, that is the first skill of the Bar. I don't want you to do it the way we taught you."

"Sorry." The little balls stopped their dance around the table.

"Let's try something less familiar." He sat back and crossed his ankle over his knee, then placed a finger to his lip and tapped it slowly.

She watched, waiting for instruction, as he took in a deep breath and very slowly blew it out. "All right, what I want you to do is form a pattern in your mind." He tossed out five more of the marbles. "You can use three

454

or more of these balls in your pattern. It should be something that moves, all the balls need to be in motion."

"What sort of pattern?"

"What comes to mind?"

Elise shrugged. "I don't know."

"Think about it, I'll wait." He uncrossed his leg and leaned back on the couch. He locked his hands together and placed them behind his head.

She pulled her attention away from him and back to the table.

A pattern.

Something simple or did he want more? There was no way to tell with this man. Whatever she chose, he would want something different. She thought of the planetary construct she had formed in the park, what seemed like ages ago, and decided against it.

Finally, she settled on moving the balls along a circle, one chasing the next. Three balls entered the loop and she added a fourth and then a fifth. She had a chain of little balls moving along the top of the table between her and the High Tender.

He tossed ten more of the marbles down on the table. "Add these, s'Lissa."

She did.

He added a few more. "Fit these in."

She did.

"Pretty simple," he said. "How about making two rings?"

She complied, splitting the one long chain into two equal parts.

"Can you move them in opposite directions?"

She did.

"Not bad." He uncrossed his hands and placed them in his lap.

She glanced at him and watched him examine the moving mass of marbles. He tossed ten more marbles on the table. "Can you fit these in and perhaps widen your rings?"

She slipped all the marbles neatly into her rings.

"How about three rings?"

Elise stared at her little construct and decided how to fit the request into her mass of twirling marbles. Two rings became three.

"Good." He leaned forward. "Can you lift it up off the table, so that it is at eye level and easier for me to see?"

"Yes, High Tender."

Elise floated the entire construct off the table. She had three rings moving in perfect unison. The inner and outer rings moved clockwise. The middle ring rotated counter-clockwise.

"Excellent. Why don't you play with it a little? Show me what you can do. Try taking it out of a single plane, or maybe weave your circles together?"

Elise stared at the moving beads and thought about what she wanted to do. It should be easy enough. The middle ring turned ninety degrees to the other two. She maintained the orientation of all three without too much difficulty. Elise wondered if she could spin the whole thing around its common center. The three rings began to rotate and then to spin. She played with the creation and moved each ring around a center point and then shifted it again. Before long she had each ring spinning and rotating in every possible direction.

"That is nice," the High Tender responded absently. "I would like you to add to it. Are you up for that?"

"Yes," she said absently as she stared at the twirling mass.

"First, is there a way to speed it all up, not too fast, just so the marbles begin to blur a bit?"

She complied, and the rotating, swirling, twisting mass became a seemingly solid set of three rings as the marbles blurred into a silver haze.

The High Tender stood and walked over to a small sink set behind his desk. He filled up a glass with water and placed it below her construct. "Pretty good so far. Let's see if you can incorporate this water. It's up to you. Either a couple loops of water, to add to the number of rings, or you can put the water into the rings you already have."

Elise looked at the water and thought.

Nothing happened.

The High Tender said nothing, and simply watched. Either of his requests was easy enough, but it was getting difficult keeping track of all the balls. They might drop if she added anything else. The memory of the park came to mind and she remembered how she had secured the first rotating mass of fruit to catch the second tossed into the air by the High Tender.

"Are you ok?" The High Tender sat back down.

"Yes, just thinking." She tried a few attempts and her rings wobbled. She stabilized them and tried to remember how she'd tied it off before. "Can I ask you a question? Sometimes distraction helps."

"As long as you keep working on it, sure."

"What makes a man a Tender rather than a master? Why don't you have a s'vlor of your own, or do you? I guess I don't know that you don't."

"I don't. Tenders train the WOR, but we don't Bind them."

Elise got her rings to stop wobbling and thought she saw how to get them to stay put. She didn't want the movement to stop, though. Talking to him seemed to help. "Why not? I kind of got the impression having a s'lor, and especially a s'vlor, gave a man, a lord, great power."

"Having a bound WOR is incredibly prestigious. It's an honor to be selected. So is training WOR. All the WOR, with the exception of the First Rank, maintain their Tender indefinitely. As I told you before, it's a lifelong relationship."

He wasn't especially forthcoming with his answers.

"Why are there no male WOR? If it's a matter of the right number of genes, there should be some. Where are they?"

"You're not making progress on your work." He waggled a finger in the general direction of her mass of marbles.

She frowned wondering how he knew she wasn't working on it. "I'm still thinking about it. Besides, how can you tell?"

He chuckled. "Distraction, right? Or are you pumping me for information?"

"Both." She graced him with a smile and a shrug. She tried a few things but couldn't free herself of the concentration needed to keep everything spinning.

"There are twenty WOR genes located on each of the X chromosomes. Very few have these genes. A woman must have fifteen paired genes to become WOR."

"Is that why there are no male WOR? It takes two X chromosomes?"

"Yes. Men have only the one X chromosome."

"So, the genes are present throughout your population, but there's a minimum number required to make a WOR. Gregor did say he left Earth as a WOR breeding ground."

"I believe you said that. He merely implied it."

"Nevertheless." She cocked a brow up in irritation. The solution to tying off the construct was almost there. She tried a few things and watched the rings wobble.

"To answer your other question," he said, "as to why I have no s'vlor, that is simple."

"Really?" She almost had it figured out.

"For men, the number of WOR-genes affects our ability to sense the WOR-skill and determines whether we're able to be paired with a WOR. That's how we guide your training. It's how I can tell that you're trying something now, and how I know when you're not working."

She quirked a brow at him and nodded. "I wondered about that."

"Men have only one X chromosome. In order to train WOR, at least

457

eleven of those genes must be active. High Tenders express fifteen. There are few Vendel with even half that number floating around in their genes. A very small number sixteen, the minimum required amount to become a 'lor or v'lor lord."

"So? Tenders have eleven to fifteen of these genes and the lords have more?" With a nudge, her construct shifted into place and she tied off her flows.

"Precisely."

"And that is what determines caste?"

"Caste is determined by birthright. In the very rare instance that a commoner expresses the appropriate number of WOR-genes, he may be elevated to Tender status, or that of the 'lor or v'lor."

Elise turned her attention to the water in the glass and thought about the next problem.

"I just described what makes a Tender and what makes a High Tender. It's very similar to how the Ranks of WOR are determined."

"The number of our paired genes? I'm assuming I have all twenty as a Fifth Rank WOR?"

"Correct."

"What else? It feels like there's more. How are the lords different? It can't just be the number of their genes?"

"It's not. They are the product of genetic experimentation dating back from the time of Vendel Rising when we left Earth. The lords have additional engineered genes located on the Y chromosome, up to five. One for each Rank. These allow the lor' and vlor' to accept the genetic material of a WOR."

"From the Blood Rite?"

"Exactly. Most lords have the required number of genes on their X chromosome. Many become Tenders. Again the combination, as well as the number of genes, determines the level of WOR the lord can successfully control."

Should she take the water from the cup, or just have it appear in place? Elise considered the best way to solve this problem. "And how do they establish that control?"

Three streams of water snaked out of the glass and wove around the three blurred strands of marbles. Once she had these in place, she added water in between the marbles of each ring.

"That's the Binding Rite."

Elise tied off the water rings and the water inside the marble rings. The glass was now empty. "Is that how Gregor expects to train me? An early

Binding and then push me past this mental block you both believe I have?"

"Exactly."

"If the Vector killed and the Activator hurt, and the Blood Rite prepares the lord, what does the Binding Rite do? What should I expect? More pain? Is there a chance that might kill me like the Activator?"

"The Vector did not kill, it selected. And while Activation is painful and we lose some, it serves a vital purpose. I imagine, for you and the Emperor, the actual Binding will be quite enjoyable. No pain at all." He lifted his brows.

I hate this man, Malice whispered.

"You didn't answer my question. I didn't ask you how it felt. I asked you what it will do to me."

"It will pacify you, s'Lissa, and accomplish what even Tender Training could not." He wiped his hands on his thighs and stood. In his coldest Tender Training voice, he said, "Now, let us finish with this assessment. I want you to stop all motion on your little work of art here. Tie it off and leave it."

Without thinking, Elise complied with the High Tender's command. Three separate rings of marbles stopped cold. Frozen in ice-rings, the mass of marbles hung in space. The three rings of pure water also froze and hovered in place. The entire structure floated two feet above the center table.

High Tender Marcus licked his lips and flicked his gaze to her. "Very good, s'vlor. Return to your master. Inform him his little experiment may continue. I will see you later."

He waved her toward the door with the fingers of both hands. She was dying to ask more questions, but when his eyes narrowed and the braklav snapped into his palm, she ran for the door and did not look back.

CHAPTER TWENTY-SIX_

Gambit, Day 260

ECSTATIC OVER THE NEWS OF HER PERFORMANCE FOR THE HIGH TENDER, Gregor took Elise to his quarters and had her show him the construct she made in the High Tender's office. Within a matter of seconds, she had the odd model complete and spinning a meter above the floor.

"This's amazing, opés. Do you realize what you have accomplished?" His enthusiasm buried her in fervent kisses.

"Gregor!" Elise wrapped her arms around him and dug her fingers into his hair, enjoying his touch more than she should. She hated him, or should, but couldn't deny the attraction building between them. Seconds turned to minutes, until even the minutes flew by as they stretched out on his couch, arms and legs entwined. Passion burned between them, igniting a blaze of desire leaving them both breathless, and leaving her terribly confused.

What are you doing? Have you forgotten about your races tonight? The lurker's displeasure filled her mind with sharp, grating sounds. *We're going to be late.*

A glance at the clock on the wall had her eyes widening.

Oh shit!

"Gregor, stop." She put a hand on his chest and pressed him back, or tried to. He didn't budge.

He laughed. "Opés, you can't refuse me." Silver eyes, heavy with lust, gazed into hers. The sexual tension sizzled between them, but as always, he kept their clothes on and their hands confined above the waist. He leaned down for another kiss.

She blocked him with a finger pressed to his lips. "It's too much."

He pressed her back to the couch.

Fine. You want to play this game? I'm all in, emperor.

Elise put a hand on his belt. "I need to get to bed. It's late and I have a very demanding schedule in the morning. If, however, you want to move this to your bed, I'm happy to follow. Otherwise, this is torture. I always thought it was the girl who was supposed to be the tease. But here we are, I say *Go* and you say *Stop*." She nibbled on his ear. "This is the last kiss, dear Gregor, unless you remove all your clothes and mine." She tugged on the belt.

He gave a deep throaty laugh. "Dear opés, I believe you would make the High Tender blush." His hand moved down and gripped hers. It shook slightly.

"The High Tender's exact words were to 'enjoy my master.' Which I would like very much to do, now in fact."

He cocked his head and lifted his brows in surprise. "He didn't say that, did he?"

She grinned and placed a finger between their lips when he tried to steal a final kiss. "Ask him yourself when you see him. It's time for me to leave."

Tonight, she was scheduled for two jump-jet races. If he didn't release her soon, she'd have to forfeit her first race.

To her shock, Gregor rolled off and helped her up from the couch. He tried to kiss her again, but she pulled away, shaking her head and laughing.

"I'm serious, Gregor. The next kiss tonight will only be given in your bed and without the interference of clothes." She jerked her head toward his bedchamber.

He gave her a low throaty chuckle and kissed her neck. "I look forward to it, opés." Gregor led her to the lift tube and kissed the back of her hand. "I'll take you back to your room."

Elise made a point of drawing her gaze down his body and below his waist. "I think you should take a cold shower. I don't think you should go out in your condition." She flicked her eyes downward for emphasis and traced his tented arousal with the tip of her finger.

He sucked in a breath and moved her finger.

She rose up on her toes and pecked his cheek. "Soon, my love, I will be

462

able to fill your desire. Until then, enjoy your shower." She flashed a smile and opened the lift tube doors.

As she escaped Gregor's quarters, she breathed a deep sigh.

Shriek unfolded from the darkness. *I hate when you kiss him.*

I like kissing him, she replied.

It's gross, Shriek chided. *Have you forgotten what he has done?*

Oh, be silent! I'll take as much pleasure out of that man as I can. It's the only thing I hold over his head. I'll jerk his chain as much as I can, while I can.

You're welcome to it, my sister. I want none of that kind of touch.

Yes, you have a different passion don't you sister?

Shriek had the worst job of them all.

Do not feel sorry for me. I embrace the braklav. Good night and good luck on your races.

Goodnight, sister.

Elise floated down the lift tube, wishing it would take her to her destination faster. She reached the Fifth Deck and raced into her suite.

On her return, she found Chandra and Aomi pacing.

"You're late. Where have you been?" Chandra cried out.

"Guess! Gregor was celebrating my success."

"Tonight's your first official race. If you don't show up its all forfeit." Aomi's delicate hands fisted at her sides and her long black hair glistened in the light. "Winning that prize money is our only hope of escape."

Elise reached out and took Aomi's slender hands in hers. "I have not forgotten what's at stake."

"At least you enjoy his kisses," Chandra snickered.

Aomi fell silent, as she did whenever they spoke of their masters' affections. Alice scared her with the sex talk and Elise and Chandra were still trying to repair the damage. Of the four of them, Aomi would be losing more than just her mind at the Binding Rite.

"Where's Alice?" Elise stripped out of her dress.

"Lord vlor'Calcask kept her over for a private dinner." Chandra rolled her eyes. "Valerius had me stay for *dinner* last night. I think they're trying to make up to us for Tender Training."

"By making out?" Aomi's almond eyes glittered coal black in the light. "Like we'd forget what they did to us. I'll never forget Talen's eyes as he put my wrists in shackles. Fortunately, he's been too busy with the High Council to pay much attention to me lately. I've barely seen the bastard." Aomi breathed a sigh of relief.

"They lost another planet, and Gregor has been pestering them to allow him to steal my mind." Elise finally managed to struggle out of her dress and the knotted ties.

Both their expressions fell at that comment.

"Cheer up," she said. "Remember what Alice said? We're not dead 'till we're dead. I still have my mind. We're still in the fight." She threw on her exercise gear and opened the bio-cart access panel. She glanced at her friends. "Wish me luck."

"Good luck!" Chandra raised her hand in a salute.

"Great skill!" Aomi said with a smile.

Elise raced down the corridor and headed to the hangar. Jeena and Dove waited for her by the *Spider Devil*. About half the black tassels remained on Dove's ship.

Jeena waved when she saw Elise. "Cutting it a bit thin aren't you, kid?" Jeena hugged her.

"I haven't missed it yet, have I?"

Dove swept her up in a big hug and spun her in a lazy circle. "Plenty of time for my *Chickadee*. Are you ready to fly?"

"I'm ready to kick butt." Elise turned to Jeena. "So, what's my strategy?"

"Kid, you're in the jump-jet circuit. You go out there and give it your all. These pilots are swift, sharp and have years of experience on you. Don't give away anything."

Elise cocked her head. "Have you seen Carek?"

Dove frowned. "No. Larkin came over yesterday. He said Carek had withdrawn your entrance fee." Dove blew out his breath. "Well, I knew that just couldn't be the case. Especially since it wasn't his to take back. Jeena and I went over and straightened out the whole mess."

Elise's stomach clenched and her breath hitched. "Yeah, well," she scratched her head, "We kind of had a falling out. He wanted to take care of my sponsor directly. Said he was a High Judicator and all and could talk some sense into him. I disagreed. Not that I didn't appreciate the offer, but I've worked really hard for this. It's bad enough to think the bastard would take this from me, but for Carek to try to take it away when he knows how hard I've worked for it was too much."

"He told you, did he?" Dove rubbed the side of his nose, leaving a greasy smear.

Jeena put a hand on her shoulder. "Kid, Carek's been burned by a lot of women when they find out his status. They see a path to wealth and power for themselves, and for their potential daughters. Carek is an easy path to a vlor'lord for an eligible daughter. Women can be like sharks when they smell such potential. It's why he avoids relationships."

"Well, he was all ready to come in and save the day for me. Professed his love and all of that. Right after that, he told me to stop racing. That's when it got ugly." So far, much of this was true.

Dove groaned.

Jeena winced.

"Give him a chance," Dove said.

"No, I think Carek and I understand each other. He wants something I don't want to give. If you could keep him away from me, I'd appreciate it."

"Come, kid, you need to get ready for your race," Jeena said. "We'll keep him away for now, but eventually, the two of you are going to have to settle this."

"I don't think that's possible," Elise said.

"Whatever, kid." Jeena walked her toward the jump-jet hangar. "Let's focus on the race. You have a timed trial up first. You have to hit the rings solid. Things aren't yet tight enough that you need to pick up any of the bonus rings. As long as the race feels good, or if you think one is easy to hit, play it safe. As for Rabbit and Fox, obliterate your opponent. Now is the time to develop a reputation. Make them sweat and keep them guessing."

Elise breathed in deeply. It suddenly got very real. Jeena's instructions continued and Elise struggled to pay attention to her jump-jet instructor's final words of advice.

"Rabbit and Fox is a triple elimination competition for the jump-jet circuit. You'll fly against most pilots several times. Based on your rankings, you'll either advance or not. Your flight today is against a pilot named Malikai."

"I know that pilot. He ran a race with Zander. He only won because Zander got cocky."

"Zander's harmless, but don't underestimate Malikai. Obnoxious and more boastful than he should be, Malikai is the real fox. I've come up against him before. He's the only pilot I lost a race to. He'll have no problem leaving you in the dust if you're not careful."

"Well, I'm up for a challenge. Which one is first?"

"Time trial," Dove chimed in.

"Good, it'll give my head time to clear before facing off against Malikai."

They walked into the hangar and, without any ceremony, Elise slipped into her flightsuit and Jeena banged Elise's helmet with her fist to wish her luck.

Elise didn't need luck, she had more than enough skill, and she wasn't being cocky.

After her time trial, which she smashed, she had a few moments to collect herself and prepare for her race against Malikai. Elise settled her jump-jet into its berth and climbed out of the cockpit. A man in a red flight suit stood next to Jeena. A shimmering mist concealed his features. Dove stood beside Jeena, closer than normal, and had a hand on Jeena's arm, holding her back.

"Well, *Chickadee*," Malikai turned to Elise, "looks like we get to face off together in the first round."

The reflective visor of her helmet hid her features, but she wished for a veil of mist. Malikai had a presence about him which had her wanting to take a step back in retreat.

Jeena spoke for her. "The kid is going to kick your butt, Malikai."

"Hardly, even you couldn't do that." Malikai carried himself with self-assurance and filled the space with his arrogance.

"I beat you," Jeena asserted.

"You got lucky and slipped through that fifth ring. Took away something precious from me as I remember it."

"It's not like you needed the win, or the prize money. I think we all know you hail from a different caste than the rest of us."

"We're all equals in the jump-jet competitions, my dear. But I wasn't talking about the prize money. I was thinking more of the other prize I lost."

"Go suck fumes."

Elise held perfectly still, content to be ignored. Dove hovered, but even he didn't move a muscle as Jeena faced Malikai.

Malikai jerked his chin toward Elise, to which she responded by taking a step back. "What about your student here? I've taken a look at some of her practice runs. Shows promise. Care to make that same wager, Jeena?"

"No."

"Well, *Chickadee*, looks like your mentor has no faith in you."

"Shove it, Malikai," Jeena said. "The kid has nothing to do with you. Play nice or leave." The muscles in Jeena's jaw clenched.

Elise had never seen her friend so mad. Jeena's knuckles were white and her face beet red. But that was nothing compared to Dove. He had both hands on her arms, restraining her from lunging at the pilot. He was beginning to breathe hard from the effort of holding her back.

"I've waited a long time, Jeena, and I always get what I want." Malikai turned and strode off.

"What was all of that?" she whispered when Malikai was far enough away and out of earshot.

"Old business, kid," Jeena said. "Dove, if you ever hold me back like that again, I'm gonna' fry you in your ship's exhaust." She shrugged out of his grip.

"Getting into a fight with a lord is poor form," he said, "even if he is veiled."

"He—" Jeena stamped her foot and screamed. Crew from adjoining jump-jets whipped their heads around at the sound. "He infuriates me."

"Why?" Elise asked innocently.

"Old business, kid. I made a foolish wager after winning nine straight jump-jet finals."

"What was the bet?"

Dove bit his lower lip. "Oh, kid, I wish I'd thought to tell you that particular story sooner."

Jeena glared at Dove, but then glanced at Elise. "I made a stupid bet with that man and I barely pulled my ass out of the fire. Custom is strict in many ways, but that doesn't mean men are content to wait around for the woman they want to want them back. Malikai took an interest in me and tricked me into betting away my security."

"How could he possibly do that?" Elise asked.

Jeena's eyes clouded over.

Dove answered for Jeena. "He convinced her to agree to matrimony if he beat her at the Imperial finals. If she won, he agreed to buy her a brand-new ship and fund her maintenance costs for life. Thus the origin of *Champions Riot*. It's a pretty snazzy little ship. Has a berth for two, although she has never tried it out." He wriggled his eyebrows.

Jeena slugged him. "Dove, someday you'll go too far."

"A man can only hope." His face broke into a huge crooked grin.

"In the end, I won the finals," Jeena explained. "The Emperor's Bet had been placed on me, so the payout was triple what I'd hoped for. I didn't need Malikai's ship or his financing. I took it though and he hasn't stopped hounding me. I jump ship whenever I find out he's close. He's kept a really low profile on this mission. Although, it finally explains why repairs to the *Spider Devil* have been delayed. I bet Malikai's hands are involved in that."

"What about the *Spider Devil*?" Elise asked. And what was the Emperor's Bet?

"Malikai holds a grudge against me," Dove said. "You saw how he acted, like I wasn't even here?" He coughed. "Luv, the kid has to get ready."

"Yes, dear." Jeena tugged on his nose. "Come kid, back up into the cockpit you go."

"But I just got back." Elise climbed on board when Jeena gave her a look.

"You're up against Malikai next. Don't blow it."

The next hour tested her skill. Malikai taunted her at every turn during their race, proving to be a formidable opponent. She did not beat him, but neither did she lose to him.

She took Fox on the first race and hit him by the forty-eighth ring, earning a single point. He took Fox next and scored two points when he hit her before the halfway mark at the nineteenth ring. In the final race, since she was behind in points, Elise got to pick Rabbit or Fox. She chose Fox and hit the rear of his craft moments before he screamed through the fiftieth ring. They tied two against two.

"You barely pulled that one off, *Chickadee*," Malikai said through the communications channel. "Doesn't do either of us any good in the rankings. Ties work against us."

"Then you should've worked harder to win," she countered, rising to his challenge.

"Hardly, you got lucky. Barely got me either time, and I never throw a race."

"No *barely* about it. I think it's pretty clear I hit you. Don't think anyone's going to ask for a sudden replay to make sure."

Malikai paused for a long moment, then he chuckled through the communications channel.

"By the gods. Sudden replay, is it? You know, I agree. I don't think anyone will ask for that, but a rematch? A rematch is definitely in order. I'm certain I can teach you a lesson you'll never forget."

"Threatening the newbie on the circuit? That's just plain rude. What are you afraid of, Malikai? Afraid a newbie will put you in your place?"

"I'm not afraid of much. How about you? What do you fear? Care to make a wager?"

"What like that stupid one you tried to pull on Jeena? No way."

"Not exactly like that one. I was thinking of something else."

"Sorry, not interested. If you're good enough, maybe I'll see you in the finals."

"The finals are several cycles away. Do you think you'll still be around?"

"Where exactly do you think I'll go?"

"Obviously, I've underestimated you." He paused. "You know, I'm dying to find out how far you make it. I'm of a mind to let this play out. Jump-jet eliminations can get pretty hairy, *Chickadee*. Watch your back. I'm going to see exactly how far you actually get with this little game." Malikai engaged his thrusters and nosed her out of her reentry glide path.

She banked hard and swore under her breath. His jump-jet entered the pick-up tube and disappeared into the bowels of the *Gambit*. She realigned her flight path and followed behind him.

Jeena and Dove stood at the jump-jet dock. Jeena's eyes were alight and she bounced on her toes. Dove stood solidly, and brushed away a tear from his left eye when he thought no one was looking. The crane lowered the jump-jet into its berth, released the clamps, and moved back to its next task. Elise popped the cockpit hatch release and climbed down.

Jeena grabbed her in a hug. "You did it!"

Elise hugged her back. "I didn't win, just tied."

"I don't care. Malikai is one of the best jump-jet pilots on the circuit and you scored two hits on him. Two!" She thumped Elise on the back and stepped out of the way for Dove to claim a hug.

"Well, I'll tell you what," Dove said, "from the way Malikai stalked out of here, you really pissed that bastard off."

"Poor loser?" Elise kissed Dove's thick nose.

Jeena leaned on Elise's shoulder. "Naw, kid, he's always been the moody type. Aggressive as hell, and moody as shit. When you go up against him later, remember that. He holds grudges."

CHAPTER TWENTY-SEVEN_

Gambit, Day 261

ELISE DIDN'T HANG AROUND TO CELEBRATE HER JUMP-JET TIE WITH JEENA AND Dove. She begged off, complaining of a headache. Sleep called to her, and with Gregor's new training schedule, she only had a few hours to revive her sleep-deprived body.

I want to fly again, Malice grumbled. *We should have beat that pilot.*

With a roll of her eyes, she ignored Malice and fell into bed. Less than an hour later, it was with great annoyance that she found someone shaking her awake. She shoved the annoying hands to the side.

The kiss on her lips came as a surprise.

The laughing eyes of Gregor took her breath away.

He sat on her bed, staring at her with an unreadable expression, and shook his head. "My little opés. Just when I think we understand each other, you surprise me."

"Gregor, what do you mean?"

She pushed her hair back from her face and smoothed out the tangles. Her chest ached from the sudden beating of her heart. Gregor's presence simply had that effect on her. Another time, another place, different circumstances, and she would be aching for so much more from him. With great difficulty, she reminded herself why she needed to hate him.

"I love hearing my name on your lips. It reminds me how far we've come, you and I. No more lying, just a wish to please me. I like that."

Elise struggled with the duality of his expression. Behind the laughing eyes, a simmering anger lurked. He was furious about something, but he was also incredibly pleased. She couldn't make sense of it.

"The High Tender was quite pleased by your performance in his office. I brought him to examine the construct you made for me." He continued, "I'm upset with him, and I wanted to tell you why, because I know how this is going to make you feel."

His eyes grew cold and flat.

Elise shivered.

He gave her a slow kiss. It was one of his possessive kisses, one he had not given her in a long time. The kiss was delivered in such a way to remind her that she was his and he controlled every part of her.

"Gregor," she said, making sure to speak his name. She had no idea where he was coming from at the moment. "What have I done wrong?"

He laughed hard. Glittering eyes fixed her in his gaze. "Opés, you amaze me, but that is not why I'm here. You need to ask what it is that will upset you."

"I don't know what we're talking about."

What has happened? Whimper wailed in the background. *What do we have to prepare for now? Shriek! Shriek? What's going on!*

Shh! He'll tell us, he's just trying to bait us right now, Shriek soothed.

Gregor traced a finger across Elise's forehead and stared into her eyes. "Do you remember last night?"

Elise sat up straight in the bed. They'd spoken of the Binding and sex. Is that what this was about? Had he received the official go ahead for the Binding Rite?

Her heart thudded in her chest.

No, no, no! her sisters broke out in chorus.

Her voice came out in a whisper, "You've been relieved of your oath? If that is the news, then it would make me happy, not upset," she lied. It seemed that's all she ever did with Gregor, except when he kissed her. Vector, Activator, Blood Rite, whatever was at work on her body, manufactured or not, his kisses felt real.

Her stomach churned at that thought. At how she'd accepted that piece of her new life.

She wasn't ready for what came next, even if she craved physical union with Gregor.

"Look me in the eye and tell me that is not a lie, opés." His tone darkened and the tattoo danced over his brow.

She shook with the chill in his voice and picked her words carefully. "It is not a lie, Gregor, but perhaps not the whole truth."

"Omission is very much a lie in my mind."

She placed a hand on his arm, and withdrew it when he stiffened. "Gregor, the Binding Rite scares me. I don't know what to expect, but once I feel your touch, I'm sure that will fade. It's difficult to think of much else when you have me in your arms."

"Then you're ready?" He cocked his head and his eyes glittered again. "Right now? You're ready to complete the Binding Rite?"

"I'll never be ready. That's the truth, but if it's time, then I will not fight you."

There would be no reason to fight. Her war against the Vendel would end in complete failure.

She silenced the wails of her sisters.

It was finally over. She had lost.

Elise touched his forehead and traced the outline of the imperial tattoo stamped over his brow. "Such a unique tattoo. I've always found it fascinating." She sighed and surrendered. Alice would be so upset. Her hopes of escape were over. "Did I do something between last night and now to anger you? I won't fight the binding."

All hope had vanished.

He gave her one of his tender, non-hurried kisses. When he withdrew, his eyes held a degree of warmth.

"I came to tell you the High Tender is ecstatic at the progress you've made and feels more exposure to the *Gambit's* WOR will only improve the strength of our Binding. He wants you to provide fresh eyes to his personal project. It's something we're looking at to combine the power of the WOR and combat the S'Lorek. He delayed my request with the High Council in hopes the bond between us strengthens, so that when we do Bind, the bond will be at its strongest. After last night, I thought you would take the news poorly, especially considering how eager you seemed to proceed?"

Wait. What? Whimper cried.

What the hell is going on? Malice asked.

Elise's breath caught. Slowly, his words penetrated the haze of defeat shrouding her mind.

We've been granted a reprieve! Shriek shouted.

Then Elise realized what happened. In that moment, she had accepted complete, absolute, no-going back defeat. It blew her away. She wasn't one to give up.

"Opés," he said, "you need to take a breath."

Elise shook. "Gregor, hold me!"

It didn't make sense to seek his embrace, but she needed the contact of a warm body. She needed to cling to someone, even if that person was her sworn enemy. Even if he was slowly becoming something more.

You turn to him for comfort? the silent unnamed sister whispered from the dark.

Gregor wrapped his arms around Elise and held her tight.

"Elise, what's wrong?" He gave her one of his tender, protective kisses.

They sat in silence while she wept.

"Are you all right?"

He smoothed her hair and stroked the nape of her neck.

Her tears soaked his shirt. "I'm sorry, Gregor. Forgive me. I thought I had it controlled."

"At least that reaction was honest."

"There's still a part of my me which remembers Earth. What I've lost. What you've taken." She glanced into his silver eyes as a knife twisted in her heart. How she ached to hold him.

He's the enemy, the lurker whisper.

Is he? It was hard to know anymore. She took a breath and it shuddered out of her, loosening the constriction around her heart. "I can't make sense of my feelings. I hate you, yet I crave your touch. How does that make any sense? I wish it would end. I crave my freedom, yet, my dreams are filled with nothing but you. I don't know what's happening to me."

He kissed her brow. "Hate is a strong emotion, difficult to maintain for any length of time. You need to accept your new life. I'm a part of it. You have to let go of your anger if you're ever to live here. What I've done has been necessary, Elise. Someday, you'll understand and accept it for what it is, and hopefully you'll let go of your hatred. You don't need to fight me. It will only cause you more pain in the end. And I wish to give you a life worth living. A life full of joy, not pain."

"Aren't you upset by this delay? I know how much you wanted this."

"I want you." He gave her the oddest look. "It's complicated, Elise, this thing between us, but I must be Emperor first. My people are my priority. My oath is to the empire and comes before my personal desires. You have a reprieve, opés. Let's see what you make of it." He shifted and lifted her off his chest. At arms-length, his eyes drilled into hers.

She felt exposed under his scrutiny.

"I want to show you the threat we face. Perhaps afterward, you'll understand why I did what I had to do. I hope it will allow you to see things differently and find some degree of acceptance to your new station."

"I'm not fighting you, Gregor."

"Yes, you are. You still think to find a way out of this and free of me. That's not going to happen." Gregor offered his hand to help her to her feet. "You have pleased the High Tender. I'm encouraged by your progress, but I'm no fool, opés. You still think you have a choice, but there is no choice left to you. You belong to me. It would be wise to remember that."

She tried to protest, but he waved her off.

"I'm taking you to the High Tender's linking program and we'll see what you can accomplish. Just so you know, that little construct you made for the High Tender in his office incorporated all the skills of the Bar and Rod, and most of the Second Rank Wheel skills. The one you made for me touches on some of the Third Rank. It's impressive that you managed to learn all that just by observing the First Rank WOR. It may not take a full sun cycle before you achieve all Fifth Rank skills. We'll proceed with the Binding Rite after that, no matter what foolish oath I gave. That is something to think about late at night, when you're in your bed hating me."

"It's the Emperor I hate, Gregor. I don't know what to think of you as a man. It confuses me, and that is the honest truth."

After Carek showed her the S'Lorek and the threat they posed, she understood what drove an emperor to do the things he must to save a civilization. She didn't like it, but understood.

The expression on Gregor's face softened. He graced her with a nod, perhaps acknowledging the truth, perhaps not. It was unclear. "I'll do whatever it takes to save my people, Elise. I'll sacrifice everything for them. I'm risking much pulling you out of conventional training. If I think anything you do would gain me an advantage, I'll take it. It would be wise to remember this. I'll Bind you, but only when it's in the best interest of the Empire to do so, personal desire has no place in it."

With those cryptic words, Gregor left her alone to dress. She tied the laces of her gown and stepped out of her room. Gregor and the High Tender waited in the common room.

Elise came to an abrupt halt, not expecting High Tender Marcus. "Good morning, High Tender," she said.

His eyes glittered and he gave her a curt nod. "Good morning, s'Lissa. Come with me. I have something to show you." He turned to Gregor. "Sire, we will talk later."

"Of course," Gregor said with an imperious nod.

The High Tender led Elise out of her suite and off the Fifth Deck. Gregor did not join them. She felt like someone had pulled the rug out from under her feet and forgot the floor underneath.

What is happening? Whimper huddled in the darkness.

High Tender Marcus took her to the Am-net Conclave headquarters. He explained the am-net and she listened with half an ear. The High Tender described what she would see and she responded appropriately with, "Hmm," and, "Yes," and other nondescript replies.

She had a moment of panic when the entry doors slid open, but the gentlemen who had watched her walk in with Carek were not manning the desk today.

Two men dressed in their dark green jumpsuits stood at their arrival. "Good morning Lord vlor'Vardhal," the first man said. "We're ready for your tour."

"Good." High Tender Marcus pressed his palm to the gel-pad.

The men ignored Elise and she was not logged in. The second man scanned the corridor behind them as if he were expecting someone else, but then brought his attention back to the display nestled into the top of the counter. The door swished closed.

"My lord, I will escort you down to the changing rooms and give the briefing."

"Will Master Varlen meet us?"

"Yes, my lord. He's already in the tank and will meet you in the soup. His assistant will escort you to the node."

"Very good," the High Tender said.

The door swished open behind Elise and she felt a familiar presence.

"I have asked one of our WOR to assist the Lady—" the first man said, stopping mid-sentence.

"That will not be necessary." Gregor cut him off.

"Gregor," Elise replied, her response automatic and contrite.

Gregor gave her a flat stare and then smiled at the two men. "I'll take care of Lady s'Lissa. No need to bother your staff."

He pressed his palm to the gel-pad, then turned his full attention to her. The dark tattoo danced menacingly on his brow. A dangerous mood had settled over him and she had no idea what she had done wrong.

Whimper, my sister?

I am here.

Lend me strength. I need to be as accommodating as possible. Rein in my temper. Watch me. I must submit to him.

I will watch and give you strength. Smile, you are glaring, and lower your eyes. Don't look him in the eyes today. I sense great danger.

Elise did as her sister instructed.

Whimper settled in her mind and watched.

Gregor put his hand to the small of her back. She smiled and he gave a bemused expression she did not understand. He propelled her through the doorway and into the am-net.

They followed the same path Carek had taken and passed through the long tunnel until they entered the changing rooms.

Three suits had been laid out on the counter. Two black suits and a much smaller scarlet suit with a decidedly feminine cut. A figure in a white immersion suit looked up from behind the counter.

Elise stared into the startling green eyes of Carek Tusel and suppressed a groan.

Carek snapped to attention. He didn't seem surprised to see her and bobbed his head in deference to Gregor, who returned the quasi-salute with a jerk of his chin.

"Sire, my lord," Carek said, acknowledging both men. "Welcome to the am-net."

"Good day to you, Mr. Tusel," the High Tender said. "We're anxious to begin."

"Yes, my lord. I have your immersion suits ready. I had thought to have one of the WOR assist." He gestured to Elise.

"I told them I would take care of it," Gregor said. "No need to bother your WOR."

Carek seemed to wait for an introduction. When Gregor did not supply one, Carek shifted on his feet, looking unsure.

"Of course, sire." Carek recovered and stepped around the counter. He handed the High Tender his suit, then gave Gregor the remaining two suits and ignored Elise.

"I'll provide appropriate instruction for my s'vlor." Gregor dismissed Carek. "You may wait outside."

Elise closed her eyes and took three deep breaths.

Whimper made her count to ten.

Gregor's strong hand cupped her elbow and lead her to a changing room.

He explained the am-net, superficially, glossing over many of the details Carek had supplied. He pulled a curtain aside to one of the single dressing chambers and drew her inside.

"Opés, remove all your clothes and your bands of rank."

The bands of rank were the symbols of her captivity. She hadn't even remembered putting them on. Had they become such a part of her morning routine that they were no longer of note? How far had she slipped into this world? How far had Earth fallen?

You must obey him! Why are you just standing there?

Sorry!

"What about the collar?"

"The collar stays, the rest goes." His face brightened and his lips quirked up in a grin. "What, no comments for me? I tell you to strip and you just say, 'Yes?' What happened to my opés?"

Elise stopped short. She ignored Whimper's words and glanced into his eyes. "Gregor, I'm sorry. I thought I wasn't to entice you. Would you rather undress me?"

He laughed. "Yes, opés, although I have to say your compliance has me wondering what you're hiding."

Elise sighed as he untied the long laces at the back of her gown.

"I'm not hiding anything from you."

The dress fell away and Gregor removed all the bands from her arms. He spun her around and raked his eyes up and down her body.

He's interested. Keep it up. Whimper coached her from the darkness.

He lifted his brows with interest. "You are a true vision of perfection, opés." He handed her the scarlet immersion suit and helped her to dress.

When she was encased in the skin-hugging fabric, he gave her a last, long appraising look before unbuttoning his shirt.

"Now wait out there, but do not join the High Tender yet."

"What? I don't get to undress you? That's not fair."

"Correct. It's not fair, but I do not think I would survive that. Now go!"

"Yes, Gregor." She exited and stepped back into the room.

Gregor chuckled and muttered about disobedient WOR.

CHAPTER TWENTY-EIGHT_

Gambit, Day 261

CAREK POPPED HIS HEAD INSIDE THE ROOM AND SAW HER STANDING THERE. HIS eyes brightened for a second before clouding over.

She ignored him.

Deep furrows creased his brow and he slipped out without making a sound.

When Gregor walked out of the changing room, she wouldn't have noticed Carek if he'd done cartwheels in front of her.

A living sculpture of masculine perfection stood before her, sending her heart into afterburner mode. The black immersion suit revealed less than the white, which Carek wore, but hinted at so much more. The pure maleness of Gregor washed over her, drowning her in sensation and undeniable desire.

Why couldn't he have been ugly?

It's just the Activator, Malice said. *It's not real.*

Except it was very real to Elise.

The corners of Gregor's lips quirked up and his eyes twinkled. "Opés, you are staring."

"Sorry, Gregor." Her brows drew down. "I wish we had come to know each other under different circumstances. I could have given you so much more."

"How can that be when I will take everything?"

"Forgive me, Gregor, but you're a fool if you believe that." Her words were not spoken as a challenge, but as simple truth.

He didn't answer, but perhaps he understood. She expected his eyes to narrow, a sign of anger, fury, or perhaps frustration, but Gregor gave her none of those cues. He shook his head instead.

"Our positions are complicated, but they are all that we have. I hope, after today, you might come to see me differently than you do now." He clapped his hands. "Come, opés, there is work to do. I'm sure High Tender Marcus is wondering what's keeping us."

"Yes, Gregor."

Carek waited outside and had probably heard every word they spoke. His expression remained downcast and he did not meet her eyes.

"Mr. Tusel?" Gregor placed a hand on Carek's shoulder.

"Yes, Sire." Carek met Gregor's eyes.

"I would like to present my s'vlor, the Lady Malita s'Lissa s'vlor. Lady s'Lissa, this is Mr. Carek Tusel. He's a level 5 Neural Mind Conclave Member, which means he stands a rank below the Conclave Master. He's also one of our very few High Judicators, a position of great prestige in Vendel society and shoulders tremendous responsibility. He sits with the High Council and is one of my greatest supporters. Master Varlen, the Conclave Master, you will meet in the soup. I'll introduce him when we arrive. Mr. Tusel is the lead designer for the linking program. If this works out today, you'll be working with him on the project."

Carek inclined his head. "It's a pleasure to meet you, my lady."

"Yes," she said, suppressing a groan as she extended her hand. "Pleased to meet you."

"Mr. Tusel, lead on." Gregor gestured toward the purple sea.

"Yes, Sire. Have you briefed Lady s'Lissa on the soup?"

"A little, but feel free to explain as you see fit."

Carek met her gaze briefly, but let the contact go. So much distance separated them.

Elise grabbed Gregor's arm. "As long as you're with me, Gregor, I'm sure I'll be fine."

Gregor patted her hand and pulled her close.

Carek's spine stiffened.

She wasn't going to make any of this easy on her estranged friend. Carek nodded and launched into a well-practiced speech.

They met the High Tender in front of the enormous tank of purple glowing liquid. Elise did her best to look impressed and pretend this was her first time seeing the am-net soup.

Carek passed out the hoods. He then pulled out a breathing cylinder and handed it to Elise.

Gregor placed a hand on Carek's arm. "My s'vlor will not use that."

"But Sire, it can be a shock without it."

Gregor gave him an odd stare. "Mr. Tusel, she has the capacity to endure much. I'm sure the sensation of drowning will not put her off."

"Yes, Sire." He turned to Elise and lowered his gaze.

How far was Carek going to let this go? He had kept his word so far. He obviously wasn't going to expose her secret. Each step he took without revealing her betrayal, however, took him further and further away from his oaths. She cocked her head, wondering, not for the first time, exactly how deep his feelings ran.

"My lady..." He gestured to the sloping ramp.

He spoke about breathing in the soup, how it would make her feel. During his explanation, she kept hold of Gregor's arm and leaned into him for support. She watched Carek's expression closely to see how he would react. His face remained a blank mask.

He'd asked her to return to her master and to embrace Gregor so that she might save the worlds of the Vendel. She did that now, flaunting it before Carek.

She didn't know which of the two men she despised more, Gregor for her enslavement or Carek for giving her love and ripping it away.

She stopped him mid-sentence. "Thank you, Mr. Tusel. I think that's enough. I'm ready to see what my master, and my High Tender, have for me to examine." She arched a brow daring him to say anything.

Gregor chuckled.

High Tender Marcus said, "Obstinate, s'vlor." But when he shook his head, there was a slight smile curving the corners of his mouth.

"I'm just anxious to see what I can do. If this helps to speed my progress toward mastering the WOR-skill, then I'm eager to begin. Besides, it'll make Gregor happy. I'm not being obstinate at all."

Gregor laughed anew. He pulled himself up onto the platform and reached down for Elise. Last time, Carek had lifted her up. This time it was Gregor. He planted a deep, penetrating kiss on her lips. She responded knowing Carek could only look on.

Gregor released her lips, but did not release her from his embrace. Her feet dangled inches from the floor. He stepped back on the platform and grinned. His heels rested at the opposite edge of the platform. Below him was the soup. There was no sloping ramp, just twenty meters of purple liquid. He cocked an eyebrow.

Elise squirmed in his grasp. "You wouldn't?"

"Oh yes, opés, I would." He looked at Carek and the High Tender who were only just now climbing on top of the platform. "See you two inside. Mr. Tusel, I'm assuming our suits are already linked?"

Carek paused and Elise could only imagine the look of dread on his face. "Yes, Sire."

Gregor tightened his hold on Elise, kissed her, and leaned back. They fell a full meter before hitting the surface of the purple liquid.

Cool and comfortable, the liquid felt exactly like water, but slippery. Gregor held Elise as they quickly sank below the surface. People didn't float in the soup. It was neutrally buoyant. His kiss became more passionate, aggressive and painful. He pressed himself against her body. Strong legs wrapped around her thighs and held her in a powerful grip.

She coughed and sputtered as the purple soup filled her lungs. She didn't think about drowning—she already knew she would not—but she certainly drowned under the onslaught of his kisses.

Feed it back to him, sister, Whimper whispered. *Something is wrong. He is testing you harder than any other day.*

Elise listened and returned Gregor's kisses. She fed it back to him, just as Whimper instructed.

Gregor's frantic kisses slowed and stopped.

She grabbed him and pulled him close. "Don't stop," she said breathlessly. "More."

Gregor chuckled. "Tell me opés, did that feel like drowning to you?"

"Yes," she said, gasping on the words, "but not in the way you might think. Am I really breathing water? Can we do that again?"

"Which part?" His eyebrows lifted in amusement.

"All of it," she replied with enthusiasm. She kissed the corner of his mouth. "I used to dive back home. We had to wear tanks on our backs and regulators in our mouths. This is amazing, feels weird but...amazing. Kiss me again, please."

"Yes, opés," Gregor complied. He broke off and said, "The am-net is a unique place, don't you think?"

"Yes. It's certainly heightening my senses. Good God, but I want so much more!"

He laughed and then kissed her.

The High Tender drifted down through the soup. Carek swam behind him.

Carek came up beside Gregor and was forced to wait until Gregor finished his kiss.

"Sire, do you wish me to escort Lady s'Lissa?"

"No, Mr. Tusel, you get to spend the rest of the day with Lady s'Lissa. I'll tow her along for now. She seems to be a bit overwhelmed."

"Yes, Sire." Carek spared a glance at Elise, which she ignored. He kicked off and headed down deep. Gregor unwrapped himself from her body and led Elise by the hand.

A few minutes later, Carek stopped at a set of four white shapes, each the size of a football. Dangling from the pods were long thin wires. Another man, dressed in a white immersion suit, spoke to Carek. She did not hear his words. He gave a nod to Gregor and the High Tender.

Carek drifted around each of them, attaching the long noodles to their temples. Gregor continued to hold her hand. She pulled away and he released her hand with irritation. When she wrapped her arm around his waist and lifted his arm over her shoulder, he appeared to be soothed again. Elise twisted her foot around his ankle, and Gregor beamed.

Carek remained impassive. He attached her leads last and she was finally able to hear the Conclave Master's voice. Carek made introductions.

The am-net conclave master appeared to be in his mid-forties. It was hard to tell exactly how old these people were. His brown eyes held the weight of age. A thin nose rested above a smiling mouth. The rest of Master Varlen was encased in a white immersion suit. Like all Vendel males, his physique was perfect.

Perfect form. Perfect musculature. Perfect proportion. Tall, strong, muscular and lean.

Weren't they all? Except Gregor. He was all of that and more. Elise stole a glance at her black-suited master and sighed at his perfection. Then frowned as Shriek kicked her.

He is not your boyfriend, sister. Remember what he is.

You don't understand.

I don't care. Your feelings for him are not real. Vendel biotech is at work here.

Elise sighed. *It feels real.*

Whimper spoke softly, *I know. I feel it too, but we must never forget.*

Elise stiffened her spine, but it did nothing to strengthen her heart.

Master Varlen, oblivious to her internal thoughts, gave her a welcoming smile. "Welcome to the am-net, my lady. What do you think?"

He gestured expansively to the glowing purple liquid. In the distance, she made out white shapes flitting around.

"It's amazing. The entry..." she gave Gregor a squeeze and a private look, "was exhilarating."

"Really? Most people find it frightening," Varlen said with surprise.

"Most people probably don't get tossed in while being held by their master. I wasn't thinking about breathing, or drowning. Gregor was kind enough to distract me and it eased the transition."

Gregor chuckled.

Carek's brows turned down.

High Tender Marcus grunted and shook his head.

Master Varlen's eyebrows shot up.

"Yes," the Conclave Master said, "it's usually only a problem the first time. After today, you shouldn't need help." He pressed his hands on his thighs and continued in a rush. "Since we're all finally here, I'll let Mr. Tusel lead the discussion, unless Lord vlor'Vardhal would like to begin?"

High Tender Marcus raised a palm. "I thought we'd start by showing s'Lissa what we know of the S'Lorek. Emperor vlor'Malita has put together his thoughts, covering what he feels is most important. I can take over after that and give an overview of the linking problem. Afterwards, the Emperor and I need to excuse ourselves for other business. Mr. Tusel can spend the rest of the day going over his theories. It might be a good time to bring in your WOR. That might give s'Lissa a more coherent picture of what we're dealing with."

Master Varlen nodded.

Gregor spoke, "Mr. Tusel, please load the program I sent over early this morning." He turned to Elise. "Think of the am-net as one big simulation room. Not too different from what you remember from Earth. The images will unfold in your mind. Are you ready?"

"Yes, Gregor," she said. "What do you expect me to do?"

"For now, not much. I want to show you to a few things. High Tender Marcus will give you a run down on the linking program. Mr. Tusel will drag you down into the details. Just like the past two cycles, listen, observe, absorb and learn. You do best when you don't try too hard. Just relax. I'm here."

"Of course," she said.

Gregor's simulation began and was nothing like the one Carek had played.

Carek had shown her the humanity of the Vendel. Gregor showed her a civilization. Images of planets, cities, colony ships and mining communities flew past in a blur. Twenty-one planets zipped by in quick succession. After he showed his empire worlds, he flashed statistics. The parade of planets flew by again. Population numbers, projected growth, major import and export details spread before her vision. The vast colony fleets

—miniature worlds unto themselves—sped by for the second time with all the pertinent data.

Elise realized how limited her comprehension of the true scope of the Vendel Empire had been. She had only a vague image of her new home, but the sheer size of the empire astounded her. A sudden, awe-inspiring feeling overwhelmed her as she saw Gregor in an entirely new light.

The empire entrusted to him was vast beyond her ability to comprehend. He was so much more than the man she thought she knew. It shamed her that she had never put him and his importance into context. Her impression had been confined to a rigid Earth worldview and then scaled down to a ship-sized slice of the *Gambit*. What a horrible mistake. He supported the whole of humanity on his shoulders.

He put up an enormous diagram with the twenty-one worlds and all the fleets of the Vendel. A spaghetti array of glowing lights connected all the worlds together. He put names beneath the planets and letters under the fleets.

Two of the planetary spheres winked out and went dark. The strands of light connecting them to the other worlds dimmed. She understood the interdependence of all the worlds. The statistics came back on screen and Gregor showed her the effect the loss of the two planets had on their sister worlds. Several fleets had also been dimmed. In the upper right-hand corner of the screen a number glowed in red.

Twenty billion dead. Twice the number lost on Earth.

Gregor didn't think on a planetary scale. He didn't serve individuals. Individuals could be sacrificed, so long as the empire endured. She finally understood a little of what Gregor faced and what he was willing to sacrifice for humanity. His passion for his people was palpable.

Carek, on the other hand, saw the empire as a collection of individuals, each with their unique contribution and a story to be cherished. His passion for his friends was extraordinary. It explained why he had risked so much. Carek gave up his professed love to save the lives of his friends, his family, and strangers he had yet to meet. Her heart thawed a little towards him at this revelation, because she understood what he was willing to sacrifice to save his family.

Gregor would sacrifice colony ships, cities, planets, all in his effort to save his empire. For him, it was the whole that mattered, not the individual.

What a startling contrast between the two men.

The simulation ended. The purple soup dissolved her tears, just like it had before.

"That was the easy part," Gregor said. "Opés, let me show you what happened to the people on Saphirah and Dunlaap. Those are the worlds the S'Lorek have visited. You will see what few have witnessed. These are the images sent back from the WOR."

Elise swam outside an underwater dome. She was s'Aartya, a WOR of the Third Rank. Darkness descended and the children paused in their game of chase. An odd sense of confusion and wrongness fell over the crowded dome and then passed. S'Aartya continued with her work. In the blink of an eye, the boiling seas came and went. Then she ceased to exist.

On the surface of the planet, it took longer to die. The WOR tried to stabilize the city spires, but they toppled as great winds ripped through the atmosphere. The wave of blistering heat bubbled and peeled the skin off their bones before the bones themselves turned to ash.

He brought her up to the orbiting stations, where the central Fourth Rank WOR watched the destruction. A massive ship, the size of a large moon had materialized above the thriving planet. A beam of devastation swept the world from the north to south pole. The cries of her fellow WOR, trapped in the firestorm, tore at her mind. She screamed for help, for her master to wake and deal with this disaster. S'Aniia sent a message to her fellow WOR moments before the S'Lorek ship turned its eye to the station. A wave of radiation annihilated everyone inside. The ship burst and twisted as superheated gases sought relief from the sudden pressure building inside. Elise felt s'Aniia die.

"Oh, Gregor," she sobbed.

The twisted wreckage of the fleet ship repeated itself a hundred times over as Elise watched the same scene across the Vendel fleet. Gregor brought the view to Dunlaap.

"Please, no more. I don't want to see any more." Elise opened her eyes. She twisted around and buried her head into Gregor's chest. "Please, make it stop."

"I have more to show you, opés," he said.

"I don't want to watch any more of that."

Gregor tilted her chin up to gaze into her eyes. His were dull silver and lined in pain. How many times he had witnessed the deaths of his subjects?

He regarded her for a long moment. "Opés, I don't like being at odds with you."

"I'm sorry." She wiped her eyes. It was a useless gesture. The tears weren't there. "I'll watch."

"You find it distressing, don't you?"

She nodded.

"So do I." He sighed. "I've watched these images again and again. Too many times. We're no closer to understanding what or who the S'Lorek are than when the images first arrived. The only thing we've discovered is the path of these aliens. They'll descend on Malbra within a few sun cycles of our arrival, if not sooner. Our estimate of their speed is a guess at best."

"A few sun cycles. You're taking us to it?"

"You would have me abandon my people?"

"But, we're not ready! The WOR aren't trained."

A sad smile filled his face. "All the Second and Third Rank Earth WOR have been Bound to their masters. It's the s'vlor who take time to train. I have only a few cycles left. We'll be using methods designed to give results."

Elise knew what methods he referred to, and knew he was wrong to think it would help.

They were not Vendel WOR. They were Earth WOR. His methods were having an entirely different effect on the Earth WOR than he intended. Every Vendel girl at least knew the possibility existed to be called to serve as WOR. Their concept of service was much different from that held by the women from Earth. For the Earth women, service as WOR was nothing other than enslavement, not some great honor. Gregor had made a huge miscalculation.

"Oh, Gregor."

He was a fool.

"Lord vlor'Vardhal," Gregor said, "we'll skip the Dunlaap feed and move ahead to your part in this."

Elise said a silent prayer of thanks. Gregor floated in front of her in the skin-tight immersion suit. She considered him from an entirely different perspective. A leader of worlds. A savior of humanity. He was much more than she'd ever considered.

He truly cared about his people and he was scared. Gregor had admitted that several times, although she hadn't had the proper point of view to appreciate what that meant to a man such as him. Gregor stretched out a hand and beckoned with his finger. Elise reached out and allowed him to pull her close.

It was the High Tender's turn. She could only imagine what he had in store for her.

We can't abandon them to this fate, the silent sister said.

I know, but how do I save them and free the WOR?

I do not know.

CHAPTER TWENTY-NINE_

Gambit, Day 261

HIGH TENDER MARCUS TOOK OVER THE SIMULATION. HIS CRISP WORDS FILLED Elise's head with pain.

"We charted the S'Lorek's course after they attacked Saphirah. They went to Dunlaap." The High Tender brought up a new simulation for Elise to watch and he continued his lecture.

"We sent our s'vlor to Dunlaap, hoping to fight off the aliens or at the very least shield the planet and attempt an evacuation. We were unsuccessful on both accounts. Of the forty s'vlor, half of which were Fifth Rank, only twenty-two survived."

He turned to her, a look of agony scrawled upon his hardened features. It was almost as if he cared about those women. For a moment, she felt his pain, but then remembered what he was capable of inflicting with his braklav. That innocent looking, slim metal rod dangling from his wrist belonged to a devil.

High Tender Marcus took in a breath of the purple soup and poured it out with his words. "When the S'Lorek turned their attention to the fleet, the s'vlor managed to hide long enough to construct a WOR-bubble. However, the effort at shielding and then forming the WOR-bubble burned out many of the WOR. The S'Lorek destroyed Dunlaap and moved on. The fleet endured, thank the gods." His gaze lifted and met Gregor's.

A look of shared pain passed between the two men.

Another gulp of the purple soup, another exhale, and his hard eyes turned to Elise. "The surviving WOR came out of WOR-space and sent back what they'd learned. I was able to see how they formed their WOR-bubble construct and the shield."

The High Tender scratched his head and the rotating mass of Dunlaap popped out of her vision. The dry scorched dirt held no life. Elise thought of Larkin and wondered if his mother had suffered as the S'Lorek killed her.

"I had already been thinking of a way to link the power of the WOR together. What those at Dunlaap tried helped me put together this."

A new display bloomed into life. She recognized the Vendel depictions of the WOR-skill. Several errors came to mind immediately. Why the Tenders had put this together, and not the WOR, defied explanation.

The blind teaching those with sight to see. The lurker, her silent sister, was not so silent anymore. But she still hadn't identified herself. *Ridiculous,* the lurker said with a snort.

The High Tender explained his theories and Elise followed his instruction, paying particular attention to the assumptions he made.

It's flawed, the silent sister said. *Do you see it?*

Shriek poked her head out of the dark. She seldom came out when the High Tender was present. *Flawed? How?*

Elise nodded. *I see it. Malice, Whimper, do you see it too?*

Malice cackled in the dark, singing about silver loops and jump-jets.

Whimper, however, paid attention, but remained silent. Of the five of them, Whimper was the least likely to speak up.

Sometime during the High Tender's lecture, Elise extricated herself from Gregor. She floated in front of the simulation and moved the wire diagrams around. The double vision of purple soup and sim-vision made her head hurt, but she felt driven to fix the errors.

Elise ended the High Tender's simulation with an irritated flick of her wrist, and drew the diagrams directly within the glowing liquid, not really knowing how, but doing it nonetheless.

Hovering in front of her, she reproduced the series of holographic plaques from the High Tender's office. After a few short minutes, she had the entire Tender depiction of WOR-skill floating in the soup.

Directly front and center, the first skills of the Bar hovered. To her left, the five rows of the Rod skills aligned themselves in ordered precision. To the right, she began with the Wheel skills, laying them out in their expanding circles with the five spokes. These she allowed to rotate slowly around their central axis.

She then took the diagrams from the High Tender's demonstration and placed them behind her, enclosing herself within a box of WOR-skill representations.

The men remained outside her construction and she had drifted some distance away. The tentacles connecting her to the floating orb, detached and dangled, forgotten.

An answer floated just beyond her comprehension, elusive and tantalizing, teasing her with its presence without revealing itself fully. She could feel the pattern shifting as it struggled to come together.

Her silent sister sat over her shoulder, nodding. *Yes! Continue!*

I can taste it, Elise said. *It's right here.*

Be very careful, sister, the unknown sister said. *What solution are we trying to solve?*

Go away!

You need me.

Who are you? Elise scratched her head. That line in the first skill of the Bar was wrong. She nudged it into proper place. The change rippled through all the skills.

I am you. You are me. Call me Alex if it helps.

Alex? Alex Comwell? You're my ghost.

Does it matter who I am? Alex hummed. *I think this is a puzzle that will solve itself. But, do we really want all of them to watch? What are you fixing, Elise? The WOR-skill or the linking problem?*

Elise had forgotten the men and turned her attention back to them.

The High Tender had gone silent.

A dark furrow creased Gregor's brow, but the corners of his mouth curled up, almost as if he were proud.

She shivered at that and stopped fiddling with the WOR-skill. With enough time, and privacy—secrecy would be the key—she'd fix the WOR-skill.

Elise remembered moments like this, back when she sat in her theoretical physics class. The answer to a particularly complex problem would hover out of reach. The solution unclear until suddenly it snapped into focus with stunning clarity. All that remained was the physical act of writing it down.

She could do that with the WOR-skill, but not with them watching.

It was too complicated to work out in her head. She needed the visual cues this soup afforded. Private time without the prying eyes of the High Tender or Gregor would be needed.

One thing was certain, the moment she solved the WOR-skill inconsistencies would be the day she sealed her fate. It would pave the way for Gregor to complete the Binding Rite and take from her a most precious possession—her mind.

The linking problem. The High Tender almost had it down.

She spun to stare at the symbols floating at the back of her little box of WOR-skill diagrams.

Gregor had his arms and legs crossed. High Tender Marcus' eyes flicked to the Bar skills. He had to of noticed the change she made in the first skill of the Bar.

Carek hovered in a modified lotus position with hands held loosely on top of his knees. He caught Elise's eye and gave a slow nod of his head. His green eyes were full of sorrow and lined in pain. He tried to smile, but failed.

Gregor's face was lit energy. His grin split from ear to ear and a sublime expression of satisfaction suffused his face.

The High Tender reminded her of her professors back on Earth. He studied, not her, but the work.

Elise caught his eye and beckoned him with her hand. "I'm sorry, High Tender Marcus. I didn't mean to cut off your demonstration. This just came to me and I needed to see it differently."

Carek floated forward with the High Tender. Gregor remained behind with the Conclave Master.

The symbols of the linking project floated between them.

"I had thought you would need more instruction to make sense of this." Brown eyes regarded her with a newfound respect. "It seems the Emperor's training has had unanticipated effects."

"I have struggled to learn, High Tender Marcus. The *Gambit's* WOR have worked hard to help me see the WOR-skill."

"It's a bit unconventional." He held up a hand to forestall her words and pointed to a line. "Why did you change this?"

Elise looked at the line he referred to. She hadn't changed it. It took her a moment, but then she realized that change had rippled through the WOR-skill modification she had made to the first skill of the Bar.

She hadn't thought such a minor alteration would have translated all the way through the skills. A quick scan of the hanging mass of Bar, Rod and Wheel skills revealed the rippling changes occurring. She quickly removed the alteration she'd made and watched the diagrams revert back to their original depictions.

She held the change in the linking solution to prevent it from slipping back to the original.

"It seemed wrong. I wanted to see how it would look this way. It's far from correct." Elise watched the High Tender's face closely.

His focus was on the linking problem and he seemed to be oblivious to the WOR-skill changes and their reversion back to their original status. "Hm." He glanced over his shoulder and beckoned Carek to come closer with a jerk of his chin. "Mr. Tusel, look at what she's done."

"Yes, my lord." Carek's eyes fixed on the first diagram. He lifted widened eyes toward Elise. "My lady, I don't know where you were going with this, but I think if we carried it over to here..." Carek stretched out his hands and manipulated the WOR-skill diagrams.

He had a reasonably good grasp of the force diagrams and seemed intimately familiar with the program. Elise watched as he traced her change through the entire series of holographs.

The High Tender grunted.

Carek leaned back, appraising his work.

Elise sat in silence. She glanced over Carek's shoulder to see Gregor. He seemed to be brooding and she remembered his odd mood. What was up with him? The High Tender asked Carek a question. The two put their heads together.

Elise swam over to her master. His brows lifted as she approached.

"Gregor?" she asked in a hesitant voice. "Is this what you wanted? Am I doing...is this the right thing? Is there something else you needed me to see?"

Gregor's eyes danced and she couldn't tell if it was with anger, amusement or something else. Her sudden inability to read this man caused shivers to run up and down her spine.

"You are an amazing woman, Elise. Continually, you find new ways to astound me. When did you learn how to do this?" He waved his hand to gesture at the soup and the floating box of WOR-skill diagrams.

The sudden image of four little holes in the wall flashed through her mind and her stomach heaved in dread. He had used her name again. "It just came to me. I haven't been hiding anything. This is not like before. I swear." Her voice dropped to a whisper.

"You swear, now, do you?"

"Gregor, what have I done to upset you?"

He shook his head and refused to answer. Gregor stared at the two men gesturing wildly at the wall of symbols floating in a purple sea. A short while later, he said simply, "You seem to have the High Tender and Mr. Tusel deep in discussion over your change. Perhaps you should listen to what they have to say?"

"Of course, as you command...master." Elise balled her hands into fists and began to turn around.

"Opés." He grabbed her arm and pulled her close. "This is not a game. It's not a sport and it's not a race. This is the future of the human race. Do you understand? We cannot afford to play games."

"I'm not—" she squeaked. "I thought this is what you wanted."

His grip tightened and he pulled her to him. "You will refer to me appropriately from now on, or I will send you to the High Tender. I am your master, but you'll call me by my given name. Is this clear?"

"Yes," she said. He increased his grip. She winced. "Yes, Gregor. You're hurting me."

"I know." Gregor released her arm and she floated free, at a loss to make sense of his actions or mood. "Inform the High Tender I'll meet him in Council. He'll give you instructions for the remainder of your day."

"Yes, Gregor." Elise rubbed her arm. She remembered Whimper's words, kept her eyes downcast and focused on Gregor's chest. She couldn't bear to watch the tattoo dance.

He motioned to the Conclave Master and swam out of sight. Elise returned to the High Tender. "High Tender Marcus?"

"Hmm," he said, distracted.

"Gregor has left. He said to inform you he'd meet up with you in council. I'm supposed to get my schedule for the rest of the day."

High Tender Marcus pulled his eyes away from the diagrams and focused on her. "Yes, well, there is that." He placed a finger to his chin and tapped. "Mr. Tusel."

"Yes, my lord."

"This is not exactly what I had planned, but Lady s'Lissa has interesting ideas. I'd like you to run through the program and perhaps..." He gestured to the linking diagrams. "See if she has any other insight with this."

"Yes, my lord."

"The emperor and I will be in Council all day. I need you to keep the Lady s'Lissa through lunch and continue afterward. It would take too much time to return her to the Fifth Deck for her meal."

"Yes, my lord. It would be an honor. I will see to it."

"Good. I'll inform your Conclave Master. She needs to be back in her quarters by fifth dinner."

"Yes, my lord. I'll escort her personally."

Elise glared at him and rolled her eyes. "Mr. Tusel, that won't be necessary. I know my way back."

Carek frowned.

The High Tender scratched his head. "No doubt you do, s'Lissa, nevertheless, I would rather have you escorted."

Elise bowed her head in acquiescence. *Gregor lets me run loose on the ship.* "Yes, High Tender Marcus."

He puffed out his cheeks and blew out his liquid breath, "Good. This has been quite productive. I'm impressed by the progress you're making, s'Lissa. Keep it up." He gave her a genuine smile and nodded with satisfaction.

She smiled back like an obedient puppy.

The High Tender swam over to the Conclave Master. The two men waved goodbye and disappeared into the purple soup leaving Elise and Carek alone.

"El," Carek began, once they were alone.

"Mr. Tusel," she interrupted. "I've been instructed to work and that is what I plan to do."

"El?" His eyes widened in alarm. "Please. Don't do this."

"This is what you wanted, isn't it? You told me to go back to my master." She shook her head, "Don't *El* me. That's over and behind us, Mr. Tusel."

"No one is watching. No one can hear us. The soup gives that amount of privacy."

His words peaked her interest. "Really?"

"Yes."

"They can't listen in, or watch?"

He shook his head. "Not unless we're hooked into the pods, which we're not."

"Good." She swam back to the WOR-skill diagrams.

"You made a pretty intuitive leap with that diagram. I think I can almost see where it leads."

"Fine. Sit over there and work on it." She meant every pointed word. "But leave me alone."

Carek said he loved her and in his next breath had told her how he was going to destroy her mind and take away her free will by allowing the Binding with the Emperor to proceed. She couldn't forgive him for that.

He cocked an eyebrow. "El, you have to work on this with me. That needs to get done."

She flipped her head. The gesture worked better with her hair free, but she'd forgotten about the hood. "I did." She pointed to the line change in the diagram. "You trace out your little theories. I want to look at this."

"Why do you want to look at the WOR-skill representations?"

"Because they're wrong. I want to fix them."

He barked a laugh. "Those have been in use for thousands of years. I doubt there's anything wrong with them."

"Men are fools."

"You need to work on the linking program. We'll get in trouble if they find out you're wasting your time on that."

She regarded him and crossed her arms. "I thought you said they couldn't see what we did."

"They can't."

"Then how are they going to know what I do or don't do? Are you going to tell?"

"El, I have some responsibility here."

"Right, and you have several broken oaths. What would Gregor think if I told him about those?"

She hated threatening Carek, but she couldn't pass up this opportunity to fix the WOR-skill. Her future depended on it.

His eyes grew cold. "That knife cuts both ways."

"That knife has already cut and damaged more than you can possibly know."

He flinched at her words.

"Please, Carek," she begged. "These are wrong and I know I can sort it out. The change I made over here..." She pointed to the Bar skill. "It reflected in your diagrams. I didn't do that. It happened by itself. Trust me. The solution to your problem lies not in working on the linking diagram, but in solving the WOR-skill."

He looked with interest. "Are you certain?"

"I feel it in here." She thumped her chest.

He chewed on his lower lip.

"I can't forgive you for what you will do to me, but I understand why you feel it's the right thing to do." She wanted to ease his pain, but needed him invested in her plan. "The worlds you showed me and the way you described them touched me deeply. You care for your people in a way that Gregor cannot envision. I'll save your people, or at least I'll try, but I'm not done fighting for my freedom. Please don't take that away from me. It's the only thing keeping me sane."

She pointed again to the WOR-skills. "The answer is over here. I need to study the WOR-skill, and I don't dare tell Gregor what I'm doing. The moment he realizes what I'm up to, or how much of the WOR-skill I actually know, I'm lost. He'll Bind me without realizing that's exactly what he can't do. I need your help. We both can achieve our goals."

"I can't help you defeat the Emperor, El."

"I'm not asking for that. I accept my fate. I'm looking for a way to save all of us. All of you seem to think I can. I have no idea why that is. I'm just a simple girl from Earth, thrust into an impossible situation, working with madmen. One foot in front of the other, one step at a time, I will continue to move forward, until I'm dead."

"That's not how this works. You can have a full life as his WOR. You don't have to fight him."

She shrugged. He was wrong. "If he, and you, and all the Tenders think I'm the solution, I'll try to do whatever you think I can do, but I won't stand by and do nothing to save myself while all of you consign me to slavery. The High Council is meeting today. I have today to work on this. I want to use my time well. Leave me alone and let me try."

"Don't hate me for wishing to save my people." Carek vented a resigned sigh. "El, swear to me that what you're doing will help with the linking project."

"I swear. The answer is over here. Or at least, the solution to my understanding the answer is somewhere over here."

He laughed. It was sudden and surprising and seemed to come from nowhere. The force of his laughter shocked Elise. His eyes twinkled. "Is it possible for a man to be triply damned?"

"I don't know."

"We call a truce, then." He pleaded. "Despite everything, one thing has not changed."

"What is that?"

Carek spoke very softly. "I still love you."

She wasn't sure if she was supposed to have heard him. Elise stiffened and held back a sob. This world was hell.

But there's a way out, Alex whispered.

I know, but will we have time?

You and me together, Elise, we can do anything.

CHAPTER THIRTY_

Gambit, Day 275

IT TURNED OUT ELISE HAD MORE THAN A DAY TO WORK ON THE PROBLEM. EACH time she made a change in the WOR-skill, the linking diagrams reflected the subtle alterations. In some way, she had formed a tie between her WOR-skill constructs and the High Tender's linking project.

The slow, but steady progress made to that project buoyed everyone's hopes. As a result, the High Tender made sure she spent most days in the am-net tank, working on his project.

Carek always joined her, but spent most of the day floating in the soup watching her work. Elise managed to complete most changes to the Bar and Rod skills over a matter of days. She also discovered several skills the Tenders had missed. On the days High Tender Marcus came to help, progress ground to a standstill. He made her nervous and flustered her thoughts.

After Carek made one or two oblique references about the High Tender's presence affecting her work, he dropped by less and less, and stayed for shorter periods of time.

Elise showed her roommates the changes she'd made to the WOR-skill. The nights she wasn't in competition on the jump-jet circuit, the four of them stayed up late practicing the new forms.

Alice taught the other Fifth Rank WOR the evolving WOR-skill, with one unique exception. The threat of further Tender Training made some of the girls hesitant, but once they understood what the Binding Rite promised, they were eager to learn, and to hide what Alice taught.

The secret code, however, remained confined to just the Elise, Alice, Aomi and Chandra.

After a long day in the am-net tank, Elise prepared for the jump-jet competition while the four of them sat around their suite comparing notes until it was time for her to slip out.

Aomi twisted in her seat, they had been talking about the Blood Rite. "Remember how the blood was absorbed into our masters' hands?" They all nodded. "Well, that's how our DNA got into their bodies. According to what Elise said about the WOR-genes on the Y-chromosome, I think I have it figured out. Our DNA turned on the Y-chromosome genes. We're Fifth Rank WOR which means our lords have the full complement of the five WOR-supplemental genes. Just like the Activator changed the chemical, structural, and dimensional connections in our brains, the Blood Rite is doing the same to the men. The only difference between them and us is the Activator was a non-specific activation for us, whereas the Blood Rite is specific for them. It links us to our specific vlor'lord. As their genes turn on, they become attuned to us, and us to them. It's a bidirectional exchange."

"So, they do read our minds?" Chandra grimaced. "According to Elise, the Emperor said Lord vlor'Delatris read Paula's mind and that's how they knew we had the code."

"I don't think it's that simple. They're not able to read our thoughts, and I think we can hide some of it from them."

Aomi lifted a finger in agreement. "Right, not our thoughts, but our emotions. The High Tenders and the vlor'lords see us working the WOR-skill because they have WOR-genes. The High Tenders are the strongest, as are our lords. The vlor'lords have the full five supplemental genes on their Y-chromosomes which means they can sense more than the High Tenders, but only with their particular s'vlor. They can't see what other s'vlor do, but the Tenders can."

Chandra looked confused. She squinted. "So, they do or don't read our minds? I'm confused."

"No," Aomi explained. "They sense our emotions, maybe even our presence. Ever notice how you know when your master is walking down the hall before the door opens? I know its Talen long before I see him. I can...*feel* him."

Alice shook her head. "If that's the case, then why hasn't Gregor figured out Elise is lying through her teeth. How come Talen hasn't figured out that you're spending all night learning about Vendel genetic technology? Why hasn't Edgard figured out that I'm training all the WOR in Elise's new WOR-skill? Why don't they know the four of us still keep a secret code? Doesn't make sense."

Aomi blinked. "I believe it has to do with intent. Paula felt guilty about the code. Her guilt, that emotion, triggered on Lord vlor'Delatris. Did you ever watch the two of them? Before Tender Training, Paula was in love with him. They didn't exactly sneak around, but I'm pretty sure his hands made a full circuit of her body. Paula feels differently now. She hates Lord vlor'Delatris with a passion. Did you know he asked High Tender vlor'-Vardhal to give her an additional day of Tender Training for betraying his trust. And not just a couple hours."

They all shook with the memories of the mass Tender Training sessions.

"I didn't know he had done that to her," Elise whispered.

She and Paula shared Master Tender Marcus as their assigned Tender. They had both endured much beneath his braklav and tutelage. Paula kept to herself. Always had. Despite that, Elise felt a special kinship with Paula, a shared misery.

Alice gave Elise a hug. "You were occupied with your Tender Training. But High Tender vlor'Vardhal made time for Paula between your additional sessions."

Chandra shivered. "Not just that, but he did it in the classroom and we all had to watch. I didn't understand why at the time."

Aomi coughed. A look of disgust crossed her porcelain features. "I believe Lord vlor'Delatris picked up on Paula's guilt and teased the rest out. It's an empathic connection, not telepathic. As long as we don't feel guilty, or give them any reason to be suspicious, they shouldn't pick up on it. They might get a sense of a buzzing or dissonance, but that's easily explained by being prisoners of aliens. We all feel that, and we're a little gun shy, so to speak, after that mass Tender Training. After the first of us completes the Binding Rite, that will be destroyed. I think. I'm still not clear on what the Binding does."

Chandra hung her head. She spoke softly. "So, what are we doing here? If the Binding Rite is coming at us, aren't we doomed? Isn't this all going to come crashing down around our heads?"

Elise looked up, realizing her mind had drifted. She'd been thinking about her upcoming race. She was slated to go against Malikai again. Regardless of the race's outcome, his point tally already earned him a spot in the semi-finals. Elise had to beat him, not tie with him, if she were to secure a spot for herself in the semi-finals. How was she going to do that?

Chandra's despair pulled at her and forced her back into the conversation. She needed to give them hope, even when she had very little to offer.

"It depends on how fast I figure it all out." She reached for Chandra's hand. "I've found a critical flaw in the linking project, but I haven't figured out how to break the news to Gregor or High Tender Marcus. I'm not supposed to know about this lobotomy job they have planned with the Binding Rite."

Alice regarded her with interest. "What do you mean?"

"Linking isn't going to work. At least not with Vendel WOR who are Bound." She scratched her head. "It's my belief the Binding Rite makes linking impossible. Binding links a WOR to her master's will. I can't link her to another WOR if she's already linked to a lord. I would have to remove the Binding for it to work and I'm pretty sure that would kill a WOR."

She glanced at Aomi. "If you have the time, I need you to take a look at it, the sooner the better."

Aomi nodded. "Sure, just give me direction."

"I left notes on my gel-flimsy. I have to leave soon, but most of it is there."

"I'll look at it tonight."

Elise turned her attention to Chandra. "If I can get them to believe me, then I might be able to delay Binding for us all. Gregor will be pissed. He can't wait. Although," she said with sudden realization, "he's been strangely quiet about it lately."

She sighed and glanced at the clock. It was almost time to leave.

"We should be at Malbra before the end of the cycle. Jeena told me the finals will be run in Malbran local space, rather than WOR-space. She's located a WOR-space capable freighter large enough to hold all of us. She was a little suspicious why I wanted such a large ship. I blabbered something about asteroid mining as a future career. We still need to figure out the WOR-drive. A few months—I mean sun cycles—later, the S'Lorek should be jumping down our throats. Maybe it'll kill us all before the Vendel Bind us."

"Elise! That's a horrible thing to say," Alice said. "We'll find a way out of this. Paula has an idea about the Binding Rite. She might be better to look at it with Aomi."

"Do you trust Paula enough to rope her into this?"

"She's different now. Paula's with us. You're not alone anymore. We're all pitching in."

Chandra added, "Yeah, the stuff you're coming back with from the

Tank is amazing. No matter what we do, and despite your comments about the S'Lorek killing us, we have to figure out how WOR-space and the WOR-drive work. WOR-space navigation and propulsion is being worked on as well. We're all behind you. Just don't get caught! We need that ship."

Elise's heart swelled. She really wasn't fighting alone anymore. The Fifth Deck had pulled together. Alice was the real inspiration. Her dogged determination to 'stick it to the bastards' brought everyone together. Elise may be their champion, but Alice had become their leader. Alice implemented and organized. Aomi and Chandra supported and solved problems. Elise just furnished the required tools.

"All right. I'm tired. I feel like I'm losing the race. Gregor is breathing down my neck, and the High Council will release his oath. I have to get it together. Or find a way to survive Binding and not give all of you away. I have to win the jump-jet circuit so I can purchase a freighter large enough for us all, and I can't fail at any step. I haven't even thought about the S'Lorek."

Alice pulled Elise to her feet and into a hug. "You can do this. You've already done so much. We have faith in you. You're our hero."

"When does the Hero get to rest?"

Chandra and Aomi joined the group hug.

"Good luck out there," Chandra said.

"Kick this Malikai's ass," Aomi said.

"Have you ever met him in person?" Alice asked.

"Just once."

"Is he cute?" Chandra winked.

"Don't know. He was in a flightsuit with the helmet on," Elise said.

After a few goodbyes and another round of hugs, she disappeared down the bio-cart tunnel. They wished her luck. She would need it. Malikai posed a serious threat to her jump-jet dreams.

CHAPTER THIRTY-ONE_

Gambit, Day 276

ELISE HOVERED OUTSIDE THE START OF THE JUMP-JET RING COURSE. IMAGES OF WOR-skill and linking diagrams invaded her thoughts. A key piece of the puzzle eluded her, and she couldn't fit everything together without that piece. It annoyed her. The Bar and Rod skills had resolved their inconsistencies under her attention in the tank. The remainder of the Wheel skills started to fall into place, but her task was far from finished.

Malikai was late. That annoyed her too.

She checked the time again.

The gray WOR-space bubble comforted her senses. It felt like a warm woolen blanket sheltering her from the cold. Outside the blanket, the real world lurked. The jump-jet finals would be fought in real space. Jeena had been practicing with her in simulations. The silver rings were a little easier to pick out in normal space, but flying the course was subtly different.

In real space, the High Council would meet and, if she didn't figure out some solution, she would lose her mind and the hopes of hundreds. The S'Lorek loomed as a very real threat. Chandra had been right, the S'Lorek had to be dealt with one way or another. If Elise couldn't link the Vendel WOR, and she didn't think it would be possible, that left only the Earth WOR to meet that threat. They still had to live in this galaxy, either hidden from the Vendel or as slaves to the Vendel.

Her head hurt from the pressure. So much depended on her.

Communication static hissed over the audio channel.

"Are you ready, *Chickadee*." Malikai slurred her name. "This is purely academic for me."

"Yes, Malikai, we've all looked at the stats." Elise didn't have the patience for Malikai's taunts. "How do you think you're going to stack up against your competition? Three of the other four finalists are women. If I beat you, that'll make four. Just two men in the top six. What has the world come to?"

He paused before responding. When he finally did, his tone was dry. "As long as they earned their positions fairly, the worlds will handle it. I've flown against them all before, but they don't really pose much of a threat."

"You're a cocky bastard, Malikai. There's no reason to be so ugly. We all fly the same ships and we all train the same way."

"Of course we do," he said with a slur. "And every year, we see novices beat out the competition and break into the semi-finals. Are we training the same way? Is that what you're saying...novice?"

"You have a lot to learn about sportsmanship. Do you forget who trained me? I've earned my place."

"I expect a clean race, *Chickadee*. A fair race."

"What's that supposed to mean?"

Jeena had warned her about this pilot, but she hadn't realized how irritating he could be.

He spoke in a low ominous tone. "Let's just say, I plan on watching very closely."

A light blinked on her display panel, signaling the course was ready.

"You do that," she said with annoyance. "Fox or Rabbit?"

"Lady's choice," he replied.

"I'll take Fox."

"Care to make a wager?" Malikai accepted Rabbit and her display blinked with his confirmation.

"With you? Never," she hissed. "Just fly your jump-jet. When I come screaming down your ass, don't be surprised."

He chuckled. "Such words from a lady."

"I'm no lady, Malikai."

"Right, and I'm no lord. See you at the finish, Fox." The timer ticked down and Malikai launched out of the starting box. The clock counted down his thirty-second lead.

Cheating? How the hell could anyone cheat? All of her races had been as clean as they came. She would show this bastard. The moment his count ended, her console blinked green. She fired her thrusters. Silver rings disappeared behind her jump-jet. Malikai secured a four-ring lead, impressive, but she was determined.

He didn't even bother to dodge as she narrowed her lead down to a single ring.

"Rabbit turns Fox in five, *Chickadee*," he called over the communications channel. "Get ready."

Elise ignored him.

Malikai dove through the twenty-first ring as she exited the twentieth. She twisted up in a spiraling right-hand arc to set up for the next ring. His jump-jet screamed forward. Malikai pushed for the twenty-fifth ring when he should have been watching Fox. Elise nailed him with her lasers as he dipped below the twenty-third ring.

Hers hit before he passed the twenty-fifth ring, earning her two points.

Elise pulled up and raced back around the torus to the start of the jump-jet circuit. "What was that you were saying? I couldn't hear...too much static."

A string of curses was his only reply.

Malikai took Fox for the second race. Elise raced through the rings and established a decent three-ring lead. Malikai came hot on her heels.

She watched him closely. Several shots narrowly missed her ship. None scored. Elise pulled through the twenty-fifth ring and pressed on the thrusters with Malikai less than a ring behind. By the time the fiftieth ring loomed into view, she had increased her lead by two full rings. Elise raced for the finish line.

Rabbit finished first, which earned her two more points.

The point tally stood at four to zero. With only one race left, there was no way for Malikai to win. She chuckled. Her place in the semi-finals had been secured.

Her communications channel hissed to life.

"Seems you've improved."

"I'll see you in the semi-finals. Thanks for the race."

"We still have one more heat to go," he said.

Elise grew still. "The race is over. I've won."

"This has nothing do with winning. I take Rabbit in the last round."

"What's the point then?"

"I'll not have you take a four-point lead. Set up for the last race."

"No," she said.

"It's my prerogative. Set up!"

"Kiss my ass, Malikai. You want it, fine. Rabbit takes Fox in the last round." That would give him three points. "You still lose three to four. I'm not wasting my time just to soothe your ego. Goodbye."

Elise accelerated, leaving another string of curses in her wake.

Jeena and Dove greeted her with ecstatic hugs. Larkin was there. His springy curls bounced over his red-rimmed eyes. His entire family had perished on Dunlaap. They had been water vapor farmers, very poor. He'd been the first in his line to go off-world. All their hopes and dreams had been placed on his shoulders. Now he carried their legacy.

Larkin gathered her in a hug and planted a kiss on her lips. He let it linger just a little too long. She hugged him back, not wanting him to feel her withdrawal.

She made quick excuses and ran off the flight deck. The last person she wanted to see was Malikai. His ship hovered above the jump-jet hangar, waiting for the crane to lower his ship to the deck.

———

THE NEXT DAY, ELISE CLIMBED OUT OF THE AM-NET TANK. CAREK FOLLOWED. It was lunchtime.

"I need other WOR, Carek. I'm close but I need to try out a few things."

She had a headache and her teeth buzzed in their sockets.

"I spoke with Lord vlor'Vardhal. He's agreed to let the am-net WOR participate."

She shook her head. "They're not strong enough. I need Fifth Rank WOR." She walked up the ramp and the purple soup drained down the tiny holes in the deck. Carek tossed her a towel.

"We don't have any of those." Gregor's deep voice made her jump.

She stepped to the edge of the platform and stared down at her master.

"Gregor! I wasn't expecting you." She replayed her conversation with Carek, wondering if she'd said anything she shouldn't. She didn't think she'd given anything away.

Gregor reached up and gestured for her to come down. She jumped down into his embrace.

"It's nice to see you, Gregor." Her heart raced.

Gregor's moods had been off lately. Darkness flickered in his steel eyes and the wavy lines of the tattoo over his brow danced.

He removed the hood from her head. "Lord vlor'Vardhal tells me he is pleased with your progress."

Elise said nothing.

Carek jumped off the platform. "Sire, it's an honor. Would you like to inspect our progress? She's been very helpful."

Gregor's eyes flicked from Carek to Elise and back again. "I expect my s'vlor to be helpful."

Carek paused but recovered quickly. "Sire, we were taking a break for lunch. Do you need the Lady s'Lissa?"

Gregor wrapped an arm possessively around Elise. "I had a free moment and thought to share a meal with my s'vlor."

Carek came to attention. "Of course, Sire. I will leave you." He gave a brief bow and inclined his head toward Elise.

Gregor allowed Carek to take three steps before speaking. "Mr. Tusel, I hadn't planned on interrupting your work. I had thought to eat here in the Conclave. Would you please join us? You can tell me what the two of you have accomplished over the past several cycles."

"Yes, Sire," Carek said, obviously overwhelmed. "We only have common eating facilities, I'm afraid, within the Conclave proper. We lack private rooms."

Gregor waved dismissively in the air. "Don't mind that. I've eaten in the common rooms before."

"Yes, Sire." He looked at his immersion suit. "Will the Lady s'Lissa be returning to the tank after her meal? If not, we can stop by the changing rooms."

Gregor squeezed Elise. "Yes, the High Tender has set her schedule. I'm just here to steal a few moments."

"Of course." Carek headed toward the dining facilities.

Gregor held her back for a moment. "Tell me, opés, who gave you permission to use that man's personal name?"

Elise froze. "I…"

"You'll refer to him properly from now on. Tonight, after your dinner, report to the High Tender for correction. Is this understood?"

Her heart skipped a beat. "Yes, Gregor. Forgive me, I…"

"Silence. I'll speak to Lord vlor'Vardhal."

"Yes, Gregor." Elise swallowed the bile rising in her throat. Shriek stretched and began to prepare. It had been a long time since she had come out to play.

Elise sat in silence during the meal while Carek explained their progress with the linking project.

Gregor placed a hand on Elise's leg. "I understand you need WOR."

"Yes, Sire," Carek said.

"Hasn't Lord vlor'Vardhal given you access to the WOR in the am-net for your work."

"Yes, Sire, but Lady s'Lissa feels they are too weak."

"Is this true, opés?"

"Yes, Gregor. I need stronger WOR."

"We don't have trained WOR on the *Gambit* higher than First Rank."

"You have ninety Fifth Rank WOR sitting idle on the Fifth Deck," she countered.

"All untrained."

"All in the process of becoming trained." She lowered her eyes and stared at her plate.

Gregor squeezed her thigh.

She suppressed a shudder.

Carek sat on the opposite side of the table, oblivious to Gregor's actions under the tabletop.

She tried not to pull away, but it was difficult.

Gregor smirked and brushed the hair away from her neck with his free hand. "How would having WOR help?" His eyebrow lifted in question.

"Sire, Lady s'Lissa feels she needs to run a few tests. The linking project is far from complete, but there are a few theories we're working on which would be nice to try out. They could provide valuable information."

"I don't know if the High Tenders would be pleased to know their charges are floating about in the am-net Tank unsupervised."

Gregor hadn't dismissed the idea. She was pleased he was thinking about it.

"Gregor, I know it seems like an odd request, but having a few of the Earth WOR will help. I'd like to try out a few ideas. They may even be able to see something I haven't seen. Is there any way you can talk to High Tender Marcus? Please?"

He leaned down and kissed her temple. "You had only to ask."

"Thank you, Gregor." She smiled at him while her stomach churned.

Carek pushed his food around with a fork. "A few WOR should be adequate. If we had a total of five, it would provide a solid circle to work with."

"You need four more?" Gregor's head tilted up.

"It would be the best number to start with. Eventually we'll need ten, but five is the minimum to form a link. We would need to run a few tests first." Carek munched on a protein bar.

Gregor glanced down at Elise's forgotten plate. "Opés, you haven't touched your meal."

"I'm not as hungry as I thought."

His eyes narrowed and silver glinted in the harsh light of the cafeteria. "Nonsense, eat up, opés. You need your strength."

"Yes, Gregor." She grabbed her fork and picked at her meal.

Carek and Gregor talked about the linking project. Carek described the progress they made and some of the things he wished to try with a group of WOR. Their conversation ebbed and flowed until they ran out of things to talk about.

Elise's plate was still half full.

Gregor pushed back from the table but did not rise. "Continue, opés. We have time to wait while you finish." He wiped his chin with a napkin. "So, Mr. Tusel, are you a jump-jet fan?"

Her heart stopped.

He knows!

You're paranoid, Alex said. *There's no way he knows.*

"Aren't we all?" Carek's green eyes flashed in the light. His attention landed on Elise then slipped away.

"Absolutely," Gregor said, "and can you believe the semi-finalists? Two men and four women. It's going to have the fans going wild."

"We haven't had a woman win since Jeena."

"Yes, what happened to her? She won ten circuits in a row and then dropped out of the races."

"She stopped racing to focus on her Pilot Conclave business."

Gregor leaned forward. "Did you know I bet against her every year but the last? I finally wised up and placed the Imperial bet on her. I guess that must have been what she was waiting for, because she hasn't raced since she won that year."

"I believe there was more to it than that."

"Do you know her?"

"My cousin knows her."

Gregor tapped his lip. "Really? How interesting. I didn't even know she was on the *Gambit* until recently. It's a shame she's not in the jump-jet circuit, although, if she were, it would skew the betting. Everyone would bet on her and then when she won, who'd be able to meet the bets?"

"She could fly veiled. Other winners have done that to keep the betting fair."

Elise pushed the food around on her plate. Her appetite had abandoned her.

Gregor scratched the back of his neck. "It's time to consider my pick and place the Imperial bet. I think all six are pretty fine pilots."

Carek coughed. "Yes, Sire."

"Do you have a favorite? Or maybe, with your connections, do you have an inside track on any of the pilots? Who is most likely to win? My picks don't always win, but I believe it spices things up when the winner is able to take home such a large prize. Don't you agree?"

"Yes," Carek said. "And it's considered a great honor to take home the Imperial bet."

"So, who do you favor?" Gregor leaned both elbows on the table and glanced at Elise's unfinished plate. "Opés, you need to eat. You're looking a little pale."

Elise stuffed a pea into her mouth and focused on her plate.

"I don't have a favorite. I'm trying to stay out of the jump-jet races this year."

"Oh, right," Gregor said, "I believe I know about that."

"Sire?" Carek's voice cracked.

Elise held perfectly still.

"Didn't you subsidize one of the semi-finalists? The novice on the circuit? What's her call sign?" Gregor tapped his lip.

"We had a falling out. I tried to revoke the entrance fee, but it was too late. I haven't spoken to that pilot about her training, or her advancement, for several sun cycles." Carek glared at Elise.

She ignored him.

"That's unfortunate. She shows promise. Why did you have a falling out, if I might ask?"

Elise shoved large pieces of protein steak into her mouth.

Gregor looked down at her. "Slow down, opés, or you'll choke."

She nodded and kept her head down.

"Philosophical differences. I felt her priorities were in the wrong place and her loyalties needed redirection."

"I see. She is still competing, however. Must not have listened to what you said."

"She heard me. She's just obstinate and wants to have it both ways. I believe she takes great risk."

Gregor laughed. "I know exactly what you mean." He patted Elise's leg for emphasis. "It's amazing the risks a person is willing to take when the stakes are high."

She nearly choked.

Gregor continued, "Well, the semi-finals start today and I need to place my bet. Perhaps I should put it on the long shot? What do you think?"

"I wouldn't presume to say."

"Please, Mr. Tusel. If you were me, and had to choose from those six pilots, would you place your money on the oddball long shot or the tried and true? I believe Malikai has won a few circuit finals in the past, although he doesn't admit to it. He flies veiled, which leads me to believe he's a previous jump-jet circuit winner or a lord. The other man, Sigour, has won once before, although he doesn't fly veiled. Candice has come in second and third in the past two Imperial finals, and she won the *Gambit* fleet finals last year. Should I bet on her? Or your girl? I'm not as familiar with the other two female pilots."

"Sire, I can't tell you who to place the Imperial bet on." Carek's eyes widened. He pushed himself back from the table. "And she's not my girl. I don't endorse her pursuit of a jump-jet prize. It's foolhardy and irresponsible."

Elise fit the last piece of food into her mouth and tried not to choke as she swallowed.

Gregor became silent. "Opés, why don't you decide?"

Elise glanced into eyes of steel that lacked any warmth. "I don't even know what you're talking about."

"It's a race. That's all you need to know. Tell me, opés, who would you bet on? An established pilot or a fresh untried novice?"

Elise followed the protein bite with a gulp of water. Malice chuckled in the blackness. Shriek was distant, she was preparing for the High Tender. Whimper had crawled away. Alex was missing, as usual.

She took in a deep breath. "I always bet on the underdog. They have the most to lose and, therefore, are willing to risk everything to achieve their goals."

After a little while, he gave an odd appraising look. "I do believe you have a point. But, the price of failure can be incredibly steep."

She held him in a steady gaze. "It depends on the reward."

Gregor turned his attention back to Carek. "I need to think about it, of course. Betting has already begun on which pilot I'll pick. Before the first race tonight, I'll have to make up my mind." He pushed back from the table. "By the way, Mr. Tusel, I appreciate you switching your shifts around to work with my s'vlor. I know nightshift can be difficult."

"No problem, my lord. It has been my honor. The Tank is relatively empty during the nightshift. It's better not having too many people around while the Lady s'Lissa works. Less distraction."

Gregor waved his hand in acknowledgement. "Yes, of course. If you will excuse me?"

Elise scrambled to her feet. "Goodbye, Gregor. Thank you for having lunch with me."

Gregor planted a kiss on her forehead. "Until later, opés. Perhaps, tomorrow night, you can dine with me in my quarters?"

"Yes, Gregor." She focused on his boots, terrified to meet the steel of his gaze.

Gregor took a step back. She didn't breathe until he exited the dining facility and disappeared down the hall.

Carek's expression became distant. He crossed his arms. "You're playing a very dangerous game, El." He jerked his chin toward the way Gregor exited. "He should not be underestimated."

Elise gave him a mulish look. "Nor should I."

"You need to pull out of the jump-jet competition. It's foolhardy."

She headed back to the immersion tank. "I'm not pulling out of the competition."

"You're risking everything."

"No. I'm here, aren't I? We're making progress. Win or lose, stay or go, don't take jump-jets away from me, Carek. It's the only thing I have that's keeping me sane. I swore to you I would work to save the Vendel, but I can't save you if I lose myself in the process. If you don't understand that, then you have no idea who I really am."

And who are you? Alex asked. *Are you strong enough to win?*

I don't know about that, but I'm determined not to lose.

I suppose that will have to be enough.

Elise stared at the surface of the glowing purple sea. It had to be enough, because she didn't have anything else to give. And somewhere out in space, an alien presence sought to destroy everything she had come to love.

"Let's get back to work." She dove into the purple sea, determined to never stop. Whether that was to save the Vendel, rescue the Earth WOR, or hold on to her sanity, were questions for later.

It was time to turn things around.

It was time to win.

THIS IS NOT THE END!

VENDEL RISING: VOLUME 4
IT ENDS WITH A BEGINNING
is next!

Follow Elise's journey with the Vendel as she seeks her revenge.

Grab your copy now!

IT ENDS WITH A BEGINNING

VOLUME 4

PART ONE_

Plans

PROLOGUE_

New Terra Histories by Malita s'Lissa s'vlor

"Make the impossible possible." These are the words my grandfather left me with. They whisper and echo in my head every day. But how do you make the impossible possible? This was my task, and I chipped at the mountain of impossibility until the first boulder fell. After that, accomplishing the impossible didn't seem nearly impossible. My most potent weapon was perseverance.

AT SOME POINT, I THINK I WAS INSANE. MAYBE? I DON'T KNOW. MY memories are foggy. Perhaps there were several times when I passed that fine dividing line stretched between sanity and that darker place of madness. It's hard to know for certain.

Tender Training.

It's an odd thing. The first time it nearly broke me. I remember a compulsive desire to please Gregor, resulting from my first experience with ten days of Tender Training.

The second time? I lost something that second time around. It splintered my identity, but I believe I gained more than I lost.

My entire goal had been escape. I fought for freedom. The fact that I faced an unsurmountable task did not dissuade me. The Vendel came to my home, they murdered nearly all of Earth's population, and they took a thousand of us as slaves. They were the very definition of evil, and I vowed to defeat them.

Revenge against the Vendel filled my every waking thought and fueled my determination to never give up. No matter the pain the Vendel inflicted, or the deaths they caused, my purpose drove me forward.

We would never make it back to Earth.

I had to find a different solution.

Not once did it occur to me that I might fail. I didn't know what to do, but I kept moving forward, one small step at a time. As long as I was doing something, I believed a solution would be found.

And that cloak of invisibility? My desperate wish to not get caught? Yeah, that had never been done before. It wasn't a wish, but rather a manifestation of the WOR skill. While I failed to learn the very basics of the mysterious WOR-skill, my subconscious took over. No one told me what I did was impossible. I just did it.

That's me . . . making the possible out of the impossible. As for my sanity, have you met my sisters?

CHAPTER ONE_

Gambit, Day 276

ELISE FLOATED IN THE PURPLE SOUP AND STARED AT THE ROTATING WHEEL OF WOR-skill diagrams. The tangled lines made her eyes cross and she rubbed at her brow. Where she had made steady progress correcting Bar and Rod skills, those of the Wheel frustrated her with their complexity. For the tenth time she changed the inner ring of symbols and came up hard against a wall.

Alex told her it was wrong, but Alex couldn't figure it out either. The silent conversations she had with her sister no longer seemed odd, but wasn't it? Speaking to yourself meant a person was crazy, right?

Why would it be odd? And what do you mean crazy? Alex said.

Can't you give me a little privacy?

Not when you say I'm odd. It makes me think you don't want me here.

I do. I do want you here.

Alex's unique perspective when it came to dissecting the WOR-skill was invaluable. They had made incredible progress fixing thousands of years of what the Tenders had messed up.

With a frustrated wave, Elise dismissed the entire box of WOR-skill diagrams. Her brain couldn't handle the challenge any more. The glowing lines faded into the purple soup. Her mind wasn't on the work, and a pinch of pain had settled behind her eyes.

A pinch of pain?

Isn't that laughable?

That lunch with Gregor yesterday, as with any encounter, had irritated her and made her uneasy. It had resulted in intense pain at the end of the braklav as well.

Gregor had hinted at things she shouldn't know, but did. Conversations of the jump-jet circuit dominated the conversation between him and Carek. They had gone on and on about the races and Gregor's placement of his Imperial bet, something she needed to win.

But what the hell?

It was as if Gregor knew about her and the jump-jets. But how could that be? If he knew she'd been escaping confinement to train in the jump-jet circuit, he would have locked that down. She would've been subjected to Tender Training for an entire Sun Cycle; thirty days of torment, if her deception had been revealed.

But that hadn't happened. Good thing too. The jump-jet circuit was her only bid for freedom.

She'd invested countless hours in perfecting her skill in the jump-jet. Her position in the *Gambit* race circuit had come at great cost and, as silly as it sounded, if she won, if she happened to win the entire circuit, she would have the means for escape. At least, that was the plan. Win the jump-jet circuit, use the winnings to purchase transport, evacuate the Earth WOR into the ship, and disappear.

Her plan had holes. Huge gaping holes, but it was the only plan she had. So far, it seemed to be working. Except for Gregor's cryptic comments over lunch.

But if he knew . . . if he suspected, wouldn't he have punished her by now? He'd done worse for far less. Gah! She didn't have the mental energy to waste on what ifs!

And it's not like she'd avoided Tender Training. Gregor had sentenced her to an hour at the end of the braklav with High Tender Marcus. Not for anything to do with jump-jets, but because she'd used a familiar address for her good friend, Carek.

Carek swam over to where she floated. "We'll be having visitors."

Elise half heard what he said. "I closed down the WOR-skill diagrams."

No one could see what she worked on. It was a closely guarded secret, known only to her, Carek, and her closest friends.

She moved over to the linking diagram. The initial three-dimensional representation had been comprised of ten separate diagrams; a mess concocted by the Tenders who sensed the fabric of the WOR-skill but failed to comprehend the true scope of it. She had condensed those down to four key nodes. She had then added a secondary layer of complexity.

The construct now extended into two additional dimensions. The fourth and fifth dimensions extended off the four nodes along several spokes radiating from each node point.

"Aren't you curious who's joining us?" His brows lifted.

"High Tender Marcus and Master Varlen visit often enough." Elise shrugged.

"Yes, but they are bringing others."

Elise stopped her inspection of the linking project. Her voice hitched. "What do you mean others?'

"Evidently, the Emperor spoke to Lord vlor'Vardhal."

Her jaw dropped. "Gregor listened?"

She barely contained her excitement as several shapes swam toward them through the purple soup. During that oddball lunch, where Gregor hinted at forbidden things, she'd made a request. It was something she required for her work on the linking project, and she'd made a valid case, but Gregor rarely took her recommendations seriously. He and the High Tender thought they knew everything about the WOR-skill and training WOR, when the truth was far different. Still, the fact he'd listened made her breath hitch.

Off in the distance, three men towed six shapes clad in red down from the surface of the purple sea. She couldn't make out who they brought, but smiled nonetheless. Gregor had listened.

Master Varlen arrived first. She looked into the faces of the two women he brought with him and her hopes fell. Not Fifth Rank WOR. With nearly a thousand WOR taken from Earth, she didn't recognize them. Both girls tried to smile in greeting, but the breathing apparatus clutched between their teeth frustrated their efforts.

The small breathing tube wasn't required. She didn't have one, but visitors to the soup tended to find the act of breathing in the purple liquid terrifying. She remembered her first experience. Her breathing tube had fallen out accidentally and Carek had been forced to restrain her as she tried to shoot to the surface over eighty feet above. For several long minutes, she'd thought she would drown, until he forced her to take in a breath.

Now she didn't think twice about breathing in the soothing liquid. The women kept one hand clutched to the small cylinder at their mouths, and one held in Master Varlen's hand. Their unease and fear paraded across their features as their gazes darted about, looking far overhead to the surface of the purple sea and across what seemed a nearly endless expanse. The am-net soup, a purple fluid which nourished the nodes of the am-net, was more than expansive. Larger than a pond, or a fair-sized lake, a sea was a more apt description.

Elise smiled at the girls, trying to reassure them, despite her frustration that they were not what she needed. She told Gregor lower ranked WOR wouldn't work.

Her frustration, however, turned to delight as High Tender Marcus swam up. He towed Paula behind him, her expression a mess of barely contained panic. Elise imagined the conversation as the High Tender instructed Paula about the soup.

Although Paula tended to keep to herself, like Elise, she shared the unenviable position of being High Tender Marcus's select WOR. He trained only five of the women, while all the other Tenders were responsible for ten or twenty. She and Paula had a unique understanding of what it meant to disobey that man.

Paula took long ragged pulls off the breathing tube. Her wide, dilated eyes broadcasted her fear. She glanced at Elise and took a shuddering breath. When High Tender Marcus released her, he sent Paula into a spin. The poor girl flailed wildly. The High Tender shook his head, disapproval heavy in his gaze. Paula's eyebrows shot up as her face drained of color.

The woman holding his other hand brought a smile to Elise's face. Chandra peeked over his shoulder and waved. When the High Tender released her, she swam to Paula and settled Paula's thrashing.

The final two arrivals were also well known to Elise. Aomi and Alice held hands with High Tender Anders vlor'Alturis. He trained Alice and had a reputation nearly as harsh as High Tender Marcus. Green sparkled from the man's eyes. The color was nearly twin to Carek's, yet where her friend's eyes held warmth, this man's eyes radiated a cold brittleness.

He stopped and hovered a short distance away. High Tender Anders vlor'Alturis did not release her friends.

"Good day, s'Lissa," High Tender Marcus said, approaching with shallow scooping motions of his hands.

She replied obediently, "Good day."

"I just had a very interesting visit from the Emperor and an odd request." He lifted his brow and continued, "He demanded I bring you four of my Fifth Rank WOR."

"Yes, High Tender."

"Do you care to explain?"

She bowed her head. "Have those women completed their Binding Rites?" She pointed to the women of lower rank.

"They have. Why?"

"I'm not sure, but it might be important."

Irritation flickered behind his eyes.

"Let me explain."

"Yes, please."

"If the WOR could listen in, I can bring everyone up to speed."

Communication within the am-net was complicated. Sound didn't broadcast through the soup, primarily because humans couldn't vocalize without vibrations of air across vocal chords. A direct connection between the immersion suits had to be established, otherwise there was no way to speak to another. Her suit linked to Carek's and the High Tender's, but no one else.

"No."

His abrupt one word response wasn't unexpected, but he was bound to do as Gregor commanded. That didn't mean she wouldn't have to jump through his hoops.

"You convinced the Emperor, now you must convince me. They will wait." He glanced at Carek. "Mr. Tusel, supervise the WOR while the Lady Malita explains all this to me."

"Yes, my lord." Carek headed toward the WOR.

"Please have Lord vlor'Alturis join me as well as Master Varlen."

"Yes, my lord," Carek repeated.

After a brief shuffling of bodies, Elise found herself surrounded by the three men. Carek drifted to the side to chaperone the six WOR while Elise began her explanation.

After an hour, Lord vlor'Alturis surprised her with the first interruption. "Lord vlor'Vardhal, I see a problem." He pointed to one of the spokes she had leading off the first node into subspace.

The High Tender moved closer and traced the line of Lord vlor'Alturis's finger. He rubbed his chin.

"Yes, I see," the High Tender murmured.

"He's not going to like this." High Tender vlor'Alturis crossed his arms.

"No, he will not." High Tender Marcus turned to her. "S'Lissa, you asked about Binding. Why is that?"

"I assume it's a form of linking." She nodded to the area which had caught High Tender vlor'Alturis's eye. "That's the key structure to linking

WOR together, or at least the keystone. I need to know how the Binding Rite might affect that piece to the linking sequence."

"Your thoughts?" High Tender vlor'Alturis pinched his brow. His gaze darted back and forth between the dimensional construct and Elise.

She took in a deep drag of purple fluid and let it billow back out. "I'm not certain, but if that portion of a WOR's mind, the subspace projection of it, is already linked, I don't believe it's possible to form another connection."

Both men turned to gaze darkly at each other. Their brows twitched furiously, leading her to believe they spoke on a communications channel separate from hers.

High Tender Marcus grunted. "Well, then it's good we brought Second Rank WOR who are bound. Answer this question first and foremost, s'Lissa. Is this clear?"

"Yes, High Tender, but it would be better to try an initial linking circle first with the other Fifth Rank WOR. Then, I can try to pull them in."

"What's a linking circle?" High Tender vlor'Alturis asked.

"Let me show you." Elise brought them back to the main body of the linking project.

After another hour, she had satisfied the questions of both High Tenders.

"This is not complete," she added, clarifying. "I see several potential errors, and a few holes where I'm just at a loss as to what to do next, but I feel there's a solution which will allow you to link together the abilities of individual WOR."

High Tender Marcus nodded. "This is far better than what we came up with. Good work, s'Lissa."

Her heart about stopped. High Tender Marcus had never praised any of her work before. "Go ahead and keep working on this. Sometimes the best way to discover what you don't know is to try what you do. Find where it falls apart, and patch the holes."

"Yes, High Tender Marcus."

He drifted off and spoke to Carek.

Sometime over the past two hours, Alice and Chandra had removed their breathing tubes. Paula had too, but from the pinched corners of her eyes and her pale complexion, her terror remained. Aomi still had hers in place. She swam peacefully, taking in the purple soup with open fascination. With a shrug, Aomi pulled the tube from her mouth, hesitated for a second, and then breathed in deeply. Her body arched for a second, but then she relaxed. A large smile filled her face.

Carek adjusted the communications channels and Elise could finally hear the other girls. She had yet to figure out how the immersion suit linking worked.

"Hi!"

Aomi turned and waved. "This is so cool."

Alice's blue eyes burned brightly. Her gaze took in the entire linking project. "Amazing."

Paula looked like she was going to be sick.

Chandra towed Paula forward. "This is where you've been spending all your time? I'm so jealous. This is awesome."

Her friends seemed much more impressed by the purple soup than Elise had been. It was awe inspiring, but Elise had been brought here and shown things her friends had not. Carek brought her first, showing her his people, and revealed their beauty and humanity through his eyes. He'd then shown the destruction wrought by the S'Lorek, an enemy which had already taken two worlds and several colony fleets. Gregor had brought her to the soup as well. His was the vision of an emperor and of his solemn oath to do whatever it took to safeguard humanity. Carek showed her the lives of individuals, whereas Gregor's view was that of a leader set an impossible task.

Two men. Two completely different views.

She was here to accomplish the impossible—find a way to link the power of the WOR and turn them into a weapon strong enough to defeat the aggression of the S'Lorek.

This was a rare outing for her friends. Perhaps their very first time free of confinement. They hadn't been allowed the luxury offered Elise, trips off the Confinement Deck, and now the Fifth Rank Deck. Nor had any of them forayed off on their own, a mini-escape like Elise. She'd escaped the Confinement Deck, although *escape* might be too grand of a term. Her excursions brought her to the flight deck, allowed her to make friends with some of the Vendel, and had set her head in a tailspin over what her priorities should be, and where to focus her efforts.

To save Earth, she would have to save the Vendel. She would have to save those responsible for killing billions, and she still hadn't reconciled what that meant.

All of her efforts, whether with the linking project or her bid for escape from the Vendel were nothing more than a race against time; a battle she was losing.

High Tender Marcus brought the Second Rank WOR over and made introductions. He explained to the WOR what was expected, then turned over the details to Elise.

The men hung in the background and watched as she explained. Only Carek came forward to join the group. He hovered on the opposite side of the diagrams and interjected only when they had disagreements over the set of force vectors and lines.

Aomi traced out the lines with her fingers and hummed quietly to herself.

Chandra shook her head and raised a hand for Elise to stop. "Start from here again." She pointed to the first sub-space divergence. "Something's not right."

Paula remained silent, but Elise watched Paula scan the diagrams. She kept coming back to the area which had caught the High Tenders' attention. Her mouth gaped, as if she saw something, but then the breathing tube fell out of her mouth. She thrashed and clutched at her throat. Her head snapped back, all her attention focused on the surface far above and the air which she didn't need.

Carek dove through the purple soup and clamped his legs around Paula before she could bolt to the surface. She kicked and hit him, struggling to find the surface and air above. As he had done for Elise, he held Paula in an iron grip. Just before Paula seemed to pass out, she gasped and the purple liquid streamed down her throat. She gagged and coughed. A minute later, her eyes widened when she realized she was not dead.

Elise laughed.

Paula glared at her.

"Sorry."

"You can release me." Paula pushed against Carek's chest. "I'm okay."

"Are you sure?" Carek gave her a long appraising look.

"Yes."

"If you surface too fast, it can be dangerous."

"Then, thank you . . . I suppose." She glanced down. "You can release me. I'm fine now."

"Everything ok?" High Tender Marcus approached as Carek disentangled himself from Paula.

Paula bowed her head. "Yes, High Tender Marcus, I am fine."

"Good." He jerked his chin toward the soup. "Now stop fooling around and get started. Your time here is limited."

In the next hour, they made little progress. The High Tenders escorted them back to the Fifth Deck without a word, but when they entered the

Fifth Deck Lounge, High Tender Marcus pulled her to the side while her friends headed to the dining facility.

"S'Lissa," High Tender Marcus said.

"Yes?"

"You may choose to eat first or accept your Tender Training. You may prefer an empty stomach."

She had forgotten about Gregor's punishment. He'd caught her speaking in a familiar manner with Carek when he'd collected her for lunch. As her stomach lurched, she accepted her fate.

"Yes, High Tender. If it pleases you, I would choose now."

"Very well." He gestured down the hall leading to her suite of rooms. "I believe the bar and shackles remain?"

Elise cast her gaze to the floor and walked to her rooms. By the time the door swished open, she was protectively encased in darkness. Her sisters had arrived.

Shriek was in control now.

Whimper waited in the wings.

Oddly, Malice crawled out to investigate.

While the High Tender inflicted horror after horror, Elise separated her consciousness from what was happening to her body.

The next hour passed in a blur as WOR-skill diagrams bombarded her in the dark.

The answer was right there, waiting to be discovered. Her screams of frustration blended in nicely with Shriek's howls.

Elise woke the next day sore and tired, drained from another round of Tender Training. At least it had only been for an hour and only for one day.

The High Tender had spent every last second of the Tender Training session working over her body with the braklav. Shriek howled and screamed until their throat burned. Raw and sore, the pain still lingered.

Quite out of character, Malice sat through the entire session. She remained silent and observed while the High Tender set their skin on fire, amongst other—more horrible—things.

Elise was just thankful she no longer had to endure those sessions.

When it was done, Shriek crawled into the darkness and Elise returned to the light.

Malice snickered and disappeared.

Whimper cried.

What she hadn't expected upon awakening was to see Gregor sitting in the corner of her room. He had pulled in a chair and sat, arms crossed, watching her sleep. What bothered her wasn't that he watched her sleep, but that she couldn't feel his presence.

His lips crooked up into his characteristic smirk when he realized she was awake. "Good morning, opés."

Elise smoothed down her hair and sat in bed. The shoulder of her sleeping gown slipped down her arm and she tugged it back into place. "Good morning, Gregor," she said hesitantly.

"How do you feel?" Gregor leaned back and gazed at her expectantly.

How the do you think I feel after a session with the High Tender?

"Sore, but otherwise fine. Thank you for asking." She chose her words carefully and then made sure to add his given name. It was required. "Gregor."

He gave a dismissive wave. Oh yes, he understood.

She regarded him in silence. Her mind furiously worked to figure out what he wanted. What he was doing in her sleeping quarters, and how long had he been watching.

Elise pushed back the covers. "Is there something you wanted, Gregor?"

"No," he said, remaining mysterious. "High Tender Marcus notified me of the progress you made with the other WOR."

He shifted to her bed, leaning over her to press his lips lightly against her temple. That contact awakened the bond between them.

"Yes, Gregor."

She placed trembling hands on his chest, hating how he drew yet repulsed her simultaneously. Desire bloomed in her mind and she fantasized about drowning under an onslaught of his kisses. Then her revulsion kicked in. Her stomach clenched and she was left lightheaded and off-balanced by the competing emotions.

"Thank you for trusting my opinion. It meant a lot that you spoke to High Tender Marcus."

"I didn't do it for you, opés. You and *Carek* . . ." He slurred the name. "The two of you have been making steady, although slow, progress. I need results, opés. Spending so much time with that man hasn't been such a good idea. You made a mistake with him."

"I forgot myself."

The imperial tattoo danced on his brow. The swirling lines moved under his skin with a life of their own.

Vendel men had three names. A given name used only by a select few: their mothers, wives, and lovers. A family name used by everyone else. And a last name. She should have used Carek's last name, but had slipped and used his family name where Gregor had overheard. That mistake had been paid with the agony of Tender Training.

"Remember who you belong to, opés."

"Gregor, I'm sorry. I allowed myself to get too familiar with Mr. Tusel. It won't happen again."

"No. It won't."

Elise leaned against Gregor and closed her eyes.

"You feel comfortable with Mr. Tusel, don't you?"

There was no point in lying. He would drag the truth out of her one way or another. "When I'm with you, Gregor, I'm forever on edge. I never know what's coming next. Will it be a soft caress? An encouraging nod? Or something worse? I don't know if it's the stick or the carrot with you. We're constantly at odds."

"That is your choice, Elise. How many times must I tell you that you chose your path?"

That might be true, but the path he wanted her to choose was one of complete capitulation. She would never be able to give him that. "You know that's not true," she said.

"And you're so certain it's not?" He spun her around, forcing her to look at him. "Fighting me and my goals will always put us at odds. You can be happy here. I wish you would embrace this new life. Work with me, instead of against me."

"Well, that's just the thing, Gregor. You don't make that easy."

His brows shot up and the tattoo danced.

"Let me explain," she began. "With Mr. Tusel, I could focus on work. He left me alone to think, never demanded, never punished. I felt safe around him because I knew he would never hurt me."

Gregor winced.

She continued, rushing to finish what she wanted to say before he made her stop. "I let my guard down with Mr. Tusel because he reminded me of Professor McCabe. All I had to do was focus on the problem and find a solution. I didn't have to fear what would happen if I didn't. I forgot myself and I am sorry."

"You don't feel safe around me, do you?" Gregor looked up and closed his eyes.

"Never, and why should I? Look what you've done to me."

"I only did what was necessary."

"To you, perhaps, but to me you've been nothing but brutal. I'm tense around you. Scared about what will happen next. I'm wary of your praise, confused with how this bond between us makes me feel, and so much more. I let down my guard with Mr. Tusel because he's everything you're not. If you ask, I won't work with him anymore."

"I wouldn't need to ask, opés. Why don't you seem to understand that?"

"I understand it explicitly. And that's my point. You've taken my free will, and yet are surprised when I don't embrace that." She shook her head.

"Your choices are limited, opés. As are mine. You understand what's at stake. I can't afford to have you going off doing whatever you want. I have the entirety of the human race to save."

"You can't stop me from working with Mr. Tusel."

"I can and I will."

A sigh of frustration escaped her lips. "Mr. Tusel understands the linking project. Gregor, he *understands* it, on a level the Tenders don't grasp. Mr. Tusel challenges me, questions me, and forces me to defend my decisions. That's stimulating and we're making progress. We're collaborating and working together. I'm not working out of fear. Please, don't take that from me."

"Mr. Tusel is not for you."

"I never said he was, and that's not what's going on at all."

She bit her upper lip, frustrated by Gregor's jealousy. And surprised by it. Although, she shouldn't be. She belonged to him. The bond between them grew every day, and if that weren't enough, she was listed amongst his personal inventory. He owned every bit of her.

"Gregor, if you *told* me to stop working with Mr. Tusel, I would have no choice but to stop. I know who owns me. But, even if you *asked* me not to work with him, I would still refuse. I'd refuse because it's the wrong thing to do. You need our collaboration because it's working. We're making progress, and you don't have time to interfere with that."

"You feel that strongly about it?"

"You know I'm telling the truth. My mistake was in forgetting my place. It just felt so normal. Like I said, Carek reminds me of my college professor. I welcomed the interaction, because it allowed me to escape the reality of my situation. I need that mental break to do what you need me to do. Does that make sense?"

His lips pressed into a thin line. Silence hung between them, full of unspoken words.

She pressed her forehead against his. "See, this is what I'm talking about. I don't know what will happen next. Will I be punished for telling the truth? Or will you reward me for my honesty? You make me crazy and that only feeds my fear."

"You shouldn't fear me."

"Then tell me what you want! I'll do whatever it takes to please you, but I can't read your mind."

Tender Training was designed to instill a compulsive desire to please. She felt the stirrings in her gut, even if she had found a way to defeat Tender Training with the birth of her sisters.

Gregor's eyes lifted. He stared into her eyes and she dared not look away from the intensity swirling in those silvery depths. For the first time, his gaze held no cruelty. Resignation filled them instead.

"Come, opés, I have something I wish you to see. Something I need an opinion on."

To her surprise, he dragged her off the Fifth Deck to Command and Control. There, he guided her into a conference room full of senior bridge officers. She glanced around at the tan and gray jumpsuits and the astonishing numbers of silver stars decorating the collars of the fifteen men present. They stood when Gregor entered.

He strode to the end of a long table and pulled out the chair. He placed Elise in the chair and the men retook their seats. Gregor stood behind her and did not introduce her to the men. Although, the emperor's WOR needed no introduction.

"Commander Eldern, bring up those images for the Lady Malita."

Commander Eldern tapped instructions into a recessed gel-pad in front of him. The far wall dissolved and a starfield appeared. The view zoomed and Elise recognized a Vendel Colony fleet. Twenty massive ships, arrayed in a loose formation, hung in a rich asteroid belt.

Commander Eldern fiddled with the displays. A singular black moonlet, enormous in size, suddenly blinked into being on top of the fleet. Oblong, irregular in shape, with multiple bulbous projections protruding from an uneven surface, it filled the view. There was no real reference to its size, except it had a sense of being massive and self-aware.

Something which kicked her heart into overtime.

A red light shot out from a circular hole at the tip of the thing's nose. It scanned the ships directly in front of it. As the beam passed over the orbital mining rigs, the outer metal hulls vaporized. Gases spewed into space and the ships imploded.

The lumpy moonlet, a creature which reminded her of a potato, for that's what it looked like, rotated slowly along its axis picking off ship after ship with that lethal red beam.

The final image showed the creature's nose? Mouth? Whatever it was aimed directly at whoever had recorded this image. The thing lined itself up. A red beam of energy surged forth. The screen went dark.

Nervous coughs punctuated the silence of the room. The shuffling of feet, and the readjustment of the men in their seats, added to the uneasy quiet. The man next to her gagged.

"First impressions, opés," Gregor commanded.

Elise jumped at the snap in Gregor's voice. First impressions of what? Horror, devastation, death, destruction? What did he want?

"Give me your first impression." Gregor's voice deepened into a guttural growl.

"I don't know what it is. It seemed curious. Excited. Ravenous."

Commander Eldern asked, "Why do you call that ship an it?"

Why? She didn't know. However, now that she thought about it, she was certain that thing was an it, not a they, or a them, or a ship at all. It was a conscious, self-aware, entity.

"I don't know."

"I demand an answer, opés," Gregor pressed.

"Can you replay the video?" she asked.

"Not until you answer the question." Gregor continued to badger her for a response.

She stood and turned to confront Gregor. "I don't know." She stared at him and put her hands on her hips. "How can I explain what I don't know? It feels alive to me."

"Why do you think you feel this way?"

"It's a gut feeling." She shrugged her shoulders. "How do I explain a gut feeling?"

"You said it was curious. Why?"

She shrugged again. "I don't know, maybe because of the way it surveyed the C-fleet."

A voice from the end of the table laughed. "It destroyed the entire fleet. Survey implies it assessed and acted upon a choice."

"But it did. Didn't you see how it ignored the processing plants?"

"It did not."

"Replay it again. It skipped right over the rocks, other moons, and the processing plants. Why attack the fleet? There were hundreds of asteroids in that system, and yet it only turned its eye to the Vendel ships. It must have found something interesting in the ships and not in the asteroids. If you were wandering around in a field and saw a bunch of ants crawling in the dirt, would you stop to look at the rocks or would you look at the ants?" She waved her hand in the air as she tried to explain something she didn't understand herself. "I don't know why, but it seemed curious."

"Thank you, opés, you may leave," Gregor's voice commanded her attention.

"Leave?"

He responded with a jerk of his chin. Her dismissal was clear. "High Tender Marcus waits for you in the am-net Tank. Try not to keep him waiting. Your contingent of WOR will be present. I expect positive results by the end of the day."

Elise's jaw nearly unhinged.

Gregor's eyes flicked toward the door.

She needed no further encouragement to leave.

CHAPTER TWO_

Gambit, Day 277

The High Tender met Elise outside the am-net. He gave a curt nod, saw to it she was dressed properly in her immersion suit, then delivered her to Carek's node deep within the purple sea. He left without a word. The rest of her day involved purple glowing soup and the company of her friends. Carek hovered in the background, watching the women work.

Paula hung back from the rest, lost in her own world.

Elise floated over. "Are you all right? I hope we aren't making you feel unwelcome."

Paula stared at the first node subspace connections. She had been sitting quietly all day, making changes to this small part of the construct.

"I'm jealous of you, and then again, very glad not to be you."

Elise paused, uncertain of how to respond.

"You've been allowed off the Fifth Deck and have been all over the ship. It's not fair. We've been trapped since we arrived, while you've gotten out and have seen the people."

Elise paused and then said, "You think I've been given special favors?"

"Yes." She sighed and shook her head. "I mean no, but sometimes I'm jealous of the freedom you've had. It's wrong, and I know this. I know what you've been through. The Emperor is the worst of them all, worse than even mine."

Paula stared off into the soup. "You and I share High Tender Marcus. They don't know what he's done to us. Tender Training was hard for all the girls, but for you and me? We suffered under a sadist's hands. I know what it was like for you. What you endured. They only think they do."

Elise's stomach cramped with the remembered pain. Tender Training had destroyed her, and fractured her mind. She was now only one of five distinct personalities. Crazy? She didn't feel crazy, but neither did she share the presence of her silent sisters. That secret was one she held very close to her heart.

Paula's breathing hitched. "How did you survive? I only had four days of Tender Training, you've had so much more."

Elise didn't answer. There was no response. She carried five different people in her head as a result of Tender Training. Her little brigade. Her sisters in war. The only thing that kept her sane and gave her strength to face each day was the presence of her sisters. How could she explain what happened to her mind and not sound insane?

Paula, in an unfortunate turn of events, had been the reason all of the Fifth Rank WOR had received that last bout of Tender Training. They'd received only a few days, whereas Elise had suffered multiple sessions a day for a cycle of ten days.

She placed a hand on Paula's shoulder. "It was easy to forget what they did to us. When Gregor touches me or kisses me, I'm very confused. You shouldn't be ashamed of how you feel."

"You feel it too? I thought I was sick. I hate my master, but crave his touch. It's a yearning deep inside of me that I can't control. How can that be? How can I want him when I hate him? Are we freaks, or is it something they did to us?"

"I've had that reaction to Gregor from the very beginning. It's an effect of the bond, but it's far more complicated than that. Have you ever heard of the prisoner paradox?"

"Yes. It's when the prisoner begins to identify with the guards. The victim will sabotage their rescue trying to defend the kidnappers. They find empathy with their tormentors."

"Exactly! When I'm here, I hate Gregor. When I'm with him, I can't get enough of him. Saying it out loud makes me sound crazy."

Paula placed her hand on Elise's. "I would have done anything for my master. Because of me everyone suffered. I don't understand why you don't hate me for what it cost you. High Tender Marcus is a brutal man. I can't begin to comprehend what he did to you, but I know what he did to me." She paused.

"No one blames you for revealing the code."

Paula sniffed and said nothing. Her attention focused back on the diagram and she shifted the conversation mid-stream. "They've made a mistake with the Binding Rite." Paula's finger poked the diagram. "See here?" She reached out and nudged a three-dimensional spiraled mass of twisted lines to spinning. "If they try linking any of their bound WOR, it'll kill them."

"Yes." Elise had been over this portion several times. The outcome was always the same.

"The link will bridge the fifth and sixth dimensions. The problem is in handling that much force. The backlash will kill any woman who can't channel her force vectors around this construct."

The construct Paula pointed to was the link formed by Binding.

"I've mentioned my concerns. Gregor wants to enhance the combined power of WOR to destroy this creature."

"What creature?" Paula twirled her little spiral of glowing lines, pushing vectors around with her finger.

"Gregor brought me to Command and Control and made me watch the S'Lorek destroy another Colony Fleet. That's what they call the enemy. He then asked what I thought. Really vague. I told him the first thing that came to mind. It was curious."

"Really?" Alice joined in the conversation. She had come up behind Elise and Paula while they were talking.

Elise twisted around to greet her friend. "Yes. He had that look in his eyes. I think it was another weird test of his."

"I wish we all could see this thing. Maybe we could figure out how to get rid of it, or kill it." Alice gestured vaguely in the air. "You know . . . first know your enemy. We're building something we barely understand to fight an enemy they refuse to show us. It doesn't make any sense."

Aomi floated into view, tugging Carek by his hand. "Sorry, late to the conversation, but we couldn't help but overhear. Why do we have to kill it?" Aomi pulled on the fabric of the immersion suit. They were all linked through the suits and could hear any conversation. "What if we could talk to it? Negotiate with it?"

Chandra bobbed over and crossed her legs into lotus position. "It kills, Aomi." She rolled her eyes and shook her head. "If it wanted to talk, it would've tried."

Alice pulled her lower lip between her teeth. She scratched at her head.

"You know, she may have a point. I used to belong to this alien simulation group. Our project was to create a creature that evolved in deep space. There were tons of weird entries. People got creative, but sentient planets and moonlets were some of the main entries."

"You believe it's sentient?" Carek's question settled over them all.

"I do." Elise shivered with unease.

Alice continued, "If we could think to make it a contest back on Earth, why couldn't it really be out there?"

Paula turned to Carek. "Mr. Tusel, is there any way we can take a look at this thing?"

He pursed his lips. "I don't know."

"Please," Elise begged. He rarely denied her requests.

"I'll need to see if I can get permission to show it to you."

Elise eyed him and arched her brow. "Can you just show it to them and skip asking permission? Blame it on me. We can ask for forgiveness later if we get in trouble."

Carek glanced at each of the women. "You're supposed to be working. So far, you haven't managed to link two of you together. I don't think side projects are such a good idea."

Chandra turned.

Elise wasn't sure how she managed it, as she made no obvious movement and maintained her lotus pose.

"Mr. Tusel, please?" She flashed him a smile. "How long could it possibly take to view a little clip of this creature? We'll keep working. Promise!"

He folded under their silent pressure. "I'll try, but you have to promise to keep working."

Paula tugged on Elise's arm. Elise glanced down and Paula put a finger to her lips for silence. She jerked her eyes toward Carek and Elise understood. They were linked and he could hear. Paula traced a finger down the center of her rotating spiral. It began to spin. She pulled four of the vector forces and crossed them into a new dimensional space. Elise gasped at the result.

One by one, so as not to draw Carek's suspicions, Paula motioned the women over. Silence settled and they exchanged glances of wonder.

Malice purred.

Alex popped her head out of the dark and yelled, *Eureka!* She disappeared again, but Elise could feel her silent sister working. It made her head itch.

"Hey, you're supposed to be working, not staring," Carek scolded.

Paula erased the last change she had made, while Alice and Chandra hid all evidence of it from Carek.

He cocked his head to the side. "What's up?"

Elise said, "I think we can try a few scenarios after lunch." Later, they had so much more to try.

"I got access to the feed." Carek beamed with delight.

Carek had them close their eyes and he played the feed of the Colony Fleet's devastation. The four women then entered into discussion about whether it was a creature or little green men. Each of them had a sense it was a single creature, but Aomi took the little green men side and began to make her case, just to argue.

Elise left the girls to their discussion. She floated a short distance away and called up an image of the Wheel WOR-skills. The five-spoked wheel rotated slowly and she examined some of her underlying assumptions.

A few minutes later, Carek tapped her shoulder. "They're really getting into it. Aomi can be quite persuasive. Chandra is giving her a run for her money, though. She's a firecracker."

"Chandra or Aomi?"

"Chandra."

"You should really use our proper names, Mr. Tusel," she said.

Carek flinched. "As you wish, Lady Malita." His brows drew down and she could see anger brewing in his green eyes. "May I ask why?"

"Gregor heard me call you Carek when we were getting out of the tank. I spent time with High Tender Marcus in Tender Training. This morning, Gregor came close to forbidding me from working with you. He's possessive, and when he heard me use your name it set him off. He needs this linking project to work. Otherwise, I wouldn't be here right now. It's too easy to be friends, and we need to remember what we really are. You need to remember what I am."

"This from the Emperor's slave who's flying in the jump-jet semi-finals tomorrow. Are you insane?"

"It's in disguise. No one is going to ask me to remove my veil."

"You're playing with fire. If Emperor Malita ever finds out . . ."

She squeezed his arm. "That isn't going to happen."

Carek changed the subject. "Why do you keep bringing up the Wheel skills?" He waved at the rotating mass.

She stared at the figures and sighed. "I'm almost finished correcting them."

"Why do you set it to spinning? It makes my eyes hurt."

"It seems like the right thing to do." She then suddenly realized why. "Carek, go help the girls, I'll be along in a minute."

"I thought we were supposed to use formal names, Lady Malita."

Elise cocked her head and ignored him.

Do you see it? She put the question out to her sisters.

The brigade in her mind sat down and stared at the rotating diagram. Alex crawled out and sat beside Whimper.

Elise spun the wheel faster. Shriek added more speed until the wheel blurred. Whimper rotated it around the vertical axis and it looked like a crazy top. Elise closed her eyes and nudged the vectors with her thoughts. The wheel flashed and a kaleidoscope of color streamed out of it. The Tenderstat came to mind, and Elise's mind exploded with sudden clarity.

Malice clapped.

Shriek and Whimper hugged each other.

Alex looked at her sisters. *Turn it off, before they notice. I have it. I have you.*

Yes, sister. Elise tucked her sisters away and closed the Wheel WOR-skill simulation. She looked up and across the short expanse of purple liquid to the four women arguing about aliens. Carek seemed to be caught right up in the middle of the argument.

It was time to work.

Elise swam over to them. "Enough about aliens. I think we can make this work, but is anyone up for lunch? I'm starving."

They responded with vigorous nods and vigorous agreement. Carek took his school of scarlet fish through the am-net sea. A single man in white followed by five incredibly powerful women. When they reached the ramp, Elise was the last to leave the soup. She made sure Carek had jumped off the platform and then dragged her hand through the liquid lapping at her knees. Eyes closed, she sent out feelers for her very special army, an infiltration of viruses she'd planted several sun cycles ago.

Bobo, be ready.

Malice sang. *Make them pay. Make them hurt.*

CHAPTER THREE_

Gambit, Day 278

ELISE AND HER FRIENDS PLANNED TO ATTEMPT THEIR FIRST LINK. ALICE, Chandra, Aomi and Paula floated around Elise as they rehearsed one last time.

"I'll take the keystone position," Elise said. "Alice, you take the conduit. The rest of you know what to do?"

Aomi nodded. "We form the construct around your keystone."

"Right, Alice will channel your power." She would bridge the gap. If she failed, it all fell apart. The Keystone position demanded the utmost control and drained strength at a phenomenal rate.

Butterflies danced in the pit of her stomach. She prayed for strength as she opened herself up to the WOR-skill and folded the first lines of force.

A looming presence filled her mind. The feeling drew near until the all too familiar sensation of Gregor's hand on her shoulder jolted her from her task. She stiffened but did not otherwise stop the exercise or acknowledge his arrival. He would have to understand her need to focus.

A vortex of shimmering light filled her vision. The constructs Aomi, Chandra, and Paula created twisted around her scaffolding. Forces pulled and tugged on the fabric of space, until it bent to her will. Space unfolded, revealing the fifth and then sixth dimensions. She pushed ever so slightly, and a sub-dimensional pocket opened up within the cracks to form a bridge.

Elise threw Paula's construct around Alice's conduit and tied off the flow. Power surged within Alice, intensifying, but Alice handled the force. One by one, Elise pulled the abilities of each woman into the fractional dimensions of subspace. Power crackled around Alice in a vortex of twisted energy.

Ten WOR would eventually be needed to bind together into a central link. It would magnify their abilities astronomically. She held a tentative hope of linking all those circles through her as the central keystone. Alex promised her they could handle the massive link, but she hadn't yet shared that hope with her friends.

She paused to examine the structure formed so far. A strained expression filled Alice's face. All the energy had to channel through her position as the conduit. They had discussed this. The ten strongest WOR would act as keystones. The next ten strongest would manage the conduits. That left nearly eighty Fifth Rank WOR to take up the remaining positions.

Carek had devised several tests for the first linking attempt. Elise ran through each of them, surprised with how easily the power flowed.

She wanted to try a few other things, but Gregor's presence loomed just behind the circle. She signaled to Alice, who then released each woman out of the linked circle. The sub-dimensional crack folded and the supra-dimensions collapsed. The five women sat together and smiled. They understood what had happened.

Gregor's grip on her shoulder released and slipped away. "Opés, is this what it seems to be?"

Elise sighed. Gregor's voice reminded her this success was as much his as hers. "Yes, Gregor." She turned around and tried to make her eyes seem bright. "I just made a linked circle of five WOR."

Silver twinkled in his eyes. He grasped her shoulders and pulled her toward him, planting a solid kiss on her lips. "Wonderful, opés." He jerked his chin at Carek. "Mr. Tusel, return the WOR to the Fifth Deck and inform High Tender vlor'Vardhal of their success."

Carek bobbed his head and gestured for the women to follow him out. They went without fuss, except Alice who flashed a look of concern.

Gregor took Elise's hand in his and held her back. "I'm so very pleased, opés." He graced her with a genuine smile. He pulled her hand to his lips, kissed the back delicately, and turned smoldering eyes back to her face.

She found herself pulled close until she was trapped in his embrace. "We have much to celebrate, opés. Come. I shall treat you to dinner." He kicked with powerful strokes and they headed out of the am-net soup.

She wasn't surprised in the least when he headed to his personal quarters. Elise glanced at the time, worried about her other task for the night. There were still several hours before her jump-jet race. She might just make it.

Gregor opened a bottle of wine and filled two glasses. Elise cast dubious eyes on the liquor and wondered how much she would have to drink. She needed a clear head for her races. It would look suspicious if she didn't join him.

"Where's your enthusiasm?" He tilted his head and his eyes pinched with disappointment.

"I'm sorry, Gregor." Elise raised her glass. "To a successful trial of a linked WOR circle." She tried to sound cheerful and failed miserably.

He lifted his glass and sipped. "Let me show you something, opés. A surprise." He walked over to the large gray wall and pressed his palm to the gel-pad. A glittering starfield filled the screen.

It took Elise a moment before she realized the gray bleakness of WOR-space was gone. She walked to the wall and stretched out a hand.

"When did this happen?"

"We folded out of WOR-space a few hours ago. I wanted to share this with you, but I had no idea you were preparing for your first linking attempt."

"I'm sorry, Gregor. Was I supposed to have told you? I wasn't sure it would work. I wanted to wait until we had it figured out before showing you. Was that okay?" Dear God, was he going to punish her for not giving a head's up?

Gregor came over and removed her untouched wine. He put both their glasses on the table. "Opés, I'm not upset. Quite the opposite. This is wonderful news."

She stared into his eyes. Lost. Confused. Terrified. And something worse.

The bond sparked between them. That incessant flare of need, want, and unbearable desire for a man she should hate danced along her nerves.

Not only is my mind not my own, but my body betrays me as well.

Gregor's eyes crinkled at the edges as he watched her reactions.

Unwilling to face the truth of her body's reactions, she cast her gaze down.

Gregor brushed his lips across both her eyelids. He retrieved the wine glasses and stooped to meet her downcast gaze.

"Toast with me, Elise. Welcome to my home planet, Malbra. It's a world beyond beauty." He gave her an odd stare. "You've traveled a long way, opés. That alone is worthy of celebration."

A long way indeed. Twisted, warped and forever changed. A journey not at all measured by distance.

He gave her a serpentine smile and licked his lips. "This is where we toast."

She snapped out of her contemplation and mutely raised her glass.

"To the true treasure of Earth. I salute you. You have exceeded my expectations."

He tilted his glass and swallowed the entire contents. Deep-set eyes regarded her, reminding her of the predator that lurked beneath.

She inclined her head. "To your accomplishments, Gregor." She filled her mouth with the bitter wine and swallowed its robust flavor.

He walked to the far end of the room, leaving her to stare out at the stars. The clinking of glassware and other plates sounded from the bar.

"Opés, come here please."

Elise turned to see a small feast laid out on the low table. Gregor tossed two pillows to the floor, one on either side of the table.

"Dinner is served."

Her stomach sank. It had been a while since Gregor had found time for them to be alone. She wondered what he had planned, perhaps even more importantly, how long it would take. In a little less than three hours she needed to be on the flight deck if she were to make her race against Malikai.

"Is this to celebrate our arrival or something else?"

He gestured for her to sit.

This was entirely too civilized. *Too much like a date.*

"I don't know what any of it is, but it's smells good." She placed the napkin in her lap and glanced at the food he had spread out.

He laughed. "I had all my local favorites delivered. I'm eager to share them with you. To start, we have a cream soup made from a crustacean similar to the crabs of Earth. I think you'll like it." He pointed to the plates on the table and described the rest of the meal.

Every plate on the table was some form of seafood. She leaned forward and breathed in the enticing smells. A smile crept onto her face and her mouth watered.

His laughter softened his features and made it easier to be around him.

The tension in the room dissipated as they talked, not about WOR or his plans for her, but about the very mundane topic of the variety of seafood found on Malbra and the many favorite dishes he cherished. He relaxed and she found herself following his lead. They established an easy banter and settled into comfortable conversation.

"Tell me about Malbra."

"It is a water world with only a few large strings of archipelagos. There are no continents. Most of our cities float on the seas, half above and half below the water. It's a world full of beauty and the seas are a garden of life. I hope you learn to love it as much as I do."

"You sound homesick, Gregor."

He filled a plate with food and set it at her place. "I grew up here. It will always be home, but now my home is all of the empire. Most of the time I live on the *Gambit*, traveling from one crisis to the next. I try to get back to Malbra at least once a year. This happens to be perfect timing. The *Gambit* has arrived in time to complete its fleet finals in the jump-jet circuit above Malbra. Do you remember me talking to Mr. Tusel about the jump-jet circuit?"

"Vaguely, I'm not much of a sports fan."

"Well, jump-jet racing is perhaps one of the most popular sports in the empire, and a personal favorite of mine." His eyes glowed with excitement, and the features of his face softened, turned boyish and genuine. "Jump-jet racing has a huge following. Competitions are held on every planet, in every colony fleet, nearly every age bracket . . . it's infectious. For those who don't race, the betting circles are just as exciting."

Elise spooned soup into her mouth and nodded politely to his conversation. She closed her eyes and reveled in the taste. What she didn't want was to engage in a conversation about jump-jet racing. Not when she was due to race in less than a few hours. She needed to hurry this dinner along.

"This is fabulous, Gregor."

"That's my favorite."

"Thank you for sharing it with me." She wiped her chin.

"I thought you deserved a treat." He gripped her fingers gently. "I hope to share much more with you over the years. You will have a good life with me, opés. Despite your feelings, I will make you happy. I promise."

Elise looked down. Her heart and stomach tumbled together into the blackness of space. His promise made her want to retch, but did other things as well. It was almost as if he cared for her future. Like it was important she found happiness. Where was he going with this?

"I'm surprised you're not more interested in the jump-jet circuit. I'm quite a fan."

"So you keep telling me, but it's not like I have time to focus on Vendel sports, not with learning WOR-skill and working on the linking project. I barely have time to breathe." She kept her voice smooth and level. The lie came easily to her lips.

"Would you like to watch some of the races with me?"

"If you insist, then, of course."

The corners of his mouth twitched downward. "I'm inviting you to spend time with me, opés. Time away from WOR-skill training, away from the am-net tank, away from the High Tender. Just you and me, doing something fun. I want you to get to know me better, outside of WOR-skill training."

She looked up in alarm. *Get to know him better?* Was he insane?

He continued, "Consider it a gesture of good will from me to you. An effort to do something pleasant together for a change."

"I'm sorry, but how is that possible?"

His eyes narrowed.

"How can you think I would want to?" She placed her hands in her lap and wrung the fabric in frustration. "I'm supposed to be honest with you, Gregor. This is me being honest, but I don't see the two of us spending fun time together and getting chummy."

"Elise," he began with a long sigh, "we'll be together for a very long time." His fingers stroked the back of her hand. "I don't want to fight you. We shouldn't be in conflict. I want you by my side and working with me. I don't want you to fight me every step of the way. You need to accept this. Hate is a very demanding emotion. We should work towards something less antagonistic. Something we can both live with."

His smile infected her and she found herself responding, because the truth of it was that she admired Gregor. His choices came at great cost, to him, to her, and to the billions who died. But he had a responsibility to the greater good. She should accept that, but she couldn't forgive the things he'd done to her, the Tender Training he'd consigned her too, or any of the rest.

Silence descended between them while she picked at her food and thought about what he'd said. "How can you demand my enthusiasm when you hand out the harshest punishments? You can't expect me to forget everything you've done and just agree to hang out and have fun with you."

He drummed the tabletop with his fingers. When he looked up, his gaze was dark and brooding. "Like it or not you're stuck with me. This is permanent, but it doesn't have to be unpleasant for you. The Binding Rite occurs in four days, opés."

There it was, that sinking feeling. Her stomach and heart both hurtled through space and were now being sucked down a black hole.

"Four days?" A quaver filled her voice.

"Yes, opés. I've been relieved of my oath."

Her spoon clattered to the floor, dropped forgotten from her hand. It splashed cream soup on her dress. "But, Mr. Tusel would've told me."

"No, I removed him from the High Council."

"Why?"

"Conflict of interest." His eyes settled on hers, an ominous darkness brewed in their depths.

"You're wrong. Mr. Tusel is your strongest supporter."

"I have reason to believe otherwise."

Anger surged in her belly. "Don't worry about him. Your little slave is very much yours. I only bring it up because Mr. Tusel is aware of the Binding problem. He would have told me. And for the record, I asked him to vote against you. He said no. Told me he served the empire above anything else, despite the cost to me."

Gregor's brows drew together and the tattoo writhed. "Be careful with your tone, opés. Tell me about the Binding problem."

Elise wiped off the fallen spoon and placed it back on the table. "I found a problem with the linking project. The High Tenders spotted the flaw too, although they wouldn't say anything to me. It was Mr. Tusel who explained the changes the Binding Rite made to a WOR's mind. I figured out the rest."

Gregor took in a deep breath. It was enough.

Elise continued, her voice rising with every word. "What you call binding is the worst kind of rape I can imagine. You will take not just my body, but my mind as well. And yet you sit here with this stupid dinner," she waved at the delicious feast in front of them, "and go on about how we should get to know each other better. It's a lie."

"Opés . . ."

Her head shook with the fury stirring in her gut. "For your information, Mr. Tusel feels I need the restraint of Binding. You removed your fiercest supporter." She pushed back from the table. Her gaze rested on the food, she didn't have the strength to look at him. "The joke's on you, though. None of your bound WOR will survive a link. It'll kill them."

"Elise, Binding is not what you think."

She turned her back to him. Her entire body shook. Tears welled in her eyes and she brushed them away, angry at her weakness. Her fingers curled into fists and she spun around to confront him.

"You lied to me. You said I had nothing to fear from the Binding. It doesn't matter how I feel about you. Binding removes any free will I have left. I won't have a choice but to be your perfect little slave. Why even bother with gestures such as this? In four days none of it will matter. I'll be your perfect, obedient robot!"

"Look at me." The force of his words snapped her eyes to his. "I admit I held back the truth of the Binding, opés, but you're wrong about many things. First and foremost, I do care about you. It would please me greatly to have you come to me willingly."

She opened her mouth to speak, but he stopped her with a single raised finger.

"Despite what you think, the Binding Rite won't turn you into a mindless slave. That would be counterproductive. It will, however, be impossible for you to lie or disobey me ever again. It accomplishes at least that much. It will also allow me to take you places even Tender Training cannot. Despite all of that, it will be easier on both of us if you stopped fighting me."

"I'm not ready to roll over and play dead, Gregor."

"Obviously."

"If you've been released of your oath, why are we here eating dinner and not in your bedroom? Why not just take me? That's what you want, isn't it? Rape my body and pillage my mind. When I think you're not some horrible monster, you go and show me how evil you really are."

He leaned forward, and his voice lowered. "I'm no monster, Elise. I would prefer if you came to me of your own accord, it's why I asked, and why I wish to share personal pieces of myself with you. I choose to wait because it's my wish to give you as much time as you need to see what is right before your eyes."

"You don't want to know what I see when I look at you, and if that earns me the whipstick or more Tender Training, I don't care." She blew out her exasperation.

He'd been breathing down her neck for months, alluding to having sex, practically promising it with every breath. Now he wanted points for telling her he was willing to wait? She might be crazy, but he was certifiable.

"I chose to wait because I know about the issue with Binding and the Linking project. High Tender vlor'Vardhal mentioned the problem to me and we've discussed it at length. He asked me to wait, and I have faith in your abilities. I have faith in you, Elise, more than you realize. Besides, I've waited long enough to have you. A few more days won't kill me, and maybe, just maybe, you'll understand what I'm trying to tell you."

"I have no idea what you're trying to tell me. You speak in riddles, Gregor, and I'm tired of trying to figure anything out."

"Arguing with you is pointless, Elise, and a waste of both our times. Now, I mentioned I'm a huge jump-jet fan. There's a particular race tonight that I'm particularly interested in. It's been generating a lot of interest in the betting circles. I'd love to spend the evening with you, sharing one of my passions. You're not going anywhere and High Tender Marcus wants you to continue to work in the am-net. In the meantime, we have a moment to take a pause, and reevaluate where we are with each other."

He came to her and tugged her to his chest. Strong arms wrapped around her as he tucked her head under his chin. She didn't want to be in his embrace, but she didn't want him to let go either. None of it made sense. He was her enemy, and yet she found comfort within his embrace.

He kissed the crown of her head and whispered, "I want you to listen and remember what I have to say. I'm Emperor first and foremost. Anything, and I mean anything, I can do to save my people I will do. The Linking project is all I have to use as a weapon against the S'lorek. If Binding with you hampers progress on that project, I won't do it. You need to understand how desperate we are. We have no weapons. Nothing has worked. My subjects depend on me to overcome this threat. I will do anything, including the unconventional to save them."

He pulled back so he could stare into her eyes. "Even if it means going to Earth and destroying everything you held dear. Or turning you into my slave. I will do it without hesitation. Not all my choices are easy, opés, but I swear they're necessary. That is my burden to bear."

Her hands shook and she felt sick to her stomach.

"Elise?" Concern filled his voice.

"What do you expect me to say? What do you want from me, Gregor? I'm a dead woman walking. Why wait any longer?" She began to untie the laces of her gown.

He stopped her hands. "Stop, opés. Not tonight. We wait. I have faith in you, in your ideas. All of them. Let's give this a few more days to play out. I need you to succeed."

She looked up, her gaze searching the glittering depths of his silvery eyes. "I'm not doing it for you."

His chuckle caught her off-guard. "I know. Now, tonight, I have a race to watch. Do you remember Mr. Tusel and I discussing my bet? Can you guess who I placed the Imperial bet on?"

She shook her head, confused by the change in conversation. *Why does he care so much about a competition?* She found the strength to answer his question. "I would guess you went with the sure thing."

"Hm." His eyes glittered with interest. "You'll find out soon enough. It's not announced until the winner's circle. Trust me, the next few days will prove to be very exciting for jump-jet fans."

"I don't care about jump-jets."

"I do, which means you do too. I want to see who wins. The S'lorek is on its way to Malbra. This is the last time for my people to relax and have fun. War is upon us, Elise."

Firm hands held her shoulders and she felt his hot breath on her neck. His body vibrated with energy. He reached down and retied the laces of her gown. She grunted as he cinched them tight.

He glanced over to the half-eaten food. "I care a great deal about you. Perhaps, some day, you'll believe me. You have much to think about, and more to accomplish, over the next few days."

Her heart felt heavy, drained of strength. "I'm too tired, Gregor. I just want it all to end. I don't want to watch jump-jet races with you."

"Go to bed, opés. Try to think about what I've said and find a path that will bring you to me."

"Within a few days, it won't matter what I think. How will you know the difference between what I choose and what you choose for me?"

"I'll know." He turned to face the screen. His dismissal couldn't be ignored.

She exited his apartments and, as the door swished closed, she felt as if a noose had settled around her neck. *Four days until my mind is no longer mine.*

Should she go down like a rock sinking beneath the waves and disappear into oblivion quietly? Or should she ignite a firestorm and explode in brilliance, going out like a roman candle, luminous and magnificent, before the darkness snuffed her out completely?

Jeena had worked hard to train her. It would be a shame to let all that time and energy go to waste. Besides, she could always designate the prize money to Dove. If she was going to lose everything to Gregor, why not spend her last days enjoying what she had left? Gregor would be furious when he found out, but by then it wouldn't matter.

I want to race! Malice hissed. *I want to fly!*

Then we will fly, my sister.

Weeeeee!

Elise had a jump-jet competition to win. Dreams of escape might be gone, but if she won, she would always know that in some small way she had defeated Gregor. She wasn't a pawn.

CHAPTER FOUR_

Gambit, Day 278

ELISE ARRIVED AT THE JUMP-JET HANGAR, ONLY TO BE SHOVED INTO HER flightsuit and pressed into the little dragonfly craft by Jeena and Dove.

"You're cutting it close again!" Jeena gave her a disapproving frown.

"I'm sorry, but it's complicated." She took the helmet Jeena handed her and shoved it over her head. The conversation with Gregor had her hands shaking and her stomach feeling light.

Dove put a hand on her shoulder and gripped tight. "Don't worry, Chickadee, you just go out there and do what you do best. In a few days, it'll all be over." He kissed her helmet.

Gregor's words still had her reeling.

He wants you to date him, Whimper giggled. *Date!*

No, Malice countered. *He wants her to come to terms with her slavery. His version of charming makes me want to vomit. I don't understand where her mind is.*

Malice, don't talk about me like I'm not even here. Elise climbed the ladder to the jump-jet and settled herself inside the cockpit. *You do realize I have a time trial to run? I need to focus on flying, not Gregor. Can we stop talking about him?*

What? I can't speak my mind anymore? Malice's words dripped with venom. *He wants you to forget every degradation, every torture, every death, and you're just supposed to learn to live with him? Have you forgotten what Shriek had to endure? He's the enemy, Elise. I'm questioning your sanity, and that alone should worry you.*

Now wasn't that ironic. The voice in her head questioned Elise's sanity.

She flicked through her preflight checklist, striking the buttons on her console a bit harder than normal.

If I don't win this competition, Malice, that's exactly what I'll have to do. Now shut up. I'm nervous enough as it is.

Malice, Alex whispered from the dark, *come and stop badgering her. She needs to focus. Whimper, you too. Come and leave Elise alone.*

Malice grumbled as Alex pulled her away.

Whimper skipped off, but Elise could hear her chant. *He loves us. He loves us not. He loves us. He loves us not.*

Shriek did not join in on Malice's taunting. Shriek was nowhere to be found.

Alex streamed her thoughts to Elise in a focused beam. *You can't afford to lose. You've trained for this. You want it. Go get them, sister. Kick some Vendel ass!*

Elise vented a low chuckle. *Thank you, Alex.*

The crane came and picked up her jump-jet and aligned it in the launch tube. As the clamps grabbed her little ship, she rocked to the side. Eager for the distraction the jump-jet competition provided, her heart thundered and her breathing sawed in and out of her chest. She closed her eyes and visualized the course she would soon fly, just as Jeena had taught her to do. The pre-race visualization helped her anticipate anomalies.

It didn't escape her notice that this would be her first time flying in real space. All her other jump-jet runs had been within the silvery bubble of WOR-space surrounding the Vendel fleet. She looked forward to the experience with an overwhelming eagerness.

Fifty rings.

A time trial.

She needed a solid run.

Malikai, who consistently scored ten seconds per ring, currently held the lead in the competition. She needed to beat his time. If he hit and scored on any of the bonus rings, his time would be cut to even less than that.

Elise traced the path of the circuit in her mind. Every ten rings, beginning with the fifth ring, she had an opportunity to catch a bonus ring. Each bonus shaved thirty seconds off her total time. In her last race, she had hit two of the rings. Malikai had hit three. That made his time trial difficult to beat.

A light flashed green on her console, and she pressed her palms to the gel-flight controls. With a roar, her jump-jet screamed down the launch tube, spitting her out into the blackness of space. Not the silver of WOR-space, but true space. She squealed with excitement.

Gregor would never take away the thrill of this moment. It belonged solely to her.

Elise positioned her jump-jet at the starting gate and lined up for her run. She was up next. For now, Sigour was on the course. He came from around the far side of *Gambit*, weaving wildly through the last ten rings. She checked his score as he pulled into the gate. Eleven seconds per ring and he hit one bonus ring.

Damn.

Elise nudged her ship forward. It was her turn.

When the light turned green, she ignited her thrusters, surged forward, and piled on the speed. The first bonus ring came into view. She considered trying for it, but her alignment was off. What she could not afford was to miss a bonus ring. That carried a hefty penalty. She left the first bonus ring behind, unchallenged.

Elise caressed the jump-jet controls and coaxed wild accelerations out of the craft. Her speed and direction shifted with nearly every breath. Ring fifteen approached and behind it a bonus ring loomed. She set her line and slipped right through the bonus ring, letting the rhythm of flying guide her hands on the gel-pad. Her palms pressed down into the gel. Her fingers fine-tuned her course. She trusted her gut and tried not to think too hard. The third bonus ring loomed in front of her. She made a break to hit it, but at the last moment it slipped to the side. She cursed, and readjusted her flight path, slipping through the twenty-sixth ring.

Jeena's words came to her. *Don't go wild out there. Stay focused and think of only the next two rings in your sights.*

Looping and diving around the course, she kept Jeena's instructions planted firmly in her mind. Two more shots at the remaining bonus rings remained. Whatever the cost, those would be hers.

The next bonus ring came into focus. Twisting and diving through the course she hit it dead on. With her focus on the last ten rings, and the final bonus ring, she didn't realize when she breezed through the last ring and glanced at her time.

Nine seconds per ring. Holy shit!

She brought the jump-jet back around to the course start. Candice and

Pauline were busy setting up for their head-to-head race. Her race against Malikai would run after theirs.

Everyone had two head-to-head trials scheduled today. Elise had three scheduled tomorrow. Elise and Malikai would face off and then she had an hour break before her race against the other female in the semi-finals, Effie. After that, she hoped to make it back to her quarters for a little rest.

Candice and Pauline finished their second heat of Rabbit or Fox. The score tied. They headed into position for the third and final race.

Malikai arrived and pulled up alongside her jump-jet.

Her head buzzed with pre-race jitters.

"Chickadee." His greeting was clipped and curt.

"Malikai," she said without encouragement.

"I bet Candice wins. Pauline's getting sloppy. Care to wager?"

"I don't bet, Malikai, but you know that."

"You should, it makes things more interesting."

"Not interested."

"Fox or Rabbit?"

Pauline, who had taken Rabbit for the last race, passed the twenty-fifth ring and raced for the finish line. Candice pursued, narrowing the gap.

"You pick," Elise said.

"I'll take Fox."

Malikai accepted Fox and Elise acknowledged her position as Rabbit. She pressed her finger to the palm pad, and their first heat was set.

Candice stopped firing at Pauline. They passed the fortieth ring with Candice half a ring behind Pauline.

"Candice stopped firing," he said. "That's odd."

"Candice is going for the finish line." The woman's jump-jet surged forward, catching Pauline's ship.

Malikai's wry voice came over the communications channel. "Care to wager?"

She laughed. "No, I do not."

Candice caught up with Pauline, passed her, and slipped through the last ring less than a ship's length ahead of Pauline.

"Pauline made a mistake," Malikai said. "She should have fired on Candice before she went through the last ring. It would have given her three points and the win. I told you she was getting sloppy. You should have placed your bet, Chickadee."

"You have nothing I want. Are you ready to lose?"

"I don't think I'm going to lose to you today," he said. "But, there is something I want."

"Not going to happen."

Elise initiated the countdown for the start of their race. When her console flicked green, she pressed down on the gel-pads. Silver rings disappeared behind her as she wove her way through the first set of rings. Just before she hit the fourth ring, Malikai began his pursuit as Fox.

She enjoyed the chase, and imagined she was riding the biggest and fastest rollercoaster in the world. Silver flashed before her eyes and rings piled up behind her. Elise was surprised when she flew through the fiftieth ring without Malikai landing a shot. She'd evaded, and he'd come dangerously close to scoring a hit on her, but her mind had been focused more on the thrill of looping through the course than on the competition.

"That's two points for me," she said.

"Don't get cocky," he replied.

She should have listened. He took Rabbit on the next race and nailed her by ring forty, earning three points as Rabbit with Fangs. He now led the points three to two. Elise cursed. It had been a mistake.

"Such words from a lady? What's wrong?"

"Nothing, I choose Fox for the last race." Since she trailed in the points, the final pick of Rabbit or Fox belonged to her.

"Key it in. I think a six-to-two-point spread will keep the fans screaming for years. Care to bet on it?"

"There's no way in hell you're going to do that again. You got lucky."

"You were distracted. If you have any desire to make it to the top three, you need to focus. It would be nice to share the podium with you. We could go out for a drink and maybe dinner afterward?"

"You're not my type. You have ten seconds, get ready."

"Oh, I'm ready." Malikai shot out of the starting block.

Elise counted down the seconds. When the timer hit zero, she went for the chase.

Malikai picked up rings with surprising speed. She tried, and failed, to lock onto his craft. There was no way in hell he was going to grow fangs and bite her again. Rabbit slipped through the twenty-fifth ring. Malakai had two options: race to the finish or turn and go on the hunt. The second choice would earn him another three points if he scored another hit.

Elise cursed.

He accelerated and headed down the course. Unsure if it was a ploy or not, she narrowed his lead and kept her fingers on her trigger, harrying him down the course.

Malikai dodged. It cost him time. She used that to narrow the gap, then took a chance and passed Malikai at the forty-second ring.

Curses blatted over her communications channel.

She ignored him and instead visualized the next eight rings. Laser fire flashed behind her as Malikai lined up his sights. One shot nearly tagged her left wing. She rolled around her center axis, without altering her course, and the shot passed between her twin wingtips.

Too close for comfort. Come on. You can do it.

More cursing followed.

The fiftieth ring rose before her, proud and glorious. This wouldn't be a win. She'd only take a single point for a Fox finish, but it would be a tie. Malikai hated tying.

Elise acknowledged the final score. There were two races before her next head-to-head against Effie. She pointed the nose of her craft back to the *Gambit* for a short rest. Malikai hung back, silent, fuming perhaps. She took a perverse pleasure in irritating him.

Effie and Pauline lined up for the next race. After they finished, Malikai and Segour would face off. She had time to regroup and rethink her strategy. Without a parting word, Elise headed back to the hangar.

Jeena jumped and Dove collected her in a bear hug. He spun her around in a circle and smothered her against his chest. When he let her down, Larkin came over and thumped her on the back. He gave her two soft kisses on both cheeks and congratulations.

"Thank guys." A little breathless from the excitement of her first races in the semi-finals, she still couldn't imagine this was actually happening.

Jeena clapped her hands. "You're doing so well. I couldn't be prouder."

"Only because I had the best instructor." Her cheeks hurt from smiling so much.

Larkin draped an arm across her shoulders. His eyes were red lined and the faint aroma of alcohol tainted his breath. The Dunlaap disaster still weighed heavily on him.

Elise envied him, in a morbid sort of way. The Earth WOR hadn't had the easy convenience of alcohol to take the edge off their pain. They had WOR-guards and whipsticks, Vendel classes and an entire culture and language shoved down their throats, with the very real threat of torture if they failed to please. She also had the braklav. None of it had dulled her pain like Larkin's alcohol, quite the opposite had happened.

It didn't seem fair.

He kissed her cheek and gave a lopsided grin. She kissed him back, on the lips no less, unwilling to hold her pain up against his.

Larkin's expression sobered for the briefest of moments. He pushed his curls away from his eyes. "You shouldn't tease a guy, El. It's not fair."

"Oh, Lark." She tousled the curls on his head. "You need to stop drinking. You reek." She disentangled herself from Larkin, and he wobbled for a moment before sinking to the floor.

He sat cross-legged, eyed her closely, and then pulled a small flask out of his shirt pocket. "Cheers, El." He dumped the liquid onto the floor of the hanger, draining the container.

"It'll get better, Lark. I promise."

"How can you be so sure?" He capped the flask and tucked it back in his jumpsuit.

"I believe in hope, even when all is dark." For the first time in days, the conviction of her words resonated with truth.

There's still time, sister, Alex said. *Gregor hasn't beaten us yet.*

What bothers me, she admitted, *is that I'm ready to let him win.* She glanced around the hangar, watching her friends. *This is my last stand. The last thing I have to throw in his face. We're beaten. Done. I can't win. What's worse is that I'm not even sure I want to fight him anymore. I can learn to live with him. I have feelings for him.*

I know, Alex said. *And I understand, but I'm telling you we're not done. Not yet. There's still hope. I need you to not give up.*

I won't. Elise vented a sigh. *I'm here. I'm still fighting. But if I lose, I'm just saying that I can accept it the end. I can accept him.*

Elise turned around and brought her attention back to the hangar.

Dove stood in front of a gorgeous man wearing a green jumpsuit with dazzling eyes which matched the hue of his Conclave colors. Dove pressed against Carek's chest and held him fast.

Carek's face was beet red. He'd put up her entrance fee then pulled it back once he'd discovered who she really was. He hadn't said anything to his friends. None of them knew Dove's Chickadee was also the Emperor's slave and soon-to-be bound WOR. He'd kept her secret and begged her to return to Gregor. Her pursuit of the jump-jet competition defied his wishes, but he held faith with her and kept her secrets. He did it because he loved her.

"Carek, we talked about this. She doesn't want to see you." Dove pushed Carek back.

"I don't care. I want to see her. El, tell this ugly bastard to let me through."

She sighed. "It's ok, Dove, you can let him come."

Dove grunted. Carek glared at his cousin and shouldered his way past.

"Now, boys," Jeena chided. "Play nice."

Carek didn't respond. He came to stand in front of Elise.

She put her hands on her hips and stared at him. "Why are you here?"

"I wanted to wish you luck." Carek shrugged and held his hands palms out in a self-deprecating manner.

"Thank you. But, perhaps it's best if you keep your distance."

He'd made it perfectly clear what he thought of the foolishness of her jump-jet goals.

He ran a hand over his hair and down the ponytail in back. "Right, well, damned if I do and damned if I don't." His eyes bored into her. He pulled her away from earshot of the others. "I just found out. I didn't know the High Council had met."

Elise put her hand on his arm and pushed him gently away. Her hand trembled. "It was going to happen sooner or later."

"Well, I wanted to see you."

"What, to say goodbye before Gregor steals my mind and turns me into a mindless slave?" The irony in her voice stung him like a bee. She arched her brow.

"El, I wish it were different. Listen, the Emperor talked to me. He wanted to know whether Binding truly affected the ability to link. I explained it to him." Carek paused and gazed into her eyes. "He asked if the others could handle linking without you, then told me I had three days to figure it out. After that, he said you'd be Bound and no longer of any use on the linking project."

"Yeah, that's sort of what he told me, too," she said.

"I wish I could make it better for you. I really do." He looked at the jump-jet. "You know he's going to find out about all of this. You won't be able to keep it from him."

"I know."

He grabbed her hands and held them tightly. "I wish things could be different for you. I wish I could have made your life easier."

She gripped his hands and then let go. "You really should leave."

His expression fell.

Elise leaned forward and kissed him. She remembered the first time he'd kissed her. It seemed so long ago. That sort of tenderness would never be hers to share. Carek left without saying goodbye to the others. Jeena arched a brow in question.

Elise scrubbed away the tears. She needed to focus. There was another race to run.

At the end of the day, the results had Malikai leading with three wins. Elise, Candice and Segour were all tied with two wins a piece. Effie claimed one victory, and Pauline had lost all of her trials so far. Elise led the time trials with an average of nine seconds per ring. Candice and Sigour tied with eleven seconds. The other three pilots would complete their time trials tomorrow.

The outcome was very much unclear. Effie probably wouldn't make it to the finals. Between Segour, Candice and herself, it was an even race. Her goal was to make it into the top two and a chance for the grand prize. In order to do that, she had to win all her matches the next day.

Without sleep that might be impossible. Elise excused herself and wandered down to the Fifth Deck. A glance at the time told her sleep would be impossible.

What the hell? Why is it never easy?

CHAPTER FIVE_

Gambit, Day 279

WHEN ELISE MADE IT BACK TO THE FIFTH DECK, SHE DIDN'T BOTHER TRYING TO sleep. A long steam shower might revive her . . . maybe. It wouldn't negate the need for rest, however, so she turned to her sisters for help.

Whimper? Are you here?

I am here.

I need you.

Whimper handled things with a gentler hand than Malice. When Elise pushed exhaustion beyond the limits of sanity, she often handed over control of their body to Whimper.

As steam filled the room, Elise's weary mind sought refuge in the dark. WOR-skill diagrams and silver jump-jet loops danced in her vision as blackness enveloped her in its comforting embrace.

An hour later, water dripped off her body.

He's here, sister, Whimper said with a shudder. *I must go.*

Soft cotton fibers caressed her skin. Elise stretched as she took back control.

Thank you for letting me rest.

Always. A flicker of fear passed through Whimper as she glanced toward their room.

Elise breathed in, filling her lungs with air and strength, and fortified herself against the man who waited beyond that door. She felt Gregor with a certainty that couldn't be shook. He was in her blood, and his presence set it to buzzing. The door swished open and she entered her small room.

"Good morning, Gregor."

Gregor reclined on her bed. "Good morning, opés." Warm silver eyes twinkled as he looked on with appreciation. "Did you sleep well?"

The broad muscular man stretched out on the mattress she had not had the luxury of touching last night. She glanced at him, frowned, and twisted the truth.

"No, I did not."

He was unfazed. "Sleep is very important for a s'vlor. I would suggest you make sure to get an adequate amount each and every night. Was something bothering you last night?"

She vented an exasperated sigh. "Nothing more than usual, Gregor. I'm going to be late to the Tank—" she paused, suddenly wary, "unless you've changed my schedule?"

"No. Go ahead and get dressed. I'm joining you today. I want to see where you are with the link. I'm hoping my presence will serve as incentive to make quicker progress."

"Not likely." Elise pulled a dark green gown down over her head.

With a flat stare, he challenged her. "I have a way of getting results."

"You're wrong. You'll just interfere and slow us down."

"Aren't you argumentative. Be careful, opés."

"There's no need to be careful, I'm being honest with you. You make everyone nervous." She gestured for him to tie the back of her gown.

He stood and began the arduous process of tying the laces. But first, he traced a line of fire down her back with the pads of his fingers.

She shuddered, and goosebumps broke out on her arm.

"Explain." He leaned close and breathed on her neck. The edge to his voice destroyed any softness from his caress.

"You say you want me to be successful—"

"Which is why I will oversee your efforts. I need results."

"If you want results, I'll give them to you, but on my terms."

If he comes to the tank we can't work on the WOR-skill, Alex's cautionary voice sounded too loud in her head. *I almost have it figured out.*

I know! Be quiet and let me deal with this.

Alex frowned and crossed her arms, but did not retreat.

Elise ignored her stubborn sister and focused on Gregor. "You can't come to the tank. Your presence is too distracting. Mr. Tusel is supervising us, and none of us feel threatened by him. You, on the other hand, are an entirely different matter." She crossed her hands under her breasts and stared him down.

She waited for an explosion. Never had she openly defied him, especially since the last round of Tender Training, but she couldn't have him in the Tank. Too much was at stake. Her entire body tensed, waiting for his outburst, but it never came.

He surprised her with a kiss instead.

Elise gasped as he pulled her to him. Her heart pounded and blood roared past her ears as his kiss overwhelmed her.

It's not real, she asserted, but the sudden need enflaming her body certainly felt very real.

It's Vendel biotech at work! Malice screamed. *Do not let it affect you!*

It feels so real. It was hard to sort out what was in her heart against what was surging in her blood.

You can't afford to fall for him, sister. Alex's soothing tones balanced out Malice's harsh screeches.

"I'm placing a great deal of trust in you, Elise . . ."

She barely heard Gregor's words with all the clamoring in her head.

"Do not make me regret the chances I take." He turned on his heels and stalked out of the room.

Odd. He left? He's never backed down like that before.

Good for us, Alex said.

But he never backs down. I don't trust him.

His presence vibrated all the way down the hall. She felt him as he stalked across the large common area and exited out the double doors which guarded the Fifth Deck.

Something was up, but for the life of her she had no idea what it could possibly be.

After Gregor's departure, Elise gathered up Alice, Chandra, Aomi, and Paula and the five of them headed to the Tank to work on the linking project. They talked good naturedly as they walked, navigating the pod circuit and lift tubes with the ease of natives. How easily they adjusted to this world. It bothered her, but she kept her thoughts to herself.

"I don't know how you handle the keystone position so easily," Alice said as they floated up a lift tube. Her mouth twisted with frustration.

Elise shrugged. "I've shown you how I do it. I don't know how else to explain it."

"I agree." Aomi clutched Chandra's hand as the lift tube rushed them up. She kept her eyes shut tight. When Elise had asked why, she had grudgingly admitted to a fear of heights.

"I was able to tie only three of us in yesterday," Alice continued, "but I struggled to hold it together." She glanced at Aomi, Chandra, and Paula. "The conduit doesn't seem to be a problem for us, but the keystone is hard."

"The keystone is the hardest job," Elise agreed. "It requires the greatest strength."

"And endurance," Chandra piped up. "I was wiped yesterday. It felt like someone had beaten me over the head with a baseball bat."

Paula huffed a laugh. Her dark eyes glittered in the soft illumination of the lift tube.

"Yes," Alice said. "We're all strong. The keystone is hardest because you have to fold everything together. I don't know how you do it so easily, Elise. It's like nothing to you."

Paula frowned. "She doesn't do it like we do."

"What do you mean?" Alice stared at Paula.

Paula focused at the empty space beneath their feet—her gaze had a distant, thoughtful cast.

Elise followed Paula's gaze and wondered what was on her friend's troubled mind. She didn't know Paula as well as the others. Only recently had Paula joined their tight-knit group. They all tried to include her, but Paula had been broken by the Vendel. She struggled to come to terms with what that meant. The two of them shared one thing none of the others had experienced. It gave them an inherent closeness she would never have with the others. They had both suffered at the hand of High Tender Marcus, and had both been forever changed by him.

"Why do you say that?" she asked.

Her friend shrugged and kept staring at the void beneath their feet. "I don't like lift tubes." She pulled her attention back to the group, and with great difficulty met Elise's gaze. "You handle the WOR-skill differently from the rest of us. It's subtle, like you're breathing it in. I've tried to mimic what you do, but I can't."

"I've shown you exactly what I do." She looked at Paula, confused.

Paula cocked her head to the side. "Not really. You dumb it down for us."

Shocked by Paula's comment, she could only stare, mouth agape.

Alice defended Elise. "That's not true. Elise shows us everything."

Paula's eyes focused downward again and shrugged. "She tries to, but she's not like us."

That's when Elise realized the truth. The image of the spinning Wheel and its kaleidoscope of color came to mind.

"I have a question for all of you."

With the exception of Paula, they all looked at her.

"When they tested you with the Tenderstat, did it change colors for any of you?"

They shook their heads.

"I only got two of the rods to light up," Alice said. "It wasn't until the Activator that I bumped from Second to Fifth Rank."

"All five lit for me," Paula said, "but no colors. Did that happen to you?"

Elise nodded.

"Must mean something," Paula mumbled. "You're not like us. You're different."

It was no accident Paula and Elise shared the same Tender. High Tender Marcus's WOR, with the exception of Elise's dismal training failure, out-shined all the rest of the Fifth Rank when it came to WOR-skill progression. He had hand-selected the strongest of the strong.

They exited the lift tube and headed to the pod circuit that would take them to the Tank. Elise thought about Paula's comments. Could that be the reason she struggled where the others did not? Did she approach the WOR-skill differently from her friends? She handed the problem over to Alex.

I need to find a way to show this to them so they can make it work. If I don't, we're lost.

Alex nodded. *I agree. She's right, by the way. We're not like them. Don't worry, I'm on it.*

Satisfied Alex would find a solution, Elise enjoyed the rest of the walk with her friends.

It still amazed her that they were allowed to walk unescorted within the *Gambit*. Each time that thought crossed her mind, however, Gregor's words came back to haunt her.

Where would you go that I would not find you?

And wasn't that the harshest truth to face. Where could she go? Where would she ever hope to hide nearly a thousand Earth WOR within the Vendel empire?

Solving the threat of the S'Lorek had become her driving passion, perhaps superseding her plans for escape. That change in priorities came as a shock.

But it made sense.

If she couldn't save herself, then at least she could save her Vendel friends.

When had her motivation changed? No longer about revenge, she fought for the Vendel rather than against them. Not that the Earth WOR wouldn't one day be free of their Vendel masters. One way or the other, she would accomplish that goal too. She just had no idea how.

Using the jump-jet winnings to buy transport and take all the Earth WOR away only worked if she had a place to take them to; a place which was also beyond Gregor's reach. That part of the puzzle she had yet to work out.

What made her laugh, and drew strange looks from her friends, was that knowing she would save an empire of billions and billions no longer overwhelmed her. It was saving a little less than a thousand Earth women which proved to be the most daunting task.

"Elise, are you listening at all?"

She shook her head, surprised to find herself floating in the purple soup of the am-net sea. *How did I get here?*

Whimper giggled. *You were daydreaming. I took over. Can I go now?*

Her sisters had never taken over control without Elise's conscious permission. This change gave her pause. *How much of me is left in here?*

There was no answer.

Her four friends, along with Carek, floated in the glowing purple liquid all staring at her as if expecting an answer.

"I'm sorry, what did you say?" Elise tried to focus. They were attempting a link. She blinked and looked at the construct Aomi had cast.

Deep furrows lined her brow marring her delicate features, even her almond eyes pinched shut.

Elise held up a hand. "Stop. Try again, Aomi. Stop thinking so hard. It just screws it all up."

"Stop thinking?" Irritation lined Aomi's words. "That's absurd." The soft melodious notes of her voice were replaced with a blaring discord.

"Listen, this is how it works. If you try to control it, force it to do what you want, the WOR-skill fights back. It builds up a dissonance. I feel it now, in what you're doing. You have to let it flow, otherwise it fights you and falls apart."

"I can't," she complained. "It's too hard."

Elise felt lost as to how to explain it any better.

Chandra rescued her by suggesting a simple solution. "Hey, why don't you try singing? Think of the hardest song you've ever had to sing. Hum it while you form the keystone."

"That's stupid." Aomi looked dubious.

"If it's so stupid, then try it. What harm could it cause?" Chandra folded her arms across her chest. Her brows lifted in challenge.

Aomi rolled her eyes and, with a glare, started to hum.

Elise played the part of the conduit. The rough edges of the linked circle formed. The fifth and sixth dimensions unfolded and then cracks widened as Aomi cracked open the sub-dimensions.

Paula fed power into the cracks, her energy melding seamlessly into the link. Elise grabbed Paula's strength and bound it to her own. Alice's thread came next. With effort, the third position was filled. Chandra was the last to add her power, but Elise slipped her into the conduit.

Aomi's face lit with excitement as she realized she'd formed her first working linked circle as the Keystone. Her grin spread from ear to ear, tweaking up the corners of her eyes. She clapped. "I did it!"

Elise smiled.

They ran through the drills Carek devised, and then, Aomi slowly released each of them.

"See." Chandra looked smug. She'd reverted to her lotus pose and floated alongside Carek. Their knees touched. "You thought it was stupid and look how well it worked?"

"Are you done gloating?" Aomi arched an eyebrow. "Because it's your turn."

Chandra's face paled. "I—"

"Yes?" Aomi mocked Chandra's previous challenge.

"I need a distraction."

"Well? What will distract you?" Aomi asked.

Chandra's eyes flicked to Carek. A slight flush brightened her friend's face.

"I'll think of something," she said.

Elise directed everyone back to work. "Ok, everyone into position. Who hasn't practiced as the conduit?"

Paula raised her hand. "I did a few tries back, but I'd like to try again."

Elise pointed to each girl in turn. "All right. Chandra is the keystone, Paula you're the conduit. Aomi goes in first, then Alice, and I'll go last. Paula, make sure you release each of us in reverse order."

They nodded.

"Ok, let's go," Elise said.

Chandra formed the bridge. The circle took shape. Paula accepted each link into the conduit without any difficulty. They did it several times over. Each of them achieving success as both keystone and conduit.

After some time, Elise stepped back and allowed them to direct one another. Her heart sank as she watched their success. It was an odd feeling. On the one hand, her pride soared as their accomplishment blossomed, on the other, she realized the cost of this achievement.

Gregor would demand the Binding.

She shrank a little as the universe swallowed her hopes and dreams.

Moving away, she floated apart from them while they practiced. She pulled up the WOR-skill diagrams. The Wheel skills rotated in front of her, blurring with the speed Shriek demanded. Alex had figured out how to hide the colors from curious eyes. Elise looked at it with an odd double vision which made her head spin, yet felt oddly normal.

She needed more WOR. One linked circle called for ten positions. She hoped to make ten complete circles with the Fifth Rank Earth WOR they had on board. Secretly, she was dying to see if Alex's thoughts were true. Could she be the keystone which linked ten fully formed circles into one giant wheel of power?

Elise motioned for Carek to join her.

He disentangled himself from the four girls and floated over. "Yes?"

"I need to speak with Gregor."

"Okay, it'll just take a second to set it up."

She sighed. "Thank you."

Carek's eyes glazed over. She recognized the look. He accessed parts of the am-net they couldn't reach. Well, parts the other girls couldn't reach. She had other access. Bobo, her viral subroutine, had been a very busy boy. There wasn't a single ship's system he didn't reside within.

Carek opened his eyes. "He's in session with the High Council and not available."

"Tell him it's important."

Carek stared flatly back at her. "He said no."

"Tell him I said *please*."

He did and gasped with surprise. "The Emperor will speak with you."

"Good, give me a private connection."

Carek did. She closed her eyes and spoke into the am-net. Gregor's presence washed over her and filled her with his power. Warmth spread through her and comforted her in an unsettling way.

"Gregor," she began.

"Opés?"

"Forgive my intrusion. I understand you're busy."

"Yes, very much." He surprised her with a laugh. "But you asked so sweetly. It means much to me that you wish to work with me. What do you need?"

"I need more WOR."

"More? I've given you several."

"I thought you'd like to know the four you've given me can now form partial links. They can fill the key positions. Before I can—" she hesitated and chose her words with care, "Before I can hand the project over to them, I need to know if they can form a full circle, and I need to observe them training other s'vlor."

"How many do you need?"

"A full linked circle takes ten. I need at least six other WOR to make a circle and I'll need to know if the s'vlor can train the new ones. However, if you would permit it, I want to try to form two circles and see if I can link those together. I need twenty total, plus me."

"If I give you the six, can you determine if the first four can carry on without you?"

She stifled a groan. "Yes, if you give me those then I can probably determine it by tonight." She knew what she was committing to—the Binding loomed heavy in her thoughts. "But, a simple circle won't be enough against the S'Lorek. Even ten circles may not be enough. I can't explain it, but I believe we need more power."

"Is this one of your hunches, opés, or an attempt to delay our Binding?"

"Yes," she said, "and no. Yes, it's a hunch. Yes, I wish to delay our Binding, but this isn't a ploy. This is important, Gregor. Please, trust me."

"How much time?"

"If you give me the full sixteen, I can start on the training assessment this afternoon. By tomorrow, or the latest, the next day, I'll know if I can link two circles. I need to make the first attempt. After I figure it out, I'll have Paula try to form the super-link. She's the next strongest, but I'm not certain she's strong enough."

"How sure are you about that?"

"I'm not. It gets complicated and the dimensions I'm talking about accessing haven't been used by WOR before."

"Hm."

"You should listen to me."

He laughed. "You're impertinent as always, my sweet Elise."

"I don't mean to be."

"I know. It's just you speak your mind so freely. It's not what I'm used to from a WOR."

"I don't mean to be disrespectful."

"I know, I believe you." He paused, as if considering her request. A long moment passed before he spoke again. "I'll send you six s'vlor for today."

"Thank you, Gregor. I'll come to your quarters tonight . . . for the Binding." Her voice hitched at that, but there was no way around it. "I still think it's a mistake to take me out of the project, but I understand your reasons. I'm not fighting you. I'm trying to become what you want."

"I know, and as much as I'd like to trust you fully, your history does not lend itself very well to believing your word. Binding is the only way to truly control you. I do appreciate your willingness, and it hasn't gone unnoticed that you're not fighting me on this." Another long pause followed. "I'll send the rest tomorrow, opés. I need to know if this super-link will work. We delay the Binding until then. Come to me after you have the answer. Do you understand?"

"Are you certain?"

"Answer me honestly, opés, are you truly the only one who can form a super-link? Is there no way for you to show the others how to do it?"

"I believe so, but I'm not certain. It's not so simple."

"Very well. I'll send you six for the afternoon and the full amount tomorrow morning. Do you need more?"

"You would give me more?"

"Only if you need them. Do you?"

She told him the truth. "No."

While she would love the opportunity to train more WOR in these skills, Gregor would sense the lie. He had to believe she belonged to him.

"Very well."

"Gregor . . ."

"Yes?"

"Thank you."

"You're welcome, opés."

Her body shook after her conversation with Gregor.

Carek laid a hand on her shoulder. "Are you okay?"

She gave a weak smile. "It's hard with him. He's sending more s'vlor so we can try to form a full circle today. Tomorrow, he's sending enough for us to try forming two circles. I'm supposed to see if they can train the others. Now that Gregor has the go ahead to Bind me, he's pushing for it."

Carek's eyes softened for her. "I'm sorry, El."

She gave a soft laugh. "I keep getting reprieves. It's so silly. I told him I think I can join the circles—"

"Is that even possible?"

She nodded. "I think so, but I don't think they have enough power to do it."

Carek cocked his head. "And you do?"

"I am much stronger than any of them. Gregor knows this. As much as he desires the Binding, he serves the Empire first. He knows if there's a chance that I'm right, he has to delay the Binding until I either prove myself right or wrong."

"Your Binding is inevitable, El. You know this." Carek's stare pierced her heart.

"I know." She bit her lip and then her expression brightened. "You know what this means?"

He shook his head.

"It means I can fly in the jump-jet finals."

"You're not seriously considering going through with that?" He looked at her as if she had grown two heads.

"I told you, I'll do what I can to save the Vendel, but I'm not done fighting for my freedom. If I can form a super-link and free the Earth WOR, then that's exactly what I plan to do."

"But, do you really want to do that? You're safer stirring up a hornet's nest than angering the Emperor."

"As long as his precious Vendel are saved, what does he care?"

"You obviously don't understand him at all. You're playing with fire."

"No. I'm taking control of my life."

And if I have to give up my free will, I'm going to compete in that stupid jump-jet competition and win! Gregor will have to live with the knowledge that I got away with it. All right under his nose. It'll make him question everything about me. That comfort, as small as it might be, will keep me sane when he steals my mind.

CHAPTER SIX_

Gambit, Day 279

ELISE HAD PLENTY OF TIME TO PREPARE FOR HER TIME TRIAL. DRESSED IN HER flightsuit, she busied herself around the jump-jet, fussing at everything and nothing as her nerves rioted with unspent energy. The concealing mist of her veil tickled her nose, and she rubbed absently at it.

Dove had already gone over the craft, as he did for each of her flights, but Jeena had instilled a rigid pre-flight discipline. Elise took her preflight check seriously. If she didn't, Jeena would chew her ass.

Elise ran her gloved hand down the outside of the jump-jet. Its smooth surface radiated a quiet warmth. Jeena had taken her through a simulation of the Malbran course. It was slightly different from the *Gambit's* circuit, but shouldn't pose a problem. Jeena sat inside the cockpit and double checked the pre-flight list Elise had already completed.

While she waited, an image of Carek flashed through her mind. They whispered quietly in a lover's embrace as he stole her away from the *Gambit* and into a new life. Larkin and his springy curls came to mind as well, a fleeting image. He would always seem youthful to her, despite being twice her age. His boyish charm radiated an innocence and carefree spirit which launched her spirit across the galaxy. In his arms, she flitted from planet to planet and enjoyed an exhilarating pilot's life. She could see the two of them settling down amidst a bouncing family of five or six.

Two other men passed briefly through her thoughts. The dark and mysterious pilot, Malikai, the lord in disguise, promised mystery and passion. This man lacked a face, the bad boy of the circuit, all the more alluring for his arrogant attitude. Would he be able to hold her heart? Could she hold his? Or did he already have a lady waiting for him at home and a family with children who giggled when their father returned each night with wild stories of jump-jet racing?

Gregor brought visions full of passionate release, tinged with domination and its partner, submission. Tenderness had no place in her dreams with Gregor. An inexplicable longing overcame her and an unresolved emotion sat back in her primitive brain. Was this a twisted love, or was it a need to be consumed? How much had she lost that Gregor might fill the emptiness inside? What did it say about her that she wanted him in her life?

She dreamt of falling into his arms. He'd brush back the hair from her eyes and plant kisses down her face, her neck, and lower still. There had to be a way to reconcile herself to him, his control, and her position.

But, that was hard when Malice whispered in the dark. *Never surrender. Keep the fight.*

Except, the fight tired Elise and she wasn't certain how much fight she had left. Exhaustion pulled at her soul.

"Hey, kid." The voice of her mentor sounded harsh and blaring.

Elise snapped her thoughts out of the darkness and searched for Jeena. "What?"

"What's up? I've asked you the same question three times. Where's your head?" Jeena jumped out of the jump-jet.

"Sorry, what did you ask?"

"You really didn't hear me?"

Elise shook her head. "No."

"Are you going to be okay for the race? You need to focus. This is it. Inexperienced pilots often dismiss the time trials, but they can make or break the final standings. It can mean the difference between first or last place, especially if the head-to-head races are close."

"Sorry. I was thinking about after the finals. The next step?"

"That's covered. Dove has a freighter lined up. Your winnings will go to him and he'll buy it for you. After that you can fly away and never look back. He secured a spot in the Omega Colony Fleet for you as a mining ore freighter pilot. Larkin may even come with you. At least, he's thinking about it."

Elise smiled. Carek would never leave the am-net. She could be happy with Larkin. In this society, a woman needed a sponsor. Why not Larkin? He would be kind to her and she could grow to love him with time. He might have a problem with their passengers, though.

Jeena continued, not realizing Elise's thoughts had wandered off again. "You've got a little less than an hour. Time enough for another simulation run."

"I don't want to run another sim. I've got it down."

"It won't hurt."

Elise's head hurt and her teeth buzzed in her jaw. The beginnings of pre-race jitters settled under her skin with restless energy.

"How hard can the course be?"

"Pretty damn hard if you've never run it before." A deep, aggravating voice intruded on their conversation.

Jeena hissed. "Malikai, what the hell are you doing here?"

"Just came by to wish a fellow pilot luck." He inclined his head to Elise. "*Chickadee,* good luck on your time trials. I doubt you'll do better than the nine seconds you had in the semi-finals, but who knows." His face, as always, was hidden behind the shimmering mist of his veil, but then so was hers.

"Get your ass out of here," Jeena said. "No one wants to talk to you."

"Do you speak for your little prodigy, now? Can't she speak for herself?"

"I choose not to," Elise quipped. If Jeena didn't like Malikai, that was all she needed to do the same. It didn't matter the man had an unspeakable presence about him.

"I came to wish you luck." He swept her a mocking bow.

"No, doubt. Good luck Malikai, and goodbye," Elise said.

"Do you remember what I said?" His head dipped and he leaned forward.

It took all her courage not to step back from him.

"About what?" She crossed her arms and was thankful she'd remembered to veil herself today. Some days she forgot. The cool mist gave her an added confidence she needed to face off against Malikai.

"About the winner's circle of course. I very much wish to share it with you. Once they pass out the prizes, I hope to bend down and give you a kiss. We can celebrate our good fortune over drinks."

"Bend down? You are full of yourself," she scoffed. "You're going to have to crane your neck to see me on the first-place block. Bend down indeed." She jerked her chin in irritation. "Jeena's right, go away."

He chuckled. With a bow to Jeena he strutted off to his jump-jet. He vaulted into the cockpit and sealed himself in.

"Shake him off, kid," Jeena said. "That's what he does. He comes over full of his bravado just to unnerve you. You were probably his last stop. He likely visited Candice first. He knows you're his real competition. Don't let him psyche you out of your victory."

"Trust me, he'd have to do a lot more than toss around a few verbal taunts," Elise said.

"Well, he's really good at it."

Elise rolled her eyes. "I'm not going to let him get to me. Don't worry. He's got the worst position. His time trial is first. All I have to do is beat his time. For once, being last is going to work to my advantage. I'll know exactly how far to push it."

"Fine, but don't take wild chances out there. If you blow the time trials and win the others, you can still lose first place. Be careful."

"I will." She placed a hand on Jeena's shoulder. "I plan to win this thing if it's the last thing I do."

"Shoot, kid," Jeena laughed. "It's a race not a death sentence."

Elise laughed. "I know."

She knew exactly what this was.

The next morning, Gregor came through with the sixteen WOR from the Fifth Deck, minus a High Tender escort. Carek employed the help of several of his colleagues, and four of the First Rank Conclave WOR, to help with the mass of scarlet-clad women in the purple soup.

Most did fine with the breathing tubes, but several had obviously never swum before. A look of pure terror marred their faces and made their limbs jerk wildly. The Am-Net Conclave WOR had their hands full pacifying the Fifth Rank women.

Solid white shapes held thrashing WOR in place until they went limp and gave in. It saddened her to see the struggles of the women end with limp acquiescence and surrender.

Her future was mirrored in these women. It horrified and exhausted her at the same time. She was ready to be done with all of it.

Malice snapped at her. *You can't give in. We hate them.*

Elise sighed, unwilling to engage with Malice's temper tantrum.

She's tired, Malice, Whimper whispered. *Just tired. Elise isn't done yet.*

But she wants to give up, after everything we've endured? After all these monsters have done to us!

Do not snap at her. It doesn't help.

Growls sounded in the dark as Malice stomped off.

Whimper cast a glance to Elise and followed the argumentative Malice, leaving Elise alone with her thoughts.

Turning back toward the struggling WOR and their mute surrender, she wasn't entirely sure how much fight she had left. Fatigue burrowed deep into her bones and settled in the marrow. It would be so much easier to serve the Vendel than continue to fight.

What she was fighting for had become blurry. Did she fight to free the Earth WOR and leave the Vendel to face the S'lorek alone? Or did she save her oppressors and potentially give up any hope of freedom?

Or . . . Alex reached out to grasp Elise's hand, *we can do both.*

Elise vented a weary sigh. *I don't even know if that's possible anymore, Alex. And I'm running out of time. You know what happens when he Binds me.*

Alex laughed. *It's not over until the fat lady sings. Until our last breath, we fight for our freedom. Trust me. Lean on me. I will give you the strength you need.*

Elise gripped Alex's hand in silent acknowledgment. Her gaze turned back to the flailing women in red immersion suits. *You would have thought they'd have chosen women who had some experience in water. We're going to lose hours just trying to acclimatize them.*

She had today, perhaps tomorrow, to make this work. Tomorrow her deadline with Gregor was up, unless he demanded she submit tonight. She pressed her hands to her head, breathed in deep, and pushed her fingers against her temples. It hurt so much.

"Elise? Are you okay?" Alice noticed her distress.

"Just give me a moment." She pressed her hands to her head and pinched her eyes shut.

Alice took over without a word. Within minutes, her friend had the new arrivals settled and separated into two groups. Alice had a flair for organization.

Alice came back to Elise. "What do you think?" Her eyes were alight with anticipation as she gestured to the women floating in two rough circles.

Elise gazed at Alice through pain filled eyes. Her teeth buzzed and the nerves on her skin seemed extraordinarily sensitive. "I think I want to cut off my head."

"What's up these headaches?"

"Lack of sleep and stress."

Whimper could only shield her from so much.

"You're not superwoman. Even you need to sleep." Alice wrapped an arm around Elise's shoulder. "You push yourself too hard."

"What choice do I have?" She held up a hand to forestall any more conversation headed down that path. Too dangerous. She asked a question, hoping it would focus her thoughts. "Who do you have in your circles?"

"I put Aomi as keystone in the first. She still struggles with that position. I'll be the conduit. For the other, I was going to have Paula as keystone and Chandra for the conduit. Paula is stronger than any of us initially thought. She has a unique grasp of the core principles."

"I agree, but put Paula as conduit. Chandra needs more practice handling all the forces and vectoring solutions."

"Okay." Alice made the adjustments. "We're ready when you are. How do you want to do this?"

"Watch and see where the problems are. Try to figure out who shows the most promise to train for the key positions. Honestly, I'm not sure."

Elise tapped out in their secret code on Alice's arm. *As you form your circles, I want to try a little something of my own. I don't want Carek to know.* To cover the secret conversation, she continued to explain. Although Alice knew what came next. "All of them need to try the keystone and conduit positions. Go through the exercises with them."

"Okay, I'll get them started."

"Gregor demands that I determine if the four of you can train the others. He knows the Binding will take me out of this and wants to make sure the project can continue without me."

Alice placed a hand on Elise's shoulder and gave a sorrowful look. Thankfully, she didn't say anything. Elise didn't think she'd be able to handle any words of comfort Alice might give.

A deep breath in and out. She pressed forward, always forward.

Just don't think about it.

Talking seemed to help keep her mind off the inevitable. "I'm not worried about you. Aomi and Chandra will be fine. Paula is more than capable, but High Tender Marcus has touched her. He has a way of leaving a mark on a person. I don't know if Paula is mentally stable."

"She seems fine to me." Alice spun around to gaze at Paula.

"True, but the way she works the WOR-skill is fanatical. It's not right."

"She's afraid of what will happen to you and her afterward. Don't worry about Paula, her head is screwed on straight enough."

Elise didn't think so. She pressed her fingers to her forehead. The incessant buzzing had returned. The dull ache at the base of her skull settled into a persistent throb.

"I'll be fine. We'll be fine," Elise said, practically chanting the words.

"We're scared. We're all scared. Paula will do whatever is required. Don't worry about us."

Elise glanced at her friend and wanted to laugh. The *we* she'd been talking about had been her silent sisters, the brigade in her mind, not her fellow Fifth Rank WOR. She placed a hand on Alice's shoulder. "Good. Just watch her, especially if I'm not here."

"I'm more worried about you."

"Ugh, don't be." She waved a dismissive hand, no need to go down that road again. "I told Gregor I wanted to try linking two full circles. I hope I get the chance to try."

"Do you think it's possible?"

"I do."

"Okay, let's start." Alice floated away, leaving Elise with her pain.

Elise took a position between the two groups of women, and watched as Aomi and Chandra began their constructions of WOR-skill force diagrams.

When the sub-dimensions opened up, she stared at the two identical structures. The twirling Tenderstat and the Wheel of WOR-skill color came to mind. Super dimensions and sub dimensions were all fine, but what about imaginary dimensions? After all, mathematics thrived on the use of imaginary numbers to solve some of the most complex problems.

The solution flirted with her mind. All she had to do was follow it through to the end. Alex traced the math with her.

Side by side, they unraveled a solution.

Elise drew an imaginary line, laughing at the simplicity of what she was attempting—technically it wasn't simple, but the elegance of what they created was stunning. Two links aligned with one another and, just like that, they connected through an imaginary tunnel, bridging all the dimensions. Her Earth professors would have been so proud.

Tension lined the faces of Paula and Alice as the strain of handling the combined power of ten mighty women took its toll. All that power flowed through their conduit position.

Elise nudged her project and the structure unfolded and bloomed into a beautiful new construct.

Got it! Alex clapped with delight.

Elise smiled, feeling hope for the first time that day.

They broke for lunch and returned to work through the afternoon.

Alice divided the women into four groups with her, Paula, Chandra, and Aomi at the head. The four of them taught the new arrivals the key positions.

The beauty and power of these women unfolded before Elise. *How did the vlor' and lor' lords contain such raw power? How can I take it back?*

At the end of the day, Chandra floated over. Carek bobbed at her elbow, looking amused with a smirk and lifting of his brows.

"Hey, Elise!" Chandra waved. "I got all of them to form a stable link by the third try. They did so much better than us."

"Well, I'd like to think we worked out the kinks for them."

Chandra blushed. Carek bumped into the blonde and set her spinning. Chandra pushed Carek playfully away. "Well, it was wonderful. I'm so proud of them. Did you see what we did at the end?"

"No, I moved on to Paula's circle, why?"

"I've got to show you. It was Martya's idea. We passed the conduit position around. You know how exhausting that is?"

It felt like an elephant kicked her in the head. The keystone felt like being a juggler, always with one too many balls floating in the air, but the conduit position physically hurt. She hadn't thought to rotate the position between each link in the circle.

"Show me."

Chandra motioned to her little group. They floated over and formed the circle. As they worked, passing the conduit position between them, Elise was amazed at the speed with which they transferred the position.

She hovered beside Carek. He couldn't feel the WOR-skill like the Tenders and lords, but he understood the mathematical basis of the constructs. If the Tenders and lords could see what they did they would all be in trouble.

Carek's eyes glazed over and Elise recognized the telltale sign of am-net communication occurring. He frowned and opened his eyes.

"The High Tenders are calling the s'vlor back to their quarters." The look in his eyes sent a shiver down her spine. "Emperor vlor'Malita has requested your presence in his quarters."

Her heart sank. "We're not finished."

"I'm sorry, El," he said.

Elise glanced around to see if any of his assistants noticed his slip. "Mr. Tusel, formal names please. I don't want any more time with High Tender Marcus."

"Very well, Lady Malita." He signaled to his assistants. They rounded up the s'vlor and the red fluttering forms disappear into the am-net purple sea.

Carek remained behind. "El, is this it then?" His face was a mask of pain.

"Does he watch what we do in here?"

"Not unless he's physically present. If you're not tied into our specific group through the immersion suits we can't be heard. Why?"

"A few times today, it just felt like he was watching."

When she'd formed the super-link and accessed the imaginary dimension, the feeling of being watched had seemed real. The headache had been real enough. When she'd closed down the alter-dimension, it faded. Both the headache and the presence had dissipated, almost as if Gregor had been there. She didn't know what to think about it.

If Gregor wanted her to meet him in his quarters, that could only mean one thing. He had changed his mind about the Binding and her freedom had come to a sudden and profound end.

CHAPTER SEVEN_

Gambit, Day 280

IT'S NOT FAIR! WHERE'S THE THEME MUSIC?

You want music? Malice sneered. *We're walking to our doom and you want music?*

It seems appropriate, Shriek chimed in. *We're headed to our doom, doom, doom.*

Yes, I want music!

Elise wanted something, like a dirge with rising notes and crashing melodies. A valiant heroine taking her final steps deserved something profound. Surely her ending shouldn't be as mundane as a simple walk down the corridor, a pod ride around the perimeter of the *Gambit*, and a final lift tube to the emperor's quarters?

Malice teased her with overly melodramatic theme music blaring in her ears. But wasn't that what she'd asked for?

You did! Malice cackled.

The doors to Gregor's quarters spiraled opened and she walked in, chin high, fists clenched—they had to be clenched—and eyes bright as she faced her final hours. This was her fate.

She walked with a purposeful stride and into . . . not exactly what she'd been expecting.

Gregor sat on a couch with a beautiful lady practically draped all over him, at least her feet were in his lap. She reclined on the couch. Gregor sat stiffly at the other end. On the woman's lap, barely visible in the folds of the gauzy, yellow fabric of her gown, a snarking pad rested.

Gregor's chiseled features seemed relaxed, his breathing soft and unhurried. He looked vulnerable, handsome even, desirable perhaps? The woman, however, appeared overly tense. Her hands caressed the snarking pad with a frantic urgency, and her facial features looked strained.

Elise grinned, because she had several snarking simulations which would light Gregor's senses on fire. Except, she wasn't supposed to know about snarking pads. The grin slipped.

This is no time for those thoughts! Malice paced like a caged beast, hissing, spitting, and growling the closer Elise approached Gregor.

The headache had returned and she pinched the bridge of her nose. Her teeth hurt as the blood in her veins hummed.

Gregor caught her staring at him. His lips curled into a predatory smile. White teeth flashed in the light.

While her fingernails bit a little too deep into the flesh of her palms, and maybe her heart beat just a little faster than normal, her gaze remained steady and level, returning his gaze with what strength remained. She waited for him to finish . . . whatever it was they were doing.

Gregor peeled the lead to the snarking pad off his palm and tapped the woman's foot.

She stiffened, and removed her hands from the snarking pad. "Ulysses dear," the woman said, "you stopped the sim. I hadn't even really begun." The pout of her mouth seemed inappropriate on such a sculpted face.

"Analindah, we have company." He gestured, and the red-haired woman twisted around and followed the sweep of his arm with her brittle gaze.

"Who, Ulysses?"

She didn't seem the least bit ruffled by the intrusion. Instead, Analindah casually wrapped the leads around the snarking pad and placed it on the floor. She lifted her feet off Gregor's lap and swung them around to place them primly on the floor. Cold brown eyes settled on Elise.

Elise ignored the woman and inclined her head to Gregor. "Gregor, you requested my presence."

"Who is this little girl, Ulysses?" Analindah's forehead wrinkled at Elise's use of Gregor's given name. "Is this your little piece of Earth's treasure? She's a tiny thing, and so thin."

Gregor looked at the red-haired woman, his gaze hardening with a flicker of irritation across his face. "Analindah del'Candlah, may I introduce Lady Malita s'Lissa s'vlor."

Analindah rose gracefully and took a step toward Elise. The redhead clapped her hands in front of her chest. "Dear Ulysses, she wears a backtie corset. You've tamed her."

Gregor's eyes darkened and Elise caught the nuance in the writhing of his Imperial tattoo. Didn't this woman know she was walking on thin ice? Wasn't it obvious he didn't like her speaking about his property in that manner. Dull silver reflected off his eyes.

When had she learned to read him so easily?

"It is nice to meet you . . . um . . ." Elise looked to Gregor for help. She had no idea of the proper form of address for this woman.

"You may address Analindah as Miss del'Candlah. Analindah has just placed a bid on me."

Analindah beamed at his comment and flashed a brittle smile.

Elise had no idea what it meant that this woman had placed a bid on Gregor, but she did feel seething jealousy radiating off Analindah in deafening waves.

"It's nice to meet you, Miss del'Candlah"

"Of course it is. Ulysses and I are quite close. You will do well to remember that."

The tattoo danced with irritation over Gregor's brow.

Analindah rubbed her hands on the yellow fabric of her gown. "Ulysses has told me so much about his little treasure."

Little treasure? Alex snorted. Does this bitch have any idea what you are to him?

I don't want to mean anything to him, Whimper spoke from the darkness. Just tell me when it's done. When it's safe to come out.

Gregor's gaze darkened and he looked to be about ready to say something when Analindah continued, "You look so pathetic. You poor thing. You must be tired and worn out from all your training." Analindah spun and placed her fists on her waist. "My dear Ulysses, this is no way to take care of your things."

His eyes narrowed.

This woman was an idiot to openly criticize Gregor. Elise couldn't help but arch a brow, surprised at this woman's arrogance, but she said nothing. The last thing she needed was to be in the middle of . . . whatever this was.

Gregor caught her expression. He acknowledged her with his trademark smirk and stood. He sidestepped Analindah. A swish of fabric followed as Analindah spun in surprise, completely ignored by Gregor. He brushed the hair off Elise's cheek, and placed a tender kiss on her brow. The back of his finger touched the corner of her jaw and he made a slow appraisal of Elise.

It made her feel all the more like property, but she did not flinch under his scrutiny. When his attention settled on her eyes, she found herself facing two silver pools of brittle light. Passion simmered there, but also something else. Amusement perhaps? Anger, maybe? A little bit of pride? She was unsure.

"Analindah is right, opés. You look a mess. You didn't even dry your hair from the Tank?"

"Mr. Tusel led me to believe you wanted me immediately. I thought . . ." She left the rest unsaid.

He laughed. "Dear, opés, thank you for rushing over. Your enthusiasm is welcomed."

"Ulysses, dear, we're going to be late." Analindah caught the subtle nuances of Gregor's affection, and his very palpable need. Her mouth twisted in a grimace.

When she placed a hand on Gregor's shoulder, he flinched.

Elise schooled her emotions and kept her features blank. If he had intended on Binding her, then what was this woman doing in his quarters?

"Of course, Analindah, but I have some business to attend to first with my s'vlor. It's quite important. You don't mind going ahead and waiting for me, do you?"

Analindah minded very much by the look scrawled on her face, but the woman had a brain. She nodded and gathered up her belongings, tucking the snarking pad into a matching yellow satchel.

Throughout the entire exchange, Gregor hadn't taken his hands off Elise.

The rich, spiced scent that was Gregor flooded her senses and fanned the simmering bond pulsing between them into a very real blaze of desire.

Analindah paused, perhaps expecting Gregor would see her to the door.

Instead, he gazed deep into Elise's eyes. "I'll meet you shortly. This won't take long." Dismissal hung heavy in his words.

Elise stiffened. Won't take long? She'd thought he'd intended to drag out his conquest.

He must have read her confusion, because he pulled her to the couch.

"Come, opés. Sit. Make yourself comfortable."

Analindah huffed and stalked out of the room.

"I think she expected you to walk her to the door."

"She expects entirely too much, practically demanded an acceptance out of me tonight."

"Acceptance of what?"

The corners of his mouth curved up. "Opés, that woman just asked me to marry her."

"And did you? Are you?"

"What?" He sat back on the couch and regarded her while he tapped his foot.

"Are you accepting her offer? Is that what the bid is?"

"By the gods, no. Taking on a wife is problematic right now. Although, it's been a really long time since I've enjoyed a woman's company."

"I find that hard to believe. You're the Emperor. Surely there are women lined up to grace your bed."

He raised his brows and suddenly burst forth with laughter.

She looked at him with even more confusion.

"You constantly surprise me, opés. It's what I love most about you, your endless capacity to amaze me. There have been no women in my bed, and won't be until you. I've been celibate since before the Blood Rite. Why do you think I'm so eager to consummate our union?"

"What?" *Celibate? No way.* She stared back, blankly.

He leaned toward Elise. "Shocked?"

"Of course. Why? You're the Emperor. You can have anyone."

"Vendel are not as free with sex as you might be accustomed to. We're not like Earth, and explore intimacy differently when not wed."

"So, you've never . . ."

Another bold laugh erupted from his chest. "Oh, Elise, we're not prudes! I've had the pleasure to sample much in my life. But, I'm saving myself for you."

"Why?"

"Your blood altered my DNA. Your genes have been concentrating inside me, increasing in potency since the Blood Rite, and changing me, specifically my DNA. DNA I'm not allowed to . . . release . . . until the Binding Rite." His finger circled above his lap, pointed downward, suggestively. "Honestly, it's enough to make a man go mad, and you wonder why I'm so anxious to get you trained. I'm going crazy with pent up need."

She saw nothing funny in his comments or his gestures.

So, this is why it won't take long? He's just a horny bastard who needs to get off and deposit his seed in me?

"I should be flattered." She tried for a deadpan tone, but it was impossible to keep the disgust out of her voice. She regretted it immediately. "Sorry, that was inappropriate."

This wasn't going to be the intimate, passionate, sexual experience she'd pictured. It had suddenly taken on a uniquely Vendel biological aspect. Her stomach churned.

Ugh, talk about killing the mood, Shriek said.

Didn't think we'd need a degree in biology for sex, Whimper said. *I'm sorry, Elise.*

He's disgusting. Malice snorted.

"So, what now?" Elise bit her lower lip, uncertain what was expected next. "You fuck me and that's it?"

He merely stared into her eyes, pinning her in place with the intensity of his gaze. "That's a piece of it, yes. If you must be so crass, but I will warn you against any further use of that kind of language in my presence. Our binding is an experience I intend for us both to enjoy. I've thought of little else for quite some time. If you accept the bond rather than fight it, you'll find it will be pleasant for us both."

She replied by closing her eyes and refusing to look at him. She couldn't, because she wanted to do exactly what he said. But she wouldn't allow herself to take pleasure in him. She would fight him to the bitter end.

After the silence stretched past discomfort, he stood and walked to the bar. "Tell me about your day, opés."

"Excuse me? You want to know about my day? What about Analindah? She's waiting for you."

"Your day, Elise," he snapped, "tell me how your day went. Did you achieve your goals?"

"Yes," she said hesitantly. *Isn't that why I'm here?* That was the deal. Achieve her goals with the linking project and report for Binding.

"All of them?"

What was up with him? Didn't he want to get to the part where he got to rape her and steal her mind?

"Yes," she answered, but then she paused. "Well, nearly all. At least the important part. They formed full circles. I had them break into smaller groups and watched as my friends trained the other s'vlor. They should be able to continue without me."

"But?" Clinking sounded through the room as he poured a drink, a single drink.

"I had hoped to have another day."

"Another day to avoid the inevitable?" Gregor walked back over and sat down at the end of the couch. "Our Binding will be a thing of beauty, not pain. It's something you should look forward to."

"If you insist, but knowing what it will do to me, how can you expect me to willing accept it?"

"Because there's no other option. And the bond is strong between us. Our attraction to each other can't be denied. I know how you feel when you're in my arms and when I kiss you, I feel your desire. It echoes within me."

She shrugged. It was true, and she wasn't going to waste any more breath on what the bond controlled.

"Did you manage to tie together two linked groups? You mentioned you wanted to try."

She lied. "No, I didn't get to practice with that."

"So, you're not finished to your satisfaction?"

"Not to mine." She spread her hands out wide. "But, I've accomplished everything you asked and I'm here as promised."

His brow crinkled. "You're here because I commanded Mr. Tusel to send you."

"I would have come on my own. I gave my word." Her eyes narrowed and her nails bit into her palms.

"My sweet Elise . . ." He leaned back and stretched. "How do you say it on Earth? You've been saved by the bell? Analindah was correct, you look a mess. Get some sleep. I want you to try your project in the morning. If you believe it will increase our chances in the fight against the S'Lorek, then I believe you're telling me the truth and not stalling our Binding. But, tomorrow night you'll be here, and I expect you to be well-rested for the rigors of the Binding. I've been waiting a long time to have you, and I intend to savor it."

"Then why not now?"

"Because the jump-jet finals are today. I have a vested interest in who wins. And you've assured me your pet project will save us all."

"What?" When had she given him any reason to think that? Her heart thudded in her chest.

He swallowed his drink. "Tomorrow we switch your schedule to proper ship time. Day will become night and I can finally get my sleep cycles back under control."

Elise closed her eyes and leaned back.

A reprieve? Alex whispered.

One day. That's all. We're still dead.

You can't say that until the very end. I'm working on something.

"Don't bother offering to come with me, opés. I know how much you'd love to join me, but Analindah has monopolized my entire day." His sarcasm made her skin itch, because a threat lay buried in his words. He expected her to want what he wanted. "I'll have to think about her offer. Although, I'm not nearly ready to settle with a wife."

"I'm so happy for you, Gregor," she said, her voice laced with enough sarcasm to match his own.

"My potential suitors are going to be quite unhappy."

She shrunk into herself, but played his game. "Why is that, Gregor?"

"Because I have no intention of limiting myself to a single night with my s'vlor. Unlike most lords, it will take quite some time before I get tired of my little opés."

"That was unnecessary, Gregor. Need I remind you that you have won?"

"I think it is I who needs to remind you. Remember what you are. Think about that as you prepare to submit to me. The time for defiance has come and gone." The expression on his face was laced with unreadable undertones.

She was missing something important.

He gave instructions for her to return to the Fifth Deck and sleep. Then he left her to find her way back alone. Only she wasn't going to sleep. She had a race to win, prize money to collect, a ship to steal, and just under a thousand women to free.

Easy-peasy simple as pie, Malice cackled and danced in the dark.

CHAPTER EIGHT_

Gambit, Day 281

ELISE CHECKED THE LINEUP FOR THE FINALS. HER FIRST RACE WAS AGAINST Candice, the next with Segour. The last race of the *Gambit* Fleet Finals would be between her and Malikai.

"You're tied with Malikai on the time trials." Jeena sat with her and discussed strategy. Her delicate fingers flew over the gel flimsy as she brought up statistics. "Nine seconds per ring on your time trial is good. The head-to-head races will determine the outcome, but it's going to come down to the last race." Jeena glanced up from the gel flimsy. "You have to beat him. No more ties."

Segour and Candice trailed in the time trials, ten and eleven seconds respectively.

"It's not like I try to tie with him," Elise complained.

Jeena bit her thumbnail and considered. "He's your only real competition, but that doesn't mean you can ignore Candice or Segour."

"I wasn't planning on ignoring them." She placed a hand on Jeena's shoulder. "I understand the stakes." Unless she completely blew her races, Elise had secured a third-place finish with her time trial results alone, but third wasn't good enough.

"Are you ready?"

Elise nodded.

"Good, you're up against Candice first." Jeena helped her complete the pre-flight checks, then fussed over her like a mother hen as Elise strapped into the cockpit.

Elise playfully slapped Jeena's hands away. "I'm good to go, Jeena. I've got it." She waved to Dove and Larkin, who stood on the hangar deck, as the cockpit canopy sealed her inside the jump-jet. Her friends waved back as the crane loaded her ship into the launch tube.

Exhilaration flowed through her veins as she launched into space. The beautiful water world of Malbra glittered like a jewel beneath her, white clouds peppered its surface, and blue oceans stretched majestically around the globe. She spared Gregor's homeworld a moment's glance before speeding over to the race's staging area.

Candice hovered at the starting area, watching the men face off against each other.

Elise's communication channel bleeped into life. "Hi, Chickadee."

With a dip of her wings, Elise acknowledged Candice. "Hi! What are their positions?"

"Segour took Rabbit."

She turned her attention to the men's duel. Segour's wild flying gave the win to Malikai when he hit the top of Segour's canopy. Malikai earned two points as Fox. Segour launched a few choice words over the communications channel. As they set up for the second heat of their race, Elise brooded.

Gregor had set her nerves aflame yet again. She could still feel his touch where his finger had caressed her jaw. Thankfully, the headache had disappeared, but the buzzing remained.

Malikai took Rabbit in the second heat. Before he hit the tenth ring, she knew he would make the finish line. How she knew she couldn't say, except to say she felt the outcome in her gut. When Rabbit slipped through the fiftieth ring, Malikai stood four points against zero. He had secured the first win of the jump-jet finals.

"Care to run the last heat, boy," Malikai taunted.

Maximum point win in Rabbit and Fox was when Rabbit grew Fangs. After passing the twenty-fifth ring, Rabbit's lasers activated. If Rabbit scored a hit on Fox it resulted in a three-point win. Three points wasn't enough for Segour to win. The fate of their race had been decided in the first two heats.

"Don't *boy* me, and no, I don't. Enjoy your win, the finals aren't over yet."

"Really? We'll see." Malikai's laughter floated across the communications channel.

Candice's smooth alto called across the channel, "*Chickadee,* promise me this, don't let that bastard win."

"I have no intention of doing that. It would be nice to have the top spots filled with the girls. Care to see who gets first place?"

Candice laughed. "Fox or Rabbit?"

"I'll take Fox." Elise accepted her designation for the first heat.

Candice acknowledged Rabbit.

The counter began its slow count down.

Candice ignited her thrusters and took off down the course. In thirty seconds, she made it past the third ring. Given the *Go* signal, Elise pressed her palms down and went screaming on Candice's heels.

The thrill of the ring circuit filled her with vibrant energy. She felt alive and invincible behind the jump-jet controls. By the end of the third heat, Elise led the point tally with a comfortable four to two. As she waited for her next race, she floated at the edge of the starting area. Malikai had left the course as he wouldn't fly again until the final two races.

Candice and Segour chose their initial positions.

The blue orb of Malbra floated off a little below Elise's left. The stars danced in the background, solid pinpricks of light, holding promise and a universe of unknown possibilities. The Malbran sun lay behind her and illuminated the first set of rings, making them glow.

Elise considered her current status. She'd always hoped to be one of the first few pioneers in space. Her grandfather said the world was hers, but the stars had to be earned.

Little did she know that she would wind up as some galactic emperor's personal slave, denied the most basic of human rights. Elise cursed the flightsuit and the sealed helmet as tears streamed down her cheeks. Her nose ran and there wasn't a damn thing she could do about it.

As the stars swirled in her vision, she traced out the cracks between dimensions with the WOR-skill. She added a few imaginary dimensions, because it amused her to try. For a second, the universe lit up with life. She heard singing and beautiful melodies, but the language was alien. If it was a language at all.

The communications channel blatted, signaling the end of the contender's race. Elise tore her eyes, ears, and mind from the glittering starfield and glanced down at the display. Segour had beat Candice.

It was now Elise's turn to go up against the quiet male pilot. She hadn't said but one or two words to the man, but then she tended to remain secluded.

"Good show, Segour," she said.

He'd won his heat against Candice five to one, earning two points in the first heat and three, as Rabbit with Fangs, in the last.

Candice's voice chimed in. "Damn. Segour, when did you start getting so aggressive?"

"Sorry, Candy, but I need some of that prize money. Even third is better than none."

"You haven't raced *Chickadee,* yet."

"No, but I've seen the girl fly."

Elise nosed her craft over to the other two.

Candice maneuvered her ship back to the waiting position. She would watch Elise and Segour while waiting for her heat with Malikai. "Whoever wins this, takes the lead. Good luck to both of you."

"Fox or Rabbit?" Elise asked.

"Lady's pick," he said.

"I'll take Fox."

Elise settled her jump-jet behind Segour's and prepared for their first heat. The words of Jeena sounded in her head; a nice, clean, non-humiliating victory. Leave everyone with his or her pride intact. All words worth living by.

Thirty seconds after Segour took off, the buzzer sounded. She engaged thrusters and headed through the maze of gleaming silver rings, the fox in pursuit of the rabbit.

Segour chewed through the rings and exited the twenty-fifth ring. He piled on the speed, showing no signs of going Rabbit with Fangs. Elise chased and passed him at the forty-fifth ring. He fired a couple of wide shots. Clean misses. She dipped below the surface of the fiftieth ring. Fox had finished first, earning her the lead with a single point.

He took Fox for their second race. The thrusters of the jump-jet pressed her head back. She wove her ship along and through the course with barely a thought. She didn't even realize she'd passed through the fifth ring before Segour began his pursuit as Fox.

Stars danced in her vision as she slipped from ring to ring. The twenty-fifth ring came and went. He fired wildly, missing her with each shot. Jeena's words rang in her ears. She slowed and allowed him to catch up and narrowed her lead. Rabbit gave Fox the finish and the race was now tied. They each had one point.

She set up for the final heat. This one she would take.

Malikai's jump-jet approached out of the corner of her eye. He set his ship to float alongside Candice.

Elise's nerves flared, nervous about her race with Malikai.

"Fox or Rabbit?" Segour asked.

"Do you have a preference? We're tied and you let me choose first."

"I'll take . . ." He paused, considering the possible outcomes. After a while, he said, "I'll take Fox. Go ahead and line up."

Elise lined her ship up in front of his jump-jet and prepared for the determining heat. She looked to starboard and the Malbran sun outlined Malikai's helmet. He inclined his head and gave her a brief salute.

Her skin itched.

The light turned green and her jump-jet launched toward freedom. Segour pursued. She weaved and bobbed, dancing between his shots, but ultimately, he was no match for her skill. Elise piled on the speed and passed the finish gate eight rings ahead of Segour. Rabbit took two points and the win was hers.

Only two races remained. Elise, Segour and Malikai tied the current rankings with one win a piece. Her and Malikai's time trial had them vying for first and second place. She had a moment while Malikai and Candice faced off.

Malikai and Candice lined up. Segour flew back to the *Gambit* to wait. Even if Candice won the head-to-head competition, her time trial standing would place her below Segour in the final standings, since she had already lost two races. Elise settled herself to wait for their race.

She gazed out at the stars and let her mind wander. Without thought, without effort, the lines between dimensions stretched and twisted. Elise followed the imaginary lines joining the dimensional constructs of the WOR-skill. She walked a path from the first dimension, a single point of infinite wonder, full of potential and empty of everything else. A long line ran off toward infinity, beautiful in its simplicity. A simple step off the line brought her to a flat featureless plane. Smooth and uniform, it held promise. Space unfolded with depth and mystery and she traveled within her universe.

Time stretched before her, and behind as well. She traced the beginnings of the universe all the way out to the end of time. Fifth and sixth space unfolded. Brilliant flowers, they were the realm of the WOR-skill. Constructs which the minds of unique women could fold into existence and form along lines they desired.

Her head spun with countless alter dimensions as they floated past as abstract realities. Cracks between the dimensions opened and transported her into a sub-world defined by the space between time and reality. This was the solid base-rock of the WOR-skill, and an area unknown to Tenders and Masters.

The stars tilted and rotated in her vision. She extended herself yet again and opened the theoretical dimensions of imaginary numbers and watched them twirl out before her.

Again, a melody sounded. A deep bass rumbled with layers of resonance piled on top one another. Within the heavy chords, individual voices sang in chorus. The lifting song rose and fell and she felt, if only for a moment, part of something much greater than herself.

She sensed a greater consciousness, a mind so massive and powerful, as to make her feel insignificant: puny, diminutive, invisible, unnoticeable, frail and trifling. In every conjugation of the word, she was small.

She reached out, and like a gnat buzzing an elephant, she was not heard. The memory of a children's story came to mind, about an elephant who heard the most amazing voice coming out of a miniature world. If only she could raise her voice loud enough to be heard.

Eventually, it all came crashing down about her; she lost control of the construct and it faded to nothing. She stared out the cockpit of Jeena's jump-jet. Malbra floated below and the stars lit the sky. She shook her head, trying to shake away the vision. Fatigue washed over her and she dismissed the hallucination as the waking dream of exhaustion.

Alex, the silent and mysterious sister, however, seemed to cock her head with intense interest. Elise let it go. She had other things to focus on.

Candice piloted her jump-jet with fury. In the end, her determination was not enough to keep her out of the clutches of Malikai. At the thirtieth ring, he shot her small craft with his lasers. Candice lost the third and final race of their heat.

Elise and Malikai, evenly tied with two wins each and identical time trials, would now duel to determine who would stand above the other on the winner's podium. She was thankful she had at least made it this far.

This race meant something. It was the last bit of defiance she aimed toward Gregor. It was something she had gotten away with, something he hadn't been able to control, and something he could never take away.

This was hers, and if she won, it would be her victory.

Even if Gregor took the rest from her tonight.

I have you sister. We are not lost yet, Alex whispered from the darkness.

Elise sighed. She was so tired of fighting.

Beat Malikai first, of course, she thought with a laugh. That still had to be done, but after that, perhaps she could spend the rest of the day rambling around in her mind and let her body go on autopilot.

Malikai's voice hissed over the communications channel, *"Chickadee,* looks like this is it. Are you ready to face off against me?"

CHAPTER NINE_

Gambit, Day 281

It all comes down to this, Alex said as Elise checked her console. *The last race.*

Elise nodded. *I can win this.*

Are you sure? Malice sounded worried. *You keep tying with this one, but you haven't beat him yet!*

Malice! Shriek crawled out of the darkness and came to sit at Elise's shoulder. *Ignore her, she's always in a foul mood.*

She's right though. I have to beat him.

"Chickadee, I asked if you were ready?" Malikai's voice rattled through the communications grid.

Elise sent her sisters away. "Absolutely." She flicked through the final pre-race sequence on the controls.

"Care to wager on the outcome?"

"You know I don't bet. You ask every time, and I always say no."

"I think you should reconsider. It's a friendly competition after all. Why not make it interesting?"

"You have nothing that I want?"

"Can you be so sure?"

"I'm fairly certain. Are you ready to lose this race?"

The Malbran sun peeked out behind his jump-jet, silhouetting his entire craft. The artistry of the sight took her breath away.

"I play to win, *Chickadee*. Never forget that."

Arrogant ass.

"Fox or Rabbit?" Elise's fingers hovered over the gel-interface, ready to accept her designation.

"Tell you what," he said, "if you win this competition, I will grant you one request, a favor. Name it and, if it's within my power, I'll grant it."

"I said I didn't want to wager."

"Hear me out. If I win, then you'll grant me one request."

"I don't have the ability to grant you anything."

"That's not true," he said.

"Don't presume to know what I can and cannot give."

"Are you always so difficult, so distant? It could be something simple, like lunch, or dinner, or drinks." He chuckled. "Or one of your infamous snarking sims."

"Sorry, Malikai, but I'm taken."

"Is that so?"

"Yes," she said simply.

He chuckled. "Fine. Then how about this? If I win, before you say no out of hand, you give your word to consider my request. If you win, I'll give you one request, whatever it may be, on my word. You can bet on those terms. It still gives you the option to say no if you don't like my proposal."

"What would you possibly want from me?"

"I'll let you know right after I win this race." Malikai waggled his wings.

"I don't know," she said, hesitating.

"Where's the harm in finding out? It's a simple, friendly bet. You can't lose and it might even be fun. Besides, if you really think you have a chance at beating me, you have nothing at all to worry about."

"Famous last words," she said.

"Then you accept the bet?"

"With those conditions, sure, I'll take your silly bet."

"Good, I choose Fox."

"I accept Rabbit."

With the first heat set, Elise aligned herself at the starting gate. She wondered what Malikai could possibly want from a novice jump-jet pilot.

Her display blinked green and she engaged the thrusters with the press of her fingers. Elise focused on the course ahead. She dipped and looped through the first ring and then dove in a spiraling arc to hit the second with just the right exit to line up the third ring.

The seconds ticked down while Malikai waited to join the race. With a hard bank, she rolled her craft through the fourth ring and came out just a little off center of a perfect line up for the fifth ring. She flicked her fingers and the craft adjusted as if it were an extension of her body. The fifth ring loomed in front of her when Malikai began his pursuit.

She kept an eye on his progress. It would take some time to catch her before he could target her in earnest. Until that time, she picked up ring after ring. Unlike her race with Segour, she was under no illusions about her ability to win. She and Malikai were evenly matched and it would be a fierce battle until the very end.

Her display alarmed as Malikai's sensors attempted to lock onto her ship. It would take a second or two to develop a targeting solution, time enough for her to dodge. She banked hard to port and then nosed her craft up, keeping a bead on the ring in front of her. His shot went wide as she found the twentieth ring.

He was close enough now to press her, and she couldn't slip from ring to ring without giving him an easy target. She began a series of corkscrew spins and banking maneuvers. He flew wide of each of her course changes and scrabbled to catch up. Ring twenty-five approached and her fingers itched to turn the tables on the arrogant bastard.

She had a plan.

He fired another couple shots; all went wide. He wasn't waiting for the computer to lock on. Tricky, at the best of times it rarely worked.

As she ducked through the twenty-fifth ring her lasers activated. With a press of her fingers, she engaged the jump-jet's reverse thrusters. All of her forward momentum stopped throwing her against the harness in her ship. She clenched her body to keep from passing out from the g-forces.

Malikai's dragonfly craft screamed over her head, barely missing the canopy of her ship. He cursed, but it was too late.

She aimed, fired, and scored a hit. Rabbit had grown Fangs and she earned three points.

Taking advantage of her new direction of travel, she headed back to the starting area.

Malikai remained strangely quiet, his colorful language absent.

She smiled. Evidently, she'd given him something to think about.

Elise hovered in front of the gate. She toggled in acceptance of Fox and waited for Malikai to rejoin her at the beginning of the ring circuit.

When he arrived, he acknowledged Rabbit and the counter started. "Nice, trick, *Chickadee,* you were lucky."

"Luck had nothing to do with that one. Admit it, you were outclassed."

"Race isn't over, luv," he said and then launched forward.

Rabbit raced down the course, swallowing silver rings with a vengeance. By the time she exited the starting gate, he was well on his way to the sixth ring. His speed was reckless, but his course true.

Malikai either needed a finish line win for two points, or he needed to hit Elise after the halfway point and earn three as Rabbit with Fangs. She didn't know which strategy he intended; however, if she didn't narrow some of his lead, there'd be no chance to even take aim, let alone hit his craft.

Her fingers flashed over the gel-interface as she raced after her quarry.

Malikai dipped through the twenty-fifth ring and accelerated toward the end of the course. Three rings separated them. The first feelings of worry began to creep into her thoughts as the end of the course drew near.

He didn't try to evade as she raced behind him. He slipped through a ring, only to accelerate toward the next. Elise swooped behind, unable to narrow his lead. She cursed as he hit the fiftieth ring with her still a full three rings behind.

He met her at the finish line. The score after the second heat of their head-to-head race now stood three to two in favor of Elise. They had a final heat to go. The two jump-jets hung suspended before a dark starfield dusted with pinpricks of light. Four of the silver rings could be seen from their vantage point, glinting with the reflected light of the Malbran sun.

Malikai's voice rang over the communications channel. "I almost wish I was in the betting circles. I can only imagine how the odds are changing for this last race. You're an interesting opponent, very exhilarating. To be honest, there hasn't been a pilot in quite some time who has given me such a challenge."

"Funny, I don't recall seeing your name among the first-place finishers in the Imperial finals."

"Right, just like you didn't throw that second heat against Sigour just to make him feel better about his loss. Winners are not always the best pilots."

His words stunned her speechless. How had he known?

"Don't worry, he's too stupid to figure it out. But I noticed. It's not fun when you win every race is it? Sometimes, it's just enough to get out there to see what the competition is like. You remind me a lot of Jeena. I can see her training in your every move, although I believe you're better than her."

"Did you really make that bet with her?"

"To be my wife?"

"Yes."

"Absolutely. At the time she ignited my desire. I've since moved on, as has she."

"And did you throw that race?"

He laughed. "Gods, no! I wanted her, and that bet was serious. I've been paying for it since, and willingly. She beat me and I'm not ashamed to admit it. She doesn't realize what she missed out on though, and that's the interesting part."

"How so?"

"Hm, I think you'll find out soon enough."

"And what's that supposed to mean?"

"Only that this race is interesting on many levels. What's your choice?"

"You trail in the points, so it's your pick," she said.

"I'll take Fox. I think it's appropriate, considering . . ." His voice faded into muffled chuckles.

She had no idea what he thought was so funny.

The green light blinked and Elise headed out into the ring circuit. His words bothered her, and her fingers trembled slightly. Elise shook her head to clear her mind.

Focus! Shriek screamed. *This is it!*

Elise steadied her hands. The fourth and then the fifth ring passed behind her ship moments before Malikai was released to pursue.

Game time.

The exhilaration of the race took control. Four more rings passed before she had to dodge Malikai's shots. He wasn't even bothering to take aim. She laughed with excitement and felt a path open up before her, beckoning her toward the finish line. Elise hit the twentieth ring, and dodged several poorly aimed shots when communications static interrupted her concentration.

"Do you know what my request will be as I stand in the winner's circle above you?"

"Race is not over, Malikai."

"Oh, I think it is. Do you want to know?"

"No, because it doesn't matter. You're not going to win."

"All I want is the answer to a simple question."

"I have a feeling no question is simple coming from you. Stop talking, you're not going to win by distracting me." Elise pulled up sharply before the twenty-third ring.

Malikai missed her course change, passed over her flight path and blew through the twenty-third ring. Fox wasn't allowed to enter a ring before Rabbit. He cursed and was forced to accept a ten second penalty. She looped around, slipped through the ring, and headed toward the twenty-fourth.

"Get ready, because I'm coming after you."

"Hardly." His penalty was up and he resumed the chase. "The question I'm going to ask, my dear opés, is how you managed to slip out all those nights without getting caught?"

Only hours of simulation practice and countless practice runs with Jeena kept her headed in a straight line. Her mind froze, but her hands knew what to do. The jump-jet slipped past the twenty-forth ring and aligned with the twenty-fifth with just a few half-conscious motions of her fingers.

"Elise," he said, "to use an Earth turn of phrase, your rope has run out."

This couldn't be happening. Not on the very last run, not now. *Dear God not now! Where has all the air gone?*

Gregor stopped firing.

The mid-way point where the Rabbit grew fangs approached. The willow began to snap in the middle of the storm.

No! The chorus in her mind screamed. Malice vented a long ear-splitting shriek. Shriek howled. Whimper burbled something low and incomprehensible. The girls went wild and she was losing control.

Alex spoke softly to them all. In a sly voice she reminded them of an important truth. *This is the jump-jet circuit. Commoners and lords fight head-to-head. Men and women duel where gender doesn't matter. Why not a master and his slave?*

Alex had always been the voice of reason, or at least a cool, dispassionate intellectual. Elise considered her sister's words as the twenty-fifth ring approached. What more did she have to lose? Wouldn't it be a wonderful moment of defiance to take this for herself?

A grin spread across her face. She pressed her palms on the gel-pad, pulling every bit of thrust the engines would give. The little jump-jet screamed toward the twenty-fifth ring.

"What are you doing?" Gregor's surprise rang through the communications relay. It was full of anger, but laced with anticipation.

"The race isn't over until it's over, and there's nothing you can do to me until after we get back to the *Gambit*. I imagine your subjects will be quite put off if you end this race. I understand they like the competition."

"Don't you dare," he said.

She noticed a slight correction to his jump-jet trajectory as he prepared to give chase.

"I don't give a damn. Beat me if you can, but you're going to have to work for it. I don't think you're up to it. I'm better at this than you."

"I seriously doubt that." Gregor actually laughed.

The display in front of her bloomed into life. Her lasers, now active, would end this competition. She looped around, executed a tight corkscrew, and locked her weapons on the jump-jet of her master.

She pressed the trigger. Gregor weaved to the side. Her shot passed through the double wings of his craft. He engaged his thrusters and turned to pursue.

Her mouth quirked up into a satisfied smile as he gave chase. Elise aimed her craft toward Gregor and set her ship into a wild spin. His shots missed as she headed straight into the nose of his craft. Her palms itched but she held her finger off the trigger. It wasn't time.

He banked hard to starboard and they narrowly missed a collision. Elise hit her rear thrusters while simultaneously pulling hard up into a long loping arc.

She lost his jump-jet to the starfield and searched frantically. Movement out of the corner of her eye caught her attention. She accelerated. Laser fire focused on the space she'd just vacated.

Both of them ignored the rings. The rings had become irrelevant. This was a battle between the two of them.

The absurdity of the engagement did not go unnoticed, but for right now the only thing she could think of was victory. This was her win, not his, not Gregor's, and she was going to take it.

The ring circuit hung behind them, forgotten. They dipped and ducked, dodged and rolled. Elise waited for the right moment. She would only fire when she was sure. Gregor, on the other hand, fired his lasers nonstop.

Elise raced after him, reason fleeing before insanity. Malice roared. Whimper held her hands clenched before herself and jumped up and down. Shriek and Alex sat down and watched, nodding occasionally when Elise avoided a close shot. Alex wrapped her arm around Shriek's shoulders and held her in a comforting embrace. Only Shriek seemed worried, but then, Shriek would be the one to pay the price when the time came.

He banked into a sharp starboard roll and nosed over into an impossible dive, attempting to loop around and get behind her.

Elise pushed the screaming Malice to the side. A stare from Whimper made the girl settle down.

Now. The time was now!

She drew in breath and fired. Brilliant green light flashed as her laser hit the canopy of Gregor's jump-jet.

Rabbit beat Fox.

Chickadee won the *Gambit* Fleet finals.

It didn't matter that she wouldn't be able to savor the win. She'd beaten Gregor and that was all the victory she needed.

"This is far from finished, opés," he said over the communications link.

She imagined the glower on his face and the dance of the tattoo over his brow. "I beat you. Imagine what they'll say about the Emperor in disguise who lost to his s'vlor in front of the entire fleet. I can't wait to see what your people are going to make of that."

"You understand nothing, opés." Over the communications channel she heard him take several deep breaths. "This is what's going to happen. *Chickadee* and Malikai are going to fly back to the *Gambit* where we will stand on the winner's podium and accept our prizes with our disguises. After that, you and I have business of a personal nature to attend to. I have yet to decide whether to involve High Tender vlor'Vardhal before or after our union."

"He can't hurt me anymore. You've lost that hook."

"But not the hook on your friends, Elise. They have very much to lose."

Elise went silent.

"Now," he continued, "pay attention and do exactly as I command. I'll dock first and you will follow. It'll be my personal pleasure to escort you to the winner's circle. I suggest you stay close. Don't disappoint me, opés. You have only just begun to see what happens when I get mad."

"Does it matter? I'll be your lobotomized lab rat within a matter of hours after you rape me. What do I care? You're the fool to think this is the solution." She couldn't help the venom lacing her words.

"Tell me this, opés, was it worth it?"

She answered without hesitation. "Absolutely! To beat you at something, anything, was worth all the worlds, to use a Vendel turn of phrase. It was worth everything to know I had something you knew nothing about. I won and you can't ever take that from me."

"Then, I'm sure you won't mind paying the price. I'm afraid this is going to be quite painful."

"And that's supposed to make me afraid? What have you done that hasn't hurt, humiliated, or damaged me in some way? I'm numb to you and your threats."

"Then I need to find a way to make you feel again. I'll see you in the hangar, *Chickadee*."

"Whatever, Gregor," she said, biting out the words.

He would make her pay, and this time he would break her. Shriek, Malice, Whimper, and even Alex wouldn't be able to shield her from the devastation of Tender Training or the Binding meant to steal her free will.

CHAPTER TEN_

Gambit, Day 281

ELISE FOLLOWED GREGOR'S JUMP-JET INTO THE *GAMBIT*. HER ATTENTION focused on his ship as a crane lowered it to the floor. Utter chaos reigned on the hangar deck as nearly a thousand people gathered to congratulate the winner of *Gambit's* jump-jet competition.

Where did all these people come from?

Pilot's red, mechanic's blue, and the dull gray of the loadmasters swarmed in the mass of people. It made her dizzy looking down upon the swirling tapestry of celebrants.

Her stomach lurched. With a gulp, she tore her eyes away and focused on the ceiling above with its mass of black cleaning bio-pods.

Your rope has run out. His words echoed in her head.

When she had imagined being caught, she had assumed a sort of freeform panic would overcome her. A racing heart, ragged breathing, trembling limbs, and other unpleasant sensations had invaded her dreams for months.

Now that it had actually happened? That rising tide of panic and heart-stopping dread were nowhere to be found. Instead, relief filled her with an odd sense of overwhelming calm.

Her breathing remained measured and smooth. She pressed a finger to her wrist and found a steady beat. No tremors shook her fingers. No quaky feeling in the pit of her stomach made her want to retch. She felt relieved. All the sneaking, training, excitement, and fear had finally come to an end. Perhaps her words to Gregor held more truth than she thought.

I am numb.

After depositing Gregor's craft down below, the crane returned and gripped her craft. A light sway jostled her as it maneuvered her jump-jet down. Another glance down showed Dove and Jeena waiting inside the red caution lines surrounding her jump-jet cradle. The rest of the cheering crowd stood behind the boundary.

Between one breath and the next, her calm turned to horror.

Her friends!

A lump formed in her throat, and a pounding beat within her chest. Gregor said he would make her *friends* pay. She thought he'd meant her Earth friends, but understood exactly what he'd meant now.

Her heart skipped when the crane released her ship. Her Vendel friends would be punished. They would suffer. And none of them, except Carek, had any idea what was coming.

When she popped the canopy, a deafening roar filled her ears. Dove grinned and held his arms to help her down. He gathered her into an enormous hug.

"You did it! My little *Chickadee*, you won!" He pecked her on the forehead and both cheeks.

It was too much. She collapsed into his embrace, her heart thudding for her friends.

Jeena elbowed Dove out of the way. "You beat him! Next step is the Imperial jump-jet circuit." Her arms wrapped around Elise.

Elise whispered in Jeena's ear. There wasn't much time. He would be here soon.

"Malikai is Emperor Gregor Ulysses vlor'Malita."

Jeena stiffened. "What? How do you . . ."

Elise continued in a rush. She had to raise her voice to be heard over the crowd. "I have no sponsor. No half-brother. I'm from Earth. Gregor is my vlor' master."

Jeena pulled away and held Elise at arms' length. Her face paled. "Dear Gods." She turned a horrified expression towards Dove. "I'm so sorry." Tears cascaded down her cheeks.

The smile on Dove's face fell, replaced by concern.

The crowd went wild, chanting her name and cheering her victory.

Paper confetti fell through the air. Amidst all the celebration, Jeena clung to Elise.

Dove gathered both of them in his arms. "What's wrong? You just won the jump-jet circuit and the two of you look like the worlds have ended."

"Luv," Jeena said, "they have." She stroked Elise's hair and hugged her tight. "I'm so sorry. You've lost so much."

"What the hell?" Dove demanded.

"She's s'vlor," Jeena said. "Malikai is the Emperor and she belongs to him."

"By the Gods." A muscle ticked in his jaw.

"He's coming," Elise warned.

Jeena released her.

Dove lifted Elise to his chest. Her toes barely touched the floor. "My little Chickadee, I'm so sorry for what we have done to you."

"It wasn't you."

His lips pressed into a thin line. "We are all at fault. This all makes more sense now." He took a deep breath, squeezing her tight.

"Dove, I can't breathe," she said with a gasp.

He let her go. "Forgive us."

"Forgive you? How can you say that after what I did? I lied to you. Can you ever forgive me?"

Jeena tousled her hair. "For beating Malikai you could be forgiven for anything." She rested her head on Dove's shoulder and gazed into his eyes. "Just think, luv, I could have been Empress. Now wouldn't that have been hysterical?"

Elise's gaze shifted between them. They were taking the news of her true identity very well.

"Thank the Gods you won that bet." Dove shivered.

Jeena kissed him lightly on the cheek. "Yeah, look what I would've missed out on."

Dove put an arm around Jeena.

Elise looked down. "About that. He's going to punish me and anyone who helped me. The two of you will suffer. You may not forgive me after he's done with you."

Jeena shook her head. "I don't think that'll be a problem."

"I'm sorry?"

"We're innocent. We can even claim to be victims. No crime, no treason. He can't do anything," Dove explained.

"Really? Is that true?"

"Don't worry, we'll be fine." Jeena soothed her with her assurances.

Larkin edged his way past the crowd and stepped over the red line. "Shoot, guys, are you going to monopolize my girl? Don't I get a little of this hugging action?" His eyes were bright and clear, his breath absent of the smell of alcohol.

Elise swept the curls out of his face. "Lark," she managed, before he too, buried her in a hug. Lark spun her around and she laughed at his enthusiasm.

When he put her down, she spied Carek looking magnificent in a pressed green jumpsuit. Emerald eyes lit up his face and he cocked his head in salute.

"Hey, I'm going to save a spot for the awards ceremony." With a wave Larkin darted off and disappeared through the crowd.

Behind Carek, the helmeted form of a jump-jet pilot approached. Gregor cut a direct path through the crowd and aimed straight toward Elise. The crowd parted before him, perhaps curious to see the magnificent Malikai concede his defeat.

A surreal calm swept through her. Whatever consequence he chose, he needed her intact. That gave her power.

Dove placed a hand on her shoulder. He leaned down and whispered, "Are you ready?"

She placed her hand on his and nodded. "Yes."

Jeena grasped Elise's free hand. The three of them faced a furious Vendel Emperor. Her teeth buzzed and she recognized the sensation.

Was this how Gregor had known?

Perhaps, Alex answered.

His body trembled. The tremors were just barely visible beneath the fabric of the flightsuit. One corner of her mouth quirked into a smirk. She drew breath, blew it out slowly and waited.

He stopped a pace away.

She inclined her head, but refused to say a word; that one word, the required greeting of s'vlor to master, his given name, would not pass her lips.

Jeena spoke first. "Malikai, looks like you lost to a woman . . . again."

He tensed.

Jeena continued, "It might have been interesting losing our bet so many years ago, but I think in the end, I got the better part of the bargain."

His head shot up. "You knew?"

"Don't be an idiot. I've known for two minutes. The kid just told us."

"You're no longer addressing a simple jump-jet pilot, Jeena. I would remind you to remember who you are speaking to and show proper respect."

Jeena gulped and bowed her head. "Forgive me, Sire."

His spine stiffened. Gregor paused and glanced at Dove. He spoke formally, "Citizen, on your oath to your emperor, is this true?"

Dove bowed and replied with equal formality, "On my word and by my oaths, Sire, it is the truth."

"Would you subject to WOR-confirmation?"

Elise couldn't make out Gregor's eyes through the helmet, but his rage radiated off in waves.

Dove's hand on her shoulder trembled. As part of her education, Elise had spent time with the Legal Conclave WOR. Confirmation meant examination by a First Rank WOR, a very unpleasant ordeal.

"You don't have to subject him to that, Gregor. They didn't know. I lied about who I was."

"Silence," he snapped.

Elise bit her lip. She stretched her fingers out wide, then curled them tight. Her eyes narrowed, but she did not speak.

"Citizen, will you subject yourself to WOR-confirmation?"

"Yes, Sire." His hand fell from her shoulder.

"So be it," Gregor said. "Now, this is what's going to happen."

The noise of the crowd soared as the people mistook the scene in front of them. They saw Malikai, the top ranked pilot, coming to the novice to offer his congratulations. They had no idea the real drama playing out.

"You," Gregor pointed at Dove, "present yourself to the Legal Conclave for WOR-confirmation. If what you say is true, you'll be fined a million marks for your part in this charade and your ship will be confiscated. If you lie, then your life is forfeit."

Dove bowed his head, accepting Gregor's judgment.

Elise opened her mouth. Gregor's head swiveled and a single raised finger kept her silent. "Not a Gods' damned word out of you."

"Jeena, from this moment forward you are relieved of your status. You have one cycle to find a sponsor. The management of your assets will revert to him. It will be up to your sponsor to determine further punishment for your role in this. I will follow up to ensure it is appropriate."

Jeena gripped Elise's hand hard and Elise yelped with the pain.

Gregor continued, "If you fail to obtain a sponsor within that timeframe, then I will find one for you. It should not prove difficult. Is this understood?"

She whispered, "Yes."

He cocked his head.

Jeena stiffened. "Yes, Sire."

He turned and called Carek over. Elise swayed and her knees buckled. Dove gripped her and kept her from falling. Carek didn't know what was happening. He didn't know who Malikai was. The noise of the crowd died down as people left to find the best seating for the awards ceremony.

Gregor unlatched his helmet, pulled it off, and cradled it in the crook of his arm. The mist of his veil obscured his features, but his eyes stared out, cold and brittle. "Citizen Tusel," he said. Gregor deactivated the mist and locked eyes with Carek.

Carek turned deathly pale. "Sire!"

"Is this not the novice you subsidized in the jump-jet circuit?"

Carek took a knee and bowed before his Emperor. "Yes, Sire."

"And how long have you known what she was?"

"Several sun cycles, Sire."

"And you chose to keep this from me?"

"Yes, Sire."

"Carek Tusel, you're hereby stripped of your citizenship, your position, and all rights. Your life is forfeit."

Elise swayed. "No!"

"Silence," he roared and stepped to within a hair's breadth of Elise.

She flinched and choked back her fear.

Steel glinted off his eyes. With a press to his temple, he reactivated the mist, obscuring his features from prying eyes.

Her four sisters clamored in the darkness. Elise drew breath and silenced them. *Give me a moment!*

He's dead, he's dead, he's dead! Whimper wailed. *We killed Carek!*

Shriek cried out, *We killed him!*

He made his own choices, Malice whispered. *It's a shame. I really liked him.*

Alex crawled out of her tunnel and turned on the light. *Malikai gave you his word if you won. Demand his word!*

Elise let out her breath and lifted her chin. She flicked her gaze to where the tattoo should be. "On your word, I make this request, pardon Carek."

Gregor hissed. "I told you to be silent."

"He sought to serve the empire." Her voice rang out strong and clear. "He told me to return to you when he found out what I was. He demanded I stop training for the jump-jet circuit and withdrew his support. He persuaded me to dedicate myself to the linking program. If it weren't for him, you wouldn't have your precious WOR-link. He serves the empire—and his emperor—in his way." She took in a deep breath and shuddered as she exhaled. "You gave your word, Gregor. That was the bet, was it not? To grant me one request, whatever it may be. Or is your word worth nothing?"

"You go too far." Gregor grabbed and pulled her to him. He yanked her arm up and behind her back.

She cried out in pain.

Then, he crushed her lips with his mouth. Elise crumbled as the bond ignited and set her body aflame.

Gregor released her and she fell back into Dove's arms. "Before you make your request, opés, consider it carefully. There may be something else, something more important, that you desire."

She shook her head. "You'll never free the Earth WOR. Pardon Carek. That's my request. Honor it or not, but you gave me your word."

"I am warning you, opés. I've given you only one request. Is he really so important to you?"

"You made the bet. Will you honor it?" She arched a brow and stared defiantly at her master.

The call came for the finalists to report to the podium. Carek remained where he was, kneeling at the foot of his emperor. All color had drained from his face, leaving a pasty gray cast to his skin. He looked up in agony.

"I would do it all again, Elise. Don't worry for me. I knew the risk." Carek turned his gaze to Gregor. "You have no idea of the strength of this woman, Sire. I ask for no pardon for my crimes."

Gregor jerked, stricken by Carek's words. "Mr. Tusel, you are very wrong. I know her entirely too well. I know exactly what she's capable of, perhaps more than she realizes."

He jerked his chin to Elise, indicating she should follow. Without a word, Gregor walked away. She glanced at Carek on his knees and Jeena standing to her side. These were more than friends. They'd become her family. She would protect them with her last breath.

But for now, it was time to go. She followed Gregor and, in an act of submission, took his arm in her hand. He stopped and placed his opposite hand over hers. He spoke over his shoulder for her friends to hear. "Mr. Tusel, at her behest, you have your pardon."

Jeena and Dove gasped.

Carek fell on both knees and sobbed.

To Elise, Gregor said, "You are a fool, opés. You could have asked forgiveness for yourself and avoided the braklav."

"At the expense of a friend's life?"

"Is he a friend? Or is he more?"

"Like I said, Gregor, he demanded I serve you, even after explaining what the Binding would do to me. We were friends to start. At one point, he desired more, but then he discovered what I was. He's dedicated to the Vendel, and to you. Despite his actions, you have the most loyal subject in that man. He's a friend, of sorts, nothing more."

"I would have given you anything, opés. You still do not understand. I would have spared you . . . you wasted your request."

"Would you have given me my freedom and that of the Earth WOR?"

He shook his head. "That is not within my power."

"Then, I made the right choice."

"Like I said, you are a fool." He jerked his head forward. "Come, we need to finish this charade."

She laughed. "It's not a charade. I beat you. I earned this."

For a moment, she thought he gave a gentle laugh, but maybe it had just been a cough. With the veil, it was impossible to see his facial expression.

In front of them, a massive crowd had gathered. A long central aisle stretched down the center of the ordered rows. A huge stage had been erected at the front and a large three-tiered podium waited for the arrival of the winners.

Gregor led her down the aisle, holding her hand the entire way. She listened to the whispers of the crowd as they watched Malikai and Chick-adee walking together hand-in-hand. Speculation would run wild and none of it would be the truth.

They reached the front of the stage and he guided her to a set of stairs. The crowd roared. Three officials came forward and greeted them.

"Sir, Miss, if you would please follow me. We'll get you set for the presentation." The man guided them behind the tiered podium. Gregor released her hand, but kept his eyes glued to her body. Segour was already there, standing behind the podium.

There was more pomp to the ceremony than she expected. After ten minutes of speeches, and the holovideo jump-jet history piece, they finally got down to the business at hand.

"Citizens and Ladies, it is now time for the prize presentations." The announcer, a Mr. Aleksi, pitched his voice to carry across the hangar deck. "All of our semi-finalists will proceed to the Imperial Jump-jet Finals to be held in three cycles." The voice of the crowd surged.

Elise glanced over. Candice approach and stood to the side with the other semi-finalists. Candice waved a hand over her head and the crowd roared.

"For our Third Place Prize, with a cash payout of five-hundred-thousand Imperial marks, please congratulate Mr. Segour Hamman."

Segour stepped up to the platform and climbed onto the lowest level. Loud applause greeted him. Mr. Aleksi allowed the noise of the crowd to die out.

"In second place, after a spectacular flight, please welcome Mr. Malikai Ulysses."

Gregor stepped up to the platform and spun in a slow circle with his arms upraised. The crowd cheered and clapped.

The noise astonished Elise. She swayed on her feet.

Mr. Aleksi had to wait for the cheering to die down before continuing. "As you know, the second-place finisher is entitled to a cash prize of one-million Imperial marks. Malikai has requested his prize money be set aside for junior jump-jet training camps around the empire." This received even more applause and a deafening roar from the crowd.

Elise glanced at Gregor and he responded with a slight nod.

Mr. Aleksi raised and lowered his arms in a shushing gesture. Slowly the sound died down. "Citizens, this has been a spectacular competition. For the first time, we have an astounding win by a novice jump-jet pilot. As many of you know, she was trained by our very own Jeena, Imperial Jump-Jet First Place finisher for an incredible ten years running." The crowd surged again, the noise level rose. "We sorely miss Jeena on the Jump-jet circuit, although, most of us are secretly glad we don't have to face off against her!"

Laughter ripped through the cheering crowd.

"What we did not expect was for her to train another pilot to fill her shoes. For the First Place Finish in the *Gambit* Fleet Jump-jet Circuit Race, please raise your voices for the novice pilot, *Chickadee!*"

The roar of the crowd before was nothing compared to the avalanche of sound rushing toward Elise as she took the topmost step of the podium. Her heart thumped as their cries filled her lungs with each breath.

Mr. Aleksi allowed the crowd's applause to stretch for many long minutes.

Elise put on a smile and waved her hands over her head. Larkin jumped up and down in the very first row and laughed as his golden curls bounced in the light.

"*Chickadee* will walk away from this competition with ten-million

Imperial marks. A cash award for her personal use. Gods help her sponsor!"

The roar built up to a frenzied fury and crashed around her ears. She crinkled her brow and wondered how much more exciting this would have been if Gregor hadn't been standing to her right. Belatedly, she remembered to raise her arms and wave to the crowd.

The sound quieted. Mr. Aleksi walked to the front of the stage. "Now, betting is a jump-jet tradition. We begin when the first pilots are selected for competition and then it gets crazier from there."

Applause greeted his words.

"This is a special competition for the *Gambit*. We don't always have our Imperial Master joining us during the Fleet Finals. However, this year we did. And, according to tradition, Emperor vlor'Malita placed his bet."

Ear piercing whistles and loud calls sounded from the crowd. Elise heard her name and that of Malikai's shouted through the throng in front of her.

"Sometimes, almost as exciting as the actual races, the Imperial bet draws intense interest within the betting circles."

The crowd grew silent.

"This year was no different, with one minor exception." He raised his hands over his head. "Citizens, this year, the Imperial betting pool surpassed the jump-jet pool for the first time ever in imperial history."

Elise made out individual voices in the crowd.

"Who was it?"

"Malikai?"

"Segour?"

"*Chickadee?*"

Elise looked to the ceiling, far in the distance, overhead. The swarm of bio-pods continued about their business of cleaning and air purification, oblivious to the human drama playing out beneath them. They looked like a swarm of ants, relentless and with a singular purpose in life. Clean, clean, clean. The mass of black pods danced above her head in beautiful harmony as they flowed around the many obstructions protruding from the ceiling.

Mr. Aleksi lowered his arms. "Do you want to know who the Emperor placed his bet on?"

The people roared their desire. She decided Mr. Aleksi enjoyed his job. He played the crowd, tugging on their emotions and fanning their desires. He waited for the sound to die down. Only the rustling of clothing, the shifting of feet, and the occasional cough could be heard.

"Citizens! Our Imperial master thought long and hard about his bet. He debated several times over which pilot to take a chance on. I know personally he changed his mind several times before finally settling his bet."

"Who is it?" a voice called out.

"Tell us!" demanded another.

Mr. Aleksi laughed. "The Emperor decided to go against common wisdom, against sanity, and against the advice of many. He bet on a complete unknown! A novice! Our very own *Chickadee!*"

At his announcement, huge bins opened up above the crowd, streamers and confetti floated down upon their heads.

Elise's head snapped over to stare at Gregor. *What?* She couldn't see his features, couldn't read his face.

He gave a half bow. "Sometimes, the long shot is the safest bet. I decided you wanted the win very much to risk so much. I did not, however, throw the race. This is truly yours, Elise, and well earned, despite the cost."

"You bet on me? Before or after you knew?"

In the front row, Larkin bounced on the balls of his feet, clapping his hands. Jeena and Dove joined him and looked on in silent wonder. Dove held Jeena's hand.

Mr. Aleksi watched the crowd and then yelled over the noise. "In recognition for her accomplishments, *Chickadee* has added an additional twenty-million Imperial marks to her First Place Finish." He turned to her, but spoke to the crowd. "*Chickadee,* you've just become fabulously wealthy. Congratulations."

If only she could do something with it, but her prize money would be going to Dove.

Oh, my God! It's going to Dove!

Her lips twisted into a grin. Gregor fined Dove a million marks—a fortune for the average citizen—and had taken away Dove's broken ship. Her win replaced that money, leaving more than enough for Dove to buy over fifty brand new ships.

Gregor's wrath had lost its sting. Carek would live. Dove was rich, and if she were any judge, he'd shortly be presented with a matrimonial offer he truly desired. And Jeena would continue on as a pilot. Her friends were safe.

The ceremony wound down. Segour, Gregor and Elise accepted their prize money. When she pressed her palm to the gel-pad, she reaffirmed the deposit into Dove's personal accounts. Jeena whispered into Larkin's ear.

His face seemed to melt and he cast a watery gaze to Elise. She nodded and pressed her fingers to her lips. She blew out her kisses as Gregor dragged her off the stage.

It was time to be Bound.

But we're not done fighting, Alex said. *I have a plan.*

PART TWO_

CHAPTER ELEVEN_

GREGOR DID NOT LET GO OF ELISE'S ARM UNTIL THEY ENTERED THE POD CAR. His silence thundered in the space between them. The tattoo over his left eyebrow did not dance, swirl or menace with the fire dancing in his eyes. Instead, he focused straight ahead and revealed nothing about his mood.

He was angry, but there was something else as well.

She didn't know if he was furious, impressed, or amused. That was quite a range of emotions. Any one of them could belong to the expression stamped upon his face. Occasionally, when she dared to peek, he seemed shocked or introspective. That look would rapidly be replaced by pursed lips and a frown. Once, he shook his head while he stared at his feet and chuckled. That confused the hell out of her. Why would he laugh at her doom? Was it possible for one man to be that cruel?

The inevitable approached. She was to be bound in the Vendel's ritual Binding Rite. From jump-jet circuit winner to participant in an intimate Vendel Binding Rite, the universe certainly had a wicked sense of humor.

"You should be frightened, opés, and yet you're not. How is that?" His cultured voice lacked any anger. He seemed more reflective than anything else.

"I am." Elise shrugged but did not meet his eyes. "You're not as angry as I thought you'd be."

Gregor led her out of the pod car and they walked down an empty corridor. She recognized the place. Down the hall, across the sweeping walkway, a public lift tube waited. Gregor had taken her in that lift tube a long time ago. It had been the first time he'd kissed her and the first time she'd felt the exciting betrayal of her body. To be claimed by him would not be an unpleasant experience. If she could forget about him stealing her free will, she might actually look forward to it.

"I've had a long time to think about this," he said. "I expected something different from you as well."

"Fear?"

"Yes, instead, you radiate confidence. You never cease to surprise me, Elise."

"You expected me to cry and beg for forgiveness? I told you, you can't hurt me." She picked at the seams of her flightsuit. "Honestly, I find myself relieved. I'm glad it's finally over."

"It has never been my intention to hurt you." He placed her hand in the crook of his arm and led her forward.

Elise and *opés*.

Those two names held meaning to this vlor'lord. Vendel were particular about names. High Tender Marcus made sure she learned that lesson early.

She hadn't quite figured it out, but when Gregor used her name, the hairs on her arms stood on end. Opés, she understood. It was meant to be possessive and defined her as property. Elise however? What did it mean when he used her name?

"You've hurt me every step of the way. You sentenced me to the attentions of High Tender Marcus. He may enjoy his job, but you made the decision. You didn't have to pass judgment on my friends, and yet you did. They were innocent."

"Mr. Tusel was far from innocent, and Tender Training is generally an effective education. Despite my personal feelings, you are still WOR. Instant and complete obedience by a WOR is vital. Tender Training has a way of shaping a WOR's mind and instilling those traits. Some of what I must ask of you will cause you pain. I need to be able to push you past and through such pain."

Personal feelings? Elise stopped that line of thought.

Instead, she said, "Nevertheless, Dove and Jeena didn't deserve that sentence."

"As Emperor, I couldn't let them go unpunished. Your little escapade will become common knowledge soon enough." He became silent for a time and then sighed. "Alas, Malikai has run his last race. I'll have to retire that identity and find a suitable story to explain why you were in the jump-jet finals. Truthfully, I hoped you'd ask for all of them to be pardoned. Instead, you only asked for Mr. Tusel. I tried to give you that concession. I had hoped you would have realized it and taken it. I'm not your enemy, Elise. I never have been."

She realized her mistake by the regret in his voice.

"Is that why you made that bet?"

He nodded. "I gave what I could."

"Did you throw the race, then, so I would win? To give me that chance?"

"No, I never lose intentionally." He said that with great sincerity. "Not with Jeena and not with you. I felt confident I'd win, but if you had beaten me, I hoped to give you something. I knew what would happen after the race; what it would cost you and your friends."

"Jeena never liked you. As Malikai, you're a real ass."

A smile tilted the corners of his lips. He glanced sideways and looked down at her. "And as Gregor?"

"You're an imperial ass."

He chuckled. "It's a good thing High Tender vlor'Vardhal isn't here to hear you say that." Gregor pulled her to him, wrapping an arm around her waist.

Oddly, it felt right standing next to him. Their bodies fit together perfectly. He kissed the top of her head and led her forward.

They came to the ramp and the circumferential park. Elise took in the view and stared down at the gardens below. She pulled away to look over the side. He stood beside her, not touching, almost as if he respected her enough to keep his distance.

"I would rather not fight with you, Elise. I don't know how to make you understand this. We don't have to be at odds. I must be Emperor first in all things. Some of what I must do, what I have done, will cause you pain. But . . ." His voice caught and he cleared his throat. "I would like to be more for you . . . I could be your lover as well as your master, maybe even a friend."

He leaned against the railing, crossing his arms as he stared straight ahead. She glanced up at him, noting how uncharacteristic it was for him not to meet her eyes.

He continued before she could respond. "We'll be together for a very long time. It would be easiest if we get along. As Emperor, I demand obedience. To be your friend, I give up my anger."

But I have not.

"I'm willing to forgive and move on," he continued. "You must decide what to do with your anger, but know this, we complete each other. If you chose to stand by my side, we can achieve great things. If not . . ." he paused and stared out at the park. Gregor took in a deep breath, swallowed, then continued as if tasting something sour. "If not, then I must still have you as my WOR."

"I can never accept being a slave. How can you expect me to ignore that?"

He didn't answer her question. He stared off, tracing the path of the park as it curved off in the distance. The muscles of his jaw clenched.

"When did you know?" She changed the conversation, needing the answer to a question that had been bugging her. *How long had he known?*

"You said a couple of things a Vendel would never say. I began to piece it together after that. A few inquiries on the hangar deck and I was pretty certain. You're memorable, in more ways than one."

"Such as?" Elise leaned against the railing and brushed against his arm. Electricity jumped between them. The bond couldn't be denied. It waited for them.

He smiled. "The very first was something about an instant replay. That is an Earth term based upon television broadcasting systems. We don't have instant replays. If a Vendel wants to see a portion of a race then we ask for a re-sim."

"Oh, I should have realized." She pushed off from the railing and headed for the lift tube.

"What do you mean?" He fell into step beside her.

She sighed. "It's the same slip-up I made with Carek. I told him I didn't need a knight in shining armor to save me. That's how he knew. We really did have a falling out. He demanded I return to you and told me he supported your bid. I know what he did was wrong, but he was faithful to the empire, if not to you. He showed me Vendel in a way very different from you, and it was through him that I learned to care for your people. I worked hard on the linking project because of Carek, Dove, Jeena, and all the rest, not because of anything you or High Tender Marcus did to me. The carrot is better than the stick, Gregor. You never figured that out."

Gregor laughed, again. "I had another clue."

"What?"

This time he threw back his head and chuckled for a good long while. "Luv, you don't realize what a striking figure you cut. Men take notice of such things." His brows lifted with wry amusement. "I can't wait to see some of these snarking sims they've been talking about. In particular, there's one at a waterfall that involves a massage . . ."

He knew about her snarking sims? Of course he did.

He snickered when he saw her expression. "I'm surprised that would make you blush, considering it's one of the tamer sims you're known for. I'm interested to see how some of them play out in real life."

"Some aren't physically possible in real life," she said, trying to get over her embarrassment.

"Well, those you can show me on the snarking pad, the others . . . well, those we'll explore together." He laughed anew as her blush spread. His chuckle turned anticipatory as they approached the lift tube.

Malice crept out of the darkness and played a funeral dirge.

Knock it off, Shriek said.

No, Malice crooned. *This is the end. We're all nothing but puppets after this.*

I don't care, Whimper said, *I don't think it's funny. Stop playing that.*

I'll play what I want, when I want, Malice hissed.

Shriek pulled Malice's hair. *Stop!*

Elise closed her eyes and counted to three. *Sisters, please? Do you really need to fight right now?*

The trio in her head grew silent.

Where's Alex? Elise searched the dark corners of her mind, but couldn't find Alex.

No one's seen her since Malikai revealed himself as Gregor, Whimper said.

"Do you remember this particular lift tube?" Gregor pressed his palm to the palm pad.

"Yes." His question pulled her out of her internal conversation with her selves.

He came to stand behind her and wrapped his arm around her waist. The flightsuit muted the effect of the contact, but his heady scent full of musk and that odd spicy aroma made her swoon. She was thankful when the lift tube door opened. It gave her a reason to take a step forward and avoid the buckling in her knees which threatened to bring her crashing to the floor.

He still had that effect on her, despite everything. Perhaps sex with Gregor wouldn't be entirely unwelcome?

Seriously? Malice sneered. *You think it will be fun? He's going to steal our mind!*

What do you want me to do, Malice? We've lost.

Unwilling to argue further with Malice, Elise turned her attention back to Gregor. "If you knew, then why did you let me continue? Why didn't you end it?"

"Would you be surprised to hear me admit that I admired you? When I discovered who Chickadee really was, I became entranced by what you had done."

"But weren't you angry?" Elise stepped into the lift tube. "That had to be far worse than keeping the code a secret."

"Oh, I was plenty angry when I figured it out. I never discovered how you slipped out, though. I still want to know how you did it. It became an obsession, if you will, and there was a small part of me that wanted to see how far you'd get. Your determination is a mystery to me, especially when I've explained why I need you."

Gregor activated the lift, and they ascended toward the inner levels of the torus. He grasped her hands.

"Two things I need you to know, and you must understand how much I give, admitting this. First, I truly wanted to see how far you'd make it. Your tenacity amazed me. Your determination left me in awe. Nothing I did kept you from your goal; that's a rare quality in any individual. In a WOR, it speaks to something extraordinary."

"You admire me?" Was it possible she'd truly affected him? "What was the second thing?"

"I couldn't bear to take any more away from you. Nothing stopped you. Even after Tender Training, you still risked everything to train. Then the entire hangar deck placed a bet on you and I had to know why. How could you get so many people to believe in you? What was it that inspired them? I couldn't take that away, not from you and not from them. It was a gift I couldn't give you because you had already made it yours. So, I decided not to—"

"Not to what?"

"Not to take it away. If I punished you, it would have destroyed the progress we'd made in your training. I couldn't jeopardize that. I must have you trained in the WOR-skill. I knew I'd have to deal with this eventually, but I figured at least I knew where you were and what you were up to, so I let it play out."

He surprised her with his honesty, but was it true? It couldn't be. Could it?

"Have you ever heard the phrase bullshit?"

Gregor let go of her hands. Evidently, he had.

"You tell me how wonderful I am, how much you respected my effort, my perseverance, determination. Am I supposed to feel something because you cared? Bullshit! Or believe you didn't want to hurt me? Bullshit. You admire me? It was a gift that you couldn't take away?" Elise poked her finger in his chest. "You are full of bullshit."

His eyes widened. "I just told you how much I care for you. The carrot or the stick? That was the carrot, Elise. Don't you realize what it meant to let you have this? Can't you see what I did for you?" The tattoo began to dance.

She rolled her eyes. "You gave me no gift. I think you liked it. You liked how I fought back. How many women do you know who have ever said no to you? How many have ever stood up to you? As long as you're dominating every facet of whatever this is between us, you're content to watch me struggle. You let me fight back because I amused you."

The wind of the lift tube decreased.

His eyes narrowed. "You do not amuse me, Elise. You amaze and astonish me. I've never met anyone quite like you. I'm in awe of you."

"Am I supposed to feel something because you admit your feelings? What exactly are you admitting? That you care for me? Or is it that you're proud of your pet?" It was a rhetorical question, one she didn't give him time to answer. "Don't think for a minute you're special to me, because I don't feel the tiniest bit of affection toward you. Physical attraction from the *callidor* aside, there is nothing between us. I despise you."

His eyes grew cold and she knew she'd said too much, but damn him, how dare he try to tug on her emotions like that? Did he really think she cared what he thought?

Don't you? Whimper whispered.

Shut up!

You know I'm right, Whimper slunk away.

"You don't hate me. You just can't see it yet. I accept your anger, but eventually you'll let it go, just as I have. We belong together. I've known it from the moment I laid eyes on you. In time, you'll understand. I'm Emperor, and you're my s'vlor, but there is something growing between us. Hate and love are two emotions closely tied together. You'd be surprised how easily one slides into the other."

"I won't ever love you. You are a fool to believe that."

"No? I'm too much in your thoughts for you to disregard me. Eventually you'll grow tired of fighting and give in. I will wait."

The lift tube stopped.

"Just finish this. Once you Bind me, I won't be the same person I am now. What you say means nothing, Gregor, not when you're set on taking over my free will."

"That's not what's happening, but you refuse to believe me."

The tone in his voice sent a shiver down her spine. Damn, how could he still affect her so strongly? Why couldn't she resist him? She lifted her chin and walked into his personal quarters.

"I'm nothing but a victim."

"No, that is not the truth. In time, you will understand, and your anger will fade."

CHAPTER TWELVE_

ELISE SCREAMED INSIDE HER HEAD AS GREGOR USHERED HER INTO HIS PRIVATE suite of rooms.

Dear God, this is it. Tonight we truly become a slave.

Alex stepped fully into the light. A strange look glowed in her expression. The darkness fled as she sat in Lotus pose. *You said the link couldn't form to a WOR already bound to a master?*

Yes.

So, my sister. The answer is staring you in the face.

There is no answer, Elise said.

Shriek, Malice and Whimper joined them, looking as perplexed as Elise felt.

What do you mean? Malice asked.

If we are linked then he can't bind us, Alex explained.

Bitterness edged Elise's voice. *We is me, sister. I can't link with myself.*

We are us, not you, Alex said with an affirmative nod.

You are constructs of my imagination, Elise insisted. *Split personalities of a crazy person.*

Shriek sat beside Alex. *I don't know about that. I earned my place. I'm not you. You could never be me.*

And you could never stomach what I will unleash, Malice growled.

Elise walked through the outer rooms of Gregor's suite, confused by the conversation going on inside her head.

That doesn't make any of you real.

And why not? Alex asserted. *We're each our own separate selves. Shriek endures to keep us sane. Whimper submits so we may fight another day. Malice keeps us strong and pushes us when we're weak. She keeps us to task. We're all here to fight.*

And what have you done, Alex? Elise gave a shake of her head. *You hid in the darkness and now you presume to tell me this?* Was she really having a conversation with her selves? Now she knew she was crazy.

Shut up, Elise, Alex said. *You're no crazier than the rest of us, a little raw around the edges maybe, but you're not insane.*

You didn't answer the question. Elise couldn't believe this conversation.

Really, Alex continued. *Where exactly do you think the inspiration for the WOR-skill changes came from? Who was it who discovered the alter-dimensions? Dimensions based outside of reality? Who figured out how to beat the Vendel? That person has been me.*

Well that got everyone's attention. All the voices silenced.

Not possible, Elise said.

Listen, it takes five to form the most basic of links. We are five individuals who happen to share the same body. We exist independently of one another as well as dependent upon one another. We are sisters! Who says we can't form a link? I'll take keystone. Malice has the strength for the conduit. You take care of Gregor. You're the only one of us who will enjoy it. And together, linked, the Binding will slip around us. We will triumph. Remember, sister, it's not over until it's over. If we don't try, then we all will be slaves. I say we take a vote.

No vote, Elise said. *I'm in charge.*

Oh no, sister, Shriek said. *I paid my dues. I want a vote.*

No vote!

Whimper spoke, her voice strong and confident for the first time ever. *I, too, have earned my place. Which one of you has the stomach to submit to these men? Which one of you can swallow all pride so the rest may live? Shriek endured the pain. I endured the humiliation. I want to vote.*

Elise, Malice whispered, *who got you out of your bed each night and pushed you to aspire to something more? I did. When Shriek and Whimper had seen the worst and were nearly destroyed, who pulled them from the abyss? It was I. Who called forth our fifth and final sister from the darkness? Again, I did that. When insanity threatened—of us all—who allowed it to claim them? Me. We are not you. Alex is right. We are us, and four of us are not done fighting. Link with us. Allow us this last chance to fight. If we don't try, then we all are lost. If we try and fight one last time, then, maybe, just maybe, we will win? How can you deny us this chance at freedom, as slim or as crazy as it sounds?*

Elise listened to their pleas. Malice's words, more so than her sisters, sounded clearly in her ears. They were not one person anymore. At some point she had gone insane. Her mind had split, but Malice had brought them back from that dark abyss. Her sisters were going to save her, yet again.

Okay. Alex, if you think this will work, then do it. Pull me in. Elise glanced over her shoulder. *I will be busy with Gregor.* She trusted her sisters to carry her through the trial ahead. *If it will work for us, then maybe it will work for the others?*

I will look into that, Alex promised.

Alex began the intricate folds of the construct forming the keystone position. Elise left Alex to the task. As a mere link in the chain, Elise didn't have to pay any attention to the rest of what they did. All she needed to do was focus on Gregor, and make certain he didn't find out what her sisters were up to. She walked into Gregor's living room and stopped short, completely caught off guard at the sight of the High Tender and the braklav twirling in his hand.

Pure fury darkened Marcus's features. His brows were drawn and his lids narrowed to thin slits. Clenched jaws ground down on teeth framed by a snarl. He glared at her and took in her red flightsuit, then his gaze flicked to Gregor.

Her knees felt insubstantial, barely able to hold her weight, and she trembled.

"Sire," the High Tender said.

Gregor was a step behind Elise and nearly ran into her. "Lord vlor'-Vardhal, why are you here?" A dangerous undercurrent laced his inquiry.

"I saw the jump-jet finals." The High Tender turned his gaze to Elise.

The flightsuit felt constricting, and she was reminded how long she'd been in it.

I stink. I need a shower.

A trickle of nervous perspiration beaded between her breasts and dribbled down her back. It had nothing to do with the High Tender, or the twirling braklav. At least, she tried to convince herself that rod had nothing to do with the nervous sweat. Gregor she could handle. The High Tender and the braklav? That made her heart stop.

Elise swallowed.

In her mind, Alex formed the link. Shriek entered the circle. Whimper waited her turn. Malice provided the conduit to funnel their power. Elise would have to endure whatever came alone while her sisters completed the link.

"I found the outcome quite interesting, wouldn't you agree?" Gregor stood behind Elise, seemingly at ease, but there was a stiffness in his body that hadn't been there a moment before.

"I told you this one would be trouble," the High Tender said with a sneer. "You wouldn't listen. At every turn, I insisted on discipline, but you stepped in, and look where it has gotten you." His voice rose in pitch.

Elise took a step back. Gregor pulled her against him, sheltering her from the High Tender.

"I have achieved results." Gregor's voice remained calm and soft, but Elise detected an edge to it.

"Bah!" The High Tender scoffed. "What results would those be? To be the laughing stock of the empire? An Emperor with a WOR out of control? A WOR who beat you!"

"You mean of course, this WOR who is with me, in my quarters, prepared for the Binding Rite? My WOR who is willing to complete the rite? I'm not dragging her in here kicking and screaming. I won't have to tie her down like some of the other vlor'lords will need to do. She accepts the Binding. Is this the WOR we are talking about? Or are you speaking of another?" Gregor's tone made Elise wince.

It never occurred to her to kick and scream.

"That's irrelevant! I'll show her what it means to serve her masters," The High Tender moved forward and grabbed Elise's arm.

She yelped as he crushed her flesh.

"Let go, Lord vlor'Vardhal." The icy calmness of Gregor's tone made Elise flinch. She couldn't see his face, but knew what she would find there. His eyes would flash silver and be as sharp as daggers.

High Tender Marcus yanked on her arm and she cried out again in pain. He ripped her from Gregor and pulled her to him. In a smooth practiced move, he pressed the braklav to her chin.

Her head exploded in a firestorm of light and agony. Alex struggled to maintain her grip on the fragile link, but then the pain vanished between one moment and the next as her world spun.

Gregor wrapped his hands around the High Tender's neck.

She found herself on the floor, gasping for breath.

The veins on the High Tender's neck bulged and his face turned several shades of red and purple.

Elise put her hands to her head as a sharp pain thrust through her head. It wasn't the braklav. Alex had forced her into the link. The circle was now complete.

Malice roared in triumph as the High Tender gurgled.

Gregor enunciated each of his words. "Lord vlor'Vardhal, do not touch my property again unless I have given permission." He shook the High Tender. "I am her master, not you. Understood?"

Rage tumbled in the High Tender's expression. On his normally cool and dispassionate face, that emotion seemed entirely foreign and terrifying. He clutched at Gregor's strong fingers wrapped around his throat. Gregor stared the man down, but did not release his grip. He pushed the High Tender back a step.

High Tender Marcus croaked out his words. "She is my responsibility, Sire. Mine! I will have her punished."

"No, Lord vlor'Vardhal. She is yours no longer."

"She has flaunted her defiance for the last time," the High Tender said with a roar. "I must administer correction. She has made a laughing stock of you, of the vlor', of the Tender Conclave and all of Vendel." High Tender Marcus turned a threatening eye to Elise. "S'Lissa, you will tell me how you managed this charade and who helped." His face turned scarlet. "To stand on the podium at the jump-jet presentations and see the Emperor's s'vlor mocking him in front of the people . . ." His words trailed off and the braklav became a blur as it spun in the air. "I can only imagine what was going through his mind."

Gregor sniffed. "I was proud, High Tender."

Elise glanced up in surprise.

The High Tender glared back and sputtered, lost for words.

"I knew what she was up to. I've known for quite some time, and I allowed it to proceed."

The High Tender's jaw dropped and he sputtered some more. He finally found his words. "You knew! You let this behavior continue?"

"Yes." Gregor glanced down and smiled. "I, Emperor Gregor Ulysses vlor'Malita, made that decision all on my own. I found it fascinating to see what she would be capable of accomplishing."

Elise recovered from her fright. A cool detached calm returned. He had only wanted to see what his pet could do when given the lead? It was always about ownership and property rights with Vendel males. She had been a fool to think otherwise.

Let them fight all night if that's what it took. She was filthy and had spent one hour too many in her flightsuit. She stood on steady legs and headed off to Gregor's bedchamber.

The High Tender growled. "Where the hell do you think you're going?"

Elise unzipped the flightsuit. Both men's eyes followed the path of the zipper as it revealed the soft flesh beneath. "I'm going to take a shower. After you're done fighting over me, the winner can come collect me." She glanced between the two men. Her eyes flicked to the silver rod. "Either to apply the braklav or . . . for other more pleasurable pursuits." Her gaze lifted and captured Gregor's shocked expression. His lips parted in surprise.

"You dare speak to me in that tone?" the High Tender took a step toward her.

Gregor reached out and gripped the High Tender's bicep. He shook his head. The message was clear.

Elise felt for the link formed by Alex. It was solid and complete, and to Alex's credit had been completely tied off.

Nice, Alex.

Let's hope it works. Alex crossed their fingers. The others held their breath.

Elise turned her back to Gregor and the High Tender and walked away. At the door to Gregor's bedchamber she said, "I believe that sim you were interested in involved a massage and a waterfall. I also remember a promise you made about our next shower together. Perhaps you should finish your tug-o-war with the High Tender before I finish the shower."

His jaw gaped as his eyes widened in surprise. Elise dropped the flight-suit near the door of his bedroom. She walked naked into his private chambers while both men looked on. Certain of the completely disparate thoughts going on in their minds, she felt freer than she had in a very long time.

She didn't hear what words the two men shared. She didn't care. One of them would win. Either way—she or Shriek—would do their part.

CHAPTER THIRTEEN_

ELISE TURNED ON THE HOT WATER AND GAVE A SIGH AS SHE STEPPED BENEATH the steady stream. Dirt and sweat washed away as the water sluiced over her body. Steam billowed everywhere, blanketing the bathroom in a fog of possibility. Her muscles relaxed and her stomach returned to its proper place in her belly.

Alex showed her the fully formed link. *Do you think it will work, sister?*

You pulled in some of the imaginary dimensions, Elise said with surprise. *What made you think of that?*

I don't know what to expect from the Binding, so I figured I had to tie this thing off. When you sleep, we all sleep, and I didn't want the link to fail.

Elise tilted her head back and wet her hair. *Do you honestly believe I'll be getting any sleep tonight?*

Just being cautious. Besides, when you have a chance, you need to take a look at what I've done, or rather, what the link has done for us.

What do you mean? Elise paused.

Only that these Vendel have no idea what they've created. Alex retreated.

Elise opened her eyes, feeling the loss of her silent sister. It didn't take long to figure out why Alex had left. Gregor stood in the doorway of the bathroom, his figure shrouded in the thickening steam.

"Did you settle things with the High Tender then?"

He laughed. "Yes, luv."

"Ah," she said.

He unzipped his flightsuit. "You made him mad."

"Well, he'll have his turn soon enough."

"No, he won't." Gregor stepped close and peeled back the sleeves of the suit.

Her brows lifted and she bit her lower lip. She was reminded of The Spot and that silly competition back on Earth when she and Alice had been judges. Back then, they'd had no worries and a bright future ahead of them. How easily things changed.

As Gregor pulled the suit to his waist, there was no doubt in her mind that had he been in that nightclub she would have picked him as the winner to the chest and buns competitions.

"I seem to remember you do a remarkable job washing hair," she said.

"You remember that, do you?"

"Not fully, I was a little out of my mind at the time, but pieces of the memory survive. You're invited to remind me."

His flightsuit dropped to the floor in a puddle of red fabric.

Dear God, what have I gotten myself into?

She gazed at the masculine perfection that was Gregor. He had no idea what he was in stepping into, and was a fool if he thought he would be in control. She intended to take what pleasure she could.

"Your mood has changed, opés."

"Anger has no place in this. I should thank you, I suppose, for making this easier to bear. I've decided to put aside my feelings toward you in private. If this is my future, and we are to be together, it might be easier not to fight in here."

"This should be a pleasurable experience, Elise, not a chore." He traced the angle of her jaw. The gesture seemed tender, almost genuine.

For a moment, she almost believed him.

A deep sigh escaped his lips and she watched as he closed his lids. His arm dropped and he stepped away from her. "I don't want to force you."

Her brows furrowed, not understanding, as he moved even further away. "What?"

"I can force the Binding and make you mine, but that's not what I want. It's not what I feel." His gaze cast downward as he brought a hand over his heart. "You see me as a monster, a man full of evil, but I'm merely a man forced to make impossible choices. I wish you could understand and accept that." His gaze skittered away.

She didn't understand what had happened to her arrogant and calculating v'lor lord.

"You killed my family, Gregor. My friends, and billions of my people, are dead because of you. What do you expect? And the women brought on board? You forced us into obedience with the WOR-guards and their horrible whipsticks. When that failed, the Tenders had their braklavs." She shrugged. "I feel what I feel."

"I know you think you must hate me, but there's a part of you that feels otherwise." His head shot up. "I know you feel it."

"What I feel is some twisted combination of Vendel biotech brought on by that stupid perfume you gave me at the Banquet. I've come to accept that I don't control my body's reactions around you."

"There's more to this than the *callidor*." He rushed toward her. Desperation thrummed through his body and transferred into hers. Like a bolt of lightning they connected as power surged between them. Lust and desire stirred in her belly, making her gasp.

"I won't apologize for what happened, because it was necessary."

She flinched at his words, because they stung and trivialized the deaths of everyone she had ever loved.

He continued, his grip on her hands tightening. "That is my burden to bear. Those deaths are on my shoulders. My oath is to protect and serve— all of humanity. Certain decisions are required of me which are difficult. No one should have been forced to make them, but I did. I had to if we're to survive. I had no choice in the matter. I believe you understand what that means. You know the choices forced upon me. Given an alternative, I would have wished we met under different circumstances."

She wanted to pull away from him, but found herself drawn to the pain laced in his words. He spoke of the deaths of billions as if they were mere tallies in a ledger book, but his voice . . . oh his voice told a different story. He grieved. It was the first time she heard him express remorse about what he had done.

He pulled her close. Their bodies touched. His chest brushed her nipples. His voice dropped to a whisper. "That you lost so much was unavoidable, but it was necessary. Deep down you must understand. You know why it was required."

He held her while closing the distance between them. His head dropped until his cheek rested beside hers and his mouth lay beside her ear. "And you also know I wouldn't hesitate to make the same decision again. If that makes me a monster, then so be it. That it was your planet is irrelevant. It was the price of survival. You know this, and you will forgive me given time. You just haven't accepted it yet."

His lips brushed the corner of her earlobe, sending a sharp thrill of pleasure shooting down her neck. A moan escaped her and she arched her neck, opening herself for him. He was impossible to resist. Whether it was the *callidor* or not, she wanted him.

Gregor nuzzled the soft tissues of her neck. "You must forgive me, Elise. What I have done since bringing you on board has hurt you, and for that I'm sorry. High Tender Marcus will never touch you again with the braklav." He kissed the soft spot at the angle of her neck and shoulder. "It's why I let you fly. It was the one thing I could give that didn't cause you pain, and I desperately needed to give you something, because I knew what I would have to take."

"Gregor, please." She tried to release his grip on her hands, but he refused to let her go.

His kisses moved to the angle of her shoulder and then his head lifted and she met the full intensity of his gaze. She expected desire to be reflected in his expression, and there was certainly plenty of that. The steam billowing around them couldn't dispel the heady scent of musk and spice emanating from the man. What caught her by surprise was the vulnerability he expressed and the raw honesty in his eyes.

In that moment, he stole her breath and took her heart. She felt herself molding her body against his, folding her softness against his strength. Like a key and a lock, she couldn't avoid the truth, and whether she liked him or not, they shared a chemistry she couldn't deny.

"I'm tired of fighting." She vented a deep sigh, because it was the truth. "I just want it all to end."

He wrapped his hands behind her back, carrying her captive hands with his. That annoying and wonderfully handsome smirk returned. With a chuckle he brushed his lips against hers, denying her the kiss she wanted. "Then, let's speak of pleasure. Tell me how does that shower sim start?"

She couldn't help but laugh as he diffused the tension with a simple question. "Oh, no," she said as she took control. "Wash my hair first, then I'll show you."

He sighed. "My opés," he kissed her deeply. "Must I teach you to obey?"

She returned his kiss, eagerly and a bit teasingly, then pushed him away. She turned and handed him the soap. "My hair, and then the rest can follow."

A shocked expression flashed across his face. His eyes narrowed and then he laughed. "So be it."

Gregor worked the lather into her hair and washed the rest of her body. For the first time, his hands explored and roamed freely. When he hesitated, she guided him with absolute assurance.

CHAPTER FOURTEEN_

THE REST OF THE NIGHT BLURRED AS GREGOR UNLEASHED HIS RESTRAINT. When he let go and gave in fully to his need, she took back control. The night dissolved in an endless sea of ecstasy. A firestorm erupted between them, sweeping her up and carrying her away with his desire, but this had become her battle, and it was time to win.

As his passion cooled from a wild, heated urgency to a slow and deliberate need, Elise turned the tables on him and the victory became hers. She shaped his responses and drove his desires until he begged for release. There was nothing sedate to his lovemaking, and while he confused her actions as eagerness, Elise orchestrated a carefully devised conquest.

Perhaps Gregor had assumed too much. She was no Vendel woman whose entire experience with physical intimacy was at the end of a snarking pad. She had practical experience in seduction and took full advantage of the education she'd accumulated back on Earth.

The number of times they came together blurred as the night drew on. The integrity of her link remained throughout the night. She checked it often. Solid as steel, flexible as a whipcord, it endured the onslaught of Gregor's DNA.

The time came when sleep finally took hold of them both, and she drifted peacefully to sleep in his arms.

Elise woke in the crook of his arm. The bedcovers lay at the foot of the bed, long since discarded during their intimate activities. Although asleep, Gregor held her possessively and breathed peacefully in his sleep. Her head rested on his chest and she took a moment to explore his body anew. She traced the contours of his chest and then traced a line down and around his navel. She outlined each of his hardened abdominal muscles with the tip of her finger before moving lower down.

"Are you still hungry, luv?" Gregor grabbed her hand and halted her exploration. He chuckled and kissed the top of her head.

"I thought you were asleep." She flattened her hand on the smooth expanse of his lower abdomen.

"I was, but your touch is electric and could pull me out of a coma. Dear Elise, I'm tired."

"You're saying no?" She draped her leg over his hips.

He moaned and pulled her leg to the side. She took the opportunity to slip her hand lower still. He claimed to be tired, but his body responded to her touch.

"Does the word 'no' mean nothing to you?" He vented a throaty chuckle of surprise.

"Not when I'm . . . what did you say . . . hungry?"

"You're kidding," he said in shock.

Elise leaned up on her elbow and moved to sit on top of him. "Not when you're awake and, it would seem, interested? Do you remember that second sim I showed you?"

"Absolutely." He rewarded that comment with a low, lusty chuckle.

She arched a brow. Some while later, she left him gasping, and when she attempted to interest him in more, he begged off.

"I'm exhausted, luv. Allow a man to rest."

"Do you mind if I take a shower?"

"When's the last time you slept?" He pulled her to him and kissed her lightly on the lips.

"I'm not tired." This statement, oddly, rang true.

She'd been up for close to two days straight, yet despite that, felt refreshed, well rested, and very much awake. *Is this a side effect of the link?*

"Gods, luv. You've worn me out. Go ahead, but don't leave our apartments. No more unauthorized exploits, opés. Those days are behind you."

She kissed him back. "As you command, so I obey."

Gregor flung an arm over his eyes, and drifted off to sleep. Once his breathing slowed, and she was certain he had fallen asleep, she took herself into the shower and washed all traces of him from her body.

Sisters? Elise searched her mind for her very unusual sisters. The girls had been silent throughout the evening's activities. *Are you there?* A rising panic threatened to drown her when no one answered her call.

Finally, Shriek spoke. *Are you quite finished?*

Yes. Did that bother you?

My tastes lie in a different direction. That was wholly unpleasant to watch.

Nobody said you had to watch, Shriek. I didn't watch when the braklav touched your skin.

That is why we are . . . who we are. You have your pleasure and I have mine.

Where is everyone else?

We are here, they answered.

Elise allowed the water to run down her body and scrubbed her body clean with Gregor's soap. The heat from the water made her drowsy. A quick change to the temperature controls and cool water washed over her, invigorating her mind and waking her tired body up.

Does anyone know how long it takes for the Binding Rite to be completed? Whimper stood to Alex's side and wrung her hands with worry. *When do the changes begin? When will we know if we're safe? If we survived?*

Silence echoed Whimper's words.

Elise hadn't thought to ask Gregor how long it took for the effects of Binding to manifest? She didn't know. How could she find out without giving anything away?

CHAPTER FIFTEEN_

ELISE EXITED THE SHOWER AND WONDERED ABOUT CLOTHES. SHE GLANCED AT her discarded flightsuit and immediately dismissed that idea. She walked back to the bedroom. Gregor was still asleep and lay sprawled on the bed, gloriously naked. For a moment she watched him and contemplated joining him.

He was hers, and yet she was the one who belonged to him. With a shake of her head, she shoved unwanted thoughts from her mind. Given another place, another time, it would have been easy to have felt some-thing real for the enigmatic man. As it was, too much separated them, too much pain divided them, and their goals couldn't be more opposite.

He didn't stir as she searched his wardrobe for something to wear. An entire row of black jumpsuits filled one wall. Another held more formal, ceremonial dress clothes, pants and tunics with silver detailing up and down the sleeves. Other uniforms of several varieties and colors, fancy coats and cloaks, filled another wall. He hadn't worn any of those in front of her. She had only ever seen the black jumpsuit.

An image of him decked out in such finery brushed across her mind. If Gregor cut a stunning figure in his black jumpsuit, then in those clothes he would be overwhelmingly devastating.

A long row of drawers lined the back wall. She wandered to those. With a sigh, she opened drawers at random, looking for something which would fit her much smaller frame. She settled on a long, dark gray, shirt. The wrists were cuffed and she rolled them back, shortening them. The shirt hung to her knees, covered all the important parts, and reminded her of all the other boyfriends whose closets she had raided in the past. None of those men were alive anymore. With a sigh, she moved on and exited the wardrobe.

The idea of climbing back in bed with Gregor tugged at her for the briefest moment. If it weren't for him being the Vendel Emperor, and responsible for the deaths of billions, she could develop feelings for him. They meshed in a way she didn't understand, but she could never forgive what had been done. She passed by the bed, but lingered to admire his sleeping form. In the living area, she stopped in front of the ugly gray wall.

For some reason, it pulled at her. A press of her palm to the palm pad and the screen activated. The gray wall of ugliness disappeared to reveal the stunning sight of Malbra hanging in space with a smattering of stars beyond it. The blue orb was in motion, or rather the *Gambit* spun on its axis. Malbra slipped off the lower right of the screen as the *Gambit* slowly rotated in orbit above the planet. Two of the other fleet ships came into view and hung as tiny silver doughnuts in the sky. The bleakness of space, the blackness between the stars and galaxies, pulled at her with an uncanny intensity.

Alex, she whispered, *are you here?*

Yes, sister. I am.

Elise touched the wall. *Do you see this? Do you see how beautiful it is?*

I do. Alex paused. *Why are you so sad? You should be happy. We've won. We escaped the bond.*

Have we?

Yes!

I'm tired, Alex. I'm tired of fighting. I don't even know what to fight for anymore. I'm caught in an indestructible web, bound by a man who has my emotions tangled into a knot so dense I can't see the individual threads anymore. I can't imagine a life without him in it, and freedom? I don't even know what that is anymore. I hate Gregor, yet I can't deny my feelings for him. Nothing makes sense. I was too eager last night, as eager as him, and perhaps more. That scares me because I can't stomach that I have feelings for him.

It's a complicated situation, Elise. It's okay to have doubts. The two of you have been through much. The callidor is only a vehicle to spark an attraction which already exists. I don't think you were ever meant to deny him.

I'm ashamed of my feelings and my eagerness last night. I enjoyed being in his arms. Not fighting him felt right. How can that be?

I don't know.

I feel like a traitor to myself, to us, to the other Earth WOR. What have I become? Have I joined the enemy?

I don't think so.

I'm lost, my sister. Did I succumb to the prisoner's paradox? Have I sabotaged my rescue by falling for my captor?

No, you most definitely have not. We have won, although not in how we thought. Alex soothed. *Let me show you what we have become, sister. You will be amazed!*

Her consciousness unfolded as Alex revealed the effect of Elise and her sisters linked in what could only be described as a self-sustaining bond. Together, they had become something new. Rank no longer had meaning. Elise marveled at their potential, dragged her fingertips across the fabric of the universe, and shuddered with possibility.

When Alex finished her demonstration, Elise sat on the floor with her legs folded beneath her. Her knees touched the wall and she pressed her hands against it. Tears streamed down her face. They weren't the tears of desperation, failure, fear, shame, or even despair. They were tears of joy, peace, and hope. They had found a way free.

Elise gazed into the darkness of space and thought again of the infinite dimensions of space and time. They unfolded in her mind, and as she had done before, she walked a path from the first dimension, a single point of infinite wonder, and stepped onto a line running with all haste toward infinity. A simple step brought her to a flat featureless plane. A graceful leap took her into space as it unfolded with length, width, depth and limitless possibility. She traveled the universe on the whisper of thought alone.

Time stretched before her, and behind as well. The fourth dimension of space, separate from the others, time tied everything together, radiating forward and back. The fifth and sixth dimensions unfolded. Brilliant constructions, they were the realms where WOR folded the fabric of space and forced it along lines they desired.

Her exploration continued. Cracks between the dimensions opened, transporting Elise into sub-space. This was a place between time and reality, the solid base rock of the WOR-skill, and an area unknown to Tenders, Masters, and even the WOR. It didn't belong to the imaginary dimensions she'd opened up previously. This was new.

Elise had seen it before. She'd been hovering in her jump-jet, waiting to compete, but didn't understand what she'd been looking at. Now, with the knowledge Alex had gleaned for them all, Elise traveled the cracks defining the dimensions of her universe.

Stars tilted and rotated in her vision. Again, a melody arose, a bass rumble with layers of resonance piled one on top the other. Within the heavy chords, individual voices rang out. The lilting song rose and fell, joining Elise with something much greater than herself.

She sensed a familiar mind. The same consciousness she'd felt before. Last time, its size had overwhelmed her, and made her feel insignificant. That had changed. Now, she was bigger, and she reached out to say hello.

Elise stretched her mind, seeking contact. The first time she had tried this she had reached out alone, and like a gnat buzzing an elephant, she had not been heard. This time she had company. The five of them, Elise and her sisters, solidly linked, had become something more. She and her sisters attempted to brush the mind of a giant. The memory of a children's story came to mind about an elephant who heard the most amazing voice coming out of a miniature world. Today they would shout.

Her mind spread its wings and said, *Hello.*

The S'Lorek answered back.

They did not use words. The S'Lorek's mind was too massive to contain such a concept. What followed was an exchange of intellect so amazing it made tears of joy turn to a torrent of wonder.

Born within the stellar nurseries of a distant galaxy, the S'Lorek evolved in the void of space. This was but a single individual, an explorer who had left its Clan to search the universe for other intelligent life. A revolutionary, it believed life would be found within the crowded and noisy galaxies, where the stars screamed, rather than in the vast emptiness in-between. The Clan disagreed, postulating any sane creature would flee the noise of the galaxies.

That beam of light, which brought death to the Vendel, was nothing more than a sensor. Like an eye, nose, or tongue, it probed the stellar systems: planets, asteroids, moons and comets looking, smelling, and tasting for intelligence deep within the stony rock. In tasting the rocks, planets, moons and other debris within the stellar systems, the S'Lorek noticed an electrifying flavor, so delectable as to be irresistible. An odd coating covered some of the worlds, a tiny film on the surface, and it wanted more.

Elise's wonder turned to horror.

Through the eyes of the Vendel, she showed the S'Lorek the brilliance of the human race. She struggled to convince the S'Lorek the biological coating on all the planets was sentient, but biology was a foreign concept to the S'Lorek.

She told it to stop.

It refused. It had tasted ambrosia and had sent the essence to its Clan who now marched toward an irresistible feast. The S'Lorek lost itself thinking about the indulgence to come. It dismissed Elise and increased its speed to Malbra. It came to devour them all.

Alex cringed in terror.

Malice straightened her spine. *We are in serious trouble, sister.* Malice rolled her shoulders and cracked her knuckles. *Now what?*

CHAPTER SIXTEEN_

ELISE SENSED GREGOR'S AWAKENING IN THE BEDROOM. HE HAD BECOME AN undeniable part of her, firmly rooted in her psyche. While the idea she could sense him gave her pause, she couldn't ignore a small part of her comforted by the connection. The dichotomy remained unresolved in her head. The Binding may have failed, but the effects of the Blood Rite—now that she recognized them—remained. She shivered as their connection solidified in her mind.

"Good morning, opés." He walked into the living room.

"Is it morning or night?" Elise unfolded her legs and twisted around to look up at him. She feigned a yawn and stretched.

He chuckled. "Ship-time or Fifth Rank training room?" His eyes twinkled as he grinned down at her. "Now that I can get you on proper ship's time, it's morning for both of us." A pair of thin, gray linen pants rode low on his hips, accentuating his abs.

As he stretched, she admired his bare chest as the muscles of his chest rippled. She closed her eyes and buried the desire rising to the surface. Now was not the time to repeat any part of last night. "I see." She turned back to gaze at the stars. The blue orb of Malbra came back into view and drifted lazily across the view screen. "Will I see any of my friends again?"

"You're WOR friends, perhaps. The others, never." He came to stand beside her, towering over he seated form. "It's beautiful, isn't it? I can't wait to show my home to you."

"I thought all the worlds were yours."

"True, but I was born here. The oceans of Malbra course in my veins. It will always be a part of me."

As Earth will always be a part of me.

She ached to see her homeworld. What had been left in the devastation? Gregor said he'd left Vendel citizens behind to safeguard against planet-wide catastrophe. Without Earth's population to man the power plants, dams, and all manner of things, Earth could have become uninhabitable. What were his plans for her homeworld?

The planet below truly was amazing, but it wasn't Earth.

Despite the heavy ache in her heart, she tried being conversational. Not knowing how the Bond worked, she had to tread carefully.

"How many people live on Malbra?"

"Close to two billion. We keep the population limited. Most of the colony fleets draw emigrants from Malbra. With nearly all the cities floating on the seas, we encourage our citizens to join the c-fleets."

"Two billion," she said with a sigh. Two billion lives at stake. Two billion lives and all life in the ocean would soon be nothing but a snack for the S'Lorek. That and the nearly thousand s'lor and s'vlor, not to mention, the thousands of First Rank WOR on the *Gambit*, its fleet ships, the hundreds of orbital platforms and stations, and those down on Malbra.

She cringed and ran her hands through her hair.

Damn, she'd found the solution to one problem, only to come up against another.

What good is freedom, if I'm not going to be around to enjoy it?

I'm working on it, sister. Alex soothed from the darkness. *Just give me time.*

Gregor ran his fingers through her hair and massaged her scalp. She managed not to pull away from his touch.

"You look tense. What's wrong?"

Elise grabbed his hands and removed them from her head.

He knelt behind her and folded his arms around her body.

"What happens now?" She leaned back and he kissed her neck.

"Now?" He laughed and trailed a line of kisses along her jaw. He nibbled at her ear. "Now, we relax."

Dear God, not more. Shriek muttered and stomped off. *Hasn't he had enough?*

"What about the High Tender?" Elise steered the conversation to more serious topics, something to dampen any amorous thoughts that might be churning in Gregor's head.

"Now that the Binding is complete, he must defer to me. You'll continue to train with him. That doesn't change, but you won't have to worry about the braklav touching you over your jump-jet escapades."

Not jump-jet escapades, but what about other things? Gregor had left that wide open, something she took note of and filed away.

"I don't understand, why not?" Elise said with confusion.

"I told you. I knew what you were up to the whole time and decided to let it play out. If I'd wanted to punish you, I would have." He released her and sat down next to her. "Don't misunderstand, opés. He's still your trainer. Second to me, he defines your life. The Binding makes it impossible for you to defy my wishes. Despite what you think, though, it doesn't strip you of your free will. You'll still have plenty of opportunity to choose your fate. Obedience will be rewarded. Disobedience will be punished. Tender Training—although exceedingly rare after the Binding—has on occasion been required."

"I don't feel any different. Is the Binding finished then?" She gazed into his eyes, searching for the answer. No glower greeted her scrutiny. Instead, she sensed supreme confidence in his gaze.

He nodded. "Unlike the Vector or the Activator, Binding is immediate."

Have we truly escaped?

"You and I are doubly blessed by the gods," he said.

"How is that?"

"I knew from the moment we met that you would be mine. It was like I stepped into that room, saw you, and knew I had found my other half."

"I don't know what to think anymore."

"Well, I believe what we shared last night was genuine. Never have I had a woman who knew me as intimately as you did. Binding has many advantages, my dearest opés." His eyes burned with passion and possession. "You have a very pleased and satisfied master; which is why I doubt you'll ever need the braklav. The Binding ties you to me much stronger than it ever could."

You're a fool. Malice chuckled.

He has no idea. Alex grinned.

Now it's time to make them pay, Malice growled.

Whimper, who had been silent for some time, spoke in a soft whisper, *No, sisters. We have a new problem to solve. This isn't done.*

Indeed. Elise stared off into the blackness of space. Out there the S'Lorek hunted, and it would devour all of humanity unless she stopped it.

"I can't go back to the linking practice. It won't work now that you and I are bound, but I think I can still help. Isn't the whole point of linking to combine the strength of the s'vlor to fight the S'Lorek?"

Gregor nodded. "You may not be able to join the link, but I would like to see if you can still train and guide the others." He scratched his chin, thinking.

Elise shrugged. "I guess we can see. If it's morning for us, then it's evening for them. They're all asleep right now."

"We have time. Until then, I have a gift for you." Gregor stood and strode off to his bedroom.

Elise continued to stare into the darkness.

He returned with an armful of billowy emerald silk.

"As good as my shirt looks on you, I can't have you wandering the decks in that. All of your gowns will be brought up here." He nodded toward the gray shirt she wore. He shook out the fabric and held it out for her inspection. "I suppose I'll have to make room for your things in my— our—closet." He grinned at the pronoun and she watched him savor the sound of it as it rolled past his lips.

The gown, as with all his selections, cascaded to the ground in a fall of shimmering silk like fabric. Otherwise it was unadorned. A tight sleeveless bodice, no corset, and a slightly flared skirt made this the simplest gown he'd ever chosen. She stood and took the fabric from him. Under his arm, he clasped a black case. This, she eyed speculatively, but refrained from asking what it contained.

At his urging, she pulled his shirt off and slipped into the gown. It fell to her feet in a shimmering cloud. He stepped behind her and fastened the long row of buttons along the back of the dress. It felt tighter than the corsets he'd routinely dressed her in. She turned and didn't need to see her reflection to assess the effect of the dress. Gregor's expression of heated lust was enough of a mirror. He ran his tongue across his upper lip and whistled softly.

"Nice." He spun his finger in the air.

Grateful he was putting clothes on her and not taking them off, she obliged his request by twirling in a slow circle.

"You look amazing, but there is something missing. I have something else to give you."

She arched a brow in silent question. He lifted his finger indicating she should follow. Gregor walked to the far end of the room and placed the case on the top of the bar and opened it.

Elise's heart sank. Inside were two items nestled in a rich chocolate-colored velvet. The first looked very much like the misted veil she'd worn on the flight deck, except much more ornate. It was a half circle of silver metal, encrusted with diamonds and emeralds. The other item was a necklace. She had seen one like it before.

It was a Binding amulet.

A large walnut sized gem encased in silver filigree hung from a linked silver chain. Inside the gem, colors swirled in a miniature rainbow.

She stood unmoving, uncertain what he expected. The fingers of her left hand fiddled with the fabric of the dress. Her right hand went to her neck. Elise's gaze shifted between Gregor and the box. His eyes narrowed briefly. Elise looked back to the box and took a step toward it, pretending interest. Out of the corner of her eye, he relaxed.

"A Binding amulet?" She raised a hand to rest on the counter, next to the opened box, but did not touch the contents.

"I thought maybe you wouldn't remember." He came to stand in front of her. "This is a new part of your wardrobe. It signifies your status as a bound WOR. You'll wear it as a symbol of our Bond. Most s'vlor chose to activate the veil only during formal occasions. Unlike the mask which we both wore for the jump-jet competition, the veil doesn't hide your features. It's symbolic only."

Gregor placed the circlet on her head. She touched the cool metal and ran her fingers over the gems. He lifted the necklace out of the box, undid the clasp, and placed the gem around her neck. It dropped and nestled within her cleavage.

She remembered an earlier conversation about the purpose of the low-cut gowns worn by the WOR. He fastened the chain and traced the links all the way down to the crystal. The light of the colors danced in his eyes.

Elise held her breath.

Gregor brought his other hand to cup her chin. He brushed his lips across hers in an incredibly gentle kiss. He groaned and then pulled her toward him. She thought he'd kiss her more, instead he whispered in her ear.

"Elise, I hope to show you the man I can be and not the monster you believe you see. Everything I've done, from the very beginning, has been for my people, for all of humanity. I hope we are done fighting. I . . ." his voice broke, "I . . . hope, not all of last night was the Bond. I would like to think some was you."

"Gregor, please." She placed a restraining hand on his arm.

"Listen," he said, "I don't expect you to suddenly change how you feel, but with time I hope you will look at me with affection and not the way you do now."

Had she been scowling?

"You ask too much," Elise breathed out in a low whisper, her words barely heard.

"We are linked. Through ties stronger than any other bonds between a man and a woman, our relationship transcends such concepts. We will be together centuries, Elise. Centuries! Can you maintain your hatred for that long? Can you sustain it? We can be so much more together, if you would only try to see me as something other than this monster you perceive."

"If it's what you want then I must obey." *You will never have that chance.* Her linked sisters echoed her thoughts.

"I don't want it because I've commanded it. Obedience, service and submission, I demand, but not your affection. What I want is a promise to consider the possibility. Don't give me your love because I command it, but rather, because you choose to bestow it upon me."

"I don't know if I can do that," she said.

"I only ask you to consider it. We have plenty of time. Enough time that it would be easier to enjoy each other, rather than not." Gregor released Elise and stepped away.

He headed to the bedroom. He didn't demand an answer, but she knew, deep down, he would eventually. Even her affection would be taken by force, unless she gave it willingly first.

A short time later, the shower turned on. Elise felt the moment the warm water hit Gregor's skin. Their link was that strong. Her entire body shuddered.

They were undeniably connected, but he'd answered her question. The Binding had failed.

They were truly free.

The next disaster belonged to her, the WOR-skill, and the linked power of ninety Fifth Ranked WOR, because Elise wasn't done fighting, not when she had all of humanity to save.

CHAPTER SEVENTEEN_

G<small>REGOR RESTRICTED</small> E<small>LISE TO</small> *THEIR* <small>QUARTERS AS HE NOW REFERRED TO HIS</small> suite of rooms. She shivered with the implication of the tiny pronoun. WOR weren't supposed to move in with their masters. They were supposed to complete the Binding Rite and reside in separate residences. Most vlor'lords had wives who found the entire Binding Rite difficult to endure. They, and their husbands, were usually happy to put the whole affair behind them.

He left Elise with an educational instruction plan and a gel-interface. With a kiss, he wandered off to a Ruling Council meeting, saying only that he would be back by dinner. She had no intention of following his instructions.

Elise sat down to the gel-interface and set up a virtual ghost. If Gregor checked in on her, he would see her dutifully following his lesson plan. Then, she checked on Bobo and the other subroutine constructs she'd planted in the am-net months ago. Despite their efforts, Carek and the other am-net conclave members had been unsuccessful in eliminating her viral subroutines. All was in place.

She needed to reach Alice. A plan had formed in her mind. Now to see if it would work. She stretched out, mentally attempting to contact Alice using the WOR-skill.

After several false starts, she brushed up against a familiar mind.

Alice.

Being nighttime on the Fifth Rank Deck, Alice was asleep. She rolled over and swatted at her ear. Elise repeated the call several times before Alice woke.

Elise? Alice sat up in bed, rubbing at bleary eyes.

It's me!

What happened? You disappeared and we were so worried.

Oh, Alice, it was glorious. I won the jump-jet competition!

Then you have the money and we'll get a ship?

Elise scratched her head. *Ah, no.* She had to catch Alice up on everything, but how much to tell? *I beat that pilot I told you about. The one that was real cocky?*

Yeah?

Well, guess who the bastard was? Elise didn't wait for Alice to respond. *None other than our favorite emperor. Needless to say, he already knew it was me. He figured it out before the finals.*

O-oh, came the halting response. *Is that what happened, Tender Training?*

Elise chuckled and her amusement transmitted through the link.

No, you won't believe what happened.

If you don't tell me right now, I'm going to scream. Are you okay?

You don't understand. Gregor took me off the winner's platform and straight to his quarters. High Tender Marcus was there with his braklav. He and Gregor fought over me. Gregor won. He dismissed the High Tender and then proceeded with the Binding Rite.

Alice went deathly quiet.

Elise didn't think it would be funny to drag out the suspense, although she thought about it for a moment.

I beat it! Elise paused for a moment to let that sink in. *I found a way around the Binding Rite. I'm still me. I'm free!*

More stunned silence greeted her and Elise wondered what Alice thought. More than likely, Alice was trying to figure out if this was a trap.

Elise proceeded to explain the link she'd formed with her other-selves. That took time because she couldn't describe the link without revealing the existence of her sisters. Describing the split of her mind into separate personalities, and eventually into five independent individuals, sounded crazy, but it had worked. She had to dredge up memories of Tender Training to explain how it had broken her mind and given birth to her sisters.

Alice did not interrupt.

By the time Elise came to the end, she felt like she'd gone to confessional and had come out the other side feeling cleansed. Keeping all of the pain and terror bottled up to be strong for the other s'vlor had taken more from her than she had realized. Finally, her words slowed and eventually stopped.

Alice, the ultimate pragmatist, gave a simple response. *I knew it had been bad, but I had no idea how bad. I understand better what you said about Paula. Tell me your plan.*

Elise breathed a sigh of relief. Alice hadn't judged her crazy.

Well, that brings up another problem. We can't leave . . . at least not just yet. We have to save the Vendel. Elise paused and gathered her breath. She began the next story, the story of the S'Lorek, of Bobo's creation, and how she would solve two separate problems at once. Only when Elise's story came to an end did Alice speak.

Very well, when do we begin?

Tonight. The S'Lorek will be here sooner than the Vendel think. I intend to go out and greet it.

How do you plan on doing that?

Elise grinned. *That, my friend, is something new. I've got something better than the WOR-drive. I just need enough ships to get us all there together.*

Show me.

Elise transmitted the details of the WOR-step, something never before devised by any WOR. Alice grappled with the intricacies of the construct.

I see it, but Elise, I can't handle that much power.

Probably not, Elise agreed, *but a linked circle can.*

Alice thought for a moment.

Elise waited patiently.

Yes! I think so. She paused and then asked, *Elise, can you handle that much power?*

Yes, and more. My sisters and I are discovering a lot of new things.

I don't understand these sisters of yours, but I would like to learn more of them. I'll go wake Aomi and Chandra. We'll be ready. Nighttime for you will be morning for us, right? Won't you be busy with Gregor?

He won't be a problem. Now pay attention. Learn this. Elise sent an image of a new construct. *When I contact you, use it to confuse the WOR-guards. You should be able to walk right by them. All they'll see is a peaceful room of s'vlor, business as usual. Bobo will take care of the gel-pads and give you access down the service corridors. Divide yourself into groups. It will make it easier to travel. I'll tell you where to go when I contact you again.*

Nice little trick to hide from the WOR-guards. How did you . . . never mind. I'm not even going to ask anymore.

Wake Aomi and Chandra. Oh, and you'll need Paula. Work quickly.

I'll be ready, Alice said. *Are you really ok? If you're worried about Paula's sanity, shouldn't I be worried about yours?*

I'm good. New. Different. More than what I once was, but still me, human and flawed. I remain committed to you and the rest, but also to the Vendel. They need our help.

I'm worried.

Don't be. We are fine. We are free. I'll introduce you to everyone later . . . when this is all finished. Don't worry for me. I am free. Have hope, because I believe all our dreams are possible.

Make me a promise.

Anything.

When it gets to be too much, when you need a break, or feel yourself slipping away, promise you'll tell me? Please.

Elise paused to consider Alice's request. Would she know when that time came? *I give you my word.*

Then let's do this. Alice couldn't hide the eagerness in her voice. *After the S'Lorek, then what?*

We take our freedom from our masters.

CHAPTER EIGHTEEN_

ELISE TAPPED THE GEL-INTERFACE AND DIALED IN *CHAMPION'S RIOT*. WHEN she didn't get a response, she put in the code for the *Spider Devil*. Dove's ugly face popped into view within the surface of the gel.

"Dove!"

His eyes widened, bushy brows shooting up with surprise. He opened then closed his mouth, twice. Dove rubbed his eyes.

"Chickadee? How is this possible?"

She ignored his question. "Listen, I need to talk to you."

"How is the Emperor allowing this?" Dove paused and gestured behind him. "Jeena, it's the kid."

Jeena pushed Dove to the side. It took a few seconds for the video feed to readjust.

Moistness pooled in the corners of Elise's eyes. It had only been a day since she'd been ripped away from Dove and Jeena, yet it felt like years. She missed her friends terribly.

"Kid?" Jeena's eyes were bright. "I didn't expect to ever see you again."

"It's good to see you too."

"How did you convince him to let you talk to us? I'd think after—" Jeena waved her hand around, searching for words, "—well, after everything, we'd be the last people he'd let you speak to."

"I didn't ask, and I don't plan to. I need a favor." She couldn't help the grin spreading across her face. Dove and Jeena exchanged glances, communicating in that silent way of theirs.

"Just so we know what we're getting into, do you mind answering a few questions?" He rubbed his nose with what appeared to be an oddly clean hand.

"Let me start with the obvious." Elise took in a deep breath. "I have endured Vector, Activator, Blood Rite, WOR-skill training, Tender Training, and more. I have worked at one purpose and that is restoring my freedom and that of my fellow Earth WOR. This explains how I met both of you. I needed a way off the *Gambit*. Sadly, that didn't work out as planned. But in meeting you, I gained new friendships and a new purpose. The S'Lorek is coming and I believe I can stop it, but I need help. Gregor doesn't know what needs to be done, or what I can do."

Dove and Jeena remained silent, heads pressed ear-to-ear. Jeena placed a hand on Dove's forearm. He placed his over hers.

"Go on," he said.

"Gregor took me to perform the Binding Rite."

She paused to assess the reactions of her friends. They knew what Binding meant, and exchanged another of their private glances. Worry and concern filled their faces, but they hadn't activated any alarms. They appeared willing to listen to what Elise had to say. She rushed to explain. Time was limited.

"Tender Training did things to me, to my mind, bad things, but some good came of it. Turns out, I can't be Bound. He has no idea that the Binding failed."

Jeena gasped.

"And how does this affect us?" Dove's eyes narrowed.

"I need your help."

"What you're asking is treason. You saw what happens to Vendel traitors. You ask too much. I'm sorry, but we're loyal Vendel citizens. We have to tell the Emperor what you've shared."

"I'm going to tell you why helping me serves the Vendel, and why Gregor and the Tenders can't know any of it. You won't be traitors. You'll be heroes. I need ships and pilots, enough to carry ninety Fifth Rank WOR out to meet the S'Lorek threat."

"Kid, maybe you didn't hear Dove. We won't commit treason."

"Let me finish. If you still feel that way once I've explained, then go ahead and report me."

"Chickadee, there's nothing you can say that can change our minds." Dove rubbed his chin.

They hadn't broken off communications. Elise took this as a good sign and pressed her point. She needed their help.

"What if I told you the S'Lorek is coming to Malbra? What if I told you I've communicated with it? What if I told you it—and it's a single entity—was coming to devour Malbra and every living thing in Malbran space? What if I told you I can stop it, but only if I get my WOR to it before it arrives in Malbran space? What if I told you the only way to do this is with Earth WOR who are not yet bound?"

"Enough already with the 'What if I told you' crap," Dove said. "What are you trying to tell us?"

She breathed out. They were listening.

"The S'Lorek is looking for sentient life. Life like itself. The fact it ran across something messy, called biologic life, is irrelevant. We're not sentient rocks. That makes us insignificant. It calls us slime and considers us pests, and unfortunately for us, we taste really, really good. It's addicted to the taste of biologic life. Even worse, it's only one of hundreds of its kind, and it shared the taste of us with its Clan. We're not looking at just one massive eating machine. We're looking at hundreds of them descending on the Milky Way. We're looking at extinction. If Gregor and the Tenders Bind the Earth WOR, we'll have no defense, but I have a chance, and I need your help."

"Dear gods," Jeena whispered.

"What do you think you can do?" Dove covered his mouth, then grabbed at Jeena.

"I'm going to fight it, but not with Gregor. He and High Tender vlor'-Vardhal don't understand, and they never listen to me. What they made me into may very well save humanity. In that small thing, Gregor has succeeded. But I can only do this without him."

"Sounds whacko, kid," Jeena said.

"I would think so too, but trust me. Gregor would never approve of what I intend, and he would never allow it. I'm going to take the WOR to meet the S'Lorek."

"And how is that?" Dove leaned forward. "Because I think this is where your favor comes in."

She took in a deep breath and blew it out before continuing. "I plan on loading up all the Earth Fifth Rank s'vlor into ships and head out to meet the S'Lorek. Once there, I plan to neutralize it."

"Stomp on one ant, there's still the rest of the clan coming, Chickadee." Dove shrugged. "Not the answer if we're just going to get buried under hundreds more of them."

"I realize that. But the S'Lorek is coming now. The Clan will take some time, a few sun cycles or even a year? I don't know how fast they travel, but it's similar to the WOR-drive. I have an idea about that, too. Although, it's not quite the escape to freedom I was thinking about." She shook her head. "First, I have to deal with the threat in front of us. In order to do that, I need you and your ships."

Dove sighed. "Chickadee, my ship isn't mine anymore and Jeena's has reverted to the Pilot Conclave. The Conclave Master has grounded her from flying until she settles on a sponsor. We don't have ships to give you."

"But you have the prize money. Gregor didn't take that from you? Right?"

"I can't make a ship appear out of thin air."

"I was hoping Jeena's ship was still available."

"Kid, my ship can't hold that many people. You'd need at least three ships that size, perhaps more."

Elise gazed at her feet and twisted her hands. "I need to get off the ship if I'm going to get out there and meet it."

"I'm sorry kid." Jeena cupped both her hands over her mouth, thinking. "I don't see how we can help." She looked to Dove. "What do you think, luv?"

Dove scratched his head. "How did you plan on getting to this thing? None of our ships have WOR-drives. The First Rank may use their power to drag us across the galaxy, but you still need a WOR-drive for them to work with. And do your WOR know how to work a WOR-drive?"

Dove was thinking of a solution, which meant he wasn't going to turn her in. "I kind of got that figured out. We're not going to drag ourselves across the galaxy."

"Right kid." Jeena crossed her arms across her chest and looked down her nose. "What exactly are you going to do?"

"I'm going to fold space around the ships and step from here to there. No drive, no machines, no WOR-space. Just a simple shift from where I am to where I wish to be."

"That's not possible," Dove said.

"Yes, it is." She stared back at him. A moment passed and then another. Finally, Dove's jaw dropped. "You're serious?"

She nodded. "You know what a Fifth Rank WOR is capable of?"

They nodded.

"Well imagine ninety of them linked together. The power isn't additive. It's exponential. But, even linked they can handle only a fraction of the power I can wield alone."

Dove tilted his head back and knocked it against the bulkhead.

"Chickadee, it still doesn't solve the problem about ships. We don't have them to give to you. Even if we did, with just two of us, we'd still be a ship or two short."

"What about Lark?" Elise leaned forward.

"Kid, I don't think so," Jeena said. "Even with Larkin, we don't have the ships. If you can just step from here to there, why do you need us at all? Just take the *Gambit*."

Elise smacked her palm to her forehead. "You're a genius, Jeena! But, I still need your help."

"In what way?" Dove asked.

"I need a place to gather the Earth WOR. The only place I know is the Confinement Deck. I wouldn't think twice about it, but the others would have strong reactions to being back in that horrible space."

"It's not like the Emperor isn't going to miss that many WOR, kid," Jeena said.

"I got that. I can shield against Gregor, the vlor'lords and the Tenders. I just need a place to do it."

Dove scratched the stubble on his head. "The hangar can be emptied out a few ships. We can arrange space in there. Pretty open."

"Can you do that?" she asked.

"Larkin and his buddies can be convinced to move their ships," Dove said.

"As long as it's done quietly. I can't afford Gregor finding out."

"When are you planning this?" Jeena leaned against Dove.

"Tonight."

"Not leaving us much time, are you?" Dove said with a grumble. He pursed his lips and kissed the top of Jeena's head. "What do you think, luv? Can we do it?"

"Let's say we pull this off," Jeena said. "Let's assume you transport the entire ship right in front of the S'Lorek's nose and either convince it to stop, or make it stop, then what? We all just shrug and beg the Emperor for forgiveness? This isn't going to end well."

"Right, I get that, and I know what I'm asking." Elise bit her lower lip. "That's the second part. Gregor is still going to need the Earth WOR. The S'Lorek is one of hundreds. The rest are coming. I plan on finding a way to stop them all. I have an idea, but I don't know if I'm going to be able to pull that one off. Gregor will have to understand, and I'll convince him letting us go is the only way to do that."

"Such as?" Dove glanced at Jeena.

Jeena stared at Elise.

"A vanguard . . . sort of. After the S'Lorek is taken care of, someone is going to have to guard, or shield, or defend, against the arrival of the Clan. That's going to be a full-time job, a lifetime's worth. It should be worth a pardon from the Emperor."

"Sounds difficult, kid."

"Yes, and I'm still working on the details, but for now we must meet the S'Lorek threat."

Dove and Jeena exchanged another set of unreadable glances, but in the end, they gave a nod.

Elise's heart soared. They would help. "I have to go," she said. "I have more planning to do. Can you empty the hangar tonight? Without causing suspicion?"

"Yes, kid, we'll take care of it. How do we get back in contact with you?" Jeena looked through the viewscreen.

"You'll sense me. Just answer, ok?"

"Like mind-to-mind? Thought only the WOR could do that with one another," Dove said.

"I'm not your typical WOR," Elise responded. "Just answer back. I'll hear you."

"Ok, kid. We'll do our part. Good luck, and take care." Jeena blew her a kiss.

"Can you really do this?" Dove asked.

"I trained for and won the *Gambit* fleet jump-jet competition while a prisoner of your emperor. I can do this."

"All right. I believe you." Dove cut the connection.

Elise sat back and massaged her temples. It was all happening too fast. Could she really break the bonds of the lower ranked WOR? Could she do it by tonight? Would she have ninety WOR or eight-hundred? She glanced at the gel-display and noted the time. Dinner would be in less than an hour, and with it, Gregor would return.

She lay back on the couch and meditated. Her mind went over Alex's new theories. The WOR-step—Alex coined the name—was intuitive. Her fellow WOR wouldn't be able to use it, as it pulled in the imaginary dimensions only she could reach, as well as slipped into the cracks in-between, but a properly linked circle of WOR might be able to. Alice would figure it out.

Elise checked the construct to make sure there weren't any limitations on size. After some period of time, she was fairly certain not only could she take the *Gambit*, but she could take something as small as, say, just herself.

She dragged her fingertips through the fabric of the universe and marveled at what she'd become. This brought back memories of Gregor explaining the origins of the WOR-skill and the very first woman to use it.

Was absolute power intoxicating? Or could she find a way to remain anchored to her humanity? The thought of becoming anything resembling the High Tender caused goosebumps to cover her skin. She would die before turning into that . . . and, she'd given her word to a friend.

CHAPTER NINETEEN_

GREGOR WOKE ELISE WITH A GENTLE KISS.

"How was your day?" she asked for lack of anything better to say. No one had given her a manual on the proper behavior for a bound WOR.

"Fine, thank you for asking." He gazed at her with soft, silvery eyes.

Elise placed a hand on her belly in hopes of silencing the swarm of butterflies dancing within.

Gregor gestured at the bar. "I'm going to pour some wine, would you like a glass?"

"Do I have to toast anything, or can I just enjoy it?"

He chuckled. "No, luv. No toasts."

He walked behind the bar and rummaged around. The clinking of glassware and then the distinctive *pop* of a cork sounded. He poured two glasses of red wine and returned to hand her a glass.

"Come join me on the couch. I want to take a moment to relax."

"You look tired, Gregor. Can I rub your neck?" She sat at the end of the couch and placed her wine on the coffee table.

He kicked off his boots. "A foot rub would be wonderful, opés."

She cringed at the pet name, and sat at his feet to play dutiful slave.

He leaned back and sipped at his wine. Murmurs of pleasure guided her hands and he slowly relaxed.

"So, what happens at these Ruling Council meetings? If you don't mind me asking."

"It's not much different from the governments you're used to back on Earth. Today we mucked around for hours trying to decide whether to evacuate Malbra or not. Many of the vlor'lords with WOR are nervous."

"This is because of the S'Lorek?" She played it cool, demure.

How much did they know? Had the Vendel picked up on the increased speed of the creature?

"Yes," he said and then vented a low murmur of appreciation as she worked on his toes.

"Can you do that? Evacuate billions of people? How long would that take?"

"Too long." Gregor withdrew his foot and offered her the other. "That feels really good, luv."

"I'm pretty good at back rubs, too. I can show you, if you'd like."

"I would like that very much, but perhaps we should eat before other pleasures occupy our time?" His brows lifted with suggestion.

"As you wish."

She managed to sound appropriately enthusiastic, but had no intention of repeating last night. Not that it wouldn't be fun, but she had something more important planned.

"So, what are you going to do?"

"The High Tenders want to take a look at the linking project. Lord vlor'Vardhal feels it's the only way to amass enough power to stop the aliens and their ship."

"It isn't a bunch of aliens, Gregor," she said. "It's one creature."

"You said that before."

"And you said all the WOR you have asked said the same thing. Don't you think that means anything?"

"Think about it, opés, how can life survive in a vacuum? That doesn't match anything we know about the origins of life."

She knew that argument well. She'd gone around and round with the S'Lorek arguing the exact opposite and all the assumptions that went with it. "It doesn't mean we're wrong. Did you ever look into whether other WOR dream about it?"

"I made a few inquiries. Little kids dream about the S'Lorek, and I'd say quite a few of the adults. Considering the S'Lorek seems to be drawn to WOR, I'd expect WOR to be more affected by it."

She finished his foot and moved her massage up to his calf. He stretched out his leg.

"If you do evacuate the planet, how much time do you need?"

He responded to her touch like she'd trained him; putty in her hands.

"Several sun cycles still," he said. "Enough time to finish the teaching on this linking project you perfected."

"It's not perfect yet." She lied, but Gregor's plan revealed the Vendel had no idea the S'Lorek had picked up speed.

"Don't worry, opés. I won't send any of you up against the S'Lorek until I'm certain we can affect them. Unfortunately, the Ruling Council isn't ready to risk its Emperor in the confrontation. They suggested I leave Malbran space by the end of the sun cycle. Closest thing to a command they can give me. You'll be coming with me, of course."

"What about the other Earth WOR? Are they supposed to fight this thing alone?"

"Not alone. They'll have their Tenders and masters. The WOR on Malbra will fight with them as well."

"But, you don't even know what you're doing with the link. That's madness, and likely suicide. After all the trouble you took to get us, how can you just throw us away like that?"

"Don't get so excited, opés. Other WOR have escaped the S'Lorek. The aliens don't seem to be able to pursue into WOR-space. If things aren't going well here, we'll have them all jump into WOR-space and rendezvous with us later. I've gone to a lot of trouble to cultivate you and your friends. I'm not going to *throw any of you away*."

"Don't the Vendel have real weapons? Something other than WOR and WOR-skill?"

"Some, but, in general, we don't squabble between ourselves. The WOR are our best weapons."

"Funny, you describe your empire as pacifists."

"That's a good word to use. The last war the Vendel fought was with swords, shields and foot soldiers back on Earth. Since we ascended to space, we've explored other, more productive pastimes. We're not a war-faring society, despite what you believe."

"Such as murdering an entire planet?"

Gregor pulled his legs away and stood. "I don't want to go over that argument with you again."

She remembered her role. Time to be the demure, timid, compliant, and Bound s'vlor. "I'm sorry, Gregor. I said too much. I didn't mean to make you angry. Can I make it up to you?"

"Let's start with food and then finish with that back rub you promised." Steel glinted off the surface of his eyes.

"We can try some of the snarking sims we didn't have a chance to get to last night." She projected an eagerness she didn't feel.

"You have more?"

"Oh, yes Gregor, several."

Gregor lifted her to her feet and kept her busy under an onslaught of kisses, which she shamelessly returned. He pulled away with some difficulty, and placed an order for their meal. Within a few minutes, several steaming trays emitting mouthwatering smells appeared on the counter of the bar via beaming technology.

Elise helped him set the low coffee table. They sat opposite each other on the floor and enjoyed the appetizing spread in a very casual manner. Gregor shared more of his favorite Malbran dishes, explaining the preparations with enthusiasm.

They spoke easily and she watched in stages as he let down his guard. It took over an hour before the true impact hit her full on as to what exactly was happening. Gregor bantered with her. He wasn't treating her as a slave, or his property, but as an equal.

Not that the undercurrent wasn't there—what she was hadn't been forgotten by either of them—however, Gregor pushed it below the surface and made every effort to be polite.

The realization he enjoyed her company came in stages. A low laugh followed a twitch of his brows. A smile accompanied the relaxing of the features of his face. Subtle changes in his body language changed the man before her into something unexpected.

She liked him; at least when he allowed himself to be vulnerable and relax. She marveled at the transformation as he ate, laughed, shared the details of his day, and, for the very first time, touched the back of her hand with fondness.

For a minute, she felt guilty for what she would soon unleash. Malice, however, chuckled in the darkness, and reminded her to harden her resolve, which she did. She and Gregor wanted the same thing, but they were not on the same side.

Before Gregor could melt her heart, she rose from the table. The glint in his eye spoke to an unasked question. Her lips twitched into a suggestive smile and she motioned for him to follow. The timepiece on the wall caught her attention, and she calculated the time required to get all the pieces in place for the battle to come. She needed to work quickly to sedate Gregor.

It took longer than she'd planned to appease Gregor's needs. He still played alpha male, and demanded her attention. It took time to coax him into lying still for a simple back rub. He had different desires, and she found herself giving in.

It would likely be the last time she would enjoy the pure maleness of the man. Her captor, enemy, torturer, trainer, master, and now lover, was a man with many faces. She would not soon forget Emperor Gregor Ulysses vlor'Malita, and he would always have a piece of her heart.

But eventually, she forced Gregor to lie down and massaged his back. She sat on top of him and, as her fingers worked the firm muscles, she trickled a thread of power into his body. Within minutes, the man slept soundly. With a quick push, she lifted off and headed to the shower. Tonight would be long and, working with the smell of him on her skin, would provide too much of a distraction.

She called on her friends. Alice reported all was ready; collars had been deactivated and the WOR-guards were oblivious to the s'vlor milling about in the common area waiting for the go-ahead.

Dove told her the hangar had been cleared. She made him clarify. Something about the odd tone in his voice caught her attention. He confirmed the entire hangar deck, tens of ships, not just a few, had all been moved. He mentioned something about Carek, toxic spills, and an evacuation of the entire deck.

She towel-dried, dressed in her freshly cleaned red flightsuit, and slipped out of Gregor's suite of rooms. Her deceptively simple use of the WOR-skill would keep Gregor slumbering for hours, plenty of time to get everyone organized and ready to fight.

CHAPTER TWENTY_

ELISE ENTERED THE HANGAR DECK. THE FIRST THING STRIKING HER AS ODD WAS the overwhelming quiet. A generalized buzz had always hung over the hangar, the result of engine noise, cargo loading and unloading bots, and the raucous voices of the pilots and mechanics filling the cavernous space. The entire hangar sat eerily silent.

Empty, it appeared to have doubled in size. Her footsteps rang on the floor and reverberated off the far walls. She craned her neck upward. A mass of black bio-pods swarmed up there, oblivious to the humans down below, or the drama about to unfold.

Several structures protruded from the smooth surface of the ceiling and interrupted the flow of the bio-pods. Where these obstructions broke the otherwise featureless plane of the hangar ceiling, the black bio-pods divided and flowed around the obstacles, where they formed a void on the backside of the structures. Several feet beyond, the little army of cleaning bots rejoined to form a continuous stream of biologic recyclers.

Turning her attention back to the hangar deck, Elise spied four people waiting in the very center of the hangar. It took some time to approach, but as she did, she took notice of the way they shifted on their feet and scanned the hangar with unease.

Lumpy, large and lovable, Dove was unmistakable. The tall, svelte, woman hanging off his arm in her pilot's red jumpsuit was Jeena. Blond curls atop a young man's head identified Larkin. Elise was surprised to see him. She arched a brow with question. The fourth man, dressed in a green jumpsuit, stood with his back to her. Carek's long ponytail dangled down the center of his back.

Jeena noticed Elise first and waved. The three men turned. Dove smiled. Larkin bounced on his toes, wringing his hands as he scanned the hangar. Carek took in a deep breath, expanding his chest, and blew it out slowly.

"Hi, El," he said, simply, and ducked his head. Carek stretched out his hands and she clasped them in welcome.

She stared into his emerald eyes and lost herself in the compassion residing there.

"It's good to see you, Carek."

"It's good to be seen. Thank you for what you did with the Emperor. I always knew the risk I took. Don't ever think I regretted it, El."

"Anything for a friend." She kissed his cheek.

Carek's eyes widened and the expression on his face fell. He would never be anything more than a very dear friend.

In a way, what she was about to attempt was the result of Carek's dedication to the Vendel. He'd been the one to envision the linking project, and he'd shown her the Vendel in a way which changed her belief of them as a people. Because of him, she loved the Vendel.

Dove, Jeena, and Larkin had a part in that as well. Their friendship and support helped her on her path to forgive. She would save their people and hopefully hers as well, because of the friendships forged in this very hangar.

Larkin gave her a hug, tearing her away from Carek.

"Sweet gods, El," he said. "When Jeena told me . . . well, I just couldn't believe it. And then, it just seemed right. I've always known you were special. I never thought . . . s'vlor! When they told me about your plans . . ." Larkin let go and brushed his bangs out of his eyes. "Well, if the Emperor's s'vlor is going to battle the S'Lorek, I'll do what I can."

"Did they happen to mention he doesn't know and wouldn't approve? I'm working alone in this, and breaking every rule. It treason for you to be here." She cocked her head, wanting to make sure he understood the risk he took standing by her side.

He waved a dismissive hand. "Yeah, but hell, I know you. You'd never do anything to hurt us, and if I can be a part of anything having to do with killing the thing that destroyed my planet, then I'm in." Smoldering flames of revenge burned within his eyes.

She remembered Dunlaad, the scorched dirt, the absence of life, and the searing red beam of energy that destroyed life. The S'Lorek had feasted on Dunlaad and murdered Larkin's family. She understood his fervor.

Behind Larkin, twenty odd shapes in a rainbow of swirling silks approached at a brisk pace. At their head, a tall blonde led them forward. Elise smiled as Alice approached. They clasped hands and Elise greeted her fellow s'vlor.

"The rest are on their way." Alice was slightly out of breath, but her eyes lit with purpose.

Elise scanned the faces of the women Alice had brought. These were fighters, her warriors. They'd come through the crucible of Vendel acclimation and Tender Training together and stood united.

"It feels good to have the collars removed." Alice fingered her bare throat. "I feel like I can do anything."

"Is everyone ready?"

Alice turned around. "What do you say, girls? Ready to kick some S'Lorek butt, and then maybe a little Vendel ass to finish it off?"

Vigorous nods were her answer.

Alice clapped her hands. "As we practiced. Form your circles. We don't know how long we have until the vlor'lords figure out we're missing."

The rustle of silks sounded as the women arranged themselves into circles.

Paula, and then Chandra approached, each with their clutch of s'vlor. They grinned in greeting, but wasted no time in saying hello. Instead, they formed up their newcomers and prepared to link together. Paula's eyes danced.

Elise watched the circles form, and her chest swelled with pride. The women held hands and snuck surreptitious glances around the enormous hangar. A sound from behind announced the arrival of another group.

Aomi brought the last of the Fifth Rank s'vlor. Aomi's face pinched with worry. She hustled her gaggle of s'vlor into place, and whispered a hurried warning to the others.

"Take your spots girls. We're going to have company shortly." Aomi turned to Alice. "I'm sorry, but Sarah woke up after you left. She's sure to have raised the alarm. We'd better figure out how to shield everyone, because all hell is about ready to break loose."

In response to her warning, booted-steps echoed from the far end of the hangar.

Elise squinted in the distance and made out black uniformed shapes coming toward them at a trot. Behind the WOR-guards, tan suits marked High Tenders racing to keep pace.

She raised a hand. "Aomi, get into position and form the links. Don't worry about the WOR-guards. I have them." She turned to her Vendel friends. "This is where it gets ugly. If you choose to stand with us, you need to move to the center of the circle. I can't shield you if you're at the edges." She turned her attention to Alice. "Ready?"

Dove shepherded Jeena, Larkin, and Carek to the center of the WOR.

Larkin eyed Aomi with appreciation as he passed. She blushed and turned away to work.

"Elise, do you need help?" Alice directed Aomi's group into place with a wave of her hands. The booted-steps approached with a thunderous roar. They didn't have much time.

"This I have, but you need to make sure every link is in place and let me know when it's done. Once you have it sorted out, I'll need you and your link to take over the shield. A single link can handle it while I form all of us into the super-link. I can't do both and I'll need you to watch the construct as I fold it, so you'll know what to do."

The black mass of towering WOR-guards closed in, sprinting. It was going to be close.

Alice gave a nod and set to work. The woman was a natural leader.

Elise felt keystones activate linking constructs all around her. They had eight full circles and one partial of eight women. It would be barely enough. The keystones pulled women into place and the links solidified. Now, to shield them all from the encroaching force of WOR-guard and Tenders.

Alex, are you ready?

Yes.

Malice, Shriek, Whimper? You with us?

Yes!

Yes!

Yes!

They answered in resounding chorus. Even Whimper sounded confident.

Good! Let's show these bastards what we can do.

Elise folded space around herself and the s'vlor. An invisible shield surrounded the women and formed a complete sphere. It guarded their feet as well as the space around and above them. She wasn't about to be surprised by an attack from below. Elise knew of the service corridors beneath their feet and the vulnerability that posed. If Gregor, or the High

Tenders, expected her to have forgotten about that facet of the shield, they'd be in for a nasty surprise.

The first WOR-guard descended upon the group. He came at them, whipstick at the ready, and running full speed. He hit the shield, bounced back, and skidded across the deck-plating. A surprised grunt followed. Ten of his fellows repeated the performance, surprise, then alarm flashed across their faces as they sailed through the air. The men nursed bruised elbows, backs, and backsides and laughed.

No.

That wasn't the men. Malice cackled with glee.

Alice signaled the completion of the nine links.

Elise arched a brow, asking if Alice was ready to take over control of the shield.

Alice nodded. She was ready.

Elise transferred the WOR-bubble shield to Alice.

They fumbled for a minute, dropping the shield. Tense seconds passed while Alice struggled to reform the barrier. Fortunately, the WOR-guards had retreated and were giving the invisible barrier wary consideration. In the meantime, Alice recovered and reformed the shield.

The High Tenders arrived a few seconds behind the WOR-guards, braklavs in hand, out of breath, their eyes gleamed with menace.

Elise ignored them. They would be treated to a unique surprise if any of them attempted to breach the WOR-shield.

She began the arduous process of weaving the individual links into a massive unified structure. The first flash of the WOR-shield sparked. Screams of High Tenders filled the hangar deck as the energy of the shield radiated back through the braklavs into their hands. As long as they held the braklav, the WOR-shield would be unforgiving. Several more flashes of energy lit the hangar. Evidently, the High Tenders were not as smart as she thought.

Forming a super-link of nine circles gave her difficulty. It was much harder than the link of two circles she'd accomplished within the am-net tank. She struggled. Minutes passed. Her first few attempts failed. Just as with learning to juggle, the harder she tried, the more balls she dropped.

Alex whispered in her ear, providing encouragement. Elise nodded, and dipped into the dimensional cracks—a time and space only she could touch. The third circle joined the first two, and then the next slid into place. Alex guided her, and together they brought nine linked circles together.

Alice glanced at Elise. Her mouth gaped in wonder, feeling a power Elise controlled that she could never touch.

Elise gave the construct over to Whimper to hold. Whimper took control, sat down, and hummed with contentment. Elise had a new task to perform. Two figures approached at a dead run. Gregor and High Tender Marcus vlor'Vardhal sprinted across the flight deck. Their boots rang out on the hard surface and echoed off the walls.

His timing couldn't have been more perfect.

CHAPTER TWENTY-ONE_

THE BLOOD IN ELISE'S VEINS THRUMMED WITH POWER.

Somehow, Gregor had defeated her pacification construct. She would figure out later how he'd accomplished that feat. By all accounts, he should still be sprawled on the bed in his quarters. Behind Gregor, a new group of men advanced. These carried weapons. Imperial soldiers spread out, forming a defensive line.

They had no idea what they faced.

She paused, relishing the moment of confrontation, and waited for Gregor to make his move. The glower in the High Tender's face promised retribution. She was done with his brand of pain. He couldn't touch her anymore. None of the High Tenders could touch the Earth WOR. He would soon realize that.

Gregor's expression was harder to read. Fury was not reflected on his features. The swirling tattoo did not promise pain like the High Tender. Silver eyes flashed in the light. A ghost of surprise and wonder crinkled at the corner of his eyes.

For the briefest of moments, he looked impressed, but then the cold steel of his gaze locked onto her. The beginnings of anger darkened his expression. Dark brows turned down and the muscles of his jaw bunched as he clenched his teeth. His eyes narrowed and he stared at her across an unimaginable gulf.

She nodded, acknowledging her adversary, and Gregor stopped short.

The High Tender made to approach the barrier, but Gregor held him back with a restraining hand.

"She has them shielded, Lord vlor'Vardhal."

Her brows quirked up in surprise. He could see the barrier?

Gregor ran his gaze around the WOR-shield. He definitely saw it. But not the High Tender? Now, that was interesting.

A new group of men poured into the hangar, singly and in small groups. The vlor'lords had arrived.

They were now complete. Emperor, High Tenders, WOR-guards, and now the vlor'lords. They would all stand witness to what they had created. As the vlor'lords neared, they too traced the boundary of the WOR-shield. The High Tenders couldn't see the boundary, but their masters could.

"You have much to answer for, opés," Gregor said with a growl. His fingers clenched, forming fists, and he took a half-step forward.

She ignored him, but did not take her eyes off him.

Slowly, the growing crowd of Vendel men encircled the women. WOR-guards formed the innermost ring. High Tenders stood beyond. Imperial soldiers spread themselves out in several configurations, and the newest arrivals, the vlor'lords, weaved between the rings of men to stand at the edge of the shield.

"Alice, rejoin your circle," Elise commanded. "Shriek will manage the shield."

Alice's eyes widened in surprise. She knew about Elise's silent sisters, but this was the first time Elise had spoken of one of them as an individual. Alice closed her mouth and transferred the shield.

Shriek grabbed the construct from Alice. Unlike their first transfer, Shriek took control seamlessly and enlarged the shield with a shove outward. Those vlor'lords, too slow in their reactions, slid backwards twenty feet as Shriek gave the WOR more room to move within their bubble.

The Earth WOR continued to hold hands in their assigned circles. They felt every move Elise, Alice, Shriek and Whimper made. Only Alex and Malice had yet to openly announce themselves to the group. A growing excitement blossomed as the women understood the full extent of what was happening.

The Vendel watched from outside the shield. Immune to the influence of their captors, the Earth WOR settled into their power.

"Everyone ready?" Elise asked.

Through the combined super-link, their response rang in her ears.

"Opés," Gregor hissed, "what are you doing?"

She turned to stare at her former master. "You will never use that derogatory name with me again, Emperor vlor'Malita. We declare our independence."

High Tender vlor'Vardhal inhaled sharply. "My lord . . ."

Gregor waved him to silence. "You won't get away with this. At some point, you will have to lower this shield. Do so now, and none of you will be punished for this . . ." he waved his hand in the air, "transgression."

"Emperor, you fail to understand your position. We have declared our independence. We are free of you and any threats you make toward us will be addressed. Touch one of my women and you will feel the full force of my fury."

"You dare speak to the Emperor this way?" High Tender vlor'Vardhal screamed.

She chose her words carefully. "Lord vlor'Vardhal, shut up."

His face turned beet red as his expression twisted in rage. He raised his hands and lunged for her throat.

Malice cackled as he contacted the barrier.

Lights flashed and his face morphed into a rictus of pain.

Shriek trickled power into the shield and held the High Tender at the edge of the boundary.

Elise gave Shriek her moment of revenge. Shriek had certainly earned it.

The High Tender spasmed in agony. His mouth opened to scream, but no sound came out.

Elise remembered the feeling well. Breath was required for screaming. How many times had he left her in a rictus of agony?

Shriek unloaded her version of Tender Training on the High Tender.

His body thrashed wildly. He emptied his bladder, and then his bowels.

Malice began to keen.

"Elise, stop it, please." Gregor spoke softly, making his words a request rather than an order.

Perhaps he realized the power between them had shifted?

"You never showed such compassion for me." She turned cold eyes on the Emperor.

"I never took pleasure in it either."

"I'm not the one in charge right now," she said.

"I feel you using the power. Stop this." Gregor glanced at the flopping form of the High Tender. He eyed her with uneasy wariness. Lord vlor'-

Vardhal's face turned a nasty shade of purple. Gagging sounds issued from his throat.

"Shriek's not done yet."

"Who is Shriek?" Gregor's tattoo finally began its maddening dance. His anger was returning.

"Perhaps it's time for you to meet my sisters, Emperor. You made them, after all." The corner of her mouth twitched up at the look of confusion on his face.

The women behind Elise shuffled, and a few made gagging sounds. Light continued to flash around the WOR-shield as the High Tender remained trapped within.

It was enough.

Shriek? She spoke to her friend.

Shriek panted with the effort of her torture, and for the first time Shriek cried.

That had always been Whimper's job.

Shriek, enough. Release him. We are not the High Tenders.

He hurt me so much and made me beg for more. Shriek sniffled.

You have to hold the shield, and I need you to stand by me with the S'Lorek. He's not worth wasting your energy. Let him go, he can't hurt you anymore.

I want to sleep, Elise. I'm so tired.

I promise, my sister, you may sleep once this is done, but we have much more still to do. Let him go.

With a sob, Shriek released the High Tender.

His body fell to the ground. Several WOR-guards pulled him back from the edge of the boundary. The purple coloring faded from the High Tender's face, only to be replaced by a deep red and then a pale, pasty gray. He was alive.

Elise dismissed him from her thoughts.

An arcing beam of energy shot through the WOR-shield.

It pinned the High Tender's body to the ground.

Elise traced the line of energy back to Paula.

Paula's face twisted in rage and torment as she finished what Shriek had begun. High Tender vlor'Vardhal, Master of the Tender Conclave, jerked and then went still. The WOR-guards assisting him flew back ten feet from the force of the blast. The imperial soldiers rushing to his side would find no pulse in that body.

Paula stared at Elise, daring her to say a word. Madness flashed behind Paula's eyes, before being replaced by a calming peace. Her friend drew breath, unclenched her fists, and stood straight.

"I take full responsibility for that devil's death," Paula said.

"We'll speak about it later, Paula," Elise responded. "Justice is an odd animal, never what you think it should be." Elise bowed her head to her friend, and fellow Tender Group member. They had an appreciation of the High Tender which only a few others shared. Elise searched for the faces of their Tender Group cohort. Clipped nods greeted her examination. Yes, they agreed, justice was seldom what it appeared.

"Emperor," Elise spoke with cool dispassion, "we have work to perform. Clear your men from the hangar."

Gregor watched the body of the High Tender being carted off by four men. He turned to Elise. "I will not."

He scanned the s'vlor. His eyes widened when he made out the four Vendel standing at the center. His voice lowered with menace. "Have you gone mad?"

"No, Emperor vlor'Malita," she said, emphasizing his name. "You collected us to deal with the S'Lorek threat. We will stop it and then we will leave you."

"I command you to stop," he said. "The Binding . . ."

"You command nothing. The Binding Rite failed."

"But you . . . we . . . you couldn't have faked all of that."

"Didn't I?"

He didn't need to know the truth. She had enjoyed it as much or more than him. Given another time and place, she wouldn't hesitate to choose him, but that was not the way of things. She shook her head and gave him a cold stare. "Remove your men."

"I can't do that."

"So be it. Interfere with what we're doing, distract us for a moment, and I'll personally treat you to the High Tender's fate. This is what you brought us here to do. Let us finish it."

"How are you going to do that?" Gregor took a step forward, but stopped two paces from the edge of the boundary. "You need us to stabilize your power."

"I don't need you anymore." She sent out feelers and located the S'Lorek within the bubble of n-space it traveled within. "We're going to fight. I trust you to leave us to it."

Alex ripped the S'Lorek out of its dimensional folding and forced it into normal space where it reeled, stunned from the harsh transition.

Elise took a WOR-step and travelled from here to there.

It was time to end this.

693

CHAPTER TWENTY-TWO_

Everyone in the hangar staggered as reality shifted. Like a rubber band, they stretched, snapped, and then wobbled before coming to a rest. The *Gambit* traveled twenty-five light-years within the space of a moment.

Elise lifted her arm and traced the outlines of a screen into the air above Gregor's head. Sitting within a field of stars, a lumpy, potato-like moonlet sat dazed and confused. She lifted the combined voices of nearly ninety WOR and spoke to the S'Lorek, transmitting the conversation for all the Vendel, friend and foe, to follow.

Gregor, and those standing with him, moved from the space below the screen and took vantage points with clearer views.

"S'Lorek, I demand you stop. We will not tolerate your destruction."

"You!" it growled. "We spoke before. Go away, pesky slime. I am hungry." The moonlet spun on its axis and aligned itself with the center of the *Gambit's* torus. It swiped at Elise, attempting to brush her away.

Elise, Alex, Whimper, Shriek and Malice deflected the S'Lorek and hid the Earth WOR from its examination.

"What is this?" It seemed surprised, and rightly so. "You have grown since our last conversation."

"And you have not. Leave now and we will let you live."

"Silly slime," it said. "You cannot stop me."

The S'Lorek completed its turn and the narrow section of the moonlet opened. Beneath its common mouth, nose and eye, a powerful beam of radiation built.

She had little time before they were incinerated and devoured. She didn't want to kill the S'Lorek. They had much to learn from each other, but the survival of all of humanity was at stake.

"Stop." She stretched her mind and swatted the S'Lorek.

It grunted in surprise, but its maw continued to open. "Interesting trick, slime. But you'll need more than that to stop me."

"We don't have to fight."

"This is no fight. Your mind is impressive, expansive, but still small and irrelevant. The universe is a big place, slime. No place for creatures such as you."

A dull, red glow built up inside the S'Lorek's mouth. It readied itself to release a wave of death and destruction.

"This is your last warning." Elise said. "Leave now and I will permit you to live. Unleash that energy, and I will destroy you."

"I savor the feast to come, slime." The S'Lorek opened its mouth and a beam of energy sped toward the *Gambit.*

"Fool." Elise unleashed the power of ninety Earth WOR bound together. A cone of protection flew forth, shielding the *Gambit* and all those inside.

The energy of the S'Lorek flowed around her shield. Radiation alarms blatted and the *Gambit* bucked under the onslaught. She held the WOR in place until the wave passed.

Alex pushed the cone forward.

The S'Lorek grunted in surprise when Alex wedged the cone into the opening of the creature's maw. Surprise turned to fear as Alex shoved it deep inside and began to expand the cone outward.

"Last warning. Leave now or perish."

Elise held the WOR as they trembled with the power flowing through their bodies. Two women staggered, drained by the energies they were forced to handle. One of the conduits failed. Women screamed. That circle transferred the role of conduit to another and held firm, but others struggled.

The S'Lorek bit down on the cone and severed Alex's WOR-construct. Elise staggered as the WOR-skill energies rebounded back to the women on the hangar deck. Three more fell, threatening the integrity of their links. Their circles closed the gaps and reinforced the links.

"Hold firm!" she shouted over her shoulder. "We are stronger than it thinks. You are stronger than you know. Trust in me."

Alice rallied the women. She had them sit to better focus their efforts.

Elise spared a glance at Gregor. He watched the screen with fascination and growing horror. He took a step toward her, reaching out to protect and support. Concern for her wellbeing stretched across his face. He stopped himself, remembering the WOR-shield, and looked on in agony.

"Elise," he croaked.

She shot another cone of energy at the S'Lorek while it readied another blast of death at the *Gambit* and the WOR inside, but it couldn't reach them. It roared as it sensed the combined power of Elise and the super-link sitting outside its reach. She kept up her attack. WOR-skill ripped through its outer shell of rock and a cloud of debris floated into space.

If it had a mouth, maybe it would have screamed. It righted itself and sealed off the breach. It came at the *Gambit*, hungry, determined and angry.

The red glow built anew.

Elise wiggled her fingers, waiting to pull the trigger. This had to be timed perfectly, or they were all dead.

Alice called out, "Do we form another cone-shield?"

"No," Elise said.

"No? But, we can't survive that." Alice's voice went cold.

"No, we can't. I need every ounce of strength, no hesitation, no fear. You have to convince them to give it all to me."

Alice's eyes went wide. In an under-voice, she said, "Not all of us are going to survive, are we?"

The red glow burned brighter.

Elise shook her head. "No. Live or die with me, or live under the rule of the Vendel. They must be willing. I'm sorry. I should have told you the price, but I wasn't certain until we took the WOR-step what it would take to finish this."

Using the WOR-skill, Alice relayed Elise's words to the WOR. One by one, and then in a flood, strength flowed into Elise through the super-link as each woman made her choice. Elise, Alex, Whimper, Malice, and Shriek drank in the combined life energy of the most powerful humans in history.

The S'Lorek fired a breath of death.

Elise caught the energies of the WOR and wove them together. She reached into the dimensions where the S'Lorek's mind resided, and redirected the energy there. In normal space, the moonlet brightened from within. Matter ignited and heated until it turned to plasma. Pressure built inside of it, until it exploded outward in a plume of molten rock and debris. Inside the S'Lorek's mind, invisible to the Vendel watching, the connections anchoring the S'Lorek to the universe shred as Elise ripped it apart and consigned it to oblivion.

Women screamed as power burned through their bodies. Elise looked on, helpless, as the reverberations of her power tore their minds to mere fragments of energy as well.

Men gasped as the S'Lorek exploded.

Collision alarms added their noise to the blaring of radiation alerts as debris pelted the *Gambit*.

Shriek staggered under the onslaught of the echoes of power.

The WOR-shield flickered.

Aomi noticed the imminent failure of their only protection from the other threat waiting within the hangar deck. She added the strength of her link, now a paltry circle of six women, to the fading WOR-shield holding the vlor'lords and Tenders at bay.

The cost in flesh escalated as women succumbed to the power ripping apart space and time. Alice broke her circle and sent her team to fill the voids in the remaining links. Seven circles remained.

Twelve women collapsed. Eight had died.

Aomi stabilized the WOR-shield.

The Vendel vlor'lords remained outside the shield.

Gregor approached as close as he dared. He ran a hand through close-cropped hair. All color drained from his face and his eyes seemed flat and lifeless.

"Enough. You did it, but this has to end. For what you have done for the Vendel, no punishments, no Tender Training, no whipsticks. Come back to me . . . Elise, please, come to me."

A tear trickled out of the corner of her eye and tracked down her cheek. She closed her eyes and extended her mind into the am-net. Bobo, and her army of constructs answered her call.

"This is not over, Gregor."

"Elise," he said in a hoarse whisper, "you can't sustain this. I promise . . . no harm will come to you. We can find our way past this."

"Will you free us?" Her fingers curled as her spine straightened.

"I cannot." His hands trembled and the muscles in his jaw twitched. "Don't make this harder than it needs to be. Lower the shield. On my word as Emperor, none of you will be harmed."

"Will we be free?"

"No."

That was not what she wanted to hear, but what she expected.

She took a WOR-step from here to there.

The world shifted and the *Gambit* stretched and snapped back into the space above Malbra. The screen above Gregor's head mirrored the view outside the ship. With the exception of the WOR, all the humans on the hangar deck reeled with the effects of the WOR-step.

She spoke low and clear, ensuring Gregor and the vlor'lords understood. "The *Gambit* is under *my* control. You have three days to evacuate the ship's crew, personnel and any citizens who choose to leave."

"Don't do this. I've forgiven you, pardoned all of you. Don't make me take that back."

She continued, ignoring Gregor. "I will not tolerate any lor' or vlor'lord, High Tender or Tender, WOR-guard, or Emperor on board."

The tattoo over his left eyebrow danced. Steel daggers shot toward her.

She deflected it all. "All life support, air purification, food production, sanitation, power relays, lift-tubes, and pod-cars, to name just a few, are under my control. Within three and a half days, the *Gambit* will no longer sustain life. Within two days, it will be impossible to walk around without a respirator. In twenty-four hours it will become unbearable. Not a problem if you are WOR. We can filter our personal air without any difficulty. As for maintaining this shield?" Elise motioned with her arm. "It's a simple matter to tie it off."

"I'm not giving up my ship."

"Not only are you giving up the *Gambit*, but you're giving up all the Earth WOR. I'm taking them with me."

CHAPTER TWENTY-THREE_

ELISE SENT A MESSAGE TO THE LOWER RANKING WOR ON BOARD. TO THESE women she gave hope and a choice. They had to be willing and know the price, the cost in flesh she would demand, before deciding their fate. She suppressed the effects of the Binding on these women while they pondered their options.

It was a simple choice. She could remove the Binding and they could join her and the other Fifth Rank WOR, or they could remain with their masters and serve the Vendel. She would not coerce anyone to stay, or to go.

"You have twelve hours to begin evacuation." She turned her attention back to Gregor, outlining her decree. "If I don't see evidence of a retreat within twenty-four hours, my WOR will transport citizens down to Malbra. Unlike your First Rank teleportation, my Fifth Rank can take hundreds at a time. I don't bluff."

"Where do you intend to go?" he shot back.

"The S'Lorek was one of many, Emperor."

She refused to use his name. Using his name personalized their exchange. His title placed distance between them, and reinforced the change in power between them. She couldn't afford to think of him on any other terms. If she did, her heart would break.

"Hundreds of the S'Lorek's Clan are coming. That thing sent the taste of us to its brethren." To prove she wasn't afraid of him, and to demonstrate her strength, she stepped through the force field and stood unprotected in front of him.

His eyes widened.

She leaned in close. "I'm taking the *Gambit,* all the WOR that will join me, and any Vendel *civilians* who care to come with us, to stand vanguard for your empire. We will protect humanity, because it is what we chose to do. Not because we've been forced to do it."

"Hundreds? You can't stand against that many. You need us. You need me."

"No, I don't." She tucked a strand of hair behind an ear. "I'm leaving, Gregor. Don't fight me. Despite everything you've done, the Earth WOR are putting our lives on the line to protect your empire. That alone should be worth our freedom."

Lines of worry edged the features of his face. He raised a hand to cup her cheek. She recoiled and he drew back as if stung. A stray glance at the ceiling far above caught the army of bio-pods, frozen by Bobo's commands.

Voids in the ceiling.

She smiled. "I have some thoughts on how to handle the Clan. You should know well enough by now, I'm nothing, if not determined."

He gave her an appraising look. Gregor struggled with his thoughts, but then he sighed and gave a low bow. "You believe you don't need me, Elise, but you're wrong. You need me just as much as I need you."

"I don't need you."

"Tell me you don't love me." Gregor wrapped an arm around her waist and pulled her to him. He kissed her before she could react. Into her ear he whispered, "You know it's true. You can't lie to yourself. You and I are fated to be together."

It felt right to be in his arms, but she refused to believe; not after everything that had happened between them.

"Let me go . . . Emperor." She placed a hand on his chest, feeling the warmth of his body radiating through his clothes, breathing in the scent of him, and wanting nothing more than to remain in his arms. But she was unable to forgive and forget everything he had done to her, to her friends, to Earth and her family. He had taken so much. How could she possibly admit to loving him? "I hate you."

"Hate is half a step away from love, Elise. You will come back to me." He kissed her and paused a moment to rest his cheek against hers. "I will miss you. I give you the *Gambit.* I'm wise enough to know when to let go."

He gestured to the shielded WOR standing a few steps away. "I have underestimated you from the very beginning."

She took a relieved breath. "On your word, you won't pursue us?"

"I brought you here to fight the S'Lorek. That is done, but understand this. I regret nothing. I apologize for nothing. I'm the Emperor of the Vendel. Before anything else—before anyone else—I swore an oath to my people to serve and protect them. That it caused you great pain is unfortunate. That we . . . well, perhaps Malikai and Chickadee could have done better than you and I. I had expected to groom the strongest WOR in millennium and save humanity. Never in a million years did I expect to fall so deeply in love with her; with you." He took her hand in his and pressed his lips against her knuckles.

"Gregor, please stop."

"Stay with me," he whispered.

"No. You need to leave." She gathered her courage and told the lie that would doom her heart. "I don't love you. It was all an act, a part of my plan. You misunderstood my enthusiasm."

"No," he said, "I know better."

"Let go of my hand."

He released her, and the warmth of his touch faded. "I need to coordinate the evacuation of my people. It will take at least two days, then you and I have more to talk about."

"No, you leave now. You can coordinate your efforts from Malbra."

"Eager to get rid of me so quickly?" His lips twisted into a smirk and her heart shattered. "It won't make it any easier to forget me. Are you afraid you'll change your mind?" The need in his voice tugged at her emotions.

"No." She cleared her head of the images swirling within.

She turned to Alice. "Transport these men to Malbra." Without turning around, she said, "Goodbye, Gregor."

"You will miss me." His words faded as Alice folded space around the Vendel. Gregor, and all the rest, disappeared in a shimmering veil.

And just like that, she and the women from Earth were free of their Vendel masters.

Silence hung in the air.

"Will you be okay?" Alice collected Elise in her arms and brushed back the hair from Elise's face.

No.

"I need to be alone. I need to rest. Can you handle things from here?"

"Yes, just tell me what you need."

"Don't leave my friends alone. Until we leave Vendel space, they need guards. Carek understands the *Gambit* better than the rest. Send Chandra with him. He can figure out what we can handle ourselves using the WOR-skill and what we'll need others to take care of. Dove, Jeena and Larkin should be our interfaces with the Vendel left on board. They'll know who to recruit. Send Aomi with them. Paula can head the departure of the ship's crew. I don't want them stripping the *Gambit*. This is our home. Either shuttle people off the ship or send them by teleport, but get rid of them. The *Gambit* is home to tens of thousands, it's a big job. Paula will need help. You handle the rest. Keep everyone organized, busy, focused. We can't let down our guard. Did you hear me send out to the other WOR?"

"Yes," Alice said. "Do you think they will join us?"

"I hope so. Someone will need to help them." Elise's head spun with all the tasks required to take over a Vendel fleet ship. How were they going to make this work?

"Elise, I'll take care of everything." Alice hugged her with sisterly concern.

"I haven't slept for days. I'm exhausted."

"You did it. All of it!" Tears streamed down Alice's face, but her lips spread into a broad smile. "When everyone started dying back on Earth, I thought the world had ended. When the Vendel brought me on board, and after the braklav touched my skin, I knew I'd entered hell. Do you remember that yoga class?"

"Yes, it seems like a lifetime ago."

"When I found out I wasn't alone, and that you were the one who devised that silly little code, I rediscovered hope. You didn't let me down. You never stopped. You kept working, and fighting for freedom. No matter what they did to you, you never gave up. I could never have done what you have done. Rest, you've earned it. I'll take care of what needs to be done."

Elise and her silent sisters retreated.

As she walked away, Alice's voice rose to shout orders.

The lift tubes were down, courtesy of Bobo, but Elise reactivated the ones she needed. In a few short minutes, she stepped into the private rooms of the Vendel Emperor. She didn't even consider the incongruity of her choice. She headed to his bed and collapsed into sheets full of Gregor's warm scent.

It was done.
They had won, but she was broken.
And she missed Gregor.

TEN YEARS LATER_

Elise stood on the Command deck and tracked the progress of the Clan's exit from the Milky Way. Ten years had passed since New Terra's liberation from the Vendel Empire. Five years they spent preparing for the Clan's arrival. The past five years they used the WOR-skill to hide the entirety of the human race while the Clan swarmed the Milky Way, looking for the feast promised by the S'Lorek.

Clan members searched for the S'Lorek, but their explorer had vanished, along with the feast promised within the shrill noise of swirling dust and light that made up the Milky Way. Instead of a delectable feast, they found a dull lifeless place full of painful noise radiating from the energies of stars being born. Black holes shrieked at them and vast clusters of stars hurled violent bursts of energy toward them.

The Clan hurried through this painful place to return to the tranquility of deep space. For five years, Elise and her sister-WOR forced the Clan around a cone of carefully crafted WOR-space. In the void left behind, humanity huddled in the shadow.

Five years of constant vigilance would soon come to an end, but it came at a cost, one shouldered the most by Elise. Exhaustion seeped from her pores. The constant state of alertness and use of the WOR-skill drained her last reserves. She didn't know if she would last until the last of the Clan exited the Milky Way.

Gregor had been correct about one thing. There was no way to fight, but fighting hadn't been the answer to the Clan threat. That swarming

707

mass of bio-pods churning on the hangar ceiling had inspired the solution to the Clan threat. Humanity would hide while the Clan passed by the Milky Way.

The cone shaped construct spanned the length of the Milky Way and required the constant attention of fifty WOR to weave the WOR-skill in linked super-circles. To keep them linked required Elise. She spent most of her time in the reclined chairs in Command and Control, overseeing the super-link. The rest of the time she spent alone, dodging the legacy of her battle with Gregor.

She didn't want to be a hero, but the role found her. It set her apart from the others. Except for Alice, Aomi, Chandra, and even Paula, Elise had few friends. Dove, Jeena, Larkin, and Carek joined her inner circle, but that was all she had. Everyone else treated her with reverence, leaving her feeling lost and alone.

Her battle with Gregor ended in a standoff really; one neither of them had won. They had both lost, in the end. After all was said and done, nearly four thousand Vendel Citizens chose to travel with the Earth WOR. Gregor placed a unique spin on the whole affair. The Vendel saw him as a hero, holding true to his oaths. He had ended the S'Lorek threat. That he lost all the Earth WOR seemed a conveniently buried truth.

History rewrote itself easily enough. The history books would claim Emperor vlor'Malita liberated the Earth WOR to stand as Vanguard for all Vendel. While he did not encourage emigration to New Terra—they had renamed *Gambit* to reflect their earthly origins—he hadn't forbidden it either.

Now, ten years later, New Terra was a burgeoning world all its own. Full of twenty-thousand citizens, it was bursting at the seams and ready to expand. Inside, eight-hundred Earth WOR had found refuge and a new home. Few had chosen to remain with their Vendel masters.

Most had made a trip back to Earth at one time or another, but all had chosen to return. Earth was not as they remembered. It was a broken, ravaged wreck. Elise had not yet made the trek, unwilling to revisit the death and destruction.

Alice had taken over as Director of New Terra. Elise had been asked to take leadership of the new colony. It was a job she refused. Only when she threatened to leave did they relent. She preferred to live in isolation from the oppressive adoration of everyone around her.

Carek was appointed Assistant Director and assisted Alice in the governance of New Terra. It took him three years to work up the nerve to ask Chandra to marry him. Larkin had no problem asking Aomi to marry him. On New Terra, matrimonial rights no longer belonged solely to women. Dove and Jeena headed the New Terra Pilot's Guild as joint Guild Masters. Jeena asked Dove to marry her the day New Terra claimed independence from the Vendel.

Her friends were happy and thriving. New Terra was self-sufficient and carried on an active trade with the Vendel Empire. Why was it then, she struggled to rise each morning and collapsed into her bed at the end of the day?

Elise sighed and rose out of the pit chair, ending another double shift holding the super link together. She walked out of the pit and into the center of Command and Control. WOR filled five of the concentric rings and were in the process of handing over their stations to their shift replacements. The other circles of command consoles were filled with New Terra civilians monitoring ship's systems. Alice stood in the center of it all with Paula who waited to take over Elise's shift.

"Ready for relief?" Paula smiled at her.

"Yeah, nothing new to report," she said.

She and Paula transferred control of the super-link. Paula wandered down to the chairs in the pit to begin her shift.

"Elise?" Alice came to stand near Elise. "Have you given thought to my request?"

"Yes, and the answer is the same." Elise hunched and ducked her head. She didn't want Alice to ask again. Why couldn't they understand?

"I want you to reconsider. I need someone I trust, someone who can negotiate for what we need."

"We talked about this. I'm not interested."

"When was the last time you took a day off?" Alice pulled Elise toward her office—Gregor's old command suite.

Ten years ago.

She dug in her heels and pulled back. "I like the work. It keeps me busy."

"We're worried about you. I'm worried. You spend all day here, oftentimes pulling double shifts and then retreat to your rooms. When was the last time you did something fun? When was the last time you ate in the mess halls?"

"I can't relax. You know that." She gestured toward the view-screen. "As long as they're out there, I can't let down my guard."

"We can handle it. Take time off. Go on a vacation. Maybe even take care of my request while you're gone."

"Where would I go? Earth?" She didn't want to go there. "This is my home."

"I need you to negotiate terms for the new colony fleet. New Terra needs room to grow. We're starting to rub shoulders."

"Then limit immigration." She shrugged. "Problem solved."

"The problem isn't with immigration, but with our birthrate. Simply put, we need new space. In another five years, we'll be bursting at the seams. Please?"

She shook her head. "Negotiations at that level guarantee a run in with him. Send Aomi, she's the one who found out about the commission of the new c-fleets."

"Aomi has her strengths, but I need New Terra to negotiate from a position of power, and face it . . . you're our strongest asset. Vendel will have a hard time saying no to their savior. It doesn't have to be him, but I doubt he would say no, not to you."

"We have nothing to trade."

"Bullshit, Elise. We, you in particular, are providing protection for their people. That's our bargaining chip."

"Gregor knows I'd never follow through with pulling that away. It's an empty threat."

Alice sighed. "I wish you hadn't forced me to do this."

"Do what?"

"You gave me your word. Do you remember?"

She damn well remembered her promise.

"I'm fine."

"You're the walking dead. You live for one thing. No one can shoulder that burden forever. The Clan can't be your life."

"I can decide that for myself."

"Not anymore." Alice grabbed Elise's shoulders and shook her gently. "I've watched you change. What happened to your spunk? Your determination?"

"My determination is what gets me out of bed each day? Don't lecture me."

"And when you go to bed, who is there to share it with you? You've pushed away every man expressing any interest. Who holds you at night? Who do you confide in? It sure as hell isn't me, and I'm your closest friend. You've pushed everyone else away. You can't go on living half a life."

"Dammit, I'm fine." Her fingernails dug into her palms.

The doors to Alice's office swished open and Alice thrust her inside. Dove, Jeena, Carek, Larkin, Aomi, and Chandra sat at the conference table.

She tried to back up, back out of Gregor's office, but Alice blocked her retreat.

"What the hell?" she said.

"It's called an intervention, kid," Jeena said. "I believe you know what that means."

"I don't need any damn intervention." She scowled at her friends.

Jeena placed a large package on the table and shoved it toward her. "Open it."

She ripped the packaging away. Inside, she recognized her old red flightsuit, a credit chit, and a snarking pad.

"The jump-jet circuit is getting under way above Segra," Jeena explained. "Dove purchased a jump-jet and secured your entrance fee. It starts tomorrow. You have just enough time for a few practice runs if you leave right now."

"I'm not going back." Her voice dropped to a whisper. "You can't ask me to go back."

Alice stepped up from behind. "Elise, you're going." She smoothed Elise's hair. "You were happy when you competed in the jump-jet races. Take two cycles and forget about New Terra and the Clan. We need you, but not the way you are now. You don't have to be our negotiator, but I wish you would consider it. Spend two cycles on Segra, if you can't handle it, come back and I'll send someone else."

Memories of flying through silver rings whisked through her mind. They were right. Flying had always made her feel free. Even after the worst training sessions with High Tender Marcus, a run though the jump-jet rings never failed to soothe her nerves.

Dove focused on her fingers unconsciously smoothing wrinkles from the flightsuit. "Chickadee," he stood and straightened the fabric of his trousers, "you're not right. A part of you has died. Work, WOR-skill training, and a hermit's existence? You've cut yourself off from the world, and now, you're cutting us out too. Do this for me." Dove wrung his hands. "Remember who you were, and who you can be again."

"I appreciate it, guys, really . . . but," she stammered, trying to find a way out.

"No, buts," Aomi said. "Even a hero needs to take a break."

Larkin stroked the first two fingers of his wife's hand.

She scanned the room. Chandra and Carek, Larkin and Aomi, Dove and Jeena, they'd all found their mates. Her heart settled as a lump in her throat and she understood how reclusive she'd become. The truth of their words settled uneasily on her shoulders. She took in a deep breath and slowly forced the air out between pursed lips.

"All right, two cycles," she said through gritted teeth. Inside, her heart soared. Two cycles of flying. No Clan. No WOR-skill. No constant struggle with the super-links. No worries of little slips and discovery.

Rest, Malice whispered. *We need rest.*

Agreed, Alex echoed. *I'm tired.*

Me too. Shriek stretched and gave a yawn. *Just two cycles of not having to weave WOR-skill.*

Yes, rest would be good, and perhaps a little fun.

"That's a girl." Dove gave his broad, crooked smile. "Everything you need is on that chit. Your ship is the *El*. Take good care of her and send us updates. Larkin already has a betting pool started."

"Really?" Elise eyed Larkin with suspicion.

He grinned back and shrugged. "The jump-jet races are quite interesting. Maybe you can bring back a few jump-jets and we can start a New Terra circuit."

"Maybe." Elise hugged the flightsuit. She picked up the other two items. "Thank you."

The bright eyes of her friends flickered as she opened up the WOR-step. Maybe negotiating with Gregor over that new fleet of colony ships wouldn't be so painful? Between one moment and the next, she stepped from Alice's office to the jump-jet hangar on Segra. A small blue and purple jump-jet, with *El* painted on the side, glistened in the light.

She walked over and peered into the cockpit. Inside, a larger brown package rested. The card on top read *To the woman I loved and lost, find yourself again and soar free.* Her teeth buzzed and a presence loomed from behind.

"I was wondering if you'd like to share a drink?" A misted veil covered the pilot's face.

Her heart lurched and her vision narrowed. Gregor Ulysses vlor'Malita stood before her, as glorious as she had remembered.

"Who told you? Alice? Carek? Dove?"

He deactivated the veil. "Would you believe, Jeena? I was surprised when I had a message from her. My surprise turned to delight when I read her words, and I have to admit, a little bit of fear. It's good to see you, Elise."

"Fear?"

"It's been a long time."

"It's nice to see you, Emperor," she said. The words rang true and she flashed him an honest smile.

He spread his hands. "My friends call me Ulysses. Emperor seems . . . too formal."

"I would call you Gregor, if I may?"

"Names are everything to the Vendel." He eyed her with speculation. "Are you sure?"

"I could never call you Ulysses. Gregor is how I know you."

"Your memories of me are not very flattering."

"Not all my memories are bad, time has mellowed most."

"If that could be true . . ." His breathing hitched. "You and I deserve a fresh start." He swept her a bow. "What do you think? Are you willing to risk it?"

"Care to wager on who will win the jump-jet finals?" She couldn't answer him directly.

"I thought you didn't bet," he said, straightening. "But, I'm intrigued. What would you wager?"

"If I win, you give me a c-fleet and a fleet of jump-jets to start a jump-jet circuit on New Terra."

"An expensive bet. What if I win?"

"Then, you give just the c-fleet."

"An unusual bet. I pay either way and win nothing. I hear negotiations are being set up to discuss just such a transaction. New Terra intends to buy the c-fleet, why should I gamble it away?"

"If you don't take the bet, then I won't race at all, and where's the fun in that?"

He said nothing, but crossed his arms with an amused expression.

"Tell you what," she said, "when I win and take my jump-jets with me, I'll see if I can't release the ban on vlor'lords on New Terra. You could race in the first New Terra jump-jet circuit."

"Hm, I'm interested, but I have a condition."

"No conditions, that's the bet."

"I have a condition, luv."

"Fine," she said. "What?"

"When I come to New Terra, I want to stay in my old quarters."

"Those are my quarters."

Gregor winked. "I don't mind sharing."

"There's only one bed."

"I don't find that to be a problem. Which brings up another point?"

"What?"

"Where are you staying on Segra?"

"I'm staying in my quarters back on New Terra. It's a simple commute . . . for me."

"Hm," he said, "that's a shame, because I have a lovely cottage on a secluded island. It's private. Besides, Jeena said you were supposed to be on vacation. I don't think you're supposed to commute back and forth."

"And how many bedrooms does your cottage have?" She poked his chest, enjoying the light banter. For the first time, she didn't feel threatened by Gregor and could enjoy being near him without risk of intimidation.

"Only one, but the bed is really big."

"Ah, then I accept."

His eyes lit, reflecting silver pools of delight.

Elise giggled, she wasn't done with him. "So, where will you be staying?"

Gregor's eyebrows dropped in disappointment, but he laughed. "Wherever fate draws me, I suppose. I've waited ten years, Elise. I can wait until after the jump-jet competition. If you win, I will hold you to your side of the bet."

"Will you throw the competition, then, to get what you want?"

"No, because if I win . . . I'll give you the c-fleet, but you and I will spend two cycles in that cottage together afterwards. I never throw a race, Elise. You can have my cottage for the duration of the jump-jet competition. I have quarters here I can use. Now, how about that drink? I plan on a highly unfair seduction of the woman I love."

"A drink sounds good." Elise crossed her arms and looked into the face of the man who held her heart. "But, seduction is the woman's job."

"My heart is already yours. I plan on convincing you to give me yours."

"We live in different worlds, Gregor, and you cannot live in mine. I can't give what you're asking."

"I'll take whatever I can get, but I intend on having your love. You can't escape from me."

"I feel like running already."

"You've run long enough, Elise. It's time to come home. Loving me will not diminish you. I'll show you the truth. We belong together, despite our beginnings, despite everything I did, we're bound—not by the WOR-skill, but by something greater. I love you with all my heart, and I intend to spend the rest of my life showing you just how much you mean to me."

Gregor's intensity scared her, but she didn't run. He captivated her completely. "Could we start with a drink?"

He laughed. "Absolutely. I'll give you the worlds . . . later."

NEW TERRA_

Carek turned to Alice. His eyes narrowed. "You didn't tell her."

"No," Alice said. "When she returns—"

"If she returns," he interrupted.

Alice blinked. "When Elise returns, we'll tell her. Let's allow her to have a little fun before we burden her with new problems."

"Was it wise to tell him she was coming?" Carek asked.

"We discussed it," Jeena defended. "Elise is slipping away and we need her now more than ever. Emperor vlor'Malita is the only person I know who might pull her back from the darkness. Madness stirs in her mind, and I'm not at all convinced she's still in charge within that head of hers. I don't know which one of her *sisters* I'm speaking to at any given time, and it scares me to death."

"He'll destroy her," Carek said.

"I don't think so, cuz," Dove said. "He loves her."

"How can that be? He destroyed her, fractured her mind and left her broken." Carek clenched his teeth. "She hates him."

"She hates what he did to her," Alice interjected, "but she understands why it had to be done. The Emperor had to save the Vendel and that meant he had to . . ."

"The ends justified the means? Is that what you're trying to say?" Carek's lips twisted into a sneer. "All of you suffered because of him. Chandra, don't you hate them for what they did to you?"

"I don't anymore," she answered. "I wouldn't have found you, and we wouldn't be starting a family together. I have a lot of things to be thankful for because of the Vendel."

"I agree with Alice and Chandra," Aomi added. "Elise needs something more than this constant vigilance against the Clan. The Emperor might just give her a reason to live again. We had to do something."

Alice braced her hands on the table in front of her. "When Elise comes back, we'll tell her. Until then, she's in the Emperor's hands. Let's pray he heals her. We need her whole for the fight to come."

EPILOGUE_

New Terra Histories

IN THE TEN YEARS SINCE OUR LIBERATION FROM THE VENDEL, I HAVEN'T SEEN or spoken to Gregor. He's not a part of my world, even if he inhabits my dreams through the long nights and lingers at the edges of my thoughts every day.

The sad truth is I miss him.

I miss our connection.

Without him, my world is empty and a profound loneliness infests my life.

Hate, he told me, is *but a breath away from love. One merges into the other when we least expect it.*

I hated Gregor, or rather, what he did to me, to my family, my friends, and my world, yet, I'm grateful for what he brought into my life. I have new friends, people who have become my family. It doesn't stop the ache, the dreams, or the constant restlessness I feel, but it fills me with contentment.

This story could have been anyone's to tell. It's not unique to me.

I hated the Vendel.

I wanted nothing but revenge.

But in the end, this is what I've learned.

Hatred is impossible to sustain when love tugs at your heart.

I love my friends, and in the depths of my heart, I love the Vendel. I may even love Gregor.

He is not my enemy.

He never was.

My grandfather's words return to me. *"Elise,"* he said, *"to understand your enemies, you must first let go of your hatred. Only then may you forgive. Only then may you understand."*

I understand what Gregor did and why. I accept it was necessary. I've let go of my hatred and I've forgiven both Gregor and the Vendel. The Vendel were our saviors, but we also became theirs.

My path has been lined with incredible pain. Never think otherwise. The day the Vendel invaded my world will never leave me.

I lived that day. I died that day.

I was defeated, broken, and the very person I was, my beliefs and faith, were destroyed.

I had every reason to hate the Vendel, but I have clarity now. I understand the terrible choices Gregor had to make. I may have made them myself if I had been in his shoes.

No longer does hate pull at me. I am free of that burden.

I love the Vendel, and I fight to keep them safe every day. I will continue to do so until I take my last breath.

They took everything from me, but what they gave me in return is something I never imagined possible.

I have found my peace.

This has been my story . . . at least for now.

END

PLEASE CONSIDER LEAVING A REVIEW_

I HOPE YOU ENJOYED THIS BOOK AS MUCH AS I ENJOYED WRITING IT. IF YOU enjoyed reading this story, please consider leaving a review, and please let other people know. A sentence is all it takes, but a book lives or dies based upon its reviews. Thank you in advance!

VENDEL RISING SERIES_

Vendel Rising: a serialized novel

Volume 1: It Begins With the End
Volume 2: Women of Rank
Volume 3: The Price of Power
Volume 4: It Ends With a Beginning

ABOUT THE AUTHOR_

L.A. Warren cut her teeth on Azimov, Pohl, Heinlein, and many other science fiction greats. Not once did she think she would become a writer, but life has a way of seeing dreams come true you never knew you had. Now, L.A. is writing the science fiction and fantasy stories she loves to read.

Website

https://jem-publishing.com/la_warren/

f facebook.com/Author.L.A.Warren

THE END_

———